PRAISE FOR TERRY MCGARRY

"Strong characters, an intriguing magic system, and powerful themes of justice, rebellion, and forgiveness . . . Highly recommended." —*Library Journal* on *The Binder's Road*

"The author's talent for world-building and sure use of language will leave fans, especially those fond of big, intricate fantasies like Robert Jordan's The Wheel of Time, feeling more satisfied." —*Publishers Weekly* on *The Binder's Road*

"Terry McGarry makes a brilliant splash of color on the fantasy landscape with *Illumination*. A fresh, unique take on magic by a true word artist." —Elizabeth Haydon

"*Illumination* is unique, a fantasy as richly complex as the sutures of an ammonite's shell. Quite marvelous!" —David Drake

"Recommended without reservation to those who take their magic, and their relationships, seriously." —Gene Wolfe

Books by Terry McGarry

Illumination
The Binder's Road
Triad

Triad

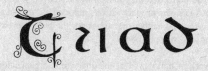

TERRY McGARRY

TOR fantasy

A TOM DOHERTY ASSOCIATES BOOK
NEW YORK

This is a work of fiction. All of the characters, organizations, and events portrayed in this novel are either products of the author's imagination or are used fictitiously.

TRIAD

Copyright © 2005 by Terry McGarry

All rights reserved, including the right to reproduce this book, or portions thereof, in any form.

Edited by Teresa Nielsen Hayden

Map by Ellisa Mitchell

A Tor Book
Published by Tom Doherty Associates, LLC
175 Fifth Avenue
New York, NY 10010

www.tor.com

Tor® is a registered trademark of Tom Doherty Associates, LLC.

ISBN-13: 978-0-765-34329-1
ISBN-10: 0-765-34329-0

First Edition: November 2005
First Mass Market Edition: April 2007

Printed in the United States of America

0 9 8 7 6 5 4 3 2 1

FOR MY MOTHER

AUTHOR'S NOTE

The book you're holding is chronologically the third of three. The first book, *Illumination,* is mainly about the craft of mages, whose power manifests as a golden yellow light. The second book, *The Binder's Road,* takes place six years later; it is mainly about a second power, which manifests as a coppery red shine in those who wield it, and concerns the adventures of an ensemble of other characters. This book, *Triad,* takes place twelve years after *The Binder's Road.* It is partly about a third power, which manifests as a silvery blue glow in those who possess it, and tells the story of several characters with that power; it is also about what happened, and happens, to all the characters we know from the previous books—including the realm of Eiden Myr. That's a lot of characters. It's also a lot of material. I hope that while you read, you'll make use of the Web site www.eidenmyr.com. It includes a detailed compendium and a complete listing of characters—their names, their roles, their ages, and their relationship to one another; a much expanded version of the glossaries found in the back matter of the previous two books; and a wealth of additional narrative.

If you're new to Eiden Myr, welcome. I conceive of these three novels not as a series but as a triangle. The way the story is oriented, *Illumination* and *The Binder's Road* form the base and *Triad* is the apex; but it's an equilateral triangle, and you can enter from any point.

And in the land beyond the mists, and the land beyond the shadows, and the land beyond the rains, is a land beyond grief, beyond hurt, beyond death, a land in which all fine things dwell, and all decencies, and all kindness; and when earth and bones and greenness are one in the touch of their flesh, when lakes and rivers and seas are one beneath the rains, when smoke and mist and flames are one within the winds and the still airs, when Eiden and Sylfonwy and Morlyrien are one within the luminous spirits of their children and the oldest of the old have returned to light the paths, then that illuminated land shall become visible, a shining beacon in the shrouded dark, and it shall be Galandra's land, Galandra's glory, Galandra's dream.

—TELLERS' TALE

NORTH

The Sea
of Wishes

The Isle of Senana

The Sea
of Charms

The Meri Isles

The
Hand

Maur Alna

The Knee

Khine

The
Boot

The
Ankle

The Strong
Leg

Th

The Heel

Maur Lengra

The Big Toe

The
Leeward
Sea

The Weak Leg

The Haunc

The Toes

Wiggle
Cramp
Stud
Curl

The Little Toes

The Low Sea

Quad

NONE'S-LAND

A roar of incandescence delved trenches in the matted clouds. The seared trenches bled light, ink into wool, a fibrous stain that veined the overcast with silver. An afterthought of thunder wrenched the viscera, seized the heart. Something nearby collapsed inward under the pressure with the crack and rumble of an explosion. Fuming balls of impossible metals burst liquid against the magewardings. Spears not wood, not metal, not fire—more quicksilver than iron, too rigid to be molten, ablaze without flame—not even spears, not really, except as light could be a spear, or terror—launched arcing from unseen, unknowable sources. Missiles changed trajectory unaided, veered in midflight on a day as still as a dead man's heart. They defied sense. They defied the senses.

Cett slammed down prone and covered. Someone nearby shrieked at the suck and crunch of rent flesh and bone and kept shrieking, then cut off with a muffled grunt, followed by a sticky spray and the patter of chunks falling. Cett bit down on a rotten tooth that she would not let the touches heal, welcomed the lancȩ of agony. It drove away the taste of iron, the taste of echoes.

She fought an arsenal of delusion. A foul dream from which the only waking was into death. A phantasm of war. It could not be real. Yet the lowland air smelled not of dreamweed but of solvents and lampblack, a bite of storm within a smoky pall.

These seeming delusions would kill you sure as the arrow or the blade you could understand.

At last a few breaths of ear-ringing quiet. Cett shook blood-spiked bangs from her eyes and shouted "You!" at a clutch of fresh visants.

One looked. Visants were cracked as a rule, and the visants willing to suffer exile were the ones with the least sense—or the least to lose. Desperate times, to resort to lunatics in defense of Eiden Myr. But visants were solitary folk, and Eiden Myr, their island home, floated alone on the briny deep, in the rising dark. There was logic in defending isolation with the isolated, battling madness with the mad. And this one, now, he might have some wits about him. The others—all sweet-faced with childlike luminance, that ageless silvery soft *something* that turned her stomach—wandered the salt marsh like three-year-olds on a field of sport: one staring gape-mouthed, one jiggling with giggles, one playing peekaboo. This one accepted eye contact, pointed to himself in silent inquiry . . . stepped toward Cett when she nodded.

An explosion out to sea hit them as a wall of air, spilled them out of the scrub brush onto the sandy crescent—shielders, menders, stewards, mages, touches, visants, the lot. Jarred from their chocks, catapults toppled. Vellum scattered, and castings with it. This one was bad. So bad that, once Cett had retrieved her face from the sand and reoriented earth and sky, she couldn't help glancing inland.

The threshold shimmered there, invisible, unshifted, the midder lowlands clear and calm beyond it. As long as her shield held, the threshold did not move. If the shield fell back, the threshold did too. As long as it was there, then so were they. As long as they were here, the world beyond it was protected. She would have known if it had moved; even deafened, blinded, numbed, she'd have sensed change or absence. She could have traced its sinuous footprint in her sleep. Was that awareness something like what a visant felt? That extra sense, like an extra pair of eyes or ears, an extra skin? Why did she never trust it?

She should have. Glancing over her shoulder was a mistake.

Naïve as turning her back on a human attacker. Blast-driven seawater breasted the maur, swelled marshland like a sponge, lifted her then sucked her down hard. Mud plugged one ear; sand gritted in the corners of eye and mouth. An afterswell slammed saltwater fingers up her nose. Spitting, blinking, she fought upright from a sucking sandy hole. Waterweeds slimed under her shirt. Fish flopped in the cordgrass. A shoulder-width block of driftwood had just missed her head.

Blindsiding was the worst. Even the smallest preview gave time to brace, or duck, or take the wave and ride it.

That was what visants were for. To see, and warn.

What she was for was to deploy them.

"Fresh casting materials!" she ordered the mages, and a steward struggled back toward the threshold, to where they'd anchored warded crates of inks, pigments, brushes, quills—what the triads would need to renew their efforts after every assault that destroyed the materials in use. "Sweep for injured!" she ordered the touches, and former wrights and farmers left their warded, weighted shelter to check the mages and the others, healing small wounds on the spot, coaxing the more gravely injured to the shelter for thorough treatment. "Reset the retorts!" she ordered the front line, and wood creaked protest and metal groaned strain and rope sang tension, as projectiles were torqued back for blind hurling into the unknowable.

Cett slogged to the visant. "What can you tell me?"

"What can I . . . what?" His voice had the high croak of some exotic frog from the jungle they'd dredged him out of.

"*Tell* me," she said. "That's what you bleeding walleyes do, isn't it? Tell futures, secrets, when it will rain, who thieved the mince pies from the sill. *You tell where the attacks will come.* So tell me! Where next?"

He was shaking his head and looked to swell into a howling wail. Weren't they initiating these clods? This one had *no* idea what he was for. Teased down from some Toe treehouse and plopped here without instructions. Bloody procurers. Half-lives, they were called, half-worlders, the only ones permitted back inside. Death's shills, they were called, too, on harsher days. Soon enough there'd be a simpler word for them, with no wordsmith's whimsy to it: *Dead.* That described them all sooner or later, all the severed: lights and lightless, killers and healers, guilty and innocent, volunteers and convicts, sane and insane. All the same, in the end and now. Damned was damned.

"The last good visant I had could tell me right before something came at us," Cett told the new one. "Might not be able to tell me what it was—I can't tell you what they are even after I've seen them—but she could point, or say 'left' or 'right' or 'seaward' or 'overhead.'"

"I don't . . . I . . . can't . . ."

"One before that could tell me where the siege devices were. We call them gibes, right? And ours are retorts. An argument to the death. You tell me where they've positioned their gibes today, I lay down cover. Get them off us for a while—long enough for you to settle in. You're in for a rough night otherwise." She would have promised him a treat at supper, but he hadn't been here long enough to hate the food more than the hunger. She had nothing else to lay on the saltgrass between them except despair: "It's not like you'll get to go home now. You're past the go-back. You might as well do what you came for."

"But I didn't come," the visant said. Typical visant gibberish. He opened his mouth to say more, then cast a glance toward a farther hump of dry ground. Cett followed his gaze to Fyldur Greasehair, the man who'd brought him. He sensed her regard and returned it. She scowled at the greased hair, the swart complexion, the white-flash leer.

Procurers had to be part visant themselves, in order to see whatever it was they saw in each other. Procurers came in all three lights, in such minute degree that they were good for nothing but seeing those lights in other people. For Fyldur Greasehair, being death's shill held more appeal than any craft. He twisted guilt and desire like a hayrope. Lights followed where he led.

He had claimed that he would put an end on this war. He had claimed that he would bring back the strongest visant Eiden Myr had ever known.

We've only known of them at all for a dozen years. Cett checked a reflexive surge of hope. Sacrifice meant nothing if there was any chance of reprieve. As long as she fought and suffered and survived—*because* she fought and suffered and survived—Eiden Myr would endure in safety.

"I didn't come," the visant insisted. "I just didn't stay."

He should have. He should have stayed perched in his jungle treehouse and never climbed down where someone like the Greasehair could catch him. "Moot now," Cett said. "You're here. You can't go home. Your knack is sight. Take a good look. Tell me what you see."

He turned a slow circle, surveying the full scene with an unfocused, nearly cross-eyed look, as though his attention were not only divided but divided into equal points around a sphere expanding from his view. As though he was focused not on something behind his own eyes or beyond the world before him, but *on everything at once.*

She couldn't guess at how many years were on him. He had the face of a child in a writhe of mist-colored hair, its clearest feature a pair of inkdrop eyes. Touches had a fleshy vitality, mages an elegant grace. Visants had that ageless softness. As though they blurred a little in the beholder's sight. Seers who could not be clearly seen.

Cett hated it. Hated them. They knew what you would do before you did it. Some said they could see the thoughts in your head. You weren't safe inside your own skin with them around. Some said that Torrin Lightbreaker made them when he killed the last mage ennead and extinguished the old light—that he opened realms Galandra's warding had repelled, and things that had been afraid of the magelight crept out and took root in the weak, the outcast, the aberrant. Others said that mages and touches drew on warm human powers and made a cold space where that warmth had been, and the visants' powers were born of that place. Powers no human vessel was meant to contain, no human mind to command. Cold powers that drove them mad, or left them hanging only half in this world.

Well, Cett would use whatever came to hand. Better the

walleyes should be here playing peekaboo than somewhere inland ruining lives.

"Shelters," her visant reported at last. "One canvas tent, the
rest lean-tos and huts and driftwood shacks. Crates. Wooden
contraptions. Cruel jumbled metal things, with chains and
spikes. Pennants on poles. Red silk people, yellow silk people,
blue silk people." Those last were the touches, the mages, the
visants; they tied on hanks of dyed silk so that those of other
lights would know their roles, and so that their own would know
them in death. "The sea, the sky, the marsh." He paused. "Dead
things. And you. And me."

Cett liked to confront a man straight on, but her eyes kept
sliding from this one. Frustrating; but no matter. His report was
poor. "Dead things"? Blood and scattered body parts, wildlife
blown from nests and burrows, touches working to heal damage
beyond their scope. "The sea, the sky, the marsh"? Out to sea,
the ghosts of ships that never landed, the shades of ships that
had sailed away from here and never returned. Above the tide-
line a snarl of twisted elders and intermittent trees she couldn't
name. Groundsel and bayberry bordering low-tide sandflats,
mudflats. The sky could at the least have been described as
"cloudy." No ripple in the air, no tail-eye glint, no sign at all of
the next attack?

You could see for a nonned leagues, you could see clear into
the next life, and if you couldn't interpret what you saw, you
were no use.

Beyond the threshold on the landward side, Eiden Myr—
whole, serene, unaffected. Somewhere out in the Dreaming
Sea—and in the other eight seas, surrounding the man-shaped
mass of earth that was their home—another threshold, beyond
which their enemies lay unseen, ineffable, their motives unknown. Twin curtains, and between the two this none's-land
steeped in nightmare, reeking of death. It was all the home Cett
Shielder had now, and would ever have.

This visant couldn't help her protect even that. *I ought to kill
him,* she thought. *I ought to earn my exile.*

She had never bedded those chandlers. Never coupled with

them in the flesh. Only in the mind. But her pledges had sensed the struggle in her, as she bushwhacked her way back to them through the thickets of her misplaced longings. Helpless, impatient, determined to divine the source of her troubled mood, they had sought the shy visants in their secret places, asked their reckless questions. Cett hadn't worried; visants were pitiful lunatics incapable of the feats folk credited to them. Soothseeing, foretelling, mindreading? Bafflegab. Then her pledges came back with wounds in their eyes and accusations on their lips, and how could she deny the names that made her pulse leap? She had betrayed them in her heart; once they knew, the hurt it caused made a crime of what had been nothing.

Although she hadn't acted, her lifemates would never again trust her. Some craven visant had spoken as if thought and deed were one, as if she'd cuckolded the both of them, and packed them home to her brimful of pain. *I love you,* she'd protested, *I controlled myself, I chose* you, *the two of* you; it only sank her in a morass of defensiveness worse than any confession. She'd cursed herself for her indulgence: she should have shut the chandlers from her dreams at the first twinge of desire. She'd cursed her pledges' weakmindedness in trusting a visant's claims over hers. But most she'd cursed the visant who'd divulged her private yearnings just as she was finding the strength to abandon them.

Where they'd lived, a secluded vale in the Heartlands, death alone dissolved a pledging. The three of them could separate, but there was only one way short of suicide to free her loved ones to pledge again.

She set off seaward, bound to join the shield. On her way, she ran those visants to ground in their earthen den, held her accuser by the throat against the rooty crumbling wall. "I'm severing myself," she told him, as his throat apple bobbed in the crook of her hand. "Not because there's nothing left here. Not because you've destroyed my love. Because severance is for those willing to kill. If longing for a thing is the same as doing it, then I have killed you, visant. If imagining an act is the same as committing it, then you are dead."

She'd left him sputtering excuses. From the inland side, the inside, nothing was visible beyond the threshold; when she stepped through that unearthly shimmer, she left the rest of it behind—the rage and the heartbreak, the empty places beside her in the night. She was as good as dead to the world, taking that step. She had died, and freed herself, and pledged anew, to death.

I could kill this one, she thought again. *It would be a start.*

A subliminal wrongness shivered the ground beneath her. She turned, and heard outcries, and saw three linear bulges in the sand converging on the tufted bank where she sat with the visant. She dragged the visant to his feet and dove, twisting in midair so that he would land on her and she would take the brunt of the fall. The narrow, straight churnings intersected seven or eight threfts on. A tumbling geyser of mud and salt and scrub erupted where they met, and a bloodcurdling shriek, as of something alive.

"Their aim is off," Cett said. "They'd have missed us even if we hadn't jumped." Part of the shield's function was to draw enemy attention. However the incomprehensible weaponry worked, it was through some ability to find living targets—homing on warmth or movement, perhaps, though after two years of this Cett was convinced it was consciousness the weapons sensed, and sought. They never went for lures, however convincingly crafted. They might not be aware, but they could find awareness, and end it.

She looked up at the visant and saw fear in his black eyes. Not fear of the weapons of madness or the field of mutilation. Fear of her.

He knew the murder she cherished in her heart.

Again there was silence, more earsplitting in its way than assault. No sound of bird or animal; most were dead, blasted from the air, their holes, their nests. No brush of leaf on leaf; there was no wind to move them. Rich and piquant odors released by gored bark, crushed leaves, delved earth hung where they'd emerged. Thick air held all still within itself—movement, sound, scent.

Move bubbled up from deep within Cett, as it came to her that she had been in the same twisted, half-risen posture for more slow breaths than she could count. One leg was bent at the knee, the other stretched out; one hand held her weight, the other lay crossed over her hip; her head was turned to the visant. He was on his rear, knees drawn up, rocking forward and back. *Marvelous,* Cett thought, with a bitter detachment. *Now this one's gone too.*

"Get," the visant was saying. He'd been saying whatever it was for a long time. *Out with it!* she thought.

But it wasn't fair, to blame procurers or stewards—any of the lightless at all, or any of the lights, either, bluesilver visants or yellowgold mages or even the redcopper touches who wouldn't lift a violent finger in their land's defense. As well fault Kazhe n'Zhevra l'Keit, who could melt weapons of iron or stone or wood but could do nothing against these. She, Cett, was the lead shielder along this ninemile stretch of the Dreaming Sea. The coordinator, meant to rally the three lights and their lightless support to hold out against the cataclysms. Salvation was down to her and the other firsts of the human shield around the coast of Eiden Myr. Some she'd heard of—Boroel Bladespirit on the Windward Sea, Kivya the Silent on the High Sea, Purlor One-Arm on the Sea of Wishes, Verlein Who Watches on the Sea of Sorrows—but most she wouldn't have known even by family names, much less the monikers of exile. She would meet none of them face-to-face. Forbidden to travel across Eiden's body, constrained to travel around the periphery, few shielders traveled at all. Severed mages circulated as they could, to trade materials and techniques around the irregular coastline. Severed touches stayed put, but kept contact with their counterparts to either side, like sleepers reaching to be sure of company and comfort. Shielders kept to themselves. They tucked in tight and dense, dedicated to each other, wary of new arrivals and their sorry odds, superstitious to a fault. Shielders had cradled the old too many times to open their arms to the new.

At first it was a battle they would win or lose. They would die unpassaged or live and go home. Moon after moon, season after season, the end was always just over the next hump, just after the next, climactic battle. But as year supplanted season supplanting moon, as futile howls of *Why?* and *Who?* and *What did we ever do to them?* ended in breakdown or grim resignation, it became this grinding attrition. Cett had long since lost all those she called her friends. Her current shielders were replacements for replacements. She was as severed here, among her own, of her own doing, as she was from home and hearth.

"*Get,*" the visant said—again, or still. Louder.

It was the job of the condemned to lay sacrifice on top of sacrifice. No one in Eiden Myr—no head of any group, no guiding body, no alderfolk, no Khinish hall—had established or enforced the concept of exile. That had grown all of its own; as if through some tacit agreement, communities had simply stopped accepting those who'd been to the coasts to defend them with violence. Killing was anathema to the fundaments of Eiden Myr society— the rule of compassion, the mages called it—and rather than declaim or debate like seekers, Eiden Myr society had done the simplest possible thing: excluded those who might have taken lives. None's-land, already on the fringe, already a ruleless world, became the realm of exclusion. Cross the threshold, and whether you killed or not, you could never go home again. Except for mage binders who harvested animal flesh for vellum and parchment—materials outlawed on the mainland for a dozen years now—there was no knowing if they *had* killed, sending their blind retorts into haze and ignorance. But because they might have, because they intended to, they would be met by stony silence in the interior. No one would speak to them, trade with them, serve them; anywhere they tried to settle, they would be gently, firmly uprooted and sent on their way.

Some stain must mark us, Cett thought. *Some shadow, like a reverse of the light in folk of power. Because they always know us.* It should not be possible to tell one of the severed from anyone else; they bore no brand, no paint, no outward sign. But perhaps it was something like scent. Cett had never noticed the smell of pipe smoke on her father until she left home, but thereafter she'd know him in the dark, the stale pungence in his hair, his clothes, on his skin. When you were close to a thing, part of it, you could never sense it. Mages couldn't see their own lights. Neither could touches, or even visants.

Only someone else with the light could see it in you. Did that mean that everyone in Eiden Myr had some killing instinct? That everyone had some murder in them, that they could smell it on the severed and drive them off?

I'm still sitting, she thought. One leg extended and one bent, one arm pushing her up and one crossing to grab hold of the visant. Her muscles trembled with the fatigue of maintaining the awkward pose, and still she was rising, not risen, and still the word *Move* bubbled up from the bottom of her mind. She tried to relax, go limp—stop resisting, let her own weight break her free. Still she was rising. Still not risen.

"*. . . up!*"

The space around Cett shattered, as though she had been encased in a clear solid block of air. The visant's voice had cracked it and the cracks had bloomed into fractures and forked and forked again until the block was only tiny fragments that burst apart and dusted the surface of the marsh. The visant had shoved her through her rising movement so that her suspended foot and hand touched earth. She staggered. The visant offered no support. He swayed away, afraid to touch her or be touched.

"A new weapon," she said. Her tongue slurred. She was still half gripped by paralysis. "Help me." He had helped all he was going to; he stood and watched while she hauled and pushed the nearest shielders out of their trance.

Then the shattered air itself attacked them. Crystalline plates spun razor edges through trunks and limbs. The winds flattened into sheets, like metal, and sliced across the emplacements, sectioning all who stood in their path. There was no ground firm enough to dig holes in. Some shimmied down into the muck. Not one of those came up again. Her folk were scythed into bloody shreds.

The visant was crawling toward a lone tree so wind- and warbeaten it was more shrub than tree, a thin, scrubby bush impaled on a stick and shoved into the marsh, then crushed and torqued and plucked nearly bare, what branches it had left splayed all askew, a fan of broken fingers. He dragged himself with dogged desperation, as though toward shelter, or safety. He grasped for the gnarled trunk like a drowning man. He craned his neck so he was looking *through* the tortured branches. Trying to obscure his view, warp it . . .

Transform it—*into something familiar.* Something like the view from among the moss-draped, liana-tangled weep of trees in his jungle home. In the dwarfed vegetation of these low, wide-open lands, he sought to . . . what?

To re-create the way he saw things at home.

It's because he's outside the swamp. He can't do what he does in a place so different from where he comes from. "That blue power's like a bloody rice plant." The words came out of her with awe—at the realization, and at herself for having it. "It won't root here on the shore. It can't grow. It won't *work.*"

She turned in the sucking blood-drenched marshy ground, trying to take stock of her forces, count the flutter of red silk thighbands and yellow, but all had fallen or taken shelter. Acid rain was singing on metal, steaming on cloth. She came farther around and saw the other visants. They stood unscathed, bare-headed, unarmored in the burning rain; no wind lifted the girls' hair, no blood drenched the boys' plain clothes. Dung-smeared scabbing visants, pus-filled reeking useless visants—

"Go home. Go back to the stinking swamp where you belong!"

They focused on her the way a crowd would on a madman. She dragged herself toward them. In brief glimpses the sight of them was overlaid by something else, something clear, some version of these folk in downy golden haze on some serene coastline. Did they stand half in some otherrealm, like the bonefolk?

She had never seen the bonefolk here. Never seen the green phosphorous glow of their feeding. *Where do the bodies go?*

She blinked hard, dragged a rough-gloved hand across her eyes, drew blood in long welted scrapes across lids and sockets, relished the reality of that pain. Still the visants wavered between this nightmare plane and some dream of peace. Bloody scabbing visants and their puking secrets—

A great, half-seen pendulum, like a spiked mace the size of a hayrick, conjured of salt and smoke, swung into her from the side. It knocked her airborne, but she stayed upright, landed two-footed in the muck, dragged one foot free to plant again and keep from falling. She windmilled balance from the solidifying air—but only in time for the backswing. The mace caught her again, spikes driving deep into bone, and this time she landed flat on her back with a sucking splash. Each gasped breath was a lungful of razored dust.

A man's face came into view. Did she know him? He looked a mage, somehow, yet not so arrogant or learned; a touch's empathy gentled his features; but no silk adorned his thigh, he was no one of hers, and there was a soft agelessness to him, like a patina on old silver.

"You see it," he said. "You see it as it is, now."

Cett could feel blood or pus oozing in her throat and was afraid of what would come out if she spoke. He was one of them. Ageless, silvered. He could hear her thoughts, couldn't he? Wasn't that one of their powers?

"*Our* powers," he said, dabbing at her lips with a plain cloth. "But no, it isn't." The linen came back crimson. "No one ever saw the blue in you."

"No," she choked, on a gush of foul fluid. "No one told me I'm . . . blue."

"Perhaps you weren't. Perhaps it was latent. Suppressed. You scorn us so. You would not have let it manifest if you could help it. Your powers are trying to protect you, Cett. They are trying to show you that this cannot kill you."

She rolled her eyeballs toward the others. They were visants. They must have heard her. But they seemed terribly far away now, receding into their land of shining peace. She could go with them, she supposed; if she had the light she must have access to that realm. But it would mean leaving her post, and she was needed here. Already some of her remaining folk were ducking from their shelters, running low along wooden planks to cart her back for touches to heal. For a moment it seemed that their planks were laid across a field of grotesquely twisted, rotting corpses, and in the next eyeblink it seemed that there were only planks, only empty planks, decaying and splintered. . . .

"You're the last one," the kindly visant said. "Can you see it now? There is no one here but you. The rest are dead of their own belief. They didn't have a mindlight to shield them. But you do. You can live, Cett. If you choose to."

He stood then, and the sun came out from behind the clouds of delusion and haloed his silver hair, and her heart broke with longing to take the hand he extended to her.

Someone has to be here to take the fall, she thought. *Someone has to stay till reinforcements come. If I'm the only one left, and I go, then the shield here will fail. I can't tell where the dream ends and the truth begins, but maybe the dream is its own kind of truth. My duty's clear. The only clear thing.*

The visant was backing away, his hand still extended, his body engulfed in light. When that faded into the familiar drifting smoke and reek of death, the other visant was kneeling beside her.

"Who were you talking to?" he asked.

Who was I . . . what?

"One of the people you thought you were giving orders to before?"

No one, she thought. *No one there. I was talking to myself. Talking to my own grieving light.*

"I tried," he said. His voice broke. So brave. So pathetic. "I tried to make it like home. I heard what you said. I don't believe you. I have powers. I do. The strongest in my region. People fear my powers. I hate it. So I let the Greasehair have me. I don't know what's gone wrong with the minds here or why the touches couldn't heal it with their hands, but I can fix it, I can, I know I can. Just give me a chance. Give me a chance to see what you see. That must be how your last visant did it. She must have watched how you behaved and . . . figured out what you believed would come . . . and told you, to warn you, before you knew yourself. People give things away, you see? They have no idea. A twitch of muscle, a tic of the eye, a nonned tiny things that only visants notice. It can't be that my powers only work at home. How could that be? It's because I don't know you. I just met you. Let me know you, let me watch you, I can help you once I learn what to look for, please, shielder, give me a chance. . . ."

She grasped the visant's wrist to halt the flood.

"What?" he whispered, leaning down.

Her lips parted.

"My name? Ioli," he said. His tongue tripped over his family name and left it where it lay. "Ioli . . . from the Toes. I don't have a shieldname yet."

"Go home before they give you one," Cett said. "Go home, Ioli. Maybe it hasn't stained you yet."

His look of accusation only made her hate him. *I can't go home,* it said. *You know that.* As though it were her doing.

"Then go somewhere else—but you can't stay here. Go on, get!" Her growl was made hideous by the terrible things happening inside her body. "You're no good to us, you puking useless walleye. Get out of here! Go!"

He just stared at her. Mindlight—hah! They were supposed to be so smart, these visants, and he just stood there, rejected, still trying to take in that rice plants couldn't root in sand. Know her, indeed. Know her innermost thoughts, her innermost fears. Did he think she would *allow* that? Did he think for one moment that she would permit such intrusion ever again, even if it meant her death? *Even if she was one of them?*

All the powers of self let you down, in the end. *Should have expected it. Only things you can trust are stropped iron and a good ash shield. And death.*

A thick vertical line bisected her vision. For a moment it was as though the world had truly split in two. Then it was as though her chest had split in two. Her arms spasmed, her hips bucked, her legs kicked out into a sprawl; she gasped; and only once she had reacted to it did she feel the penetration, a numbing punch, an agony of impact. Death had courted her for a long time, but she hadn't expected to be swept to climax with such abruptness. The spear that pinned her stretched six feet up, like a rope deployed to haul her cloudward; when she raised her head, its shaft, scant fingers from her nose, gave the world a left side and a right side, a right side and a wrong side. Which one was she on? Those who killed were on the wrong side. Those who killed were sent to the wrong side, expelled from Eiden Myr, made peripheral, exiled to none's-land and thence to death. Those who came to the wrong side became killers. *Had* she killed? She wished she knew. Had she answered delusion with murder? *If I did,* she said to the spear that impaled her, *then I deserved you long ago.*

Cett knew there was no spear. But the spear was real. The agony was real. The guilt was real. The two-sided world was real—both sides of it. Now, because all things of power came in threes, she would be treated to a view of the third side. That was the least her death could buy her. That glimpse.

She saw the visant staring at her mouthing pleas of forgiveness *too late too late beyond that now save your rancid breath you worthless scab* and a touch hurrying to her side *too late too late you cannot get to me in time it pierced my heart no more no more no more* and a triad taking note of her *too late too late I'm a haunt already how could children have the wisdom to cast passage.*

Then they, too, were gone, the remnants of her shield and her belief, and Cett Turnheart drew her last breath alone in a lowland marsh on a gently overcast day, with seasparrows bickering in the bayberries, a pair of sand rats packing food into a burrow, dowitchers sailing the inverted sea of clouds, and the edge of none's-land a gossamer scrim, her distant home secure beyond it.

The last thing she saw in the realm of flesh was the soft shimmer of the threshold, fading away.

1

Aiden's Eyes

❧

On one knee beside the shielder's body, Ioli reached tentative fingers to slide her eyelids down. The irises were a vivid cerulean, set in pale skin under blue-black bangs. It was sad to shutter them. Worse to leave them staring.

"Did you *see* that?"

The younger girl. He saw the tic in the muscles over her cheekbones without raising his gaze. As if her skin, stretched tight by hunger, kept trying to shrug back into place. It gave a blinking, dazed impression, made worse by a perpetual gape. He didn't remember her name, though the Greasehair had told him. She'd been the last to join them. He didn't remember the others' names, either, the older girl who wouldn't stop laughing and the boy who kept running off and coming back. Now they were the only ones left.

"I saw it," he said. *There were six people alive wearing colored bands, and four with no bands on them, and two bladed, and then us. Now we're alive, and those dozen are not.*

"I mean, did you *see* it? Do you *see* this?"

Those dozen, and dozens more already dead. Carnage was everywhere. Bones were everywhere. Bodies in all stages of decay. He'd seen it all earlier. He saw it now without looking. Looking made him dizzy. He swallowed his gorge against the stench. Whatever madness claimed this place, it kept the bonefolk off. No corpse had been passaged here since the war of the coast began.

The corpses were whole. Animals and weather had scattered some of the oldest bones, but even those showed no sign of violence. No nicks from blades, no dismemberment. Berserker palsy, walking marsh fever? They'd had touches, and mages. No illness came on so fast that touches couldn't cure it. Injury, then? A skull cracked open when a fall bashed it on a crate, a fall taken in a headlong, blind-terror dash for safety? The way they looked at the sky, ducked down, covered themselves, hid behind things when they could . . . they were terrified. Hearts could fail so fast no mage or touch could save them. Terror strong enough, suffered long enough, might do that to the strongest heart.

I'm not a seeker, Ioli thought. *I'm not a mender. I don't solve mysteries. I don't care what happened.*

The other girl had paused in her incessant giggling. Her eyes went wide and her hands came up to cover her mouth. "*We* didn't do this, did we?"

It was hard for Ioli to speak before he was ready. It wasn't complete in his head yet. He didn't like saying snatches and fragments. He grated out, "It was an illness of the mind. Our minds are different. That saved our lives."

The girl pressed her lips together hard, then burst out laughing. "Different!" she cried. "Different!"

Ioli dug nails into his palms. She had the blue glow. She was like him. She shouldn't make him speak before he was ready. He hated people laughing at him. But she wasn't laughing at him. She was laughing at a world so mad that it was the only response she could give. She wasn't like him, not at all. No more than the boy was like him because they were boys.

You bleeding walleyes, the shielder had said. *Puking useless walleyes.* And, *Go. Before it stains you.* There was nothing they could do here. They were visants, good for nothing but seeing truths that made people hate them. They couldn't *do* things, like touches or mages, make or heal or ward. They couldn't make sense of things, like menders or seekers or scholars. They

couldn't fight like shielders or build like crafters and they even
made animals skittish. They were useless, here as everywhere
else, and they should go, now, quick, before none's-land
stained them.

The younger boy, the one who could never bring himself to
run away, was trying again. Creeping from bank to tuft to
crate to tent. Mumbling to himself. Ioli felt his light; it was
dark in hue, darker than the one girl's robin's-egg and the
other's evening sky. Ioli would have seen him anyway, from
the edge of his eye, but anyone looking toward him would
have noticed him, too, because he hid so large and mumbled
so loud.

The gaping girl whirled toward the hideabout boy. "Do you
see that?"

"Yes, I see it!" Ioli shouted, starting to rise, and the insides
of his head turned upside down and his stomach lurched, and he
sat hard on the waterlogged ground, between the shielder and a
fly-haunted corpse.

Being here was like being blind. Like waking up in someone
else's body. He didn't feel right in it. He didn't know how to
move and do and *be* in it. At home, he could *see*. Interpret his
surroundings without thought. Here there was so much to
watch that he couldn't see at all. Distance was an assault. The
jungle was a close, crowded place, a place with heights and
depths. This flat land under flat sky had only extent. It made
him close down into himself. To stand and look around was too
much effort. He wanted to hide, cling, burrow. He would fly
free in the windless air, nothing to anchor, nothing to orient; he
would be crushed under the heavy plate of sky, consumed by
the unspeakable sea. How did the sky stay up with no great
trees to support it? What kept the sea at bay? Why didn't the
expanse of landscape curl up into itself? Earth and air and water were incomprehensible in this configuration. They made no
sense.

He looked at the shielder. He felt all right when he looked at
her. She had lived in this landscape for a long time. It was as familiar as her own limbs. She had seen things that he could not

see, and seeing was the only thing he *did*. She'd died before he had a chance to learn them through her eyes.

The girl he had shouted at was poking him, then dancing away. At the next poke, he flung out a spastic arm, but failed to hit her. She took it for response, and said, "Maybe if we stay here long enough, we'll start seeing things too."

The hideabout boy crawled out from under a stained canvas tarp and hid behind Ioli.

No, he thought. *We won't.* They were immune to the delusions that killed these people. Because they were visants.

He looked at the shielder's corpse as if it might tell him something, but it was cooling and still. So wrong, that stillness. He averted his eyes to a collection of bones sunken into the marsh in the shape of a human body. An older death than hers, and not so hard to look at.

She could have conquered her fear of the delusions. She had started to reach for something. Someone she thought was standing by her. Someone not him; he was on the other side and past arm's length. She had reached for that clarity. The bluesilver light had flared in her—very dim, nearly below the threshold of sight, but visible. She had denied it. Let her splayed hand fall limp. Denied him, too. Ordered him away. That was when the convulsions took her. She'd gripped life so hard that it killed her. She'd driven her light so deep that delusion had claimed her. Her body had reacted so plausibly that he could almost see the weapon she believed had pierced her, and he had never seen a blade or anything else kill a person.

At the last, just before her eyes glazed over, he'd seen the glow again.

As death dissolved her will, her thought, the bluesilver glow had surged.

Knowing wasn't thinking. Knowing wasn't feeling. Knowing wasn't figuring-it-out. Knowing wasn't even seeing, not really, not completely. Not the way people said. What Ioli could do, what Ioli could know, there was no term for. It was a wordless thing. It couldn't be explained. It couldn't be described. It couldn't be taught.

It couldn't be forced. Pressing your mind against a thing made it slip away, soap clutched too tight. Concentration brought you down to a point, made you dense and hard and tiny. Knowing was suspension, dissipation. Knowing was a mist of awareness hanging in the air.

The shielder had glanced inland from time to time. What had she been looking at? Or for? Folk spoke of a threshold, as if they knew how close they could come to the coast without tainting themselves. As though there were some kind of wall, invisible but sensible.

Looking at the sunken bones, with the shielder's body at the edge of his vision, he *knew*. "We have to close the ranks," he said, raising his head to the others so abruptly that they flinched. "We have to tell the shield to either side that this section has failed!"

The older girl looked at him google-eyed and then laughed so hard she had to hold her belly, as if her guts might burst out. He wanted to shake her, give her a slap, and was appalled at the impulse. No wonder visants were scorned as idiots. Some of them *were*. He got to his feet, fighting vertigo, and snatched at the scared boy's sleeve. "You." He tried to make his voice like the shielder's, full of menace and command, a voice you obeyed. He cleared his throat hard, pushed authority through it: "Go Heartward. That way, along the maurside. See? Tell them the shield here has failed. Tell them they're all dead. Tell them they have to close ranks. Do you understand? Do you see what's needed?"

The boy cowered away, elbows up and forearms pressed to his ears, hiding, blocking out Ioli's words. *I can't see you I can't hear you I can't see you I can't hear you.* Ioli recognized himself in that, and bit his lip as the boy wrenched away to clamber behind a listing catapult.

"I see," the gaper offered. Her mouth fell open again after she said it. Possibly her mouth just never closed. Her dark eyes were grave and committed.

The other girl pointed Legward and turned a tear-streaked, beaming face to him, as though her gesture indicated something so funny she couldn't even speak.

"Yes," he said, "go that way, give them the message. Close ranks."

"Ranks!" she gasped, hands flying to cover her mouth, as though he'd uttered an obscenity. Then she erupted into laughter that sounded like pain.

"Yes. Ranks. Close ranks." He had to raise his voice to be heard over her hilarity. "Send more shielders, whatever they can spare." *Send more shielders to their deaths. But they'll die where they are just as surely. And that's their sworn duty. To protect. To be a human shield.*

Suddenly dead serious, the giggler said into a shock of quiet, "Two leagues, two miles, half a nonned feet each way Legward. Two nonned nonned steps for us, two nonned nonned steps back for them. Maybe more Heartward. Not in time." Done with her gleaning, she began to laugh again. "It won't be in time!"

Herded here by Fyldur Greasehair, they had passed several downleg shieldposts. Her visant's eye would have gauged the distance to every one, down to the fingerwidth. "Go anyway," he said. "It's all we can do. Go on, both of you. I'll see if I can find help inland." *Become a procurer, like the Greasehair. That was worse than summoning shielder reinforcements. That was pulling the unstained over the threshold. But the shield could not be allowed to fail. He had pledged himself to that when he went with the Greasehair.*

Where *was* the Greasehair? Where was he when you needed him? Maybe he'd gone to get more people, effectual people, not visants but mages or touches or blades, people who could *be* of some help, if only to become fodder for madness.

He wasn't here now. Ioli would have to go for help himself.

I don't want to save the world. . . .

"Go," he said, and the two visants took off at their best pace in opposite directions, leaving only him and the hideabout boy.

Ioli tried to turn toward him, but the boy kept moving to stay behind his back. Over his shoulder, Ioli said, "I have to go too." After a moment, he added, "We both have to go. You can't stay here. They'll want to use you, any others who come, and neither of us is any use here." He could feel hesitation like heat against his spine. Then a hand took hold of his tattered tunic sash. To make sure Ioli didn't trick him and turn him out of hiding. "I won't hurt you," Ioli said. "But I can't take care of you." He felt the smaller visant shrink further, but couldn't tell what it meant. Ioli wished he would let go. He didn't like being hung on to. Gritting his teeth, he said, "I can't help you."

The hand slid away. When he turned—slowly, because he didn't mean to scare or trick—the hideabout boy was gone. His dark blue glow was like a scent with no obvious source. For the first time, he'd actually managed to hide.

"I'm sorry!" Ioli called. "I'm sorry I'm not the kind of person who could look after you! I hope you'll be all right!"

There was no answer. Only birdchatter and seamurmur, the grainy hiss of loose sand through cordgrass, the hollow sound of distance and vastness, as though only he remained in all the empty, alien world.

The salt marsh was a blur. Details refused to cohere. He could focus on immediate things—the flooded ditch, the vole's burrow, the tree whose unique shape could restore lost bearings—but he could not hold all of it in his mind at once, and so he could not let it fall below conscious thought.

All right, then. Be conscious of it. But walk. Move.

He made his way, step by concentrated step, to where the shielder had looked every time she glanced back. He didn't feel any difference there, even when he was well past the point where her eyes had focused. With each step he got a little better at the marsh, a little less hobbled by unfamiliarity, but it granted him no more sense of delusion's boundary than he'd had of delusion itself. With each step he could hold one more blade of saltgrass in his mind without thinking on it. With each step the weight of flat sky infinitesimally eased. It helped to leave the sea behind. The sea was more than he could bear. Here, a little inland, at least most of what surrounded him was based in earth, not water. The tendrils of sea that came in were not so vast or unpredictable. Earth held them in their place. He could treat them like swamp rivers, and navigate among them. It didn't turn his insides over to see a lone saltmonger plying his trade on the water's edge.

What did turn his insides over was the choice he had to make. Procure the man, conscript him into none's-land, lure him or coax him or bully him over the threshold, to hold the line until the shield closed ranks?

He stopped, uncertain. He dared not go much farther inland; he'd lose sight of the coast entirely, and never know when the ranks had closed. But the girl had told the number of steps to the nearest shieldpost. It would take the rest of the day to make all those steps. He didn't have to choose this one. He could go on—to one of those sod cottages up there, with smoke rising from their chimneys. Give them his news, ask for their aid, let them take the burden of choice, of sacrifice, upon themselves. He was no talker. He would never talk anyone into exile. But he could tell them what he knew and let them choose.

The saltmonger started to raise a hand in greeting, then frowned and let the hand fall. He didn't sniff the air, but he might as well have. He could scent the stain of exile on Ioli as though it were the rankest midden runoff. He hefted his tool, considering whether to send Ioli back coastward, considering whether it was his place to bother with runaway exiles. He decided that Ioli was too far away to be herded, and glanced back toward the cottages on firmer ground. Someone there would catch him. He was too old-boned to hare after deserters, too busy earning a day's honest living to chase down cowards.

Ioli had never been scorned as a coward before, for all he'd run from his own village into self-imposed exile in the jungle. For more than a breath, it made him reconsider his decision to overlook the old saltmonger. He might walk right up and tell him the truth—dare him to prove how brave he was when the safety of his own land was at stake, when there was no shield there anymore to sacrifice itself that he might stand in contempt of it. Would he have the courage to sacrifice himself like that, if forced to the choice?

The saltmonger twisted and let out a shriek.

No, no, Ioli thought. Seeing what, knowing how, not yet arrived at why.

Cottagers were stopping their work, calling others out from inside, pointing. Consternation, not fear. Curiosity merging into concern. Not terror. Not the horror that twisted the face and body of the saltmonger as he raised his ineffectual tool against some phantasm Ioli could not imagine.

The man thrust forward and upward with the dredging tool, then swept the air before him. He was a wiry old man, strong with a lifetime of work, and fierce, but his old heart would not withstand this sort of battle. Ioli's foot came down, his other foot went past it, he was moving toward the man to tell him *no it isn't real don't fight it don't harm yourself,* moving to reassure, his arms opening with some notion of capturing those wiry limbs and holding him still until the assault abated. Something, he must do something. The man was flailing, panting. Too many threfts between them.

Two of the cottagers set off running. One to aid the saltmonger, one to intercept Ioli, because as far as they knew he was the cause of this, and good folk reacted to emergencies, good folk took action, good folk didn't cower in their jungle trees and say *I don't have to save my neighbor today.*

Ioli ran, too. He was closer to the saltmonger. In the space of six running steps all of his guilts swept through him. His cowardice. His anger at an old man who was fighting now for his life and defense of his home as bravely as ever any bladed shielder had.

The marsh betrayed him. A sunken wet spot sucked his leg down. He went to his knee. Grass sliced his hands. His palms slapped flat onto a surface of muck. His own struggle to rise drove him deeper into the sinkhole. He could only watch, trapped, as the old man fought the phantasms. The man shouted over his shoulder for the cottagers to take cover in their homes.

The two would-be rescuers stopped halfway. Confusion. Indecision. Continue forward, or go back as ordered, defend their families closer to home? They looked to each other for guidance, failed to find any. "Go back!" Ioli yelled to them, despairing. He knew they would not heed him, and they did not.

The old man went down under a flurry of invisible attacks. He twitched, moaned, then was still. His heart had given out.

The rescuers were still threfts away; Ioli could not gauge the distance, but they were far enough that the delusion had not affected them. They were reacting to the incomprehensible behavior of the saltmonger, the tainted stranger's shout. They were safe, where they were. Far enough inland to be safe.

"Go back," Ioli moaned. He could not push or draw good living souls into this madness. He slowed down, extricated himself from the morass, scooted back onto solid ground. All the while watching the rescuers and the cottagers beyond them as if his will alone could keep them from crossing the invisible line.

As if watching, alone, could ever do any good, had ever done any good.

He nearly cried when the rescuers, a solid young woman and limber young man, went still in shock, faces drained of blood, jaws fallen slack. Their dawning horror was so genuine that Ioli, even knowing better, nearly twisted to look over his shoulder at the sky. He would see nothing there. Whatever they saw, hurtling toward them, doubled the man over and then knocked him onto his side in a writhing ball, and drove the woman to the ground.

Tended ground. Inland ground the delusions of none's-land had never touched. The madness was moving inland.

Ioli gained his feet and walked to the edge of the tended beds. He walked between them with as much care as he could, not sure where he could step and where he couldn't. He had to try to help. He was helpless, but he had to try. If he could save these two, if he could save *one* of these two . . .

He made it to the woman, but she was dead before he turned her face to the sky that had not attacked her.

He stood on shaky legs to wave the cottagers off. *Back!* his desperate arms said. *Back! It's not safe here!* Two men caught another man in their arms and hauled him away from an at-

tempt at rescue. Ioli turned, and stumbled, and crawled to the
young man, who lay on his left side, curled around his middle.
Blood dribbled from the corner of his mouth. His eyes, when
Ioli knelt beside him, were terrified and pleading. He did not
know if Ioli was friend or foe. "I want to help," Ioli said. Oh, he
was not good at words. The young man scented the taint on
him, but it seemed to make him hopeful, as though Ioli, experienced in battle, might help him survive this. To his senses, the
taint would seem salvation now that he realized the war had
overflowed its banks.

Ioli could do nothing. The young man died curled against his
thighs, on a gush of blood and the reek of effluents.

Helpless. Useless. Every movement a supreme effort, Ioli sat
the dead man up, leaned down to take him over his shoulders.
The cottagers were digging in, putting their panicked energy into
collecting makeshift weapons and sandbagging the field's home-
ward border. Making a new, inland shieldwall, Ioli saw as he began the agonized trudge to bring the first of their dead to them.
The only thing he could do. Fetch the dead, like a boneman.

He stopped in his tracks when the first of them pointed past
him.

They all covered their heads at the same time, then looked
behind them at their homes. One ran to fetch a bucket; another
followed; a water brigade formed. They began drenching their
sedge-thatched roofs. Roofs that stood serene and untouched by
flame. In their world of blooming delusion, balls of fire had set
their homes ablaze.

It should have been ludicrous. Ioli should be laughing the
way the giggling girl had laughed, uncontrollably, past articulation. He understood now why she had laughed, just as he understood why the gaper had gaped and the hideabout boy had
hidden. In a moment of queerest clarity, he understood why
folk gaped at visants, and laughed at them, and avoided them.
To ordinary, common folk, visants' words and deeds appeared
as mad as these, because they were reacting to things that ordinary, common folk could not see.

He laid the heavy body down gently and girded his resolve against despair. He could see himself chasing just behind the inland-sweeping boundary of none's-land, crying out that it was not real, crying out not to let it kill, always too late, always unheeded, always in vain. He was not a seer of futures, he didn't think any visants were, but that future was clear enough in his mind's eye. Even if he outran the front of it to bring advance warning, nobody would believe him.

He turned one last time toward the coast, wondering if he might better serve by going back and convincing the shield of what he knew. Then he turned again. The shield had held for three years; these cottagers might hold for long enough for him to convince them. They had seen the effects of delusion from the outside. Forearmed, they might fight them off from the inside, with someone to make it clear to them. They'd seen him try to help the old saltmonger, wave them back from the danger, start to bring their dead to them. They'd forgive him the stain because they'd be stained now, too; none's-land had engulfed them. They might heed him. He might be able to make them see.

He stood for a long time, unable to decide which course to take. He watched them fight their fires and win. He watched with increasing hope as they mimed a successful defense against impossible odds. They were beginning to think they might survive till nightfall. They were beginning to believe these weapons didn't always kill them. That was a foothold. That was a grand foothold from which to persuade them that what killed them wasn't the weapons but their own belief that they were dying.

He might have a chance.

They faltered. They let their weapons drop. They stood up behind their sandbagged wall and looked about in wonder. He almost broke into a run, to warn them—sometimes the assaults subsided for a while but they must not lose vigilance—and nearly barked a laugh. The insanity of it! Entering into the delusion. Warning them that the things that weren't happening had only seemed to stop but might soon start not-happening again.

They turned in bewilderment to their whole, unscathed cottages, touched wet thatching that flame had never touched, ran hands over solid walls they must have thought were breached.

Their sight had cleared, all of its own. Could ordinary folk summon immunity to the madness? Could others learn it?

He turned reflexively back toward the coast, as if to compare in his mental landscape the two different scenarios, the cottagers recovering versus the shield failing. Looking for the similarities, looking for the differences, as if he would find them in the blank flat distance of the marshland itself.

And then he saw.

Small human forms, just at the limit of vision in the coastward direction. What he took at first for an enormous, walking tree draped in vines like something out of his jungle home. Flaming balls and spiked iron whipchains arcing high into the sky. *It's got me,* he thought. *I stayed too long, and now I'm seeing things.* But the weapons arcing into the sky were on a seaward trajectory. The monstrous walking jungle tree was the rigging-draped mast of a ship. The human forms were the shielders the ship had delivered, in half the time it would have taken for them to take all the gaper's steps.

The shield had closed ranks.

He looked at the cottagers again. Looked down at the dead young man he'd laid on the ground, at the dead young woman, the dead old man. Too late for them. Death did not ebb like madness. But the cottagers were free of it now. And running toward him, and their dead. Taking him in hand. Wailing over their loved ones. Treating him roughly, demanding explanations they did not believe when he gave them. "Those are the weapons the outerlands send," he said, "weapons of delusion, weapons of madness, and what kills you is your own fright of them," and they thrust him loose in response, shoved him off and his taint with him, told him to go back to the shield, take his mad visant ravings and leave them to make sense of the terrible palsy that took their folk.

Ioli went off as he was told. They were coarse, not cruel. They didn't vent their grief and bewilderment in more than harsh words and a shove or two. But he stayed, for a bit. Hidden off to the side. Watching the shield reassert itself in the distance, with its missiles of spike and flame, the drifting smoke of its incendiary powders, the distant sound of orders shouted over an imaginary din. Watching the cottagers react to none of it, as they piled their sandbags off to the side in the event of flood come storm season, returned their sometime weapons to their toolsheds and forges and hearths. Watching, as dusk came on, the green glow of bonefolk feeding, passaging the three bodies to some otherrealm for safekeeping against no one knew what day.

Before he lost the light, he found his landmark tree, a twistedness in the gloaming, and climbed it, handhold by weary handhold. The night wind blew the clouds to sea. It was Candlenight tonight, a time for spirits to roam, and nearly the spirit days, with the moon carved to a sliver by the darkness; in the Toes, tomorrow would be the start of winter. Up here, he didn't know, except that it was harvestmid, and would remain so until Longdark.

Sound carried clearly from shoreward in the nighttime quiet. Catapults sang thunder. Ranks of bows twanged in a humming unison. The sky lit with unnatural fire. The screams began.

Hidden in his alien, inadequate tree, Ioli looked out into darkness and distance.

The shield had closed the gap, and the delusion had dissipated as though it had never been, save for the bodies of the three its first shock had taken, and those the bonefolk took, though they'd left three years' worth of dead to weather and wildlife less than a mile coastward.

The shielders were taking an arrow for Eiden Myr.

All fighters vowed to stand between the enemy and their home. All fighters vowed to die for Eiden Myr. This was more than that, different from that. Had they brought it on themselves through some perversity of the stained? Had they manufactured the deaths they'd promised? No; the cottagers had fallen, the saltmonger had fallen. The delusions were no doing of the shield.

Ioli remembered when the first mirages were reported. A dozen years ago, just after the revelation of touches and the rebirth of magelight—just after Jhoss n'Kall had betrayed the visants. Ioli had been a boy then, but tellers told the stories around every village fire. On the coast of the Fist, a young shielder girl saw a ship that never made landfall; her commander saw invasion that never arrived. In the Fingers, a pair of boys saw banks of oared vessels rowed by monsters. Nonneds saw the tall black ships with black silk sails come at the mouth of Maur Lengra belching fire. Every village on the Sea of Charms saw the fleets that massed there, the gleaming blades of their prows, the bone white of their hulls, their jeering, deformed crews.

None of them real, none at all, at least not real enough to threaten, always veering off as though at the last moment Eiden Myr had moved. Seekers were wild with theories, menders wild with frustration; scholars could find nothing like it in the old records. The sightings continued, unexplained except as shared hallucination, and neither touches nor mages could heal madness.

Then the attacks began.

They did not come from the mirages. They came from nowhere, or otherwhere, all at once. No ninemile stretch of coast was left unscarred.

No ninemile stretch of coast was caught unguarded. The shielders had maintained their posts since the magewar. They evacuated the shoreline. They reinforced their emplacements and called up their reserves. In response to siege, they built siege retorts. They mobilized with astonishing speed.

Such speed, Ioli realized, that no one had understood that the attacks were only on their minds.

The shield had waited twice nine years to fight. The shield expected to fight. Everyone expected the shield to fight. The shield fought, and did not yield. It gave no ground, no matter the losses. It held the line.

The leader of his fallen section of shield had kept glancing back, as at a threshold.

Inlanders conceived the border of none's-land as a point of no return: cross it and you were tainted, stained. That repressed visant shielder, from her viewpoint on the far side, conceived the border of none's-land as a threshold of safety.

All fighters were trained to stand their ground. If the monstrosities on the mirage ships ever landed, only the shield would stand between Eiden Myr and their blades and fangs and claws. But the missiles of delusion were aimed at the coast. They ravaged where they fell and did not pursue. Why not fall back beyond their reach?

The shielders stored materials beyond the threshold—Ioli had seen that. In their delusion, crates stacked far enough back were left unscathed in each attack. They tethered their riding and draft animals there. But the shield never fell back.

There could be some obvious reason he failed to apprehend. He was not a shielder. He was not a mender or a scholar or a seeker. Perhaps some mender, even some visant, had calculated the arc of attacking missiles and determined that the shield's archers and catapults could reach the missiles' point of origin only if positioned at the sea's edge. Perhaps their delusions sometimes included attacks that blades and arrows could parry; that would be a crueler weapon, teasing them with intermittent victories.

Or perhaps their shielder honor forbade it. Perhaps their training instilled in them such pride that even to think of yielding became anathema.

Perhaps some shielder, at the outset, in the first days of the war of the coast, had designed that training with full awareness, realizing what Ioli realized now: The shield created none's-land, and maintained it. If the shield fell back, *the threshold would go with it.* The attacks would follow them inland.

The shield here had failed, and the attacks had come inland, mind by mind, seeking consciousness, seeking sentience and warping it. When the shield re-formed, the inlanders' delusions evaporated.

The attacks stopped at the first minds they found. As long as the weapons of delusion found minds to harm, they sought no further.

The shield must hold, or village after village would fall to delusion, until Eiden Myr was ravaged from coast to coast. It would be worse than giving ground to a berserker horde. A physical enemy could be routed. This enemy could only be appeased.

Shielders did not come in infinite numbers. They were dying too fast for replacement. As the ranks of those stained by previous battles thinned, as procurers drained the land of those who could be coaxed into exile, the well of sacrifice would run dry.

His section of shield had fallen. Other sections would follow. The shield could not hold.

Those weapons had to be stopped another way.

Ioli slept in his bent tree, and at dawn, with the bent moon still hanging in the Headward sky, he climbed back down into the world, to save it.

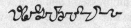

THE LEAD SHIELDER raised her left arm high. "First retort, two hands Headward, release on my signal!" Her hard gaze tracked the incoming mass. From afar it appeared to be a billow of smoke around a core of flaming solid, but it moved like an insect swarm. She had been watching these things half the night. It would sweep across her field of view, hover, come back partway, then rise abruptly and launch itself at a steep downward angle.

Trying to come in over their heads. The visants she had arrayed along the lip of her seacliff post, contrary to every instinct to place only shielders at the battlefront, were the cause. A brilliant strategy, until it failed. But the lead seeker had observed that the weapons failed to learn. Different each day, sometimes different in morning from in afternoon or night, they were nevertheless, for a short time, predictable.

And they did not have a taste for visants.

The weapons, though they had seemed imbued from the beginning with an ineffable intelligence, could not adapt to changes in tactics. Her people had only to survive one incidence of each new assault, or two, or three—however many it took for her menders to divine weakness and develop a best-guess response. Then it became a fight rather than a slaughter. Then, each day, each noon, each night, they had another fighting chance to live.

"Now!" she shouted, signaling with a downward sweep of fist.

The torsion engine launched with a mighty crash, ash beam into a cradle of tarred flaxwool folds on a bonewood brace, the frame magecast for flexibility and shock-tolerance. The projectile it delivered to the attacking mass was magecast as well.

Her lips pulled back in grim satisfaction as the retort sailed directly into the path of the mass's dive. Just before retort met gibe, ties around compressed coils gave way inside the simple burlap sack. It burst into a spray of simple wood chips, blooming to fill the billowing swarm.

That ought to give it some indigestion.

The first fireswarm had swept straight in at midnight, resolving on impact not into smoke or tacks or drops of acid, but into needled flame that pierced and charred any flesh it found. Two shielders and a scholar lay dead to prove it. Their corpses were a mangled mess of black and red five threfts away. Their screams still echoed in her mind.

Their deaths would not be in vain if the shield learned from them.

Mages firewarded homes and smithies and forests as a matter of rote. Mages had cast durability into tools and walls for generations. This night her lead mage had led his triad in a brand-new inversion of those castings. The chunks of pine that spread to fill the fiery needled swarm were steeped in vulnerability.

An invitation to be pierced and set aflame.

The lead shielder did not understand how it worked. She did not understand the medium of spirit through which the mages cast, any more than she understood how the touches worked through their medium of matter, or anything the visants saw. She understood weapons and how to use them.

This fireswarm spent itself on the sacrificial offering; the gibe attacked and consumed the retort in a violent pop and crackle of eye-searing flame, devolving into a spectacular rain of sparks, then a harmless shower of spined charcoal spinning to ground like a flock of child's whirligigs.

A second swarm was massing at the limit of sight, maurward this time. To her left, launchers were partway through the process of resetting the retort, the rhythm of their low chant blending with the groaning torque of the skein. Behind her, she did not yet hear the sound of bindsong rising as mages cast on a second sack of pine chips. The time that castings took was a persistent logistical hindrance. But they'd had time for two castings before that last swarm had arrived. She had not wholly trusted in the reliability of the first retort. She raised her right fist. "Second retort!" she called to her archers. "On my signal!" The creak of yew bending and horsehair singing tight was a melody more beautiful to her shielder's ears than bindsong.

"One hand maurward," she called, eyes fixed on the approaching swarm. If it moved Headward just so far, then doubled back, and dipped, and hovered . . . "Two fingers up!" she cried suddenly, and, fist plummeting, *"Let fly!"*

A flight of magecast arrows tore the sky, and took the swarm before the breakpoint of their arc. Too soon, too fast—they'd fly straight through before the swarm could react, she should have positioned her bowfolk farther back, she'd been wary of stray arrows hitting her visants but she hadn't reckoned the speed of flight when increased by the forward speed of the diving swarm—

The swarm contracted down to a dozen writhing spears and whipped away as though jerked on tethers—or as though the arrows had caught on something like fabric and dragged it with them over the water. It was the swarm, reacting faster than any living matter possibly could have. Pouncing on the arrows, irresistibly attracted by the magecast quality of wooden heads and shafts and tender fletching, all begging to be pierced, begging to be burned.

Fewer in number and lesser in mass than the pine chips, the arrows left no ashy cinders to twirl groundward, but went out in silver-white streaks over the sea, nothing left but a puff of dark dust that drifted onto the waters.

Now came the bindsong from behind her, a queer, gut-turning sound, magecraft done upside down and backward. This magecraft-in-reverse made her uneasy. It was ill use of a power meant for gentler things. She believed the advent of battle magecraft was at the root of their exile, not the shield's blades or retorts. But that was not her province; darkcraft had been available to mages since the days of the old Ennead. She had to trust her mages to wield their powers rightly. Here on the edge of doom the only right was what kept the shield alive to defend another day.

"Ready to load!" came the call from the reset retort. She didn't need to look; she heard the clacking of sacked wood chips placed in the sling. "Loaded!"

Her eyes had not left the newest mass as it swarmed in from its unknown senders. There was something subtly different about this one. She let it dance its way across, double back, called an adjustment to the retort; her raised arm twitched, her fist clenched; but something made her wait. The swarm veered sidewise, then far to the right, dipped down, swept up, doubled back high—

"*Now!*" she roared, and the retort kicked its answer into the sky. The coil released, the burlap disintegrated, the pine decoys spread high and wide . . . and just as they began to fall, just as it seemed she had misjudged this one and called the launch too soon, the swarm of flaming, needled death stooped like a flock of raptors—and obliterated the spread of wood chips in a glorious, glittering spray. Beyond it, the night sky was clear of threat.

A cheer went up from the shield.

She let them shout, congratulate each other, dance their jigs, hurl their taunts and ugly gestures seaward. She let them laugh their tension out, howl their victory and contempt at an enemy they would never see. Meanwhile, she watched the horizon as she had watched it for a dozen years.

She ignored the mirages. Night or day, they were always there. Strange, alien craft in raft-ups larger than towns. Lone vessels sailing under the stars, steering well clear of the raft-ups; drifting hulks with tattered sails and skeletal masts and spars; fast, wicked warships, maneuverable as coasters and propelled by oars under billowing square sails emblazoned with cryptic sigils. Fleets and flotillas and solitary wanderers, a sea full of mysterious craft that went about their mysterious business. Haunts of another time, some said.

She knew otherwise. She had been the first to see one.

In the far distance, dotting the shores and hills of the nearest of the outerlands, bonfires burned, so large they could be seen even from here. She did not know what it meant.

The mirages had not attacked in years, and when they had, it was an attack of insane trajectory, as though they were heading for a land off-kilter, a land that lay not quite where Eiden Myr lay on the sea. They were no threat, though the shield had kept watch on them through nine years of peace and safety in the reborn light, its only reason for not disbanding during those years. And a good thing, that, for when the true war of the coast began—the siege launched in no relation to the seafaring spectres and no doing of theirs—the shield had been there to meet it.

The mirages were no more than seemings. Her eye had long ago learned to screen them out unless she was on spectre watch. Death didn't come from them. Death came from beyond them, from beyond the limits of sight, from an unseen foe. Death was no mirage.

Only when nine slow breaths had passed her lips and no further swarms massed out to sea did the lead shielder on the Forgotten Sea call her visants in from the brink, and turn to deliver to her folk the praise they'd earned.

"Well done!" she roared, with a grin to split her face; they would see the white flash of it even in the old moon's dimness.

Silently, she thought, *I thank the spirits for the gift of your life,* a silent benediction on each and every woman and man who shared this rocky promontory with her—who fought beside her on Galandra's ground to beat the darkness back from Eiden Myr.

Then—alone, as always, refusing all aid—Breida Shipseer carried the bodies of their dead to the cleared space at the border of the living, and delivered them out of horror, back to safe ground, where the bonefolk would come to passage them.

She always brought them home.

Breida n'Geara tore free from the shieldmaster's shocked grip on her shoulder and ran so close to the edge of the cliff that to an observer she would seem bent on hurling herself off.

Home. She's come home. She's come *home.*

No one else had seemed perturbed that her sister, seven years older, was the first to leave Eiden Myr by ship to see the outerlands. When the belated farewell message came, it held no secret, special words for Breida. No words of wisdom to guide her through her growing year . . . no apology for leaving her.

No goodbye in lieu of the one she had never come home to say.

It was five years, then, of repairing the war-torn village of Clondel, and rebuilding their family's public house, burned to the ground in the magewar; backbreaking work during the lightless years when every traveler might carry illness, any injury might fester into death. There was no time to watch for her sister as they raised a new Petrel's Rest from the ashes of the old. But Breida had never given up. Though the Petrel's Rest was a legacy of daughters, the summer she turned two nineyears of age she chose the shield. She watched for storms and she watched for invaders, because it allowed her to watch for Liath.

And so she had come here, to this rocky, forlorn place, to the very ground where the last triad had vanquished the old, corrupt Ennead—to Galandra's ground, where the first mage had cast the warding that isolated Eiden Myr from the outerlands. Here the Lightbreaker had broken that warding. Here, Verlein Shieldmaster believed, invasion would come from the old world, across the Forgotten Sea from the land that the persecuted mages had fled. The outerlands were all around them, as far as anyone knew, and Liath might arrive from any direction. But if you were a mage, Breida thought, and you were returning to the haven that mages made, this was where you'd land.

"It's her!" she cried to Verlein as the shieldmaster came up beside her. Her olive skin was blanched to gray, her green eyes narrowed to a hard squint. "It's her, it's my sister, look, the red hair at the tiller!"

"As red as yours," Verlein allowed. She had expected some longship manned to the rails, propelled by sweeps, bristling with spears. She'd said as much only breaths ago. This was a single vessel, rigged in a familiar style, a snub, deep-draft two-master such as they'd built along the High Arm before seagoing became a one-way trip and shipwrights fell to producing only coasters.

It wasn't the ship that Breida had imagined. But it was a ship that one could sail, and there was only one on deck, and her red wind-whipped hair was like a flag, the long wiry body unmistakable.

"It would be her," Verlein said, with a dark light in her eyes that Breida barely registered in her pent excitement. "And she would pick the hardest shore. Looks like she hasn't changed a bit." Turning to gesture a set of commands to the guard back in the post-house, she said, "She'll have to sail round to the cove if she wants to come ashore. Catch her eye, wave her round the point."

Breida was so busy jumping up and down and waving that she hardly cared when the shielder said, gazing out at the little ship, "And to think I didn't see the resemblance. What will the mageling make of her bladed little sister, and under my command?"

Breida could not get Liath's attention. Why wouldn't she look up? The Lightbreaker had died here, this was the cliff that crumbled and killed him and her friend the halfman, and she'd *loved them both more than life. Perhaps she'd set her gaze against it. Though drawn to Galandra's ground, perhaps she couldn't bring herself to look up at just that spot. Breida moved toward the cove and redoubled her waving.* "Liath!" *she shouted.* "Liath!" *How could she miss the sight and sound of someone leaping and waving and calling, how could that fail to catch her eye on a calm Ve Eiden with the sun just past noon?*

As if she's ignoring me on purpose, *Breida thought, then was ashamed. Perhaps neither of them had changed at all, perhaps Liath was still the girl who paid attention to her baby sister only when she wasn't caught up in her own concerns. But they were both grown now. Breida was as old as Liath had been when she first left to see the Ennead. She had proven herself. She would be a hero, too, one day, just like Liath, saving Eiden Myr from darkness.*

Why wouldn't her sister see her?

"Liath!" *she called, and called again, and refused to acknowledge the shieldmaster's frowning tension, refused to believe what her eyes told her: that the little ship, after tacking twice, was coming about.*

Heading back to sea.

"LIATH!" *she cried, despairing, a cry that would have carried over all the leagues and all the years right back into the old world itself, down through all the fathoms to the rocky bottom of the sea. A cry of disbelief and bereavement that had been building in her for years, ripped from her as though she were casting her own tormented heart out on the waters.*

The snub, two-masted ship caught a breeze off its aft port quarter, sails filling, boom extending till the mainsail stretched like a great white wing. Like a shard of shell set upright in the sea. This, now, was the ship Breida had imagined, one sail visible, one woman at the tiller.

In her vision, it had been sailing home. This ship was sailing off.

She didn't realize she had shouted herself raw, didn't understand why there were iron arms around her, crushing her own arms in tight, pulling her back from the cliff's edge, stopping her from harming herself, turning her, muffling her unshielderly sobs, until she heard Verlein's string of growled obscenities lower into gruff murmurs, felt Verlein's hand cup the back of her head the way Liath's used to. The winds must have been wrong, the shieldmaster said. The headwind off the point must have been too much. Like as not her sister would try again tomorrow.

Breida pulled herself together. Stepped away from the shieldmaster's incongruous, disquieting comfort. Turned for one last glimpse of sail as it pricked the horizon and was gone.

"She'll come back," the shieldmaster said. "If anyone can, it will be her."

Breida nodded. She wiped her face with a cloth wet from her water flask. She kept her eyes on the sea, taking up her shielder's vigil once more.

That was when they saw the second ship. The one Verlein had feared.

It was no more real than the first had been.

All illusion. The expectations of their hearts given shape; fears and longings given spectral form.

Liath was not coming home.

Breida Shipseer roamed her encampment, dispensing brandy and tea, soothing the troubled, cheering the desolate, encouraging the last of the victory celebrations. Good-humored and ribald, edged and stern, she maintained discipline with a grin and a ready fist. She encouraged ingenuity and demanded inspiration, met fear and grief with firm, unyielding sympathy, rewarded even the most minor courage. She inspired futile heroism, though it sometimes robbed her of the best of them. She had kept them mostly alive, and mostly sane, for three years. Clawing survival from impossibility, day after grinding day.

This post was where the war began and rumor held it would end. It was the place ambitious shielders came to prove themselves to the silence of the ages. But what made the Forgotten

Sea the most coveted posting in the shield was the leadership of
Breida Shipseer herself.

Long swaths of shoreline were losing a battle of attrition.
Anonymous deliveries from home were their only contact with
the inside, and those no contact at all, casks and crates left like
boneday tithes by unseen folk who would not come at all if
there were exiles near. Few inside cared for their plight or
worked to aid or save them. All shielders knew that. Unlike
other shielders, who had pledged themselves to sacrifice and
thus to doom, Breida harbored a fierce belief that there was a
way to defeat this craven, invisible foe. She didn't know if they
would discover it in time. The assaults might overwhelm them
first, the shield might fail for lack of numbers, inadequate logistical support, a host of other reasons. But she knew there was a
way to win, somehow. As she fed her folk and jollied them,
rested them and comforted them, encouraged their games and
entertainment, never let them stop being human, never let them
stop remembering what life was and why they had loved it
once, she never let them stop working toward that victory.

She ordered the watchfires banked in the approach of dawn.

The old moon had only one more night to live, after tonight;
it dangled from stars behind her, a sharp crescent over Eiden's
drowsing head, as she went to relieve the watcher by the cliff.
Thus far no attacks had come in the thin predawn hours, so she
always took that watch alone. There would be time for sleep
when she was passaged; like most shielders, she had learned to
catch winks here and there throughout the day, sometimes
standing propped by a spear or her kite shield. She took comfort from those familiar weapons, though they were of little use
here. On watch, she strolled the railed cliffside with only her
blades for comfort.

That railing wanted work. She'd have stewards on it at day-
break. Her lead steward was concerned at the dwindling tithes
of casting materials and other goods that were collected here
and dispensed to the four subordinate shieldposts on each side.
He'd suggested they procure a procurer, not to bring them more

lights or stewards but to petition local villages for better support. Breida didn't like the idea. She was proud that they attracted more volunteers than they could use, proud that they lost so few, proud that this was the glory posting and she could forgo the loathsome procurers. But it was a good idea. The locals had shunned her for two years. She was lucky they still sent firewood and flour. When they discussed the guardrail, she'd tell her steward to go ahead.

Running an absentminded finger along the braced banister, she found scored marks where the visants' fingernails had dug in. They'd been very frightened to be put at the front. She was proud that they had obeyed her orders without hesitation. It must be hard for them, unable to see the attacks. To be so miraculously sighted that they could count a bucket of stones at a glance and tell tomorrow's weather from the cant of a bird's wing, yet blind to the siege weapons . . . if it was agony, they bore it well. They'd been with her since the beginning, strange but stalwart Fist folk she'd befriended when she was first posted here under Verlein. Once they'd stopped denying the attacks and understood that the danger to others was real, they'd become the shield around the shield. They ringed mage triads to protect them with their siege-immune bluesilver light; they were the touches' extended hands and arms, pulling the wounded out of blast and flame to get them healed in time. They had been their village idiots and madmen, and she'd made them heroes; she did not know how she would bear it if a weapon ever came that could do them harm, but she put them in the fire's path every day. They feared only the cliff, the brink. This night she had posted them at that brink, and they had gone there for her, and hung on.

She gazed out over the dark waters, wavecaps paled by predawn glow, a growing chop that testified to a rising wind the visants had foretold. Where she stood, now, was where she had almost fallen from the unrailed cliff in her distress when Liath sailed away. Where Liath had almost fallen after her lost triad, and pulled Kazhe Blademaster, the Lightbreaker's bodyguard, back from the brink. Now Breida Shieldmaster had put a railing here to keep her people safe. It seemed a fitting though futile barrier against her private siege.

The ship was not there. Not on this watch. But it often appeared in the gray hours, the midder times, the breaths that fell between night and day. Approaching the cliffs, turning about at the last moment. As though Liath simply could not bear to bring herself home.

Or as though Breida could not bear to believe that she was not still trying.

Everyone saw the mirages. Even visants. She and Verlein had been the first, and both their visions—errant sister returned, invasion launched—had come to nothing. But thereafter other folk saw other ships, including the Eiden Myr ships that had set sail for the outerlands, full of exuberant explorers, seekers and journeyers free at last to sail beyond Galandra's shield. For six long years after the breaking they had not come home—and then they did, or tried, or seemed to try, but like Liath's ship their ships always turned, as though fighting a wrong-angled headwind or sighting on land that was not there. Thereafter other folk had seen other ships—attack ships, ships out of nightmare, bristling with weaponry, seething with monsters.

Everyone saw them. But they were not real. No invaders' arrows ever hit shielder targets; no invaders' flaming projectiles ever burned on Eiden's shore. Breida knew the difference between things that could kill you and things that could not. All the years of waiting for the outerlands to find them, of fearing, on some deep level, that the persecutors of old lurked out to sea and would swoop in and destroy them, had induced a sickness in the mind, an illness of the eyes. Death and madness were the only things that mages and touches could not heal, and visants were madness itself. The three lights could do nothing. The mirages were a collective insanity. The sum of all longings and all terrors given form.

And to her, a private torment. Time and again she had watched the ship draw near. She knew its lines, the rake of mast, the sweep of hull, the blunted prow with its battered figurehead. But it was only another spectre. Another ghost ship on the waters, making for land, never making landfall.

She bore her visions stolidly, alone in the slender hours, and never spoke of them. Not even to Verlein, though her mouth had opened at their parting, when Verlein had ceded this command to her and gone to take charge on the Sea of Sorrows. Letting Breida keep her watch. It made no difference; the visions would have come no matter what sea she looked out on. The convictions of Breida's childhood were long abandoned.

Liath would never come home. Wherever she was, drowned in the Forgotten Sea or lost in the outerlands, Liath could never go home.

Well, neither could she. At least in that they were together.

Breida had come to the end of the guardrail, near the tree-girt stony path that switchbacked down to the cove. So obvious, so unsubtle, the unconscious mind that had drawn her toward the moorings when she could just as well have patrolled the guardrail to the other end. She shook off her dark reverie and scanned the Forgotten Sea. Alien ships were drifting as in a drowse, unanchored. Distant bonfires were paling as dawn loomed over the back of Ollorawn's hills. The choppy sea had gone a pure, light blue under the wind-cleared sky. This was the sweetest time of day, this blush of dawn. This moment of stillness before the next assault came in under the rising sun.

Wearily, she turned for a glance at the encampment, to see if her relief was making his way to meet her at the center of the rail.

Her eye caught on something standing in the shadows of the cove path.

She caught herself with blade half-drawn, and stared.

Liath stared back at her.

Breida swallowed her heart, blinked hard, and said, "Well, this is a new one. No ship this time?"

The apparition made no reply. It swayed, as though not certain of its footing or its balance—or of her.

"My imagination's aged you," she said. The seeming was a sea-brined woman garbed in foreignness, hair cropped short to the skull, one eye skirted by a livid slash that dwarfed the older scars; this time her mind's eye portrayed a sister roughened by the years.

A cruel trick. This wasn't Liath. Breida slid her blade home with a click of guard on metal scabbard band, the only sound in the still air, while her heart cried, *Answer me, Liath! Prove me wrong!*

It seemed the apparition leaned toward her . . . twitched, as if about to open its arms for an embrace of love and apology. But in the end it made no move.

All illusion.

Breida turned her back.

Took a step away.

And if by wildest chance it *was* her sister, successful after twice nine years of failing to make landfall? What would that battered woman see as, weary to the bone, she made her slow disbelieving way up the rocky path? Her own sister, turning away. Flippant, scornful. Emotionless. No joy to see her, no shock blooming into wonder. A turned back, a cold shoulder, a blank rejection. Not even the respect of a drawn blade.

The thought pained Breida so deeply that she nearly changed her mind and went to give greeting. Wouldn't it be better to suffer the pain of being wrong than to risk the one-in-nine-nonned chance of cutting her sister dead?

One chance in nine times nine nonned.

She'd been taunted enough. Shared mirages out to sea were one thing; this was torment past bearing. Delusion so grave threatened her command. She could not protect her folk if she was seeing things.

She gripped the guardrail, dug her fingernails in so hard they scored the wood, and hauled herself another step back toward her post.

The little girl in her cried out. The little girl in her never gave up. The little girl in her struggled to turn, determined to welcome her sister home. But little girls could afford to hold out hope. Breida Shielder could not afford to indulge it.

She walked away from the apparition and greeted her relief. When she chanced to glance in the direction of the cove path, the apparition was gone. She snorted derision, and returned to her encampment to stave off death for another day.

SOMEONE NOT FROM here. Someone he should remember but couldn't. Someone all winks and elbows, bulge and leer, someone with just a drop of color. Not trying to be quiet but not able either. Not where the ground wasn't but muck and wet and hole and splash and rot and sometimes spring but mostly sink and always tricks.

Someone not from here. That's who was coming.

Mauzl was not from here. Mauzl could still know things here—most had to be *from* or were eyeless noseless earless, but it wasn't that bad here for Mauzl because Mauzl's *from* was earth and distance too, just dry hard earth where livewood kept its arms to itself and things didn't croak and scream, and that was very far now, but here was safe because it wasn't there and Mauzl could still know—but Mauzl couldn't know enough. Mauzl couldn't know as much as there. Mauzl needed someone who could help.

Someone from here might hurt. When people were in their *here* they sometimes hurt. Someone not from here might also need help. Someone not from here might also be afraid. Someone afraid, someone who needed help—someone like him— might befriend. But when people were afraid they sometimes hurt. When people needed help they sometimes hurt. They got so angry when he couldn't tell them what they wanted.

Mauzl tried to know if it was sage or fool to show himself. Bubbly vinegar tumblebelly said show. Mauzl couldn't know food or safe water. Here, Mauzl needed someone else to know those things. That's why it was fool to flee from there. There, he knew things by himself. But there was very bad. There he knew too many things, and too many people knew. Throbshoulder swellrib fruitflesh said don't show, don't show, don't show.

He tried to open the paths. Paths were everywhere, no here or there to them at all, only when and whether. But it was hard to open them on purpose. That's why he was never any good. Paths opened when they wanted to. They knew when it was sage or fool. More than he knew, here in his prickly hedge.

The hedge shifted, tilted. *Tore.* Mauzl was silent, so silent, cats' paws and silkwings and holdbreath and stillness, but the hedge reared back and peeled away from leer and bulge and hook and jut, and winks and elbows leaned past thick partings into the heremost hidden here, and now no show don't-show, no from-here not-from-here, no more. All choices punched into *this,* into *now,* and that was the least right thing of all.

Mauzl gaped, then croaked, then screamed.

Rekke snarled from a half-doze inside the hollowed spoilheap. His forehead slammed a crossbeam and he fell back. Now there was a ringing in his ears. But the shriek still rang there, too, underneath the layer of daze. He had not imagined it. He did not imagine things.

"No," said a voice, and a hand fell on his arm. "Stay. Don't."

In the dark, there was only the silver outline of a form filled by soft azure. It crouched beside him, a teller's notion of a ghost, human-shaped with shadowed gaps for eyes. But this ghost's hand was fleshy and firm.

He shrugged it away. "And if I'd stayed this morning? They'd have had you and all. He's at it again. That was his doing."

"You can't see him. He's too dim. He's a pinprick, a marble, a droplet. Hardly more than a blunt."

"A stinking rotting blunt I'm going to kick back to the

Crotch where it belongs." Rekke twisted onto all fours and backed out of the sleephole, to where he could sit up to get his boots on. He snagged his sleeproll on the way and stuffed it into his canvas pack. A nice sojourn, this; a pleasant tumble in the dirt to repay his protection, with a silver-blue ghost whose curves and moans were substantial enough when she lay beneath him. But she was a vole, here in her burrow, with her vole companions. Visants were voles, burrowing, hiding. Rekke had no use for holes or mounds or caves, beyond what he could loot from them or stash in them. As long as these voles were more careful where they ventured and what they saw and what they told of it, they wouldn't need him again. Others would. That one out there did.

"The one he's got is bright," said another voice, from across the central chamber of the abandoned saltern, as Rekke tied off the bindings on his boots. "Too bright. Let him be caught. Let him be stained. We'll be the safer for it."

Visants, betraying each other, sacrificing each other.

Rekke slung on his pack and groped for the trapdoor. "No," he said, to all of them, all the spectral forms that lurked in their living grave. They laid hands on his leggings, the hem of his tunic, but he was far too big and strong to be restrained. He wriggled them off, slid the bar from its mounts, and pushed out into the bufferway.

The tight passage gave only room enough to crawl, half a turn widdershins around the hill of leavings, to the laddered tunnel that led up to the exit hatch. Any who'd come down the ladder from the entry hatch, farther on, would have crawled in the same direction, so would not fetch up against him and stall them both. But few went in or out in the daylight hours. At the top of the ladder, he peered through the peeping tube and then, reasonably certain that this side of the mound was unobserved, he opened the hatch, moved the turf covering away, and pushed himself out onto the moundside. A bit up and over, the least trammeled-looking way so as not to further imprint their trails, then down to where he could jump. He landed flex-kneed and moved off in a crouch.

Absurd, complex precautions, when one ill-timed entrance or exit would betray their hiding place, and one good flood would drown them all. But they were afraid. They had been used too hard and too often to trust in the aboveground places where ordinary people lived. Fear made voles of them. Rats.

Rekke would never be a rat. But he could not abide the tormenting of rats.

He'd have seen the lights under that mound if they'd been buried at twice their depth. They were sapphires in the earth. Through the thinner medium of air, the two lights he sought vibrated with clarity. One a blue so intensely dark it seemed to radiate without glow, the other a pinprick, a marble, an all too familiar droplet.

There. By the clump of untended bayberry hedges grown wild into a snarl of thickets.

"Fyldur," Rekke growled, too low to hear, as the procurer sensed his light come out of nowhere and his greasy head began to turn, "I am going to thrash you within a breath of your stinking life."

Someone not from here. That's who was coming. Someone long-limbed, loose-legged, lank-boned, looming. Someone with big smelly feet. Not trying to be quiet but well able, someone trying to make noise, to scare and cow. But walking, not running. Striding, still not running. Not coming fast enough.

The oily cruelhand was all hurt and hatred, all throatgrip hairgrip shakebody, all rage at being hurried. And fear. It was always fear. He needed help. He wanted to find. He wanted to send. He wanted the paths, though he didn't know they were the kind of paths he wanted, and they were far too many for him to choose among if Mauzl could even tell them all. The paths opened, dizzying stomachdrop rushfall, paths within paths beside paths under paths, all the paths here and away from here, from places that were to all the places that could be. Long loose lankbones was on a good path, more good paths branched from it than bad, but bad paths branched from it, too, and that was cramplimb heartseize. Mauzl whined as his eyes rolled back and he could no longer see the cruelhand, but he didn't have to see with eyes to know the cruelhand thought the terror was of him, or that he liked it.

"Tell me." Rage and hate and leer and jut. "Where will he go next, you stinking walleye?"

If the cruelhand crushed his throat, he couldn't tell. That would be fool. But every breath still left one path where the next breath was the last. With every breath that Mauzl ever drew, there were countless paths where he died in the next, or fell to harm, or fell to terror. Every step was taken on a cliff's edge, every step by every person in the world. He knew those paths even when they weren't open. Those paths were always there, known or unknown. Knowing them was terror, knowing them was anguish. Wrenchheart numblimb clutchgut, that was how paths opened. It was the curse of sight. No likely or unlikely, no might or maybe. Just *will.* All paths were always possible. All paths were equally possible. Everything could always happen and always would. Until the next breath. Until the next set of everythings.

"Everywhere." Choking, begging, telling. "Everywhere he can."

He waited for the paths to close. He'd told. He'd told the *truth.* He'd told the paths. But they stayed open. All the long loose lankbones pausing, staring, walking, striding, trotting, plunging headlong shouting madness, falling turn-ankled, falling heart-stopped, giving up, turning away, a countless horde of long loose lankbones, a hot mist of them roiling boiling along the paths. Cruelhands fled and cruelhands killed him and cruelhands dropped him and clashed with lankbones, lankbones won and lankbones lost, and every one of those birthed more paths, mounds aid-bursting and mounds tight-closed, Mauzls saved and Mauzls strangled. Countless paths, every one of them spined with branchings, a warp and weft of fates that squirmed and heaved on their forever frame.

Long loose lankbones knew the cruelhand. Long loose lankbones didn't expect the cruelhand to hurt. Then long loose lankbones saw the cruel hand, the yielding throat.

Long loose lankbones plunged headlong, and though there were paths in which he fell and paths in which he failed, there were no paths in which he didn't plunge to help.

Mauzl looked down the fixed paths of the past and knew that he had never seen anything like that before.

He shuddered in surprise. His body came back. The paths closed, and there was only here. Only now.

Only the cruelhand's fingers and thumb digging between soft neck parts and hard, between airway parts and bloodway parts, and the sparkle-snow of no-breath. Poor heart, trying so hard to pump blood to his sore brain. Poor lungs, trying so hard to get him air. Mauzl had seen the paths that branched from here. He didn't have to see them now to know that most now led to death, most now had long loose lankbones' big smelly feet too slow in wet and muck and sink to stop the cruel claw hand in time.

Why did people get so angry when he couldn't tell them what they wanted? He wasn't why the answer wasn't there. He was looking, too, and not finding, and he was supposed to be the one who knew.

Rekke could not believe his eyes. Whatever Fyldur wanted from the runt he held, why *throttle* him?

He knew the Greasehair, knew his methods. Knew he seduced them into exiling themselves. Knew he took pleasure from the act. But minds had layers that Rekke could not penetrate, and visants were all mad—Fyldur no less so for the dimness of his light. All that Rekke knew was that he'd sent the Greasehair packing and the Greasehair had come back, and with his first glimpse of Rekke had dropped his wheedling wiles and gripped his prey in a stranglehold.

"Thwart me and I'll kill him," called the Greasehair.

Rekke had gone layered. One of him was white-blind rage, one of him was fled to a far realm of calculation; one was still able to see, and speak, inasmuch as he ever bothered.

"Kill him and I'll *kill* you."

Someone not from here. Someone long-limbed, loose-legged, lank-boned. Someone with big smelly feet.

Long loose lankbones crossed the distance, outran the too-lates, slid past oops and ouch. Threaded the unthreadable, fought sheerstrength and strongwill into the only now he would accept. Brought loomings and intimidations, brought base metals in his fists, brought righteousness, brought things small fainting Mauzl could not know in words.

Someone who was here now. That's who had rescued Mauzl.

Rekke swiped Fyldur's fending arms aside and cocked his fist. It was a strong, massive fist, meaty on the end of his arm, heavy, a knuckled mace on a chain of muscle. Fyldur had dropped the bright runt to protect his head. Rekke had a long time between inhale and exhale to choose to smash that head, or not.

He released his fist, then clenched again to scare the relief off Fyldur's face, and giggled.

"I swear you're one of *them*," Fyldur said. Lashing out. Watching him, eyes veiled and angled, to see how he'd react.

It was a punch, a fist of words. The damaged visants, that's who Fyldur meant—the wrong ones, the broken ones, the stunted ones, the ones with minds as weak as their lights were bright. Not the blunts, the lightless. Rekke laughed right down into his belly. "That makes three of us then. A veritable triad!" He was pleased with that rejoinder; their kind could not form triads, and the foolish ones took pride in it. Fyldur was one of those.

On the ground, the runt sobbed in breath, scrabbled at the

turf with spasming hands and heels that made no serious effort at flight. Passive. Weak. Rekke stamped down hard to release the kick that tensed in his leg, and grinned when Fyldur was the one who flinched.

Contempt engulfed the grin. Through gritted teeth and curling lips he felt with the part of him that watched but could not control, he said, "I told you to be gone. Procure your offerings somewhere else."

"This one's already stained," the Greasehair said. "He stained himself, but he's forgotten."

"Then he's of no use to you."

"He knows where one of my runaways is."

"Find him yourself. Somewhere else."

"You drive me from all the somewhere-elses."

"If only I could." It was a pain on him, that he could not be everywhere, that he could not flit at will from one end of Eiden to the other, rousting Fyldur and all his ilk, making their days a misery, herding them the way they herded their own into exile. Fyldur was stained before he ever found his niche in none's-land, yet contrived to remain at large, pretending to the mark of exile when what stained him was only hatred of his own. But Rekke had never seen him come so close to dealing death.

"You can't foster them all," Fyldur said, watching him. Misjudging him. Rekke was the only one Fyldur could not wind on his spool. "You can't protect them all. In the end I have the ones I want. Give me this one. Look, he doesn't even have the wits to run now that he can."

The runt had propped himself sitting and looked blinking from one of them to the other. Rekke snorted. "I *will* thrash you, Fyldur, as well you know. You won't do much wheedling with a broken jaw."

"Mended at one touch of a touch. You can't beat me, Rekke. You can't be everywhere. You can't save them all."

"I can save this one," Rekke growled. He moved into another part of himself, the part that saw this all as a delightful game.

"And I have!" he crowed, hauling the startled runt up and yanking him close. "He's mine now, till I'm sure we're shut of you. Shut and locked!" He laughed, made a face at the runt, laughed harder at the runt's wide-eyed recoil, and pointed to him, looking at Fyldur as if to share the joke.

Fyldur backed off. He knew when he had lost. But his devious squint bespoke a calculation of angles by which he might retrieve his stolen tool. Rekke went layered, vertically down the middle. He threw one loose, companionable arm around the quivering runt, pulled him in close, looked down on him with affection. The eye he kept on Fyldur burned with soulless hatred, and the fist he raised ached with the unrealized potential of violence. Fyldur shrank from it, from Rekke's palpable insanity, and all the words he threw as he retreated were foiled by futility. He knew how dangerous Rekke was when he layered himself. Touches or no touches, Fyldur wouldn't chance the agony of broken bones.

He wanted this one, Rekke thought, in the clear, calm part of himself the madness never reached. *He wanted him for more than tracking a worthless runaway, and if he couldn't have him, when he saw that I was coming to take him away, he wanted him dead.*

Why?

He held the runt up by the scruff to examine him in the colorless light.

"Hmpf," he said.

The runt squeaked.

He pawed grass off the runt with his free hand, turned him left, then right, to take the measure of him.

Not much, from the outside. Washboard ribs, slug-pale skin, a gangle of wrists and knees. A pointy rodent's face that deprivation had deflated to leave little of note but its enormous, pleading eyes, indigo irises so deep that purple lurked in their depths. Couldn't be more than nine-and-eight. Surprising he'd led Fyldur such a chase, and Rekke didn't meet much that surprised him.

From the inside, though . . . that was a different pail of rocks. A blue so subtle it glared. An indigo blue so deep that purple lurked in its depths. A kind of darklight so intense it shimmered.

Rekke dropped him back to earth. The runt hunkered down between his own knees, covered his head with knobby arms, and said, "Don't hurt. Don't hurt."

He'd already forgotten that Rekke had saved his life.

Weakness. Craven weakness. He despised it. It demanded he rise above himself when all he wanted was to cuff it into submission and go find someone who deserved to be thrashed and would put up a decent fight.

Rekke was an Ankleman, a stones man, body too tall for a miner, fingers too coarse for a cutter. He was also a depths man—a layers man. He'd made a trade of locating veins and deposits. Saved his neighbors years of wasted digging. He pointed, and there was garnet, there carnelian; there was opal. All the stones for all the tavern games in the world, and then more still when the seared magelight sucked the old superstitions down with it, because crafters began using them for decoration. His knack kept him in stew and ferments for two lengths of years. But it was uncanny. Unsettling. It had *implications*. The blunts got worried that it extended to more than minerals. That it might extend to the veins and deposits in their heads. They idolized the gold light and welcomed the copper once they could see it, either of which could destroy them in an eyeblink; but the silver light, no threat to them at all if they left it be, *that* they feared.

The people of the third light had known better than to show themselves. They'd stayed mute and safe and separate. Then Jhoss n'Kall had come along, with his theories and futures, his fevered fantasies of a new world order based on intellect. Jhoss n'Kall had seen the blue glow, and there was an end on safety then.

Rekke hated the blunts only slightly less than he hated Jhoss, and only slightly more than he hated Fyldur and his procurer ilk. Both Jhoss and Fyldur were his enemies; both Jhoss and

Fyldur sought to use the lights that Rekke sought to shield. They made a pair, the two of them, and Fyldur had been with Jhoss before he found an excuse for his own stain in none's-land, and made that his trade, keeping his liberty in the bargain. Rekke had been with Jhoss, too. It was Rekke whom Fyldur sought to punish, as he sought to punish all lights brighter than his own by wheedling them into exile. He'd like to trick Rekke into staining himself, though not if he was the victim. But working Rekke into a murderous fury wasn't the only reason he'd threatened this puny, dark-lit visant.

"Why did you cross into none's-land?" he asked. That had to be the source of the stain. Gentle, helpless creatures like these did not have it in them to kill.

The runt blinked and said, "To follow. It was the only almost mostly good path. To follow."

"Who?" Rekke asked. He had the queerest feeling, depths opening beneath him, layers gone hollow, the solid gone shifting.

The runt pondered for some while, then said, "I don't remember."

Rekke spat his unease onto the turf. He was considering whether to turn the runtling loose or consign him to the saltern's doubtful care when the runt looked up and said, in a hush of awe, "But which way—that's a kind of path, isn't it? Mauzl can hold those longer. Mauzl can know which way."

Fyldur's eyes were keen at distance. With a meaty hand, Rekke covered the trembling finger the runt extended, and said, "All right. Let's go and find him."

Before Fyldur does.

Before the alternative opens up and swallows us.

Someone big. Someone strong. Someone who could know food and safe water. Someone with harsh fists that never fell and a glow like warm blue stone.

That's who would help Mauzl find out what he was looking for.

ORIANE N'MEGENNA L'NOLE lay on the slanted roof of the Petrel's Rest, watching daylight ebb from the dome of sky to collect in liquid fire at its rim. A splash of violet leaking into brilliant crimson over rivulets of molten gold. Her fingers closed over a brush that wasn't there, her body reaching for inkpots and sedgeweave even though her mind knew that leaf and pigment could never do justice to that flaming sunset. It was made of light. Just as she was.

She unlaced the fingers at her middle, uncrossed her ankles, and propped up on her elbows. The Frostfire twilight was already leaching warmth from the shingles underneath her. Across from her, the fullers' and the smiths', flanking the mill road, were darkening silhouettes with warm golden squares for windows. One by one those windows were going dark, as folk closed up the affairs of the day and came across for the celebration. Beyond them to either side, the weavers' and the potters', the stables and the saddlers', had only nightlamps lit over their front doors. The Clon was a silver ribbon holding the last of the light, arched by dark stone bridges framing the cottars' row beyond. Where the village gave way was a charcoal fuzz of spruce and softer frostwoods, the tinkers' field a lake of open ground.

She could hear the brooms as children whisked the road clear of drifted leaves for dancing, and the last tap of hammers as the coopers to her right and the cobblers to her left finished one last job before breaking for the night. Hardworking folk, the wrights and crafters of Clondel, and Iandel, its sister village, and Drey and Orendel just down the road. She had worked hard in the last year to ward their buildings against fire and rain, to shepherd their weather, to ease their babes safe into their arms and their spirits safe into pethyar when it came time. Her mistakes had been few and thankfully harmless, her triumphs fewer but exhilarating.

She had earned more than a few somber words of ritual praise. She had earned a triskele, and she would not get one. She had to remember that the pewter pendant in itself meant nothing. What she had earned was the honor of continuing her work, the pleasure of serving her home village as illuminator for the rest of her life. With Delf and Sorilyn, binder and wordsmith, at her side.

It's what you wanted, she told herself. *You're a mage now. Act like one.*

But she was only two nines of years, and though she'd come of age in a demanding craft, this was her last night in the bosom of her family. The morning would be time enough to move the packs and crates from the room she shared with her sister Tegan to the room she'd share with Delf in the triad's cottage. The morning would be time enough to grow up.

She sat up, bent her knees, braced her feet. Just a moment, and she would go in. The sky had gone indigo, its sunward rim bloodred deepening to the hue of a darkwine grape. The chill of the harvestmid evening was setting in; she should be sipping hand-warmed brandy, dancing up a sweat with folk celebrating the harvest. She felt the tug of custom, even after all this time, felt she should be down in the greatroom pouring ale, telling stories, or out fetching kegs from the coolhouse. But that was not her job anymore. Tegan and their father would have it well in hand, with Gran Geara and Gran Danor to watch over them. She was a guest here tonight, one of three guests of honor in this special Frostfire celebration. Even though, for one more night, this was still her home.

Again she touched the hurt place inside, probing it the way she'd probe a bruise: to no purpose, nothing to be learned, unable to resist. Triskeles were an archaic tradition. Magecraft was full of traditions, and half of them were ludicrous. To think that in the old times, mages' trials lasted a scant three days! You couldn't tell anything from three days of contrived castings. You had to practice the craft in earnest for a year before it was clear whether you could be trusted over time, whether you'd be up to a lifelong commitment. So what if there was no triskele for her? The old light was dead. The old symbols were antiques. She needed no sigil to proclaim her skill; her light proclaimed it to mages, and her castings proclaimed it to everyone else.

But Delf would get his mother's triskele tonight, and Sorilyn would get her uncle's, which she'd saved among the keepsakes that were all she had left of her family dead in the High Girdle plagues. Oriane would get an armclasp. "And three become one," they would say, time-honored words. But only two would wear the symbols of their achievement. Even if Delf and Sorilyn removed them later—in solidarity, or their own exasperation with old fashions—for tonight it would be only the two of them, not the three.

Oh, what difference whether she got someone else's hand-me-down pendant? She was a mage. The brightest from this region since the searing. Trained in childhood by her great-grandfather, Pelkin n'Rolf himself, then five years more in the crucible of magecraft in the Haunch. She had served this village well for the requisite year, and now would serve it always. She was a mage. Nothing save coring and sealing could ever make her not-a-mage again, unless another Galandra cast another colossal shield and another Torrin broke it and seared them all, and Oriane had it in mind to develop wardings against both. But *that* was something she hadn't told even her triad yet. Not even Delf, who would be pledged with her in sowmid, when all this triskele-bestowing nonsense was over and they were settled in the cottage Befre was leaving them.

Still and still, it galled. There were not enough secondhand triskeles to go around, not available ones, and no one permitted to cast new ones yet; but it was childish of her to feel slighted because she wasn't one of the few to get one. She just couldn't silence the spoiled ingrate inside, grumbling that if she had to cede this house to Tegan, the least she could get was a bloody piece of pewter. The Petrel's Rest was a legacy of daughters, and Oriane was the firstborn. Though her father ran the house because both her aunts had skyved off on adventures, she was the eldest, and it should fall to her.

But that was tradition. She couldn't disparage it with one side of her mouth and claim rights of it with the other.

She loved this place. She loved the feel of it, the sound and smell, the warmth, the light. Three stories of love and family and community, company and camaraderie and cheer. She could feel its pulse, laughter and dancing feet ringing in the beams and joins, the murmur of conversations, the clink of mugs. She and Tegan, a year apart in age, had spent their toddlerhoods vying to be the center of house life. But once Oriane turned six the race was lost. She and Delf saw each other's lights, and went into training, and Tegan always knew the house better than she did after that. Tegan knew where things were. Tegan knew what the regulars ate and drank. Tegan knew more jokes to charm travelers. The legacy had slipped through her fingers. Though those fingers were better at drawing kadri than pints, though she knew she could not be both mage and publican, though her love for Tegan was stronger than her jealousy . . . still there was the bruised placed where her publican's pride had been.

She gritted her teeth and crawled up to the unshuttered dormer. When she dropped down inside, Befre was waiting for her in the attic shadows.

"Done feeling sorry for yourself?" she asked, stepping into the sunset glow to sit on a crate of old stored blankets. Her head was cocked, attentive and curious, and with her angular features and short thick ruff of russet hair she looked like a fox. She was as good at sniffing things out.

"I think so." Oriane sat beside her. "I can't have my triskele and be a publican too, and I can't have anyone else's triskele either. I'll live."

"As will I," Befre said quietly. Her crystal eyes held no reproof, but her face went flat. Befre was about to give up the only thing she had left of a power that had defined her in the world. Lightless, former mages never wore their triskeles, but few would allow them out of their keeping.

"Oh, it's all right, child." Befre's tone gentled, but Oriane saw her hand caress her breastbone, where the pewter used to lie. "I want him to have it. I can't wear it anymore; what use is it tossed in a dusty box?" In fact, it had been kept in a soft drawbag under Befre's pillow, but Oriane wasn't supposed to know that. "And I can't see him wearing anyone else's. As far as I know"—she flashed her lopsided grin—"his father wasn't a mage."

Oriane managed only a sickly half smile in response. Befre was as bad as Gran Geara's sisters, lusty and ribald, never pledged, taking her pleasure where she would in her roamings. She had no idea who Delf's father was. *Perhaps I'm not cut out to be a publican after all,* Oriane thought. *I never could get the hang of that bawdy humor.* Oriane had loved one boy all her life—Delf, the boy up the road, the boy who was like a brother to her until they grew old enough for him to become something more. Delf claimed he could see the future in her clear gray eyes, count their days in the countless freckles across her nose. Silly nothings, but they warmed her. Oriane knew she was no beauty. Her littlest sister, Milis, was the pretty one, and Tegan's robust vitality made delicate beauty look wan. Oriane, too tall for herself, all joints and angles, felt beautiful only when she cast, only in the regard of those who could see her light. But Delf loved her. Delf saw the future in her eyes. That was beauty enough for her. She could not imagine lying with anyone else.

Befre was a wanderer. She'd triaded for a while, her wordsmith brother Graefel and Hanla, his Khinish pledge, but gave her binder's place to her brother's son as soon as she'd trained him, and went off a journeymage. She'd come home only after the searing, when the magecast freedoms failed and she came with child. She brought Delf back to Clondel, swept and aired the abandoned triad's cottage, repaired the fallen bindinghouse, and made her living laying sedgeweave with reeds from the town's twin rivers until her son showed a light at six. Then the village, in prospect of one day having a binder again, perhaps a triad, began to tithe her as it had once tithed the mages. That gave her time to train the boy and gather casting materials, and the wherewithal to trade for what she couldn't collect or grow. She filled that bindinghouse the way prentice binders had once worked to fill their journey trusses. She had no light, but she had hands, and craft, and knowledge. It would be a long time before Oriane and her triad used up all that Befre had produced in those early years—and afterward, too, after she and Delf had turned nine-and-three and Pelkin had taken them off to the Haunch for broader training.

Oriane didn't know why Befre had stayed, those five years, trading her sedgeweave to scribes and runners, filling and filling the bindinghouse. For love of her son, Oriane supposed. To be there when he came home, to supervise his year of trial. A former mage had to supervise, or they'd have had to do their year somewhere else. But as soon as the triskeles were bestowed, Befre would be off. They'd be on their own. A real triad, with inescapable responsibilities. No teachers to run to. No Befre.

No Pelkin. Oriane missed her great-gran. She hadn't seen him all year. She knew his wartime duties in the Haunch were too pressing to permit a visit, even for her celebration. And she knew that Gran Geara, his daughter, missed him more than she did. She was trying hard to keep other people's hurts higher in her thoughts than her own. That was what a good mage did. Mages had been pillars of the community in the time of the old light, the folk people turned to for advice, to settle disputes, to render judgment. She would have to earn that respect. Magelight wasn't the only light in the world anymore. She would not be granted deference because she was special. She still had a lot to prove. Pelkin, lightless, ran the Haunch holding, respected and heeded by all. Befre, lightless, was a pillar of this community, for all she'd tried to live a quiet sedgelayer's life in her modest cottage. They had earned their places in the world. Losing their light could not rob them of that.

"My mind's all over," she said, when she realized that Befre had been speaking. *So much for respect,* she thought. The ruddy light that had bathed them was gone. This was the time last night when they'd seen the arc of golden light span the Heartward sky and thought the siege had come inland upon them. But it was only some last gasp of Candlenight sunshine, a trick of the light.

"I said it would be different if there were reckoners who could cast you triad." Oriane saw no point in being cast triad, when they were a perfectly functional triad without the casting, but she kept that to herself. "I cannot describe the . . . the insight, the vision, of being cast triad, not so you'd believe me. A sublime experience of joining. If you were celebrating that, or even an old-fashioned three-day trial, exhausted and proud and happy, you would feel this more. I hope you can be satisfied with being the brave vanguard of a new generation, enduring hardships so your successors will be spared them."

Oriane sat up a litte straighter. "Will it really be a dozen years before we can start casting triskeles?" No mages were permitted to forge triskeles for one another. You couldn't cast a triskele for a peer. There was something in the quality or method of the casting itself that resisted it. She'd like to take a crack at that. See if they could develop a new casting.

"At least. Triskeles are cast for one's prentice. There are no mages or triads experienced enough to take a prentice. Soon, though. Soon we old weary lightless will be able to turn the task of training over to you lot, and stop being tormented by having to teach what we can no longer have the joy of doing."

"I'm so sorry, Befre. I'm so selfish. I forget."

"You're young, my girl. It's how you're meant to be. Leave the guilt and worry to your elders. We're better at it." She clapped a callused binder's hand on Oriane's shoulder. "Now let's get you down for your nine nonned toasts, eh?"

Heart lightened, Oriane stepped over to one of the two trapdoors—there were two iron stairways outside, as well, for escape in the event of fire—and slid it aside, admitting a surge of tavern noise. She'd have joined her celebration in genuine good spirits if she hadn't turned, on the upper landing, after the trapdoor slid shut, to see why she didn't hear Befre's footsteps behind her, and found her lingering, hand still on the ladder, looking at her. Looking at her in what she thought was one last private moment. Looking at her with *that look,* more insulting than any usurped tavern or triskele denied.

The look that said, *You're so like her. It's like having her back with us.*

The look became a wink and an encouraging twist of the chin the moment Oriane turned. But she'd seen it, from the edge of her eye. She'd seen it on Clondel faces since she was six. The day she showed a light, it had bloomed there, in amazement and poignant ambivalence, in shared glances among the family, among the villagers—and worst of all, between Befre and Pelkin.

As though we've been given another chance.

Oriane was familiar with the myriad haunts of the Petrel's Rest. Folk who'd never walked these floors or touched these walls. Folk who'd lived and loved and died in the old house, haunting this one just the same. Countless ancestors, their joys and griefs. Her great-gran Breida, dead of a broken heart when Pelkin put duties as mage over duties as mate. Her aunt Breida, named for that great-gran, lost to the exile of the shield. Oriane loved her too, and missed her too. But she was grieved here like a ghost, when she wasn't dead at all. She was off being a hero. Off on a grand adventure. Just like the other, the worst ghost of all, her other aunt—the one whom Oriane had never met, would never meet, unless she looked into a mirror to see herself as they all saw her.

It's like she's been reborn to us, with the reborn light.

What a barrel of backwash. Oriane was herself, no more and no less. The physical resemblance with her father's sister owed to shared blood, simple as that; her aunt's light and illuminator's talent owed to Pelkin, just like hers. If Liath bloody Illuminator were around to hear people imply that she'd been poorly trained and Oriane was a chance to make amends, she'd have a thing or three to say about it, and the fists to back it up.

I'm not like her at all, Oriane thought, as she let Befre's slip of the face pass unremarked and continued down to the second landing. *I'm no good with my fists. I can't drink anyone under the table. I don't go on quests. I don't save worlds. And my light isn't as bright. It's the brightest hereabouts, among the brightest in the Haunch, it's brighter than any three of the old lights . . . and still it's not as bright as hers was.*

She came down the last flight of stairs, to the smoky, crowded greatroom, to the roar of cheers and applause. She plastered a huge grin on her face. She embraced Sorilyn at the foot of the stairs, and winked over her shoulder at Delf, and thought, *But I'll be thrice the mage she ever was.*

Befre n'Brenlyn l'Traeyen sat at the top of the stairs and watched Clondel celebrate her children. She thought of all three as her children, though Delf was her only progeny and daunt-less, cheerful Sorilyn resisted everyone's attempts to foster her. They stood on the cusp of adulthood, those three, and her pride in them knew no bounds.

But it wanted sharing. She regretted Pelkin's absence, and was concerned at the lack of messages from him; in wartime that could bode ill, though he was nowhere near the coast, nearly as buffered from the conflict there as she was in this peaceful valley. He'd approve of his daughter Geara's staunch efforts to support the shield. He should be here to pat her on the back for that. He should be here to see his great-granddaughter take the triskele.

Alas, there was no triskele for her to take. Befre had tried every former mage she knew, but none could bear to part with theirs, even the folk who'd returned to their family trades and put magecraft behind them. She'd gone so far as to petition the Strong Leg holding for one of their hoarded triskeles, the ones left by the bonefolk after the Triennead fell. When they denied her, claiming it would dishonor the ancient dead, she bit the belt and messaged her brother in the Head. Plenty of lights lost there in the magewar. If they did not consider use by a living mage a higher honor than some lifeless display, perhaps Graefel himself would make the offer? Delf was his nephew, after all. Graefel was all scholar now, head of the scholars' holding; surely he had no need of a metal symbol to prove how high he'd climbed. He'd forsaken his silver proxy ring and never acquired the golden Ennead ring he'd coveted; what loss could mere pewter possibly be? But he had messaged back, with brusque terseness in his impeccable wordsmith's hand, that it was out of the question. No reason, no pretense of apology. Just no.

He'd known that though she'd requested a triskele for Delf, sending one would mean that Befre's would go to the publicans' daughter. He'd helped train the last daughter of the Petrel's Rest who'd shown a light, and she had failed him and defied him. Graefel never forgot a slight, let alone a betrayal. As relentless as he was arrogant. Some things never changed.

This public house was one of them. That was a happier thought. Less than a year after the magewar she'd returned to Clondel with infant Delf on her back to find the shingled Petrel's Rest gone and a blackstone structure in its place, one story higher and half again as deep. It was the same Petrel's Rest. The same center of village life. The same brawls, the same easy friendships. She drank in air piquant with pipe smoke and redolent with stews simmering in the cookroom, the scent of fresh rushes on the floor and fresh drink spill just wiped from the tables. Except for the hint of cool Aralinn Mountains exhaled by the stone walls, it was as she'd always known it. A few folk gamed with painted wooden slats or moved carvings on boards of colored squares, but most still rolled raw stones by hand, the same piles of tallysticks beside them. A couple of gray-clad scholars and a Heartlander or two, but otherwise all locals, with hillwomen and mountainy folk come down special for the celebration. There was one Souther off to the side, a Heelman judging from the wide-browed shape of his gaunt face but with unusually pale flesh, regarding the room with eerie pink eyes. An odd man, and no Southers had passed through in some time, but Clondel served a major road to the Head, and saw just about every kind of traveler there was. A chant rose around the great trestle table—Nole, the head of the house, being goaded to arm-wrestle a burly Drey ironsmith. Nole's trembling forearm had just recovered from a certain pinning when a voice said, "She looks so like the other, doesn't she?," and Befre startled to find the Souther right beside her. He was looking away from the match. At Oriane and Delf and Sorilyn in a cluster of friends.

Abruptly she knew who he was. He hadn't had his unpigmented flesh healed by a touch. He wanted to be recognized as Torrin Lightbreaker's mysterious albino Jhoss n'Kall. Working legend to some ends of his own. "Yes, she does. But don't tell her that, if you want to keep your nose in the middle of your face."

"I would not presume." He gave the suggestion of a bow. He looked frail, as though he were only partly in the world of flesh, or had suffered a prolonged fever. "Is she as bright?"

"That's a personal question for a man who was never a mage."

"You are no longer a mage."

"The craft remains. But I no longer have a light. I can't tell you how bright she is."

He nodded, as though she'd answered. Perhaps she had. Oriane n'Megenna was one of the brightest mages in a generation in which the average light was thrice the average light of old. Things it would have taken an ennead to do, Oriane's triad mastered in a day. But Befre had tasted Liath Illuminator's light. She'd known what Liath Illuminator was capable of. Oriane was a candle to that sunrise. Liath had been an aberration, not unlike this albino here, and the young Liath whom Befre had known had a long way to go before she was qualified to wield the power she'd been gifted with. Even if she lived, tossed on the nine seas, that grand light was gone. A grieving pity, that— but perhaps safer in the end. Oriane and her peers were more than enough power for Eiden Myr.

"Have you any message for your brother?" the albino asked.

"On your way Headward, are you?" Befre cocked her jaw and grinned, stroking a back tooth with her tongue as numerous possibilities occurred to her. In the end, she huffed a sigh and said, "No. But I wouldn't petition him for anything. I can't imagine what you want of him, but whatever he's doing up there, he won't be budged from it. My advice, turn around and go back to the Heel." Her shrug told him that she didn't give a tick what he did.

"Oh, far too much depends on me for that," he said, with a closemouthed smile. "You shielded the warm heart the old Holding froze in him, Binder. I cherish the privilege of having seen you."

He left her with a queer frisson, and the sense that he knew it, and that by "see" he meant much more than a chance encounter. The frisson became a shiver as he slipped into the crowd and out of sight. She'd heard of a visant or two down in the next valley, but they had none here. It was disturbing to realize that she'd just met one, passing through this place like a ghost, there one breath and then gone into the night.

Whose heart had he meant? Her own, or Graefel's?

Well, if she'd just unwittingly provided insight that would aid him in some power game, fair play to him. She stayed clear of the sluggish ebb and flow of political tides across Eiden Myr. And whatever he'd meant, the last thing Graefel her brother had ever needed was her protection.

She had loved him as long as he would let her. She had triaded him once, subsumed into a soul-plundering oneness, then dissolved that triad, a casting she still felt as though it had cut off her limbs. She hoped the scholar's life suited him. She hoped that gaining his cold heart's desire, control of that Head holding and the codices it held, was all he'd dreamed.

Befre watched her son and his wordsmith and illuminator be toasted, carried around the room on shoulders, pulled down into an endless series of embraces, armclasps, back thumps. She watched the greatroom full of wrights and hillfolk, crafters and dairyfolk, farmers and wranglers and sheepherds, celebrate their palpable joy at having a triad in their midst once again. They'd had touches to help them, this last dozen years, and they'd always had their own strong arms and common sense to see them through the worst times, but the Neck had valued its mages, and two nineyears without had not dulled that appreciation. Clondel and Iandel remembered. Drey and Orendel remembered. They rejoiced in the light's return, and Befre, though she felt her own dark core like a weight in her chest, rejoiced with them.

This was the last night of the old moon. Three days of darkness, and then the new moon would appear, no more than a curved white line at first, waxing slowly into a fullness.

Beyond the door, dancers' bodies flashed by, spinning and stamping in sets and couples, driven by drumbeats and now and then a hesitant skirl from some newfangled noisemaker of reed or string. Befre sat on her stair and looked across the packed, sweaty greatroom at that door, at the cool, clear night beyond it. She had not been on the road since Delf was born. She had drowned the yearning so deep she feared to find the pleasure gone.

Soon I'll know. Six nineyears and five—she was old for it now. Perhaps too old. But come morning she'd be off, all the farewells behind her in the night. Time only to lift her stout walking stick, raise the pack to her shoulders. She could already feel the miles beneath her feet.

When a runner appeared in that doorway, dressed in black with a nine-colored holding cloak swirling from shoulder to calf, she sat up as though someone had pinched her. *It's the call,* she thought, before she caught herself—the old Ennead was dead these twonine years and would never call anyone as proxy again. Then she thought, *Sweet spirits, it's Graefel or Pelkin, something's happened.* Ordinary runners did not wear those cloaks. Congratulations would have come in a scheduled, daytime delivery. Pelkin head of the Haunch holding, Graefel head of the Head—a holding runner could have come from nowhere else, the Strong Leg would have sent a bird and the Strong Leg had nothing to say to the Neck. Befre was off the stairs in the next breath, eeling through merriment, pressing a path to that doorway and that runner before anyone else had noticed him. He stood blinking in the lamplight, a boy no more than nine-and-five, shy of all the revelry, unable to bring himself to step inside.

"I'm Befre n'Brenlyn," she said "Who is your message for?"

If he said Geara's name, then it was Pelkin—injured, ill, even lost to them. Keen-eyed Geara was making her way over, with Tegan in tow and concern on both their faces. But he said, "You."

Graefel, then. She took the drawbag the boy held out to her with a small sedgeweave scroll. She felt the weight and warmth and shape of a triskele through the bag's velvet, and thought, *He's relented, that's all. They haven't sent his triskele to announce he's dead.* But her hands trembled when she broke the wax seal, and she welcomed Geara's steadying hand as she unrolled the sedgeweave.

Her eyes, expecting Graefel's efficient hand, could not resolve the shape of the glyphs at first. She had learned to read in adulthood, and sometimes the knack deserted her, so that scribing seemed meaningless lampblack trails on plant leaf. Then, at last, she recognized Pelkin's mark at the foot of the message. The ornate curls of his illuminator's Celyrian came clear, and the words sounded out, a poignant song in her binder's mind.

This token is for my grandson's daughter Oriane, at the successful completion of her year's trial. It was my own. Bid her wear it long and well, and mind its history. Some traditions are worth keeping; but let this begin a new one, of gifts passed down through the generations. With love, Pelkin n'Rolf l'Liath, Haunch holding, harvestmid in this ninth year and four of the new light.

Befre clasped the soft drawbag tight around its precious contents, glanced across the greatroom to where Oriane and Delf and Sorilyn were straightening in notice of the huddle at the door, and said to Geara and Tegan through a brimming smile, "Call for quiet, if there's any hope of that. It's time."

Geara n'Breida l'Pelkin watched her father's triskele bestowed upon her eldest granddaughter. So much moaning and groaning about secondhand pewter—she'd heard them in Oriane's room, when they didn't think she was near—yet it ended like this. Next thing you knew, they'd all be begging family heirlooms; when they were allowed to craft the things fresh no one would want them, and they'd be grumping when there were no hand-me-downs for them.

In truth she'd never had much use for mages, though the Neck was always thick with them. Most, for most of her life, had just been there, like any other crafters, useful when you needed one but nothing to crow about. Reckoners, though—she had always hated them. She'd been none too happy to see that cloaked black lad at the door, until she found out what he carried. Then she'd sat him down with a bowl of thick lentil stew to warm the chill from his bones. He looked to be enjoying it, as well he ought. She used to serve them week-old bread. She had hated reckoners because her father was a reckoner. She had hated black because her father wore it. And her father had abandoned them, left her mother to die of a broken heart, loved his bloody proxy circle more than them.

But she hadn't known. She hadn't known that he was the head reckoner, as he was head runner now. She hadn't known the weight of secrecy and duty he shouldered. Until her oldest daughter came home scarred by the Ennead's tortures, she had not known the depth of evil her father fought. He had refused to forsake the ring and surrender to darkness. He had trusted her and her sisters to be strong enough to carry on in his absence. It grieved her, now they had reconciled and all truths were told, that she had been so hard on him. She'd banished him after her mother died. She'd sent him away without even seeing his youngest grandchild, when young Breida was a babe in arms. Liath had shown a light the year before and prenticed to the Khinishwoman. That light would take her daughter from her just as surely as it had taken her father. For a time, she could not abide the sight of either of them.

She grieved the pain she'd caused, and the pain she'd felt. But it was many years ago, and now was now. Worse griefs were there for the crying, now: one daughter lost at sea, one daughter lost to exile.

She would yield to neither. Each nineday she sent her shipment of food and drink Fistward; with Nole and now Tegan running the house day-to-day, she and Danor could devote themselves to the relief. Any surplus over the Fist rations, they sent to the shield in Shrug, then other shores. They'd got folk at the Curlew in Orendel doing the same, and the Iandel innkeepers and Drey publicans were considering it. There was plenty to go around, in these prosperous times. If she could harden her old bones for a journey, she'd petition farther; but deeds spoke stronger than words, and the deeds were spreading of their own.

No one leaves a daughter of the Petrel's Rest down a midden without a shovel. No one leaves a daughter of this house to burn. And the world is full of houses, and their daughters, and their sons. Eiden Myr had abandoned its defenders with a hypocrisy that shocked her, though she'd seen her share of fanatical insanity—it had burned this house to the ground, once. But this Petrel's Rest was made of solid Aralinn blackstone, touch-strengthened and magewarded. There would be no more burnings. And if her youngest daughter died, she'd die a hero, not a casualty of a world that turned its bloody back.

This was a time for fighting, not for griefs. For stubborn endurance. And for blessings. Nole, her gentle son, grown into a red-bearded bear just like his father, beaming as his eldest accepted her honors; her pledgedaughter Megenna, petite and comely still, clutching his strong arm, bursting with love of her firstborn. Young Milis, plump and pretty at nine-and-two, arguing the merits of various gruits with an astonished brewer from Drey. Tegan, all ample-bodied grace, already a jolly host at nine-and-eight, a fine publican to inherit this house one day. And Oriane, face shining as the triskele settled into place, the spitting image of her Liath. Her Liath, who had taken on the cursed nine who scarred her, and destroyed them.

Good on you, my girl, she thought. To both of them, daughter and granddaughter.

It felt for all the world as though Liath herself were here. This was so like her celebration, all those years ago—two nines of years and one, just one year longer than Liath had then lived.

She was Oriane's age then, and Khinish Hanla had slid the triskele over her head with no one seeing, off in the alley while old Drolno Teller, dead of a palsy in the plague years, recounted the myth of Galandra's birth. Geara hadn't minded that; she hadn't wanted to see that chain go around her child's neck. But later, when Hanla had torn it off in a fury at her prentice's rebellion, Geara had knotted it back in place. She could almost forget the hard year between, when they'd had no idea where Liath was—but she didn't want to forget, because she had no idea where Liath was now, and she must believe that she would come home.

Father had come home. Oriane had come home. Her merchant sisters had come home. Even Befre had come home. Not always to stay, but they came home. Liath would walk in the door from nowhere, just as she did in the magewar. She would push back the hood of her cloak and call a round of ale for the house, and then she'd ask where her sister was, and when they told her she would go fetch Breida home. The two of them had always been the best at putting a stop to brawls when they got out of hand. That brawl at the coast had gotten out of hand, and the two of them together were just the ones to put a stop to it.

Ach, she was an old woman, with an old woman's dreams and fancies. She hauled herself back to earth and cast a practiced eye around the room. It was no longer down to her to see their growlers and their bellies filled, but the habits of a lifetime clung, and to this day she sometimes caught things with her old eyes that Nole or Tegan missed—an altercation brewing, someone cheating at stones, a traveler slipping off without leaving a tally for his meal, a lonesome regular too polite to beg attention—and mentioned it on the quiet so they could sort it. Tonight all seemed well, until her gaze chanced across the doorway.

Oriane was standing in the spill of light through the open door. Had she slipped out for some air? She looked pale, as though after a long weary night, and inexplicably sad. But Oriane was walking toward her, flushed with drink and excitement, putting off the well-wishers, coming straight toward her to show her Pelkin's triskele before her parents or anyone else. Geara glanced back to the block of light beyond the door, and Oriane was still there. Just standing, looking in, a tall gray-eyed girl two nines of years with short red hair and a spray of freckles across her nose.

A wiry girl with arms more muscled than Oriane's had ever been, with Tegan to lift the heavy kegs, and years away from tavern life while she studied magecraft in the Haunch.

A pale girl with shadows on her, losses and yearnings that Oriane had never suffered.

A girl dressed in the colors of flax and wool, none of the dyes that were commonplace now, the dyes that Oriane wore.

It was Liath standing just outside the door.

"Oh, my girl," she said, her chest cracking at the sadness and the longing on that face. She moved to the door, arms already lifting to draw the gangling frame to her breast, to hold her as when she was a child and came home furious after some tussle or injustice, fighting with all her spirit not to cry. "Oh, my girl," she said, "come inside, love"—but then Galf n'Marough's hulking son swept her up into a dance, taking her outstretched arms as invitation, and Galf was extricating her before the boy tripped over his own feet, and Oriane was laughing and turning her and asking for the next dance as an excuse to bear her off to show the triskele, and by the time she was able to twist round, by the time she got free of the grip of revelers, there was only a drummer in the doorway, head stuck in to call for the next set, and no sign of Liath in the road outside.

Twice more that night she saw her daughter in the shadows. She was old, but not daft, and she had never been prone to visions. It *was* her daughter, by the pantry, by the stairs. But she looked confused, out of place in this rebuilt house that was not the house she'd known, and Geara could never get to her in time past the dancers and the gamers and the clumps of conversation. Someone would stand up, her view would be obscured, and in the next breath the girl would be gone.

It *was* her daughter. But her daughter as she had looked at two nines of age, before the Ennead scarred her, before her hair grew out, before she'd learned that her mother still loved her and always had and always would.

Liath was a Frostfire child, a child of harvestmid. She would have turned four nineyears of age and one today. Scars could be healed, hair cut, clothes left undyed—but she would never again wear the face of that child, the look of private longing that she'd borne at two nineyears old.

Geara could not explain it. But she would not believe her daughter was dead. If she was dead, she would haunt the sea she sailed off on.

Liath was trying to come home.

IN SOFT, MISTY morning light, Ioli took one step to the side as a leaf fluttered right, then left, then settled on the spot where he had been standing.

Without conscious awareness, he had sensed that the dying leaf was about to fall. Without thinking, he had gauged the air's flow, the leaf's shape, calculated angles and resistance, and known that it would land where he stood. The simplest thing at home, though if he tried to *think* about it, to hold in his mind all the leaves and bark and ground and sky and clouds and air currents and humidity and temperature and sounds and movement and scents and sights . . . he could not. Here in the open Lowlands, far from his dense jungle, it had all been too new for him to manage. But stay in the new for a while and it became old. Stay in the unfamiliar for a while and it became, just passably, familiar.

He'd returned to the world and found it unnavigable. He hadn't realized how the procurer had guided him on the way here. Alone, he was overwhelmed. Not quite so helpless as in

none's-land, but incapable of making any sort of speed. He'd
stumbled on this apple orchard, plucked clean of most of its
fruit but still bearing a few late ripeners. He'd eaten them and
his stomach cramped. He'd slept rough, shaking with chill,
whining as the damp soaked into his tight-curled bones, but
sheltered from the worst of the showers that came through in
the wee hours, shepherded by mages to water the world when
most folk were sleeping. The orchard gave him space to think.
Time to look.

His was an edge-of-the-eye talent. He just knew things, felt
things, saw things. He hadn't known that the eyes could be conditioned to see, the senses conditioned to know. He'd spent the
long breaths between dawn and noon, noon and dusk, just
watching the landscape. Here, on the edge of the Haunch, letting the Haunch seep into the edges of his eyes. The way the angle of light shifted as the day wore on, revealing shape and
depth, delineating dimension in shine and shadow. The way the
nameless birds flew, the way their flying revealed the movements of the wide, intimidating air, its warm places and its cold,
its risings and its currents. The shape of earth, the lay of stones.
He spent the sleepless, miserable breaths between dusk and
midnight, midnight and dawn, just listening, just feeling. The
way the leaves resisted and surrendered to the breezes. The way
the earth breathed under his body. The sounds the night creatures made, so peaceful, so sleepy compared with the dark activity of the jungle, soft rustlings and lowings and only a couple
of sharp hoots to knife the stillness. The way the trees around
him shored themselves, distributing through hard flesh the
strength they'd drunk from sunlight during the summer. His
mind did the same, when he slid into a blessed drowse, dreaming deep into its folds and crevices all the shapes and textures
he had drunk in while waking. Making them part of him.
Shoring him against the cold, the strangeness.

His was an instinctive talent. It could not be explained. It
could not be taught. He was surprised to find it could be
adapted. He could learn this alien world. For the turn of a day

he had kept to his orchard and learned the world. This morning he had risen, and extended his eyeless sight, and felt the imminent fall of leaf, and stepped aside.

All he knew, now, was this orchard, not so unlike his world of trees at home; and the hawthorn hedge that protected it, and the pastures that surrounded it, and the animals that grazed in them. He would be good at apple orchards hereafter, less good at hedges, less good at pastures. Still it was a start.

The urgency came back on him, the fear, as he stepped through the rickety gate in the inland side of the hedge and out into the open. He controlled it. He must take care. He must be the loris making its slow way up the spiritwood trunk, invisible to predators, seeing all through its night-huge eyes.

He had to reach the runners' holding. That holding could send runners out to warn the world. That holding had the power to save the world. If the runners only heard what he had seen, and believed it. If just one runner, the head runner, heard, and believed, and bade the others carry the message.

It would be a kind of warding. A shield around their minds instead of a shield of flesh around Eiden's body.

He would walk into that holding, and they would feed him and treat him kindly and let him say his piece before their head. He would relax there. He would be able to *see* there. He would not look frightened, or insane. He would stand collected before the head runner and tell him everything he had seen. How the madness crept inland when that section of shield had crumbled, then withdrew again when new minds massed on the shoreline for it to feed on. He was an eyewitness. The old man would give credence. The old man would see that he had no twisted motives, that his words were not the ravings of a lunatic.

The old man might order a test to see if Ioli's account bore out a second time. It would. Pelkin—that was his name, he remembered now, Pelkin n'Something, the head runner—would nod in grave acceptance of the task. To send runners to every village, every herd band, every enclave in Eiden Myr, and persuade the people that the delusions could not kill them.

It wouldn't matter, then, if the shield fell. The shield could

not fall, then, not if they believed they would live. They had
been dying for a long time. They took pride in their dying. It
would be harder to convince them. But runners could do it.
Runners wore black. Runners ran messages. People believed
what runners said. Runners carried the authority of the old
times.

The shield was failing. Those weapons had to be stopped another way. Making every mind in Eiden Myr as immune as a
visant's to the delusions—*that* would be another way. A better
way. There'd be no more dying then.

There'd be no more none's-land then.

I can save the world. I truly can. He broke into a trot to cover
the last pastureland, to leap the low gorse and thistle that ran
along the dawn-quiet roadside, to get his feet on flat raked
ground that would carry him quickly to Sauglin, famous
Sauglin, he even remembered that name now, Sauglin in the
Haunch, where the runners' holding was.

The earth was not at the height his foot expected it to be. He
came down in soggy grit, several hands below ground level. A
trench beyond and below the gorse. He yielded, twisted into the
fall to avoid breaking his neck. Pain spiked through his ankle.
Hauling himself from the drainage ditch and onto the drier
road, he cursed roads and flat ground that needed draining. The
rain-soaked, tree-dense Toes had neither. They had sturdy
stilted walkways and swingropes and ladders, they had
breeches slings to carry you across the flooded places and between the treetops. Everything was vines and handholds and
laid sisal and hemp ladderways. There was always something to
grab if you slipped.

There was color, raging color—in frogs and flowers, birds
and moth wings. There was scent, thick and delicious; the air
had substance. There were hoots and shrieks and chirps and
chatters, there were fliers and creepers and crawlers, slow tor-
toises sunning on logs, lizards startle-stopping and snakes sinuous in the understory, there was life, there was fullness, there
was *dimension*. Ioli sat hard on the hard flat road and bound his
ankle with his handcloth and the drawstring from his empty

carrypouch, and let the flat land drink his tears in payment for its tricks and ditches.

Then he got up, and limped on.

He was stained. He could not go on. The inlanders would not let him.

A touch he met on the road healed his ankle, then made him promise that he would go back to the shield. Ioli pretended to go, but forged on when the touch was out of sight. A wagon driver stopped him; he escaped only because when he ran off-road the man wasn't willing to leave his young team to pursue.

Time after time, he was turned. He could not skulk well enough, could not hide well enough, not with the stain on him. They sniffed him out like brindle dogs. "We can't have killers wandering loose here," the frightened ones said. The righteous ones said, "You went to the shore to serve. You can't leave them like that. They need you. You have to go back. It isn't fair, for you roam here safe while folk are dying there." The craven asked him for a gleaning before they sent him off, and sent him off more roughly for denying them. Starving, he stooped at last to trade on his powers. "I'll tell you where you left that lost spade, if you'll share that meal with me." A fair exchange, but it sullied him.

No choice. He could not go on without food. He must go on.

He could not. No matter how far around he went, there was no way through. Folk were out ploughing their fields under. Folk were out traveling the roads. Villages were everywhere. None of them would abide the stained. He'd wondered why no visants had tried before to do what he was doing, tell someone inland that it was all delusion. Now he knew: They couldn't *get* inland, even if the shield let them go. He'd heard shielders say that deep inside, in Heartlands and Belt and Girdle, the stained were left to travel as they would. Here they would not let him travel any way but coastward. If he pushed past them, or tried to run, they'd gang on him, they'd ride him down, they'd turn him around and boot him on his way. There was a second shield within the shield that guarded Eiden Myr, and it defended against the stained.

He wondered what they would do if bladed shielders decided to bring their stain inside. If they left their posts en masse and drove inland, turning trained violence on any who tried to stop them. He wondered what would happen if he did manage to get through, and get the runners to arm people's minds against the imaginary assaults, because the shield would no longer be needed, then, and what would happen to all those stained? Would they be left at the coast to rot? Suppose they wouldn't lie down for that?

Terror grew in him, worse with every setback. Terror of half-glimpsed futures, terror of failure, terror of success. He'd have to move at night, creep across those harvested fields when they were unattended, but he feared this land at night, in the spirit days, under lowering clouds, no moonlight to show his way. Even the sky was trying to keep the stain from Eiden's insides. He'd be lucky if it didn't pour. The spirits conspired against him.

I didn't kill anyone! he wanted to scream. *I haven't done anything!*

He would have to find a way to use his powers. Could he threaten to reveal folk's secrets? Small thefts, betrayals, infidelities, resentments muttered behind backs, secret longings, humiliations? Everyone had something they did not want someone else to know. Couldn't he use that? Rise up in all his fearsome strangeness and cow them into letting him pass?

He couldn't do it. He couldn't ruin lives like that. There were things he could tell that people would never recover from, things that could destroy friendships, pledgings. He couldn't bluff; he'd have to be prepared to make good on any threat, and they'd know, they'd sense it on him, that he would never bring himself to tell such things.

They put him in the care of a man in black, running messages coastward. "He'll see you get where you're going, mostways anyway, and then it's not our problem anymore." The runner boosted him onto his horse and said he'd best go quietly or they'd only truss him.

"Aren't you afraid of me?" Ioli said. "You say I've killed. I'm already stained. I have nothing to lose. Aren't you afraid I'll knife you in the back?"

"I've no fear you'll kill your own. But Eiden Myr can't abide killers. Surely you understand that. The magewar, the battle in the Strong Leg—those aren't forgotten. Terrible losses. That must never happen again."

It made no sense, any of it. Such good intentions, but look how they applied them. It was homegrown madness.

If he'd killed, he could understand it. If the stain were just, he might accept it. He didn't know what he would have done if some real warrior had stood in flesh and blood over that shielder and poised to plunge a spear through her breast. Hide, probably. Scream and duck. You couldn't know a thing like that until it happened to you. Maybe he'd have thrown himself across her. But what if he'd had a spear in his own hands?

What if any of these people did?

He didn't know, he didn't know, he couldn't know. He remembered one time Jalairi fell. He didn't want to remember; he'd been doing well not remembering; it flashed into his mind the way the fall had, too fast to prevent. He *saw* the slick spot on the branch before she reached for it, he *saw* her fail to notice it and reach there, he *saw* the grip slide off before it did. He saw her fall the way he saw the leaf fall at dawn, before it fell. He could have stepped aside. Had time to step aside. Had time to call out, too, but no guarantee of staying her hand. What he did was gasp and brace and reach, and he knew the weight of her before it hit him, he knew the wrenched muscles in his arms before they caught her, he knew the rocks below him before they jammed into his ribs and spine, he knew their mass and sharpness and every bone that they would break. He was nine and she was three. He caught her. Not without thinking. Full knowing. Knowing all before it happened, except what he would do. That was his choice. There'd been no hesitation.

That was nine years ago and two, and he could still feel the plump weight of her, still smell her hair, her skin. Still hear her cry ringing in his mind. Still see her swinging off for help, a touch to heal his bones. *Don't fall, don't fall, don't fall*, he'd thought, until she'd returned safe in the care of the local touch and they made him whole again.

Jalairi.

He must not let the shield fail. He must not let delusion reach its killing hands into his jungle home. His sister was there, lost to him as surely as if he'd fallen from a great height where she still perched, but there, whole and well and safe, up in the canopy where sun could kiss her in his stead.

He *must* reach the Haunch holding.

He pushed off the runner's back and vaulted from the loping horse. Rolled knees over head, tucked close. Came up uninjured by the cursed flat road. The horse was skidding, turning on a pinpoint. No animal that large should move like that. He'd watched them in their pasture, but hadn't known what they could do under command of legs and reins. No one rode horses in the jungle. He burst into a sprint, daring the treachery of ground over the certainty of capture. The horse had him in the end, ran him down and circled him; the runner hauled him back aboard, he was a big man and strong and he just pushed back over the lip of his saddle and hauled Ioli up in front of him. "I hope we don't have to do that again," he said, voice as flat as the road.

"Take me to the holding," Ioli said. "I beg you. Take me to your head runner. I have a message he must hear. News about the shield. *Please.*"

"My route is around the maur," the runner replied.

Ioli held his breath, encouraged by the lack of resistance in the iron arms that imprisoned him. The man had listened, despite the trouble he'd just caused. He'd given honest answer. He was still thinking.

"You're stained," he said, after a while during which the only sound was the creak of linen stretched tight over the saddle's frame, the clop of the horse's hooves, the snort of its breath. "I couldn't take you to the holding were I bound there.

You must return to the shield." Ioli bit his tongue to still it. "Find a procurer," the runner suggested. "Send your message that way."

Ioli spoke from a memory of sidelong glances, leers, dark satisfaction: "There are no procurers I can trust."

The runner chuckled, deep and chesty. "Good on you, lad. Can't stand the louts, myself. All right. I'm stopping at a scribe's place next to pick up whatever scrolls he's sending late. After that I turn for the Girdle. I'll leave you off there, and you can have him scribe your message to the holding."

This was the best the man could offer. It might not be a bad idea. Besides being stained, he was on foot and unsure of his route. A morning rider could have his message in Pelkin's hands by tomorrow's eve. Pelkin might send back some scroll of safe conduct for him. Something with the authority to get him through. *I've sedgeweave here with the mark of Pelkin himself,* he would say. *You must let me pass.* If he could persuade the head runner that what he had to tell was important enough to summon him. If he could find the words.

Perhaps the scribe would help. Making words was what they did. They trafficked in the languages of tongue and glyph. Most had been wordsmiths under the old light. They were good at making words powerful—making words *do* things.

"Thank you," he said softly.

"You're all right," the runner said. "It must be quite a message, for you to chance a tumble like that."

I know how to fall, Ioli thought. *I've been falling my whole life.*

The scribe lived among a cluster of sod cottages roofed in cane. All were dark save his, leaking light around door and shutters, and one alive with dancing shadows and rowdiness. "Spirit house," the runner said, tying his horse to a ring in a post under the window. "Take no notice." Ioli imagined the sod house filled with cavorting haunts, but he could smell the distillations from three doors down. In the Toes they fermented palm sap. Here it was cane, a sweeter scent.

He stood in the doorway while the runner and the scribe completed their business and the runner explained Ioli. Then, to give the runner room to get out, he moved inside, past sedgeweave baled like squares of hay, shelves of inkpots, sacks of quills. The scribe was a heavyset man seated with incongruous primness at a lamplit table by the hearth. Ioli could smell the waxy lamp oil, a mustiness of feathers, leeks and carrots from a stew long eaten, a charcoal tartness that must be ink. His stomach turned. This place was too close, too cluttered, too smelly. He jumped when the runner clapped a hand on his shoulder on the way by and leaned down to say, "Behave yourself and he might let you stay the night. Spirits shield you, visant." Then he was alone with the sharp-eyed, chestnut-bearded scribe.

"Sit," the man said. He angled a fresh sedgeweave leaf in front of him. He unstoppered a jar and dipped his quill, testing it on an offcut. "Tell me your message."

There was nowhere to sit except a narrow bed strewn with scrolls. Ioli took the floor. It made him feel like a child at his father's knee. He didn't like it. This didn't feel right.

The scribe would not help him with his message. He asked, but the man said it must come out in his own voice. Ioli wondered if it would be different if he had something to trade. He was afraid to offer a gleaning. This man kept himself very close. Perhaps put all of himself into the glyphs he scribed, leaving nothing to show on his face. The way he held his body was all restraint. He considered himself a medium. A tool, like the scribing tools that filled his cottage, no room for ordinary living there.

Ioli closed his eyes and delved his mind for the best words to frame his account. He changed his phrasing here and there, asking the man to emend words already scribed, and he heard irritation in the scratch of the quill point. He stumbled over his name—would his family name make him sound more genuine, or should he concoct a shieldname here on the spot?—and said at last, in conclusion, "Just Ioli. And the name of this place, I suppose. Or Maur Sleith. My section of shield was partway round it, I don't know the town names there, there was a salt marsh . . . It doesn't matter."

The quill had stopped after he said his name. He opened his eyes. The scribe was holding the sedgeweave up at an angle. Shouldn't he sprinkle sand on it? Wasn't that what they did? It wouldn't dry in this humid air.

The scribe was reading the glyphs on the leaf. Ioli felt a surge of protectiveness, as though the message were private, even though he had just said it all out loud to this very man. But the scribe was a medium. A tool. He didn't think about the words while he rendered them. He thought about proportion and clarity, the lay of the sedge, whether his supplier was giving him the best cuts, whether the quill point needed dipping or sharpening.

Now he was reading the message, and Ioli wished he wouldn't. He found himself scrambling to his feet.

The scribe didn't scroll the leaf or reach for wax or seal. He tore it down the middle, then tore the halves in half.

"What are you *doing?*" Ioli cried.

"I won't send such ravings to the holding," the scribe said, and blew out his lamp. "I have a reputation to maintain."

"But—"

"You've paid me nothing, only cost me good ink and sedgeweave. I took your message as a favor to that runner. I've no obligation to pass it on, and I will not."

"But—you can't—"

"Begone," the scribe said, rising, dropping the torn fragments to the floor. They caught on the air and angled down like dying leaves. "Take your stain and your ravings and go. Back to the coast or anywhere else you like, it's no difference to me. Though from the sound of it you'll be no aid to the shield, if they'll even take you back."

Standing, he was large, and his approach drove Ioli backward and out of the cottage. Following him into the road, the scribe turned and worked a key in the door lock, then pocketed the key and swept a shooing arm in Ioli's direction. When Ioli just stood staring, he muttered something about visants and strode off to the spirit house. Its door opened on a roar of laughter and a blaze of profligate lamplight, then engulfed the scribe, and closed.

Ioli waited. He waited for them to drink their senses dull. He waited for the noise within the spirit house to surge to a climax of revelry. Then he pried the shutters open, stood on the hitching post, and slid through the window, down onto bales of sedgeweave, into the cottage.

In the embers' light he found the pieces of his message. The ink was somewhat smeared, but dry now; he could not tell whether it had smeared past reading, but he'd get the runner to tell him. Whatever runner he found on the road, whoever he could waylay on a legward course and press his torn words upon. The runner tonight had been almost sympathetic. He'd find someone like enough. Maybe even the same one, bound back the way he'd come. No matter how long it took. He would hide at the roadside and wait. There was water. It would be a nineday before he starved.

He crawled back out the window and dropped to earth to find the scribe standing in wait, an array of drunken neighbors around him.

He saw himself as they saw him. Ragged and filthy from sleeping rough. Wild and intense with an urgency he could not calm into conviction they would heed. Just another raving lunatic, with thieved sedgeweave in his hands. Stained with the deaths of none's-land.

Madness, he thought, when the first blow fell. Some of them hated him because of things other visants had done or said, or things they'd heard they'd done. Some of them hated visants because they were queer, they were slow, they were different. Some of them hated him because he'd been brave enough to join the shield, what they could never bring themselves to do, then turned its heroism to gibberish. One of them simply could not abide thieves and thought a good thrashing a sound lesson. Those at least made sense. Those at least had reasons. The others were in it for the pleasure. They wouldn't kill him. They'd never kill him. That would stain them. But the pleasure of lashing out against the stain, there was no harm in indulging that, and he was stained, he was a visant, he was fair game. Serve him right, for abandoning his post. Serve him right, for thieving off a scribe. Serve him right, for being queer.

Thoughts not Ioli's cluttered his head with sickening pleasure and reeking impulse. As his will flagged, he felt he was more them than him, more fist than bruise. That was the worst of all. To lose the knowing that was himself and become the knowing that was the mob, all mixed together, one raving mind with one raving purpose.

Madness, he thought, as thought slipped away. *This is the true madness.*

The wild roar that pierced the madness made no sense to him. The force that flung the mob away seemed invisible, preternatural, the runner's exhortation to the spirits made manifest, Sylfonwy herself sweeping through the madding throng to scatter them like cut cane. Too fast for his swelling eyes to see. He caught a glimpse of fist, a flash of boot. He should have felt them land. He was still as much the mob as Ioli. He only felt the ground heave up, the cursed flat land achieving dimension at last. He only felt their helpless outrage. He knew it as theirs, not his. The part of him that was him, curled tight inside itself, deep down where no bruises could reach, sensed a warm bluestone glow.

Reached out to it, as he fell. The longest fall he'd ever taken.

Felt it reach back.

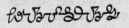

REILER N'GRAEFEL L'HANLA hefted his worn pack to a sore shoulder. The pack was all that remained of his long-ago binder's truss and the healer's bag that had replaced it. Its canvas was stained and frayed, but molded to his body, shaped to it—part of it. It slung onto shoulder and back like a companion.

Nowadays it carried only water and his midday meal, and only across his own modest acres. He'd acquired another dozen head of cattle, and a donation of lumber, and he faced another day of digging post holes to fence a new paddock, reclaiming one of the Legward meadows for pasture. The steers were aging and ornery and wouldn't tolerate crowding long.

What possessed me to refuse that last batch of prentices? he thought, with wry amusement. *Youthful hijinks beget extra chores. I'm failing to exploit a prime source of labor.* In fact, those who hadn't pitched in willingly hadn't stayed his prentices long. Whether they embraced farmwork and livestock was a means of gauging them, one of many he'd developed to compensate for the lack of the true means—a magelight of his own, with which to see and scent and taste the quality of others'. He'd worked blind for a long time, and been profoundly wearied by it. Now his first crop of young mages had passed their trials. There would not be a second. He would rather shoulder the load of maintaining this stead alone than spend one more breath training lights he couldn't see.

Light should train light. He'd done his part, in these transitional years. He was four nineyears of age and three. Old and tired enough to have earned some peace. Young and strong enough to fence a paddock by himself.

The geese and goats were fed and watered at dawn, before he broke his fast, but as he left his four-bay cottage—quiet now, with no sounds of vocal practice, no wrestling or horseplay, no spats over who took whose things—hooves clattered on the roof and three goats dropped down to accost him for head rubs. At the same time Snarl crept out of his sidewise barrel chocked by the door and came to heel, resolute in his refusal to yield his place to any presumptuous nanny. Dogs had never been bred for the binders' harvest, but some were unwanted just the same. Keiler didn't know who'd turned this one mean, though he'd have a chat with the fellow if he ever found out, but whatever the reason, the gray sheepdog wouldn't abide men. "I'd be grateful if you'd take him off our hands," the Sparrowhawk's taverner had said, at her wits' end, the last time he'd walked to town to indulge in ale that tasted of home. "We wouldn't hurt him, we've fed him and all, but he's bad for business and I've never seen him come out of that barrel for anyone till you." Keiler had called the dog to heel and rolled the bloody barrel the threemile home. Snarl had made a fine herder till his old joints seized. No female touch with the healing knack had been by since then.

"Not today," he told the dog. "I'm bound too far for your old legs. You keep those geese in line for me, eh? No snacking from the windowboxes."

With a sigh, the sheepdog found a sunny spot where he could warm his bones and watch for errant geese. The geese were old, too; it wouldn't tax him much.

Keiler moved down the gravel path with a rake, grooming as he went, then exchanged rake for spade and sledgehammer in the shed by the stone wall, and went out onto his land. A quick headcount of the near pasture proved that he hadn't dreamed the green glow in the window last night; one of the cows had passed. Touches kept them in good health, but the years were taking their toll. He said a soft prayer for the placid spirit and moved on. He eased their dotage as he could, and was content that in these days of the new light, there would be no more to take their place.

Only new batches of the old. There were only a few places like his—places of penance for the old binders' ways. If he were head of that Haunch holding, he'd see that every teacher, every hedge school kept some of these animals, while they lived to serve as a reminder. No good for breeding, no good for milking, no good for anything but being slaughtered and flayed for parchment or vellum, untold numbers of them were left when the magelight died. Many fell to disease and injury during the dark years, and more, of no use to anyone, even after there were touches who could heal them. A few former mages, like himself, had begun collecting them. Some had been bred by binders for the binders' harvest; others had been a binder's tithe from local dairyfolk and woolmongers. Now they were fed by binders' tithes. And by this binder's pastureland.

Magecraft used sedgeweave now, and newfangled materials or forgotten ones rediscovered—pressed rice mash, bamboo flitches, even bark and slate and canvas, once considered fit only for practice. It had changed the craft; they could no longer heal ailments of the flesh. It took materials of flesh to do that. But touches made mage healings obsolete. There was still plenty left to do, and material to do it with. You didn't need goatskin to fireward a building. You didn't need calfskin to wrangle rainclouds.

Keiler's first binder's harvest had changed him forever. Drugging the calf, trussing the legs, slitting the throat, draining the blood, removing the flesh. Harrowed and inconsolable, he couldn't bear to go home, where only mages dwelled—his mage parents, and the mage aunt who'd trained him. He'd hiked up the old binder's road behind the public house, to sit cradled by the roots of an ancient tree and nurse his hurts. He'd turned snarling on his best friend, his secret love, when she followed him. She'd intended only comfort, dismayed by his pain, and he'd turned on her like an angry stranger.

Funny, how the memory still stung after so many nineyears. Liath had forgotten it within a nineday. He remembered the first thought that had sounded in his head after the magelight had been ripped out of him: *Now I won't have to kill anymore.* He hadn't known what had happened, or that it hadn't happened only to him. He'd had no idea what it would cost him. He felt only profound relief of the burden he'd carried since childhood.

It was no wonder darkcraft had arisen, from a craft that routinely took life. He was glad that darkcraft had been routed. He had supported the rebel mage who routed it, though it had cost him his triad and the love of his parents and his intended pledge. He had cheered Liath for aiding that rebel, though she'd lost her heart to the man and that meant he could have no second chance at it. He was not sorry to have shed the romantic illusions of his youth, and he'd long ago recovered from that heartbreak. But the price for darkcraft's routing was the searing of the light, and from that he would never recover, any more than he would recover the lives his hands took in service of that light. Six years as a journeying healer had made barely a start. A dozen years training new binders in the kill-free magecraft the searing had bought them had made barely a start. Every head of livestock he saw to a gentle end—*that* was a start.

Reaching the track and the fence he'd begun yesterday, he set his pack and tools down, slugged some water, and took his spade to the seventh marker on the string that measured out the planned fence. Few travelers passed here, and fewer neighbors. He was alone with bee drone and birdsong.

Now I won't have to sing alone—that had been his second thought after the magelight died, when he found out it had happened to all of them. The prohibitions on singing and scribing and patterning would be lifted, and voices would join in song for the first time in generations. Now he found he rarely sang. He told himself that he preferred to listen to the earth's song. Birds and brooks had voices far more versatile than his. The truth was that he missed the power of singing to change the world in a casting. Worse, he missed the singing of his prentices. He'd encouraged them to sing for the joy of it, so long as they didn't strain their throats. He'd encouraged innovation, improvisation. He'd promised it would only improve their castings.

He'd told them true. They had passed their trials with outstanding results, surpassing binders trained only in rote canon. He was proud. He could not have done better by another batch. If you were going to release only a handful of new mages into the world, best they should be the best you could produce. He had done well. He could let go.

But now he would always sing alone.

Six holes dug by midmorning, his sweat-soaked shirt spread to dry in the harvestmid sun, he distributed the strain to other muscles by driving posts. The sledgehammer felt good in his hands. Swinging the weight over his head was exhilarating. The ringing clunk gave deep satisfaction. The rhythm of swings and impacts became its own song, and he smiled, happy in this task that most folk hated. Binders' work was the most grueling in all magecraft, but it was not as grueling as this. He reveled in a body hardened by hard work. In this, he was all flesh, no light at all. For this not even the memory of light was required. This was the sort of simple work he could dedicate the rest of his life to.

Only when he stopped for a drink and to mop his chest and brow did he hear the hoofbeats on the dirt track. He swore under his breath and wished the water cast into beer. Neighbors rarely came on horseback. This would be a runner or an aspirant. When would they understand that he wanted nothing more to do with magecraft? He would need a drink when this was over, no matter who it was.

The man who appeared, leading a mare strangely tricolored in bay, blue roan, and gold, was not the father of some six-year-old perched nervous in the saddle, nor was he dressed in black, save the coal-thick hair that tousled into his eyes and over his collar. Keiler, though he'd enjoyed his share of men after the romances of his youth, would never have described a man as beautiful, but this one was. Beautiful, and powerful, in ways Keiler had not seen since his magesight was blinded.

Steer clear of this one, something inside him said, wary and primed. *He's lost his way. Give him directions and think no more on it.* He leaned on his sledgehammer and waited while the man drew near, willed him to pass by, though there was nothing up this road but fields and farmhouses.

He did not pass by. Although his tunic and leggings were dusty with travel and his eyes shadowed as if he'd ridden through part of the night—ordinary signs of a human journey— it seemed as out of a dream that the man approached him, and halted on the other side of the fence-to-be. He gave the suggestion of a holding bow.

"Fair day to you," he said, in a quiet voice that blended with the birdsong, the bee drone, and raised the damp hairs on the back of Keiler's neck.

No introduction, no statement of intent, no request for directions. This was a man who waited to see what he was dealing with before he proceeded, even when he had broached the contact. There was the mark of one of the holdings in that, clearer than the bow, clearer than the air of authority so ingrained it had become casual. Keiler said, "The road to Sauglin's back behind you. You needed to bear right at the fork." The Norther Highlands accent burred his speech more than it had in years. Surprise flickered in the eyes of the man, who must have taken him for hired help until his bloody accent betrayed him.

"I doglegged at the fork. I've come from Sauglin. At Pelkin n'Rolf's behest. He requested I prentice myself. To you."

Pretty men looked younger than their years, but the difference between this man's age and Keiler's was no more than the span of a young child's life. There was only one grown man in Eiden Myr who had a magelight. "You're Louarn n'Evonder," Keiler said.

Dark blue eyes dipped down below their lashes. This time only the head bowed, briefly. The eyes came up first, to gauge his reaction.

"You took the wrong turn," Keiler said, his voice gone flat and cold as his father's, and as accentless.

Louarn's head cocked. "I know I've—"

"There are no mages here to prentice to."

"Perhaps the—"

"You've had a dozen years to learn your craft."

"And so I have."

"Then Pelkin sent you on a pointless errand."

"On the contrary. He hoped you could help me."

"I'm a farmer. A lightless steward of aging beasts. The man Pelkin sent you to see isn't here."

"I apologize for misjudging you at the first. It was arrogant of—"

"You judged correctly. This is what I do."

"Build fences? So it would seem."

"You've missed your calling as a wordsmith. Play your games with someone else." Keiler's anger mounted as he was drawn in by the verbal twists. This was wordplay typical of mages, holding mages in particular, an example of just what made him resist the Sauglin holding. Pelkin, who'd known him in the Neck, had tried to lure him here a year after the magewar, exhorting him to teach, to keep the binder's craft alive. When the light returned in the children, he'd acquiesced, but come only as close as this farmstead, a day's ride from Sauglin. He refused to be embroiled in holding intrigues, and once he dedicated himself to training the best mages he could, he wouldn't let his prentices near the place till they went off for their year of trial. Holdings bred mages like this one, pretentious and manipulative and full of schemes. There was no manipulation in a fence post. There was no scheming in the earth.

"You are the most revered and most sought-after teacher of binding magecraft in Eiden Myr," Louarn said. "The brightest lights fought for entry to your school, and some of the most troubled, whom no one else could teach. You changed lives and ennobled the craft while maintaining independence from the Sauglin holding. Or so they say. Teaching is a worthy craft. A pity to bury it."

"Earth is the craft I ply. Go ply yours, Binder."

"I promise you I did not come here to play wordgames with you. Binder."

Losing his temper, too? Good. If Keiler could get him angry enough, he'd stalk back the way he came and vent it in complaints to Pelkin. Maybe that would stop the old man sending aspirants down here. "There's a stream runs along the road back toward Sauglin. Your mount will be thirsty in this heat."

Louarn seemed to be trying to control himself, but as Keiler picked up his spade, the effort seemed less against irritation at Keiler's rude manner than against some impulse of his own. It seemed, in the strangest way, that he was struggling *not* to hide his reactions. Keiler dismissed the entire question and walked to the next marker on the string. Louarn said, "The head runner left it to me to discover what will persuade you to make one exception in your retirement. I've spent rather a large portion of my life persuading people to do what I wanted them to. I'd much rather you just tell me."

"Nothing," Keiler said, plunging the spade into the ground

and heeling the blade's shoulder to turn over a clod of turf. "No more games. Yes, I'm Keiler n'Graefel, and no, I no longer train binders, and nothing you say can change that. Go on your way."

Louarn stood still as a midday shadow for a long time. Keiler worked the ground hard, pouring sweat in the noon sun, his anger only fueled by the frank consideration he felt from the motionless form by the fence. He dug his anger into the hole, piled it along the miniature earthwork accumulating along the string, moved on to the next marker. He almost managed to forget the bloody lingering irritant pondering his fence-in-progress.

Then Louarn stepped over the string.

The mare, loosely ground-tied, shifted across the road to forage along the bushes. Louarn, as Keiler straightened and hefted his spade, unlaced his plain linen shirt and pulled it over his head to drape on the third post down. With a glance at Keiler and his spade, he picked up the sledgehammer still standing on its head. Expressionless, he turned, and in a pale, slender arc swung the hammer over his head and drove the nearest post, left half-driven and forgotten in Keiler's annoyance, solidly into its place.

Keiler could only stare as Louarn fetched the next post and set it in position. When Louarn paused, as though waiting permission, Keiler shrugged. Again the pale arc of wiry strength, the ringing clunk of impact, and again, and a third time, to drive it home. No grunt of effort. No complaint, no chuckled excuse of being out of trim. Louarn assessed the lack of progress Keiler had made on the next hole, then moved three pieces from the lumber pile into place by the driven posts.

With a few tools fetched from his saddlebags, some twine from his pocket, and the use knife from his belt, Louarn mounted the rails. Not banging them up with the iron nails Keiler would have brought the next day, but joining them, pegs through wood into carved seating. He worked effortlessly but with total concentration. Keiler had never seen craftership like it, in years of helping neighbors build pens, both here and at home in the Neck. Eiden strike him, but it was . . . beautiful. Almost the work of a touch whose talent was wood.

His eye strayed back to the horse. He did not think too much on the strange coloring, but he marked its implications. He continued digging, doubling back to drive posts when his digging muscles flagged, and when the shadows lengthened toward evening there was two-thirds of a fence built. Louarn had taken only one break, to pour water of his own into his hat for his horse to drink, then drink himself.

"Come back with me, then," Keiler said at last, retrieving his shirt to pull over the cooling damp of his flesh, watching Louarn do the same and cursing himself—for the watching, for the offer, and for being a bloody fool.

Louarn led his horse around the fence and shouldered the sledgehammer while Keiler was slinging on his pack. Keiler took the spade, and, without words, they started the journey through the pastures, to his home.

Keiler paused at the gate for the dog to slink into his barrel at sight of the male stranger. Instead he rose, stretched his front legs with a yipping yawn, and came to meet them. Louarn, laying a friendly hand on him, stifled a sound and went to one knee. The dog laid his chin on the other knee and let the hands stroke down his shoulders and legs and over the bony points of his hips. Then he let out a contented whuff and trotted around to Keiler's heels.

"I'm not strong with flesh," Louarn said quietly, shifting under Keiler's gaze but not returning it. "I did what I could."

"Have you all three lights?" Keiler asked, to have out with it. Not that any light or shine or glow would explain the dog's behavior.

Louarn frowned. "You didn't know? You knew the name Louarn n'Evonder."

Keiler snorted and replied, "Your fame fails you." He took the mare's reins to lead her around back.

"Yours doesn't," Louarn said, in a low tone of respect, urging the mare on with a hand on her flank when she balked, head down and wary, at the unfamiliarity of scooting geese.

Embarrassed to receive sincerity in trade for scorn, Keiler bade the man go in and have a seat, thinking, *"The name," he called it. Not "my name." Not as if it should speak for itself, but as if it wasn't quite a part of him.* After he'd made the mare comfortable, he found Louarn sitting in the path, grinning, surrounded by goats all butting in to be the one he petted. Upon Keiler's return, the smile shut down—hidden, too genuine to be risked in company—and he said, "What you've done here, it's a fine and gentle thing."

Keiler nodded, and gestured him into the cottage, and pressed down firmly on the swell of his heart. "Tell me, then," he said, pouring the ale, setting out a board with bread and cheese. "You say you've learned your craft. Why come to me?"

Standing to slice food for them both while Keiler busied himself at the woodbox, Louarn said, "My craft is flawed. Unreliable."

"You're a touch. That's hard to countenance."

"Something in my light, then? Sometimes it works, sometimes it doesn't."

Keiler was abruptly and unaccountably stabbed with the memory of Liath's magelight failing her the night of her own celebration for passing her trial. Of Ferlin's voice, sweet and selfish, calling him away over the millbridge, purposely preventing him from giving comfort. He'd seen other magelights fail in trial. He didn't know why that memory rose with such painful vividness. "If it's your light, you're in the wrong place. I'm quite blind to it."

"Young mages in two holdings pronounced my light more than adequate," Louarn said. No pride in it at all; simply a statement of fact, a piece of a puzzle he'd laid out for countless others. "And frequently it does the job. The question is when it doesn't."

Having laid a cookfire under the stewpot in the hearth, Keiler struggled with strikers and recalcitrant kindling. Louarn knelt beside him; their fingers brushed as he took the metal in hand, and he drew into himself, forcibly, before he touched a piece of wood and then struck a flame with the first spark. "The wood doesn't mind," he said, in a vague tone, then took himself back to the table and stood as though uncertain what to do with his hands.

This is ludicrous, Keiler thought. Two adults; they would make short work of it, and move on. *If it were anyone else—* He cut the thought off hard. It wasn't. Pelkin had sent him a remarkable aspirant, and the least he could do in return for an afternoon's work was divine the problem, whether or not he could solve it. No dalliances.

"Sit down, Louarn," he said, all brisk business now. "Eat something. Drink up. What sort of castings does it fail in?"

"Every sort, and none. There is no pattern." Louarn sat slowly, as though wary of assuming a place here, even though that was precisely what he'd been sent to do. *I feel it too,* Keiler thought. *Set it aside.*

"Different wordsmiths and illuminators each time?"

"The same, at different times; different ones at other times."

"When you're weary or overtaxed?"

"Or fresh and rested. Cheerful or irritable, centered or distracted. It's been a year of this. I'd have distilled the commonality if there were one."

One side of Keiler's mouth pulled back in a grin. "You should always be centered, never distracted. Never irritable." He chuckled at the flash in the man's eyes. So there was craft pride there. Good. There should be. "All right," he said. "I get the gist. Just one more question, and then we'll have a look at you while the stew warms. Does it fail you when your other lights are roused?"

It was a key question. Few folk possessed two lights, and none all three so far as Keiler had known before today. In some seared mages, a second light emerged to fill the void, but that was rare as well, and a disappointment to many whose hopes had flared at the discovery of touches and visants. One of his early prentices, however, had shown a copper shine as strong as her bright magelight; one had interfered with the other to the point where she gave up the rigors of magecraft and contented herself with working wood. Keiler had seen what Louarn could make of a pile of lumber and some posts. It could be that every time he touched a binding board or sedgeweave, some part of him shone in response; Keiler could not imagine the complication of a visant's glow.

"No," Louarn said, with perhaps too sharp a promptness. "I've grown adept at managing . . ." That was more than he'd meant to say, but he forged on: ". . . my different . . . selves."

Keiler waited, giving him space to continue, finishing his snack. He'd just drained the last of his ale and was drawing breath to speak at last when Louarn said, "But sometimes, when *I* am roused . . . when I . . . care about what I'm doing, when the casting has a personal importance, or . . ." He faltered, frowning; muscles worked in his jaw as he ground his teeth.

That was odd. Putting one's heart into a casting strengthened it. To spare the man further obvious discomfort—and himself further talk of rousings, which he would very much rather avoid—he said, "No matter. We'll sort it in the bindinghouse. Come on."

Taking charge, donning with ease the teacher's cloak he had hung up for good. Well, it was safe garb, and it was why the man was here, not to gall him with his holding manner or fill a space at Keiler's hearth he had not known till now was empty. He crossed the yard under a moon-dark sky, and hung three lanterns from their hooks in the rafters of the bindinghouse, bathing the ample, cluttered space in golden light. He hadn't decided yet what to do with the building's contents—trade it to journeymages over time, or pack it all off to Sauglin and convert the building to some other use. A fair head of stock could be sheltered in here.

He tried not to look as Louarn caressed the fine lay of sedgeweave, the smooth richness of charcoal, drank deep of the scents of iron gall and linseed oil and paint. Keiler loved the smell of this house, the piquant perfumes of magecraft; the reek of lime and the stench of rancid lard had never touched this place, and no blood had ever stained the ground beyond it. He permitted himself a gracious nod as Louarn complimented the materials, and said, "Most of it's the work of prentices." Before Louarn could return some politeness crediting the master, he said, "You've all the raw goods here, if you can find them. I want the items required to cast a barrel watertight. From scratch." They might as well do Snarl an overdue favor while they were at it.

Louarn cleared a space at the large worktable in the center and set to his assignment. He brought the same relaxed concentration to this as to the fence. He chose the right kind of leaves for the sedgeweave, and set them to soaking while he chose a different kind of reed for the pen, putting accuracy above efficiency, the right decision. He ground a variety of pigments, in small measures, then before proceeding further asked what sort of wordsmith and illuminator he would be casting with. Keiler didn't know—if it proved necessary, he'd send a bird for some tomorrow and hope they made good speed—so he invented a traditionalist wordsmith difficult to please, and an illuminator expansive with her knotwork and sparing with her powerful kadri. He startled when Louarn looked up at him for the first time. "What?" he said, bemused; not a little unnerved by the intensity of the dark-lashed sapphire gaze, not a little peeved by his body's reaction to the eye contact.

"Your pardon," Louarn said. "It's nothing."

As Louarn returned to his work, preparing oak-gall ink in addition to the lampblack a less picky wordsmith would default to, and enlarging his selection of pigments for the illuminator, Keiler realized with a start that he had invented his father and Liath. Louarn had sensed it.

Bloody visants. They rattled his teeth. This situation was charged enough without that kind of insight. He didn't let himself think what else the man might glimpse in him. He was managing the only thing he'd prefer to keep private. Attraction was an irritation he'd set aside enough times before.

The sedge Louarn laid was impeccable, creatively woven to

echo the cooper's work without compromising the mat, and when he stood back, a perfect array of materials lay on the table before them, neatly arranged in the order they would be requested.

"Well done," Keiler said, though it deserved higher praise. The man was an instinctive crafter, aided by shine and glow Keiler couldn't begin to comprehend. In this, he'd passed. "Now I'll ask you to sing for your supper."

For a moment, the shadow that crossed the pale, boyish features made Keiler believe he'd found the trouble. This man had grown up, as he had, in a time when singing was forbidden outside the binding circle and mages' practice rooms, and he'd taken up the art of voice as an adult. It must have been some effort to shed the inhibitions of a lifetime. But Louarn obediently ran through a series of wordless canonical melodies, then demonstrated proficiency with two newer lyric songs. His tongue wasn't tangled by the curls of Celyrian, his throat blended the unmusical Ghardic into the melodic line without choking. His voice was lower than his speaking voice, and richer, and well trained; it was as beautiful as he was, and Keiler's command to stop came just short of rude. A teacher's perquisite, to be brusque, unpredictable, to keep his pupils off balance. He'd never indulged in those games, he'd been a warm and affable mentor; he'd taken care not to become his father. But he was too relieved when the singing ceased to care how he had ordered it.

Its only flaw was a tight sense of rote performance. That was common, in tests and during practice. It would pass, in the heat of a casting, when the magelight was in use, warmed by blending with the wordsmith's and illuminator's.

"I'll send a bird to Sauglin at dawn," he said. "There's nothing wrong with your craft. I regret the necessity of putting you through your paces to confirm what we already knew."

Louarn smiled for the first time without hiding it, a soft smile, like a moonrise blurred through tears. "It's all right," he said. "I love the craft."

Nothing wrong with this binder at all, and far too much right. Keiler started taking down the lanterns. "You can sleep in one of the prentice bays," he said. "I haven't dismantled them yet." *It doesn't mean I'm taking you on,* he thought, as they left the darkened bindinghouse and Snarl escorted them to the cottage. As they spooned sunroot stew into themselves in silence, he thought, *Tomorrow we'll solve your problem and you'll be gone with my blessing on a productive career.* The stew would be better tomorrow, twice cooked. It was still too fresh. Tomorrow night this man would take his three invisible lights and go, and leave Keiler to the peace of his empty cottage and uncompromised principles.

Tomorrow night he would not sit up late by the fire, Snarl come into the house to lie at his feet, listening to soft breathing through the open door, the sweet, eerie sound of the binder's low voice murmuring in dreams.

The wordsmith and illuminator arrived toward late afternoon, while Louarn was down at the stream washing off the day's fencing labor and Keiler, having opted for a bucket of cold water over a head upon which the metaphor did not fail to register, was setting the stew to cook again. For one breath of suspended memory, he thought to suggest they cast a few neglected preservings in his pantry and his cellar while they awaited Louarn. Some days the craft was like a phantom limb. He hid the twinge and made the mages welcome.

They brought news and holding gossip, to which Keiler attended only vaguely. Who was in, who was out; some blinding arc of light they all claimed to have seen crossing the sky a few nights ago, no doubt just a freakish manifestation of the pole aurora. Pelkin himself had been talking about retirement for some while, as he took more often to his bed with various ailments of his age, denying the healing of any touch and accepting only a few mender's herbal easements; so Keiler didn't worry overmuch when the one item that caught his ear was

Pelkin ailing. The young mages didn't seem worried. They considered Pelkin nearly immortal, and Keiler suspected they were right.

Louarn returned fresh and groomed with Snarl gamboling around him. The dog got one whiff of the male wordsmith and crawled into his barrel. That was a problem Keiler hadn't foreseen, considering that he'd planned to have them cast the leaks from that barrel. Then Louarn coaxed the dog out and into the barn, and their way was clear to complete the casting before they lost the daylight.

All went well, too well, as they prepared. Both boy and girl were instantly smitten by the older man; they went tongue-tied before his handsomeness and the quiet power he exuded, awed to meet someone nearly the sum of both their ages who showed a magelight. Their gaping awkwardness threatened to undo any casting they might attempt; but Louarn put them at their ease with an effortless charm, and in seeing it applied Keiler was struck by the understanding that Louarn had refrained from applying it to him. He charmed these children, and they adored him; he made them feel wise, and important, and secure in themselves. They responded to his casual authority without knowing it, and they relaxed in his hands like stiff joints gone supple.

They'd have done anything for him. It had taken Keiler years of firm, warm kindness to earn that kind of loyalty from his prentices. What he inspired would last a lifetime, and what Louarn produced would likely fade as soon as they left his company. But for the duration of the casting, it was a remarkable thing to witness, and made Keiler's job of suppressing his envy all the harder. Their lights would join with Louarn's, now. Keiler had grown so weary of watching these joinings, forever outside the circle, the eternal observer.

Just this once, this last time. As a favor to Pelkin. In repayment for daywork. Just this one more time, he'd bear it.

He noticed that neither mage had responded to Louarn's light, only to him. It was amazing that a man of his age should have one at all, their reaction said; you couldn't expect it to be very bright. Yet Keiler had expected Louarn to be very bright indeed.

When he cast, all of that changed. Subtly at first, as his only tasks were to offer materials or supply them on request, and as the wordsmith applied himself to his scribing, the illuminator to her painting. They knew this was a test of their skills as much as of Louarn's; Pelkin never sent them anywhere without their trial in mind. But as Louarn's turn came, it was as though the sun rose where he sat and was reflected shining in their young faces. As he laid the inscribed, illuminated sedgeweave on the battered barrel in the center of the casting circle, and took their hands in his, the swell of light affected the young mages with such intensity that numb Keiler would have sworn he felt it.

Then Louarn drew breath, and closed his eyes, and sang, and Keilèr understood everything.

"It was caring, just as you said," Keiler told him as they ate. The mages, bewildered and humiliated and unwilling to believe the failure wasn't theirs, had chosen to ride back at night rather than stay in one of the prentice bays. "You developed a fondness for the dog, possibly as a result of some kind of bonding when you healed him, and that affection thwarted you in trying to make his refuge comfortable."

Louarn had waited with expressionless patience for Keiler's verdict. He made Keiler wait now, in turn, as he cleaned his bowl with a scrape of wood on wood, soaked up with the last of his bread the last, unspoonable remains of stew, chewed and swallowed the bread, washed it down with the last of his ale, then arranged bowl and spoon and cup neatly on the table, wiped his mouth, wadded the cloth, tossed it into the bowl, and sat back.

"You're lying," he said.

Keiler met his stare. "Only by omission."

"Tell me, then."

"Can't your blue glow illuminate the truth in me?"

Louarn's blue eyes flickered as he saw far more than was comfortable for him, but there was nothing of the visant's sight in it. "I don't have that kind of light."

"What kind is it, then?"

"That's not the question."

"It is if I'm asking it. Answer me."

Dark hawk's-wing brows drew together. "I see patterns," he said to the table, grudging. "I solve puzzles."

"And make them."

Again the gaze came up before the head did. "That's a good guess."

"I've had a lot of practice with unforthcoming prentices."

"I'm not one of them."

"No. I haven't taken you as a prentice."

"And now you won't."

"I don't have to. You don't need a teacher. You had a masterly teacher. Your craft is flawless."

"And therein lies the problem."

"No. Flawless is flawless. No blemish, no imperfection. What you are capable of defies measure."

Louarn's fists were clenched to bloodless knuckles in his lap, where he did not realize Keiler was tall enough to see. In a measured, level voice, he said, "Then what prevents it?"

"What does prevent it, Louarn?"

Louarn rose snarling from the table and strode to the hearth to stare down the rivulets of light running in the embers. The dog rose under the table and stood with hackles spiked; failing to find the source of alarm, he settled back to the floor, eyes slitted.

"What prevents it, Louarn?" Keiler pressed, from his seat.

"Don't work me," Louarn said.

"I won't give it to you."

"Then I'll go."

"No. You won't." Keiler released a shaky breath and rose to stand behind Louarn. He'd hoped it wouldn't come to this as much as he'd hoped it would. "You won't go with the other unfinished."

Louarn laughed, a full-bodied release of tension from the belly through the chest, the throat. *So close, so close to what he needs to understand,* Keiler thought, and cursed the part of him that wanted to show him the other way. "Don't seduce a seducer," Louarn said. "The irony is unbearable. And so bitterly unfair, when I refrained from doing the same to you despite every temptation." He drew breath; it came in ragged. "And unethical besides."

"You're not my prentice. I wouldn't have you. The answer's too easy. It's in your fists. It's in your laughter. Listen to yourself, Louarn. You don't need me."

"On the contrary," Louarn said, still with that vestige of the holding, keeping sentiment at safe distance with rhetoric. "Quite the contrary, I'm afraid."

"I'm not your teacher." He stepped in closer; he was a head taller; his breath brushed the hairs over Louarn's ear. "I'm no one's teacher anymore. Just an ordinary, lightless man with a singing voice I'm not afraid to use."

It was so quiet he could almost hear Louarn blink. "Is that the answer, then?" *But I sing,* Keiler imagined the internal voice protesting. *I sang for you. You were so roused you silenced me. I sang in the casting. It was the right song for the task, and I performed it . . . flawlessly.*

"Come inside," Keiler said. Only his own rigorous vocal training got the words out without breaking. "We can take care of this in there."

Louarn's voice tightened to a whisper. "I can't."

"Why?" Keiler asked, feeling the heat of Louarn's back, feeling him tremble. "Why, Louarn? You want this."

"Too much. I want it too much. It's something I use, a way that I get what I want. I've learned, over the years. I learned how not to use it. That mattered to me. Matters to me. A great deal. I don't . . . know how to . . ."

"Come to bed, Louarn," Keiler said, stepping away. "We'll find out how."

He left him standing by the fire, and went in, and turned the covers down; removed his clothes with care and folded them on their trunk; slid into the bed and warmed it with himself. Only then did the firelit rectangle of the doorway fill with the shadow that was Louarn, limned in the color of magelight.

It had been some while since either of them had indulged in this, but both were adept; either could have led, both tried. Keiler's hands and weight and purpose were adamant. Louarn was unaccustomed to relinquishing control, but Keiler took control, gentle and insistent, working him and opening him until the greater pleasure lay in surrender. He gritted his teeth against his own release, and equally against his instinct to be tender. He waited for the moment when Louarn's face turned reflexively away. "Look at me," he said. Louarn, who until now had been completely silent, responsive flesh the only indication of when Keiler had it right, mumbled something inarticulate that was *no*. "Look at me," Keiler repeated, harsher; still moving, unrelenting, increasing pressure, friction, pleasure. He cupped the pale jaw in his strong binder's hand and turned the head to face him. It strained to turn back; Louarn's hand caught his hip, to belay him, then fell away, not wanting it to stop, just wanting to keep the end close within himself. "Open your eyes," Keiler urged, his voice gone hoarse; he held the jaw firm, but he was slipping into ecstasy, he couldn't stay the rhythm. "Open your eyes, Louarn. Share it with me. *Louarn*—" He cut off with a cry, he'd passed the brink, it was too late. While he was lost, Louarn had flung his face aside; Louarn was following him in shuddering echo, but into a realm inside himself, closed off behind his closed eyes. Still, the groan that wrenched out of him was a wanton, raw, abandoned thing, and Keiler was swept through an afterswell of climax to hear it. "That's your answer," he said, as his neck went boneless and his head sank. "*That's the song,* Louarn. But you have to share it."

The young mages were back at dawn, contrite, begging permission to try again. Keiler welcomed them saving him another bird, another request, a new set of mages. He set the three of them around the barrel, and this time when Louarn's turn came he moved around to stand behind him, to lean down and murmur low in his ear, "Open your eyes, Louarn. Share it."

He wanted to chuckle at the involuntary response that elicited in the slender body. It did not interfere. It went into the casting, became as much a part of the binder's song as his compassion for a mistreated dog and the pure love he felt for this craft he'd embraced.

They'd spoken long into the night about Louarn's lad-of-all-crafts past, about the tortuous road that had led him at last to the binder's craft, the one he was bred for. About how he bound the three lights within himself. About the history that bound the two of them: people they had both cared for, broken illusions that littered the trails they left, the harrowed little boys who dwelled within them both. "But there's the trick," Keiler had said, draping a loose arm across Louarn. Louarn stayed of his own choice, the culmination of years spent learning not to walk away from what he loved. "Binding isn't always about binding. Binding is as often about release."

Now he moved around the periphery of the casting circle to watch Louarn open his eyes and release his bindsong into the sweet morning air. Dissipating the sedgeweave; sealing the cracks and mending the leaks. Putting into it all the feelings that he felt, large or small. Opening his soul.

"That's the song, Louarn," he said softly. He was nearly as awed as the astonished young mages.

Never before had a hoop-sprung old tavern barrel been mended so well.

That night, when the mages were gone, and the paddock was finished, and the supper was eaten, and the dog, unimpressed with their casting, had forgone his barrel for the foot of their bed, Louarn took control, with a mastery and tenderness that robbed Keiler of breath. At the end, Louarn's eyes were open, fierce and glazed and powerful, staring naked and adoring into his, and in the blending of ecstasies Keiler felt what he'd only ever felt before from the blending of lights, and far surpassed it.

* * *

In the slender hour before dawn, Keiler found the bed empty, pulled a robe on against the chill, and padded out into the common room, where Louarn sat at the table, wrapped in his cloak, staring at a single guttering candle.

Keiler sat where Louarn had sat at supper. "That was fresh-dipped when I put it in the holder. Have you been staring at it since you lit it?"

Louarn nodded from a place far away, but summoned a tired smile for him. "I didn't like to leave your side. It's a warmer spot, though sometimes bony."

Keiler smiled in return, and said simply, "Tell me."

"I have . . . dreams. They hold great power. I believe they are the product of the three lights inside me, working as one. They can transport me from one place to another, one realm to another, through a sort of tunnel, like light, or crystal. When I was a boy, they brought horrors into this realm, razored shadows, dark things from a . . . bad place. Unchecked, they can kill. They've been known to turn on me. In these dozen years I have learned to control the dreams, inasmuch as I can now sometimes get a half night's sleep without waking up somewhere else. Or destroying the world. Or endangering the person I . . . love, beside me."

He paused, and Keiler nodded. This was the power he had sensed in Louarn when they met. It wasn't the risk of a broken heart that had raised his hackles, though his inner sense, with its deep mistrust of love at first sight, had warned him against that too. It was the power of three lights combined, a power so intense that even the lightless could apprehend it. Or, more likely, Louarn's control of that power. A heady attractant, that kind of control.

Keiler had breached it.

Louarn feared what opening himself might have opened the world to.

"You think perhaps you should go." He said it before any rancor could rise, any panic, any weakness.

"I've been a wanderer for a long time."

"I was one too, long ago." Keiler thought of his days as a journeying healer, and his mage journeying years before that.

The call of the road. He still felt it, now and then. But not enough to follow. Not for a lifetime. "I understand."

"Don't be so quick to." Again Louarn smiled. It was grand to see the ease with which he smiled now. "Half my heart lies here. Half my heart lies with three young women in Gir Doegre. I'm responsible for them, though they've almost grown up. They're very powerful, and very dear to me, and I fear they'll need me in what's to come." He paused. "But I need you. I'll always need you, now." He raised haunted eyes to Keiler and said, "Other people are going to need you, too. Consider that a visant's gleaning."

Now Keiler felt the surge of pleas and denials. He bit down on them. Two grown men, old enough to know the bond of a lifetime when they found it. Old enough to know that lives did not always follow the same paths. They'd have made short work of lust. If only that had been all it was.

He would not let pain sully this joy. "It's not so bad," he said, "having two places to hang your heart." He grinned. "And you say you can travel through dreams? That's convenient, eh?"

"There are grave perils in it. I shudder to think of the risks I took in my youth."

"As do we all." Keiler left his reply at that neutral acknowledgment and waited. He would do much waiting, in a cottage the darker for having been lit so bright. The peace he'd cherished seemed a dull thing, and gray, from this vantage. He must trust that it was still there, waiting for him to reinhabit it, as he must trust in Louarn's return.

When he could no longer bear to wait the parting sorrow, the rustle of clothes as Louarn dressed, the creak of the saddlebags slung over his shoulder, he did the Norther thing: he got up and put the kettle on. The banked embers of the cookfire were easily stirred. He hoped that was another metaphor.

When he turned around, Louarn was still at the table, stock-still, muscles tensed into ridges, staring into the darkness of the open doorway to the first of the prentice bays. Keiler bent his knees without thought, without haste, to grope an iron from the hearth.

"Keiler?" said a hesitant voice. A voice that reached into his past. Into his soul.

It seemed an eternity in which his body swiveled toward the doorway where Liath stood. "Li?" His own voice sounded nineyears younger, lips and throat shaping a name he hadn't said in all that time. "How did you . . . ?" He must have made as if to lunge into an embrace; she stepped back into a fighter's guard and reached behind her head, found the grip of a long-blade nestled in the folds of her cloak's gray hood. Keiler pulled up, looked at the iron in his hand; looked back at her, blinking. He carefully replaced the iron in its wrought stand, and showed his empty hands.

She looked at them, uncomprehending, and then looked at Louarn, risen to stand by him, calm but for the hand that fisted in Keiler's robe. It caught some skin as well, and Keiler winced. At least he knew he wasn't dreaming.

"Mellas?" Liath said. Surprise, then pain, then relief crossed her face, only just visible at the flickering edge of candlegutter and fireshadow. "Mellas. I tried to find you."

"I went far," Louarn said quietly. "But I survived. I have a new name now."

Her gaze went lost, unfocused. He'd used to read the changing weather in those gray eyes. "So much is new," she said, and staggered.

Over the gulf of years, Keiler reached to steady her, then drew her into his arms. She was no dream, no haunt; real tears dampened his neck. He'd forgotten she was as tall as he, remembering the child who'd lagged two years behind him in age. But the young woman who drew back from him, though her scarred face attested to brutal experience beyond her years, was barely a year older than his oldest prentices.

The last time he'd seen her, she'd lain fevered in a tent after the magewar, delirious with grief for her wordsmith and bindsman. He'd been delirious with freedom, no idea yet what losing his magelight meant. She'd known. She'd sent him away, as though she couldn't bear to see him. Later on, he'd understood the way she'd looked at him. But she was gone to sea by then.

Now she was standing here. That same young woman. Still dressed in the black boots and breeches she wore then, the loose white shirt, the dove gray cloak. Holding attire, a mix of reckoner and warder and vocate. The breeches were torn in the same place, showing a pale flash of knee.

"Sweet spirits, Liath, *where have you been?*"

"Sailing," she said. "Surviving. There are horrors out there, Keiler." She looked up at him as if startled. "They've taken triskeles at home. Befre's son. Nole's daughter. Oh, Keiler, they look just like us. But happy."

How could she have seen that? Oriane and Delf would be celebrating their new magehood only now. "I'm glad," he said, not knowing how else to respond, not knowing what to do with this young woman who couldn't be. "I'm glad there was no Graefel to stand in their way."

"Graefel?" In an instant she was her old self, ready to defy his father as he'd never had the stones to. "I could have had you but for *Graefel?* Eiden's bloody . . ."

"I'm sorry, Li." The same words, over and over. Maybe she was a haunt—or a dream in which regrets echoed forever. But he'd touched her. Could some new healing or casting turn back the years like that?

Of all the questions, the one that squeezed out past his resistance was "Is there a light in her, Louarn?"

Louarn shook his head, squinting. "She was seared in the magewar. It is her, but . . ." He shook his head again.

"Mellas," she said, with the affection you'd show a younger brother. "I've been trying to find you, but you're so changed. Funny to find you here with Keiler."

Keiler had the strangest, saddest feeling that it was Louarn she'd been looking for, not him. Not the fool boy who'd let his father drive them apart. They'd been inseparable as children, but it was the Ennead runner boy she'd sought on her return, and only found him by accident when she gave up and came to Keiler instead. Then he didn't know why he'd think such a thing.

"I tried to see Pelkin, but I couldn't get in. Something—"

She halted, confused, then shook herself. "I'm glad you survived. We lost so many. Tolivar . . . Bron . . ." She choked on the other names.

"You don't get in from the back," Louarn murmured. "There is no back. You get in from the top. Or the sides."

Liath grinned. "You can't get in from the top, either. Though I'd have tried if I could." She took in the sight of Louarn's hand on Keiler, the candlelit cottage, their state of undress, and her grin widened. "Well, that's the last thing I'd have expected. Fair play to the both of you."

They both started to answer at once, but Liath whirled, looking into the darkness behind her, then said, urgently, "Keiler, Pelkin's dying. You have to go there. You have to cast passage."

Keiler's stomach went cold. "Have you been there?" She'd said she couldn't get in. What had they told her? Pelkin was ailing again, the young mages had said as much, but . . .

I should have heeded them more closely.

Liath said, "I don't know where I am." She frowned at him. "What's happened to your light?"

"Liath—"

"Where's Hanla? Maybe she can . . ."

"My mother's on Khine. But Liath—"

"I have to go," she said. "I've lost . . . I have to find . . ."

"Liath!" he cried, somewhere between an order to a prentice and a plea to his first love, and he reached for her, but she'd retreated into the darkness, and when Louarn followed with the candle she was gone. Doors and windows were all shut tight against the chill. She had been flesh and bone and tears in his arms, but she had fled into darkness like a haunt.

"What in all the bloody, raving spirits was that?" he said.

"Something extraordinary," said Louarn, moving to fetch his clothes from the bed. "But I don't know what." Snarl lay asleep under the table, as though nothing at all had happened. He didn't mind women. There was no telling how he felt about haunts. "I do know that she spoke the truth."

"The truth?" Keiler followed, dropping his robe to the floor. He pulled on fresh silks and socks, then the shirt and trousers he'd folded on the trunk. "She thought I should still have a light. She looked as though she hadn't aged a day in two nineyears. What kind of truth is that?" He didn't even know why he was dressing. To follow her? To search? His mind was stunned. He couldn't think.

"The truth about Pelkin. The rest is a mystery that will have to wait, but she was certain about him. Pelkin sent me here as though performing his last act. I took him for a master patterner playing feeble to bend me to his designs. I won't disregard this too. I've got to go back to the holding, Keiler."

Keiler stamped into his boots and reached for his pack.

"You can't," Louarn said, lacing his shirt, then sat to pull his own boots on. "Who'll look after your stock?"

"I've neighbors who'll pitch in for a few days."

Louarn looked doubtful, but accepted the answer, and it was dawn by the time they'd packed materials and rations and abbreviated the morning chores and saddled Louarn's tricolored mare and Keiler's bay, and the nearest neighbors were up and about their own work, and willing enough to repay Keiler for past times he and his prentices had lent them a hand.

A family emergency, Keiler had told them. His father in the Head, his mother on Khine, his aunt and cousin in the Neck, his brother in Shrug; all estranged, or made strangers by distance. He hadn't thought he had family anymore.

He hiked his worn pack higher on his shoulders, and reined his horse around beside Louarn's, and doglegged onto the Sauglin road.

WARM BLUE SLATE cooled by rivulets of quicksilver. Supporting, soothing; preventing the fall. Another feeling, too. Buoyancy. Submerged but not drowned. Held but gently drifting. Unconfined. Dark blue that was limitless and incomprehensible as the sea, the night sea, but not to fear; to bask in. Blue so dark it shimmered. Mysterious, ancient, and deep.

He'd felt that glow before. He did not know when. It was timeless. The other was placeless. He didn't know what his was. He couldn't feel his own. He didn't know what color he was, or what quality; only that he was blue and silver. Visants told him so, and he knew they spoke the truth. That knowing was his glow. None had ever told him what kind of blue it was. Just blue. The stone was blue. The sea was blue. That made him happy. He had not felt happy in a length of lonely time.

Slate. Indigo. He knew those lights.

He knew them.

Ioli surfaced gasping. His body came back on a wash of agony. His bones came back with an unbearable ache.

"You were in a far realm," a solemn voice said.

Someone laughed, in the same voice.

He couldn't see. Lamplight fractured into rays and starbursts and would not focus. He thrashed. Warm hands touched him, consternation. "I can't see I can't *see*!" His head burst into jagged fragments. He fell. There was nothing to grab.

"Waking . . ." Voice. Warning.

"You're all right." Hands. Pressing. "For spirits' sake, no more seizures. You can see. It will come back. You took a blow to the head. Your brain's jiggling like a jellied clam. Leave it be."

"I," he said. "I'm. I'm Ioli. I have to get to the Haunch."

"You're in the Haunch. Or near enough. Be easy, now."

"A touch . . . I need . . ."

"One's sent for. Sleep now."

"I'll fall."

"You won't. I've got you." A chuckle, as though someone else had taken over speaking: "Should stay awake after a conk on the head, but he didn't, did he? And he didn't die. He won't now. He's a stubborn fellow."

Two, even three speakers in the same voice. Concern; mockery; grudging respect. All from the slate-and-quicksilver form that leaned over him like a haunt, no body inside it, only glow.

"No turning," came the cautionary voice, from argent indigo. "No moving. No looking."

He could look without his eyes. He could know without seeing. That wasn't possible. Except . . . the orchard. The jungle after dark.

All was confusion. Glows that didn't match the voices. Comfort that didn't match the pain.

He listened to the first voice, the kind voice. He went to sleep on sun-warmed stone in a depth of moon-delved sea.

Healing raised him again. Healed again. He'd never been healed so much in all his life. Only that once, when Jalairi fell.

"Jalairi," he moaned.

"Who?" A touch drew her hands back, drew breath in to the very bottom of her. She looked a Haunchwoman, big and thick, hair like applewood. She was exhausted. He'd been badly hurt. The exhaustion wasn't from healing him, though abruptly she was so hungry she couldn't think. It was the pain of feeling the damage that other human hands had caused.

"And that doesn't stain them," Ioli said. Soft disbelieving scorn. It came from her, not him.

"What?" she said again. Sharply this time. Then, dismissing his echo of her unarticulated thoughts, "You're not making sense."

"He's a visant," said the voice that went with the slate blue glow. "He's not supposed to."

"Better," said the voice that went with the silver-shot indigo. "Better."

It couldn't be. Ioli looked around the space—a lamplit cellar, littered with stained sleeping pallets, packed tight with crates and barrels, piled high with burlap that bulged with tubers, brimmed with grain, who'd keep grain in a root cellar, who'd *sleep* there? The only people besides the touch were a lanky Ankleman with a lazy eye and an oafish grin, and a boy with his head ducked down, wrapped around his own knees between two grain sacks.

They could not be the owners of those extraordinary lights. They could not be the source of the glow that had sustained him through delirium and pain. He could sense their glow now, and it was strong as glows went, but a faint blush of what he'd felt as he went in and out of consciousness.

He *did* know them both. He just couldn't place them.

The ceiling creaked, and then more lights were coming down the ladder, a stream of blue lights like a waterfall, pooling in the cramped cellar. All dressed in mismatched castoffs, old clothes with no dye in them. A chunky girl with a soft blue glow at odds with her earthy Haunchness handed wheatcakes and greasy fritters to the touch, who set upon them with relief. She hadn't complained, but she'd expected to be fed. It was how you repaid touches when they healed you here. They didn't trade on their powers, they kept their own ordinary trades, but when they did a working for you, you fed them after.

He was surprised to see the touch break each item of food in half and offer it to the clustered visants. Wordless, they declined, and for a moment there was only the sound of her chomping.

Then the girl said, looking at him, "He can stay with us, now he's well." There was a hunger on her, too. She was as hungry as the touch. A different kind of hunger. Her hands absently knotted and unknotted a piece of string.

"We'll look after him," said another.

"Tell him the places he shouldn't go."

"Who he shouldn't thieve from."

The Ankleman rose from his crouch with a looming suddenness that made everyone cringe—even Ioli, who had sensed it coming. He knocked his head on the low ceiling and let out an obscenity. "Bloody holes," he grumbled. "Bloody rats."

I won't leave him to the likes of you, he was about to say, or more or less; the words hadn't formed, but the thought was there, in the sour pinch of cheeks and lips, the loose exasperation of limbs.

He didn't say it. He became someone else, someone dangerous. Flat, unfathomable—Ioli had never seen this man before. As though another man dwelled just within, and surfaced in reaction to nothing Ioli could make out. "Keep him then," he said, "so long as you keep him away from the Spotted Tern. I've banged enough heads there. Next time I'll have to break a few."

He had moved past the ragged visants to the ladder when the touch said, with her mouth full, "I didn't heal any broken heads in Yorl."

Yorl, that must be the scribe's village, the Spotted Tern the spirit house. Ioli's eyes went wide. This dark shifting man was the fists, the boots, Sylfonwy's wind sweeping the mob away.

The man turned, hand gripping a ladder rung, big knuckles unscarred, only dust on his boots. A white smile knifed the darkness of his face. "There's still time," he said. He started up.

"No!" Ioli cried, in a terror of being left behind. "I have to get to the Haunch!"

"You're in the Haunch. I told you." The man was only a pair of legs now, his voice coming muffled down the ladderway.

"We'll look after you, now you're well," said the girl, moving toward him with her hands out, stopping before she touched him. Visants didn't like to be touched. Ioli hadn't known that; he didn't like it much himself, but he hadn't known that many visants, there was only one other at home and the few he'd met in his upleg journey with the Greasehair, and—

He cast a wild look around. The visants were creeping in on him, strange and unknowable except for the hunger that came off them like a stench—and a strange compulsiveness, like a tic, a need to always be arranging things. Most of them wore small objects on strings around their necks or wrists, dangly things and beaded things to occupy their fingers. It seemed important, but made no sense to him. His eye fell on the touch, sitting relishing her food, calm and unruffled, and he knelt on the dirty straw mattress and leaned toward her, beseeching. She shrugged, and took another bite of fritter. *No accounting for visants.* That diffidence let them trust her, let them reveal their hiding place, this cramped dank cellar, the empty safe house above, where no one else knew they dwelled. She didn't care enough either way to betray them.

He didn't want to know these things, he didn't want to feed their hunger or compulsions, he didn't understand any of this, he had to get to the Haunch holding, he couldn't let the lank man leave with the only remote chance of safe conduct.

"The Haunch *holding!*" he cried, scrambling to his feet. "The runners' holding!" He swayed as the flood of words burst forth: "I have to tell them! The war of the coast is illusion, the shield will fall and the war will come inland and everyone will die but if the runners can convince them it isn't real then there's a chance! The shield can only hold on and take the arrow for us and they can't hold on forever there aren't enough of them, but if everyone is armored against the illusions, if everyone truly believes that no matter what they see coming it can't kill them, then nobody will die at all, the war of the coast will be over! But it only works if everyone is armored, it only works if the holding sends runners everywhere in Eiden Myr. People trust runners, people will believe them, I have to tell the head runner, I have to get to the holding!"

The visants recoiled. Were there none like him among them? Was there no one who could have seen this on him, known the thoughts before they flooded into words, had no one seen, had no one *known?* What did they *do* with their blue glow?

The ceiling creaked as the Ankleman stopped, and turned. His weight, his decision shifting.

In the frozen silence, the hangdog boy with the darkest light slipped out of his sack-padded corner and elbowed through the shocked visants to put himself behind Ioli.

It was the hideabout boy. His silvered indigo was that dark blue glow. Ioli had forgotten him. How did he get here from the coast? He was stained too, if Ioli was.

Legs dangled through the ladderhole, supported by elbows on the floor above, and then the Ankleman dropped down, landing with lithe grace. Not much of a drop for him, less than his own height. He stood slightly bent at the waist, and pivoted to stand sidewise.

"Out," he said. He glared the visants into obedience when they hesitated, but left Ioli, who didn't budge, and ignored the hiding boy. Gallantry welled up as he looked at the touch, and making a gracious bow of his cramped hunch he said, "Even you, I'm afraid."

The touch shrugged again and lined up behind the visants filing out. She offered Ioli half of her last piece of wheatcake, and at his headshake popped both pieces in her mouth and chewed them, smiling. "No doubt I'll see you again, Rekke," she mumbled through crumbs as she hauled herself up the ladder. "Always another one to save, isn't there?"

Ioli was left with Rekke standing before him—bent, hipshot, arms akimbo, an old woman administering a scolding—and the hideabout boy cowering behind him. Slate, and indigo. Their glow had been the strongest in the cellar even when other visants filled it. He could still feel it touching his. There was no hunger in it. Only . . . offering.

It bore no relation to their behavior. As though their glow had sense and motive independent of their will. Why hadn't the hideabout boy's reached out to him in none's-land?

"You won't reveal these visants," Rekke said. His lazy eye looked at the wall.

"I might," Ioli replied, *if the threat of that will make you take me there.* "I'll tell them everything I know, to make them believe me."

"I don't know that I believe you. I've heard that sort of prattle from other walleyes. No one believes it."

"Who have they told?"

"Besides each other? I have no idea. They don't talk to blunts if they can help it. Blunts only use them. Or hurt them." Puffing with pride, gone from harridan to buffoon in an eyeblink, he crowed, "And then I thrash them!" His left eyeball rolled toward Ioli and then down as he laughed. It moved without the other eye moving at all. Ioli felt queasy.

A bird hooted, somewhere in the distance. The hideabout boy hooted back softly, as if unaware that he was doing it.

"They want you," harsh Rekke said, scowling. His back hurt, bent like that. "I should leave you to them. But you're the kind of light they'd rally to. Who knows what you'd do with them."

That hunger he'd felt . . . He was a stranger here. He was no one. Barely a man, at two nines and two. Not the kind of person anyone rallied to. "That's crazy," he said.

Mad Rekke jeered, "That's walleyes for you!"

"I don't want to rally visants," he grated out. "You don't need to . . . protect them from me. Just see me safe."

"I'll see you safe back to none's-land."

"I'm going to the holding."

"He is," said the hideabout boy, then grabbed Ioli's sash and buried his face in Ioli's back.

Ioli had the queerest feeling, as though the boy had *seen* him, though he showed no sign of sharing Ioli's particular knack. As though, somehow, he'd seen what Ioli would do before he did it.

No—all the things he *might* do. He sensed it as he turned and took the boy by the shoulders and shook him so his head came up. His eyes were rolled back to show only white. His glow had gone so dark it was tinged with violet, shimmering with a silvery not-light. He was *gleaning*—and though Ioli could not know what he saw, Ioli could know . . .

Terror. Amazement. *Sometimes he fails and sometimes he dies and sometimes later he wants to give up but there isn't one where he doesn't try.* There was only one other like that and he was here. Ioli wrenched around, wrenched away from the overwhelming act of gleaning the boy, and found Rekke braced on a support post, one agate eye fixed glittering on him and the boy, the other angled down in horror as at a dirt floor gone to quicksand.

There isn't one where he doesn't try.

One what?

One future. "He can see through time," Ioli breathed. He was trembling. He only realized it when the boy wrapped bony arms around him and squeezed in tight, as if he were trying to hide inside him. Visants didn't like to be touched. He didn't know why the boy kept touching him, or why he allowed it. "All the ways that things might go. All the ways that things do go, depending on what happens next."

"There's only one future," Rekke growled. He put his other hand on the post, bent nearly double now, as though winded from a sprint, or as though he might throw up.

"Not the way he sees it."

"He's mad."

"Yes. Seeing what he sees would drive anyone mad." Ioli made himself look hard at Rekke. An Ankleman, a stones man, a layers man. Seeing sapphires in the depths of earth. Bluffing to keep them safe, bluffing with his knuckles and his boots and his size, his scary eyes, his shifting madness. Sheets of blue slate, sliding on quicksilver . . .

Ioli felt tears well up and dashed at them viciously. *I don't care I don't care.* He never let himself feel anything for what he saw. He'd seen tragedy and ugliness and heartrending courage just by staring the people he lived with in the face. He'd fled deep into the jungle. He told himself it was because they might try to use him. He would become a danger to Jalairi. They would try to get to him through her. He told himself it was to protect her, to protect them all from the things he saw that no one should ever see. In truth it was because he couldn't bear it. He'd exiled himself long before he joined the shield. He'd let the Greasehair have him because what difference did it make? Exiled here, ex-

iled there. Maybe there, he'd thought, he could do some good.
The Greasehair said they needed all the most powerful visants.
He'd hardened his heart and shut his eyes and gone. He hadn't
let himself feel for the shielder dead of her own fear. But he was
kidding himself. He felt for them all. Now his cursed gifted eyes
spilled over with tears, that there should be such lights as these,
such powers as these, such gifts, and it should only drive them
mad.

"Tell me," the Ankleman said, voice gone low, eyes very still.

"I see through the veils of mind. Not to hear in words. I make
the words, I think, with some of me in them. But I know. Folk's
hurts, their wants, their prides, their lies."

Veins and deposits in people's heads. "You're a dangerous
fellow."

"You didn't think there was anyone like me."

"I thought you were what they accused the rest of us of being."

"I didn't think there were any visants who could see the future."

"Maybe there aren't. Not if there are as many futures as you
claim. Not if he can't tell which one will happen."

Ioli felt drained. He wished he could eat some fritters and
wheatcakes and be good as new. But he wasn't a touch. Whatever his sight cost him, it couldn't be put right with food.

"Someone's got to watch a dangerous fellow like you," Rekke
said. When his lips said "watch," the rest of him said *watch
over*, but every tense muscle spoke mistrust. Ioli might reveal
them. Ioli was not damaged enough; Ioli, someone might heed.

The bird hooted again, closer. More urgent.

The hideabout boy whined, and burrowed in tighter.

"Someone's after me," Ioli said, stiffening, puzzled.

"Dug that from my head, did you? Or the runt's?" Rekke was
pale under his swart skin. He'd broken a sweat. He'd been seeing, too. Seeing places far away, places that made no sense to
him, just balled into one huge danger in his mind. What was his
gift? To see through layers. To see through earth. To see
through the walls between realms? When he was seeing, there
were as many places around him as there were times around the
boy. Ioli could make no more of it than that.

"Going now," said the boy, hopeless and miserable.

"Yes," said Ioli, with no conviction. "We should go now, while it's day." He wanted to curl up on the floor. "You'll take me to the holding?"

"Not while my bowels are trying to come up through my nose."

He would. He had relented. He would see Ioli safe there. But not feeling like this. It was their alien lights, leaking into each other. If they moved apart, the nausea would ease. But that must have been worse, in the end, than if they stayed together, because the hideabout boy still clung.

Three birdcalls sounded in a row, query-response-acknowledgment, and it came to Ioli that they were human sounds, not bird sounds.

The hideabout boy sprang to the ladder, then ran back to hide behind Rekke as Rekke raised his head and his left eye rolled straight up. A moment later Ioli heard a commotion above. The sounds of things being hidden in haste. A cold feeling gripped him.

"Mauzl," Rekke warned, trying to shoo the hideabout boy away.

"Mauzl?" Ioli echoed dully, so confused, so weary. Was Rekke speaking in some ancient tongue?

"This runt, you puking woolhead." An exhilaration of fear flooded Rekke's limbs and propelled him up the ladder with no more thought of his queasy belly.

What was coming? What had frightened the visants? Some drunken Yorlmen, come to finish the job? Ioli's heart pounded. He could hide down here while Rekke fought them off, whoever they were. He didn't have to go up. He didn't have to risk his life. *If I can't see them they can't see me.* He could hide here, burrow among the grain sacks, bury his glow too deep to see.

The hideabout boy hissed at him and tugged him toward the ladder. "Moving now!" His face looked like an angry rat's. "Climbing now!"

Weak with trembling nerves, Ioli started to laugh. The boy was so . . . cute, under the filth and the smell, with his tiny mouth and enormous eyes. A ferocious mouse, driven out of passivity by the lankbones' influence. Rekke Lankbones! This was how people got their shieldnames! "Have you no name for me?" he asked, through laughter that was bringing tears. Like the giggling girl in none's-land. *Sweet spirits, I have gone mad. . . .*

"*Climbing!*" the boy insisted from behind him, and pushed him toward the ladder.

"I have to get to the holding," he whispered as the rungs came under his hands. Climbing, like at home. Talking to himself so that he would remember how. "I can't go mad until they've sent the runners out to save the world." He must have paused; Mauzl's hands shoved at his rear. He laughed again. Mauzl. His name. The hideabout boy. "Climbing now," he acknowledged. He could climb. He was good at climbing.

He could not climb. On a rush of quiet feet, like a mass of vermin, the other visants were pouring down the hole. They swept him back. He fell, scrabbled up. Mauzl still clung. He couldn't choose between shaking the boy off and hauling him close. Together they were shoved up against the piled grain sacks. A small tear in one widened under the impact, and released its contents in a liquid whisper, the only sound in the close cellar. He couldn't even hear them breathe. Someone doused the lantern, and there was only dilute gray light through the ladderhole, gleaming from the visants' eyes where they huddled in the shadows. A glowing mist of blue filled the cellar. They were trying to glean what was happening outside. Completely still, completely silent, they were all using their powers. He felt their glow reach for his, trying to use that too—trying to be *guided* by it. They didn't know that was what they were doing. Their powers were doing it all on their own.

They failed. Blue glows could not combine. Not theirs and his. They wanted to, but couldn't. But his and Mauzl's, his and Rekke's . . . when he was hurt, when he was floating . . .

He couldn't bear it. He had to get out of here. He struggled past the visants to the ladder.

A thud and whuff and creak and jingle of horses came from outside. Low voices, rising toward argument.

Mauzl hauled on him. *"Too late!"* he whispered, pleading, then spasmed as someone pinched him into silence. He wrapped his arms around Ioli's middle and tried to hold him back. Ioli peeled the hands away and climbed up quick as a monkey into the emptiness of a deserted barn.

All the footprints in the dust—how did they expect those to go unnoticed? Following Rekke's matte blue glow, feeling Mauzl's silver indigo surge up behind him, he went outside into a blazing, blinding afternoon.

In a dirt yard as unkempt as the cellar, no troughs or hitches to tempt travelers, only abandonment and dry weeds and encroaching brush, Fyldur Greasehair stood with two bladed shielders.

Rekke stood between them and the barn. Between them and Ioli.

"Here's our runaway now," Fyldur said.

Not good, Ioli knew from the tension in Rekke's shoulders, the tap of a heel. *Not good, that he brought armed aid.* He was angry that Ioli had shown himself. *How was I to know?* Mauzl had told him. He hadn't listened.

"Now you've found him," Rekke said tightly. "Now you can go."

"Yes, I can," Fyldur said cordially, as though thanking him.

Ioli couldn't understand the Greasehair. Fyldur made his face do things at odds with whatever happened inside him. Right now it wore that leering smile: he'd discovered a secret, was winking at them to show he knew. But shock had blanked his eyes before they crinkled. There was outrage in the hands that clenched as he hid them behind his back. It made no sense.

That's visants for you, said the memory of Rekke's voice.

Fyldur said, "I procured a powerful visant for the shield at Maur Sleith. They'd like him back."

"I didn't run away," Ioli said. "The shield there fell—"

Rekke silenced him with a curt gesture. Not to spare Ioli wasting his breath. To keep this between him and Fyldur.

It had been only a few days since Ioli had seen the Grease-hair, but he was surprised to realize how much he looked like Rekke. Rekke was from the Ankle, Fyldur from the Crotch, but they had the same dark Souther skin, the same white-flash smile, eyes the same black inside vivid white. They were of an age, roughly, toward the end of their fourth nineyear. Fyldur was shorter and broader by a hand, his black hair long and oiled; Rekke was longer in body, like a rangy horse, and his hair was a black tangle on neck and brow. But they had the same square jaw, the same malleable features, a superficial resemblance that went deeper in some unknowable way. Ioli could not keep up with Rekke's shifts of personality, and Fyldur was as hard to see past his unctuous pretenses, but he could sense some . . . bond of opposites. As though they were bound snarling to either end of a pole, past arms' reach, circling each other endlessly.

Fyldur's glow was so dim, so pathetic, that Ioli didn't understand why Rekke bothered. Rekke tried to hide his glow, but it was powerful and deep. Ioli could find no basis for rivalry between lights so unequal.

"Why the blades, Greasehair? Did I scare you so badly?"

One of the shielders moved his feet, uncomfortable. Neither of them liked this. "The procurer's moving inland from here," he said. "We're to take this one back."

"The gap on Maur Sleith has been closed," the other said. "He should have stayed where he was."

"It's not safe to travel stained," the first said. "We'll see him back to the coast." He blinked. "The other as well, he's stained too. You didn't tell us there were two, procurer."

"There's just the one, for you," Fyldur said. "The small one. The Toeman will go with me."

They'd come for *Mauzl?* Ioli stared at Rekke, trying to understand.

Rekke was shifting like mad. Indecision. The instinct to protect them from bladed shielders. The knowledge that they were stained, they belonged to the shield, the coast was the only place for them now. Deep down, the disturbing sense that they belonged with him. Confusion as to why Fyldur would want Ioli, shifting into suspicion as he began to figure it out.

Ioli couldn't see what Rekke saw. "You can't take Mauzl!" he found himself saying. "He never agreed to join the shield, he only followed us to the coast."

"He's stained," a shielder said. "It's too late. He can't survive inside now—look at him. He's got to come with us."

Hearing the shielder speak from his own conviction, Ioli saw him with sudden clarity, and knew that everything both shielders had said before had been the Greasehair's words, the Greasehair's oily reasoning.

"You can't take him back there. He's small. He hides. He's no good to anyone!"

"They'll train him up," the shielder said. "Come on now. Mauzl, is it? Come along, you can ride behind me."

He started forward, to reach around Ioli for Mauzl. Rekke's hand fell on his arm, Rekke's body blocked the way. The shielder pressed forward, trying to stare him down. Rekke pressed back. Something happened with their arms, too fast for Ioli to see, a blur of grips and holds. The shielder wrenched away and swept his blade out. The other shielder drew his more slowly and stepped around to trap Rekke between them.

Beyond them, Fyldur was smiling.

He wanted this to happen. Rekke would die or Rekke would stain himself. Fyldur would be happy with either.

"No!" Ioli cried.

"I don't know who you think you are," the nearer shielder said, "but this is shield business. Stand down."

We could run, Ioli thought. *I could grab Mauzl and run. But they'd hurt Rekke and then they'd only ride us down.* He could leave Mauzl. But he couldn't get to the holding without Rekke.

"You'll take both to the coast, or neither," Rekke said. "The procurer gets nothing."

"You have no say in it," the farther shielder said, and came within a blade length of Ioli and Mauzl. What would he do if they ran? Slice out at their legs? He could cripple them just long enough for the healer to come back, then sling them off to the coast. . . .

"He's using you," Ioli told them. "The Greasehair's using you. What do you care if visants run off? Don't you have better things to do back on the coast? Suppose we only run away again? You can't force people to stay there. You can't spend all your time haring after deserters."

"It's for their own good," Fyldur said smoothly. "Now that you're here you might as well bring the small one back. He's very powerful. Invaluable. He can tell you when the next attacks will come."

"How can you know for sure?" Ioli asked the shielders. "How can you know he's telling the truth about anything?"

The shielders looked at each other, doubts cutting the oily reasoning. The stain would drive these two back to the coast in its own good time. They did have better things to do. They didn't like the procurer, they didn't know why they'd let him talk them into this. Their blades were meant to defend, not subdue inlanders. They didn't want to hurt this daft Ankleman. They weren't meant to come in. It wasn't their place. They were stained. They had to go back. Their comrades could be dying, and them inland herding walleyes.

Fyldur saw that he had lost them. Rekke would not be killed or stained this day. In a sweet voice, he said, "I only want to train the Toeman as a procurer. He'll come with me, given the choice. Won't you, Toeman?"

Ioli was too shocked to answer.

"We'll get your message to the holding," Fyldur said, straightforward and sincere. He'd talked to the Yorl scribe. He knew what Ioli had tried to do, and what had happened to him. "No need to hide and starve, risk further beatings, the runners' rejection. No need to put your safety in this madman's hands. You have my word on it: Your plea delivered, if you prentice yourself to me. You won't find a better bargain."

"He's lying," Rekke said, but Rekke didn't want him to go to the holding, Rekke wanted him returned to the coast, where he couldn't rally visants to some cause Ioli didn't even understand; Rekke didn't want Fyldur to have him. He would accuse Fyldur of lying even if he wasn't.

Ioli couldn't find the lie on Fyldur anywhere. Fyldur was a masterly liar. Could anyone *be* that good a liar? So good they could fool someone with his gift? Could that mean he was telling the truth? Mauzl would be safer on the coast; delusions couldn't harm him, but stain-fearing inlanders could. Rekke might only take both of them back there anyway. What difference did it make what happened to him after, so long as the runners heard his tale? He would make a good procurer. He could tell when people were sincere in wanting to join the defense, and when they were going for the wrong reasons. He could save people like himself from making terrible mistakes. And Fyldur could persuade the runners. Fyldur could talk anyone into anything. . . .

"No listening," said Mauzl, so low that only he could hear.

Mauzl was right. Fyldur was handling him. He'd known he was being handled, in the Toes, when he let the Greasehair have him. He hadn't cared. He cared now. He couldn't desert the lights reaching out. He couldn't let Rekke be twisted into staining himself. He couldn't leave Mauzl to be terrorized and used—

"And for a bonus, I won't tell your little sister about your cowardice. Dereliction of duty, breaking your vow to serve, the headlong flight the very first day. She needn't hear that her brother was a craven deserter."

Jalairi would laugh in the Greasehair's face if he told her a thing like that. Wouldn't she? He hadn't seen her for a long time. A whole season, before he took to the coast. He'd hidden when she came calling, seeking, begging him to come home. He'd hidden high in the trees. She must have known he was there somewhere, that at some point he'd heard her voice and never answered. She might be angry with him, hurt. That might open her to belief. . . .

"No *listening*," whispered Mauzl, but Mauzl was the hideabout boy, Mauzl had attached himself to the Greasehair's party as they traveled up the Leg, lurking about their campsites, until it was as if he too had been procured, and no one had cared, wrapped up in their own miseries, their own reasons for letting the procurer have them. What was he to Ioli? A clinging vine. He saw it in Fyldur's face, dismissal that didn't even stoop to being scorn. . . .

No. Fyldur knew Mauzl's powers—not what they were exactly, but how strong. He was letting Ioli see the dismissal so he'd miss the hatred.

He saw Ioli see through him. Relentless, inexorable, he turned Ioli from the truth, presented more attractive truths before Ioli could plant himself to refuse. "Surely you don't think the runners would permit someone like you an audience with their head. Look at yourself. Ragged, homeless. A raving lunatic. I'm not unknown to the head runner. He'll see me. He'll listen to me. We'll deliver your message, fulfill your quest, and be on our way. You never wanted to save the world, did you? Let someone else save the world."

How could he know the weaknesses of Ioli's heart? His glow was too dim, his gift too small, to see things as deep as those. Guesses or not, glow or not, his words had power. So much easier, to leave the world to those who wanted it.

"How much longer are you going to let this go on?" Rekke said to the shielders. Ioli had been so fixed on Fyldur Greasehair, trying so hard to find the lie in him, that it took effort to drag his gaze to Rekke. Why would Rekke wait on shielders at all? Always claiming that he would thrash things, but he never did. Rekke was the liar, always lying to himself—

He looked at Rekke, and saw no lies. There were infinite Rekkes, but every one of them was genuine, and though they obscured each other, layer on layer, not one of them was evil. The difference made him blink, made him see, by comparison, the seductive evil that was Fyldur Greasehair.

Tempting lights to destroy themselves.

His field of view expanded. Staring at Rekke, he saw the change in Fyldur's eyes, saw cold hatred slither behind them where Ioli wasn't supposed to be looking, and he *knew:* Fyldur hated him, Fyldur hated Mauzl, Fyldur hated Rekke, because when they'd come out of that cellar hole they'd come out brighter than any one of them had been before, alone. That was the secret they'd been keeping. What happened to their glow when there were three of them. Fyldur wanted them all consigned to exile. Fyldur wanted all the bright lights gone.

He wanted to punish them for being brighter than him. It wasn't enough to kill them, though he'd do that if it came to it—that's what stained him, not none's-land. He wanted to see them suffer.

I can tell him how much they're suffering.

That was why Fyldur wanted him.

He couldn't have known that when he dumped me in none's-land, or he'd never have left me there.

Someone had told him. One of the other visants, when Fyldur went back and found Ioli gone and a new shield in place.

He'll work on me until I'm his. He'll tell me whatever I most want to hear. That's his knack. That's the power his thread of light gives him.

He knew all this in the space of time it took Fyldur to take a breath, and, seeing it, Fyldur changed the words he used that breath to say.

"Take them," he said to the shielders. "Take them both, and we'll sort it out on the coast. I have orders from Barumor Breakneck himself."

"And you didn't tell us that before?" said the shielder nearest Rekke.

"He didn't want to involve himself," Fyldur said, as the shielder behind Ioli said, "Barumor's not head of *our* shield-post, I'll take no orders from him," and as Rekke, hearing none of it, dove into a sidewise roll at the feet of the first shielder, to topple him.

The shielder leaped up in lithe reflex. His comrade snagged Mauzl by the neck. Rekke bounced to his feet behind the first shielder and lunged at him. The shielder was expecting it, was turning, too close to bring his blade into play, instead aiming to drive a forearm into Rekke's neck. Rekke ducked his head down and flung his arms around the shielder's waist to lift him.

The shielder hooked a leg behind Rekke's knee and would not be lifted. He brought his elbow down on Rekke's back. Rekke bellowed, and they crashed to the ground.

The other shielder flung Mauzl at Fyldur and moved to break up the tussle and take Rekke in hand.

Run, Ioli thought, *run,* but where he ran was to pull Mauzl from Fyldur's clutches, and then there was the strangest sound, a rumble from underground, a sound like rushing water, the patter of bare feet on dusty boards, and the barn erupted with visants. They overwhelmed the shielders, overwhelmed Rekke, overwhelmed Fyldur and Ioli and Mauzl. No fists, no violence, no hurting, just sheer numbers, a mass of bodies that the shielders couldn't fight unless they hurt them. They disgorged Ioli and Mauzl, pressing them among and through themselves until they stumbled out the side of the throng, and Rekke with them.

"The horses," Ioli said, straining toward them, but Rekke said "No time" and Mauzl said "No thieving," and the two of them were fleeing with him between them, and they were through the brush and halfway across a fallow field before the sound of Fyldur's raging orders faded.

"You made them reveal themselves," Rekke growled. "I'll thrash you within a breath of your life if you ever do that again."

"It wasn't me!" Ioli protested. "Those shielders would have let us go if you hadn't started a brawl!"

Rekke humphed, and fell into a brooding silence as they crossed the field, climbed over a bank, and started into the next field, corn scythed to a stubble.

No shouts followed them, no commands to halt in the name of the shield. The visants hadn't hurt the shielders, but they wouldn't be taking any more orders from Fyldur Greasehair. The shielders did not ride after them.

Others did.

Rumbling hoofbeats rose like grounded thunder from behind them. They turned. From beyond the screen of trees by the visants' barn, from behind the visants' barn, two dozen horses came at a gallop. Some of them had two riders. Though he hadn't expected the visants to defend his quarry, Fyldur hadn't trusted the shield to back him up. He'd stashed reinforcements out of sight.

"Eiden's puke," Rekke said. "Get behind me. Stay there. If I go down, run if you can. Watch for holes. We'll only have one chance."

"They have horses . . ."

"I'll take care of that. Do as I say."

It was the Yorlmen. Ioli recognized two or three of them as they came close. One who hated visants because a visant once told him something he didn't want to hear. One who thought thieves should be beaten. One whose face still struck fear into Ioli's heart, because he just liked an excuse to feel his fists and his boots land in stained flesh.

They came up and rode three circles around Ioli and Mauzl and Rekke before they dismounted and closed in.

Mauzl went to his knees and covered his head, saying, "Shh, shh. Shh, shh." He'd gone fuzzy. Ioli's eyes couldn't bring him into focus. He must be gleaning. He must be gleaning all the futures in which they failed, and fell, and there was no use in getting up, or hiding.

"Get him up," Rekke said. "Stay with me."

Ioli dragged at Mauzl, got him to his feet, but he was limp, his eyes rolled back. Rekke breathed an obscenity, one eye on the villagers, one eye on Mauzl. He turned Ioli and draped Mauzl's arms over his shoulders, boosted him onto Ioli's back. Ioli scooped his scrawny thighs in tight, hiked him up higher. He staggered, but didn't fall.

The villagers were closing in, mumbling threats, obscenities. They'd left their horses with reins draggling over the stubbled corn. The horses were mildly winded, had no desire to go anywhere. They started cropping at the stubble.

Rekke crouched, touched the ground, then leaped high into the air and let out an earsplitting, bloodcurdling shriek.

The horses shied, heads snapping up. Rekke had come up

with a stone in each fist. He winged them between the villagers, taking one horse, then another in the rump. They bolted. The other horses startled farther off, some milling in confusion. All well out of reach of their riders.

Rekke grinned at the villagers, sauntered toward them as if to jeer, then burst at the two nearest. He planted a boot in one man's belly and shoved the next into his fellows. It made a hole, and in an eyeblink he was through. Ioli, taken equally by surprise, was only just lumbering after him, weighted down by limp, lolling Mauzl. Arms blocked his way, hands grabbed at Mauzl. Ioli leaned forward, straining to hang on, to get to Rekke.

With an oath, Rekke was back, kicking and pounding at the legs and bodies that went with those arms and hands, and dragging Ioli free, dragging Mauzl off his back so that Ioli could run and then whirling, with Mauzl cradled in his arms, to whip a kick into the groin of the closest pursuer.

Far in the distance, back on the other side of the field, Ioli heard the shielders' voices, shouting commands for this to stop. If they came, he and Rekke and Mauzl might get away, they might run away just long enough for the shield to save them.

Rekke struggled up beside him, keeping pace despite the unwieldiness of Mauzl in his arms. "Do you hear them?" he panted.

Ioli tried to reply, tried to nod, couldn't do either and run at the same time, so he just kept running. Behind him, the vicious calls of the villagers; beyond that, the clear sound of the shielders' horses. They were riding. They would get here in time. Their gleaming blades would put a stop to this. All they had to do was come around in front of the mob and draw them. They were older men, veterans of one of the ground wars, deeply stained. Theirs was no dilute none's-land stain, no taint by association or intent. They had killed, for real. The villagers would wilt before them, cower off with their tails between their legs, ashamed of what they'd let themselves become.

We're getting away, he thought.

The first rock took him in the small of the back. He didn't comprehend the sharp bloom of pain until the next took Rekke behind the knee and crumpled him. A third hit Rekke's left shoulder blade. Bone cracked. He howled. Mauzl tumbled into the shorn stalks.

Ioli fell to his knees and pulled Mauzl's head into his lap, covering it with his chest. Rekke stood up with a roar, a rock in his right hand, a rock that should have broken the blade that plowed this field, and pivoted to fling it at their attackers. Ioli heard one yelp, then a curse as someone tripped over the man who was hit, but the rocks kept coming. Stones peppered Rekke, small and large; he ducked and weaved and bent for more stones, but he kept himself between the mob and Ioli and Mauzl, he was too stationary a target, and he was only one against more than two dozen, with only one throwing arm. In four breaths he was sinking back to his knees, turning with his temple pouring blood.

He tucked Mauzl up tight between them as the mob encircled them. He pushed Ioli's arms in, pressed Ioli's head down, protected as much as he could with his broad back. But there was no hiding from stones. Even the smallest were battering now. Another laid open the back of Rekke's head, and his body went loose. "I'm sorry," he slurred, in Ioli's ear. Sorry that he'd given them the idea of rocks. Sorry that he was a stones man and was taking them down to his stony end. All Ioli could do was forgive him, and hope to be forgiven in return. Ioli could feel their glows, mingling. Reaching for each other and finding. It was no good. It was sublime, it was like nothing he'd ever felt before today, but it was no good for anything. It couldn't stop rocks in midflight. It couldn't stop the hands that threw them. *Useless . . . useless walleyes . . .*

Ioli and Mauzl had escaped exile, and the mob had thought of another kind of exile, and it didn't require wars or procurers.

He could not believe they had come to this, but there was no arguing with the truth of stones. They hit him in the head, the arms, the legs, the hips. Most were small and badly flung, but they were sharp and there were so many. Rekke's blood was smeared on him, Rekke's arms spasmed with every impact, he felt one of Rekke's knuckles smashed where the hand cupped the back of his head, broken by a rock that would have killed him.

Protecting. That was what he did. Rekke was an agony of failure, weak under the hail of stones, trying to make himself iron, make himself stone, make himself a barrier to shield them. Trying so hard to hang on until the shielders came. But the shielders had come. The whack of blade flats on backs, on thighs; curses and commands, the thuds of bodies flung away to the ground; still the rocks came, the shielders could beat two-thirds of the mob off them and at this distance the remainder could still kill them. Were killing them. Ioli's tears soaked Mauzl's hair.

There's nowhere we can go. No escape, no appeal. Sylfonwy's wind would not come to sweep the ugliness away. No rescuing the rescuer.

Jalairi, he thought. *I love you. I tried.*

He was dying.

He knew because he felt the welling of their glow, the sweet delusions of delirium. He was losing consciousness under the hail of rocks and hate. Falling. Falling into moonlit depths, an indigo sea, gentle drifting oblivion. Embracing quicksilver slate, buoyant stone that slowed his fall, eased it, but still fell with him. Sinking, away from pain, away from sight, into a place of easy currents, restful darkness, a place where he didn't have to think. Living was thinking. Dreaming was thinking. In life there was never rest from the workings of his own mind. No peace, no letting go. Now there was. A warm blue peace. Silvered indigo depths. All the paths, open to him, open to them. All the walls dissolving. No more barriers. Only peace. Silver, indigo, slate blue peace.

The battering had stopped.

He could feel his body. Again, or still. But different.

He could feel Mauzl's body, Mauzl's trembling. He could feel Rekke's hand on the back of his head. It cupped his head. It should not have been able to do that; it was broken, it could hold nothing. But it held him. Held him too tight, clawing in surprise. He cracked an eye open, peered sideways, thought he caught a glimpse of impossibility: hills of purple and dark pink, a grassy sward as a blue as a visant's glow, in the distance towering white stalks wreathed in rainbow, vaulting under a nacreous sky. There was no pain, no brokenness. He turned his gaze inward, let his lids slide closed. He was weary of seeing. Life was seeing. Death was rest from all that. He would rest now.

"No," Rekke snarled. His glow surged into theirs. A brutal domination. Taking the power he needed. "This is not the right place—"

There was pain again, there was brokenness again, and they were back in the horror of life—but when Ioli lifted his bleeding head free of Rekke's smashed hand and blinked the stickiness away, what he saw was not the stubble of the cornfield, or shielders beating back a mob, but a hill, topped in ordinary grass, split open and peeled back to reveal an incomprehensibility of innards, gnashing metallic beams, melted slag, wooden beams propping up an entryway. Hoists and winches. Crowds of workers, some turning to point at them, shouting. What he felt was the agony of Mauzl wriggling free to sit beside them hugging his legs, rocking back and forth, whispering, "Shh. Shh. Shhhhh." What he heard was Rekke's groan as he folded into the earth, passed out or dead Ioli couldn't tell, and someone crying, "Sweet merciful spirits, *what is this?*"

He groped Rekke's chest, felt the heartbeat. The glow was diminished, but still vibrant. "You saw us safe," he whispered. "Sylfonwy's wind. . . ."

"Get a healer," someone said, and "Fetch Oreg!" someone cried, and Ioli wondered what oreg was—a sweet liquid perhaps, a healing draught to soothe the throat and dull the pain? The pain was terrible. His body was all pain.

"No touching," Mauzl said, as concerned folk clustered around them, and someone said, "He's right, don't touch them, wait for the healer, these injuries are terrible, what could have *done* something like this?" And some were asking who they were and some were asking Mauzl their names and some were asking where they came from and were they injured inside the mound and a blue glow hovered near and said that they were visants, and Ioli raised his head very slowly, very carefully, and said, "What is this place?"

The blue glow crouched down before him in a blur of kindliness and replied, "This is Sauglin. This is the runners' holding in Sauglin, in the Haunch."

Rekke had brought him where he needed to go.

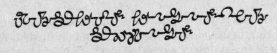

PELKIN N'ROLF WAS well aware that he was dying. He had lived for over a nonned years. There was a great deal still to do, and he would have liked to see how it all turned out, but younger hands would make better work of it—and now, at last, for the first time in his long life, he felt safe in leaving the work to others.

He felt safe in leaving the world to others.

It was an unsafe world. Beset by horrors, stained by exile, haunted by spectres, it was a world that needed a good deal of saving; it was a world under siege. But he had made arrangements to end that siege. His plans waited only on the completion of Graefel's work and the readiness of nine mages under the supervision of his master of prentices. If he delayed his departure much longer, his plans would see fruition and the way to his destination would close to him.

It was time to go.

Pelkin had fought wars most of his life. The grinding years of covert work against two—no, three—corrupt Enneads. The magewar between the last Ennead and Torrin n'Maeryn, so lyrically and unjustly dubbed the Lightbreaker. The diplomatic battle he had fought to forestall the Khinish invasion and prevent the bloodshed on the Menalad Plain. He had not always succeeded. But he'd done his part.

He'd pledged his life to vanquish an ancient evil, and it was vanquished these twonine years; all that remained of the old Ennead was scattered aides, stewards, lackeys, aging and purposeless. All were stained, and the ones he'd identified and watched had been driven into exile from the land they'd tried to subvert. Any who had escaped both the shield and his notice—and they would be few, for he was thorough—would find no power to rally them, and age and die in bitter anonymity.

He'd fathered three fine children on a beloved pledge and watched his legacies of flesh and light extend through three generations. He'd trained a prentice whose diligence did him honor, and sent her his triskele. That gift, and his ingenious solution of binding two difficult binders, had been his last acts as head runner, and he was pleased with himself on both counts.

His life's work was well and truly done.

He had considered permitting touches to let him linger, allowing his family to travel to his side for the final breaths. He would have liked to see them one more time—but in their element, at home, not here in a roughhewn barracks amid bustle and strangers.

And not with the others missing. Not with Liath and Breida, his granddaughters, pledged to exile and the sea.

He could not wait for them to finish fighting their battles and come home.

He would not wait for the rest of his family to travel half a world just to see his body fail.

He would not wait until it was too late, and the way closed.

His pledge had waited a lifetime for him, though she'd chosen to spend more than half of it in pethyar. He had things to atone for. Much pain lay in store. Much reckoning, for this old reckoner. But oh—oh, glorious spirits!—what joy would follow.

It was long past time for him to go home to Breida n'Onofre's arms.

Karanthe couldn't bear it. Outside, two stories below, the stamp and snort of horses, the reports of runners, the calls of prentices freed from a day's labor, shouts and clanks from the digging site—sounds of activity and life, however subdued by Pelkin's state. In this veiled, airless sleeproom, only the rasp of breath into deflated lungs, the rise and fall of the sunken chest, the wasting flesh, the scent of endings.

The anguish of the runners who had been his reckoners and his aides.

Karanthe flung the shutters open.

"What are you *doing*?" Laren cried.

"Letting in the sunshine. Letting in the light. He was an illuminator. He thrived on light. If he opens his eyes one more time before the end, I want the last thing he sees to be the sun."

I want the last thing he sees to be me.

Pelkin, who was going at last to join his beloved pledge. Pelkin, who was leaving them to run this holding. Pelkin, who was leaving them to receive Graefel Scholar's imminent decoding of the message hidden in the wordsmiths' canon, which would complete the instructions they needed to recast Galandra's warding, and return Eiden Myr to safe isolation.

Pelkin, who was leaving her. Going where she could not follow.

"I'll see what's keeping the triad," Jimor said, but when he reached the door to the sitting room he did not go through.

"They can't decide who it's to be," Chaldrinda said. "They're desperate for the honor and terrified of failing."

"He should have picked them out himself," said Laren. "Saved a lot of trouble."

Annina said, "He picked the nine for the more important—"

"Shh," said Herne. "Not here."

"He wants them to choose." Chaldrinda kept the subject off the one that wasn't safe to discuss with touches and stewards in earshot. As master of prentices, she would clearly have rather done the choosing. "It's a test."

"A rite of passage," Laren punned, with a sour expression.

"It should be Oriane's triad, and blast the rules," said Chaldrinda.

It should be me, Karanthe thought. During the magewar, she had joined with other reckoners and Pelkin to form a group of nine to cast a warding around the last triad. She had felt

Pelkin's light, through the casting leaf, through the joined circle. It had not been enough. She had not been close enough. She had not *touched* it. Now, with both of them lightless, she never would. Not even if, as some believed, they would regain their lights in pethyar.

She looked out the window, and her eye caught on a striking tricolored horse being led with a leggy bay toward the stables.

"Louarn!" she cried, and pushed past her startled colleagues. "We've got our binder. Chaldrinda, come help me escort him past that cordon of mages downstairs." She hauled the woman out and down the long hallway, thinking, *This is what he wants, and I will see to it.* On the landing she nearly ran headlong into Louarn. He had Prill Wordsmith in tow. "No illuminator?" she said.

"Your young mages want shepherding," Louarn said. "They seem to be done answering to you, their lightless masters. You may have a bit of an uprising on your hands when Pelkin passes. Keiler n'Graefel has taken charge of them for now, but he can't see to choose an illuminator."

With an oath, Chaldrinda continued downstairs. Karanthe led the way to Pelkin's rooms. In the sitting room, pausing to check the hooded birds waiting to carry messages, already scribed, to the Head and the Strong Leg and Khine, she asked Louarn, "Have you materials?"

Louarn patted a worn canvas pack hanging from his shoulder. Karanthe hadn't seen one like it in years; it looked like part of some binder's journey truss from the time of the old light.

Herne stood before the inner door, blocking Louarn. He minced no words: "Your light is unreliable."

"Pelkin sent me for . . . polishing," Louarn said. "The problem is solved."

Karanthe said, "He came with Keiler. That old recluse wouldn't have brought him unless . . ." She frowned. "How did you know to come?"

"Does it matter?" Louarn said. "I've known Pelkin n'Rolf since I was a child in the old Holding. Keiler n'Graefel will vouch for me."

She barely knew Keiler except by reputation. She'd known

Louarn since the battle of the Menalad Plain, but he'd only just begun studying magecraft when she left the Strong Leg. While Pelkin held him in high regard, they had never seen him do one of the major castings. With all three lights, would his magelight be compromised, or even enhanced in some unpredictable way?

"Pelkin knows this man, and trusts him," she said to Herne. "This is our binder. Show him in."

She went back out into the hall to watch for the illuminator and bid the remaining touches be patient a little longer; two had already allowed themselves to be called to some other duty. Until the casting was under way, they had to be prepared to save him. They could not let him languish as a haunt, separated from his pledgemate into eternity.

When four figures turned the corner from the stairwell, she thought that one of them was Liath.

She rubbed her eyes, and there were three: Chaldrinda, the illuminator Earil, and a tall russet-haired Norther with a rugged authority. Keiler. It must have been Keiler she had mistaken for Pelkin's granddaughter. She had not seen Liath for more than two nineyears.

When she'd gestured them inside—Keiler was Graefel Scholar's son, and as close as family to Pelkin, with as much right to attend his passage as anyone here—she still felt some extra presence in the hall. A familiar, isolated longing from half a lifetime ago. That same reaching-out she'd felt when she and Dabrena and Tolivar healed a stray vocate's sprained knee and the vocate's blocked light tried to join with theirs. As though the place where that light had been was trying to reach out to the gaping emptiness inside her, to see how that absence felt.

It feels the same, she told it, as she turned to go in. *It feels like death, and I cannot bear it.*

Louarn sat on a stool at the foot of the bed, wood-backed sedgeweave on his lap. Prill Wordsmith sat to his right, Earil Illuminator to his left. The bed had been moved far enough from the wall for him to chalk the casting circle around it. He used white chalk from the Oriels, the Spirit Range. This was the last of the three spirit days. Prill's eyes were closed as she centered herself; the tension smoothed from her features, eased from her fingers, and when she opened her eyes she looked to Pelkin first, with affection and respect, before she turned to Louarn for materials.

He passed Neck sedgeweave and wychwood binding board to her. He passed first to the right; in a birthing they would have reversed positions so that he was passing first to the left. Deasil for the entering of the world, widdershins for the leaving of it. Motions as ancient and powerful as time.

Prill let him choose, so he provided an ink of bonewood bark and powdered mica; it would dry as she scribed to an iridescent silvery gray. The quill was one that a touch had revitalized, after age had dried and cracked it, so that the penknife angled through smooth as silk when Louarn trimmed it: the quill that Pelkin and his reckoners had used to cast Keiler's triad, saved by Keiler for all these years and carried as a keepsake in his bindsack. All of these were Keiler's materials, some made with light, some made with craft, all made with love; the strength of their bond would carry that power into the casting.

As he passed the materials, their lights began to join. His flowing toward the wordsmith's, hers flowing toward the illuminator's, the illuminator's flowing toward his. Gradually he began to sense the wordsmith, too, as *toward* became *into,* as her scribing flowed in long unbroken lines across the leaf. He could not see what she wrote, and he still did not read well after all these years, particularly not the stylized scripts employed by wordsmiths. But that added an archaic flavor to the casting that perhaps balanced the new-grown craft of the younger mages. Under the old light, neither binder nor illuminator would have been able to read a word the wordsmith scribed. Pelkin was a man of the old light. Perhaps this would suit him.

The leaf filled quickly; the wordsmith worked fluidly, with a sure hand, relaxing as the work took her out of herself, out of the shell of a girl overconscious of scrutiny. Louarn tested a reed point, then a quill point, on the pad of his thumb, letting his touch's sense assure him that they were cut correctly— letting his touch's power mend an infinitesimal flaw in the well of the reed. The stronger he grew in all three powers, the less certain he became of which he was using when, and the less it mattered. They were all good and decent powers. Awake, he had no fear of them combining adversely.

His pigment pots sat ready on the floor around his stool. He tried to anticipate the illuminator's needs with customary pigments, cobalt and antimony and ochre bound in resins, wax, casein. He'd drawn no hair from Pelkin's silver head, no blood from a pricked finger; except for birthing fluids and moonflow, blood was a forbidden material, harking too much to darkcraft, and in casting passage the goal was to prompt the spirit to move on; materials of flesh would be counterproductive. Flesh and spirit were knit close, and the spirit clung fiercely to its home. He had wandered for half a lifetime, and Pelkin had roamed far and long from home in his reckoner days. There should be no obstacle to this dissolution. Pelkin was desperate to be freed to join his pledge.

He realized that he knew that not from being told, but by some other means. Was this the beginning of the vision these castings brought, or some flare of his bluesilver glow as he looked at Pelkin? His mind left off observing itself as the word-smith passed the board and the inscribed leaf across Pelkin's body and the illuminator received them.

Here his work grew harder. The illuminator, a gentle girl but a demanding mage employing varied techniques, required different inks for kadri and knotwork, different paints for borders and historiations. The swell of their light carried him through preparations and provisions. A tune seeped into the folds of his mind. A golden tune, a melody of magelight, a warm flow of honey in sunshine, a sinuous spill of golden hair over a young girl's shoulders. A song of sweetness to open the way between the realms.

The inscribed, illuminated leaf came into his hands. He laid it on the sunken chest, a magnificent portrayal of Pelkin's spirit. The mages' hands slid into his as his lips parted. The glide of tender skin across calluses, silk on sand; the sensual pleasure of flesh and power blending. He drew breath, inhaling light and life. He opened his eyes and looked on Pelkin's face. He opened his heart and their shared song poured out. A great spirit was passing from the world. He sang it to its end with admiration and with hope.

He saw something, as he sang. Something at the edge of the eye. A bitter darkness entered his melody, a counterpoint, a syncopation. Salty as an unwept tear, shot through with discordancy; he wove it into the binding and then lost the thread of it. The bindsong warmed into fullness, completion. He pressed the last drops of melody through the cracks in his soul.

The casting circle seemed to float inside a sphere of its own making, the result of focus so intense that it numbed the edges of vision. The leaf on Pelkin's chest was sharply delineated, every line and ornament, the only remaining clarity. The last note of Louarn's song elongated into an otherworldly drone. The casting leaf swirled into a brilliant mix of color, spreading instead of dissipating, swelling instead of contracting. It smeared pigment across the world; hues and tones separated and resolved into cyan, magenta, lemon, then circled, faster and faster, around the blurred periphery of vision, until they had blended into a crystalline scintillation.

This was not the casting vision. This was enclosure, not expansion. The other mages had gone dim, diffuse; the room was gone, nothing solid remained; Louarn and Pelkin were suspended in a whiteness that might end at arm's length or extend forever. The drone continued, the only sound in a white silence.

The sum of all colors, Pelkin said, his eyes opening. He sat up as though healed. The casting leaf was gone. They sat on nothing, as though inside a vessel, riding a dream.

Pelkin, Louarn said, while somewhere else his song went on, and on, and on. *Pelkin—I fear I'm dreaming.*

Louarn the White, Pelkin said, with some affection. *Where have you brought us?*

The wordsmith and illuminator appeared in a gossamer shimmer; they cast panicked glances beyond the sphere, speaking in mute voices to the shades that moved and shifted beyond the white veil. Then they were gone.

This isn't the vision, Louarn said.

Isn't it? said Pelkin. *No one remembers, after. I remembered white. This place is white. But I don't recall sitting in conversation with the dying.*

I saw . . . I did see . . . a woman, crying . . .

Pelkin crossed his legs with supple ease. He folded his hands in his lap. His eyes were the color of pewter. A triskele glinted dully in the fold of his shirt, graven silver flared on a ring finger; then both were lost to sight. He said, *You saw me sick with a fever, racked with rage and guilt. They were flaying them alive in the Holding. I hadn't known. I knew they were corrupt. I knew the head warders opposed them, but I didn't know . . . I wanted to race up there and batter down their walls and kill them all.* He produced a terrible smile. *They'd have crushed me like a leaf.*

Yes. That was what Louarn had seen. The night that Pelkin learned the truth of the Ennead's darkcraft. The night he and eight reckoners cast against them, and lost. The night that Pelkin believed he had stained his soul.

You were helpless, Louarn said. *Defeated. Emasculated. Grieving. You met death by making life. There's no shame in that.*

I was sick with complicity and afire with rage. I had been away from Brei for years. The cool cloth, the cool hands, the soft mouth . . . I lost myself.

It was comfort, Louarn said. A woman from Elingar, in the Belt, where Pelkin's reckoners cast their defiance at the Ennead and were destroyed. One left alive, found raving in a field after the bonefolk had been and gone; she tended him. She had no face, in Pelkin's memory. Only shape and softness on which to vent the madness of his grief.

It was rage, Pelkin said. *I used that comfort, and not gently.*

You were not yourself.

I was wholly myself. Didn't Keiler teach you anything? I was the self I am when I have lost control of myself.

We're many selves, all different. Sometimes they stand in opposition. Don't presume to think you are the only one.

Pelkin looked through Louarn, down the dark byways of the past.

Louarn said, *Your infidelity persuaded the Ennead that they had broken you. Even the deaths of your eight reckoners could not do that. They conceived your integrity as based in an unbreakable bond to your pledge. Once that was shattered, they believed they'd turned you. Only then could you continue in their service and subvert them.*

Pelkin raised his silver eyes. *It was too great a price.*

And new life a reward so great, for such a sin, that it verged on punishment?

I did not deserve her. My family in Clondel did not deserve for her to have more of me than they had ever had.

You should have told her, Louarn said.

I was a terrible father. She didn't want a father. She had a father. A solid man. His name was Jebb. I learned that later, and her mother's name. Farine. I left that night before I learned it, stumbled away to retch in the bushes, make my way back to the tatters of my proxy circle.

You had your reckoners keep watch on her.

No. I didn't. But she found me. She scaled the old hierarchy rung by rung, unstoppable. I could not be shut of her. Of course I loved her, though I was no fit father for anyone. It was my privilege to be her teacher and her friend. Don't tell her, Louarn. Don't let those young upstarts tell her.

Your pledge forgave you, Pelkin. Or she will, in short order.

My Brei cared not a whit what seed I spilled. Abstinence was my choice. A gift I tried to give her, or perhaps myself. She was proud of our daughters. She won't be sorry to know I left another to carry on for me in this world—in my own work, as our eldest carried on for her.

The space flared silver-blue as Louarn struggled to define the invisible trespass. His own light—he shouldn't have been able to see it. *What, then, Pelkin? What keeps you from going on?*

Pelkin raised a brow. *You do, my boy. This is no doing of mine. It's your dream we're inside, your power we inhabit. I admit I'm fascinated to see it from within, but I have somewhere to be, if you take my meaning.*

I must have needed to know the truth of you. I must have expected it from the casting, and made it happen when it didn't.

His eyes gone dark and hard, Pelkin said, *Then know that what Breida must forgive is the sick madness that came over me in Elingar. I became the Ennead I fought, that night. I have amends to make to two spirits in pethyar, and only when they've absolved me will I forgive myself and rest easy in my pledge's arms. Is that enough for you? Is that what you wanted to know, Louarn the Black?*

It was Louarn who had trespassed. He had no right to plumb the heart of Pelkin's shame, and Pelkin had no need to unburden himself—expiation awaited him in pethyar, not in dialogue with some acquaintance. Pelkin's admissions barely moved him; he had no stake in them, and now that he had heard them, he wished he hadn't. He didn't want entrée to someone else's mind. His own was trouble enough. *Why did I bring us here? What is this place?*

Pelkin rose and stood beside him to survey the formless white. *I believe it's your mind, Louarn. Do you hear that?*

Loaurn did: the drone, continuing unabated. The sound of his own voice, still singing the final note of Pelkin's passage. The casting leaf had dissipated, the casting was complete. The way to pethyar should have opened to them. Pelkin should have gone on. Instead Louarn had somehow dreamed them here.

I don't dream while waking, he said.

Apparently you do. If it wasn't something you wanted of me, then what?

I don't permit it, Louarn thought, and spoke, at the same time, because there was no privacy in dreams. *I don't. When I'm conscious, I maintain . . . control.* A deep terror bloomed within him. Keiler had mended him too well. He had opened heart and mind and spirit, and this was the result.

I'm afraid, Pelkin, he said. *I've lost my way.*

Yes you have. And so kindly thought to bring me with you. Pelkin's clothes had drained of color when all colors combined into the whiteness; when he moved to try the boundaries of the space, he seemed to blend into it, his head and hands the only solid parts of him. *Well, let's see what last adventure fate has contrived for me.* Feeling no barrier, he stepped through the veil of white.

Pelkin, wait! Louarn lunged after him. *Don't get lost here—*

Pelkin stood on a platform of shadow within a vast, silent space. His arms windmilled as he tried to catch his balance from the void. Louarn grabbed a handful of black tunic and hauled him back to center.

Bloody, raving spirits, Pelkin said, and looked around.

There was nothing. Louarn stood agape. He knew this place. It was the birthplace of shadows. The place inside him where he made the razored shadows that killed people while he slept. The depths had been filled with unbearable things, griefs and failures, punishments and threats, shrieking and gibbering. Mellas had come here with Liath and plunged down into the tortured depths, and harrowed them. He had forgotten that, when Mellas died. For six years he had not slept long enough to dream, for fear of releasing those horrors into the world. For a dozen years now no shadows had come when he warily let himself sleep. This was why. Those depths were swept clear.

Or perhaps the shadows were just fled to other quarters. There were worse things than shadows, in the depths of dreams, in the places where you fell when you fell the wrong way into sleep.

I should be able to dream us clear of this, he thought. *I should be able to dream us anywhere I want to go.*

We can't always control ourselves, Pelkin said, in wry allusion. *And this isn't your ordinary dream, whatever one of those is like, which I'm quite sure I don't want to know. We're still bound by the casting. I can still hear you sing.*

Louarn stepped backward off the platform, drawing Pelkin with him into the blur of white. This time he led, without letting go. With nothing to orient him, he struck off in a random direction. He wondered vaguely what would happen if they walked back into Pelkin's sleeproom. Would the body still be lying there on the bed? Would his body still be perched at the foot, voice raised in bindsong? Would they be haunts? Pelkin's forearm was skin and muscle and bone within his grip, the arm of a healthy man in his prime. But that could be a substance of the mind's creation. He had not passaged Pelkin's body. He was not a boneman. As long as that endless note sounded, his own body sat back in that room. Pelkin's must be there as well. Their sojourn here was occupying the space between one breath and another—between his last sung breath, and Pelkin's death rattle.

He had to send the man to pethyar. They had completed the casting. The passage must be open. They had only to find it.

It had seemed that they were sitting in the center of a room-sized sphere, and reached the shadow void in no more than five or six strides, but they walked through white for a long time before it thinned, like a mist, and then was gone. They stood in a murky attic under angled rafters, among spare tools and old draped furniture. A pigeon feather went skittering as though blown by a breeze through a door behind them, where there was only mist and slanted roof. Louarn banged his shin on a crate.

"How odd," Pelkin said, his voice rich and real in the wooden space. "This is home."

Not home as in the runners' holding. He meant home in the Neck.

A high, round window at one end glowed with burnt-orange sunset, casting a ray of smoky light through air the color of brown Norther tea. The shadows were deep and quiet, as though they'd bided here longer than memory. The diffuse ray of light never shifted; the sun never set. A trapdoor lay open on its hinges in the center of the floor. Pelkin walked over to it, looked down, then hauled the trapdoor up by its pull string and dropped it closed in a puff of dust. The pigeon feather spun into the air with a blue sparkle.

"That's not the way," Pelkin said.

"What is this place?" Louarn asked.

"It's the attic of the old Petrel's Rest. My pledge's public house." He raised one end of a linen sheet that draped the outline of a chair. "This was her favorite rocker. My eldest probably couldn't stand the sight of it after she died, and banished it up here. She was doing a lot of banishing in those days." He let the sheet fall. "I didn't do this, Louarn, before you start that nonsense again. Brei's not here. From the looks of this place, she hasn't been here for years. I've no cause to go into the past. I want to move on."

"We'll keep looking, then." Louarn pondered whether to go through or return to the milky center and try another direction.

Liath stood in deepest shadow at the other end of the attic. Facing outward, shoulders slumped. "She didn't want to know me," Louarn could hear her murmur.

"*Liath?*" Pelkin breathed, and she turned.

Louarn had not told him how she'd appeared in Keiler's cottage this morning before dawn. It would not have mattered if he had. This was a Liath profoundly changed from the young woman who'd come seeking Mellas and fallen into Keiler's arms. Her hair was shorn to a dark red bristle with a rat-tail lock at the nape; the webwork of triangular Ennead scars was slashed, on her face, by a more recent scar from temple to lip, just missing her left eye. She was four nineyears if she was a day. Her body rode the attic planks like a ship's deck. She looked harrowed, as though she'd seen a ghost on the other side of the attic wall.

This was the Liath who should have barged into Keiler's house; the hauntlike girl they'd seen there belonged here, in the sepia past.

"Pelkin?" she said. Her voice came strong, from deep in the chest, the voice of a woman hardened by long years at sea. But there was reservation in it. As though Pelkin might not want to know her. "Gran?"

"Liath," Pelkin said, and moved to embrace her.

Louarn looked away; it was too poignant and private a moment to be observed by eyes like his. Let them have their brief reunion and farewell. Where Pelkin was going, neither a living Liath nor a haunt could follow. Louarn did not know how long they had before the droning note died out. He was itchy to move on, to find the way to pethyar. Once he had sent Pelkin through, he could concentrate on the puzzle that was Liath.

"My girl," Pelkin said, squeezing her shoulders, pressing her out to arms' length. "Where have you *been?*"

"Sailing," she said. "Surviving." As though she hadn't said those same words to Keiler a matter of hours ago. Her gray gaze fixed on him. *"Mellas?"*

The old Liath, the younger Liath, would have spoken to him awkwardly from where she stood. This Liath strode across the attic to pull him into a rough hug of relief. "Thank the spirits," she said. "I didn't know what had become of you, after you went into those tunnels. I couldn't find you after the magewar."

"He's called Louarn now," said Pelkin. "A tale we don't have time for, more's the pity. It's quite a piece of knotwork."

"We have to go," Louarn said, shrugging almost rudely out of the embrace. He'd trusted her, once; he'd cared for her as he might a sister. But that was two lifetimes ago, and they stood on dangerous ground, halfway to the realm of death. He did not know what she was.

Liath chuckled. "Same old Mellas," she said. "All right. Where to? So long as it's not out to sea, I'm with you."

"We're looking for pethyar," Pelkin said, eyes twinkling, as though the whole thing had become a grand game. "We're in the middle of a casting in the Haunch, and our binder here, who has all three lights, has spirited us off into some otherwhere. I don't suppose you know where the passage is?"

Liath frowned. "There's a hole," she said. "But it's not what you want. It's a . . ." She looked at Louarn. "A bad thing."

Marvelous, Louarn thought. "You don't remember seeing Keiler?"

She frowned. "Keiler's in the Haunch." Startled, she said

"Pelkin—" and then whipped her head round to look at him. "I don't know what's happening to me," she said. Harsh, uncomfortable. "I've seen some bloody strange things in the last two nineyears, but this is the capper."

Louarn started across the attic, negotiating piles and crates, giving the trapdoor a wide berth, and whatever Pelkin had seen when he looked down there. They would go straight on. No backtracking. No detours.

He gritted his teeth and walked directly at the attic wall.

Though pale mist engulfed him, he flinched, his head expecting to bang the rafters. He went through where the wall had been, but it was harder to walk than it had been. Each step grew more labored. Liath and Pelkin came up beside him, then moved ahead. Whatever the impediment was, it did not affect them as it did him. Liath, in turn, could not keep up with Pelkin. Her motions grew logy, dragging. Where Louarn felt as though he were moving through fast-curing mortar, Liath looked to be fighting the failure of her own bones.

The whiteness began to thin. Louarn glimpsed a complexity of shapes ahead, rock formations, perhaps, and a coruscation of colors. His progress halted at the edge of white. He could not press on. The mist did not clear away, but hung behind him in a formless, depthless curtain.

Before him was a realm of wonder.

Graceful structures of impossible height swept upward in sinuous columns to flare out into blossom-dripping canopies. Grown or crafted of unknowable substance, pale as seashells, curved as driftwood, they might be dense as stone or springy as fungus, or they might shatter at a breath. Their surfaces were sheened in rainbows. The air itself was opalescent; the sky was a gentle coruscation of rose, cerulean, pearl, mint, and though soft shimmers of fire flirted in its depths, no sun was evident. The ground at Loaurn's feet was a velvet mat of plum and turquoise moss; feathery broom and fern brushed the trunks of the upswept structures with vermilion and citrine, and smooth landscaped pathways wended among them, banked in peach and apricot flowers. To the left, atop a hill quilted with lavender and mauve, turreted pavilions glittered like spun sugar in the sourceless light, a confection of architecture. To the right, a crystalline river delved an undulation of azure grass.

It was a breathtaking world—but there was no life in it. No breeze stirred the nodding fronds or caressed the delicate petals into a flutter. It was airless, empty, abandoned. The ghost of a sublime, crafted beauty.

His heart ached to look on it. A few steps away, Liath stood bent with her hands on her knees, then bowed her head between them, fighting nausea or sending blood to fight a faint. Pelkin was turning circles of wonder, drinking in the colors, lost in awe. His tunic and hose had gone black again and taken on a silvery sparkle, like mica in the nightstone of the Aralinn Mountains. Liath's alien vest and leggings had gone matte and lost detail—they must be tanned animal hide, Louarn realized, the scholars spoke of such material, and it would not be recognized by any reflection of Eiden Myr.

We must go on, he tried to say, but he couldn't work his mouth. He could move, a little, but as though trapped in a weight of mud. He eased back a step; the whiteness yielded. Back would open to him. He could get out. He could breathe. But he could not follow, and he could not speak from here.

Pelkin spoke to Liath. She drew herself upright and replied. Louarn could not hear them. Pelkin pointed at him, Liath turned to look; he could not gesture that he was all right. They conferred. Liath came toward him, feet sinking into the delicious mossy mat, while Pelkin struck off down the nearest path.

Don't wander too deep, Louarn thought. The inability to communicate was intensely frustrating.

Liath pressed him back a few steps into the mist. The pressure eased. She flexed her joints. "Ah," she said. "It's better here."

"Don't let him wander," Louarn said. Every word was an effort, as though his tongue and lips and jaw were numbed by strong drink.

"He won't go far, he just wants to see what those giant

mushrooms are made of. I can't go far. The deeper I go, the weaker I am."

"We do not belong here."

"Any idea what 'here' is?"

"The ghost of a world," Louarn said. It had the eternal quality of the bonefolk's realms: sourceless light, constant skies, incongruous colors and textures. He wanted to tell her that, but in so doing he would have to explain the bonefolk, the waiting places where they passaged the bodies of the dead, and it was too many words to produce through the winter sap he stood in.

"It looks like the Haunch," Liath said. "Near Sauglin. The river, the shape of the hill. Pelkin thought so too. Do you see it? I think in some strange way you're still where you were."

The ghost of a Sauglin-that-was. Yes. It made sense. An idea struck him, and he knew what Pelkin intended. To put his hand on it. To see if it felt anything like the substance they were excavating from the Sauglin dig. To see if this might be the Triennead holding in its prime.

It was an exciting notion. But this was no human world.

A deep foreboding took hold of him. A fear that if Pelkin touched this place with his bare flesh, flesh that represented his roaming spirit, it would take him, and keep him. "Go fetch him," he said.

"Suppose this is pethyar? A peaceful reflection of our world, a shining place for spirits to spend eternity? It has the scent of forever in it."

Suppose it was? How would he know? He had botched the casting. How would he find the way if it was not?

With a groan, he drove himself forward, plunging deep into the transparent substance of the barrier. He would drive through. He would force his way. He was young, strong, alive. He would push through and follow Pelkin, to save him or to join him, whatever chance decreed. He was responsible for the spirit walking down that curve of path. He would not let it go alone into the unknown.

The barrier froze him in place. The mortar cured around

him, just beyond where he had stood before, and there was no movement, there was no breath, there was no feeling in his body at all.

There was only sentience and sight. He could only watch as Pelkin went up to one of the pale trunks, dwarfed by its immensity, and reached his hand through the rainbow sheen, and touched it.

A darkness seeped up into the sky. Something terrible took form beyond the vaulted towers. Sniffing, questing. Sending out a wisp here, a tendril there. A thing of pure malevolence, both alien and hideously familiar. It knew this place. It hunted here.

Pelkin's hand sank into the pale substance before him, and he snatched it out and stared at it, then reached again. Wary. Fascinated. Unheeding of the thing that loomed beyond the ancient tower grove.

Liath saw it, and tried to spring forward, and fell to her knees, then her hands. Braced on the yielding moss, she struggled to heave herself up, raised her head to shout, and couldn't.

Louarn could not cry warning. He could only watch as the rising malevolence sniffed, and found, and rushed down the curving paths toward Pelkin.

Pelkin stopped with his hand extended toward the indescribable chill substance his hand had sunk into. Before his head had turned, he felt the terror swooping down on him. He caught only a glimpse of writhing darkness before the prismatic sheen of the tower engulfed him, and sucked him stumbling in.

He found himself gripped by the arm, staring into the face of one of his reckoners.

"Liath!" he cried, and twisted out of the grip, whirling to plunge back out and race the darkness to tackle her into the safety of Louarn's white mind.

Black arms caught him from both sides, black-clad bodies hauled him away from a wall of living, undulating rainbow that his eyes could not make sense of.

"She's all right," said an old, known voice. "Turn around, don't look at the wall, it'll make you sick till you get used to it."

He fought the weight and grip of his reckoners with all the strength of his spirit, but they bore him back, farther from the incomprehensible wall, farther from his granddaughter, and he had to yield, the nausea was too acute.

"You see, I told the truth about the wall, now give it up, Pelkin, Liath fled back the way you came." A man with tousled sandy hair and storm-green eyes came into view as the reckoners cautiously released him. Agroed, Tinion, Coldur, and the rest . . . all eight of them, the eight he should have died with in casting against the Ennead that doomed night. He was too overwhelmed to greet them, but his eyes must have shown it, for they gave shy smiles and murmurs before they made way for the sandy-haired man to come up beside him.

"Evonder." He managed a bow of genuine respect to the only member of the Ennead whose authority he'd recognized. When Torrin left the Ennead's Holding to form a triad to fight the Nine from without, his friend Evonder had stayed to fight them from within. Joining them. Not, it seemed, at the cost of his own soul, since it was here. But not without cost. "Evonder n'Daivor."

Evonder sketched only a brief bow in return. Unlike Pelkin, who was still unbalanced by strangeness, he was all business, a man with concerns in a realm Pelkin could not begin to understand and wasn't sure yet that he believed in.

"My granddaughter . . ." he said, still doubting what he could not see. Looking at the shifting colors in the wall was like looking down into a whirlpool from a great height.

"She had more sense than you, Pelkin n'Rolf," Evonder said. "Better to be a disembodied haunt in the realm of flesh than risk annihilation here. You're new. You'll learn."

"How do you know?" Pelkin said. "How can you *see*?"

"You were an illuminator. You'll acquire the knack soon enough. You can see between the colors, once your eye has found the patterns." He paused. "There are more pressing things you need to know."

Pelkin turned his back to the wall and regarded the vastness that extended from where they stood. It was empty. The sheen of the walls lit tiers and balconies arrayed within them, and suggested the towering, vacant heights above; entire villages could have been housed in here. But there was nothing.

"They're gone," Evonder said. "They made what they needed when they were here, but now they're not, and so there's nothing. Now, there are th—"

"Who?"

"Its makers. Pelkin, you—"

"This structure is made of light."

"Something like that. Now—"

"Is this the Triennead holding?"

Surrendering with some irritation, Evonder said, "This realm is where haunts go when they aren't haunting things. In the world, we're disembodied spirits. I wander the Holding. I watch it heal. It's my hobby. Here, we have a semblance of ourselves. But no one knows for certain what this realm is. I believe it is itself a haunt. I believe it's the ghost of the place the original crafters made—the bonefolk, before they fell, before whatever great crime they believe they committed razed the land and rendered it barren. The ghost of Eiden Myr before it fell into ruin and became the wasteland that Galandra reclaimed for her exiled mages. Ancient Eiden Myr in its prime. A place so glorious, so vibrant that its own spirit survived its passing from the world of matter. All who die unpassaged find their way here. Now wave hello so we can move on."

Pelkin focused on the other figures standing around them. There were more than he had realized at first. As he looked, others joined them, as though sliding into the darklight from some otherwhere. Family, old friends, stewards from the Ennead's Holding. Too many to greet, too many familiar, beloved faces for his heart to hold. Brondarion te Khine, looking through the wall as though he wished very much to go out to the white veil but was restraining himself. Drinda Baker, Leoryn Tailor, the others who had planned and carried out the stewards' uprising. Warders and reckoners who had been vocates with him a lifetime ago. Folk who had become dear to him in his years of traveling. A human rendering of his long life, his loves and losses. An illumination. He did not know what to do. He did not know how to be with them again after so long.

After a few breaths, they faded. Were they only the shades of his past, some step in a reckoning he must endure on his quest for pethyar?

"You'll see them again," said Evonder, when they were alone. "They felt you pass through. They only wanted to pay respect. It's how it's done here. There's all eternity for reunions. All will come in time."

"I don't have time," Pelkin whispered.

Evonder did not hear him. "I'm sorry to see you here," he said. "You should have had some years before you were consigned to haunthood." He looked through the wall. "And sorrier to see her. She looks to have died hard."

"She's not dead," Pelkin said. He composed himself, shrugged his tunic straight, adjusted his belt. "At least, I don't think so. Neither is the lad."

"That answers some questions and raises more." Evonder's gaze sharpened in evaluation. "Who is the lad? Do I know him? He seems more man than lad."

For one breath, as the shifting patterns of light passed through some configuration his mind could grasp, Pelkin caught a glimpse of him, frozen in his struggle to breach the barrier. "He is your son."

Evonder went very still. "My son," he said.

"The babe you got on Lerissa, the one we took to Bron for fostering. He escaped the Holding eventually, though it was a twisting journey."

"In life I longed to see him again, just once before the end. In death, I couldn't find him."

"His name is Louarn. Louarn n'Evonder; he took your name, once he'd put the pieces of the past in place. He takes after you."

"He has Lerissa's eyes."

"And nothing of her soul. He's a remarkable man. You can be proud of him."

I have to be going, he thought. He could no longer hear the last note of the bindsong. He must trust that it was still sounding, within the portal of Louarn's white mind. *I have to get back to the casting and find my way through. I can't dally here.* He would have liked to explore this realm, to hear Evonder's concerns, to find out what that writhing darkness was that could annihilate the dead. But this was not his destination. Evonder's concerns were not his.

"Can we walk back out through this bloody headache of a wall?" he asked.

A hint of smile curved Evonder's lips, but was quickly weighted down. "I wouldn't venture into the open till you've learned to move yourself from the shadow's path. But yes, you can."

"Good," he said. "Come meet your son." Before Evonder could resist, he pressed them both back through the chill alien light.

Louarn could not even struggle in his paralysis, but he never gave up trying to find his limbs, to drive them forward with sheer force of will.

Liath had collapsed beside him after scrabbling backward, out of harm's way, when Pelkin was drawn into the tower. The malevolence had swept across the paths and mossy sward, a shapeless thing like a hole in the world, a gaping hunger made visible. Where it had passed, the world was briefly drained of color and substance, but when it had gone, sinking out of this realm like a blotted stain, the vivid changelessness reasserted itself. Liath rose out of the misty border and made for the towers. Her foray ended with her panting on her knees.

Louarn could not help her. Louarn could only watch as a tall figure in tunic and hose of robin's-egg blue emerged from the tower with Pelkin.

He could only stare in recognition at his own face.

* * *

"I can't," Evonder said, grinding to a halt on the curved path. "I can't go too near the living, not in this form, not here. They shouldn't be here." He stared at Louarn, his sculpted features hard but the fixity of his gaze implying a reluctant fascination with the sable-haired likeness of him, frozen as though in ice in its struggle to reach him. "I couldn't find him in the world," he said in a low voice. "I didn't know him." *I wish I had,* Pelkin heard, between the words, and between those words all that knowing him would have meant.

The man Pelkin had known in life had rarely displayed genuine emotion, even among those he trusted. He feigned everything, all the time, and became so used to feigning that he found it difficult to be himself. Here, it seemed, he was wholly himself—and held that self on as tight a rein as his son did his own in the living realm. They were more alike than they knew.

Liath was struggling to drag herself to them. With an upraised palm, Pelkin bade her stay. She didn't like it. She had been more than fond of Evonder, and she had questions of her own to ask. They would have to wait.

Evonder said, "How did they come here? I have to know if there's some breach the shadow might exploit."

The shadow, Pelkin thought, and then: *No. Not my concern.*

"Your son has all three lights. That white light is the proof of it, and the fact that we lightless can see it is proof that in combining his light becomes something greater than its parts. He was casting passage for me, but his powers surged and . . . opened more than we'd bargained for. I can't explain it, or how Liath joined us. We made our way through as we could, and now we're here."

"They'll have to go," Evonder said. His gaze dismissed them as irrelevant to his situation; he was a commander dismissing personal concerns to scan the surroundings for threat. "A hole like that might let in anything. Tell . . . my son to take care how he uses that power. Our spirits are at stake here. Our existence, if you will. We're under attack from a great evil."

Pelkin felt a plummeting hopelessness, and great anger in its wake—an old, banked rage that he tried to put aside, and couldn't, and despaired. Slowly, painfully, he said, "What is the shadow, Evonder?"

Never ceasing to scan the distance for it, Evonder said, "It is the thing the leading triad of the Ennead became when Torrin's triad vanquished it. They fought the passage cast for them and went into some otherwhere. Like any other unpassaged, they found their way here eventually. The rest of the Nine died unpassaged as well, and they are also here, aiding it, feeding it. Using it as a weapon of terror. Still trying to manipulate to their own ends whatever realm they find themselves in. Still trying to wreak vengeance somewhere. Our struggle with them isn't over, Pelkin. I'm glad you're here, though I regret that you died unpassaged and too young. We have need of you."

Pelkin watched his dreams of absolution and reunion seep like tears into the earth.

He had yielded himself freely to every minor ailment, every fever, every cough. He had let arthritis sieze his joints, weakness claim his heart. He had staved off menders and healers and eagerly embraced what he felt was a natural death. The end his body would have come to, left free of light's interference.

Because Graefel had found a partial description of how Galandra's ennead cast the warding that severed Eiden Myr from the outerlands, and believed that once they had cast another like it, they would be severed from pethyar as well.

There was no other way to stop the war of the coast. Whatever the outerlands had become, it was not a realm of mercy. Whoever or whatever dwelled there was still bent on Eiden Myr's destruction. Eiden Myr could harrow the outerlands; Eiden Myr was a place of great power. But it would require darkcraft, which they must never use again. Casting another warding was the only solution. To cast it properly—to cast it better than it was before—would mean total isolation. No more Great Storms, as there had been. No breach, no hole, like the one that had allowed Torrin's outlander mother, Eilody, to ride the Storm through the warding and make landfall on Eiden's shore. Total isolation.

Graefel believed it would cut them off from all the realms. The outer realms, and the otherrealms. The bonefolk's realms, where the bodies of their dead lay. This realm of haunts, presumably, though he had not known of it until now. And pethyar, the realm of spirit.

It would be cast before the next cycle of the moon. If Graefel was right, it would block his way to pethyar and to Breida. He had chosen to die before the casting, in trust that his eight masters would see it through to completion. His life's work had been to vanquish the old Ennead and set Eiden Myr on a safe path, and he had believed both to be accomplished. He had chosen not to gamble that Graefel was wrong. His work was done. He'd earned his eternity.

Oh, Brei. Oh, Brei, I so wanted to touch your sweet spirit again.

"I'm not unpassaged," he said at long last. "I'm not a haunt." He gritted his teeth. "At least, not yet."

Evonder stared at him in harsh incomprehension. "Your casting failed," he said. "The lad's powers surged, and—"

"They haven't finished casting passage yet. That white veil is . . . my choice, made visible."

"You must go back!" Evonder said. The voice of authority, the voice of the Ennead—it had not left him even in death. "You were not meant to come here. You were meant to go on. This is a mistake." He tried to usher Pelkin toward the veil, but within three steps he doubled over. "Bloody balls," he said. "They're too alive. It's wrong. It hurts. I can't go with you. I can't force you. Go!"

"I'll go," Pelkin said. "But only to say farewell. Watch me safe into the veil if you choose, but wait for me, Evonder. We're going to have to defeat that Ennead remnant more quickly than you may have planned. Your access to this realm is only temporary now. When I come back, I'll tell you why."

Ignoring Evonder's angry objections, Pelkin crossed the ground of the afterlife with bitter purpose in his stride and his heart cracking in his chest.

* * *

Louarn grunted as Pelkin bore him back into the borders of his mind and the suffocating pressure of the ghost realm eased.

He'd read the grim decision on Pelkin's face.

"It's not too late—"

"No, lad. I chose to die. Now it's only a matter of what I do with it."

"You could truly die here," Louarn said. "For good. Forever. That black thing that passed—it can kill the dead."

Pelkin cocked his head. The brief blue tinge of the mist around them gave his face a glaucous cast. "You are a visant, aren't you? Bloody eerie, that knack is. Yes. I can die forever, here. Consumed by an evil I thought was soundly thrashed. It only took another form. But if we can die here, so can it."

Liath struggled to her feet behind him, blanched and drawn. Pelkin told them that the battle against the Ennead had only shifted to new ground.

"I fought them my life long," Pelkin said. "I thought we'd stopped them. It seems I was wrong. I wasn't finished."

Liath's expression was hollow. "I thought you were going to pethyar."

"I was."

"Gran Breida is there."

"Spirits willing."

"If you get killed here, you'll be leaving her alone forever."

Pelkin closed his eyes. "I know." He looked at Liath. "She'll understand. Tell her, will you, if you get the chance? Tell her what became of me."

"I will, Gran."

Louarn looked through the misty curtain at the lone figure on the pathway. Evonder, though worried into anger, stood in wait. Louarn had seen his body, perfectly preserved in the bonefolk's realm. The difference of animated features was remarkable. Haltingly, he said, "I'd like to see my father, before we go."

"There are a lot of unpassaged I'd like to see," said Liath, and abruptly Louarn understood that her brutal struggle had been to reach, and find, far more than just Evonder. Lost in paralysis, he'd failed to recognize her private anguish. From the hard look on her hard face, she meant to keep it that way.

"You can't go close," Pelkin said. "You're too alive."

Louarn lifted a hand in greeting and farewell.

Evonder raised his in salute.

Louarn did not watch Liath say goodbye to her grandfather, or watch Pelkin walk away, or watch to see that he and Evonder made it to safety unbesieged by shadow. He turned and waited for Liath to come up beside him. The lad-of-all-lights and the publicans' daughter made their way back through the sum of his powers. Memory's attic awaited her, patient in its dusty time-lessness. Where she'd started her journey, two nines of years ago and one. The night she'd taken her illuminator's triskele. Or not quite that night; it was still sunset. It was forever sunset here. The light had not yet gone, in the refuge of Liath's heart.

"Are you dying, Liath?" he said, before he left her.

"I don't think so. I was too alive to touch Evonder, or to look for . . . Wouldn't I remember dying? I don't . . . remember . . ."

"Then where are you? What are you?"

"I don't know. I only know that I'm still trying to go home. There's something . . . I have to tell them . . ."

"Come with me," he said, a sudden impulse. "Come and tell them. Come and say goodbye to Pelkin in the flesh. Karanthe is there. You knew her, didn't you? In the Holding, when you were vocates."

"I knew her." Liath's voice sounded the way a haunt's would sound, dry as a husk of leaf. Without interest, as though reciting an old and obvious tale, she said, "She was everything I wasn't. Beautiful and confident and full of light. I'm glad she lived."

She lives, and bears your blood, and you are all she is, and always were, he thought. And was glad that in this shadowed sunset attic thoughts did not come out aloud. *Your line is strong, Pelkin. I'll keep your secret.*

Liath picked up the pigeon feather and traced a shimmering blue design in the murky air. A kadra, Louarn guessed, but illu-mination was not his craft. "I made my farewell," she said. She was distant here, restless, disturbed. "Pelkin won't be there when you get back." She dropped the feather to the floorboards in a soft blue sparkle. "I'll find my way. Don't worry."

I'll always worry about you. "If I can ever help you, Liath. Wherever you are, whatever you are . . ."

"I don't know where I am," she said, her expression slack and vague. She lifted her head. "If I find out, I'll let you know."

In three steps he was gone, back into his own mind, or his own powers, or into the casting. He was tense, and afraid, half certain he would cast himself into pethyar in Pelkin's place. He was not ready to go there yet. He loved too many things back in the world. He was not ready to make that kind of sacrifice, not even for Pelkin n'Rolf, who had just made the greatest sacrifice of all.

He found what felt like the center of whiteness. His doubts cured around him like mortar. He sat on nothingness, closed his eyes, willed himself back.

Nothing happened.

The last note of the bindsong still sounded. He'd lost it, from time to time, grown so accustomed that it didn't register on his conscious mind. He concentrated on it now, delved its richness, accepted the subtle quaver that indicated its decay. His breath was running out; to work a note to that point was a powerful tool in the binder's craft. It was strange to hear his voice from outside his own head, though he might well be inside his own mind; the tone's quality was higher and less nasal absent the resistance of sinuses and the resonance of skull. He set himself to plumbing its essence, defining its characteristics, and the quaver only grew more pronounced as the last of the breath left his lungs. He was still sitting on nothing in a world of white.

You're thinking, Mellas's voice said from within. *Stop thinking!*

He'd been lost in tunnels then, as black as this was white. Trying to sleep so he could dream himself free.

He feared to sleep within this waking dream. He feared to dream within the dream. But perhaps Mellas was right.

Or perhaps it wasn't sleep itself, but the state of acquiescing to sleep.

Open your eyes, Louarn. Open your eyes and share it.

He opened his eyes, and leaned back, and let the light of all
colors pillow him, and he let go of striving and let go of will,
and opened his throat to sing the note that his body was singing
somewhere far away, or far outside; he blended his voice with
that voice, matching the tone until his breath ran short and he
was matching the quaver, too—

—and felt his body ease into place around him, as he let the
bindsong die away into a hoarseness, then a memory in the utterly still air of the holding room.

Pelkin's throat closed over his breath, and he was gone.

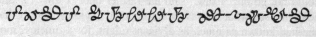

IOLI CLIMBED LIKE a bug from the iron fire ladder in through
the window.

The grief in the crowded sleeproom knocked him against the
wall, tilting a framed map on its nail. It was more of a blow than
any outrage could have been.

He was too late. The head runner had passed.

Rekke clambered in behind him, and after a few breaths
came Mauzl, slipping down to huddle by Ioli as though trying to
make himself even smaller than he was. In those breaths no one
said a word. Eight folk in black just stared at him, unable to resolve what they saw into anything that made sense. Untriskeled
mages sat to each side of the bed. A redheaded Highlander had
moved to one of the runners, an auburn-haired woman who
pulled away from comfort and sank onto the bed to lay hands on
the body of a man she'd loved without realizing he was her father. The man on a stool at the foot of the bed, a mage's position, showed a glow as blue as deep ice. He looked at them; he
saw them, saw their glow, and their glow seemed both absorbed

and reflected by the dark blue of his eyes. Then he looked down, and pulled over a battered pack, and took out sedgeweave to lay on the board on his lap; with an inkpot nestled into one of its wells and a fresh quill from a box beside him, he began to draw.

"He's been to a far realm," Rekke murmured, not even realizing he spoke. Mauzl was humming, low in his throat; Ioli could feel the vibration of it where the boy's shoulder pressed into his arm.

"Did he make it?" the auburn-haired runner asked the mages. "Was she there? Did you passage him?"

"She was there . . ." the farther mage said vaguely, and the nearer one said "So much—longing—forgiveness—" and then could not go on. "I saw," said the farther one. "I *saw* . . ." She could not say what she saw, and Ioli could not know it, only that she had known as much as a visant might, for a timeless moment, and could not hold it. The man at the foot of the bed had looked up blinking. Ioli, without understanding why, knew that he was surprised and somehow hurt that pethyar had opened during the casting, even though that was what the mages were there for. Then he pulled a seeming over his brief openness and said, "He was passaged, Karanthe. He went where he wanted to go. And he loved you dearly."

"Of course he did," Ioli blurted, so deeply was he plunged into the knowing of them, "he was—"

He clapped a hand over his mouth, like the giggling girl in none's-land, as the man's blue gaze pierced him like a blade.

"What?" the auburn-haired runner demanded. "What did you see?"

The man broke eye contact with Ioli to pass a minute shake of his head to the Highlander, who laid a callused, dye-stained hand on the woman's shoulder. "Say goodbye, Karanthe," he said. "Then send your birds. The rest can wait."

"The bonefolk can't," said one of the other black-clad runners. "We'd better all say our farewells. They won't come with us clustered here."

The man with the blue glow said, "One will," then returned

to his drawing as though nothing else mattered but capturing in inked lines whatever was in his mind before it faded. *The way you'd capture a dream by telling it to someone, quick, as soon as you woke up,* Ioli thought. He was glad; he didn't want that man's blue eyes on him again. They had seen him, and seen him seeing, and he had to brace himself against the vertigo that tunnel of seeing had brought on him.

Though the Highlander was formidable, that glowing man was the most powerful person in the room. But he might not be the one Ioli had to speak to. More likely it was the one waiting to take the woman's place at the bedside, letting others go ahead of him, hanging back so that he would be the last. Not to be the most important, but because for these few breaths, until he'd made it real by paying his last respects, he could delay the leaden yoke about to settle on his shoulders. He was filled with knowingness, twined and knotted in it, a skein of messages and information. He was unmistakably the head runner's heir. Ioli would make his case to that one, and hope he could leave this place without ever having to treat with the other at all.

Oreg Holdingmaster burst huffing into the room. "They just appeared on the bloody dig site, out of *nowhere,* I tell you, like bonemen they are, it was uncanny, and beaten near to a pulp, no one had any idea they'd come tearing—"

"It's all right, Oreg," said a petite, mouse-brown runner, speaking over the holdingmaster's continued apologies. "You'll make it worse by fussing."

Oreg slowed to a halt as the mousy runner's quiet words got through, but one of the other runners, a thin, dark man, said, "They're stained."

"And when did we ever turn the stained from here?" the auburn-haired runner said, taking hold of an old debate like a lifeline.

"Karanthe," said the head runner's heir, a low reminder of gravity, and she said, "He's gone from us, Herne. He's not *here.* We've said our farewells, all but you anyway. We could dance a set in here and it wouldn't make the first bit of difference to him."

Herne, Ioli thought. The heir's name. *I have only to say it. "Herne, there's something you must hear—"*

"We're needed downstairs in any event," Oreg put in. "I don't know what's taken hold of those youngsters, but I had a snail's time getting up here."

"They're hatching an egg," Ioli said, or those were the words that came out of him, despite his thinking the other words as hard as he could.

"What?" snapped a black-clad Haunchwoman.

"Plotting," said the man with the blue glow, standing up and laying his board and drawing on the stool. "You had better see to it, all of you, though Karanthe and Herne may want to wait here for the bonefolk. The visants as well."

He wants to see what we'll make of a boneman, Ioli thought, and this time he said, "Herne, there's something you must hear, I came here to make my case to the head runner and now he's gone and I think it's you I have to speak to, I know it's a terrible time but this is important, this is important enough to—"

"Slow down," Herne said. "I'll hear you. There's time."

"But—" He stopped as Rekke moved from his side. It seemed for a moment that he was pulled in the wake of the departures, Oreg ushering away the folk beyond the door and clearing room for the runners and young mages to leave. But Rekke was not following. He sank cross-legged onto the floor, staring at the inked sedgeweave, drawing it down into his lap. The auburn-haired runner—Karanthe, they'd called her—went into the outer room to release three great mottled birds. As she came back in, Herne asked the man with the blue glow about the bonefolk, something he hadn't wanted the others to hear. The glowing man started to answer, then noticed what Rekke was doing.

Rekke had turned the sedgeweave over, and was inking in the back. The glimpse Ioli had of the front was a rough sketch of a place, an approximation of shape and structure that could not exist. What Rekke was bringing to life, in trancelike strokes, as though someone else's hand worked the quill, was a dimensional rendering of a fantastical realm in impossible depth and detail. Looking on it was like looking through a window as fog lifted. The realm that came to life on the flat sedgeweave was the one they had glimpsed as they traveled here through what Ioli believed, though he had not yet had time to think it through, was Rekke's power.

They were the same place.

"Louarn?" said Herne, frowning.

The man with the blue glow looked at Mauzl and said, "Why are you humming the bindsong I sang in the casting?"

Mauzl went silent and as still as a rat caught in lamplight.

"He didn't know he was doing it," Ioli said, helplessly, because he had to say something. It was better to have those awful blue eyes on him than on Mauzl.

"He doesn't speak for himself?" Louarn asked—curious, not harsh.

"Sometimes," Mauzl said, pressing closer to Ioli and dropping his head so that his matted hair obscured his face.

"We're going to have a lot to talk about," Louarn said in a quiet voice, and added, as though hearing Ioli's own thoughts, "after you make your case to Herne, who is head runner now." He paused. "And after Lornhollow has moved Pelkin through the ways."

A boneman, as tall as the room was high, thin as a vine, clothed in shreds more tattered than Mauzl's, had emerged like a great pale mantis from the wall Ioli leaned against. A wall outside of which was only air and a three-story drop. Ioli clutched Mauzl against him as the creature moved past, taking care in the small space, too tall and too thin on its stalks of legs, and stood at the foot of Pelkin's bed. But it wasn't Mauzl he needed to worry about; the hideabout boy drew clear of him and shook his hair from his eyes and stood as tall as he could, as though in respect for the creature that had barely noticed him. "Far," he breathed. "Pretty." It was Rekke who cringed away, scrabbling backward into the corner, his lazy eye wild.

"I am Lornhollow, in your naming," the boneman said. Ioli's jaw dropped to hear a boneman speak. The words were slurred by a mouth not designed to make human sounds, the tone dry as windblown sand, the voice as alien as the place that Rekke had drawn. But it was speech. "You have the ways," the creature said to Rekke, "but those ways are strange to me." Rekke looked at the creature the way he had looked at the glow coming from this room before they climbed up, as though he saw a hole there and feared he would fall through.

"Pass through, Lornhollow," said Louarn, as if in greeting.

"I do not know these," the boneman said. A jitter ran through its insectile body.

Louarn's hands moved, and the boneman's hands moved in reply, far too fast for Ioli to follow, a blur of movement. Then the boneman stepped around to the side of the deathbed and leaned over.

"I told him who you are, as best I could," Louarn said. "You can stay. That's a privilege, by the way."

As though the body weighed nothing, the boneman scooped up the sunken, vacant shell of Pelkin's flesh and cradled it tenderly, like a beloved infant. Its long head fell back on a neck so spindly it seemed it must snap, the small lipless mouth opened but made no sound, the great dark eyes seemed to brim with tears. It stood in an attitude of great pain, or grief, or joy; the body in its arms began to glow, a phosphorescent green like Galandra's fire in the deep swamps, intensifying until the bones were visible through the flesh, until it seemed the glow was coming from the bones themselves as they dissolved within the body. Then the green glow became too bright to look on, and when Ioli could open his eyes again, Pelkin was gone, the boneman's arms were falling back to its sides, and the room was filled with the sharp clear scent of rain.

To Ioli, it smelled like home. Though he could not glean the boneman, though the creature was opaque to his sight, he had the profound, calming sense that he had just witnessed both transformation and healing.

It was known that the bonefolk sent the bodies of the dead on to some kind of waiting place. No one believed anymore, as in old times, that they consumed them. But he'd had no idea that the passage granted by the bonefolk could be . . . beautiful.

"Pass through," Lornhollow said. This time Ioli did not pull into himself as the boneman came near. He stepped from the wall with polite deference, and watched in awe as the boneman simply sank into the wood, walking through solid stavewood back to wherever bonefolk dwelled.

"You saw where he went," Louarn said to Rekke, speaking to him for the first time. "You've seen that place before."

Rekke came up and out of the corner with an angry groan, flinging board and sedgeweave onto the bed. "Pus and guts on all of this!" he said, and whirled on Ioli. "Make your case and have done with it so we can leave this den of inkmongers and death."

"You are extraordinary folk," Louarn said, "and evening draws near. Won't you stay the night? Have a meal, a bath, speak with Herne more comfortably and at your leisure?"

"Especially a bath," Herne said acerbically, and Karanthe said, "Oreg told us they'd been beaten. Go easy. The world treats roughly with visants and worse with the stained."

"Stoned," Rekke corrected, with a horrible grin, and then turned a writhing face on Ioli and gestured urgently for him to speak up.

"The shield is failing," Ioli said. The words came hard at first, but then faster, unstoppable: "You must know that, you're runners, you must know a lot of things, but I can't tell if you know that the war of the coast is all delusion, what kills the shielders is their own belief that they're being killed . . ." He told them all of it, in a headlong rush, and made his bid for help.

There was a long pause when he was through. Then the High-lander said, "Belief makes its own truth." Ioli didn't know if that supported his claim or dismissed him as a madman.

"You've come a long way to tell us this," Karanthe said. "Endured hardship to deliver a solution to a threat that can't touch you."

"There isn't one where he doesn't try," Mauzl said, as if that would make sense to anyone besides them. Rekke grimaced: "He's a puking do-gooder, and he's putting visants at risk, telling you a thing like this."

"We can save the world!" Ioli cried. "We can stop people dying for nothing! Does it matter if those people are us or them?"

"We already know the siege weapons don't affect visants," Herne said. He was scowling. Ioli saw him working his mind like a visant's mind, making his slow lightless connections between all the flutters and shreds of information the webwork of runners carried. That scowl meant he was coming as close as someone lightless could come to gleaning. Ioli felt a queer surge of pity. If only Herne had a visant's glow in place of the magelight that had been seared from him . . . what he could do, with a glow . . .

He felt Louarn's eyes on him, those eyes he had never wanted to feel on him again. Louarn gleaned the pity in him. That swayed him as no words could. "I believe him," he said. "I think you should consider it."

Herne nodded. "I will. I am receptive to this. It could be a great hope. Salvation, even. If we could do something like that, instead of . . . Well."

"Instead of cast Galandra's warding again," Ioli blurted as it came clear, from looking at all of them at once.

Rekke danced a jig of frustration, his lazy eye fixed on Louarn despite his body's mad gyrations. "Enough!" he said. "You've made your case. They can take it or leave it. Let's go."

"Where?" said the Highlander, knowing there was nowhere.

"Stay awhile," said Herne. "Tell me more. I want to listen."

"He's said all he has to say," Rekke said, one eye warily tracking Louarn as he moved to the bed. "That one with the blue glow was trying to grease us into staying. That's the sort of thing procurers do. I don't trust a single one of you."

Ioli had seen through Louarn's attempt to charm them, and seen Loaurn acknowledge that and desist. He got a strange feeling, hearing Rekke say it. As though their glows were bleeding into each other. The nausea was gone, ever since they'd stood together against Fyldur and the shielders he'd brought to Denglin. They'd united themselves, somehow, or fate or chance had, and now the things they knew were mixing together. He wished he had a chance to sit and think it through. If they stayed, they could rest, they could eat, they could think. Too much had happened, too fast.

"You're not stained," the Highlander said to Rekke—to distract him as Louarn picked up the sedgeweave Rekke had drawn on.

"So?" Rekke tossed his head like some half-tamed beast.

"You protect these two. You defend them from people who attack the stain, even though there's no stain on you. Why not walk away?"

Rekke made a series of faces and finally folded his arms, standing hipshot. "You need not persuade me of Ioli's altruistic motives by analogy," he said, a mockery of holding articulation.

"Don't try to hide behind madness," the Highlander said.

"But I am mad," Rekke said, with a wide-eyed grin, rolling his lazy eye. Then, quick as a cat, he sprang onto the bed on all fours and said, "Leave that."

Louarn raised the sedgeweave out of reach as Rekke swiped for it. "I need the aid to memory I sketched on the reverse. But I'll copy it, and return this to you if you like."

Rekke hawked phlegm as though to spit, and turned away. "It's nothing," he said. "Forget it. A picture of a dream I had."

"A dream?" Louarn said, with a smile that chilled Ioli. Then a puzzled frown crossed his brow. He moved to the window. "Someone's casting. Should there be castings during a period of mourning?"

"No," said Herne. He opened the door to the empty sitting room. "I'll see to it."

"Chaldrinda will do that," Karanthe said. "It's probably just prentices who don't know any b—"

A muffled shout came from below, and the whole building shuddered with the impact of a slammed door.

Ioli only realized he'd been hearing a binder's voice, faint with angles and distance, when Mauzl, who had sat on the floor and become engrossed in spinning a child's top he'd found under a bureau, began humming again. A different tune. Whatever this casting was, it was almost complete.

The Highlander was already across the sitting room, the runners right behind him. Louarn stopped in the doorway and turned. "Please stay," he said. "You have wondrous powers, and are linked to each other in a way I have never seen. I've been to that place you drew, Ankleman. I've traveled in something like the manner you traveled here. Don't hide from us. We're on the same side." Leaving the sedgeweave on a dressing table, he followed the others.

"We could go," Ioli said, tasting the idea with his tongue. He looked at Rekke. "You brought us here. You could take us away."

"I didn't bring us here. I can't do that. No one can do that."

"The bonefolk can."

Mauzl said, "Far, far back. So pretty, that far back."

Rekke rolled his eyes in different directions. "That cursed creature had naught to do with me. I can only see through things. Rock, and mounds, and bone. I can't . . . I can't . . ."

"Yes you can. You did."

"It wasn't me!"

"Then it was us."

"There is no us."

"There is. That's why we're here. Our lights . . . when the end was coming, they . . ."

Abruptly Rekke was all writhing fury, slamming walls with the fleshy sides of his fists, snapping vicious kicks into the air, stamping the floor when that wasn't enough, falling to hands and knees to pound on it. "Cretins!" he raged. "Grieving murderous stained cretins!"

"Shh," Mauzl said, spinning his top. "Shh."

Shutting out Rekke's raging release of all that he'd held in since the Yorlmen tried to kill them, Ioli asked Mauzl, "Does he ever travel that way when he's alone?"

When the top slowed and tottered, Mauzl raised enormous glinting dark eyes, eyes the same color as his glow, and said, "Alone?"

"By himself." Ioli sat next to him. "Without us. Before us. Has he ever . . . realmwalked . . . by himself."

Mauzl righted the top and gave it a twist. "I don't remember."

Rekke's tantrum subsided, leaving him sprawled on his back. "I didn't bring us here. And if I had, I wouldn't know how. Grieving spirits . . ." He flung his arms across his face. Ioli realized he was crying; his chest shook with silent sobs. There was no madness on him now, only exhaustion, soul-deep, and infinite bewilderment.

I'm not a seeker. I'm not a mender. I don't solve mysteries. I don't care what happened, only that we're safe. "We'll figure it out," he said. "I'll figure out how we can do it again."

Rekke waved him off with a boneless arm that thudded on the floorboards. Then he barked a bitter laugh, and went limp. Every few moments he would twitch or jerk as different Rekkes rose and fell.

Voices drifted up to them from outside. Orders and demands.

Ioli looked out the window, down on the confrontation between the young mages and the lightless masters. It was like looking down from a tall tree. He knew how to see, from a height like this. Dusk was creeping in, but there were nightlamps lit. He could see well enough, and hear well enough, to glean.

The young mages had cast a warding around the dormitory. Ioli saw the wreckage of a stool someone had swung at it from the inside. They were trapped.

Ioli had pinned all his hopes on the runners' persuasive powers, and they could not even talk their own prentices out of a youthful rebellion. The mages called them stewards. Said that no mages' holding should be run by runners and they should go back to Maur Gowra where they started. Some of the runners thought that reestablishing their own holding wasn't so bad an idea. They didn't think that the disciplines of light should ally exclusively with the human disciplines—that the menders in

Gir Doegre, also lightless former mages, should leave the holding there to the touches. But the mages here were young, headstrong, inexperienced. They were here because they could not yet be trusted to work magecraft out in the world. They could do harm without knowing it.

Asrik, the young mages' leader, a belligerent Weak Legger, said, "Harm is precisely what we plan to do. For three years Pelkin n'Rolf didn't lift a finger to save Eiden Myr. We've had a dozen years of training now, and we're ready, and Pelkin isn't here to see his failure brought to light by our success. We're going to stop the war of the coast. We're going to harrow the outerlands. We'll have your promise to cede this holding, to stand aside and let us end that siege, or you won't come out of that warding."

Ioli paled at the horror and old grief he gleaned on Asrik. He'd lost a brother to the siege, and someone else—a friend. Another mage. He was from the coast. He hated the siege. He wanted it ended.

Could the young mages do it?

On the Highlander he gleaned the answer: With enough of them together, they could destroy the world.

The masters told them that such use of their light would be darkcraft. Galandra's warding was broken when Torrin Wordsmith battled the old Ennead to *stop* them using darkcraft to harrow the outerlands. They said that they would not allow it.

The solution contrived by Pelkin, the head runner, and Graefel, the head scholar, was to ward Eiden Myr again. Recast Galandra's warding, only properly this time. The new warding would not be breakable, the way the old one was. It would last thrice nine nonned years.

The masters did not tell these young mages of that plan.

One of the masters was the head of the stables, another the head of the dig; they were excavating what they believed had been a Triennead holding—that was the innard-spilling mound he'd seen when they first arrived here. Their stablehands and their diggers came and took the young mages roughly in hand. They were going to force them to uncast the warding. The masters said there would be no violence. They would spend the night in the mages' sleephall. Let the mages bed down in stable hay and consider the consequences of rash action. In the morning they would speak again.

The masters came inside. A bar clunked across the front door, others against the back door and side doors. Ioli told Rekke what he'd gleaned. Rekke shrugged. Mauzl said, "Hungry." Rekke looked at Mauzl and said, "Smelly." They went downstairs and joined the masters for a meal. The masters talked about recasting Galandra's warding in four ninedays. About how ultimately they were helpless to stop any mages determined to strike at the outerlands first. Mauzl had a bath and then sat drowsing against Rekke, and Rekke allowed it. Ioli watched the masters, and the Highlander, and Louarn.

Jimor, the scribemaster, smiled at Louarn. "We *can't* get out of here tonight, can we? You can't cast us through that warding, or break it?"

"I never learned the other two triadic disciplines," Louarn said. "I can't break their warding without a triad."

"You could dream yourself free, though," Karanthe, the birdmaster, said.

Rekke must have tensed like a bowstring, for Mauzl startled up blinking. Several of the masters also sat up. Karanthe was unabashed. "We should all know everything we're capable of," she said. "The world's at stake here. No secrets."

"Then yes," Louarn said. "If it comes to that, I can." He shifted on his seat. "In the confluence of my three lights, I can move myself from place to place through dreams. Physically move—I wake up where I want to go, for the most part. But it's very dangerous, and I seldom risk it, and thus improve at it quite slowly. And I can't take anyone along." He looked at Rekke, and Rekke looked back, one eye seeking escape, one eye defiant and unyielding.

"We traveled here like that," Ioli said, to get it out. "We don't know how, and we don't know if we can do it again, so there's no point asking." To Rekke, he said, "They all saw us go, in Denglin. Shielders, Yorlmen. Fyldur."

"Folk will say they're mad, and forget about it, if we don't keep spreading it around," Rekke said. "It wasn't our doing. It just happened. I don't know how. I don't want to know."

Softly, Louarn said, "You know the ways you can fall, if you step the wrong way through."

Rekke went hard, layering himself in stone, impenetrable even to Ioli's sight. He was getting better at that. But Ioli could sense his glow surge, and that meant Louarn could too. Rekke's knack was seeing through the veils between realms. Where was he looking now?

"Oopses and ouches," Mauzl said. "Slips and crumbles."

Louarn considered that, then said, to Karanthe, "No secrets."

Ioli was astonished that he could look her in the eye and offer that when he was keeping her own paternity from her. Louarn could not be trusted. There was too much of the procurer in him. He handled, he charmed. He had as many seemings as Rekke had layers, and Fyldur's gift of persuasion, magnified by his trebled, brighter powers. Louarn was not only the most powerful person in the room; he was also the most dangerous. He was the most dangerous person in Sauglin—perhaps in the world, although Ioli would rather not find that out by meeting his better. He'd heard rumors about the touches in Gir Doegre . . .

"No secrets," Karanthe agreed.

Louarn said, "Pelkin did not go to pethyar."

Flat silence. No exclamations, no protests.

"Pelkin went into a hauntrealm. Its denizens—well, Evonder my father, in the main—have a theory that it is the ghost of the makers' realm. Eiden Myr as it was in its glory, before the bonefolk fell from grace and became the . . . scavengers of flesh. It is a realm of incomparable beauty, surpassing the bonefolk's realms—the one I've been to, at any rate. Haunts find refuge there, moving at will between that realm and ours. Pelkin chose to stay there rather than go on to pethyar. I had hoped that when my three lights surged I had fouled the casting and made that his only option, but the other mages confirmed that pethyar was open all the time. Our detour allowed Pelkin to learn that the realm of haunts is threatened by the haunts of the old Ennead. He dedicated his life to destroying them. He found that his work wasn't done, so he stayed there."

Karanthe had not cried when Pelkin died, although she had loved him. There were tears in her eyes now.

Laren Stablemaster said, "We'd be cutting our unpassaged dead off from the afterlife, by casting Galandra's warding complete."

"Pelkin knew that," Louarn replied. "He will present the unpassaged with the choice of staying there or staying here."

"Still better than destroying the bloody world," Oreg grumbled. "Why couldn't they leave us alone? What is *wrong* with them, why are they forcing us to this?"

Serafad, the digmaster, said, "We have to assume we'll never know."

"There is one other way," Louarn said. "Ioli's way. If his solution can be effected quickly."

"We don't have to get out of here to brief the runners," Herne said. "I can call them over and talk through the warding. We'll start tonight."

Herne believed him. Herne was willing to try.

Ioli had done all he could do here. Louarn and Herne and the rest would convince the runners and send enough of them out in time to make folk everywhere immune—or they would not. They would implement Ioli's plan before Asrik's mages cast destruction upon the outer realms or the other masters cast the isolation warding, or they would not.

He feared they would not.

Rekke grabbed Ioli's arm and thrust his wild face in close and whispered, "He wants to use me, that one. He's procuring me. He's so layered I can't find the bottom. I won't be greased. I won't realmwalk for him. I won't guide him to his hauntrealm. I won't look beyond the sea for him. I won't, Ioli."

Mauzl roused, and found his top in his hand. He set it on its spindle and gave a twirl. The wooden toy skittered across the table, veered wildly toward a corner, flirted with an edge. Mauzl didn't reach to catch it. It didn't fall.

"Is there an almost mostly good path, Mauzl?" Ioli asked. It wasn't fair, to ask him. He didn't like it, and he couldn't see on demand, and when he did see it looked horribly painful, like a palsy. But Ioli felt defeated, and Rekke would not take charge unless something threatened them.

"Sleep," Mauzl said.

Rekke took his turn in the tubroom while Ioli and Mauzl found unmade beds piled with folded laundry in a second-floor sleeproom. When Ioli woke, the air in the room was freezing. Rekke was asleep in a mound of blankets on the floor, and Mauzl had crept off his horsehair mattress to curl up in his own blankets next to him. Ioli laid a fire in the hearth, then went off to find one rainbarrel still full, and had a cold bath by candlelight. When he got out, a glowing form stood in the ink-dark stairway. A glow as blue as deep ice.

"Help us," he said. It just came out of him, when he wasn't thinking, while his eyes were filled with that cold glow.

"Herne will help you. My road lies elsewhere."

"Help us find a faster way. A visant way. I can't see past your seemings, you're too good a pretender, you protect yourself even better than Rekke does. But I know you have the power. You could do anything."

"Not alone." The voice that came from inside the glow was melodious and controlled. It told Ioli nothing. "And I don't know what to do, or I'd have done it, if I could."

"You don't know the visant side of you. You know your copper shine and you know your magelight now, I saw that on your pledge, but it's the glow we have to understand to stop the siege."

"Jhoss n'Kall studies mindlight. He's in the Heel. Go ask him."

"Mindlight, you call it. The siege attacks minds. There has to be a way to ward them, the way the mages warded this building."

"Galandra's warding will do that."

"A way to ward just the minds, so we won't have to cut ourselves off."

"Like a firewarding on every building in Eiden Myr, all at once."

"Yes!"

The blue glow before him surged, so cold and intense it burned. But the man inside it said, "I would not know where to begin, in seeking such a thing, unless I began with you."

Ioli sagged. "I don't know how."

Hands of blue ice reached past him for the door. He eeled away, to avoid their touch. Louarn stepped through the space he made. "Think on it. I'll do the same. We'll speak more of this come daylight."

He still had business with the masters in the common room. Distracted, he let that much brush past Ioli's awareness as he moved through the open doorway. He was not thinking about visants yet. He wanted Ioli to do that thinking.

I don't know how! Ioli thought, and wished his powers let him send his thoughts on a beam of light to that other mind, that mind so much more powerful than his. *I don't know how to save the world! I need your help!*

But he would not have Louarn's help, not this night, not anytime soon, and he could not wait. He could not wait while runners ran and mages cast. He had to find someone who could help him find a visant way.

He padded silently up the narrow stair. In their sleeproom, the fire snapped and popped. Rekke had lifted Mauzl back into his own bed.

Ioli took a black tunic from the pile of laundered clothes they'd set off to the side. "We can travel in these," he said. "They're all black, even the silks and socks. There are boots in the bottom of the wardrobe."

"Pretend to be runners."

"You can. I'll have to pretend to be a procurer to excuse my stain."

"And him?"

"They gave him those plain clothes. I'll find him a cloak."

"Tell him that's a gift too. He doesn't like thieving."

They stood for a long moment, both staring into the fire,

nothing decided but what was unspoken: that they had to leave. Then Ioli went to rummage in prentices' wardrobes for outerwear while Rekke tended the neglected hearth.

"I don't know how to do it again," Rekke said when Ioli returned with a thrice-shrunk wool coat. Rekke was hard, unknowable; he'd put up walls, fortified himself against Ioli's sight. "And I don't think you're going to figure it out. I think you're a lost jungle boy with no idea what he's about."

"We could be stuck here for days otherwise."

"Those young pups will yield, and if they don't the muckers and shovelers will force them. We'll be out of this box by noon."

Ioli was changing into black clothes, trying and discarding till he had a decent fit. Rekke kept his own buff tunic and leggings on; he'd scrubbed out what blood he could and stitched the tears while Ioli slept. He'd also found a pack somewhere, and laid it by, full of bread and hard cheese from the cookroom.

"We can't be sure what will happen," Ioli said. "These people are all at odds. We have to find a quicker way. A visant way."

"To persuade all of Eiden Myr not to believe their eyes. In four ninedays." Rekke stabbed a poker at the fire, causing a collapse and a fountain of sparks.

"We have to try!"

"You have no plan. Nowhere to go."

"I'm going to go to Jhoss n'Kall."

Rekke dropped the poker. It was so hot from his pestering of the fire that it burned into the floorboards, making the room smell like a signmaker's.

When Rekke didn't speak, Ioli sat by the wardrobe and said, "He has a place in the Heel." He tried on a boot. Too big. "I know he was the betrayer, but that was a long time ago." He pulled the boot off and set the pair aside. "He might know something about the way the glow works. Some way to use it." He tried another boot and couldn't even get his foot in. He pulled it off and set that pair aside too. "He might make something of my idea." He tried another boot. This one would fit only with extra socks. He reached for the next.

"The Heel's a long way from here." Rekke was very still.

"I'll beg a horse from the runners. I'll learn to ride it on the way. I'll get to the Crotch somehow. I'll travel the coast of Maur Lengra so I won't have to worry about the stain." Too small, too small, too big; that was it, all the boots there were. He'd have to settle for the ones he had to pad.

"You don't want Jhoss."

"I don't know where else to turn."

"Don't turn to Jhoss."

"He knows about visants. He studies them."

"I know." Rekke closed his eyes. "I was one of them."

"You what?" How could he have missed seeing this on Rekke, in Rekke? Because that Rekke had never surfaced. Rekke buried that layer deep. Even now he was only referring to it, like a teller. Skimming on top of it. Why?

"The glow was already there, and blue folk had already seen each other, but they kept it to themselves." With his agate eyes closed, his brow took on more prominence, his features looked longer, his hair bushier. You didn't realize how the eyes dominated, until they shut. "They didn't know what their power was, and they didn't want to know. They were mad, half of them, anyway, and not much for gatherings. Jhoss gathered them. Recruited them. As many as he could find." Rekke gave a harsh sigh. "I helped him."

"When?"

"Long ago. A few years after the magewar. In the last dark days before the magelight was reborn. You'd have been a child. I was only two nines and some myself."

"You joined him."

Rekke nodded. "Left my village to follow the strange Heelman with the pink eyes and the blue glow. The mines killed my mother and father, when there were no mages or touches to stop it. I wouldn't go into the mines, so I went with Jhoss."

"What did he do with all of you?"

"He tried to make menders of us. Scholars. He had us learn symbols, along with a gaggle of blunts he'd already been working with. Not scribing, though he taught that too, but symbols to represent counting. He had strange words for large numbers, and stranger ideas about what we'd do with them. Measure things, build things somehow. He thought it would make us think better. Learn things. I never understood it. He's a madman, like the rest of us. He grilled us, tested us. He was trying to *figure us out*."

Now Ioli saw. "He couldn't. You can't figure out what light is or how it works. Touches can't tell you how they do what they do; they show each other, they learn by feel, they learn by doing. Mages train by grueling years of practice—but in the end not one can tell you why their castings work. No one knows what light is. No one can know."

Knowing was what visants did. Seeing beyond the ken of ordinary folk was what visants did. In the pause, in the silence filled by the pop and crackle of the fire, Ioli saw Rekke look into some far realm, and thought it might be the realm of light itself. If anyone could see the source of light, it would be Rekke. But Rekke pulled his gaze from there. He dared not look too deep.

"Jhoss tried to craft a system to channel the powers of sight. He thought that sight was the same thing as brains. He thought madness could be harnessed."

"I guess he failed."

"Smart visant." Rekke's eyes opened, and glittered. "Smarter than most of them, and saner. That's why they wanted you, in Denglin. You're the sort who could rally them. You're the sort who could give them purpose."

"I'm not smart, and I'm not brave, and I don't want to save the world. I want someone else to do it."

Rekke threw back his head and laughed, big square teeth a white flash in the firelight. "You go on telling yourself that, little monkey." In one of his sudden, dizzying shifts, he leaned over, his face a stranger's, and said, "But let me tell you something. Jhoss never *figured us out*. Jhoss couldn't make us smart, only afraid. He saw what we were, what he was, and it *made him afraid*. Then he went off to Gir Doegre to tell the menders and the runners about it and make them afraid too. After that there was no safety for us. The *word* got out. Words are dangerous. Words are powerful. Ask a mage sometime. Words change things. After that anyone who could see a little better than his neighbors and didn't have the wits to hide it might have *power* over them. After that our neighbors weren't neighbors anymore. Because of Jhoss, trying to *figure it out*."

Ioli couldn't follow the complexities of Rekke's resentment. When the three of them were together, they had the potential to do powerful things. He could feel it. He knew Rekke could feel it. Why was Rekke afraid of it?

Visants were more afraid of themselves than anyone else was. That might be what kept them useless, not their madness. Visants feared what they could do, and so did nothing. Visants feared each other, and so they never triaded. That didn't mean they couldn't.

The three of them had realmwalked; it had happened, they could not deny it, they could not unmake the memory. Wouldn't Rekke rather figure out how they had done it, so that they could do it again? What else might they do? Didn't he want to know?

Puking, useless walleyes. They didn't have to be useless anymore. Not if they could *do* things. But all Rekke could do was tell stories about other people's failures.

"What happened to all the visants Jhoss gathered? What happened to you?"

"Me? I went home. I wouldn't go into the mines, not even then, but I could see inside mountains. I made a trade of dowsing stone, until the *word* got out and folk started fearing I could dowse minds. Don't let them know you can do that, Ioli."

"Sometimes people don't know their own minds. Sometimes it helps them."

"You're a fool. Leave people's minds alone."

"I do. Mostly, I do." Mauzl murmured something, then sat up

blinking. Ioli poured him some water. "What happened to the other visants?" he pressed.

"There were only a handful. Most were truly damaged or truly mad. They could work wonders with those numbers Jhoss made up, but to no purpose, or they could repeat long lists of words after one hearing, but to no purpose. All they wanted was safety and a predictable life, all they needed was minimal care. Jhoss is not a nurturing fellow. But there's still a nest of them there, in the Heel. The original rathole. The source of all vermin."

"He doesn't work there anymore?"

"I heard not. I don't know." Snarling-dog Rekke surfaced briefly, and said, "I don't bloody care."

"There's something else. It's important. Say it."

Rekke's mouth twisted and his eyes narrowed. "He wanted to triad us," he said. "Visants can only see alone. Each trapped inside his own head. Jhoss put us into threesomes. It was . . ." He wouldn't finish.

"Our lights are blending, Rekke. We're not so mad when we're together. We walked through realms together."

Nonchalant Rekke said, "A fluke."

"It was us. Together. Three of us. A—"

"Don't say it."

"A triad. When we were scared enough, and close enough, it happened."

"So it happened!" Irritable Rekke got up and paced, a looming shadow. "And you want to make it happen again. Well, we've got two good feet, each one of us. Walking's been good enough for me for a dozen years. I've been from one end of this benighted land to another. I see no reason to change my ways, unless someone gives me a horse. That's as far as I'll go."

"Let's try," Ioli urged. "You could prove Jhoss wrong. You could do what he could never get anyone to do. You could . . . be what he wanted you to be."

"Don't grease me," dangerous Rekke warned.

"Don't pretend you haven't considered it."

"Stop delving my head."

"Stop hiding in it!"

Mauzl made a noise of protest, looking from one of them to the other. He was a helpless mouse. He couldn't change the paths. He could only see them, sometimes, and follow, sometimes, and wait to find out which one came true.

"Delving your pet runtling, are you? Ask him what we should do." Rekke turned on him, and Mauzl cringed. "Do we form a triad, runt? Is that in any of the futures you can see?"

"You're scaring him."

"He should be scared! I'm scared! We should all be scared!"

"Mauzl can't make the paths open," Mauzl said, very softly.

"You see?" said Rekke. "It can't be controlled. You can't control what you can see and when. No one can. Not even Jhoss."

"Jhoss isn't here. Only us. We have to try."

"Fine." Rekke plopped himself down in the center of the floor. "Let's try. Our very best."

Ioli pulled Mauzl down so that they were sitting in a circle, like mages. He sensed Rekke's disgust at the eager way he jumped on what was meant as mocking consent. "Just concentrate," he said. "Look inside yourself. Find the common room, and take us there. We'll help you. Draw on us."

With a great sigh, Rekke capitulated. He closed his eyes. He suffered Ioli to put Mauzl's hand in his and take the other. When Ioli closed his eyes, all he had to know the others by was the flesh of their hands, the sound of their breathing, the sense of the space they occupied, subtle clues of air currents and echoes of the sounds the fire made, the wind angling off the shutter louvers, a bird's soft call beyond them, the swoop and chitter of bats. All that, and the pool of their lights. Warm slate and swelling sea. A blue that wasn't even color anymore, but substance.

Nothing happened for a long time.

Nothing happened at all.

"That's done then," Rekke said at last, withdrawing into himself. "And for the best. We'd have left this fire burning untended. How irresponsible."

Ioli's disappointment was bitter. "Do we have to be under attack? Do we have to be . . . dying?"

Rekke crabbed back to lean against the side of the longwise bed, reaching up and behind to pull a blanket down around his shoulders. "Maybe so. The next time we are, remind me to have my pack on my back, will you?" Without even glancing at the shuttered window, he said, "Three hours till dawn." As though the rotation of the convex disk of the world were a thing of realms, not a thing of time—his precinct, not Mauzl's—and he could sense it without looking. "I need more sleep before the sedgeworms go at it again."

"Sleep," Mauzl agreed, but he got up and put his feet in the smallest pair of boots Ioli had tried, then put on the coat Ioli had found for him before sitting down beside Rekke and closing his eyes. Ready to jump up and leave as soon as the sun rose?

Ioli put his black coat on and sat beside Mauzl. He would wake, and watch, and think this through. There had to be a way.

Rekke pulled the blanket tight around him and through one slitted eye watched Ioli let the fire die to embers in his effort to glean the impossible. Every few breaths the pale head lolled forward and he caught himself, firmed his jaw, set his will to the task again.

I could go anywhere, Rekke thought. *Be anywhere. I could save them all.*

Too close. Far too close to what he'd longed for.

He layered himself, found a measure of control in observing his own reactions. Muscles tensed for headlong flight from the terror of what they might do. Muscles clenched against the tension of kicks and punches undelivered, a rage of desire to thrash the two who brought this terror on him. Pride, exhilaration; an impulse to stride bellowing across the length and breadth of Eiden until he'd routed Jhoss and shown him. Tears and hysterical laughter threatened in equal part. It felt he would shake into all his component selves, shake loose in sheets like slate or shingle.

He found a layer that was safe, a layer that was quiet. The layer that used to surface when he dowsed stone. His mind went still when he dowsed, blessedly still. The battling parts of him stopped struggling and vying for position. If only he had some stone to dowse. An ancient stillness of stone, deep and patient. Here there was only a flagstone hearth, thin and flat. He could not hold on to stillness. Would weariness do, in its place?

Arming the world against delusion by telling it not to believe in its own death . . . it might be daft, it might be brilliant. He hadn't been to the shield; he didn't know. But he was wary of the fragile structures of belief. They were spun crystal, woven mist; they shattered, shredded at a breath. Still, shouldn't the jungle boy have his chance? It was a bitter thing, to be defeated by time and distance.

It was galling, to feel for the pathetic monkey, to fear for him, to fear him. Fear dripped like condensation down stone walls. He wanted to pull indifference around him like this scratchy wool, press sympathy into the floorboards the way he pressed the hard points of his tail. He couldn't. This weary, this drained, he was only ordinary Rekke. Not dangerous, not demented, not attractive, not insane. A dull man with no special talents, who felt every year of his three nines and six, every blow, every inadequacy.

Every terror. Every failure.

Trying to manufacture a gleaning, engineer a transit through realms—now, *that* was madness. The places they might land, if he erred, if he misstepped. He'd had no idea what he was doing. He saw other realms in glimpses, never clear enough to *go* there. Certainly not clear enough to bring two other souls safe through. They were lucky to be alive.

He still reeled at the memory. Through an accident of despair they had stumbled upon something that Jhoss, with all his resources, hadn't found. There was a lesson there. Something to do with having nothing left to lose. But poor Ioli was the picture of despair, hunched into himself, and still they were here. If despair were enough, he'd have given Jhoss what he wanted a dozen times over. He'd believed in Jhoss with all the fervent idolatry of youth, and Jhoss had used him. Procured him and used him. Done things to him and the other visants, to bond them into his projected triads. Manipulated their hearts, their bodies. Their failures were a feast of humiliation, a harvest of despair. It hadn't brought them any closer to Jhoss's goals.

That cocksure, credulous youth was still inside him. Still raging to prove himself. Still open to belief. He hadn't surfaced in years. Perhaps he should let him. He and Ioli could wallow to their young hearts' content in rage and despair and impotence.

Poor Ioli, fighting invisible battles in the dying fireglow. He would help him, if he could. He would walk him through the realms this very moment, brave their perils for him, shield him, bring him safe to his destination and give him the chance he deserved. But he had no destination. He was lost.

In his drowse he giggled at going softhearted, then growled at being unmanned, then forgot both until he startled out of a snore.

Brave monkey, he thought, floating between indigo deeps and dawn skies, rising into dreams. The boy had the clearest glow he'd ever seen, the cerulean intensity of morning on a bright, sweet day. *Blue monkey,* he thought. *Sky monkey. I'd take you, if I could. I'd bring your dawn-bright glow down into that nest of vermin and watch day break there.*

Those two lights soothed him, centered him, relieved the torments of his shifting layers. What peace it would be to surrender. If only it were possible. If only it weren't a dream, a whisper, a hope spun of mist and crystal.

I would take you there, he thought, suspended between sea and sky, mesmerized by flames. *I would take you there, brave hopeless shining monkey, if there were any way. If I only knew where there was.*

Going. Falling. Rising. Hurtling headlong, soaring. *Folding.* Unfolding.

Paths opened into dizziness and cliffdrop. Paths opened on

strange byways his small mind shied from. Some had always opened there, the paved past-paths showed, but blurry, nosense, look-past. Shadows and stick things, shiftings and murmurings, weird glows and worse glooms. Bad things, bad ways, bad paths. Some good paths, too, but few, so few. The lankbones must be very certain of his footing. Gaps and holes and hazard. Trip and loss and crumble.

Don't fall, don't fall, don't fall . . .

Don't fall!

Mauzl closed his eyes and held tight to keep from flying apart.

Ioli became aware of a dank chill. He must have let the fire die. He'd tried so hard to stay awake. Working their previous transit in his mind, trying to find what he had missed, the key to repeating it. Mulling over Mauzl and his paths, Rekke and his layers. Trying to see their glow instead of them, insinuate his sight into the glow and plumb its secrets. He didn't jerk awake as from a doze, but when he opened his eyes the fire was—

Gone. In place of its glow was lamplight, a buttery sphere. The walls were not stavewood but stone. The black stone was aglitter with eyes. Long stretches of it were covered in things that looked like carpets, so that walls seemed to be floors and floor seemed to be wall. There was only one bed, and in the wrong place, made of the wrong wood. He felt he'd flown across the room, but it was the wrong room. Was it even a room? Was this what a cave looked like? A slight, white-haired form sat hunched over a table that should not be there, part yellowed by lamplight, mostly in shadow, its back to them, oblivious. A haunt had materialized in their room; or he was dreaming.

He was not dreaming. He groped to his right and touched rough stone. Mauzl had his left arm in a deathgrip, cutting off the circulation. Rekke was on his knees beyond Mauzl, fists clenched on his thighs, color flooding his dark cheeks. His right eye was fixed on the haunt; Ioli couldn't see the left.

A shiver ran up the haunt's spine. The bone-thin hand that set the reed pen in a holder was pigmentless, like a night frog.

Albino, from a place where folk had skin as dark as ebony.

They don't find the places they know, Karanthe the birdmaster had thought when she sent her messages. *They find the people they love.*

"Rekke," said the man with a corpse's face. His stool scraped the stone floor as he moved himself from between them and the lamp to get a better look. Ioli had sat in the light, but the man's shadow had fallen on Rekke. He'd known him even in darkness. "So you managed it, in the end. Congratulations."

Rekke hissed something inarticulate. It might have been Jhoss's name, or a curse, or both. The expression on his stone-hewn face was unspeakable.

Mauzl scrambled behind Ioli, hiding his face between Ioli's shoulder blades. Ioli rose to his feet with Rekke, dragging Mauzl with him, then staggered. It was too different here.

He had to hang on. Adapt. It would make sense, if he waited, if he let it seep into him. The strangeness would wear off.

Jhoss n'Kall's glow was blue as the pulp of a spiritwood fruit, thick and sickly sweet. Translucent, like the gelatin preserves Jalairi put up. It was hard to see the man inside the viscous glow. Every visant was an oddity. All visants were harder to see than other folk. Ioli's gleanings were built on years of unconscious observations; each visant differed from the ordinary in his or her own way. It took time to see a visant. This one's body and mannerisms were so strange that Ioli could see almost nothing in them.

He waited for something to make sense.

Rekke stared down at his mentor and tormentor, wasted with febrile visions, nothing like the potent figure of memory, the man who'd held the future in the glint of his eye.

He'd meant to bring them to the nest of visants in the Heel. He'd meant to do it overland. Suspended between waking and sleep, he'd lost the way.

Below them were fathoms of silver-flecked black rock veined with lightstone. Veins of lightstone ran inside these walls, beyond the tapestries. Their whispers swelled to a muffled roar.

They were inside the Aralinn Mountains.

He had brought them to the Head. To Jhoss.

What realms might they have passed through? He had no memory of it. Had they come straight here? Had he been dreaming?

He had no idea. Grieving spirits—*no idea at all*. Running blindfolded along a crumbling, jugholed cliff. Insane, brazen recklessness. The places they might have gone, the ways they might have fallen . . .

He laughed. The blasted monkey was right. It could be done.

A shadow darkened him, fears too old, too ingrained to deny. *Eiden's spleen, we were half asleep, we were* helpless—

He raged to see Jhoss watch the layers rise and subside within him. Always watching, nineday after nineday. Observing him, testing him, gauging him. He was never free of those pink eyes. The eyes of a cellar rat. There in the corner when he least expected it, assessing his reactions. There when he slept and when he woke. There even when they weren't there, when Jhoss had locked three of them together for days, starving, thirsting, no light, stale air, the terrible cold. To force them to use their powers. He'd believed that if he did as Jhoss bade he would triad those other walleyes and the world would open. Then he'd broken. He was big, he was strong, he was young, he could endure whatever Jhoss required, but he could no longer abide the tormenting of the others. He set them free.

They wouldn't go. The grieving puking walleyes wouldn't go. His rebellion meant nothing. Jhoss wasn't there. No eyes gleaming from their holes and niches. No eyes to perceive his defiance. No eyes to witness his failure. Jhoss had given up and gone. Abandoned them to court the new redcopper shine in Gir Doegre. It was all for nothing. Jhoss had discarded them.

His fists were bleeding. His head was bleeding. He had battered himself on stone. A tapestry lay trampled under his feet. A needlework depiction of the Cor range of peaks. The proportions and perspective were all wrong. He stepped off the heavy folds of wool and kicked the mountains into a corner.

I am insane as the most damaged walleye pitching a mindless fit.

Mauzl's top whirred across the rocky floor. "Shhh," Mauzl said to it, "shhhh," sibilance blending with the lightstone's whispers and the soft scritch of the wooden spindle. Rekke fell into a crouch and gripped his knees to keep from booting the toy to pieces against the wall.

"You did not fail me, Rekke," Jhoss said, his voice a dry whisper, as he returned to his seat. "But you left too soon."

I left too soon?

Jhoss was thin, aging. He must be nearing the end of his seventh nineyear by now. Rekke could break him over his thighbone.

"What are you doing in this holding, Jhoss?" he said.

"I might ask the same. Of you."

"I need your help," Ioli said, in his sudden way. The first leak. Any moment the dam would burst and all his thoughts would come pouring out.

"I may need yours, as well. Perhaps we might strike a bargain."

"No bargains," Rekke said. "No promises."

"The promises are already made," Jhoss said. "This mountain as a sanctuary for any visants who would seek it. A stronghold the equal of the mages in the Haunch and the touches' in the Strong Leg. To keep them safe. So they can teach themselves to do what they are capable of. I was wrong, Rekke. What I asked of you and the others. It can't be forced. But it can be learned. Look at yourselves. How you came here."

Rekke had stopped listening at *sanctuary*. "Another bloody burrow," he said. "You're starting it all over again!"

Jhoss inclined his head at an odd angle. "It never ended. I have only to issue the invitation, and they will come."

Rekke snorted. "The Head scholar won't share his holding with you."

"You haven't even seen him yet," Ioli said, blinking. So he'd cracked Jhoss's shell. Good on him. "He's busy. He's kept you waiting days."

Jhoss raised his brows in something like a shrug, and shifted his thin bones more comfortably on the stool. "It won't be long now. You will come with me. The first visant triad. A token of what we can accomplish. How we will end this siege. You've timed it well."

"We're not a triad," Rekke said.

"End the siege?" Ioli said.

"With all three lights combined," Jhoss said. "Once the blue light has equal standing with the yellow and the red. A grand triad of the powers of light."

"What will you do with your triad of triads?" Rekke asked. Suspicion drove the weariness from him, drove him to his feet.

"Anything," Jhoss said, looking through him. "Anything we choose."

He was the maddest of them all.

"It's time to go, Ioli."

Of course the monkey wouldn't listen. Hadn't he told him what Jhoss was like? Hadn't he told him the story, ripped it out of his own guts to strew on the floorboards of that other holding, to keep him from doing precisely what he was doing now? But there the monkey went, jabbering on about delusions and immunity, as though Jhoss knew anything that could help him. Jhoss had done nothing in these dozen years but dream of futures he would never see, make promises he could never keep to frightened, gullible visants.

Holdings were burrows. Places to hide. He had to get out of here. He had to go back to his rounds, find out what rumors Jhoss had been spreading through the interior while he was trying to keep the coastal visants out of none's-land. He had to mend whatever damage Jhoss had done. They'd follow Ioli. He hadn't needed Ioli's gift to see it on the Denglin visants. They'd rally to whatever mad scheme Ioli concocted for stopping the siege before the mages made a cockup of it. Rekke didn't care about the siege, he didn't care about the outerlands, he didn't care about mages' plots or touches' plans. He only cared about keeping visants from procurers like Fyldur. Procurers like Jhoss.

He flung open the iron-bound oaken door of the chamber and found a dozen bladed men standing along the lamplit corridor. Behind him, he heard Ioli falter to silence. Mauzl whined.

That rope pull, by the tapestry, beyond the scribing table. Jhoss had yanked it, while he was raging in his tantrum. He'd barely noticed.

It was an alarm.

Of course. This holding was stormed by a rebel horde, once. Its new head would not have forgotten that. The Head was mostly coastline, and the coast was under siege. He'd have installed safeguards. Magecrafted, touchcrafted. It didn't matter how it worked. It had summoned bladed aid at Jhoss's bidding.

"Please continue," Jhoss said, to Ioli. "They won't hurt you."

They weren't stained. The blades were for show, though no doubt they were trained in the use of them. It was a perverse world, where secondhand stain could mar the blameless like Ioli and Mauzl, and leave bladed men untouched.

Rekke moved his body a quarter turn so that he could look at Ioli through his right eye while keeping his left on the men in the corridor.

"That's—that's it," Ioli said. "I don't know what we should do or how. Only that it has to be visants, and it has to be soon. The siege attacks minds. Our power's been called mindlight. It's down to us. I thought—that you . . ."

"If I could," Jhoss said. "Alas, I cannot. Our salvation will require all three lights combining to white. That is the task at hand. You three will help. You are the first. The first visant triad. You are a gift."

"We're not a grieving *triad!*" Rekke shouted.

"Only a bound triad could have moved as you did. Did you know that each of you shows a tinge of the others' glow?"

Ioli wanted them to be a triad. He wanted the world saved. Jhoss would offer him both on a stinking platter of promises and lies.

Of all the ways he could have misstepped, to bring them to this man instead of where he'd meant to go . . .

I must have needed to know. I must have needed to see for myself that he hadn't changed and he couldn't help the sorry monkey.

Bloody, grieving fool.

"No listening," Mauzl said, to the top clutched tightly in his hand.

Good lad, Rekke thought. To the bladed guardsmen, he said, "We won't trouble you. You can see us out the Heartward gate."

"No," Jhoss said, "they'll be staying for an audience with Graefel Scholar. Find them separate chambers, please, and walk them separately to them." His smile was like a corpse's death rictus. "Best you not leave the way you came until we've had more time to discuss our options."

Jhoss was completely certain of their obedience. Jhoss hadn't been there to see Rekke's rebellion. To Jhoss, Rekke was still the gangling youth who tried with all his heart to do whatever his master asked. Jhoss believed that Rekke had turned up here to *show him what he could do.* A trained dog, a pet rat. Jhoss turned on his stool and leafed through the sedgeweave on his table, expecting them to do as they were told.

One of the guardsmen gestured Rekke out into the corridor.

He could take them, on his own. If he had only himself to worry about. Bowl one into the next, spin them like toys; the narrow passageway would make it simple for him and hard for them. But not if he had the others with him.

He would not leave them in Jhoss's hands.

In two steps he had Jhoss's neck in the crook of one arm and the sharp reed pen in the other hand. "Stay behind me this time," he told Ioli and Mauzl. "If he goes into one of his faints, Ioli, smack him, shake him out of it." His right eye saw Ioli's blinking nod as his left caught the gleam of drawn blades.

His arm tightened to cut off Jhoss's choked orders. He ignored the long nails scoring the flesh of his forearm, then the fragile battering of elbows. Jhoss was light as a feather, bones thin as a bird's. "Back," Rekke said to the bladesmen. He jerked his head. "That way. Down the passage. Farther." He slipped through the door with the others huddled close. He delved the layers of rock, found an openness with a switchback rampway, rows of rectangles. Stables.

He made for an iron spiral stair at the end of the corridor. Half the bladesmen followed; the other half went to cut him off. He shifted his grip on Jhoss to let him breathe, but tightened it around his chest whenever he tried to talk. Twice the bladesmen ventured too near, and he shouted them back. They were high and centered in the holding. Heartward, the passageways blurred and shifted as he delved them. This was a tricky mountain, alive and duplicitous, veined with ancient memories and whispers. But in this section there was a dullness to it, a lethargy. It would keep its crafted configuration.

Two levels down, up again, and over, and he'd lost the bladesmen entirely. He went straight down to the level he wanted. As they came into the smell of hay and horseflesh, he told Jhoss, "Two fast horses and you're shut of me."

Jhoss conveyed the orders to the astonished stablehands. Rekke saw Ioli mounted securely in a saddle he could hang on to with Mauzl behind him controlling the reins, and both of them up the first stretch of ramp, before he deposited Jhoss at the bottom and urged his own horse up behind them.

"It will still fall to you, Rekke," Jhoss called after him. Rekke was mildly surprised that he was not calling for pursuit instead. "You can't evade the world's demands forever."

Maybe not, Rekke thought, pressing layers of betrayal and pain down deep, like flows of moon-pale magestone. *But I can bloody well evade yours.*

By full light they were making good speed on the new Shrug Road. Mauzl was at ease on horseback, like any Girdleman, Ioli miserable, like any Toeman. Firs and blue spruce were a balm to the eye, and almost compensated for his rumbling belly. The first visant enclave he knew up here was outside the town of Crook, at the inner point of Maur Leryn, where Neck met Shoulder. They were good folk. They would tell him what promises Jhoss had made. They would listen to his response. They would consider the alternatives.

He'd lost his way, in the dark, in the confusion.

Now he knew where he was going.

Ioli had thought he was getting better at being in strange places. This bouncing ride through too-straight trees with needles instead of leaves, no canopy, no understory, all cold dry space between and rocky ground beneath . . . he didn't know how he would hang on. "Is this a good path, Mauzl?" he asked, staring at his own white-knuckled grip on the saddle.

"This is a good horse!" Mauzl said happily.

Ioli groaned.

"You want the visants to save the world, yes?" Rekke said. "Cheer up. I'm taking you to some. They're better than that Denglin lot."

"There has to be someone else to turn to."

"There's only you, Ioli. We'll find the ones you need."

"You only want to go undo whatever Jhoss is trying to do."

"I'm out for my own ends. So are you. So is everyone. That's the world. Good ends and bad, all of them our own."

"Maybe what Jhoss is trying to do is the right thing."

"Maybe what the mages are trying to do is the right thing, or maybe what the other mages are trying to do, or maybe the runners, or maybe someone else. What else can you do, Ioli, but what you believe is the right thing?"

He didn't know what the right thing was anymore. He might not know it if he saw it, and seeing was what he did. But he'd come down from his tree. There was no going back.

GRAEFEL N'TRAEYEN L'BRENLYN moved one molten triseme from its canonical position into the fainter glow of an array toward the bottom of his view, then moved it back. The temporary array receded as he turned his attention to rearrangement of the strophes that hung before him as though on transparent sheets. His eyes flicked to and fro; certain glyphs brightened while others faded. He read the spread-out words they formed. In response, a word off in the upper left flared, then another to the far right—a corollary. Between and above them glowed an inversion. No meaning emerged. He rearranged the strophes again; luminous glyphs writhed and crawled in the still, black air, combined and parted, small slithering Celyrian worms casting blank trails of insignificance. He failed to conjure consequence from the elements wherein he knew it dwelled.

He let his mind's eye rest.

He still considered himself a wordsmith, though the triskele hidden beneath his tightly laced shirt and high-collared coat lay dull and lifeless on his breastbone. His title had changed—his name, if you would—but that meant little; in his youth he had been Graefel the chandlers' son, then Graefel the mages' prentice, then Graefel Wordsmith, Graefel Vocate, Graefel Reckoner. It had all come round to Graefel Wordsmith again, when he had lapsed from the proxies. For two nines of years he had been Graefel Scholar, a title he had invented for himself and those who worked under him. "Wordsmith" was as precise a term as any for the man he had remained, unchanged, under all those names.

He worked words the way an ironsmith worked iron. As mage, he had heated them in the fires of his burning light and laid them on the anvil of his will, to bend, to combine, to shape into whatever he required. As scholar, he ignited them with the fires of his intellect, and watched to see which ones flared bright, noting and assessing the patterns that emerged. He had only to look once at a scribed leaf to etch its image permanently into his mind. He recalled every glyph he had ever seen, every word, every line, every strophe, every verse.

Seeking a return to a pure tradition after his stint as reckoner, he had worked through the entirety of the wordsmiths' canon, handed down from mage to mage for twice nine nonned years. He had dug constants from the morass of regional variations, teased clear threads from the tangle of time's adaptations and distortions. He had flensed from canon all creeping, propagated error, all personal style, all ornamentation and addition—all evolution. Comparing the work of every wordsmith he had known in the time of the old light, comparing reams of samples scribed for him by wordsmiths seared of magelight but not memory, he had found the roots and trunks, trimmed off the flowering branches. Learning all the ways the quill could stray, the mind could substitute, the will could disregard, had made it possible to deduce the original verse, even re-create it. Removing all modifications, intended and inadvertent, left the pristine Celyrian of the founders, distilled to perfection.

At first, that was all he had wanted: to hand the Ennead the heart of their craft, renewed and refreshed, purified and uncorrupted. Earning his way into their ranks with his accomplishment had always been a tertiary goal, despite what Befre believed. Cleansing the craft had mattered most to him, then being justly credited for his work; if it earned him a golden ring, so much the better. A place on the Ennead would have given him the authority to see the illuminator's and binder's crafts cleansed in their turn, would have enabled him to personally oversee a more sweeping protection of the revitalized tradition. But he had trusted that the Ennead would see to those things when the time came. He had had no way of knowing that Torrin n'Maeryn would destroy both craft and Ennead in one catastrophic rebellion.

He would not have been in time in either event, but he had refrained from presenting his cleansed canon when he realized, in one night of glowing vision, that there was more to those original verses than practical use. They transcended the words of transformation, the inscriptions of power that could shepherd weather, cure ills, ease births, pledge lovers. They carried secret words from the dawn of time. Deep in their structures was embedded a message, a shadow scribing straining to come to light.

It was the variations that had made him wonder—precisely the variations he had worked so long to eliminate. Why had the syntax of a certain line been cast a certain way by the founding mages, when the verse worked equally well with some words reordered, or other words in their place? The canonical verses were meant to be building blocks for inspiration. Wordsmiths were meant to imbue their castings with their own artistic spirit. Originality and invention were critical to success; magelight was a creative power, magecastings were an actuation of spirit, and wordsmiths were far more than scribes or copyists. Why, if variation did not compromise the craft, had the founders chosen to express their power in this particular configuration?

The obvious answer harked back to his initial assumption: The original verses were the most efficient, most elegant, most powerful phrasings. But in looking deeper, in delving the very essence of their form, he began to sense a double meaning in their structure, in their order. He came to understand that they were not only pure, not only potent—they were genius, for within the epitome of poetic form they carried a hidden message for the ages.

He had set himself to deciphering it. At first it seemed a credo, an expression of the fundamental tenets of magecraft itself: service, expression, compassion. A subliminal embedding, a continual reminder to be true to the craft's intent. Examined another way, it seemed a teller's tale of an age long forgotten, of realms long passed to dust—an age when giants walked the earth, omnipotent beings who wove the very matter of existence to suit their whims. The origin myth of the earliest mages, their craft founded in the ashes of an ancient world fallen into shadow even then. He had hoped for a true history to unfold, believed the story of their craft would be revealed through the encryption. What he found was either metaphor or misapprehension.

Once he had solved the puzzle and put aside his disappointment, neither message held his interest. He gave the origin myth to the seekers and the credo to the runners for their archive in the Haunch, pap for Pelkin n'Rolf to suck on. In the years after the searing, he had let the burning glyphs of vision sit idle in his mind's recesses, devoting himself to organizing the scholars and delving the permanent, tangible glyphs of the codices the Ennead had kept under lock. Jhoss n'Kall had fought to have those codices removed to the Isle of Senana, far from any vengeance wrought in the name of Torrin Lightbreaker; Graefel dismissed Torrin's claims, but he agreed that the danger was real enough. He and Jhoss saw the codices safe to Senana, and into the dubious care of Nerenyi n'Jheel, a seeker woman Graefel never could stomach; Graefel set about founding the discipline of scholarship. Once the Lightbreaker's transgression had faded into legend and the menders were seduced away by their so-called Triennead holding in Gir Doegre, he returned the codices here, to the true holding where they belonged, and settled his scholars in around them.

Foundings and relocations were pragmatic tasks requiring methodical attention. But when the magelight was reborn, the old verses began to itch, scratching at the back of his mind as if they were not yet done with him. Though they were a discomfiting reminder of his seared light, he began to meditate upon them again. The most powerful things came in threes. There might be a third way of looking at those glyphs, a third embedding to tease free.

Of course there was. Examined a third way, the pristine verses revealed a set of instructions for what they heralded as magecraft's most exalted application. A recipe for the casting of all castings, to be undertaken only at the end of days, when all was redeemed and all darkness come to light. The message was shrouded in allusion and resisted his efforts at every turn, sliding from sense just before it came clear, thwarting him with exceptions and contradictions, daunting in its size.

It stretched across the entirety of the canon. There were a nonned verses in the core canon, and nine times that in the extended canon; the verses of the major castings could run to nine strophes. There was good reason a wordsmith's training took so long. The task of sifting through those verses was enormous. He had applied himself to it for a dozen years now—the same number of years it had taken to earn his triskele. Though he still administered this holding, and saw to the finishing of young wordsmiths who came here to research the codices, he had undertaken the work of decipherment to the gradual exclusion of all else.

He had only one section left. Yesterday he had messaged Sauglin that he was nearly finished. Soon he would have it: the warding Galandra had intended to cast, the warding as it should have been cast, unbreakable by upstarts, unbreachable by storms. The warding that would save Eiden Myr from a siege it could not withstand. That the defense was flagging he knew from evenings spent on the holding balconies that faced the Windward Sea, watching the dwindling shieldpost that occupied what had been the village of Crown. The shield would not hold another year. It could fall before Longdark. It could fall before dark.

He must complete his work today.

Perversely, perhaps, he eschewed leaf and quill. The twinge of a muscle, the cant of an arm, the inadequate integuments between hand and eye would compromise the clarity of vision. Any minute flaw in tabletop or scribing board could send the stroke of a quill awry. He would not waste his time playing copyist when he could hold it all unsullied in his mind. In the time of the old light, before permissives like Pelkin n'Rolf and Dabrena n'Arilde let ink stain any hand that reached for them, scribing outside of a casting was strictly forbidden. He had done his work in his head for most of his life. He would not stoop to shuffling sedgeweave now.

He closed his eyes, allowing the cool, damp air of the dark chamber to soothe their dry lids. He kept this chamber bare of all accoutrement save the unpadded chair he sat on; he did not let the holding mages ward the stone against damp, or the holding stewards blanket it in colored tapestries. He was a hardy Norther, accustomed to brutal cold, and found the constant temperature of these caverns perfectly comfortable. The visions of his mind's eye burned best in this cool, stone-scented darkness, unmarred by wardings he couldn't sense and illuminated tapestries his heart still decried as sacrilege.

Slowly, without his willing it, the glyphs came to burning life once more, suspended in the black chamber air, in the cavern of his mind. There whether he closed his eyes or opened them.

The passage strophes. The last learned, and the most difficult. Those strophes were where the warding instructions were completed. Designed to separate the spirit from the body and guide it safe and whole into the realm beyond, the passage strophes did not precede or follow each other naturally, and could be cast in any order. They were shrouded in mystery; their language worked on a level below consciousness, and the process of scribing their words was a meditation, a journey through shape and substance into the sublime. Passage was the casting in which a wordsmith, required to be of rigorous mind, found himself most at odds with his craft. The very act of memorizing the strophes rendered them null, and every casting of them was a rediscovery. A looking-away. Allowing the memorized words to surface, line by line, as though they came from another realm, as though the wordsmith were reading them for the first time as he inscribed them. Subjecting them to this sort of scrutiny was exhausting. They did not want to be examined in the cold, burning light of intellect. They did not want to be seen.

Graefel opened his eyes and drank them into his cold soul.

As a scholar, Jhoss n'Kall l'Sirelyi appreciated the solitude required for intellectual pursuits. As a seeker, he respected the silence of others. As a beekeeper, he had long ago learned patience and the advantages of a slow approach. But he had been in the Head for days. He would wait no longer for Graefel Scholar to offer audience.

He was not a superstitious man in the strictest sense, but he believed in the interrelationship of elements. The associations between the luminaries and the human lights were more than symbolic. The moon was the visants' luminary, as the sun was the mages' and the world was the touches'. Today a new moon was angling into view around the rim of the world's disk. There was power in that.

At least, he thought with an arid amusement as he made his way through the silver-flecked passageways, he now knew a back way to the stables, available should his interruption send the famously prickly head scholar into a rage.

It would not be his first error of the day. He had badly misjudged the visants who'd appeared in his chamber before dawn bells. So engaged with seeing the middle one, the mist-haired Weak Legger, that he'd ignored the signs of intractability in his old charge. Considered his madness spent after the tantrum. Rekke n'Gerst had never been his prentice. Jhoss had never been Rekke's master. Together they had strived toward a common goal: understanding the power they both had but could not share. Rekke had never viewed it that way. Headstrong, young, afflicted with a host of personalities he could not control, grieving a mother lost to a grisly mine collapse and a father dead of black lung. Mad enough to lock himself in an airless, lightless, unheated shed with two other visants for days, determined that they would *glean* their way free, then claim that Jhoss forced him to it, when it was only his own desire to please.

Jhoss had told him a dozen times that he would return after he learned more of the new rumored copper shine. That it was only the dream of applied symbology he was giving up, only his vision of theoretical discovery, not his commitment to the bluesilver light. That commitment had been secondary for years; now, he promised Rekke, it would be his sole pursuit. The day he left, Rekke occupied himself in "liberating" the other visants. A ludicrous, unnecessary act. There was no captivity to liberate them from. Rekke had only wanted to hold him there. Rekke had always done whatever he could to get his attention. Rekke was the engineer of his own captivity. Jhoss was incapable of coddling. When he'd returned to the Heel, as he had promised, to work exclusively with the visant powers, Rekke was gone. A pity, Jhoss had thought, but he was unmanageable. He had dismissed the miners' son from his mind, and refused to readmit him, these dozen years later, despite the extraordinary implications of their reunion.

Rekke had seen his way free of the box he'd put himself in. *And he came to show me, and I looked only at his companion, because he was the one gleaning me.* Worst of all, he had failed to take the measure of the small one, whose light was both darkest and brightest—so dark it was light. Older, bigger, more functional, the lanky miner had dominated, with his earthy vigor; the mouselike boy, though he craved diminution, had the most intense glow; but it was the middle one who had drawn his eye. It was not only the human tendency to return perceived regard, which was sometimes trebled in visants. The Weak Legger drew the eye of history. He bent the fabric of probability like a lead ball suspended in a cloth. Jhoss had known others of that sort. Graefel n'Traeyen was one; Torrin n'Maeryn had been the weightiest. Whatever destiny wreathed those visants, it was circling closer, faster, whirlpooling around the middle one. Jhoss was caught in those currents now. He should not have sought to swim in them, or divert them to his use.

He must relax, and let them take him.

As soon as he concluded his business here.

"I'm afraid this time I must press the issue," he told the gray-clad underling in the lamplit outer hall of Graefel's chambers. Day never dawned here beyond the imputation of bells, and the noon clangor had ceased long since. "I can no longer await his emergence. He will want to see me, I promise you."

Aides dispatched to him at intervals had contrived all manner of excuses for the unconscionable delay. This one at least told the truth: "It's my skin if he's pestered. You might protect me while you're here, but I like my work and I have to live here. He comes out when he comes out. No one goes in."

"It's my skin," Jhoss thought. *How freely they employ the metaphor. In this of all places.*

He drew breath deeply into his thin chest, and shouted Graefel's name. His effort produced a cracked rasp, but it was sufficient to carry through the wooden door.

The copyist regarded him impassively. "It's warded against that. He won't have wardings on the inside, but he never told us not to do the outside. As I said, it's our skin."

Jhoss pressed his lips into a thin line, and was considering his options when the door swung silently inward on oiled hinges and Torrin's illuminator looked out at him, then back over her shoulder to say, "There's someone here. Didn't you hear him calling?"

Graefel squinted against the lampglare, deeply startled, trying to make sense of the silhouette in the doorway. He saw an aide scrambling for the outer exit, but could not see who it was. No matter. There was only one way into this chamber, and the figure of a young woman stood inside it—had drawn the door open from within. One of the Gir Doegre touches? Though Prendra's daughters were not known to him by sight, he was informed that in extremity the bonefolk would transport the girls through their realms. What could possibly have gone wrong in the Strong Leg that would require something of him?

He stood too fast, and had to clutch the back of the chair. In darkness, the chamber had oriented to his perspective, asserting only Eiden's downward pull. The light beyond the doorway hurt his eyes and skewed his balance. "What is it?" he said, brusque.

"I don't know," replied the clear female voice. "You'll have to ask him."

The albino stood staring in what appeared to be fascination, seeing not the individual before him but vast tides of human history and endeavor. It had taken Graefel some time to understand what lay behind Jhoss's pink eyes. Now he had the queerest sense that Jhoss was looking through the figure in the doorway, at him—not as he was now, but as he had once been, as he had once connected to and influenced events larger than himself.

Graefel stepped into the light to have a look at the girl.

It was Liath n'Geara, the alemongers' daughter Hanla had prenticed. The girl they'd crafted a triskele for, two nineyears ago and one. Not that girl inside a woman's body, not that girl grown up—that very girl.

"What are you?" he said. "Are you a haunt?" He and Hanla had drilled a profound respect for tradition into that girl. He had never been able to explain how she was turned. She had run off to this holding to seek a cure from the Ennead for her failing light. Perhaps that girl had died here, in some metaphysical sense, and never left. Still clear-faced, fair-skinned, freckled . . .

"I don't think so," she said, touching her triskele.

"Where did you come from?"

"I was in the attic," she said vaguely, and with a frown touched his triskele through his coat and shirt, pressing the pewter into his chest. "Your light," she said. "Your bright light."

He moved past her into the antechamber. "What is this about, Jhoss?"

"I do not know," the albino said. "Not six hours ago, three visants appeared in my chamber in similar manner. I did not witness their entrance, therefore I cannot describe its form. That they . . . gleaned themselves into my presence, I have no doubt." His weird eyes remained on Graefel as the girl wandered off to touch the wall, apparently drawn by the glitter of mica in the nightstone. "Their glows had blended."

Graefel tensed. "Three, you say?"

"The first visant triad, to my knowledge."

"Is that how you came here, Liath?" Graefel asked, not least to cover his discomfort at hearing that term applied to a power other than magecraft.

Liath turned, and the years turned back. It was uncanny, to see the adolescent who had studied with his pledge, mooned after his younger son, defied his authority. He had been determined to see her cast reckoner, to force her from her fantasies of domestic village life into full realization of her providential light. He had put a stop to her puerile romance with his son; it would only hinder her progress. When her light had failed her in a healing, he had viewed it as one final, vicious act of defiance, retribution for forbidding Keiler to court her, retribution for the Ennead runner come to call her to her future, a willful rejection of his plans for her—because they were his, because he had never coddled her as Hanla did. He had broken tradition only hours before to hint to her of the destiny in her name, and she had failed to grasp the metaphor, failed to grasp the import of what he had said—or she had grasped it too well, and flung it from herself in one spectacular act of failure. Only one thing in the world could have appalled him more than what she did that night. Like a resentful child, she had run away and found it. Whoring her powers to the Darkmage. Using that blazing light to bring an end on light itself. She had humiliated him, and then betrayed all that he stood for.

And then she had seared him.

This young, freckle-faced, red-haired girl from Clondel.

"I don't know where I am," she said, a reply that was no answer to his question. "I came to tell you . . . there's a hole . . ."

When she faltered, looking pained, Jhoss said, "A hole?"

She winced aside and gripped her head. "I don't *remember!*" she cried, as though she had been badgered. Then her head came up and she fixed her gray eyes on Graefel with a chilling clarity. "Stop hiding and help me."

"This is madness," Graefel said. "She's acting like one of your visants, Jhoss. What's wrong with her? What *is* she?"

"I cannot fathom it," Jhoss said. "She is the girl I met in a rebel encampment more than two nineyears ago. The girl who resisted Torrin's truths with all the stubborn conservatism you instilled in her."

Graefel swore under his breath. He would not have this debate with Jhoss again. They had long ago agreed to disagree in the matter of the Lightbreaker. He moved to summon an aide through the bell cord. "She can stay with the mage prentices in the old vocates' quarters. I'll see both of you when I've finished my work." The glyphs scratched at the back of his mind, chafing for attention. Visant threesomes, fleshy revenants, and impossible transits could wait; the casting of all castings could not.

"The answer you seek will require all three lights," Jhoss said, ignoring his dismissal. "The silver and the copper as well as the gold. Gold and copper have their strongholds, their places of fertilization and discovery. Menders and touches draw on each other's strengths, runners and mages on theirs. The human powers support the powers of light. Scholars and visants are a natural match. Blossoms and bees. 1 would make of your scholars' hive a visants' sanctuary, to give them equal standing with the mages and the touches. I require your permission."

The glyphs itched madly—burning, escaping their confines to hang in the lamplit air of the antechamber. The passage strophes, milling, disordered. He must find the right order. He must find the arrangement that would bring the hidden connections to blazing light. "Only one light is required," he said, distracted, irritated. "The reborn light. Magelight." The only light that mattered. Visants were mad. Touches were a step away from farmers, stewards, wrights. Magelight was the only light that had ever mattered; the molten Celyrian that streamed in the air around him, dimming the lamplight to insignificance, was the closest he would come to ever seeing it again.

"Only one light," Jhoss agreed, then said: "The combination of the three. Three primary pigments combine to black, three primary lights to white. The white light, Graefel. What is required is the white."

White.

The strophes broke apart. Tristichs and nonastichs loosened and divided into their component parts; the curling lines slid free of the bonds of symmetry and syllable, concatenation and copula, the weaker links of enjambment and caesura; the organizing staves burst into a glowing disorder of single lines, an undulating weave of fire—then shifted, inexorable and sinuous, into a new configuration. The correct configuration. Centered, balanced on that one word: *white.*

"Scholar?" an aide said, coming to stand in the doorway.

Graefel gestured him to silence.

White.

He had conceived it as a metaphor. Part of a lyrical conceit. He had taken it to mean bright, or fine, or high, or noble. It was the defining word for the casting of castings. But it was literal. It was the key. It was the spindle on which the message turned. The white casting.

The three lights.

"That was why it didn't work," he breathed. "That was why it wouldn't translate, wouldn't fall into place. I assumed it would be mages."

This changed everything. Everything he had told Pelkin and his aides. How would he verify it? How could he be sure? "Galandra's triad were mages," he said, "but we don't know who the other six were. We know from the Gir Doegre codices that when they combined into hein-na-fhin it made a blinding light, as bright as the sun. We conceive the sun as yellow and equate it with magelight, but the brightest sunglare has the quality of whiteness . . . the mention of the three luminaries, there and there . . ." He reached out to the glyphs he could not touch. "She may have cast that warding with only one mage triad, not three. If we could speak to someone who was . . . one of the mages who . . ."

One of the mages who cast her triad's passage in the breaking of her warding. His eyes went to Liath.

"She does not remember," Jhoss said. Liath was watching Graefel with the wariness she'd shown him as a child, always presuming antagonism when all he had done was try to guide her. "This is not the Liath who cast that passage."

Visants. They made his teeth ache. "She will have to remember. Whatever's happened to her, whatever alien healing or casting has returned her to this youthful state, it can be undone, uncast. The mind of the Darkmage's illuminator is in there somewhere, however clouded." The glyphs were vibrating in the lamplight, sucking the light into themselves, drawing on it, darkening the room around the edges of his vision, like the encroaching cold of shock. He strode to the table, wiped hardening ink from a dish, poured in black powder from a vial and distilled water from a pitcher. The aide who'd fled had left his quill to dry; Graefel took another from its vase of liquid and trimmed it without thought. "Yes," he said while he prepared. Abstracted, careless. Still reading the glyphs burning in his mind. "Fine, Jhoss, bring your visants here, do whatever you like. There's room for all of us, we occupy barely a third of this holding as it is, scholars and stewards and mages and all. Bring them here. I have an urgent message to scribe to Pelkin."

"Pelkin's dead," Liath said, straightening to a commanding hardness so at odds with her girlish looks that it pulled Graefel from his purpose. "He died late yesterday afternoon."

"In the Haunch," Graefel said, flatly.

She scowled. "I don't know. He wasn't in . . . Clondel . . ."

"You cannot possibly know what happened in the Haunch late yesterday afternoon."

"She cannot possibly be here," Jhoss reminded him.

Irrationally angry, Graefel sent the waiting aide to fetch the birdmaster and inquire after messages from Sauglin. Then he inked his quill and drew a sheet of sedgeweave from the pile.

"I can't be here," Liath said, the vagueness coming upon her again. "I don't know where here is."

"Be silent," Graefel snapped. "I must phrase this with care."

"There's a hole . . ."

"Be silent, Liath!"

"Stop hiding and help me!"

Exasperated, Graefel said, "Jhoss, take her somewhere else and wait for the birdmaster," but Liath backed away at the albino's approach, reaching behind her head for something that wasn't there, then faltering, blinking. "Jhoss?" she said.

Jhoss fixed his penetrating eyes on her and said, "You do not know me."

"I do," she said. "You're Jhoss, you helped . . ." She tried to say a word, perhaps a name, and could not find it. "I think in colors," she said, "and you have no color."

Babble worthy of the daftest visant. But Jhoss seemed to perceive the reference; he said, "I did not then, not that we knew. I do now, but you cannot see it. Which part of you knows me, Liath? That is where you have to go."

"I can't!" she cried, and appealed to Graefel: "Why are you here? Where's Hanla? Why isn't she in Clondel? Your nephew took the triskele. Befre's triskele. My niece took Pelkin's . . ."

"Enough!" Graefel said. "Hanla went to Khine. Keiler is in the Haunch—if you'd been there you would have seen him. My pledge and my son are farmers now, scrabbling in the dirt to grow in a season what they could have cast into fruit with the stroke of a quill. Because you tore their light from them. Be silent or by all the spirits I will have bladed guards remove you from this chamber."

A cold, feral grin spread incongruously across her callow features. For a moment she looked like the most stained of shielders—she looked like the young woman who had returned to her home village scarred by the Darkmage's depredations, forged into a blade-wielding monstrosity even her family barely recognized.

The expression passed, replaced by horror. "I have to go," she said. "I have to find . . ." She stumbled back into his darkened workroom as the aide returned with the birdmaster, scrolled sedgeweave in hand. Graefel took the scroll and broke the seal, and when he looked up from reading the message, Jhoss was emerging from the workroom and replacing a clay lamp on a side table.

"Pelkin n'Rolf is dead," Graefel said, feeling a greatness pass from the world, the head reckoner he had served under long ago, the man he'd known in childhood in Clondel. "Sometime yesterday. They must have scribed the message before his passage was cast. It doesn't specify a time."

"She is gone," Jhoss said, of Liath. "She left as she came."

Graefel turned to the black-clad birdmaster. "Who runs Pelkin's runners now?"

"Herne n'Kaye," she replied, staring at the ink-dark workroom.

"And the mages?"

"Chaldrinda n'Poskana is master of prentices in Sauglin."

Graefel drew fresh sedgeweave from the pile, re-inked his quill, and started again, with a new salutation.

IOLI'S SUPPER, THE day after they left the Haunch and then the Head, was dillisk boiled over a driftwood fire and mashed with orange lichens. The fire's smoke was sucked up into the high holes leading out from the tidal cave; outside another hole, farther back, their horses were tethered on the border of none's-land. Twilight blued the cave mouth. Seawater lapped at the ledge they sat on. When it ebbed, those who lived here would climb down the slippery rocks and pick the long slope clean of the gifts the sea had delivered. Overhead raged the war of the coast, silent but for the cries of those who believed in it. Now and then someone would duck or shudder, as though the cave had been rocked by an explosion, and be patted and soothed. Here, among visants who had lived alone for years, they were considered the mad, the damaged—the folk who must be cared for. Some of them were mad, or damaged, but that didn't make them different; being lightless did. Feeling the war did.

"Can't you tell them?" Ioli asked the slim, ginger-haired visant girl who'd led them here after Rekke recognized her in Crook. She glowed, but was afflicted by none of the tics or palsies that beset her parents. Her parents never spoke; they communicated through some system of silent touches, as most of these people did, and Ioli was uncertain how the girl had learned to talk at all. "Can't you tell them that it isn't real?"

She shrugged. "What's real?" she said. "The sea, the stone, the things the sea brings to eat and burn. I trade for clothes for us, in Crook, and iron and whatever else the sea keeps, but sometimes the people seem like haunts."

Though they dwelled right under none's-land, not one of these folk were stained. It had come to Ioli as they rode here that he couldn't see Mauzl's stain at all, and never had. Maybe he couldn't see anyone's.

Rekke asked the ginger girl about Jhoss n'Kall. She only shrugged again. Others answered, pressing their fingers into her arms, her legs; she spoke their answers aloud. We'll be shown, they said. The madness will end, and we'll see a place for us. Rekke grumbled, "Visant prattle." Ioli asked if they would go live in that place, and they laughed and said, Why would we leave here? The sea brings all we need. When Rekke asked if Jhoss would cure their madness, they said, The ones above will stop falling dead. A woman caressed the hair of a lightless, crying child and pressed her other hand into the ginger girl's back to say, And the ones like this will cease their weeping.

Ioli could see the words form on Rekke's lips and be swallowed before they were spoken, washed down on clover tea: *He'll give you nothing, he'll cure no one, don't believe anything he told you or anything you heard about him.* There was no point to the words; these people would bide here unaffected by anything Jhoss did or didn't do, or the mages, or the touches, or anyone else. They were lights and lightless, mad and sane, living contented side by side, raising their children, harvesting the sea, tending the miniature goats that roamed the ledges and squeezed in and out of the holes. They knew the siege was delusion, inasmuch as they cared what was delusion and what was real. They took life as they found it, accepted each other as they were, and were not afraid.

As they made their way into the Heartlands, he began to wonder whether the ugliness he'd experienced wasn't something alien to Eiden Myr, and nothing to do with the stain at all—or whether the stain was not exactly what they thought. No one threatened them, no one bothered them—no one looked at them with veiled hatred, he gleaned no desire to pummel them or stone them or hurt them at all.

The visants they met lived mainly in enclaves, but because they felt easier around each other than around the lightless, not because their neighbors feared them. Many could not speak, but like the ones near Crook they'd found other ways to communicate. Some drew pictures; others used pantomime, still others a sight not unlike Ioli's, able to know each other, glean each other's needs and preferences, simply through long familiarity.

The locals didn't mind their small communities, and some even showed charity, providing food and goods with no expectation of gleanings in return. When Ioli asked a woman why she'd left a pile of blankets at the back of a visant cottage at dusk, she said, "It's what we used to leave out on the bonedays. But the bonefolk don't need clothes or blankets. Your folk are touched by the spirits." He shivered, and brought the blankets inside. His body bore the memory of stones. He could not reconcile the two.

It was hard to think on stains and ugliness inside a cozy Heartlands cottage, smearing acorn butter on sunroot bread. He'd never eaten so well. Rekke was known to these people, and respected; though routine was important here and Rekke had dropped visitors on them without warning, they put their best foot forward and spared no effort. Ioli was used to the confines of solid structures now, and inside, away from the rolling, flaming landscape, he could hang on to his bearings, even start to glean a little.

The leader of this group of visants was warm and open. Her glow was serene, her sanity firm. She was wonderful with Mauzl, touching him with kindness rather than flesh. She found the grittiest, sharpest, stinkiest cheese in their larder, and Mauzl munched it ecstatically; Ioli saw that the food he'd gotten till now had seemed tasteless, that his tongue would respond only to tangier flavors and sandier textures. She demanded the shirt and breeches the runners had given him, turned them inside out, and had him put them on again; Ioli hadn't understood that scratchy seams on oversensitive skin were what had made him wriggle and pluck at himself since they'd left Sauglin. She said to a dour-looking man, "This fellow's name is Rekke, isn't that a good name?" To Rekke's profound disgust, for the rest of the evening the man would call his name at random moments, happily, as though he'd remembered he had a sweet. "He collects tasty sounds," the woman said. "Words that are round and sharp in just the right places." What Ioli saw in this woman was her own gleaning, the way she intuited the strange needs and compulsions of the visants she looked after.

Most of them had eaten quickly and moved off to amuse themselves around the cottage. Some were drawing, some were placing and replacing stones and marbles and old bent nails in lines and rows; some were mesmerized by the flickering fire, some by Mauzl's top when he left the table to spin it on a clear stretch of floor. Ioli's eye was drawn by a tin crescent on a string, meant to hang as some decoration, he thought, but dangled now by a visant who kept twisting the crescent between thumb and forefinger to wind the string so he could watch the crescent twirl into a shining sphere as the string unwound. Their glows brightened when they relaxed, entertaining their visant eyes with trinkets and motion and arrangements. He couldn't glean them when they were engaged that way; they absorbed themselves wholly in idle play, and went opaque.

He tried to glean the glow itself. He tried to know it, the way he knew people's hurts and wants from minute shifts of gesture and expression. He tried to delve what it might be capable of. In one of these enclaves were the visants who could confer immunity from the siege weapons. Could their caretaker be one? Could she see the itchy seams that caused the death throes of none's-land, could she find the thing they had to turn inside out to prevent them?

"You're looking in the wrong place, Ioli," she paused in some debate with Rekke to say. Because she wasn't looking at him, he didn't know she was addressing him until she said his name. "You have better eyes than that."

"Tell me where to look," he said, trying to see her see him.

She would not glance over. She started clearing the table,

thumping Rekke to make him get up and help, setting some to washing and others to stacking and others to wiping the tables, each according to what would satisfy an itch. Handing Ioli a broom, she said, "You've already seen all you need to." She would not meet his eyes—not even in parting the next morning.

Mauzl grew more recalcitrant the closer they came to the Belt. He'd been happy at first, riding the horse, eating his way through the Heartlands, and no gleanings had come on him. He'd picked up whatever fingerspeech Louarn had used with the boneman in the Sauglin holding, and was passing it on to the visants they stayed with; he would hold animated and prolonged conversations with speechless visants, and come back increasingly reluctant to move on.

Just as Ioli got used to one landscape, they'd come into a different one. None held an answer. Louarn could not help him, Jhoss could not help him, and he wasn't sure himself what he sought. He was wandering aimlessly, with Mauzl growing more resistant by the day and Rekke more irritable.

Rekke would never sleep at the same time they did. He sat watch when no watch was required, keeping company with the waxing moon, and that was a Rekke thing to do, he was wary by nature; but it was because he didn't want to fall through the realms again. He knew that it had something to do with them drowsing by the fire, losing consciousness under the hail of rocks. *It has something to do with letting go,* Ioli gleaned from him in an unprotected moment. He kept strict control of himself, and nothing Ioli said would move him to try again.

When he'd lost count after nine days of journeying, they topped a hill and saw the lakes of the Belt spread out before them like a chain of many-colored beads, and came down into a village of cidermakers and chandlers to find that they were expected. "The seers will be wanting you," said a grizzled shopkeeper. Two boys left off a kickball game to run over and say, "You're the ones they want on the isle!" The grizzled man pointed them to a farrier's where they could leave their horses. Someone would row them out to the isle.

"I don't like this," Rekke said, on a path down to an amber lake with a forested island in the center. "The *word's* gotten out about us. Who's carrying tales? Your runner friends?"

No one was carrying tales about them, as far as Ioli could make out from the man who rowed him to the island and the visants who met them there. No runners came here, no visants from other enclaves. They had no one with Mauzl's knack. Their glows and their gleanings were subdued and simple, focused mainly on their wooded isle. They expected nothing of Ioli and Rekke and Mauzl except their presence. They only wanted to be near them. To look at them.

Yet they'd known that they were coming. Ioli's skin prickled. It was the first time he'd found the gleaning of visants to be uncanny, eerie; this must be the way it felt to the lightless, to be gleaned, and Ioli had to admit he didn't like it. They couldn't tell him what they saw, and whatever they said to Mauzl, as they seized on the speechless language of fingers he brought them, Mauzl could not or would not translate.

"Staying," Mauzl said stubbornly, after they'd eaten their fill of oilnuts and truffles and treebark bread.

They sat on a plank platform in the central clearing, surrounded by visants engaged in their typical habits. One of them had a collection of gloves, every conceivable sort from work gloves to the heavy metal gauntlets of a shielder, but got upset when Rekke went to try a pair on. One proudly showed them a box full of candle stubs, every color and substance including tallow, which only mages of the old light had ever used; she showed no interest in the subject of wax or dippings or the idea of prenticing to a chandler.

"*Staying,*" Mauzl said, more urgently, and Rekke said, "We're not staying more than the night. There's nothing here." *There is,* Ioli thought, *but we aren't seeing it.* Rekke added, "They're safe as they can be on this drowned nub of hill, and they've never even heard of Jhoss n'Kall."

They hadn't; Jhoss had never been here, nor any folk of his. They didn't even know there was a war of the coast. They had the same notions as the visants in Crook and throughout the Heartlands: that a madness would lift from the world, that someone would show them a special place, a visant place, a place they could go. How did they come by such a notion, if no one ever came here?

A place they could go—yet they were happy on their island and had no intention of ever leaving it. Mauzl said, "Staying!" Tugging on Ioli's sleeve.

This was a pretty place, a woodland place, just reaching its full harvestmid glory when the leaves had already fallen up in the Head; the island was a haven of peace in the midst of calm waters. *He's the hideabout boy,* Ioli thought. *This is a nice place, he wants to hide here.* But some part of him knew that wasn't right, that wasn't what Mauzl was asking, or trying to tell him.

"Bloody spirits, let him stay then," Rekke said. "You can wander through the interior to your heart's content, Ioli. Eiden take your grieving quest. I'm going back to the coast. Let the runt stay here. You do what you like."

Ioli fought a frantic despair. Mauzl grown stubborn, Rekke grown bored and impatient—and him unable to make sense of what the visants were trying to tell him, by clustering near with their toys and their stacks and lines and rows.

"Just see me through the Girdle. As far as the Crotch. Then you'll be back on the coast where you want to be. I'll find it in the Girdle. I will, Rekke."

"He will," Mauzl said, from inside the screen of his hair, in sulky resentment.

"No he won't," Rekke sang, a tune of contempt. "It isn't there to find."

"You said you'd take me to every visant enclave if I asked!"

"Little monkey. Never believe what people promise you, least of all me. I didn't know what I was saying. I didn't know how blind they'd gone in here."

"It's you who's blind! You blind yourself to what's possible!"

"And you've become a procurer, and in helping you I've become one of the cretins too. Trying to make visants into something they're not. All they're good for is being sent to the coast, and I should be out there putting a stop to that. This was a fool's errand from the start."

"It wasn't, Rekke, truly. There's something . . . they're trying to tell . . ."

"They're not trying to tell it to me."

"I think they are," Ioli said, staring at the visants staring at them. All staring at them now. Gleaning them. Seeing the way their glows blended. The tinge of each of them in the others. Wanting to be near it, learn the feel of it, maybe find something like it among themselves. They'd all been clustering near like that. Using the powers that were like sight, but weren't. "I think they're telling all of us something, whether they mean to or not. We haven't seen it yet. We just . . . aren't, yet, what we could be. We stopped trying."

"It's too dangerous. Visants don't work together. Every one of them works alone in his own head, and when they try to work together half the time they work at odds. Betray each other. Thwart each other. I brought us to the Head, Ioli, because I wanted to feel a mountain under me again. But *you* brought us to Jhoss. You're the reason we landed in that chamber. Now you've taken me from the coast where I can do some good. You keep diverting me. I won't let you keep doing that. I've had enough. I go on alone."

"Alone," Mauzl said, as though he might weep.

"Just to the coast," Ioli pleaded. "Don't split us up yet."

"It's the grieving runt who wants to stay here!"

"Not here," Mauzl mumbled. "Together."

Rekke flung his head back and his arms out. "Bloody grieving helpless dependent runts! Bloody walleyes!"

He wanted them to be dependent on him so he could save them. When there was no saving to do, he went mad. But when they needed him, he hated them.

He rounded on Mauzl as though he would strike him. Mauzl hunkered between his own knees and tucked his head between his upper arms, defending it with pointy elbows. He made a low, awful sound. Rekke thrashed the air around him in grotesque contortion. His feet pounded the platform with all the weight of dense bone and muscle; the other visants scattered, like stones jarred off a hammered table. Mauzl kept completely still. Rekke's fists and boots passed so close they brushed his clothes. All his strength and speed was behind every blow, he followed through on every strike, no pulling up, no pulling back, no feinting—if Mauzl moved a hair he'd be broken, crushed. He only trembled. Rekke roared.

Ioli cried out, and snatched up Mauzl's toy to fling at Rekke, to snap him to his senses. Rekke saw it, saw him rise, and turned on him. A crazed berserker, body warped into deformity, face blackened, ugly, unknowable. Ioli drew his missile back. Rekke's pupils contracted to inhuman pinpoints.

"Rekke, no," Ioli breathed.

With an anguished cry, like a sick animal, Rekke sank to his haunches and buried his fisted hands in his wild hair.

The visants crept back onto the platform, crept near again. All their little bits and pieces had been disturbed. They set about restoring their neat arrangements. Ioli gleaned Rekke's miserable revulsion: His fit had only given them something interesting to do. Perhaps they all had fits, at one time or another. Fits probably passed here like thundershowers. You ducked for cover till they were spent, then went about your business.

Ioli's arm was still cocked with the top in it. Mauzl unfolded himself and groped in a circle, seeking it. Ioli whispered his name and handed it to him before he could get agitated. Mauzl set it directly in front of Rekke. When Rekke didn't acknowledge it, he picked it up and moved it closer.

Rekke reached down and gave the thing a twirl. It spun perfectly in place, no wobbling, no veering. Just spinning, serene and balanced. The patterns carved on it blurred into an undulation.

Rekke was defeated. He'd defeated himself. He was repulsed by himself, repentant, but he would surrender not a word of apology.

"Just to the Crotch," he said. "Just to the coast of Maur Lengra."

Mauzl plucked his top from the platform in mid-spin and stuck it inside his shirt. Ioli did not see it again. Later he heard Mauzl crying.

Rekke would return them to the shield. Then he'd go back to his old, known ways. In the end he was just another visant, craving the routine he'd graven into his life over the years. In the end, he was only trying to line his days up in neat rows, collect his victories in boxes like candle stubs.

They left the mist-wreathed island at dawn, no farewells from the visants who dwelled there like forest creatures, no leader to speak for them and bequeath cryptic visant words in parting. Just the sleepy villager at the oars, and particles of fog condensing on brows and lashes, and a soft round blur of waning moon, one day past full, that refused to set; and Mauzl clutching his pack to his chest and whimpering, Rekke weighing down the stern like a cold stone.

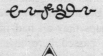

HANLARIEL TI KHINE rose to face her adversaries across a pillared, open-air hall of oceanic marble.

It was the largest hall on the island of Khine, perched at its highest elevation, crafted out of the stone beneath it, quarried in the leveling of this peak. The journey here was a twoday spiral. Several nonned had already made the ascent, hiking with their food and water on their backs, or riding donkeys surefooted enough to be left to graze the precipitous slopes. Such a hall was convened for only the loftiest of purposes. Gathered within the colossal pillars were all the significant landholders on Khine.

They'd reached consensus, in the Khinish way. It had taken days, and most of it had happened in her absence. They'd have eaten in place, walked at will to stretch their legs while still attending, suffered only brief adjournments for sleep in the open air. Hanla did not know how many had originally sat at this end of the stone-terraced rectangle, how many had sat neutral along its sides, or what configuration had prompted them to send the call for her. Summoned here, all unknowing, she had waited on the floor of the central well for the ongoing debate to come clear. Once she'd understood the topic and the terms, she'd seated herself with a handful of hereditary antagonists on a middle tier at the sunward end. By the time the sun had moved behind the opposition, she'd sat alone, abandoned even by her enemies, and the tiers to either side had emptied. Now there was only standing room at the sunward end.

All were agreed. She stood to answer the charge they would lay on her.

The moon was in the second day of its waning, only a hint of shadow at the edge of its fullness. Its light flooded the central depression of the hall as the furnace of sunset cooled to indigo in its blue-pillared portal. Hanla stepped down, tier by stone tier, until she stood in that veined pool of light.

"Hanlariel ti Khine, daughter of Geiordinel and of Aldharasil, last of your line to bear the honor of Khinish title unless and until your sons shall join you on this island and take up the duties of your holdings, you are called by consensus of this hall to—"

"I will not serve."

Silence fell. No gasps at her unthinkable statement. No indignant exhalations at the rudeness of its delivery. They turned to stone, three nonned Khinish like so many statues on stepped pedestals. Somewhere among them were the shades of her unpassaged parents; she did not know whether they would have argued in her favor or against, but in her mind she heard the creak of their thawed hearts refreezing. Somewhere at the edges stood her cousins, very much alive; one by one they had claimed the lineage of pledged or bonded lines, as the ambitions of her parents failed to bear fruit and the fortunes of her family whittled to a splinter. She was that splinter, an only child, whose status had shot skyward as proxy under the old Ennead, then plummeted when she pledged out of her reckoning in a roadside village. If she accepted the charge consensus had laid on her, those cousins would scramble to reassert the blood connection. She was ashamed at the spiteful urge to make them beg. She was startled at the fierce surge of ambitions doused long ago. Banked, it seemed, not extinguished.

The kadra Duty flared molten across her mind's eye, and faded.

She squared her shoulders, lifted her chin, stood firm.

She would not serve as headwoman of Khine.

"You must," the speaker said at last. Salmureg, who had been amanuensis to the headwoman who succeeded Strelniriol te Khine after his Midsummer's Folly nine years ago and three. Headwoman Guldrierel had served well but not long, and it shocked the island to its fundament when she stepped back. Salmureg bore this new shock with equanimity. "There is consensus."

"Not while I dissent, there isn't."

Another insult, to address a speaker in hall with Neck-roughened informality. To remind them that she was part mainlander still; that she was among the most minor of landholders here, and only because she'd come home in time to salvage what cousins had not carved from her aged parents' estate and added to other holdings. She was garbed in outdated mainland fashion, plain woolen shirt and breeches, no wide Khinish pleated pants or short silk blouse or quilted satin coat. To remind them she was lightless, no Ennead cloak on her, no silver proxy ring on her finger, no black tunic and hose. No triskele around her neck. To remind them that she was no more than an exile come home disgraced, still marked by the Neck where she had lived for nearly threenine years, shed of all the trappings of accomplishment.

"You are a child of Khine," the speaker said, calmly ignoring her effrontery. "Birthed in polity, steeped in it. You heard the song of the vines. You heard this murmured in the wind."

She had not. She'd had no idea, when they had called her to

this hall. She had believed herself summoned, a minor land-holder, the only remaining representative of her family line, to add her voice to other smallholders' in easing a deadlock; when a hall could not reach consensus, they enlarged the hall, seeking lower in the ranks. More voices meant more arguments, but more thoughts yielded wiser decisions. The method had worked for generations.

It had not worked here. It had chosen her.

She saw snow-haired Guldrierel amid olive growers on a middle tier. The older woman had been the first to issue invitation when Hanla returned to Khine, welcoming her into her home, encouraging her to tell the tales that welled up inside her. The first and, as time passed, the only. Hanla owed her debts of gratitude, and the largest was that, if this was in the offing, Guldrierel had not put her name forward. It must mean something that the woman had tried to spare her this. But she could not fathom her reasons for leaving her post. It was grave dis-honor to do so without good reason, worse to do so without suggesting a successor. Guldrierel was lucky to be accepted in this hall.

"Do not pretend to oblivion, Hanla," the speaker said, drawing Hanla's eyes back to him. "You assessed the standings in your Khinish mind, and recognized how all might devolve on you." Mild reproof, as though Hanla were a dissembling child. "You knew a former mage would be required, in this time of the new light. You knew it must be someone tried and tested in a time of war. You knew it must be a child of Khine, however minor. You heard in every grapevine the rustle of candidates' names. Your failure to answer the call-to-holders was calculated to bring atten-tion on you. You bided in your persimmon groves, awaiting a call-by-name, full knowing in the end it would be sent. You sought to make an entrance. Do not insult this hall with further display."

She had done nothing of the sort. But the speaker's accusa-tion neutralized any potential attempt to play coy. At least the brief summation confirmed what she had gathered from the tail end of debate. The hall had determined that Guldrierel's replacement must have a working knowledge of magecraft and some direct experience of battle. Her experience of battle had been abortive and embarrassing—the botched attempt of her roadside village, Clondel, to defend itself against the rebel horde in the magewar—but it was more experience than anyone but Strong Leg veterans had. Most of them had joined the shield, and none had been mages. She had been a higher-ranking mage than most before she lapsed, and unlike the other Khinish former proxies she still held land. She *should* have seen it—perhaps would have, if she'd taken any interest in the purpose of this hall, if she'd listened to the winds and murmurs, the singing in the vines.

She was the fallback of mediocrity, the best of a hard lot. The kadra Honor flared and died behind her eyes.

Almost gently, the speaker said, "Why did you come home, Hanlariel, if not for this?"

Because with Graefel gone, my sons gone, the Neck was home no longer. I have no other home but Khine.

She could have gone to the Head, after Graefel followed the codices to Senana and made of it a scholars' isle. She could have aided Dabrena n'Arilde in the founding of the menders' craft, moved to the Strong Leg, and avoided Graefel's triumphant return to the Head holding he'd always coveted. But menders were former warders; she had been a reckoner. No one who had proxied for the last Ennead ever outgrew the rivalries and grudges it had fostered.

She could have joined the runners under Pelkin n'Rolf. She'd known him in the Neck and served under him as reckoner; he'd have welcomed her into his fold. But she would not wear the black again. Forsaking it, for love of Graefel n'Traeyen, had hurt her. Black dye would chafe the scar raw. Pretending to rank in a vestigial hierarchy, she would never be free of the ache of her seared magelight. She would never be free of the fame and infamy of having trained the Lightbreaker's illuminator. In the Haunch, she would always be Hanla n'Geior, once Hanla Illuminator, abbreviated and fallen. Here, by leave of her few acres and the crops her own diligence harvested, she was still Hanlariel ti Khine, as she'd been born seven nineyears ago. No searing could take that from her.

Why not be Headwoman Hanlariel? It has a silly euphony, like the sound games Befre used to play with my boys. My son Keiler would be amused.

She gritted her teeth. *Because they can't call me to serve all Khine when I wasn't fit to dine at their tables before.*

As the thought echoed off the inside of her skull, a kadra formed there, burning red as her cheeks—a kadra she had never drawn, born of itself for this occasion. The kadra Spite. It was shameful and unworthy. A Khinishwoman served. A Khinish-woman did her duty, without thought to fickle cousins or social slights. Fortunes changed, and opinion changed with them. Stigmatized one day, idolized the next; that was the way of it on Khine, where they forgave as readily as they denounced. If she was going to be bitter about that, she might as well pack some cuttings and plant her persimmons in the Boot.

Why did I come back, if not for this?

Nonneds stood in wait on the tiered seating, motionless but for the rise of breath, ghostly in the moonlight. The invisible shades of her parents were joined by those of her grandparents and all their forebears, all the way back to the original settlers of Khine, mages and their families who'd come in ships from the outer realms to join Galandra's Ollorawn refugees and other seafolk and overlanders. They'd come from a sun-soaked archipelago, bringing seeds and livestock that thrived in the warm clime at this southmost tip of Eiden's body.

Was Eiden Eiden then, or had he grown with the mainlanders' belief in him? The Khinish had always believed mainly in themselves, and though they participated in the mainland's mage-built hierarchies, they retained a steadfast, self-sufficient independence. They observed their own holidays, convened their own halls; they raised a headwoman or headman to oversee them while the mainland thrived in gentle anarchy. They kept the old ways that suited them, and packed the ones that didn't in camphor and cedar against a day of need. They embedded in their new culture the best of the old, to see them safe through generations of forgetting.

Graefel Wordsmith, her lapsed reckoner pledge, had believed wholeheartedly in such embeddings, to the point where he conceived of the wordsmiths' canon as one grand example. Sometimes she'd wondered if what he loved in her was the taste of ancient origins—not her foreignness or strong dark body or dauntless courage, not her shining golden light or the inspired illuminations with which she empowered his scribings, but her existence as proof incarnate that the old ways lived hidden inside them all. For love of the light she had left Khine, for love of her ambitious parents she had heeded the vocate call, for love of Graefel, the first vocate she met in her proxy training, she had forsaken her silver ring and become a village mage at the foot of the black mountains whose heights she had scaled, whose summit she might have reached from within one day.

Like her Khinish heart, her light was always partially hidden, but when she cast with all her powers she knew how bright she blazed; she knew that with her talent and her discipline she might have risen to head reckoner, even ascended to the Ennead. All the shades of her ancestors implored her, in moonlit supplication atop this Khinish mount, to take the offered alternative. She had slipped from the summit of ambition at the world's head, to find herself hauled to the summit of Khinish ambition. She had merely to say two words.

I accept.

She choked on them. Two words, and she could stand as high as Graefel did at the other end of the world. Two words would redeem her parents' hopes.

She could not say them.

Why? Because of *spite*?

Because in the end she always chose the route of failure and ignominy?

Because she'd always gauged herself by her shining magelight, and without it she did not feel fit to live, much less to lead?

It could be any of those, or none. She had pleased her ancestors, she had flouted them; their yearnings and their whims had no more hold on her. It didn't matter why. Perhaps she just didn't feel like saying yes! She was happy on her terraces, content to put her strong back into simple work with simple rewards. She had no stake in polity, wasn't fool enough to tangle in its thickets. Knotwork had never been her strength as a mage. She'd been strongest in kadri, the idealized triangular symbols drawn from deep within the illuminator's spirit. She had cherished the meditations that formed them. The Khinish way was to look outward, to good works and proud results. But placid farmwork turned you inward. That was where she wished to turn.

She opened her mouth to say *I will not be moved, find someone else.* She told herself the words and told herself they were the right ones. After that she need never speak again. She could fade into peaceful obscurity in her terraces and groves.

One figure stood out from the waiting crowd. One familiar, impossible figure, dressed in black breeches, blowsy white shirt, dove gray cloak. Red of hair, darkened in moonlight to the color of old blood. A murmur ran through the crowd as they noticed this strange mainlander. Hanla had not seen her before now, yet surely her eye would have caught on that pale, scarred visage, that tall, whip-thin Norther body in the midst of broad and swarthy Khinish.

It was her prentice, Liath. Geara's daughter. Dressed as she had last seen her, looking just as she had then, during the defense of Clondel in the magewar. The day Hanla had torn the triskele from the neck she had draped it around a year before, and ground it under her boot.

She approached like a spectre through the fall of silver light. There was no golden light in her, though on that day there still had been. The spirits of dead mages, Hanla believed, must have been seared of their light as thoroughly as the living. But it was no haunt who gripped her arm, hand to elbow, in the greeting and respect of the Neck.

"Are you come home, then, from your long journeying?" Hanla whispered, feeling she spoke from a dream. She remembered a young red-haired girl just past her trial, heartsick to leave the boy next door for her journey year. The girl hadn't thought that Hanla knew—when the boy was Hanla's son, and the girl her prentice. Hanla had fed her platitudes about magecraft, about duty.

Liath shook her head. "I've lost my way. Don't lose yours."

"What are you doing here?"

"What are you?"

"This is my home."

"I've sailed toward home for twice nine years. Home is a gift. Don't refuse it."

Hanla looked past her and up at the murmuring crowd. Fingers pointed, heads turned to speculate and comment, but the speaker made no move to intervene, and Khinish halls were patient. When someone took the floor, they granted audience. Consensus was not valid until all voices had been heard.

"What do you want?" she asked Liath. That staunch, heartsick girl she'd prenticed from childhood was gone these two-nine years. The woman who stood before her, the woman she had trained illuminator, had allied with an insurrectionist and seared the light. Hanla had always mistrusted the excuse of darkcraft. "What in the world possessed you to turn up in a place like this? You speak of home. You should go home. Your mother forgave you long ago."

"As you have not." A bitter smile twisted the white scars around Liath's mouth into a knotwork complexity.

"Were you so easily turned?" Hanla had said, so far in the past, a world away, before tearing the triskele from her neck.

"No, Hanla," Liath had said. *"It was not easy. And the Ennead carved its kadri from one end of me to the other, lest I ever forget how hard it was."*

Only darkcraft could have wrought such scars, whether it was the Ennead's or the Lightbreaker's. Only the war could have kept Liath from Eiden Myr so long. Only strange powers rising could have kept her from seeming to age. Contemplating persimmons, Hanla had lost sight of larger things.

That's what I wanted—to forget. That was the bloody point!

"This is neither the time nor the place," Hanla said. Brisk, dismissive. Forced. The kadra Remembrance burned molten behind her eyes, like a guider. She blinked it away.

Liath looked around, unsure where she was—as if for a moment she'd thought she was back in the summer cornfields where they'd practiced drawing in the rich soil of the Neck. Then she said, "It seems it is," and turned on Hanla a dark gray stare that raised the hairs on her arms. "Pelkin's dead."

"What? When?"

"I've just seen Keiler in the Haunch. He was hiding on a farm too. But then he was in the holding. I couldn't follow him in to see them cast Pelkin's passage, so I came to see you."

"Liath . . ."

Again Liath seemed to blink herself back from some far place. "Jhoss n'Kall is courting Graefel in the Head. Young mages are planning to take over Pelkin's holding. Powers are massing. People who understand such things are going to have to be in positions where they can act. If you hide on your farm, you're as bad as Graefel was, hiding in Clondel all those years."

Her pledge. Her son. Pelkin, who had cast her triad. Too much to take in. Let her just say no, and she could leave this place. "You should be telling this to the Khinish head," she said, and Liath said, "I just have."

How much of their dialogue had carried to the hall? Closed halls carried murmurs like shouts, but in this cold, airy space there was no telling. She looked at the landholders, trying to gauge them in the stark and shadowed light, and when she looked back Liath was three steps away.

"I just wanted to see you," Liath said, a ghost of that young prentice hovering behind the scars. Hanla had mothered her for years, when Geara couldn't bring herself to love what she would lose. "I hoped you might have forgiven me. I understand why you didn't believe me. I fought tooth and nail against the truth."

"And the Ennead carved its kadri from one end of me to the other, lest I ever forget how hard it was. . . ."

"There are horrors out there, Hanla," Liath said, still moving away. "Circling these shores. Waiting for a chance. A hole. A breach." She was nearly to the other end of the floor now. Puzzled landholders made way at her approach. "Don't let them in," she said, and melded into the crowd.

Hanla wanted to call her back. She wanted to embrace her, absolve her, forgive and be forgiven in turn. She wanted to grab her and shake her and demand details of what she'd claimed. She wanted her prentice back, she wanted her sons back, she wanted her pledge back, she wanted her light back. She wanted her ring on her finger, her triskele on her chest. She wanted the world to be as she had believed it to be, safe in the Ennead's keeping. Because she could never have those things again, she hid through years of war, and powers rising. Now every fiber of her cried out to *do something*.

To lead.

Her eye fell on Guldrierel, standing quietly not far from Salmureg on the lowest tier. Guldrierel's shadowed gaze caught hers, and held. She laid her hand over her heart in salute.

Guldrierel had stepped aside for *her.* She had not put Hanla forward. That would have aroused resistance. She had simply resigned her post, no explanation, and let consensus choose. She had disgraced herself so that the hall could find their way to Hanla on their own. Salmureg's accusations were a portrait of Guldrierel's strategy, not Hanla's. Guldrierel found herself inadequate to the task of a world so changed, a world at war with mirages, a world of blooming lights. Guldrierel, chosen for serenity and wisdom after Streln's martial disaster, had found herself too Khinish to proceed. She had opened the way for the only possible replacement—and trusted consensus to choose her.

It had worked. They had chosen Hanla.

Hanla had thought to spend her remaining years looking inward, not outward. But when she looked inward, now, she saw what the hall had seen: a woman who could recognize dark powers if they rose, a woman who knew not battle but the fevered madness that gave rise to it; a woman with sons on the mainland but feet planted firmly here; a woman with experience of the old world, young enough to have the fortitude to ward the new against the old mistakes.

A woman they trusted. Not the default of mediocrity, but the convergence of required strengths. A Khinish woman who knew the mainland. A skeptical woman with no desire to take power for its own sake.

A woman who would say no before she said yes.

Kadri flared and faded before her eyes. Some flared but did not fade, rising in succession, one behind the next, to separate and drift on the night air. The kadra Fidelity. The kadra Humility. The kadra Endurance, the first her prentice ever rendered. Three circles touching at their edges within a triangle—that had been the proxy kadra, graven on their silver rings. Magecraft's kadra, the shape of a triskele within that triangle, replaced in the same angled borders by the crescent of a sickle or cupped hand, then by an oval between two circles, resembling an eye. Lines and mazes and spirals supplanted those, idealizations of the lightless disciplines. The last to rise, after Duty, after Honor, and hang suspended in the starry pillared portal over the landholders' heads, was Acceptance. It subsumed the stars beyond it, then became them. A permanent kadra, graven in pinpoints on the fabric of sky.

Hanlariel ti Khine strode across the floor of oceanic marble. Her final answer was better expressed in action than in words. When she reached the other side, Salmureg the speaker said, "I give you greeting, Headwoman."

Hanla laid her open hand over her heart, and said, "I pledge my service to all Khine." Then, raising her voice, stepping backward into the center of the hall, she said, "I pledge my service to all Eiden Myr, and call upon Khine to do so." It came to her as she spoke: what they must do, the lot that must fall to them. "Our realm is under siege. A third of our island is denied us. Our ships languish in harbor. The mainland's shield can barely hold the line. Powers rise on the mainland, disorganized, in conflict with each other, incapable of mounting an effective counteroffense. The situation is unacceptable."

"This we know," someone said. "What would you have us do?"

"Take the war to the attackers."

There was a murmur of unease mixed with wary approval. They all knew what must be done, had known it for years, but no one had ever dared to voice it.

Hanla dared. "Call Evrael te Khine," she said. "Restore his fleet to him. Rebuild what can't be refitted." He was eight nineyears of age and three, but still spry, still masterly—and still a shipbuilder, with the skills to effect the required repairs, the resources to build new ships, the authority to command them. "All Khinish will be called to battle."

"You were a mage," someone said. "You would flout the rule of compassion?"

"It would stain us all," someone else said.

"It may kill us all," Hanla said. "Undertaking that risk is the greatest gift we can offer the world Galandra made, that let us drowse in peace and safety for twice nine nonned years. We must repay that gentle respite. We are already stained. We wallow in ancient stain without employing the arts of war that stained us, and so we die. We were conquerors once. Seafarers. Warmongers. Our blood remembers. Our weapons and armor are stored in trunks in every home. The time has come to don them again. Not to conquer Eiden Myr, but to save it. We must reclaim our heritage. Lift our bloodied hands in defense of a precious realm. Death, should it come, will honor us. Our victory will be our glory. *This* is what we were born for."

"None of our ships ever came back," someone said.

"The ships Eiden Myr sent into the outer seas were explorer ships, ill equipped, and few of them were Khinish. This time it will be Khinish ships crewed by Khinish warriors. Bristling with weaponry, like the phantom ships that have haunted our shores these dozen years. None will return unless as victors. We have sat long enough in our groves and on our terraces letting homegrown defenders flail helplessly against horrors they were not bred to fight. We are conquerors. We are Khinish. We will stop the siege, or die."

The roar of approbation enflamed her blood even as it humbled her.

"There is consensus," said Salmureg. "The hall favors the headwoman."

"Then I suggest we adjourn," Hanla said. "We can be halfway down the mountain by moonset."

Liath had disappeared in the crowd, and Hanla did not sight her again in the torchlit procession that wended its way down the spiral path, ringing the mountain in fire.

IOLI BARELY BLINKED and they were in the Girdle, a wind-stroked ocean of long grasses in as many shades and colors as the Belt's lakes. It undulated, like the sea. It didn't look solid. It didn't look safe.

"I won't go chasing herd bands," Rekke said. "There's only one visant band in all this region, and I don't know where they'll be this time of year. We ride straight through." Straight was a relative thing, in the Girdle, where rivers curved and forked at will and there were no roads to guide you to the fords. There were no bearings at all in the sea of grass. Rekke could glean the earth itself; Rekke could find his way in the most complex of unfamiliar places. Rekke was everything Ioli wasn't, and Ioli didn't know what he'd do without him.

Mauzl, at least, was home. It didn't make him happy the way the horse had. Sometimes thundering herds swept past, horses with coats of all colors shining like satin. Mauzl brightened then, took interest. But he didn't seem happy to be home, or calmed, or able to see any better. He only rode more slowly, sometimes stopping the horse entirely until Ioli took the reins and urged it forward, and even then it would some-times balk, getting one command from the weight and the legs of the rider it trusted, another from the irritating madman in the saddle.

"There's an encampment up ahead," Rekke said. Ioli couldn't see it, blinded by the rippling, nauseating grass. "Come on, Mauzl, stop dawdling."

Mauzl would not let the horse move. When Rekke swore and grabbed the horse's halter, Mauzl vaulted off to land hip-deep in the fluid grasses. He had his pack hung on the front of him instead of the back, and he clutched it, defensive, mutinous.

"Eiden's teeth," Rekke said, and released Ioli's horse to gig his own forward. For a moment it seemed he would leave them both behind and just make for the coast on his own. His horse swept into a lope. Then he reined around and came straight at them. Ioli's horse shied, seeming to drop straight out from under him and sidewise. He was left clinging to its neck, only one leg over the saddle. *Oh, spirits, he's cracked, he's going to run him down!* But Rekke rode to the side of Mauzl, who stood defiant and unflinching, and leaned his long body over to scoop him up in one arm. Ioli had forgotten how strong he was, how mad he was. He didn't even put Mauzl on the horse, just held him in that one arm and carried him, arcing around to their original path, cantering off into distance.

Ioli pushed and scrambled back into the saddle. He flailed with the reins and kicked the horse's sides, panicked at being left behind. The horse bucked in irritation—it was used to following the other horse, it would have followed it anyway, he was only aggravating it. He dropped the reins and hung on. In a few breaths of unbearable pounding he'd caught up with Rekke, still swearing, Mauzl limp in his right arm, and he could see the peaks and domes of the herd band's tents resolving from the swell of grass.

People were running out to meet them.

They were calling Mauzl's name, in joyful voices.

"He's like a changeling from the lands-beyond," Mauzl's mother, Ziyel, said, scooping peppergrass stew from the com-

munal pot with a thick crescent of black bread, then adding a
dollop of green grass jelly to the end before she bit it off. Chewing, she said, "Sylfonwy carried this beautiful alien child to me
on the winds, put him in my belly, and I carried him and birthed
him and loved him, but none of it was enough. None of it was
enough to make him love us back."

"He loves us," said the older sister, Thandra. When she saw
Ioli's eyes tear after his first bite, she passed him a crock of
mare's-milk yogurt to cut the burn of ninespice. "It just took us
a while to understand how he says it."

"You couldn't have told me that when he was toddling,"
Ziyel said. She sat on her hip, instead of cross-legged on the
carpets like the rest. "He'd never let me hold him. He'd never
let me touch him and cuddle him. He'd hardly look at me. I
thought it must be my fault, that I hadn't loved him enough, caressed him enough. But I did. I loved him with all my heart. We
all did."

"He liked it when Granna hugged him," said the little
brother, Chez, through a mouthful of food. They all talked and
ate at the same time. "She hugged too hard. None of us liked it
but him."

"We should have held him a little harder," said the father,
Shefen, a bandy-legged man with a perpetual squint. They all
had that squint. Eyes so accustomed to vast distances that they
had trouble resolving the closeness inside their tent. The tent
had three chambers separated by beaded curtains, and was built
in cloth layers over a curving wooden frame. It was as layered
as Rekke—even the floor, which was six carpets deep to keep
the ground chill off, and required a step up when you came
through the entry flap. Scented braziers warmed this outer
chamber; there was no fire, and the food had been prepared
elsewhere in the camp, for everyone to share. To Ioli, the chamber was a dizzying confusion of pillows and tassels and beaded
brocade, nothing solid to it but the implication of ground under
all the padding. That didn't keep him from eating. Shefen finished, "Might have stopped him running off like that."

Mauzl seemed a world away. He fixed his gaze on a new toy

he'd traded his top for, an oblong bonewood box with a groove-seated front panel that slid out to reveal five colorful grape-sized beads dangling on strings within. Drawing an end bead to the side and releasing it to swing into the rest produced a satisfying woody impact—and sent the bead at the other end flying out, leaving the ones in the middle unmoved. When that bead fell back, the first one swung out again. The toy would keep clacking indefinitely—or until Rekke threatened to smash the maddening thing if it wasn't stopped. The mother had Mauzl still it, but she let him keep it on the dining cloth to look at.

"We're grateful you brought him home," said one of Mauzl's aunts. Aunts and uncles and cousins filled the tent. All hearty horse folk, they smelled like the stables in the Head holding.

"No we're not," said Thandra, the sister. Though as lightless as the others, she seemed to see him better. "He doesn't want to be here. He wants to be with his own folk. They're his family now."

"Thandra!" the mother cried. "We're his family!"

"Well, you can't take him with you to the Crotch." One of the uncles looked at Rekke. "That's where you're bound, you said?"

Rekke's lazy eye glanced sidelong at Ioli. "Yes," he said, and fingered more pepper onto his next bite of stew, eliciting approving glances from some of the cousins, who considered spicy food a test of strength.

"The Crotch isn't safe for him," the uncle said. "The blue-lights there keep on about some . . . event that's going to happen. That kind of talk makes people nervous."

Ioli's belly went cold. Rekke's ears pricked up. *He'll go this afternoon,* Ioli knew. *That's his calling, that's his life's work, to protect them from people who don't like that kind of talk. He'll go as soon as we've eaten.*

"Mauzl stays with us now," said the father, casting a look at Rekke that dared him to contradict, even though Rekke was the one who'd carried their runaway home to them. Rekke shrugged.

"He'll go to the Zhemar band if he wants to," said the mother.

"He won't stay there," the little brother piped up. "Not even if it is all bluelights. He'll sneak away again."

"He should go where he wants to go," said the sister. "He wants to go with them." She cast a soft, pleading look at Ioli, startling in its clarity: *Don't leave him here. He belongs with you. Please, please take him with you.* She couldn't watch him suffocate here, crushed in the embrace of their overprotective love. She'd helped him leave in the first place, Ioli saw. She was the one who had the horse waiting for him, the horse he must have lost somewhere along the way; she was the one who packed rations, the one who'd distracted the family so he could slip out from under their watchful eyes; she was the one who'd known that he'd had to go, that something out there called to him, even though he couldn't tell her what it was.

He'd left here because the paths, or his own longing, had told him that there were glows out there that would blend with his. He'd left here to be with Ioli, traveled all that way down into the Weak Leg to find Ioli's glow, and fate or accident had added Rekke's glow, and together they had traveled through impossible realms. They were already a triad, in spite of themselves, though "triad" was a mage word and there was no word for what they were. There was rarely a word for any visant thing; that didn't make visant things less potent. If Rekke refused to accept what they became when their glows worked as one, there was no point in them being together. Without their glows, they were just three Southers thrown together by circumstances. The circumstances had changed.

Rekke's departure might make a space where another glow could fit. But without Rekke, Ioli couldn't bear the burden of Mauzl.

It wasn't safe for him out in the world. He'd been in a terrible state when he attached himself to Fyldur's conscripts. He was starving and dirty, he'd been beaten, his clothes were rags. He couldn't take care of himself. Ioli couldn't take care of him alone. If they left him anywhere else, he'd only run after them again. This was the only place Ioli could leave him where he'd be both safe and unable to follow—both loved and restrained.

The sister was still staring at him, pleading silently while the family argued. They argued because they loved him; it was painful to hear, not because Ioli had any affection for them but because it was so jangled, so unresolved, so contrary to sense. He had only to say "Mauzl, you've got to stay here with your family while Rekke and I go on to the coast" and all would slide firmly into a rightness, a solution. It was a rightness that was wrong, because it wasn't what Mauzl wanted, but it wasn't what Ioli wanted either and it was the best he could do. Rekke would not yield. Rekke would not triad them. Rekke would go back to his routine, jump on this news from the coast with fierce pleasure in righting the wrongs he knew how to.

Before Ioli could stop the argument and break the sister's heart, a head popped in through the entry flap and someone said, "I was told there's a runner in here. I have another one outside who'd like to talk to him, if that's so."

For a moment Ioli had no idea why everyone fell silent and looked at him. Everyone except for Mauzl, who was looking at his toy. Then Rekke snorted, his lazy eye raking Ioli up and down, and Ioli remembered his own black clothes, stolen from the Sauglin holding. He felt caught out. Then he leaped to his feet, thinking, *It's the mages, they're going to cast the warding, or the end of the world*—and then he faltered, because no runner would have been sent to tell him anything. For a moment he'd thought he was important. Remembering that he wasn't, he didn't know what to do.

"Well, monkey?" said Rekke. "Go see what the crow wants."

The black-clad runner waiting outside was a chunky woman, staring into space, one leg jiggling with impatience. She took one look at him and said, "You're not one of us."

"No." He didn't know what else to say.

"I have a message to pass to the Effai band before I can head back. I guess you won't be taking it." She squinted. "You're one of those visants who can walk through wardings."

He started to say no. Then he said, "We didn't walk."

"The mages are mad to know how you did it."

"So am I," Ioli said, his mind leaping miles between each word. He was accomplishing nothing out here. He was useless. Roaming aimlessly. Learning nothing except that he didn't understand his own kind at all. Maybe if he appealed to Louarn again. If Louarn had finished his business in Sauglin and had time for him now. He was pledged to that Highlander, the teacher who was a day's ride away from Sauglin. He might be there. Ioli might find him again, if he went back. Jhoss said that the three lights combined would save Eiden Myr. Louarn combined the three lights within himself. His blue glow was intense. Ioli had done nothing of any use except wander and look and learn how much he didn't know. If he went back, he could tell Louarn what Jhoss had said. He could find out if Herne had made any progress. Maybe they'd thought of some use for him, some way he could help. Some way he wasn't finding, out here on his own. Some way he wouldn't find, going Crotchward with Rekke.

He asked the runner if he could go with her.

"If you like," she said. "Can't really let you run about in runner's clothes. Shouldn't let you run about with a stain like that. But I'm leaving right now, so you'll have to be quick. You do have a horse?"

Ioli nodded. Going with her was better than going with Rekke into a place that feared visants. Better than trying to be with Rekke, two-thirds of a whole, always reminded of what it had felt like when it was three of them together, always resenting Rekke for what he had cost them, what they could have been. Better than roaming, stained and glowing, through a world he couldn't understand. Better than deciding, later, to go back; he'd never find the way by himself, he could hardly even ride his horse, this runner was going to be peeved when she saw that. He'd be safer with her. She knew the way.

"Hurry up then," she said. She was still squinting at him. "As soon as I'm tacked up, I ride."

The moment he was through the tent flap Mauzl was plastered to him, whining horribly. "We can't do it, Mauzl," he said, helpless, no good at making his voice sound kind and comforting when he knew what he was doing was a cruel thing. "We can't do it without Rekke, and he's going to save those visants in the Crotch. That's what he does, that's his way, that's how it is. I can't look after you. I can hardly look after myself. You have to stay here, where it's safe, where they love you." Every word a hammer, smashing.

The father and uncles pried Mauzl away. The little brother tried to console him with some tongue-blistering treat. The sister stood with her cheeks silvered by tears. Rekke hopped to his feet and said, "I'm off then. Thanks for the food, though it was a tad bland." He barged past Ioli at the entry, and didn't look at Mauzl at all.

Ioli followed him to where their horses were staked. "This is wrong," he said. "You know it's wrong."

"Don't be a puking baby," Rekke said. "The runt's better off here. I'm better off on the coast. You go find whatever it is you're looking for, Ioli."

He had his horse saddled before Ioli could get near his own, as it backed to the length of its tether to avoid his nervous approach. The runner came over to do the job for him. Useless visant, couldn't even saddle his own mount. Didn't even know which saddle it was, in the row of saddles that all looked the same to his eye. Rekke called back "It's the black one with the double girth!" Ioli watched him ride away. He wouldn't even have known that way was Crotchward.

The runner gave him a leg up, then mounted her black horse and took his horse's head when it turned to follow Rekke's. "Keep your leg on him," she said. "How did you get here if you couldn't ride?"

He was a child in the world, a lost child. He despised himself. Not for being a fool, not for being useless. For the cracked, hideous cries that were coming from inside the tent where Mauzl's family dwelled.

It looked like every other tent in the sprawling encampment. All the layers of fabric in buff and brown, the peaks and domes that blended into the grasslands themselves. But that one tent had a heart of indigo, so deep it shaded to purple, shimmering with a silvery darklight. Beyond it, a heart of warm blue slate was flying into distance. Each glow was discrete, identifiable— like colors in a fabric, like one of Jalairi's scarves, knotted and dipped into different dyes to produce a dappled mottling, but still one piece of silk; like dyed flax threads in a weave, turning over and under and back on themselves, tricking the eye into seeing one piece of linen in one color.

The fabric stretched and went tight.

Ioli forced himself to turn and look where he was going. The runner was still leading his horse, which didn't want to go, and saying something curt to him; he realized that he was sitting back, the way Mauzl did to tell the horse to stop, and pulling on the reins. He let them go slack. He let himself go slack. He let go of the tight-stretched fabric of their glow.

It was rooted in him. Rooted deep. Rooted in his soul.

When it tore, he screamed.

The sky was pain, the air was pain, the earth was pain. Vision went to crystal, and shattered. Flesh was nothing—a seeming, a construct, a temporary dwelling. He was consciousness, and identity; he was Ioli, and he was torn, shredded, rent. He was Ioli, Ioli, Ioli, he was a name, he was these thoughts he was thinking, he was beingness, he had awareness, he had self.

He came back gasping into his body, collapsed over the horse's neck. The runner had a handful of his coat and was dragging him upright. His head lolled. He lifted it. He took possession of his flesh. He blinked back into his eyes, swallowed back into his guts, tensed back into his muscles. His skin was clammy. The runner was wiping drool from his face with a coarse cloth. He shook free of her, and almost shook free of himself; with an effort of will, he hung on to his body, and made the horse turn.

Seeing isn't looking. Seeing isn't pressing your mind against. Knowing was suspension, dissipation. Knowing was a mist of awareness hanging in the air. He had been a mist of awareness hanging in the air, knocked free of his body by the shock of their glow ripping apart. He came back into himself on a gleaning:

It's us. We're the ones they've been talking about. We're the ruckus in the Crotch. We're the ones who'll lift the madness and stop the war. Everyone knew that, every visant. They all knew it together. They came to know it as we moved from one of their groups to the next. There's some pool of visant knowingness, and when they stare at their rows and lines and stacks and sparkles and toys, they blend with it and they know what it knows. They learned to do that because of us. Because we were blended. Our blended glow showed them. It spoke to them in a language they could understand.

We're the visants I've been looking for.

"Aee shaa," he slurred to the runner, then started again: "I'm sorry." He was already pulling away. "There's something else I have to do."

We're the visants we've been looking for. But only if there's an us.

He drew plains air in deep and shouted, *"REKKE!"* He collected the braided hemp reins, dug his heels into the horse's flanks, and hung on.

Mauzl shot out of the tent and stood in the trampled grass. His sister came out behind him, pushing his bonewood box into the little canvas pack, then guided his arms through the straps and settled it securely on his back. Rekke came up at an easy trot as Ioli's confused horse skidded to a stop by the tent and he dismounted in a tangle of reins and stirrup. With his horse still moving, Rekke threw a leg over its back, kicked free of the near stirrup, and pushed off to land lightly on his feet, the horse coming to a neat halt beside him.

We're so different, Ioli thought. *Maybe that's what makes us strong.* The blue glow was a draught of healing liquid, narcotic and stimulating. Warm blue stone and depths of indigo sea. Streaks and shimmers of silver. A glow that wasn't light at all. A glow that was just them.

"Staying?" Mauzl said, eyes downcast, screened by a fall of hair as silken as the grasslands.

Rekke shrugged. "It's better than ripping my brains out through every pore of my bleeding skin."

That wasn't good enough. Rekke was harrowed, under that dark skin. He'd felt the same thing Ioli had, the same thing that had turned Mauzl's wails into a shriek. Ioli stared down the tall loose insolence, the layers of diffidence and scorn, until Rekke eased, just for a breath, and let him see the weary, angry, frightened man inside.

"All right," Rekke said. "We'll try. Because it's important." He sighed: "Because no one else can." He reached out to tousle Mauzl's hair, which Mauzl hated, and Mauzl squirmed away to hide behind Ioli. With humorless grin, Rekke said, "It's down to us, isn't it?"

"Yes," Ioli said, as the family surrounded them demanding explanations he couldn't yet give, intentions he hadn't yet formed, decisions they hadn't yet made. "Yes. The three of us."

NERENYI N'JHEEL L'CORLIN stared down the ruined limestone slope to her right. The way was fissured, blackened. Too cracked and tumbled, too steep, too jagged to descend. Kelp-slicked, smashed by storm, and nothing at the bottom but the tongue of the sea. She ran her eye along the curve of naked stone that carved the dour sky to her left. Nothing there but a sheer drop to thunder and seafroth. A sound persisted into her awareness, cutting through the ceaseless wind, the crash and whisper of the sea. *Crack. Crack. Crack.* It had been going on for some time, or perhaps had just started. She looked down. Three spotted gulls were dropping mollusks on a jutting slab of rock to break them open. The slab was littered with broken shells. The shells were lurid in the dingy light.

"Come away," someone said, though she stood alone on the wind-lorn precipice. "Come away from the edge."

It was not her own voice. It was not Gisela's voice, though it might have been. Gisela's voice was that steady, that toneless. Never a hint of unease, whether a boat was taking on water or a gale was tearing the doors off. The folk of the isle were like that. They never raised their voices, even when projecting them through a shriek of wind. Gisela's father was an islander. Her mother had become one. The islanders endured, through searings and scholars and storms and sieges. They spread their compost and sand and seaweed on the rocky shelf and grew potatoes in it. They raised their hardy donkeys where there was only bramble to graze. They had fields to plant barely enough rye to keep two nonned of them in bread through the winter; if the crop failed, they ground and baked the tough weeds that grew between the rocks. When the magelight went, they went without. When the scholars came, they built them halls, for stone they had in abundance, and the skill to lay it dry and tight. When the scholars went, they used the stone for other things. They wasted nothing, not even their breath. When the shielders came, crying onslaught, they told them that it was delusion, then let them be. When the shielders died, they blessed their bodies to the bonefolk. After a while, the shield forgot them, and saw to its High Arm shore. They went on, as they always had. Gisela stayed, as she always would, and Nerenyi stayed, because she loved her.

They would grow old together, gray heads nodding by the fire, oblivious of its stink when there was only kelp and manure to burn. In the deeps of night, curled close in the comfort of old wool, they would startle awake at some queer windy whine, then ease back into dreams as the wistful breath of Korelan's distant flute soothed the restive haunts and spirits. On clear mornings they would hike to the cliffs to scribe and paint the rockscape, and the sea; hiking slower each year, up the stony way, until their aching bones and seizing joints said it was time to scribe and paint the landscape of their hearts instead, safe by the hearth. Gisela's poetry would mellow like a fine wine as she aged. Her black hair would go iron gray like her mother's, her sea-colored eyes would peer out from fissures of crow's-feet, her hands would gnarl and cramp, but the sweet black wine would still flow from her quill, fermented by the passion her steady voice never surrendered.

"Come away," said the voice. "Come with me."

Nerenyi looked over the edge, and down, to where Gisela lay broken on the jutting slab of rock.

"The bonefolk won't come if we watch," said the voice. Steady. Calm. Sensible.

Yes. She must go before the bonefolk came.

One breath, one step. There was no other way to get down to her. On one side, the jagged slope; on the other, the frothing sea. Neither would take her where she wanted to go.

"Is it nice, to be a haunt?" she asked. "Is it beautiful and free?"

"I don't know," Liath said. "I'm not dead."

"Ah," said Nerenyi. "A dream, then. I'm dreaming you, in my grief. Longing for my old friend, in this hard time."

"You haven't felt your grief yet," Liath said.

She had only to drop herself, and she would break open on the rock, and free herself to join Gisela.

"You love life, Nerenyi. Don't throw it off a cliff."

"I've done my share of living while you were gone."

"You're a seeker. You can't have answered all the questions yet."

"There will always be questions. There's no end on questions. I can't answer them all. But I can answer this one."

"Ask again when the time comes. She has forever now. She'll wait for you."

The tide was turning. The sea was coming. It already had the shielder. It would lift Gisela in its cold, dark arms. It would carry her away.

"No," Nerenyi said, reaching for her, "no—"

And Liath was bearing her back in muscled arms, driving her

from the brink on sailor's legs that should not have been that strong, she was stronger than Liath, she would not be stopped, *Gisela*—

"You're stronger than this," Liath said, low and hard. "Let her go."

"You fool," Nerenyi snarled, breaking free, stumbling back. Her heel caught her paintbox and sent it clattering. "This is what killed her!"

Reaching for that lone daft shielder, fighting his phantasms on the edge of disaster, not content to tell him once and let him die if he wouldn't listen, not content to let him cast himself into insane oblivion on the tides, she was always like that, bloody stubborn hardheaded woman, always trying to stop their mad vain heroism, always trying to *save* them. So few came now, so few believed there was anything worth fighting for on this smudge of land, but this one came, this one and his boatload of brave doomed friends, and wouldn't listen; and one by one they died, till only one was left; and Gisela couldn't watch them die anymore. What did she think she was going to do if she pulled him back from the brink? How did she think the two of them would stop him from going back to fight for them again? Why hadn't she waited for Nerenyi, why did she have to be the faster runner, why did they have to hike up here today with their sedgeweave and their inks and quills, why couldn't they have stayed safe at home and let the menders and the runners and the mages sort it out? Why did Gisela have to be such a bloody *islander,* trying to save strangers from themselves? Why couldn't she be islander enough to let him be?

"I won't let it kill you," Liath said.

Nerenyi looked at the shorn head, the twice-scarred face, the alien vest and leggings and boots. Her visant's gleaning was detail; her affliction was truth. "What an *outerlander* you've become. Did you know they banned the binder's harvest? Grieving spirits—you're wearing *animal skin,* and what that shirt's made of I can't even imagine. They're barbarians out there. They're *monsters.*"

"Yes. They are. And they're coming, Nerenyi. Help me stop them. Help me do what I have to do."

"I don't bloody care what you have to do." She lunged for the cliff, to do what she had to do.

Liath blocked the way. She was fast—faster than flesh could be. But she was flesh; Nerenyi had felt her. To reach Gisela she'd have to bowl Liath over the edge.

"She's gone," Liath said. "The bonefolk will have had her. They won't have you as well."

Vain, foolish heroism, futile in a world of darkness, of siege. The only certainty was home and hearth, and the only home seekers ever had was with each other, and home was gone, gone forever, gone to the sea, the winds, the bonefolk.

Nerenyi went to her knees, hard on the cold, hard stone. The paintbox had weighted a sheaf of Gisela's sedgeweave against the wind. When she'd kicked it loose, the sheaf had scattered, but one half-inked leaf had caught in a crevice. The wind took it now, sent uncompleted lines unread out into distance. It was gone too fast to catch. She did not reach for it.

The sea had the last of Gisela now. The bonefolk came for the drowned, found them and took them; perhaps they'd recognize that leaf as part of her, and take it too, and if the mystics were right and one day all spirits returned to the flesh the bonefolk passaged, perhaps Gisela would wake up to find her own words on her breast, and ask someone for quill and ink so she could finish them.

"Maybe she will," Liath said, from her knees beside her, gone pale as a ghost, staring at the limestone dropoff. "Maybe he will too." Nerenyi thought wildly, *She's read my thoughts,* and gleaned her, thrust her mind's hands deep to probe for a bluesilver glow. Finding none, she said, through tears she hadn't felt her eyes produce, "What *are* you?"

Liath pulled her harrowed gray gaze from the edge and said, "Your friend, Nerenyi. I'm your friend."

Then Nerenyi understood that she'd been sobbing, babbling every mortifying thought out loud, as always when she was roused, when she was *feeling;* then Nerenyi glimpsed the chasm of grief that opened before her.

"I can't bear it," she said, in the cottage, in the dark, in her empty bed.

"I know," said Liath. "Neither can I."

"Why?" she moaned. "Oh, spirits, *why?*"

Softly, with all the sadness of the ages, Liath said, "Because."

Days came and went. Nights came and stayed. Sometimes Liath was there, sometimes the other islanders, bringing food, memories. Sometimes she laughed; sometimes for a space of breath it was as though the pain had left her, and she thought that maybe she'd be all right now.

She knew better. She'd seen Liath through something very like, after the magewar—she and Gisela and Imma. She saw the grief on Liath still.

It was not going to go away.

"There's somewhere I'm supposed to be," Liath said, looking out the window at the chill harvestmid day as though she'd just remembered she left her gear outside. But she had no gear.

"You're not entirely here, are you?" Nerenyi said, taking the serving dish Liath was holding and wiping it dry. It belonged to Bansel, who lived up the road. "You come and go like a boneman. Where do you sleep?"

Liath looked startled, as though she'd never thought to wonder, then winced and raised three fingers to her temple. "I . . . don't know. There's something wrong with me. There's a hole. There's something I have to do. Someone . . ." She drifted toward the door, like a sleepwalker.

Nerenyi barred the way. "We'll go together."

"No. You can't . . . go where I go."

Nerenyi didn't know what that meant, and Liath seemed unable to tell her, but she was telling the truth. That much Nerenyi could see. "Then you'll go where I go," she said. "I'm sick of cleaning this spotless cottage, I'm sick of rooms that are empty even when they're full, I'm sick of my neighbors' food. I want to know more about the bonefolk. I know where to go to find out. Come with me."

"The bonefolk," Liath said, frowning. Abruptly she turned and stared hard at Nerenyi, as though willing Nerenyi to look through her eyes and see what she had seen. "There was a place, Nerenyi. Pelkin thought . . ." She couldn't finish. She swore, and turned away.

Nerenyi went to a trunk by the door and flipped back the lid. "You've been gone a long time. A lot has happened. I'll fill you in, while we travel. I suppose I'm stained, and you as well, but we won't know till we try to cross the Hand. The shield controls Maur Alna, so we'll be all right there. We can walk across their seawall if we have to."

"I have no idea what you're talking about."

"And I have no idea where you've been, or how you got back when no one else could, or how you came here when no one rowed you over and there's no boat to be seen. You can tell me that, and together we'll learn the rest. Come on. I'll find a pack for you, and see what we can carry across to trade for horses."

"I tried to run away from grief," Liath said, hugging herself, as though the chill of the sea had come back on her. "It doesn't work. It comes with you."

"It'll be with me wherever I am. You didn't run away. You found a thing you could bear to do. I was here, remember? You and Korelan built the boat. This is a thing I can bear to do. I'm going to find out where they took Gisela."

Liath's head snapped around. "That's daft."

"I'm a visant." Nerenyi moved from one end of the cottage to another, piling items on the old scarred table in the center, more than they could bring. As she spoke and worked, the pile grew, and became a mound of things to give away to neighbors. "We're all daft. I'll tell you about that, too. We have a lot to tell each other." She smiled, remembering a rift of old, long mended. "Imagine what we'll learn."

"You've put down roots here."

"My roots were in Gisela, and she's gone." Her voice cracked. She ignored it, and began sorting. This for Korelan's family, this for Bansel's . . . Then she thought, *They know what they need. I'll leave the choosing to them.* "If I make it back, her haunt will be here. She has forever now. You said it yourself." For trading, she packed a set of silver-wrought spoons that had been hidden through generations of old superstition but would now be valued for their antique craft, and a bag of one-of-a-kind playing stones, like nothing she'd ever seen on the mainland—Gisela's father's lucky stones, which had won many a game for him at long winter-night gatherings.

At last it came down to objects of sentiment. Everything her eye fell on had significance. Every crack in the floor, every dent in the table. . . . In the end, she put only three keepsakes in her old pack—their triskeles, and Imma's, poured in a tangle of their chains into a flannel drawbag—then changed her mind and tied the drawbag on a thong around her neck. Her good coat and gloves and hat she gave to Liath, who was her size. She wore Gisela's. That they were a shade too small made their embrace more intimate.

Twice Liath seemed to forget where she was, what she was doing here; she seemed to wake from a dream without waking at all, and dropped whatever Nerenyi had handed her, and walked toward the wall as if she'd keep walking straight through it. The second time Nerenyi stopped her, she said, "I'm so bloody lost, Nerenyi," and Nerenyi said, "You can't be lost. You've found me."

Could years alone at sea drive the mind to such fits of distraction? Or something she had seen, or something that had befallen her, wherever she had gone in those lost years? Nerenyi had to bite her tongue to keep from asking. What was out there, what she'd experienced, what it was like. She had a nonned questions. The islanders, in their wisdom, waited for Liath to explain herself, or not, but in the blur of grief, clutching at anything to claw free of the unbearable, Nerenyi had started asking—and every time, Liath had grown irritable, even agonized, and disappeared into the night. Nerenyi had a horror of being left alone, and knew she must rise above it; if the time came to ask hard questions, she must ask them; but in the meanwhile, for Liath's sake, she must allow her to tell the tale on her own terms.

She did not say farewell to the island, but she told Fensa, Korelan's pledge, where she was bound and asked if a couple of her sons would ride over with them and row the boat back. "They're already at the landing," Fensa said. "Korelan and our eldest. He saw you here. He means to see you back."

They'd already known. They'd known before she had, with their ineffable, lightless islander sense, the keen eyes of their hearts.

At the top of the steep path that led down from the plateau, past the scythed fields to the coracle landing and on to the foot of the island, Liath said, in her steady voice, "Pelkin's dead."

A deep, soft jolt went through Nerenyi. Another link to Gisela severed. Pelkin n'Rolf had come to Senana after the magewar, to pledge Gisela and her. Liath had asked him to come. The light was seared, there were no more pledges cast, but he enacted the ritual for them anyway. It had moved her deeply. Jhoss n'Kall had followed Pelkin there, seeking someone to lead Eiden Myr into a new age, and recognized the island as a haven of spirit and good sense, and that was how the Head codices came to Senana for safekeeping. Pelkin had rejected Jhoss's bid to put him in charge. "I'm sorry," she said. "He was a fine, wise man." *And full of grief, just like ours, though his pledge stepped off a different cliff.*

"My niece has taken the triskele. She reminds me of myself, all those years ago. What I might have been, if it hadn't all gone to ruin, if I could have had home, and my light, and Keiler too. And Hanla's headwoman of Khine. How do I know that? It's as though I dreamed it, or lived it in some other life. . . . Keiler's pledged *Mellas,* of all bloody things. I was so sure he'd pledged Ferlin, with her stinking chrysanthemum hair, and Mellas . . . I thought he was lost, inside the tunnels, I thought he'd only dreamed himself back into his prison. . . . A dream . . . Is this a dream? You're alive, Nerenyi, aren't you? You're real. Tell me you're real. You *are* real, I can feel you, you drive the shadows back the way you did when we were young . . . this isn't a dream . . . I'm not dead, this isn't pethyar, or some vision of . . . coming home . . ."

"I bruise easily, for a dream," Nerenyi said, prying Liath's fingers one by one from where they'd gripped her arms. "If you're a dream, you're a strong one. Why would you dream yourself to a home so changed? You'd dream yourself to the home you knew, or the one you wished had come to be. This is real, whatever it is. It's real, and whatever's wrong we'll set it right."

"Why can't I remember, Nerenyi?"

Nerenyi wuzzled the dark red fuzz on Liath's head, then gave the nape-length tail of hair a tug. "Don't ask why," she said—meaning to help, meaning to soothe, then blinking to hear those words come out of her own mouth.

Liath froze in a sort of shock, confounded by the utterly unseekerlike advice. Then she burst out laughing. "By all the blessed spirits," she said, striking off down the path, shaking her head, "I have missed you, Nerenyi."

Nerenyi turned to whisper a private farewell to Gisela, a benediction on her steadfast spirit. Then she followed Liath down the winding, stony way.

"WHEN I WAS hurt," Ioli said. "When I was going in and out of consciousness. Your glows were brighter."

Mauzl set his clacking-ball toy in the center of the vacated hut's outer chamber, aligning it with the carpet's pattern.

"Dozing off in the Sauglin holding," Rekke said. He sat with arms clasped around his long legs, closest to the brazier. "About to die, in the cornfield."

"You were passing out. I suppose I was too, maybe. Mauzl

was gleaning. Or he might have come out of that and just been scared."

Mauzl shrugged. He didn't remember.

"So if I conk us all on the head," Rekke said, "off we go. Wouldn't that be just like a flock of cracked walleyes, running around bashing themselves on the head. Leave that grieving toy alone, Mauzl."

"It can't require that. It can't be so unlike what mages and touches do when they're wide awake."

"If it is, we're jaxed. I won't be caught half-asleep."

"We'll only do it in safe places, like here with Mauzl's folk looking after us." When Rekke's lips drew back in a grin that wasn't, Ioli said, "Well, how else then, if not dozing? You're not bashing me on the head."

"It's something to do with having nothing left to lose." Rekke fixed one baleful eye on Mauzl, freezing him as he reached to start the toy clacking. "You said that shielder's glow flared right before she died. I've seen that happen with other visants too."

"It's something to do with letting go. Drowsing, losing consciousness . . . dying . . ." Ioli swore, then blinked at Rekke, because the obscenities were Rekke's words, whether they came directly from him or not. "We're blending more all the time."

"Part monkey and part mouse. My life's complete."

Mauzl watched Rekke and slid his hand toward the toy. Rekke held a forefinger in front of Mauzl's nose, drew it down to the toy, then held it up straight and waved it back and forth. Mauzl nodded vigorously, pointing at Rekke's finger. Rekke looked at his finger, found nothing wrong with it, and made a face at Mauzl. Mauzl sighed, and made an act of slumping. No one noticed.

"You've got to take this seriously," Ioli said.

"Oh, I do. We're sitting in a nice safe place with a nice warm brazier and pillows and carpets and nice people to cook for us, trying to *figure out* how I can drag you and this runtling into the ninth circle of horrors."

"You won't, Rekke. You won't let us fall."

"Just get on with it." With his left eye on Ioli and his right on Mauzl, he said, "Letting go. That doesn't have to mean passing out or falling asleep."

"Or having nothing left to lose."

"No. I nearly killed myself trying to give Jhoss what he wanted. I tried too hard. It's the opposite of that. Don't ask me how." He put on a high, nasal voice, part seeker and part scholar. "Perhaps if we endeavor to meditate upon the irrelevant . . ."

Ioli started to smile, then said, "If we think about something else. Gleaning is an edge-of-the-eye talent. The front of the eye is a callused spot, the edge is where gleaning happens. Peripheral vision is the most intense."

Mauzl's hand crept toward the toy, then paused. If he left it still long enough Rekke might forget it was there, and it could creep a little closer. His expression dared Rekke to see.

Rekke said, "A star is brighter if you don't look straight at it. Mauzl's hand is two fingers from disaster, but then I can look at two things at once."

Mauzl's hand stayed where it was. His eyes stayed on Rekke.

"We were sitting in a row, leaning on the bed, in Sauglin," Ioli said. "We could see each other from the sides."

"We've become a shell game, have we?" Rekke said. "I wasn't in the center in the cornfield. It was the runtling. Who will lose a limb if he touches that contraption."

Mauzl's hand slid infinitesimally back from the toy.

"We weren't in a row in the cellar, although we didn't go anywhere then. But the glow was strong."

"And I was ready to upchuck."

"That went away."

"Yes. Now it's only when I try to get shut of the two of you. Like a man who gets sick the first time he gets drunk, and then becomes a drunkard and gets sick if he stops drinking."

"You're stuck with us. Stop griping. Concentrate."

"That's what you said in Sauglin. 'Concentrate, think about the common room, bring us down there.' It worked so well."

Ioli murmured, "Knowing isn't pushing your mind against things . . ."

Mauzl touched the toy, and Rekke snatched it up and held it high enough to smash even on carpets, and Mauzl squealed, and Ioli cried, "No! Rekke, no, put it down! That's *it*!"

"Nine times nine nonned pieces," Rekke threatened.

"Put it *down*. That's it. The toy. All the sparkly things and whirligigs, the spinning pictures that blurred into moving shapes . . . the way they knew things . . . it wasn't just to calm themselves, it wasn't just a sedative . . ."

"You're babbling."

"I'm a visant." Ioli got the bonewood box away from Rekke. It took both his hands, and two tugs. "This toy," he said. "It's mesmerizing. So was that top he had. Mauzl's been trying to tell us." He pulled one ball away from the others and let it go. It knocked the middle ones. The end ball swung out and back and knocked them from the other side. The first ball swung out. It knocked into the other ones. Left, right, left, right . . . The movement was like a rocking cradle, but faster, and focused on stillness. No swaying, no vertigo. Balanced.

He stopped it, then tried two beads at once. The center ball never moved. Three balls were always stationary while two swung together through their arc.

The objects at the edges moved. The center remained still.

The motion and the muted, rhythmic sound were hypnotic.

Rekke rolled onto his back, covered his ears with his hands, and thrashed his feet in the air, wriggling and moaning piteously.

Mauzl laughed in pure delight. "That's a good toy," he said.

"Because it galls me," Rekke growled, sprawling flat. "Wretch."

"It's a tool," Ioli said. "As much as a mage's quill or a touch's hand."

"All right," Rekke said with caution, rolling upright and sitting cross-legged. "Now someone tells me why."

"Because it occupies the front of the eye and the front of the mind. Because it's stillness in the center of motion. Because it keeps going, it doesn't wind down, at least not right away; we don't have to spin it or crank it or twirl it. Because . . . it makes you calm. It gives you a calm, still center."

"It makes me insane."

"You're already insane. You have to find a part of you that can settle down and appreciate it. Someone in there must be able to do that."

Grumbling, Rekke came over and sat between Ioli and Mauzl to have a look at the maddening toy. He felt the part of him that watched but could never control. That part of him was the middle bead, the spindle of the spinning top. He knew that. He endured the irritation of the clacking until it faded into a background rhythm, like the beat of his heart, the rise and fall of his breath. He let his left eye go, stopped forcing it to focus on the blasted toy when it wanted to be roving. Beyond the liquid fall of smaller beads that screened the entry to the next chamber, he saw—

"No!" he said, scrambling back. "No. It's too dangerous!"

Ioli gripped one ankle, Mauzl the other.

Oopses and ouches, Mauzl thought sadly. *Crumble and cliff-drop.* The lankbones was afraid. Mauzl was almost always afraid. He knew how the lankbones felt. But the paths were there, open or not. You couldn't avoid them by scooching away. They didn't stop when you closed your eyes. You couldn't hide from the paths.

"You're the sanest one of us, Ioli," Rekke said. "You can't ask me to take you through there."

"You're the strongest," Ioli said. "You're the only one who can. We know we can realmwalk, because we did it. We only have to do it on purpose now. Then we can find out what else we can do."

"We have only to live through it," Rekke said. "We could die. We could be lost forever."

"Tell him, Mauzl," Ioli said. "Tell him that there are paths where we stray and paths where we fall but there are no paths where we don't realmwalk again. Tell him it's inevitable."

"It's not," Mauzl said, lowering his head to let his hair fall down around his face. It made a ripply screen, like the strings of beads in the doorway. It made the world into countless little slivers of itself. If he shook his head, it shimmered. That was pretty. When Rekke moved, all the slices of Rekke moved in fascinating unison.

Rekke put himself in front of the clacking bead box. "My choice, then," he said. "No fixed future to go fill. No fate, no prophecy to tell me what to do." *No Jhoss. Only me. It was only ever me.*

Ioli sat to Rekke's right. He let the rhythmic sound and motion draw his attention. His gaze fell naturally on the bonewood box. To look away would be an effort. To rest his eyes there was the easy thing. He was aware of Rekke beside him, a dark-skinned, white-eyed mass of doubt and strength and fear and courage, an aggregate of unpredictable moods. Rekke sat up straight, but the tension drained from him on a profound sigh. He sank into his spine, his tail, the grasslands earth beneath the layers of carpet and groundcloth. The slate of his glow slid on quicksilver, took on indigo shadows, a tinge of darklight. Ioli sank into that glow as into fathomless liquid. Rekke could feel his glow, and Mauzl's. His was bright blue, to Rekke, dawn-bright, sky-bright; that was a revelation. Mauzl's was a blue so dark it was almost purple.

The walls dissolved. Their glow filled boundless space with an aqueous twilight. Shimmering strands sifted down, sinuous and sedate, a long slow fall of silver. The glow was buoyant, soothing. They floated gently free of matter's moorings. It was easy; much easier than hanging on. They were a bubble, drifting. Rekke maintained the cohesion of the bubble while Ioli and Mauzl filled it. It was an eye, lensing. Rekke focused the eye, and drew the surface inward, and turned the bubble inside out. Contraction and then expansion of the infinitely malleable, vitreous glow. He brought them back into their flesh, and they were sitting in wind-stroked grasses, by a strand of silver river.

"You did it," Ioli breathed. He crawled toward the river and retched. Near death the first time, half asleep the second, he hadn't fully felt their transit. This time he had. His body convulsed, then went clammy with shock. *We did it,* he thought, triumphant, ill, panting on all fours by the rush of water.

Rekke cast his eyes in different directions. "Two leagues from the runtling's band. Not bad. Not bad. Better than a trip downstairs to a common room." Abruptly he was too jubilant to contain himself. He leaped to his feet, crowed at the sky, punched his arms into the air. *Mine,* came the fierce thought. *All realms are mine. I am their master now.* Then he giggled, clapped his hands like a child, and drummed his feet on the hard Girdle ground. *Mine, mine to travel as I will, mine to travel at a whim.* "Where next?" he said. "The Hand? The Fist? The lands-beyond? Anywhere you like, Ioli. Anywhere!"

Ioli had heard that sort of promise from him before. He pulled himself together. Two leagues from Mauzl's home could be anywhere. All these grasslands looked alike. He stayed on his knees, afraid he'd fall if he tried to stand. "Back," he said. "Let's make sure we can get back, before we try anything else." His shins made long wakes through the grass as he kneed his way back to Rekke.

Rekke sank cross-legged in front of the bonewood box, parting the grass so they could see it. The focus had made the transit with them, but the journey had stilled its motion. Rekke laughed as he set it going again. And to think he was going to smash this. *The runtling will find something else to get my goat.*

Mauzl was still in his place. Mauzl still kept still. No moving till they'd come safe again through seadepth and skywide. No jostling, or they might fly loose. One time safe, maybe, even two, but this last made three, unless he'd forgotten. It was possible he'd forgotten. He never knew how much he forgot until he remembered, or the past-paths opened and showed him, and then it was gone again, and no knowing it had been. But he was bigger in the big glow, he could hold more. Four was where the lankbones might step wrong. Three made you believe. Four was what tricked you. Mauzl kept very still.

Through the rhythmic motion-and-stillness they entered the aqueous, boundless sphere again, and swam, or floated, or flew, or drifted; Rekke collapsed the sphere, sucking it into its own center, which was them; sent it through them and back out; then released it to fill the hut's interior, and restored their flesh to them. Seated in the brazier-scented, carpet-buffered warmth of the outer chamber of Mauzl's family's hut.

"I got out of the shed, Jhoss," he whispered, then stilled his voice. The moment of return—so much like the moments between sleep and waking or waking and sleep, an unguarded crevice truths might slip through. He said the rest in his mind: *It took more than a dozen years, and I had to be led to it like a bull hooked through a nose ring, but by all the grieving spirits, I got out.*

Ioli patted himself down. He patted the carpets. He poked the beaded pillows, the tasseled throws. He sniffed the aromatic fruitwood among the coals, smoothed his hand down the silk-hung walls. *We're back.* They had not deformed the world. They had not lost themselves. Only now could he admit the wonder of it. No accident. No act of desperation. No other-worldly power looking out for them, moving them, saving them. They had done it. The three of them. Combined their glows, and walked through walls. Transported through impossibility; or warping the realms around them, until the center, which was them, was somewhere else. He didn't know. He didn't care. He wasn't a mender or a seeker. He didn't need to know. It worked. They had done it. They could do it again.

They could do more.

"This calls for a spectacular act of inebriation," Rekke announced, unfolding his long frame for a luxurious stretch. "How much of that spiced wine do you suppose I can put away before I wear out the runtling's welcome?"

"No," Ioli said, staring at the bonewood box.

"I warn you, I'm a madman when I'm in my cups, but I'm a madman anyway, who'll know the difference? The first visant triad. Balls, that's a mages' word, we'll have to petition the scholars for a better one. Three visants, doing the impossible. If that isn't cause for celebration, I don't know what is."

"No," Ioli said again, and Mauzl said, "Ioli now."

"Ioli what? What are you on about, you stinking woolheads? Mauzl, where can I get a jug of wine in this forsaken huddle of huts?"

"You can't," Ioli said. "Not yet. We've only just started."

Rekke threw up his hands. "We just did, at will, what can't be done! What else do you want? We've been at this for three days. We did it. We're done. We rest now. The sun will set in less than two hours. When's supper, anyway—nightfall, or before? I plan to have a nice head on before I fill my belly, half a jug of wine and I'll be chewing those blinding peppercorns like candied . . ." He fell silent under the rhythmic clack of bonewood beads.

Ioli lined the box up with the pattern in the carpet. It had come back slightly askew. He didn't know what that meant.

"Ioli's turn," Mauzl said.

"When you lead," Ioli said, gazing at the swinging beads as if gazing deep into a fire's embers, "we walk through realms. What will we do if I lead?"

The question had crossed Rekke's mind. He didn't want to know. Not today. Not before he'd savored vindication to the fullest—warmed his tongue with spiced stew and his belly with spiced wine and his bed with a grasslands girl.

"Save the world," Mauzl said. It answered both Rekke and Ioli.

Save the world, Ioli thought. A better way than mages isolating Eiden Myr forever, or mages casting destruction upon the outerlands, or the three of them returning to Jhoss to be combined with mages and touches into some kind of white light. Immunity for every mind in Eiden Myr. A visant's immunity to delusion.

"Save the world tomorrow," Rekke said. "Tonight we celebrate."

"We'll celebrate when we've done our job," Ioli said. "Sit down, Rekke."

They argued. They always argued. Mauzl hid inside knees and elbows until it was done. The only thing about them that agreed was their glow, and that was in spite of every effort to break apart. Even when Ioli was weak, even when Mauzl couldn't remember, they ran up hard against each other's wants and fears. But in the end Rekke always did what Ioli wanted. He didn't know what he'd do without a none's-land to shield the visants from, but he'd think of something. The only way to be spared Ioli's nagging demands was to complete his task.

Ioli sat in the middle. He let the rhythmic motion still his mind. He occupied the front of his eye so the edges could expand. Their glow filled the space, became its own space. A portal to anywhere. A portal to minds? He couldn't find the minds. He couldn't see beyond the glow. How did Rekke do it? He saw beyond the veils of realms. Veils like the silk draping the walls of the hut. Ioli saw beyond the veils of mind. But only when he was looking at people. He couldn't look at everyone in the world at once.

He shook out of it. He stilled the beads with a fingertip. "I can't."

"Just look," Rekke said. "Use your sight. This is what it's for."

"How do you see between the realms when you can only be in one place at a time? I can't see the minds unless the bodies are in front of me."

"I don't know. I just do it. You can do it too."

"I don't know what I'm doing."

"I think you're a lost jungle boy with no idea what he's about." Ioli remembered those words. Rekke remembered them, too. He'd said them in irritation, in fear, rejecting the blending he could not resist.

"You have to go home," Rekke said.

Rice plants can't root in sand. He'd climbed into a twisted marsh tree to make the world look more like home. So that he could *see.* Among alien apple trees he'd learned that he could learn. He could adapt, slowly, to alien landscapes, soak them in, make them part of him so he could function. But it would take all his powers to do what he'd set out to do. It might be possible only in the place where his powers developed.

Home. Jalairi.

Abruptly he couldn't bear the thought of going back there.

"Maybe we need to be closer to the center," he said. "The middle of the Midlands. We're too far south. I won't be able to reach them all from here."

"You can't reach even one."

"We'll try again. I'm getting used to this hut, to the grasslands."

Rekke sighed. If he deferred to that reasoning, Ioli might find his way clear in a few days, as he settled into this environment. Rekke could have his glorious three-day binge. He wanted that. He was tired, and triumphant. He'd earned that. But the monkey had convinced him that they couldn't wait. He'd agreed; he'd committed; he wouldn't back off from it now. No one knew when the shield would fail. It might hold for another three years or another three days or another three hours. Only one section of shoreline need fall, with no one left to fill the gap, for all the world to fall. Rekke didn't care about the world, not the way Ioli did; he didn't have the monkey's idealism, he was older, jaded. But he liked his comforts. He liked his adventures. He'd liked the world the way it was before the siege. And though he did his saving one by one, visant by abused, misunderstood visant, he could see the logic of extending the saving to all. Night was coming. None's-land was worse at night. If Ioli was going to do this, he had to do it before it was too late. Because they didn't know how late would be too late, they had to do it now.

"You need to go back to your swamps," Rekke said. "I can take you. They have tasty ferments there. That's worth the trip."

"You've never been to Curl."

"I've been to Stub, and Wiggle. It doesn't matter. I don't need to have been there to go there. I'll take you home to Curl."

Thick, humid, perfumed air. The embrace of spiritwoods, the nod of palms. Moted shafts of golden sunlight through rich, vine-draped darkness. A sharp, sweet pain went through Ioli's heart at the thought of home. But how would he face Jalairi? He'd abandoned her. He'd changed. She might have changed too. She might not want to know him.

He wouldn't have to see her. Rekke couldn't put them right

in his village. Just somewhere in the Toes. Somewhere in Curl, a place he knew as he knew his own breath, his own skin.

"All right," he said. "Take me home."

They thanked Mauzl's folk for the shelter and the privacy, and accepted food and a change of clothes—Rekke even got a watertight, magewarded linen bladder of their best spiced wine to hang on his pack. Mauzl endured hugs and farewells. Their horses had been sent back Headward with passing runners; Girdlefolk would not keep stolen mounts. The lumbering animals would have been no use in the jungle anyway. The harvestmid sun was sinking toward the horizon when they hiked out of sight onto the plains; it bathed the grasslands in dusty gold. They flattened a spot for themselves in a curve of river, and sat, and filled the world with their blue glow, and floated into it.

Ioli tried to watch what Rekke was doing. Tried to glean him, as they made their transit. To see through both his eyes, understand how he turned his gleaning of all realms into specific transit to a chosen place. He could not. Whatever Rekke did was instinct so deeply embedded, or power so integrally part of him, that it went past Ioli's ability to glean. Glow was self; Rekke was Rekke, and he was Ioli, and they could only join, never merge.

He could not see what Rekke was doing, only support it. That was why he didn't see when Rekke misstepped.

Rekke felt it the moment it happened, but there was nothing he could do to stop it. In the same moment, he felt Mauzl's glow retract, as he clutched tight to himself, reflexively; and he felt Ioli lunge to catch him, just as reflexively, with a memory of other falls, long falls through trees, the swish of leaves, the thwack and crunch of branches. This was not a kind of fall Ioli knew how to stop. This was not a kind of fall Rekke knew how to roll through.

He flailed loose into emptiness. Realms gaped like chasms, one within the next, no end on them. Layers of realms, coexisting, space within space, space without end. This was no tail-eye glimpse of alien landscape, such as his left eye often saw between a fire's flames, between blades of grass, beyond the shadows of a close room. Other realms impinged on the ordinary world at every turn, unperceived by all save those like him. A hint here, a glimpse there, always in the interstices, the cracks, the betweens. Now he saw them all. Now they yawned before him, each visible through the others, one behind the next behind the next. No limit to them. No stopping them.

He saw realms full of bonefolk. Realms of earth, realms of air, realms of water. Skies of amethyst over hills of coal and trees of gold. Forests of impossible trees, melding and changing, turning back upon themselves, groves that were as close to each other as thought and as far as forever. Sea-deep realms of crystal caverns, coral grottoes; airy realms with no up or down to them at all, just mists and clouds and colors he could not have named, and moorless structures fragile as belief, downy as seeds drifting on the wind, gossamer as spidersilk. Realms that incarnated the essence of air, of water, of earth. Some of the bonefolk saw him, and jittered: *Do not come here.* Beyond their realms, a realm he'd fallen through or into once before, drawn on a piece of sedgeweave in a trance—pale turrets, cerulean hills, fluted towers wreathed in spectral sheen, vibrant and as dry as dust. The realms surrounded him; he was in them all, and yet in none; he was the center, but he was the crack in the wood, the niche between the floorboards, the wrongness in the air. Realms spun into infinity; of the ones he could comprehend he perceived only monstrosity, abomination— sere wastelands, twisted ruins, the aftermath of apocalypse. Were those the outerlands? *We must not go there.*

He writhed; he torqued himself; the luminous blue glow within the bloom of realms twisted with him; he must kick them clear of this, claw his way back to familiar planes. Curl. The Toes. He knew them; he had delved them; he had delved all Eiden Myr, he knew its heights and depths, its roots, its trunk, its limbs; he could feel his way into its parts the way he could feel his own hand or foot, simply by allowing it to come into awareness. But he was twisting, torquing, falling. He could not find the way. He could not find anything he knew.

Mauzl was a shrill whine swelling toward a shriek. Shamblings and stick-things, spines and shadows, bad, this was a bad path, and there was no fleeing or hiding, the lankbones had lost his footing and all was crumble and cliffdrop. Ioli was a despairing moan, a vibration like sound that wasn't sound at all; they were falling, life was falling, falling through the present into the future, falling through existence with nothing to grab on to but yourself.

Rekke seized upon their flesh to stop the fall. Rekke delved their bodies, and put them back inside.

They sprawled in deepest gloom. Mauzl groped for the bonewood box and couldn't find it. What they felt under hands and knees as they pushed themselves standing was not soil, or metal, or wood, or anything of earth; it gave under their weight, and held their weight, yet did not seem to be there at all.

It had substance enough for friction. The air had substance enough to carry sound. They heard the dragging, limping steps of something coming toward them. Something that clicked and rustled, something that barely held together. Something with fetid breath, the stink of carrion, decay and death and what came after death, the desiccated emptiness of void.

This was no void. This was a cesspool. What had seemed at first to be vacant obscurity was filled with . . . things. Shreds and tatters, spines and billows, viscous ooze. The air dripped a noxious black oil. The stink was choking. Guilts and terrors, unspoken words, dark impulses, crushing remorse; grief, horror, desolation. It all collected here, the dregs and leavings of hearts and minds, the detritus of broken dreams.

The thing bore down on them. No bonewood box to center on, no clacking motion-in-stillness, only the clacking of the horror that approached out of the gloom, a miserable, hulking snarl of hatred and missed chances, agony and bitter failure, dried to a husk, a click and rustle of senseless malevolence.

Stay behind me, Rekke tried to say, but there was no speaking in this place, this was a realm past speech, past articulate thought.

Before Ioli could reach for Mauzl, he felt himself engulfed

by something huge, something chill and greased and oozing, it was webbed with pulsing veins of anguish. Surrender. Despair. The abysmal rejection of hope and life.

He fought it with all his heart and all his will.

For Mauzl there was no hiding. Rekke was lanced and stick-torn, all tearing and pounding, no getting close. Ioli was gone into bleakness, just thrashing glow within black ooze, no reaching. Nothing came for Mauzl. Nothing wanted Mauzl. He stood alone, exposed to gloom and dark and whispers. No one to shield, no one to hide behind, nowhere to go.

No one—that's who was coming. No one. No one at all.

Rekke roared, and rended the stick-thing. He broke it, smashed it, dismembered it. There was always more. No matter how much he crushed and ripped apart there was more of it behind, more to shred him, stab him, break him. He could fight it forever and never win. He might fight it forever; this might be his sorry end, eternity locked in battle with the sum of all vicious hatreds and the rage of all miserable failures. He felt scraps of himself inside the thing, deep in the spiked and writhing thickets of it. His own grand expectations and grander errors. But he'd *won,* he'd walked the realms, he'd proved it could be done. Yet it brought them to this. Eternal failure. The one spectacular misstep.

He would not let it have the others. He might fight for a nonned years, a nonned times a nonned, forever; but at some point the others would find their way free. The monkey was smart. The monkey could climb. The monkey would figure the way out of here, for himself and his pet runt.

All Rekke had to do was fight the monster off until they'd fled.

He focused all his will on its destruction. All he'd ever wanted was something to thrash, something that could put up a decent fight. Now he had it. He had the fight of all fights, the thrashing of all thrashings. He tore into the relentless assemblage with a raging madness for all time, his layers fused into one act of will: to hurt the hurting thing, and save the others.

He tore into the center of it, and found his own.

Mauzl found his, a lonely center that was only Mauzl, and could be enough if it had to be, could stand alone if there was nowhere to hide—could stand alone even if there was.

Ioli found his, a burning kernel of will at the heart of him, a fierce refusal to surrender to despair.

Their blended glow surged, aided by inattention. Focus on survival was stronger than focus on an object. Strong enough to crack the shackles of this realm. Consumed by will, they left their powers free to complete the gleaning Rekke had begun. They were subsumed by indigo darklight, dawn-bright sky, bluestone slate, by the colors of water and air and stone, and came through and out into nightfall in the swamps, frog twang and treechatter, a swoop of bright feathers, a golden flash of fur, the weep of vines.

"Merciful Morlyrien." Ioli sobbed to feel home coalesce around him.

He was covered in something putrid and black. Rekke was torn and bleeding, scored with punctures and gashes, his clothes in shreds; one arm dangled, broken. What had attacked them had been real. Where they had been was a real place. Only Mauzl stood unscathed, but he stood alone, no cowering, no scramble to hide behind Rekke's bulk or Ioli's sanity. His hands were empty; the bonewood box was lost somewhere between the realms. They probably wouldn't need it again. Anything could be a focus. Anything that drew the eye. Anything that absorbed the front of the mind. A butterfly's wing, or the fight to survive.

"Your village," Rekke said, through split lips. "It's—"

"I know where it is," Ioli said. "I know where I am now."

He didn't want to go there. He didn't want to face Jalairi—not like this. Not until he'd done something to make her proud of him, and forgive him.

Rekke's injuries required a healer. There were touches in Edva-Gani-Teka, the string of treehomes where Jalairi lived. There was a healer in Anju-Rinka-Lais, the next string Heartward, but he was not a touch. Still, he might do; he could set broken bones and suture torn flesh. But Anju was a long way, with sinks to swing over and climbing to do, a journey more through trees than along the ground. There were walkways between here and Teka; a stilt-raised bridge crossed the sucking fen. Rekke could make it to Teka.

"You're practically in none's-land here," Rekke said, a teeth-gritted slur, as they walked. Trying to keep his mind off the pain. "What possessed Fyldur to drag you all the way to Maur Sleith?"

"He claimed the coast here had enough visants," Ioli said, straining under Rekke's weight. Rekke was leaking blood, and would only get weaker. Mauzl lugged Rekke's pack, which was the heaviest of all yet somehow had not come off him in the fighting; Ioli's pack was gone, swallowed. Rekke carried only the wine, hung around his neck; at intervals Ioli would reach over and squeeze some into his mouth. "He said they needed us up the coast. He said . . ." Ioli shifted Rekke's arm so that it wasn't pinching his spine. "It doesn't matter what he said. It was only his greased truths. He dragged us to Maur Sleith to destroy us."

"Taking you off your home turf made a good start."

"I'm back now. We'll get you fixed up, and then we'll do what we came here to do, and then . . ." He didn't know. What sort of life would they have, after this? Where would they go?

Well, if their fall into the dark place had taught him anything, it was to take life as it came to him, and stiff-arm doubt away before it consumed him.

Night lay thick on the shrieking swamps when he saw the hanging fires of Teka—pitch torches hung on chains in iron baskets. Each basket lit a rope ladder. Life was lived overhead, and only work was done below. Dredging the silty rivers for metals, cutting the forest to burn for charcoal, collecting herbs and edibles. Export was the chief trade of the Toes. Things that grew here grew nowhere else on Eiden's body. There was little husbandry, for those things grew in abundance on their own. The jungle provided necessities; the rest they took in trade.

Self-sufficiency was a kind of exile, Ioli mused, his profound relief to be in familiar environs offset by the estrangement of absence.

A city of monkeys, Rekke thought, looking up at the rope-ways, the suggestion of dwellings built ingeniously into the trees. *It'll be a job climbing those floppy ladders with one arm.*

The jungle announced them before they came into the flickering torchlight; even Rekke and Mauzl could hear it, every screech and squawk crying *strangers, strangers, strangers.* They could feel the eyes on them from up in the trees.

Instead of anyone corning down a ladder, or any human voice greeting or accosting them from above, Fyldur Greasehair sauntered into view, his arm around the shoulders of a slim girl a bit younger than Mauzl. A pretty girl with ash gray skin and brimming inkdrop eyes and a mist of soft white hair to her shoulders. A girl the very likeness of Ioli.

"Jalairi," Ioli said, too shocked to summon any other words.

She jerked forward as though to embrace him; the Greasehair held her firm. "What's that he's covered in?" Fyldur said. "He's stained inside and out."

"So are you," she spat bitterly, but she didn't free herself. Her face bore the tormented sadness of someone gazing on a loved one who had done a thing beyond forgiveness.

"Jalairi," Ioli said again, in a misery to find her in the Greasehair's clutches. Then he lifted his head and called to the trees, "We need a touch. Is Caerle here, or Trebor?" When no response came, he said, "My friend is hurt. There's no stain on him. It won't harm you to help him."

As if to prove it, Rekke went abruptly boneless, sinking onto the leaf-spongy path. It wasn't a ruse. He tried to get up, tried to sharpen a remark to cast at Fyldur, but he'd lost too much blood.

Ioli and Mauzl maneuvered him to the base of a spiritwood tree. Ioli tore blankets from Rekke's pack. Even in warm Souther swamps, trees and ground would leach the warmth from human flesh at night. "Caerle!" he called. "Trebor!

Please! He isn't stained. We'll go if you like, Mauzl and I, but please come down and heal Rekke. He's done nothing but protect people all his life. He got these wounds defending us. It's your calling to heal the injured. Please!"

"They won't come down," Fyldur drawled. Stepping closer; drawing Jalairi closer. He knew her nearness would torment Ioli. "I've warned them about you. What I saw in Denglin. Your dark power to appear and disappear."

Fyldur didn't even have to lie to cast aspersions. He had only to fling truths out at the wrong angle. He'd come here straight from Denglin. Made a beeline for Ioli's home, on a hunch that sooner or later he would come back. He could have been here for as much as a nineday, maybe more. Insinuating his oiled truths into the minds of Ioli's neighbors.

"If we have a power like that, why don't we just wink out and go someplace where healers do their job?" Ioli asked bitterly.

"Because it's Rekke's power, and he's ripped to shreds for his pains," Fyldur replied without effort. "He won't be taking you anywhere."

He'd have an answer for everything, and every answer would be the truth, unanswerable.

"Gleaning now," he heard Mauzl murmur from behind him, holding up Rekke, who would topple without support. Ioli didn't know what Mauzl meant. "Jalairi," he said again. *I'm sorry I fled, I'm sorry I left you, let me explain, please don't listen to this man, please, I'm your brother, I'm Ioli, the one you love.* He couldn't choke out a single word; was his face speaking for him? She hadn't a glimmer of bluesilver glow, but she'd known him all her life. . . .

He looked away before he could glean her.

That was why I ran, he realized, as though gleaning his own heart. *That was the truth behind my exile. I was afraid to look too deep into Jalairi.*

How could he ever think he would see anything in Jalairi that would compromise his love for her? He'd love her if she were stained. He'd love her if she were damaged. He'd love her if she hated him.

He looked straight into her face. She was frightened. She'd humored this odious, oily man because he'd teased her with news of Ioli. She'd endured his allegations, even let him think he was swaying her, because she knew that it was safer to keep him among them until they sorted this out. He hated her brother. That was clear enough. Left to lurk in the swamps, he might do Ioli harm if he came home. And he might know where to find him. If she played along convincingly enough, it might come out. If she listened very carefully to his version of the truth, she might find contradictions, and deduce from them a more accurate truth—a truth that would enable her to track Ioli down.

You're only nine-and-seven, Ioli wanted to say. *What did you think you were going to do, go roaming the besieged, stained world to find me?*

She was called to be a seeker. Jalairi had always questioned. Jalairi had always reached for higher branches than she should. She was discovering her own way, a seeker way, and had been now for a year or two, and he hadn't seen it because he'd tried so hard not to glean her. In his mind he had some vision of her, some construct that was not who she was turning out to be. The little girl he had to save from a fall. The little girl he had to keep safe. In her turn, she'd tried to conceal it from him, knowing that his overprotective heart would balk at her taking up a seeker's nomadic, inquisitive, contentious life. Knowing that he wanted her to stay safe and known and understood in a world that made sense to him—the sane child, the normal child, the one who wasn't cursed with visant sight. The child who would make up for him.

The safe, predictable sister he wanted always to be able to come home to, even if he never came home again.

Jalairi, I have wronged you. But I see now. Oh, I see. . . .

Her keen, dark, lightless seeker's eyes saw him see, and glowed with their own light.

"Caerle, will you come down?" she said. "You left it to me, and I've decided. They're all right. It's the procurer who's got to go."

The touch Caerle slid down a rope and started toward Rekke.

Fyldur started toward him too—and took Mauzl by the throat, and backed half into shadow. A knife came out of a side sheath, far too curved and wicked for a use knife. "Heal that one and I'll cut this one's throat."

Folk dropped like a flight of spiders, from treehomes, from ropewalks, from ladders where they'd clung to watch. The understory filled with treefolk. All the good folk of Teka, and some from Gani and even from Edva, more coming behind them as word spread along the vines that one of their own needed aid. But all the folk in all the Toes could not have wrested Mauzl from that oily grip before the blade swept through his throat.

Rekke groaned horribly, trying to rise. For the first time in his life, his strength and muscular virility failed him. He drew upon their glow, trying to walk himself through the tree at Fyldur's back to break his neck, walk himself *through* Fyldur. Realmwalk his big body right inside the Greasehair's and destroy him from within. He only swayed to the side, barely able to catch himself on his good arm. He could not even roar out his rage and impotence.

Fyldur laughed at orders to unhand the boy. Fyldur was already stained; what difference would killing make? No one could tell the difference between the stain of death and the stain of exile. How could they see the stain at all, unless they were stained themselves?

"I'd have made a procurer of you," the Greasehair said to Ioli. "That was all I asked of you. To tell me how they suffer. You denied me. This is on your hands. Rekke n'Gerst will bleed to death, and I will enjoy every slow breath of it. What a fool, to have a gift like his, and squander it. He was everything Jhoss wanted, everything I couldn't be, and he ran away. After that it was always what Rekke would have done, what Rekke could have done if he had stayed. Jhoss n'Kall rejected me because I wasn't Rekke. Well, there's his Rekke, bleeding out into swamp muck and nothing anyone can do. No saving the savior. You're going to watch him die, Ioli, and this one who sees the future, he'll watch him die nine times a nonned times while it comes to pass. And maybe you'll kill me, or maybe you won't—but it won't matter anymore, because I'll have rid the world of you and your 'triad.' I'll die happy, knowing that."

Every stinking word the truth, and none of it stanching the blood that stained the spiritwood roots, and none of it halting the cut of that curved blade. *That's a binder's blade,* Ioli realized, irrelevantly, insanely. *That's a blade that mages used to use to cut off their lambs' skins.* In his horror, he could not tear his eyes away from the torchlit glimmer of that blade.

Bluesilver glow expanded to flood the space like water. Their useless glow, surging as Rekke died, surging as Mauzl's death flashed over and over before his visant's eye. He was still, so still in the Greasehair's grip, all holdbreath and limplimb and stillness. No jostling, no cutting . . .

"Gleaning now," Mauzl's voice echoed in Ioli's head.

Ioli could glean them all. He could see them all, encompassed in the aqueous bluesilver glow, which made an undersea realm of the liana-draped jungle. The folk of his home—they'd never have turned on him, never have used Jalairi to get at him. Why hadn't he just gleaned them and found that out? Because he feared to discover things he did not want to know. He feared to justify their fears. It was his fear that drove him out, not theirs. He gleaned all that, all at once. On a reflexive, remorseful, heartbroken surge he showed them, through the bluesilver glow, how sorry he was that it had come to this, and how much affection and respect he bore them. It was only the truth. It wasn't hard. It was the easiest thing in the world, to show them that. He had only to open himself a little, through the glow, and it all went out to them.

That's it, Rekke thought, receiving the apology with the rest, receiving the flood of comprehension. *That's it, monkey. You've done it. Now do the rest of them, before I die and it's too late.*

He couldn't send the concept through to Ioli. Ioli seemed unable to grasp it on his own. He wasn't yet ready to see what he had just done. He was fixated on that rippling silver blade, the curve of that honed edge. He wasn't gleaning Rekke, wasn't looking at him. He wouldn't even look at Mauzl. Only at the blade.

The paths opened around Mauzl. Bad paths. Sad paths. Sometimes he died and sometimes Rekke died and sometimes both of them died, and in every one of those paths the world died shieldfailed and mindkilled, and there wasn't but one where no one died, there wasn't but one hairthin needlesharp thread of no-death path, and that one forked . . . that forked . . .

The blade bit deep, and Mauzl's mind went white with panic, and lost the paths.

Ioli, in his fixated horror of that blade, delved Fyldur's mind.

He went straight in. Carved through skull and tissue like a binder's blade through fruit. Took the pulp in his hand. Kneaded it. Worked the barbs from it, picked out the spiny thorns, and then, although he'd rather fling it at his feet and leave it there to rot . . . put it back. Whole, and spineless.

Fyldur's blade arm went limp. Mauzl darted away, quick as a mouse. The touch flung herself down beside Rekke. Fyldur said, "What in all the weeping spirits was I doing?," and dropped the knife into the jungle loam.

Ioli stared at Mauzl. Mauzl stared back.

"What have I done?" Ioli breathed.

"It was the only almost mostly good path," Mauzl breathed back.

The treefolk seized Fyldur and would have borne him off into the jungle to meet whatever fate the spiritwoods decreed, but Ioli begged them not to, and when Jalairi added her voice to his they grudgingly relented.

"Take care of him," Ioli said. "I've done a terrible thing. I don't know how long it will last. You'll have to watch him, if he stays. Or let him go, let him make his own way. But don't cast him out into the jungle at night."

"I don't understand," Fyldur said, frowning. "Why was I . . . ?"

"It's all right," said Ioli, sick and miserable. "Go away. Go to sleep."

He felt no sympathy for Fyldur. Only horror. "I mustn't ever do that again," he breathed.

"Save a life?" Jalairi said. "Stop a madman? Come home?"

She slid into his embrace, and he inhaled the clean aroma of her pale hair, cherished the familiar weight of her in his arms. *I don't deserve you.*

"I twisted a human mind," he said.

"It looked to me like you untwisted it," Jalairi said, and drew back. "You've grown up while you were away. Don't ever run away like that again."

"You're the one who's going to leave," he said. *It makes me afraid for you, but I wouldn't stop you even if I could.*

"I'm not old enough yet," she declared. "Anyway, there's still too much I want to know about the jungle. And now I want to know all about you."

Rekke was standing solidly now. In the exuberant flush of restored health, or in payment for the healing, he swept the touch Caerle into a passionate kiss, from which she emerged bemused and pleased and famished for food.

"You did it," Rekke said to Ioli. "I don't know why we can't discover these things sitting safe and warm in a hut somewhere, but I'll take it. I could do with a meal and a drop of palmheart wine, but let's finish this."

"I can't," Ioli said.

Rekke made a ludicrous face. "Of course you can. You just did. You—"

"I know what I did. I can't risk it again."

"No saving?" said Mauzl.

Ioli said, "No saving."

Rekke exploded. Cursed him, cursed the jungle, cursed all bleeding rotting puking scabbing walleyes. Ioli endured the tirade in silence. He watched the touch run hands over Fyldur, feeling for damage, and did not respond when she told him that Fyldur was fine, he'd recovered his wits, all the malice was gone from him. Ioli knew that. He'd gleaned the thorns in Fyldur's mind and removed them. He might heal madness itself, Caerle said—no mages, no touches could do that. He might smooth the pain and confusion from the most tormented minds.

Ioli listened, and felt the pulp of Fyldur's mind in his mind's hands, and said, "No one, *no one* should have power like that over another person."

"I have power over you," Caerle said. She cupped his cheek in her hand, and felt his jaw clench under it, and didn't pull back. "I could kill you now. I could rupture vital organs, stop your heart, tear your lungs open to fill with fluid. I could scramble your brains, Ioli. With this tender hand on your face."

"It's not the same," he said. "It would kill you to do that."

"Nonetheless, I can do it, and if it were worth it to me to give my life to end yours, you couldn't stop me."

"I could," he said. It hurt so much he couldn't even feel it. He couldn't feel anything. "I could stop you from wanting to do it, and you'd never know you ever had. I could see the urge on you before you ever touched me, and stop it." He raised his gaze. "I could make you want to kill me even if you didn't."

Her hand drew back. Tears flirted at the corners of her pale eyes. It was an awful thing, to learn you had that kind of power. She had wrestled with it since she was six years old. "I'm so sorry, Ioli."

"Stop coddling him." Rekke hauled Ioli up by the scruff of the neck. "Why don't I put my fist through your face? I feel like it, right now. Glean me. It's true. I'd like to thrash you to the far side of tomorrow. Why don't I? Have you stopped me? Have you untwisted the knots in my head?"

"No!" Ioli shouted. He shook free of Rekke's grip. "Because it's wrong! Because you have to learn to control yourself on your own!"

"Then learn that, Ioli. Learn it fast."

"I have learned that," Ioli said. He'd have to go back into the deep jungle. Tear himself from their glow again—that would be agony, but they would live through it. It was the only safe choice. The runners would convince the world of the delusions. They would convince the world, or it would fall. The world was responsible for itself. He couldn't go groping in its mind to force his beliefs on it. " 'Leave people's minds alone,' you said. That's what I'm going to do. They have to learn the truth for themselves."

Mauzl would not hold the paths open. He could now, and that was new. With the lankbones and the monkeylimbs near, he could keep them open once they were. But it was fool. It hurt his small scared Mauzl-mind, it hurt his small weak Mauzl-eyes. Too many ways, too many whiches, all which ways—too many. But he remembered. He remembered the paths he had seen, partway anyway, parts of paths, the nearer clearer paths. He remembered the needlethin threadsheer no-death path the monkeylimbs had found. Most of that was a past-path now, fixed tight. But he remembered the fork in it. He watched the monkeylimbs come to that fork.

It had only two tines.

The monkeylimbs went down the wrong one.

Was there another fork beyond it? A way back to the mostly good path? Another choice, another whichway, a better thisway?

Mauzl could not remember.

DABRENA N'ARILDE L'DESARDE read out the last words of the bedtime story and closed the borrowed teller's codex. Mounded to each side of her was a warm slumbering lump of six-year-old. Dobran had burrowed deep under the covers, only a spiky tuft of pale hair visible in the serene lamplight. Andri had the fleece tucked up to her nose, but she would push it off her later in the night, as though to free herself to move without constraint through the realm of dreams, then half wake and call that she was cold. If Dabrena or Adaon didn't hear and come tuck her back in, Dobran would snuggle her in close. If Dobran had one of his falling terrors, in the moments between sleep and waking, Andri would be there to soothe him—and even in her sleep she'd reach to keep him from rolling out of bed for real. They always woke facing each other.

Dabrena had the codex under her arm and was sliding out from between them when she sensed someone's regard. The corner of her eye caught a shape in the doorway. Adaon, returned without her hearing, looking fondly on her and the twins. But the shape was a wrongness. Too tall, too thin—a stranger in the doorway, staring. A deep startle shuddered through her, and she put herself between door and bed, hefting the heavy stonewood-bound codex.

A tall, pale girl. Just a prentice. Some idiot prentice who'd gotten no answer at the outer door and barged right in.

"Dabrena?" the girl whispered. "Don't you know me?"

She didn't, and at the moment didn't care to, beyond finding out her name and section to see she was dosed with extra chores. She pressed a finger to her lips with a withering look, then blew out the lamp and herded the girl into the sitting room. Her own sleeproom and the workrooms were closed off to give the hearthfire a chance. Drawing the door just shy of shut and placing the codex on a nearby pile, she said, "What in blazes do you think you're about?"

"I had to see you." The girl turned a circle to survey the room—brimming shelves, piles of sedgeweave, cushioned chairs, tumbled stacks of volumes, a strew of toys, a snack of cream and biscuits half consumed on an end table, brandy in a crystal decanter on the end table opposite, a sparing fire in the grate—as though she hadn't just walked through to reach the inner doorway. "I didn't know where else to go. I keep getting lost."

Dabrena frowned. Maybe she did know this girl. She put Dabrena in mind of Tolivar for some reason, though she didn't have the look of his folk. "That's three answers," she said. "Pick one. And I'll have your name, please."

"I'm lost," the girl said. "It's worse than that bloody shifting labyrinth of passages in the Holding."

Dabrena folded her arms to cover a weird frisson. "You're in the holding, and the hallways are perfectly straightforward. What is your name?" One of the new prentices? Quite a blunder, to wind up in the head mender's private rooms. She might have been misled by some other prentices, but if so it was a cruel trick. She seemed not to be all there.

"I'm looking for help," said the girl, completing her circle.

Pale Norther skin, thoughtful gray eyes, shoulder-length red hair. By all the— *"Liath?"*

"Can you help me, Dabrena? You healed my knee. You tried so hard to heal my light. We always helped each other, as we could. We helped more than we hurt, I think."

Dabrena hadn't thought about Liath in years. They'd been friends for such a short while, as vocates in the old Ennead's Holding—was that the holding she'd meant? Had she taken a crack on the head? Or had aiding the Lightbreaker, all those years ago, done some damage to her mind? They *had* tried to help each other back then, though none of them knew what they were doing—though in the end Dabrena had betrayed Liath to the Ennead, and their friend Tolivar with her. So young, all of them, and courageous for the most part, despite the grievous errors. Liath looked that young still. It brought a pain onto Dabrena that she'd never expected to feel again. Tolivar might almost saunter in, say something saucy to the both of them—

Adaon came through the door with the chill, damp-dry scent of earth on him. He'd been at the dig. They were excavating the last of Gir Doegre's eight hills, under which was the last of the Triennead holding's eight marble halls; if there was a ninth structure, they hadn't found it yet. Dabrena drank in the sight and smell of him, the rightness. Adaon hung coat and cap on a peg and rubbed his ears and bald head vigorously, with a puzzled, interested smile for the late visitor.

Liath backed up as though to take refuge in the twins' room. "Whoa, whoa, whoa," Dabrena said, grasping her arm firmly.

"You're not going anywhere. Sit down, have a brandy. This is Adaon n'Arai Seeker, my pledge. Adaon, this is Liath." She couldn't remember Liath's family names. She got her seated by the fire and took the facing armchair. "We were vocates together."

Adaon, pouring Finger brandy into three chunky crystal snifters, raised a pale brow. Dabrena shrugged at him wide-eyed. While two nineyears of authority had matured her, she would always look younger than she was; but she knew it seemed impossible that she and this freckle-faced girl should be of an age.

"Liath," Adaon said, coming around between the stuffed chairs to serve the brandies. "Word was you'd sailed to see the outerlands."

"I sailed," Liath acknowledged, with some caution. "Perhaps I've come to the wrong place."

"No, I think the menders' holding is exactly where you need to be." Adaon cupped his brandy in his palm to warm it and leaned on the mantel with the casual air that always hid his most intense curiosity. Dabrena was bursting with questions, too, but Liath seemed by turns so forlorn and so unsettled that she hesitated to push her. Adaon would glean more, with his glow, than any blunt interrogation could elicit. "You came alone?"

The way he asked it made Dabrena think he suspected not. If the explorers were starting to come home, they would carry news, knowledge, perhaps even the secret of who was attacking the coast. Her menders and Kazhe n'Zhevra had been working for three years, with mages and seekers and touches, to craft a counteroffense, thus far to no avail. Kazhe, a kenai blademaster, was a touch with the unique ability to destroy any weapons she could extend her awareness to, focusing her workings through a near-legendary magecrafted blade. But her powers were ineffectual against the siege weapons. If they had more information—how the weapons were launched, who was launching them, what they were made of—they might succeed in their attempts to neutralize them.

Liath winced and said, "No. Yes. I don't know." Then her face relaxed into a wry smile that reminded Dabrena painfully of her grandfather's. "Not much use, am I?"

"Neither are we, as yet," Dabrena said. "Tell me what kind of help you're after."

The last time Dabrena had seen her, Liath was dressed in stewards' clothing, battling the Ennead's forces in the depths of their black mountain. It was the last time she'd seen Tolivar, too. Later on, Liath had told Karanthe how Tolivar had met his end, and much later still Karanthe had told Dabrena. Now she found herself possessed of a perverse temptation to demand Liath's eyewitness account. What he'd said, how he'd seemed. She knew the answers would undo her. She had seen what the Ennead did to the mages it used. She knew all she needed to of Tolivar's last days in the realm of flesh. But an unresolved piece of her past had come back with Liath, and she was besieged by emotion. *We went to save you. Bron Steward called Tolivar and me to help, and we went down into that chamber of horrors to cast you free, and Tolivar died for it.* Tolivar had died because the Ennead had killed him, not because they'd gone to save Liath, not because Dabrena had divulged their location to save infant Kara's life. But still there was the irrational surge of rage. *Look what happened the last time I tried to help you. Do you think I'd risk that again?* Threaded through it all was guilt. She'd made her amends to Tolivar's ghost, but Liath was alive, and Dabrena hadn't seen her since the day she had betrayed her. It was hard to look her in the eye, remembering that. It was hard to keep her mender's objectivity, when she felt compelled to do anything to atone for that craven betrayal.

"I'm not sure," Liath said with a frown. "Some kind of healing? There's something . . . wrong with me."

Wrong with your mind, perhaps—you hardly seem yourself— but that's not my bailiwick. She glanced at Adaon, but he was unreadable. "You look sound as a bell, and two nineyears younger. I'd like to meet the touch who managed that."

"I'm hard to kill," Liath said, as though it were an answer.

She was also, it turned out, unaccountably informed and very hard to understand. Though she'd come asking for help, she rose several times to leave, with vague allusions to someone she had to find. She knew that Pelkin was dead, but didn't seem to grieve him. She knew that her sister was lead shielder in the Fist. She knew that Hanla n'Geior was the new headwoman of Khine, her first act to pull the Khinish fleet out of mothballs to attack the attackers, news that had come here by bird only today. She knew that Jhoss was in the Head, petitioning Graefel n'Traeyen for a scholar-visant alliance, though Dabrena had tried to talk him out of it on his way up there—though Dabrena herself was racking her brain for ways to extricate her menders from the touches, concerned at their increasing dependence on the touches' powers, their decreasing invention. There were great gaps in Liath's understanding of the current state of Eiden Myr, but she possessed what seemed certain knowledge of things Dabrena had not known: Louarn had pledged Graefel's son Keiler, the former binder and renowned teacher—not quite what Dabrena had envisioned for him when he left for Sauglin to work the kinks out of his inconsistent castings. Graefel had broken some sort of code he was working on, something hidden in the wordsmiths' canon. Nerenyi Seeker, the former keeper of codices, had left the ghost of the scholars' isle and was coming, of all places, here. Dabrena hardly knew what to make of it. Could any of it be true? How in the world could Liath know? If she had a blue-silver glow, Adaon would have mentioned it. He only shook his head at Dabrena's silent appeal. He was as perplexed as she.

Liath spoke of a hole, but couldn't say in what. When asked about the outerlands, she grew agitated and spoke of indeterminate horrors, and when asked repeatedly how she had gotten home, she clutched her head in pain and snarled, *"I don't remember!"*

"Three hours shy of midnight," Adaon said at last, with his visant's unerring sense of time. He eschewed the clunky device in the corner, which lost more time than it kept and which they sometimes forgot to wind altogether, but both he and Andri found the rhythmic clicking of its escapement soothing. "Perhaps we ought to find a bed for our guest."

"Is that a bonewoman, Mama?" Andri stood in the doorway to her room, blinking in the light, fingers twisting the legs of her flannels. "She won't stay if she's a bonewoman. The bonefolk never stay."

"This is Liath, an old friend of mine, and you're a little girl who should be snugged in her bed."

Dobran's head peeked out from behind Andri's as their father moved to shepherd them back to sleep. "I want to see the bonewoman."

"She's not a bonewoman," Andri told him. "Mama said. I think she's a haunt."

"I'm not dead," Liath said, with a dash of irritation, as though she'd had to make that point before.

"Adaon, hold on a breath," Dabrena said, and he rose from bending to scoot the twins inside only to have them slip past him to stand in front of Liath. "Did I hear your key in the door when you came in?"

He cast a speculative look at Liath, understanding before he answered. "Yes, I locked up when I went out after supper. The shutters were all closed against the chill, and barred."

Almost no one locked their homes anymore, in Gir Doegre town or within the halls of the holding, but Dabrena permitted herself a few small vestiges of overprotectiveness where her younger children were concerned, and Adaon made no objection. She said, "How did you get in here, Liath?"

"I needed to see you," Liath replied. To the twins, looking up at her with curious eyes, she said, "I'm not good with children, and I'm not very interesting. You should probably go back to bed."

Dobran said, "How come you don't show a light? You're old enough." He pointed. "That's a triskele. You're supposed to be a mage. I'm going to be a mage. I'm going to be a wordsmith."

Andri turned to her mother with an air of firm conclusion.

"She's a haunt, Mama. Some new kind you can see. They can go through walls."

"I'm not dead," Liath insisted, exasperated, and pushed off the padded arms of the chair to stand at her full, quite corporeal height.

The twins scrambled back toward their room. "You should get Pelufer," Dobran declared on the threshold. "Pel can even talk to the haunts you *can't* see. It makes her nose bleed!" He grinned with grisly relish.

Adaon saw them back into their bed, then drew the door almost closed and, in a lowered voice, said, "Her glow flared, Dabrena. That was a gleaning."

Dabrena didn't have to see the child's glow to know that. Her grown daughter had once claimed to know a haunt, and Dabrena had dismissed it as a product of loneliness and overactive imagination. But Kara had told the truth. Dabrena wasn't about to dismiss a similar claim from a visant daughter.

"Adaon," she started, and Adaon said, "I'll send for her," already moving toward the door, and Dabrena said, "Don't let Kazhe keep her."

"Kazhe," Liath breathed. "I can't . . . I have to . . . go . . ."

"Oh, no you don't." Dabrena set her firmly down in the seat. "I've seen a lot of strange things while you've been gone, Liath. I don't know why you'd come to me, why you'd trust me, after what I did to you and Tolivar. But he forgave me. Maybe you have too. I couldn't help you when your magelight was blocked, but that was a long time ago. Things are different now. I have resources here you may not know about. Wherever you've been, whatever's happened, we'll sort it."

"There's a hole, Dabrena. There are horrors out there. . . ."

"Yes. So you've said. Now, you sit tight. You came to me for help. I'm going to help you."

KAZHE N'ZHEVRA L'KEIT itched to feel her blade come into her hand. A dozen years since she'd taken a life with it. Far too long to live with an itch that never stopped. Worse than swearing off drink, swearing off death. She clenched her right hand, gouging nails into the itch. Pain helped, a little.

Stars more than the sickle moon blued the trampled field where the Kneeside shantytown used to sprawl between Tin Long, Highhill, and the forest skirting the Knee Road. The shanties' denizens had found work and proper homes long ago, leaving the space to her use as a training ground. Fairs were held here twice a year, and in daylight the field was occupied by folk with horses to school, children with kites to fly and balls to kick, crafters with projects too large for their workshops; she worked around them, and taught her prentice to do the same. In the dark, it was theirs alone.

Not quite dark enough, tonight. Never dark enough, in this populous town. Her prentice fought well from under a blindfold, but there was nothing like the full dark of the spirit days, out in the grasslands, leagues from any lamp or hearth, to test a fighter's intuition. Blindfolded, eyes surrendered and other senses took the fore; open, eyes felt they should see, strove to see, and blinded the other senses. Kazhe could still feel the aching sting of her father's longblade on the backs of her thighs. He'd given her the flat, a calculated insult that burned deeper than the pain that had crumpled her. That blade was on her back now. At the end of this moon, come the spirit days, she would find a place as black, to test her prentice in that final drill.

The traders' daughter would be kenai, and soon. Though the girl had prenticed late—Kazhe had started from age six, like any crafter, and this girl had been nine-and-two—she'd had her dozen years of training and it was time for her to go use it.

She'd be wasted in none's-land; all blades were wasted there, and kenaila were their blades. The same word meant both blade and blademaster. The girl already had a mage to serve, assuming those Sauglin sprinters didn't break him in the fixing. She lacked only a blade. The like of Kahze's longblade, mage-crafted in some manner lost to the ages, would never be seen again. A kenai passed to the prentice upon the master's death, and Kazhe did not plan on dying in the near future. The girl would have to make do with the blade she had.

Or the blade she could craft. She never stopped applying her touch's powers to all the bladesmithing she could learn. Dozens of her castoffs had gone to the shield. This new one was a thing of beauty, wasp-waisted with three fullers and a tri-lobed pommel. Starlight ran like water off the flat; the edge caught the moonlight and tore the shadows with silver. Pretty. Very pretty. Kazhe wondered what it would take to prove it was a waste of time. The best blade wasn't the longest or the shortest, the lightest or the heaviest. The best blade didn't balance toward the strong or toward the weak. The best blade wasn't a cutting blade or a thrusting blade. The best blade was the one you could kill with—and for Pelufer n'Prendra, any blade was the best blade.

She swept through flourishes as though engaging a flesh-and-blood opponent. She drilled as though fighting for her life. It made for uncanny realism. Eight cuts, and the killing thrust that made nine; eight directions of movement. The ninth direction was down, into death—but with the insolence of youth her prentice had rejected death and decreed the ninth direction to be up: a leap over a swipe to the legs, a leap forward to deliver a flying thrust.

When Kazhe had trained Verlein, she'd allowed her to adapt her training to expediency, and Verlein had diluted kenai technique past recognition. When Kazhe had trained a rebel horde for Verlein, then trained an army to defeat it six years later, she drilled with rigid discipline and got a horde of fighters who couldn't think on their feet. They led to the same end: a shield that was nothing but siege fodder. She'd learned from both mistakes. This prentice was as rigid and as flexible as her own blade; she would bend and always come back to true. As she developed her own style, Kazhe pushed her hard to defend it. She wanted to leap? Kazhe made her leap until she could barely stand, then attacked with full intent. The fighter who didn't give up was the fighter who won. The fighter who could think past exhaustion and pain was the fighter who won. Kazhe drove her mercilessly. Kazhe made her kenai.

Soon she must go and be kenai.

Then Kazhe would throw off the fetters of her vow, and see about ending this benighted siege once and for all.

Pelufer danced with the shadow.

Move and live; rest and die. Hit; don't get hit. Deceive; don't be deceived. Don't get killed. Kill.

Finish it.

She had never killed. The first time she killed, she would lose one sister forever, and perhaps both.

She didn't see how she was going to avoid that, if it came to it. She didn't know how she was going to bear it.

She didn't know what it would feel like, to be stained by another's death. To carry the burn mark of a life she had turned into a haunt. She had communed with haunts since she was nine-and-two; named them since she was five. She knew a lot of haunts who had killed; she had sensed their relish and their remorse. She knew some living who had killed, too, though most of those had gone to the shield. Yuralon had hated it. Risalyn had shrugged it off as necessity. None of them, living or dead, could tell her how it would feel for her.

I should have gone to the shield.

Distracted, she nearly took a thrust to the kidney, failing to pass through after her last cut. For a fraction of a breath she felt the old freeze of indecision, not knowing what to do when Kazhe broke the timing of routine repetitions with some unforeseen assault. "Anything!" Kazhe would shout. "Do anything! Move!" She would do something awkward, something ugly, and be praised for it, when her ambition was to move as fluidly and beautifully as Kazhe did. "Death is ugly," Kazhe would say. "Living is uglier. Be ugly. Be alive." Slowly, she had learned. Now she let the remaining momentum of her cut carry her around, and stepped out, and brought her blade up under the shadow's thrust, and closed, grinding her new blade down the shadow's until they pressed guard-to-guard. She could smell the shadow's breath, dry as the inside of a stone.

She'd forged herself a hooked guard. She used it to lever the shadow's blade out of its hands. The blade sprang out into the air and dissolved. She hacked down, from the elbows, to cleave the shadow from crown to breast.

Pelufer grinned as the shadow re-formed to come at her again. It was grand to have a new blade. It was grand to be young and strong and trained. It was grand to dance with shadows.

But they're only shadows. I should have gone to the shield.

Kazhe was stained black with all the killing she had done. By rights she should be in exile with the rest of them. But she'd gone to the strip of none's-land along the Knee, and her blade—her shining crimson blade, which had destroyed the weapons of three armies—had no effect. Shielders, mages, touches, stewards had fallen all around her while she stood burning with useless crimson fire. Her blade could not hack through explosions. Its edge could not slice acid mists. She had returned to her prentice and forbidden her to go to the coast.

Kazhe had lived inside the exile of her own stain most of her life. The shield had suffered for three years. Their exile had only just begun. They still believed they had each other for comfort. Eventually, they would learn that they had only themselves. Each one exiled within that shell of stain. Just as she was. Just as Pelufer would be.

"He's good, that dark one," said a familiar voice from right beside her, where no one had been standing. "But of course he has nothing to lose. He's giving your prentice a good run. That is your prentice, isn't it?"

Kazhe stiffened. She kept her eyes on the bladework. "There's only my prentice there. She drills so hard you think there's a real opponent."

"Oh, there's an opponent. But he's a haunt. Or something worse."

Kazhe turned. Took in the bladed back, the scarred visage, the dark red hair, the amusement in the hard gray eyes. "From the looks of it, so are you."

Pelufer took peripheral note of her master going ramrod-straight, of the tall, travel-stained stranger beside her. They were exchanging low words. Kazhe's body sang tension to Pelufer across the practice ground. But Pelufer couldn't call a halt to the bout. The shadow was unrelenting. If she put up her blade, she'd lose a limb. Kazhe couldn't see the shadow, didn't believe in it; no one could, or did. The shadow, however, was very real, and would kill her without hesitation. She could spare only a fraction of her attention for whatever was going on at the edge of the field.

She set the shadow blade aside and sliced to the neck.

"I'm fairly certain I'm not dead. I am interested in talking to a couple of haunts, though. I hear your prentice has a knack with that sort of thing."

Kazhe's teeth clicked together and ground sideways, molar on molar.

"You must have considered it."

Kazhe stayed well clear of her haunt-sensing prentice when she was working that side of her powers. What would it get her? Forgiveness, for letting him fall to his death on that rocky headland? She unlocked her jaw with effort and spat into the dirt. "The dead should stay dead. So should the past."

Liath bared her teeth. "And so should I?"

* * *

The shadow voided the slice with a bursting step to her dead side. She ducked the arc of its black blade and drove straight up at its groin. It sprang away, raising its blade into high guard, inviting her in. She feinted in, then dodged sidewise as the shadow committed to its strike, and sliced at its middle. It writhed away, more supple than any human body would be, and tried to take her on the upswing, a rising false-edge cut that would have severed her hands if she hadn't lifted them clear to come into hanging guard.

For one breath, they held that position—Pelufer in hanging guard, shadow in high guard, neither moving a muscle. Reevaluating with each shift of weight, hitch of breath, angle of eye. A nonned engagements were fought in that breath.

At the same instant, both struck.

"Why aren't you dead?"

Liath chuckled. "I've been asking myself that question for twice nine years. Why aren't you?"

"I've been asking myself that question all my life."

The shadow banked on being faster than Pelufer was accurate. Pelufer banked on nothing. The shadow lost an ear and took a slice to the shoulder.

Before it would have bled out if it were alive, it came at Pelufer with all the cold ferocity of the damned.

"There are horrors out there, Kazhe."

"Mirages. I've seen them. They're not the threat."

"Are you so sure of that?"

"Don't play with me. What do you want?"

"To get home in one piece."

"Don't we all."

* * *

Pelufer finished it with a sweep across the shadow's knees. The shadow toppled, blurred, then re-formed, and stood to salute the victor. Pelufer walked to within six paces of the scarred stranger. She did not put up her blade.

"I'm Liath n'Geara," the woman said. "You probably know me as something along the lines of 'that bloody illuminator.'"

Pelufer darted a glance at Kazhe.

"That puking alemonger who won't stay dead," Kazhe growled.

Pelufer nodded, wary. There were no politenesses around Kazhe, no "Pleased to meet you"s. There was only caution and respect. Kazhe might pull a blade on her at any moment without warning. In the middle of a meal. In the middle of the night. In the middle of an introduction to a legend. More dawns than she could remember, she'd dragged Kazhe stumbling from a tavern only to find a cold-sober dagger against her throat. Caille had threatened to leave her scarred afterward, thinking to make Kazhe ease up. Pelufer stared at the skin of the stranger and thought that if Caille had healed not a single one of the countless cuts bestowed upon her by Kazhe, she would still not look like that.

Liath Illuminator's voice was quiet and low, her intonation burred with the Norther Highlands. "There are two dead men I'm looking to speak to."

Kazhe said, "They're in the Fist if they're anywhere, in none's-land, and she's not going."

"She is if I take her," Liath said.

"I killed you once, Illuminator," Kazhe said. "Don't think I won't do it again. Don't think I won't keep killing you till it sticks."

The woman grinned. Pelufer's hand tightened on her blade. She'd seen the same grin on Kazhe's face too many times. The grip of a longblade gleamed in the starlight, the scabbard nestled in the gray hood of Liath's cloak. Her stance was deceptively relaxed, her joints flexed, ready. If she had killed, Pelufer would not be able to tell unless she touched her. She couldn't see stains.

Yet.

"She's not a haunt," Pelufer said, suddenly. "But she's not . . ."

Two sets of cold, clear eyes, ice-blue and gray, pierced her, waiting.

She swore. "I don't know. There's something wrong with you, Illuminator."

Liath laughed, a harsh sound in the clear night. "I don't need a hauntspeaker to tell me that."

"I'll find your haunts for you." Pelufer didn't know why she offered; legend was nothing to her, and she had other things to do. But it was her craft. "They may not be as far as Kazhe says." Sometimes, if the bond had been strong and the parting unexpected, threads joined the dead to the living like cobweb—so dry and dead that a breath might collapse them, but enough *there* for Pelufer to sense, and sometimes follow. Usually there was a place that haunts came back to again and again. It wasn't always where they'd died. She'd made a trade of finding those places, and reconciling the living and the dead. That was her business, not Kazhe's. Kazhe couldn't stop her. Kazhe didn't own her.

"But I'll have to touch you," Pelufer said quickly, sheathing her blade. With someone this dangerous, it was important to give warning. Hands empty, she took a step forward.

Liath stepped back. "I have some things of theirs, if you can work with those," she said. "A pack, a codex, spare clothes for the one. They've seen some years and countless leagues, but there might be something of him left in them. For the other, some blacksmith's traveling tools. Will that do?"

Will that do, to keep your hands off me?

Pelufer didn't see those things anywhere on the woman, and when Liath looked around, as though they should be with her or on her, she didn't find them, and she frowned. The not-rightness of her surged. Her body twisted into frustration, anger. Kazhe felt it, and came up on the balls of her feet, ready to sweep her blade into play.

Drawn by the tension, the trembling metallic vibration of edged weapons seeking release, shadows filled the empty field around them. Bladed, dancing.

Pelufer abruptly understood that she could, in fact, see the stain very well indeed—on the dead. What surrounded them was the stain of countless fighters who had died here. Fighters who were defined by their stain the way touches were by their shine. So that when they died, their lifeblood seeping into this earth under her boots, their bodies taken by the bonefolk, their personalities fading to a dry rustle over all the nonneds of years, what remained viable was the stain. Black, human-shaped, agile, deadly.

Eiden's spleen, Pelufer thought. *I've raised the puking dead.*

Her shine, when she raised a weapon of death, gave half-life to the stained, black shades of killers.

She'd been sparring with the stain itself.

"It's all right," she said, trying to keep this from escalating. Kazhe had hated Liath for more than two nineyears; Pelufer had heard the tale often enough when Kazhe was in her cups. She was primed for goading. That would stir the shadows. Pelufer couldn't control the shadows. "We won't do it now, we'll think of some other way, we'll get Dabrena, she's the head here—"

"What do you want with their haunts anyway?" Kazhe said. "Some new mission, some new torment, some new place to take them where I can't protect him? *Torrin's safe where he is.* Leave him be."

"You don't know where he is," Liath said. "He might be in pethyar." She looked ill, unsteady on her feet. "I have to find . . ."

"You leave him alone, Illuminator."

Liath's head snapped up and she blinked as if shocked to find Kazhe n'Zhevra standing in front of her. Shocked, then possessed of a fierce relief. *Wrong,* Pelufer thought, *this is so wrong,* she's *so wrong, what's wrong with her?* Liath lunged to grab Kazhe by the shoulders, lifted her onto her toes. "Kazhe! There's a hole. They'll find it. *They're coming, Kazhe.* You have to—"

Kazhe's doubled fists swung hard into Liath's diaphragm. She sprang back, her blade coming into her hands too fast to see, a silver whisper in the starlight, as Liath doubled over coughing.

"No, Kazhe, leave her," Pelufer begged, and fumbled her own blade out, keeping the shadows in the corners of her vision. They were dancing. They were gleeful. They loved this. They craved this. *Oh, spirits, what have I done?*

"I will not let you plague him," Kazhe said. "If this last protection is all I can give him, then I'll give it, and spirits strike that grieving vow."

Pelufer opened her mouth to say she wouldn't go near the haunts—but Kazhe drew her blade. Liath was a fighter; when she saw a naked blade she drew her own. Kazhe had been itching for a fight these twonine years and Pelufer hadn't been enough for her and not-killing hadn't been enough for her and this field was steeped in stain, alive and roiling with stain, contagious with it, and Kazhe's blade came down, a full-arm swing from the shoulders. The clang as Liath's blade met it was deafening, and smashed the night open.

The shadows gave a silent roar, and rushed in.

They're both mad, Kazhe thought, in the part of her mind that stayed clear and calm and easy in the midst of the most ferocious battle or raging drunk. Liath's scarred face twisting in bizarre horror as she fought; Pelufer whirling *away,* through bleeding *flourishes.*

Liath was better than she'd been when Kazhe had fought her last. Her style had been blunt, defensive; all her practice had been in keeping herself alive. Now she was devious and vicious. Canny on the attack. Why should the difference be startling? Because she looked exactly the same as when Kazhe had left her in that tent on the grounds of the magewar? Because she was dressed in *exactly the same clothes*? The gray Ennead-spun cloak floated around her, blending into the night. Black breeches showed a pale flash of knee, a rip in *exactly the same place.* The dust of that Fist headland was still ground into them, still shadowed the front of her white shirt. Slashing at her from cutting range, putting a new tear in the billowy sleeve of that shirt, Kazhe noticed things she had not seen while standing next to her. Fighting her in the bind, pressing, releasing, sliding the strong of her blade to the weak of Liath's, she saw no age on that mutilated face, not one year of age past the two nineyears and one she'd carried then. Her hair was cut the same. Her body weighed the same. But she fought as though she'd battled unthinkable horrors for a lifetime. She fought close, as though used to close places. She used the leverage of solid open ground with a relish that bespoke familiarity with treacherous footing.

What are you?

Liath wasn't seeing her anymore. She was seeing phantasms, monstrosities out of some other realm. *There's a hole,* she'd said. *They'll find it. They're coming, Kazhe.* In pupils so dilated that the irises were pressed into a thin gray line, Kazhe saw the horrors that Liath saw. The horrors that were coming.

"Stop," she said, springing out of range. "Enough, Liath."

Liath drove in, forcing her to counter and counter again. As Liath shifted for a killing thrust, Kazhe gritted her teeth and said, "I yield, Liath. Stand down. *I yield.*"

Where Liath had been, there was no yielding. She'd learned the one sure way to finish a fight. Kill the opponent.

"Pel," Kazhe called, "I need you to hamstring this one. . . ."

But Pelufer had gone mad. Pelufer, too, was fighting things that weren't there. It seemed she danced against an army, single-handed. As though beating something back from Kazhe and Liath, clearing the field for them to fight.

Insane. Kazhe thought. *This is insane—*

Liath lunged off line and whipped into high guard for the strike of wrath. Kazhe half-bladed to take the blow full on the flat, and snapped a boot up to drive Liath back. Then she slid past Liath with a low sweep of her feather-light, indestructible, razor-sharp blade. She took Liath's foot off just above the ankle.

A straight cut through straight bones. Easy enough for a touch to heal. Easier than sliced viscera or punctured organs. She sheathed her blade—it wasn't blooded; it drank blood—

prepared to bind the leg and keep Liath from bleeding out before she could be healed.

Liath was coming at her again, on two good feet.

Kazhe came up under the charge with her belt knife. She plunged it into Liath's belly, twisted, and pulled back. Liath turned, the wound healing even as Kazhe's blade withdrew. The blade was bloodied, but the only blood in the rent fabric of shirt was what the blade smeared there.

Kazhe rolled over her own shoulder and came up brandishing her longblade.

Liath had become one of the monsters she had battled.

She can't be killed. All sensation drained from Pelufer's limbs. The shadows had withdrawn at first blood. They'd only been playing with her, exulting in the fevered aliveness of battle in their midst. They'd only been dancing along. They made her fight them, all right; she'd wound the ribbon as Kazhe had taught her, trailed them behind her in a sinuous line to keep them from massing on her or the others. But they should have had her. Now they had put up their black blades. They clustered behind Liath.

Liath, who could not be killed.

Pelufer had attacked a boneman once. He'd taken her little sister away, and she had clawed and gouged him, stabbed an iron tool into his face, his eyes, his chest. The wounds had healed as they were made. He could not be killed; he could not even be harmed.

It was because the bonefolk existed in two realms at once. The realm of flesh, and their own realm. They were not entirely of this world.

Liath was not entirely of this world.

Kazhe's magecrafted blade could hew stone. She parried Liath's old-style longblade edge-on-edge, and the impact ran up her arms in a sickening vibration. She summoned her crimson power, and Liath's weapon did not melt, though Pelufer's did— served her right for not doing as she was told. When they grappled, Liath was flesh and bone; yet Kazhe cleaved her to no avail.

Kazhe had better things to do than fight some daft, transformed alemonger until she dropped. She'd seen the horrors in those gray-limned eyes. There was a bigger fight on the horizon. She couldn't join it if she was dead.

"Run," Pelufer begged her. Kazhe barked a laugh, lost the toe of her boot to Liath's longblade, and said, "Get help. A lot of help."

Liath staggered, and stared at her blade, and stared at Kazhe. The horrors ebbed from her eyes. She put a hand to her head with a groan.

Kazhe stepped in fast and took the blade away from her. "I thought we'd have to pile on you and truss you. *What in all the raving realms have you become?*"

Liath murmured, "I don't know," and at that moment they heard running steps in the silence of Copper Long, and watched a young boy come up breathless with urgency. "The head mender wants Pelufer in her rooms."

"Tell the head mender to come here."

The boy stared at Liath, then looked from Kazhe to Pelufer and back, desperate not to be sent back with that message.

"I have to go," Liath said, and turned as though there were a doorway behind her, as though she weren't standing in the middle of a field in the middle of the evening—as though there were somewhere for her to go.

"Not so fast, alemonger." Kazhe snagged her arm. To the boy, she said, "Tell Dabrena we've got her old friend Liath Illuminator here."

With an agonized look, he trotted off the way he'd come, back down the long toward the path that led to the residences up beyond the woods.

"Dabrena?" Liath said, sounding vague and lost—and then turned snarling on Kazhe and spat, *"Let me go."*

Kazhe released her. No horse in evidence, nowhere to go. Let her stumble off a few threfts if she felt like it. She looked about to retch. Too ill to be going anywhere, and she'd just fought a bout that left Kazhe soaked in sweat and short of breath.

Liath moved into the night as into a dream, and began to disappear.

"No!" Pelufer cried out, and lunged after her. The shadows massed behind Liath, an unearthly blackness in the midst of starlit night, and she was walking right into them. They would swallow her, take her whole—

Pelufer plunged half into shadow herself, wrapped her arms around the tall woman's waist, and hauled back.

Her body seized. Names burst into her mind, the names of the dead, the names of all those Liath had killed, and some were human, and very old, and some were not. She screamed.

They tumbled to the ground, locked together. Pelufer could not let go. She was stuck—lint to rubbed wool in winter, a tongue to a frozen iron bar. She'd been stuck to Louarn like that, glued to him by the shock of his hauntedness. This was different. This was terrible. Agony convulsed her. Those names, those terrible names, nothing human, nothing of this world . . .

And something else. Something gentle. Something soft as cobweb, sticky and dry and old. The haunts she wanted. Not *in* her, not the way Louarn's haunts were, the boys he'd been before he crafted himself into the man he was, boys struck as good as dead by traumatic amnesia, but still inside him. Not in her the way Pelufer's mother had been in her, haunting her the way you'd haunt a place you'd loved in life. They were on her, still part of her, connected. Pelufer could find them for her, trace down the sticky gossamer strands—

Liath twisted and scrabbled and broke free to crawl away from her and kneel, panting, bent over, hands on her thighs, in the patchy grass.

"I'm sorry," Pelufer said. Sorry to find out more than she

wanted to know, sorry to have touched her when she didn't want touching, sorry to have intruded on her private haunts. She didn't do her workings without permission.

But the shadows would have had her.

They were gone now. Pelufer didn't know if they'd recoiled from the contact with whatever this old adversary of Kazhe's had become, or if they'd gone because the fighting was over, and battle was all they had left to want, after all the silent ages.

"It's all right." Liath rose with effort. "Not your fault."

Kazhe offered no hand up. "What's *wrong* with you?"

"This is the right place," Liath said. "I'm close, I think. But it hurts. It hurts so much more." Her eyes scanned the field, the trees.

"Don't go," Pelufer said. "I can find your haunts. I felt them on you."

Kazhe looked past her and said, "Here's our head mender now."

Pelufer looked with relief on the petite woman striding up Copper Long in a sphere of lanternight. Dabrena moved with purpose and authority, ready to take charge. Adaon was with her, short and thick and strong as a stump. And someone else, a bit behind them, someone tall—Karanthe? Had she come in person from Sauglin, was there some message so important that . . . ?

Pelufer blinked, then blinked again, and a third time when her eyes didn't clear. The upward angle of light cast by the lantern swinging from Adaon's hand, the swaying shadows of their bodies—

As the three drew near, the tall, spare figure resolved into undeniability.

"By all the grieving spirits," she heard Kazhe murmur.

In front of her, Liath gripped her head as though it would burst into bloody shards, then fell, unconscious or dead, to the ground of the field.

Down Copper Long, the other Liath did the same.

A SCREAMING MASS of molten metal smashed through the top of the cliffside fortification. All they had here in the Fist was stone, and it was no bloody use at all. Coughing out dust, hip-deep in corpses, Breida reared back on her haunches and drew her blade. "Launch, you benighted, forsaken thing!" she shouted at the jammed retort, and swung her blade through fouled lines. The arm swept into the air as the counterweight plummeted. The sling caught on a jagged end of rock that had jammed in the trough. The linen weave tore with a sound of despair. Its contents of rocks and powders spilled out. The arm hurled nothing but a flutter of canvas and a stub of rope.

"Listen to me, Ioli." Rekke's eyes seemed to be all whites, his pupils contracted to pinpoints. Ioli didn't want to listen. He wanted Rekke to go away. Take Mauzl and go. Tear their glow apart, so that he wouldn't have to do it.

Rekke took him by the shoulders and squeezed until the pain made Ioli look up. "Listen to me. Look at me. Glean me. *I can feel it.* The shield failing. None's-land is a realm. It's a realm of threat and delusion and poison, a danger I've shielded visants from for a dozen years. It's always with me, do you understand? It's always there, it's my horizon, always pressing in on me, trying to swallow the people I swore to protect. *It's failing, Ioli.* You cannot sit here in your tree and ignore it. Your runners failed. Your plan failed. Your shield at Maur Sleith, where they closed the gap? Gone. The shield down the road there, that snatch of seacoast defended by your Toefolk? Gone, Ioli. Gone. They're tumbling like standstones on a tavern board. You waited too long. You waited for someone else to do it for you.

They failed. They didn't have time. There's no one else now. Only you, and me, and the runtling. *You've got to do it now, Ioli, or there won't be anyone left but us.*"

Ioli stared at the madman in front of him, and felt the pulp of another man's brains in his fingers. He writhed out of the crushing grip, hugged his shins, ducked his head between his knees, and sobbed.

The two new retorts were smoldering hulks, crushed and seared by the molten balls. They still had the three smaller retorts—

Make that two, Breida thought, as another palpitating globe reeking of sulfur and hot metal arced from nowhere into the Headmost one, demolishing it in a ninefoot-wide molten spray that sent stewards running, shrieking, beating at their clothes and skin. *Make that none*—a rain of molten missiles took out the rest. The air was thick with smoke and the stench of charred flesh. The burning globes broke into smaller globes on impact, and bounced crazily around the emplacements, no avoiding them by reflex, only luck.

Call the retreat, a voice within her urged. *Send them to safety.*

No. No retreat. No surrender. If they fell back, her visants told her, the attacks would follow them. The interior would stay safe only so long as they held the coast.

They would beat this. There was a way to beat this.

"They tell me you've cured me of an illness." Bathed and groomed, Fyldur was the Greasehair no longer; his smooth, shining locks draped him like rain. "I thank you, visant." He knew Ioli had been in his head. He felt no violation. Only hesitant embarrassment.

Ioli had seen to that.

"Don't thank me," Ioli said. "I did you harm."

"No harm," Fyldur said gently. "You righted me. I led glows from their homes and cast them into terror. It shames me to think I did that, though I have no memory of it. It was kind of you, to bury that memory. I vow to make amends for what I've done. I'm grateful to you."

Ioli pushed away. "*I made you feel that way.* Those aren't your thoughts. Those aren't your feelings. I created them in you. I wronged you terribly. Someday you'll figure that out, and then you'll hate me again."

"You've wrought a marvel," Fyldur said, "but I fear you flatter yourself. Visants spend their days arranging trinkets in ranks and rows. Putting things in their proper place. Making their worlds what they ought to be, sorted and tidy. You only did the same. Aligned me, with the brightest bits in front, the darkest, twisted bits behind. You only moved what was already there."

Fyldur believed that. Ioli gleaned it; he could not help but glean, he could not stop the gleaning, he could not shut his mind's eye or halt the workings of his mind. There was no surcease from it. Only exile to the deep jungle would relieve him. There he could glean trees and leaves and droplets, the coming of the rains, the flight of colored birds, and do no harm at all.

"I'm glad you believe that," he said. "But I put that belief in you. You're telling me what I want to hear, just as you always did."

"Then I am what I have always been. Only rearranged. Untwisted."

"It was a crime. Every gracious word you say makes it worse."

"No crime. Achievement. I left you no choice, Ioli. I tried to take a life. You saved me from myself as much as you saved your friends from me."

"It was wrong."

"Then don't do it again. But don't punish yourself by punishing the world." Fyldur took hold of the rope ladder. Ioli didn't watch him start down, but in looking away he noticed how much brighter Fyldur's glow was. He'd compressed it to a marble, in his hatred of himself. It had expanded into a soft azure blur as wide as his chest. Now it surged. Ioli closed his eyes tight, but couldn't shut it out. "Your greatest fear is of yourself," Fyldur said. That was his gleaning. "The world needs you to stop hiding now."

Still coaxing me down from my tree, Ioli thought. *All the*

*miles, all the leagues, all the suffering, and here I am, back
where I started, the Greasehair calling me to save the world.*

He would not be greased. Nothing could mitigate his crime.
Not even the fact that he gleaned nothing of himself in
Fyldur—only Fyldur, glowing Fyldur, tidied Fyldur, Fyldur
arranged and sorted into what Ioli had decreed, in his insuffer-
able pride, was the proper order.

Breida crawled past smoking shadows, blackened, human-
shaped silhouettes like so many scorched Eidens mapped out
upon the stone. No bodies left for her to carry to the border for
the bonefolk. She found a triad. "Can you freeze spearheads?"
she gasped out, between explosions. "Can you cast ice coldness
into something we could throw?" The mages nodded. She
ringed them in visants while they cast on a sheaf of javelins.
She took one up and stepped toward the cliff.

A javelin was a shielder's tool. A human weapon. Her hand
and arm became one with it. She gloried in the tangible. She
stood her ground, letting her target find her. Before long she
was flanked by shielders and stewards, each one armed with an
icehead javelin. They formed a line in front of the handful of
surviving mages and touches.

They knew this was the last stand.

From the smoke-heavy horizon, over the heads of oblivious
mirages, hurtling past the indifferent stars, came the next
molten fusillade.

Not one, or two, or three. A battery, filling the sky.

Ioli said nothing as Jalairi slipped into her hammock, leaving
him to blow out the lantern. She'd done the same every night
since their parents had died in the lightless years. The comfort
of old routine speared his heart with pain.

*She knows the truth. The delusions won't harm her. She'll be
all right.*

He'd told them all the truth when he'd apologized to them. All the treefolk. So that they would understand why he'd done what he'd done. There were no partial truths in an opening like that. It was all or nothing. He'd opened himself and let all his knowing out. A gleaning in reverse.

He put out the light. As the dark closed in, he saw the waning moon tangled in branches overhead, like a white eye opening just a slit.

"They're very disappointed in you, Ioli," Jalairi said. Her sisal hammock creaked as she settled in. "You showed them why, and they understand. But they don't like being the only ones you've saved." Softly, she said, "I don't want you to go. But they're right. I don't think you can stay here, after this."

Abruptly he didn't care. He didn't care what the treefolk thought. He cared very much what Jalairi thought, but even that didn't matter. He sat up straight, then got to his feet as he realized that it didn't matter at all.

What mattered was that they were rejecting him. What he'd shown them hadn't manipulated their minds. If it had, they'd want him to stay here, because this was where he wanted to be. They'd be trying to talk him out of exile.

He didn't have to manipulate minds to show them the truth. Only show it to them, and let them decide for themselves.

Not a sending. Not a forcing. Just an opening. An offer.

"Where are you going?" Jalairi said, louder, on a note of panic as he swung onto the rope ladder. "You're not *going*, not now, in the dark? I didn't mean tonight, no one meant tonight—"

"I'm just climbing down," he said. *Climbing down from my tree.* "I'm just going down to get my triad."

One for each of you, Breida said to the oncoming horrors, javelin in hand. *An icy, tasty treat. Come and get it.*

Breida chose hers, or it chose her. The one in the middle. The largest. The hottest. She fixed on it. She felt it fix on her. Rippling, quivering through the air, shedding molten mass without diminution, oscillating without deviating from its arc. Hurtling toward her.

She cocked her spear and sighted on its blind, burning eye.

"It's too late," Rekke groaned. Perverse Rekke, balking now that Ioli had acquiesced. "And we have no focus."

"We don't need one," Ioli said. They'd realmwalked out of the abyss while fighting for their lives. What they could do, they could do anywhere.

Ioli stood beside Rekke, who was twitching and mumbling, agitated by the jungle and the violent gleanings of his realmseer's eyes. Mauzl stood beside Ioli. With himself in the center, they were arranged by size and age and hue, biggest to smallest, oldest to youngest, darkest to lightest.

The surge of their glow filled him with peace. Slate sliding on quicksilver, deeps of moonlit indigo . . .

"It's bad out there," Rekke warned, jittering.

"Show me," said Ioli.

Breida hurled her javelin into the molten eye of death.

Globe and weapon exploded with an earsplitting crack. A hissing burst of steam buffeted the line, knocking them all flat. A few other javelins were loosed before the ground reared up to brace the shielders for the scalding. Explosions shook the stone under their backs. Steam billowed across them. Breida couldn't hear herself scream.

They'd taken out the first rank of missiles, but the backlash had broken the line, and more hurtled past in searing trails of afterglare, shedding mass in a rain of fire. Too many to count. The stone of the Fist bucked under every impact, battering their scalded bodies. A wave of molten spray drenched them.

Fight, Breida called to her shield, from the blank darkness of her mind. *Keep fighting!* The shield would not fall so long as there was one shielder, one mage or touch, one steward left. But there was only her, in all the silent world. A lone ember of consciousness, trapped in a blistered, useless body.

One more breath. One more eyeblink. But she had no eyes to blink, no lungs to fill. She must stave off death for one more instant. Just one more instant . . .

The public house burned.

Mother had sent her away from where the fighting would be. She'd sneaked back into the house, up to the top, where she could stack crates up to the high attic window and look out and see the battle. She wanted to be in the battle, fighting by her mother's side. But now the house was burning, and the trapdoor wouldn't open, and she couldn't fit through the window. She took an axe to the wood around it but the crates collapsed from under her and the smoke sanded her lungs raw and she couldn't breathe, she couldn't see, and it was so hot . . .

She came to wrapped in a soaked blanket, being unwrapped from it, freed into the sweet clear air, pulled into her mother's arms, stroked and caressed and checked for injury by those strong brewer's hands.

"I wanted to see the battle . . ."

"Ach, you stupid, stupid girl . . ."

She couldn't see the battle. She couldn't see if her shield was hanging on. No eyes, no breath, no sight, no body, no sense. The world had collapsed from under her. There was nothing to hold on to.

I'm sorry, Mama.

Delusion radiated deathlight inward from the coast of Maur Sleith. Villagers tore shrieking out of their beds, snatching up children, snatching up stewpots and hearth irons and old farm tools hung on walls, fighting for their lives against every night terror come true. Shepherds jerked in a panic from their drowse as fanged, ravening shapes out of nightmare tore through their heedless flocks and came for them. Along the river deltas between the Toes, dredgers beat back great clouds of stinging nettles with blankets, fans, whatever came to hand. From the rivers themselves rose serpentine malevolence, scaled, silver, eyeless things that coiled to strike at them. The seawall at the throat of Maur Alna fell, and tides of horror swept along the High Arm and the Brisket Mountains and Headward into the Oriels. Swarms of metallic wasps descended on towns along the Thumb. Smoking boulders smashed through the roofs of loggers' cabins. Riverfolk dozing on their tethered rafts woke to colossal waves looming overhead, limned with roiling froth and weighted as stone. Chalk miners woke to billowing white avalanches rushing down upon them.

Between the vines, the leaves, Ioli saw it through Rekke's eyes. *It's not real!* his mind cried. *You're fine. You're safe. None of it is real! Don't hurt yourselves!*

For a moment he was again the helpless walleye stumbling out of none's-land, unable to negotiate the marsh, watching saltmongers sandbag their homes against nothing, douse their flameless roofs. No matter how loud he shouted in his mind, he could not reach them all, he could not beat back those horrors. How could they fight this? How could anyone fight this? Who could possibly deny the overwhelming evidence of their eyes?

"No pushing," Mauzl said, and then Ioli was seeing the shadow reflections of Mauzl's sight, as well: shepherds and ferryfolk and loggers, miners and hillfolk and cottars, falling to delusion and fighting delusion and *letting delusion go*. Dying, and not dying. All paths were possible. All paths were true, until the next step forward into time collapsed them into one path from which countless new ones branched. There was a way, a route to that letting-go. It was there, in among the blooming, writhing blur of futures.

It was here, inside himself. He had only to relax. Stop fighting his own power. Stop struggling. Knowing wasn't pushing your mind against. Knowing was suspension, dissipation. Knowing was a mist of awareness hanging in the air.

He had only to open himself and let the glow do the rest. Make available, through all the realms and all the paths, everything he knew, everything he'd seen, everything he understood.

It was just the truth. It wasn't hard. It was the easiest thing in the world. No pushing. No forcing.

Release.

Ioli opened himself. The aqueous glow brightened and swelled. Expanded past the limits of conscious thought. Filled the world. Quicksilver and moonlight, indigo and slate, the clear pure depthless blue of morning skies, of truth, of peace.

I'm alive.

"Oldor," Breida said to the shielder beside her. He looked whole. The molten globe must have hit her and missed him. Maybe a few others had missed as well. A few left to see the dawn, to stave off death for another day. "Oldor. You're all right. Get up. Find a touch. Survivors . . ."

She could hear her voice, but he did not respond.

Maybe she was a haunt. Maybe she was speaking out of some hauntrealm, some between-place, and he couldn't hear her at all.

"Oldor!" she barked. "Acknowledge my command!"

He convulsed upright. "I don't . . ." he said. He fell back.

At least he'd heard her. She wasn't dead yet. She turned her head to seek out someone else to get them regrouped before the next barrage. The sky that rolled across her vision was clear and dusted with stars, hooked on a falcate moon. Had wind swept the smoke away? Her nose worked; she could smell the sea. . . . The shielder on her right was gone. No—a pair of boots, just above her head. Only boots. Fioral, cremated where she stood. But there were legs in the boots. Fioral had gotten to her feet. A hand came down in front of Breida's face. Not severed. Offering to help her up.

She grasped the wrist. Felt the hand, meaty and callused, grasp hers. Fioral hauled her up. She surveyed her emplacements with no comprehension.

The retorts stood whole and undamaged. Fresh lumber gleamed in the starlight. The fortification wall that had replaced the wooden railing spanned the cliff edge, mortared solid— three layers of it, as though each rebuilding had been addition, not replacement. Beyond it, the stars paled against a lighter blue. She twisted to find tents and sheds and crates in perfect condition. Shielders were rising as from a sleep of horror to find the headland calm and undisturbed by anything save the dawn wind off the sea.

"Sweet, merciful spirits," she said.

"Are we dead?" Fioral said. "Is this a dream?"

Not all of the shielders were getting up.

As the night skulked off Heartward, Breida got a better look at the battleground. It was strewn with bodies. She went down on one knee by the nearest one, to check, though she knew death when she saw it. This was Hilsig, who had stood three shielders down from her in the last assault. He wasn't charred, he wasn't scalded, he wasn't crushed. She felt his head for a crack taken in a fall to the stony ground. Nothing. "Touch!" she called, sliding the eyelids down. A young touch made her best speed over, avoiding corpses, still unsteady on her feet. "Can you tell me what killed this man?" Breida asked her.

After a moment with hands pressed to Hilsig's chest, the touch said, "Nothing. There's no damage in him."

"There's something. He's dead. Could you tell if his heart had seized?"

"There's a . . . a taste, to a seized heart," the girl said. "His doesn't have that. There's no . . . constriction in his lungs. No fracture to his skull under the skin, no harm to his organs, no blood in the wrong place, no poison in it. He just . . . I think he just stopped being alive."

"Just stopped being alive"? What sort of bloody way is that to die?

"It was the madness killed him," said an older steward, picking his slow way over through the dead. "And her. And him. All of them here."

"Do you see it now?" asked a visant, as Breida's remaining folk began to gather round her in blue morning. "You all see it now, don't you?"

"Or don't see it anymore," said another visant, and giggled.

"There was a great gleaning," said a third visant, standing well off to the side. "Someone showed them. The ones we felt."

The other visants nodded. Breida gave a harsh sigh. She'd sort it out later. A new assault might come at any . . . time . . .

With the sense of realizing something she'd already been aware of, just learning something she'd always known, remembering something she'd never forgotten, Breida Shipseer understood.

"This is no dream," she said in wonder. "We just woke from the dream."

No scorched, smoking silhouettes graven into the stone. No batteries of flaming death. No needled fireswarms. No explosions, no missiles, no gibes.

"A siege of illusion," said a shielder, torn between awe and rage.

"It was all one weapon," said Fioral.

"All one attack, for *three years*," said Oldor.

"All these dead," said the touch. "All these people dead . . ."

"We died for *nothing*," a mage spat bitterly. "My wordsmith, my binder—"

"We held the line," another shielder cut in. "That was our job."

"We held the line," still another shielder affirmed, "and someone found out how to end the siege, and they did!"

"It's over!" two or three others cried at once, and before Breida could rein them in, they were dancing, crying, hugging each other, hugging themselves.

It was over.

Ioli stared into nothing, stunned. "It's over."

The treefolk cheered. Mauzl ducked away from their back-slapping, but he smiled despite himself, and Ioli smiled to see it. Then Jalairi was embracing him, kissing his cheeks and his forehead, dragging him to his feet to dance around the clearing. Soon others were dancing, too, and anyone who wasn't dancing was beating a rhythm on the nearest tree trunk, and someone pulled out a nine-hole flute and struck up a sprightly tune. Then Ioli was laughing and shouting at the treetops, and pounding his feet on the springy ground, and spinning Jalairi until her feet flew free and her pale hair streamed out behind her. It was as though they were children again, spinning until they dropped.

There was no speaking such joy aloud. There were no words for it. Ioli had felt the minds receive him. He'd felt them accept his offering. They understood now. They believed. The weapons of delusion could no longer harm them. There would never again be such weapons. They would teach their children, they would pass their understanding on. They were immune. They would stay that way.

Ioli danced until the sky above the canopy paled to blue and the sweet misty glow of dawn filtered down into the shadows.

They had survived. Breida could barely bend her mind around it. If they'd fought nothing, they'd killed nothing. The stain was delusion too. They could go home. *I can go home—*

She pulled herself together, hard. None's-land had tricked her before. A painful count showed a nonned dead, but almost that number left alive. "Calm down," she said. "Spirits willing, yes, it's over. But we're still the shield. Godill, Simry, on sentry duty, now. The rest of you, help me carry the bodies to the bonefolk." She didn't know why the bonefolk wouldn't come into none's-land, but she wouldn't bank on that changing until she saw it, and she wouldn't have gulls or crows or flies pestering their dead. "Move."

Godill called to her from his post. While the others lifted the bodies of their comrades in exhausted arms, she went to look where the sentry pointed.

The mirages were still there. Floating quietly in the peaceful blue of dawn. Oblivious, or unconcerned with anything that had happened here. If all was illusion, they should have vanished with the siege; but the siege had been no doing of theirs, and in all these years no missile launched by a seagoing apparition had ever found Eiden's shores. They hadn't even appeared to attack in years. As far as Breida was concerned, they could stay out there forever, drifting on their inexplicable currents. She told Godill not to mind them.

In somber procession through blue morning, the shield carried their dead to the edge of none's-land. It took two trips; on the second, as they arranged the corpses in gentle postures of sleep for their trip to the bonefolk's realm, they found themselves face-to-face with gaping locals. The long row of the dead marked the border. A barrier between their comrades and those they'd defended.

"Is it true?" asked a blinking boy. "Is it over?"

It was the first thing a local villager had said to Breida in two years. "I hope so," Breida said, and turned her back on them, and returned to her post.

Her shielders followed. A few breaths later the last vestiges of night were illuminated by the green glow of bonefolk taking the dead.

Rekke should have been whirling and stamping in wild abandon, roused by the manic glee of the treefolk, hurling himself into the fierce release of the drums, the flute, the dance. But he was more perturbed than he'd been before.

Mauzl, too, had withdrawn.

"What is it?" Ioli said, moving toward one of them, then the other. "What's the *matter* with you? Can you never be happy? We did it! Together! A visant triad! *We* ended the war of the coast!"

"There's something wrong," Rekke grumbled. "The runtling feels it too."

"Well, what? What is it? Show me. We'll fix it."

Together, we can do anything.

Rekke rolled his eyes. One came to rest on Ioli. The other looked Fistward, boring straight up the coastline with its visant sight. "Cocky monkey. Thinks he owns the world now."

Chastened, Ioli glanced over at where Fyldur stood amiably chatting with some treefolk. Victory had swept his ill deed right out of his thoughts.

Fyldur looked happy.

"I need your help." Rekke gave him a shake. "I have to look."

Ioli's head was still spinning from the dance. His heart was still bursting with triumph. "At what?"

"I don't know, you grieving cretin. That's why I have to look. I saw something . . . in the corner of my eye . . ."

"Just now? When we were gleaning?"

"Or whatever you call what you did to clear their minds."

"I didn't clear their minds. I'm never doing anything to anyone's mind ever again. I gave them a choice."

"Don't raise your hackles at me." Rekke drew them deeper into the shadows where Mauzl had stood, around the back of the pale, striated trunk of the spiritwood tree. It was wide enough for the three of them to sit cradled in its roots, unseen by the treefolk. Rekke sat in the middle. "I saw something, when you opened yourself. It was a different view of the world. Like a bird's. There was something at the edge. I need to get back up there and look."

Their glow, which had become as much of a background sensation to Ioli as the sounds of the jungle, surged through him so suddenly that he had to steady himself on the tree's roots. And then he was . . . flying. Suspended high over Eiden's body, vistas opening all around him . . .

Something was terribly, terribly wrong.

"Shieldmaster!"

Breida raced to join her sentry at the wall. She nearly flinched to see the molten globe rising out of the sea. It was just the sun, the ordinary sun, lifting itself up the sky.

"The ships, Shieldmaster."

Most of the ships were far away, small craft drifting anchorless and alone. Nearer, a vast raft-up floated quiet in the dawn, too early for waking, only just speared by the light of the sun. But nearer still, just this side of the raft-up, a black-hulled ship was raising sail, plunging oars into the water. Its deck was a seething mass of monstrosities. Breida's fingertips scraped bloody on the stone. The prow was aimed right at them.

"It came straight through the raft-up. Rowed straight through as if it wasn't there. *It's seen us, Shieldmaster.*"

It can't have done, Breida thought. For nine years and three, the ships never made landfall. They'd given up. They were haunts, or reflections of some other time and place. A conundrum for seekers to muse on. A taunting display to break little girls' hearts. The ships might come, but they never arrived.

The first arrow struck sparks off the stone a foot away from her face.

"*Down!*" Breida said. "Back! *Now!*"

She plunged through a hail of arrows, shoving stragglers back to the encampment, where there was protective gear. How many on the ship? Two nonned? And she had barely a nonned here, and a third of them were mages, touches, visants, menders, stewards. The stewards could handle weapons. The touches wouldn't. Maybe mages would be willing to operate the retorts. She sent word of the attacking ship to the shield-posts on either side. She strapped her armor on, her blades. She kept one eye on the progression of arrows.

Through the clear dawn air came the jeering calls of blood-lust. Was it the siege all over again? Should they stand their ground and chant *"This isn't real, this cannot kill me"*?

She snatched up a fallen arrow. It was cold in her hand. Real enough.

They didn't have the luxury of doubt.

"The siege is over," Breida Shipseer said. "Now the war begins."

2

Eiden's Bones

❧

Caille surfaced from gossamer dreams into a body sprawled like Eiden's on a downy sea, one arm alongside and one out-flung, one ankle turned and one straight. It was only just light, the boy wouldn't be in the glade this early, she wasn't due at Greenhill till midmorning, and she didn't have to pee. She could lie abask, listening to them breathe, feeling their hearts beat.

They sensed her waking. Some stirred, but only to flop over or curl in tighter. One hunkered on the pillow, by her left ear, close but not touching; sometimes the old ones only wanted to be near, not to be touched. Another lay upside down in the crook of her arm, back legs a silly sprawl, front paws tucked beside the chest he was deeply engaged in grooming, an act of meditation. Dogs draped her shins and cats her knees; curled in the center of it all, atop her stomach, the great tom produced a low rumbling purr. The prim calico lay on Caille's chest, greengold eyes attentive and inscrutable. Caille closed her own eyes and opened them again, a blown kiss; the owl eyes blinked back.

Covered in warmth, weight, breath, heartbeats. This must be what it felt like to be Eiden.

She hated to leave this freedom. At night, in her bed, she was just her. Not powerful, not awesome, not famous. Wanted, not needed. Loved, not obliged. Just a comfortable, happy body, luxuriating in sweet, warm bodies snugged close.

She missed the way her sisters had slept warm and mumbling on either side of her when they were small. She missed their wayward, tatterdemalion childhood. She had been lonely then, denied friends, terrorized into hiding her powers, but there had always been the three of them, together, tighter than tight. Now they felt a world apart, though she was only up here on Wood-hill, and they were only down the path and along the road in Gir Doegre town. Elora had her trade, her pledge, the baby on the way, and oversight of the training of young touches in the hold-ing. Pelufer had her haunts and blades.

They didn't like her moving up here on her own, though they'd already moved into their own lives, away from her. Sometimes she thought they feared her as much as feared for her. They'd kept an eye on her since she was born. Though she was nine-and-eight and no longer anyone's child, they still weren't sure what she might do, left to herself. Sometimes she felt like doing some-thing just to spite them. But she couldn't think of anything.

Everyone who knew the extent of her powers was afraid of her. Most were polite enough not to say so. Revealing the shine was supposed to make her and her sisters safe, and mostly it had. But it hadn't made them ordinary. It hadn't made them just three more touches in a land where touches were everywhere.

They were the most powerful of their kind. Three touches to-gether couldn't work wood the way Elora did. Three touches to-gether couldn't do what Pelufer could do with iron. It had to do with how they'd gotten their shines, at such a young age. A boneman, Lornhollow, passing their mother's life force into them instead of passaging her body to the bonefolk's realm. Be-cause he'd done it in a forest, and because Elora loved the for-est, she got her knack with wood. Because he'd done it in the hauntwood, and their mother had haunted Pelufer, Pelufer got a knack with haunts that no one else had yet developed. Caille had been a baby, much smaller and newer than her sisters, so her share of their mother's power went farther. Except for the hauntsense, Caille got some of every knack.

Nine touches together couldn't do what Caille could do.

Pelufer joked that she'd like to be as feared as Caille was.

Caille couldn't touch Pelufer anymore. She'd gone cold as a corpse, hard as a blade. A trained killer who talked to the dead. Pelufer had become more dangerous than any shielder or any fighter or anyone at all save her master Kazhe.

Pel is the scary one, yet it's me they fear. And Elora doesn't scare them at all, and that's their worst mistake. Pelufer could kill, and Pelufer could speak to the dead, and Caille might do almost anything—but Elora was the one to reckon with. Elora, willowy and so beautiful it took people's breath away, was a formidable woman: a leader, a teacher, a hardheaded trader. It was Elora who could change the world. Caille was fairly certain it suited her that no one recognized it. Folk took Elora for granted, like the earth and the rains and the trees, and relied on her in ways they weren't aware of.

Elora was also a nagging, annoying parent who needed constant reminding that she was *not* her sisters' mother. Kara, Caille's best friend, had escaped her doting mother by becoming a master mapmaker, which justified frequent travel for surveys. She was off right now on a yearlong journeying to complete her self-imposed training; Caille could barely wait for her return. Caille had left Elora and Nolfi's fine home in town for this grotto in the woods as much to be free of Elora's mothering as to have a place to be herself.

She loved the woods. She loved the world. If it weren't for the siege, and the stain, and none's-land, and the explorers lost at sea, Eiden Myr would be a finer place than any teller's landbeyond. She wanted to heal those things, with her lauded powers. But it wasn't something she could do.

On that thought it came to her, like a dream just ended but forgotten till something trivial jogged it:

The siege was over. It had ended in the night.

Someone had ended it. The way she had ended the storm when she was five. Not someone with a copper shine. She'd have felt that; a working that great would have woken her. And the siege wasn't something a touch could touch.

Now she knew why. It wasn't a thing of matter. It was a thing of belief. Someone had given them something truer to believe in. Caille could feel the choice she'd been offered: believe in life, or believe in death. She'd made the choice in her sleep. With everyone else in Eiden Myr.

It was over.

Her breath quickened, her heart raced. *I have to tell the boy.*

She told him everything, though she'd no idea if he understood. She talked to him the way she talked to lost, shy animals drawn up here by her shine. Just talking, till they knew the murmur of her voice, till they were used to her. All animals loved her, but the lost ones, the scared ones, took a while to trust even her. For three days she had brought food to the hauntwood glade, set it by the edge, sat still and unthreatening in the center, and talked to him, whether he came out or not. Yesterday, he'd come out.

Would he be there? Each morning she feared he'd have gone during the night, slipped away with her never knowing who he was, what he was, where he came from. Why he haunted her wooded hill.

Did he unshroud the siege? Was that his doing?

She knew he had power. He was too beautiful and mysterious not to have power. But it wasn't a shine, so she couldn't see it. Which power could pull the veil off delusion like that? Mages did what they wanted, usually without asking. Visants didn't seem to do much of anything. But the boy . . .

She was up and washed and dressed in moments, hair tidied with four quick brushstrokes and a twist of silk. The dogs were all writhing, wagging joy to have her up and about, and bolted out the door the moment she opened it. She took a basket of food, packed the night before. She didn't think he ate if she didn't bring him things. There wasn't much to eat in these woods in harvestmid. Truffles, if he could sniff them out. Late hazelnuts. Stonewood nuts. Yewberries were delicious, but you should spit out the kernels—did he know that? He seemed so new to the Strong Leg, so uncertain. He looked a Heartlander. Did yew grow in the Heartlands? The boy loved to eat, though he tried to hide it; every flavor of local fare seemed new to him. He loved to eat almost as much as she did.

Her home was built right into the back of the hill, exploiting a shallow cave hollowed by the drainage of rains under ancient roots, where she and Kara used to come when they were children, to hide and eat sweets and giggle. She swung the basket as she hiked up the path, feet whispering through golden leaves. Inside this hill was Woodhill Hall, one of the eight marble halls of the Triennead holding. Some of the other halls had been completely excavated, the earth piled up to make new hills in other places. But this hill was crowned with the spirit wood, the hauntwood where the dead were taken to the bonefolk. It was a sacred place. The storm a dozen years ago had torn off the front of the hill, exposing the front of the hall. Dabrena's menders had only cleaned up that accidental excavation, leaving the hall accessible but still embedded inside the earth that covered it when the Triennead fell. Caille wasn't interested in the doings of mages generations ago. She was glad they'd left the bonefolk's glade alone. It was where her shine had been quickened when she was a baby. It was where she'd stopped the storm and healed Eiden's body, with her sisters, and Louarn and Dabrena, and Kara, and the bonefolk. It was a place of ancient serenity. She'd have gone there every day, just to sit inside the circumference of huge old hollow yews and bonewood brakes. Even if there were no boy there.

The glade was grassy and peaceful, dusted with pink and yellow asters, brightening with the day, but when she came into the center of it and put her loaded basket down, the surrounding wood seemed darker. This was when she usually saw him—not at the crack of dawn, but while the deep evergreen of yews was still in half-light and he could lurk among the golden hazel stars.

"I've brought buttered primrose tips today, and Ulonwy cheese, it's very soft and mild, and berrybread, my favorite," she said. "And I don't know if you felt it during the night, but the siege of the coast is over—it was all a ruse, the attacks were the delusions themselves, not any real flying or burning things. That's why our shine was no use against them."

She went on speaking without knowing whether he listened; now and again she stole a glance between the yews, but wild things could sense your stare, and stares made them nervous. She didn't want to start eating without him, but her stomach was beginning to grumble. She still ate enough for three, even though she wasn't constantly using her shine to keep her sisters healthy. She checked Elora's belly every day, but the baby was growing well and didn't need any help from her. It would be a boychild. She hadn't told Elora yet. She told the woods now, but didn't know if any human ears received the news.

"Caille," he said, in a breathless, husky voice that carried across the glade as though accustomed to projecting over distance. Walking straight out of the forest as her head turned to find that it *was* him, not a daydream of storm-tossed eyes and black-tousle hair. "Caille," he said, and knelt beside her, and took her hands in thickly callused fingers that sent a tingle up her arms. "I'm sorry, I didn't want to scare you, I wanted to wait till I was sure of you, but something's happened. I need your help."

"You're an outerlander," she breathed, feeling the foreignness on him, feeling the sea on him. She'd thought he was some orphan Heartlands boy—

"From the outer seas," he said. "Yes."

His accent was a strangeness, but she wasn't good with accents, it was Elora who could tell where you were from as soon as you opened your mouth. She felt the years on him, the same number as on her, and he was human through and through—no apparition. She'd heard of the ships circling the coast like sharks, crewed by horrors. This wasn't one of them. Her hands twitched out of his, and closed, so intense was the tingling contact.

"You can't scare *me*," she said. "I've been trying not to scare *you*."

Worry shadowed his stormy eyes, but he flashed an almost-smile, a sweet curve of lips that startled her with a desire to kiss them. "Then we'll promise to try not to scare each other. You're a healer? The strongest in all the land?"

"Well, yes," she said, surprised enough to pause in packing

food back into the basket. She'd told him everything—resentments, frustrations—but down deep she'd believed he couldn't hear her or didn't understand. Finding, suddenly, that he knew everything about her pulled her up short, even though she'd told him herself. Wrapping the berrybread snug in its cloth in a corner of the basket, she said, "Did you end the siege of the coast?"

"Is it ended?" He stood up, a queer mix of hope and panic in his eyes. Though his face still held wary reserve, his eyes told almost as much about him as her prattling mouth had told about her.

"I suppose that means no," she said, and flipped the basket's lid closed.

"Will you come with me?" he asked, though it was obvious that she would, she was packing up to go. Was he that uncertain of her?

"Of course I will," she said, and ignored his proffered hand to stand up on her own. "On one condition."

"If it is in my power to meet, and begets no harm or danger," he said.

She blinked, then huffed out a laugh and hefted the basket into the crook of her elbow. "I only want to know your name!"

His tension eased. Had he expected some trick or impossible demand? What sort of place *were* these outer seas?

A place where monsters crewed black-hulled ships with spiked prows. A place where horrors drifted upon the deep.

All right, she thought. *I suppose I might learn equivocation too, in that sort of place.*

"Eilryn," he said, as though gifting her with the greatest trust.

This time she took his extended hand, and let him lead her into the shadowed wood.

Caille couldn't imagine what lay under the piled boughs in the hazel thicket, but when Eilryn pulled them off to reveal a hideously scarred woman mounded in tattered blankets on an ancient waxcloth tarp with a scabbard weighting the covering cloak, head laid open by a gash, body convulsing, she gasped and pushed past him, nothing in her mind but the need to heal this.

Eilryn deflected her hands so fast she didn't see him move. His expression was flat as death. She drew back, hugging herself. The wild danger drained from him, but he didn't apologize and he didn't stand aside.

The woman's convulsion subsided, but she didn't regain consciousness. "How long has she been like this?" Caille didn't know how to handle the fierce unpredictability that stood between her and the problem.

"I don't know how you reckon time here," Eilryn said, brows drawn down. "The moon was old. It went dark two nights later."

"*Candlenight?* That was more than three ninedays ago!"

"The seizures only started in the night. Last night."

Another was starting now. The woman's back arched, her jaw locked half open; froth bubbled from her mouth. Again Caille tried to go to her.

"No," Eilryn said, a kind of plea. He wanted her to help, he'd brought her to help, but now that she was here he couldn't bring himself to let her near. There was more to this than he would say. There had to be, if that gash hadn't healed in a full turn of the moon. There was something shifty about him under the reserve, anguished and contrite and defensive. She couldn't force it from him. It should be left to come out on its own. But there just wasn't time.

The seizure passed. That damaged body couldn't withstand another.

"Eilryn, if you want a healing, you'll have to let me touch her. That's why they call us touches." Gently, she added, "I won't harm her. I promise. You don't even have to take my word for it. Let me show you." She rolled up her sleeve to display the tender flesh of her inner forearm. Held her hand out for his arm. He gave it to her. She turned it, laid her fingers lightly on the inside, and made a bruise, black and purple and nasty. Turned her forearm up to show an identical bruise. He probed his, frowning, perhaps thinking she'd smeared him with dirt, then lifted his fingers with a hiss. It hurt. It was real. He touched hers, harder, suddenly, and she jerked away with pain reflex that couldn't be feigned. Grudging belief came into his eyes. She brushed her hand across his arm and smoothed the bruise away. The bruise on her arm stayed. "You see? I can't heal myself. If do something bad, I'm stuck with it."

His eyes narrowed at all the ways that this could still be a trick. But he stepped aside.

Caille knelt on hazel boughs and blankets and laid hands on the unconscious woman. The gash was as fresh as though it had just happened. Eilryn, or someone, had done a good job cleaning and suturing. No infection was setting in—discoloration in the surrounding flesh was contusion—but there was a skull fracture underneath, and below that blood vessels had been twisted and torn by impact, injury that went deep into the brain. Whiplash had made the neck a complexity of tears and swellings. Caille worked with great care from the inside out. She slid her hands over the close-cropped head, picked the sutures from the brow when the knitting flesh disgorged them. This body was scored and gouged with old injuries, as battered within as without. Most had healed on their own, some badly; some had the mark of imperfect magecraft on them. The fingers . . .

When she moved to run her hands down the rest of the body, she gasped and recoiled. Death—old, dry, violent. She'd touched a vellum codex once, and it had felt like that. It was the clothes her palms had brushed. Her gorge rose. The woman's vest and leggings were the flayed skin of living things.

She had to go on. The woman still foundered deep in unconsciouness. Caille had never heard of anyone being under that long, not since the dark years, and those people, the menders said, had rarely woken.

The hand with the oldest injury—healed by some hurried mages, she thought, leaving knuckles to swell and joints to stiffen—was draped with the other hand on the scabbard. She put her hand on top, not touching scabbard or vest, and straightened the bones, smoothed the joints into a suppleness. Then she returned to the head. She didn't have to touch each body part to heal it; she could work through hands laid on any spot. With an array of old and new hurts as complex as these, she liked to put her hands where her attention was. But the clothing was too much impediment. She cupped the woman's face, and sent her shine in a warm flow down the length of the body.

Broken ankle, broken ribs, perhaps two nineyears ago—healed on their own, not too badly, but she made them seamless. Other breaks, not so old, not so well healed. Shadows of trauma to skin and muscle from numerous small blades; scars from tears and strains in muscles and ligaments, some bone deposits in the joints, a history of hard use with little rest. A wrongness in one kidney extended straight through the viscera from back to front—a longblade wound that should have killed her, also healed by magecraft. Mage healings had only approximated what touches could do; it was good that they'd given up using their powers on flesh. The puckered external scars took nearly a breath to smooth away; they'd extended in a webwork over the entire body, and felt more deeply embedded than they were, as if they resisted being healed. Finally, small colonies of tiny, foreign, opportunistic lives gave way before the shine. She left that for last, because the multitude of minuscule deaths sapped her strength. When she drew back from the mended flesh, now glowing with health, she felt more tired than she had in recent memory. It shouldn't make her tired, putting flesh back the way it wanted to be, and the colonies hadn't gotten that strong a foothold. She didn't know where the weariness came from. It was as if the scars and old injuries had become an integral part of that body, and it hadn't wanted to let them go.

"She's all right now," she said, rubbing her brow, her neck. The bruise on her forearm ached. She was famished, but the sight of those repugnant clothes turned her stomach; she had to turn her back for a few deep breaths before she could even think about reaching for the food basket.

"Why doesn't she wake?" Eilryn said. He was staring fixedly at the woman, but his expression revealed nothing.

"Give her a chance," Caille said. "She was out cold for all

that. Her body barely knows it's healed. Her mind might take a moment to understand that it doesn't have to protect her from the hurt anymore."

She opened the basket. She should have eaten before she started so her stomach could be digesting it. But she'd probably have thrown it all up when she touched the vest and leggings. *Don't think about that,* she told herself, and crammed berry-bread into her mouth, forcing herself to chew before she un-corked the wine and washed it down straight from the jug. "Eat," she told Eilryn.

He sank down cross-legged, all lithe grace, facing her across the basket with a clear view of the woman. He ate the sweets first, the berrybread and some maurmallow from Jiondor's stall, simmered in birch sap, and then moved to the primrose tips and the cheese. Every bite filled his eyes with awe, as though he'd never tasted real food before. That didn't seem so strange, now.

This wasn't how she'd envisioned her morning meal with the mysterious boy. They were meant to experience this first shar-ing in the enchanted glade, bathed in golden sunshine in a peace of benign haunts, asters fluttering in the scented breeze, birds warbling in the woods. Not in a close hazel thicket under a dark canopy of stonewoods, with a stranger lying insensible on the ground, a chill, shaded silence vibrating with unan-swered questions.

"Who is she?" Caille asked at last, when all the food was gone except the little Eilryn had saved against her waking.

"Liath n'Geara l'Danor," he said quietly. "Liath Illuminator."

Caille couldn't help glancing over her shoulder. *This* was the famed illuminator? She'd seen the silver-gray chain around the neck, but the triskele must have slid around back. Why was she still wearing it, if she'd been seared? She had no interest in the time of the old light, less interest in legend, but even she had heard about this woman. Dabrena and Karanthe had known her, Kazhe had known her, Louarn had known her; she had vague recollections of their reminiscences, but it was all from a long time ago. Judging from the scabbard and the injuries, she'd been on the shield all these years. Why hadn't the touches in none's-land healed her? Why had Eilryn dragged her inland in that state? Had the blow to the head come when she was already inland?

"What did this to her, Eilryn?"

He stood up and turned away. After a long moment, he turned back, and looked her in the eyes, and said, "I did."

"You clubbed her on the head?" Caille said in horror.

"No," he said. But that was all he'd say. He wanted to trust her; he was desperate to share his inexplicable burden. But when the moment came, he batted his own reaching hands away, and wouldn't let himself go near.

Caille didn't know what to do. *I should be afraid of him. I don't know him. I'm out here alone. I'm a fool. I can't defend myself. If I hurt him it will kill me.* But she couldn't even talk herself into fear. She wanted to hold him close, be held by him, learn who he was, touch and be touched. She couldn't bear the way he looked—utterly alone, lost in a world he didn't understand, tormented by a burden he couldn't share.

She was in love with him. She'd never been in love before. She loved the woods, she loved her animals, she loved her sisters, she loved Kara; she loved Louarn, and Jiondor and Beronwy, and Dabrena and Adaon, all the people who'd tried so hard to make up for her lost parents. She'd never felt what it was like to be *in* love. She'd fallen in love with this boy days ago and hadn't known it any more than she'd known his name.

You love too easily. You love everything. Every stray animal that comes under your hand, you love. Every tree in the woods, you love. Every cloud in the sky. Every person who does someone else a kindness. You love everything.

It was true.

But not like this.

How can I love someone I don't know? He was guarded, he was evasive. But he came from a hard place. And she'd touched him. There was no evil in him. Only power. So much power. More power than he knew. Maybe power he'd recently gotten a glimpse of, and scared him down to his soul.

That was something she could understand.

I'm not afraid of you, she thought. Then said, a breath later, "I trust you, Eilryn." Words that meant more than *I love you.* "Will you trust me?"

He looked at her for a long time, face impassive, doubts and decisions passing through his storm-gray eyes. "I already do," he said at last. Then he cried out and said, "Why won't she *wake*?"

She should have woken by now. It was a very bad sign. She couldn't stay out here. It was getting colder every day. "How is she even alive?"

She hadn't meant it as a real question, but Eilryn said, "She doesn't seem to need to eat."

"That's not possible."

The woman convulsed again with a choking sound. The scabbard slid into the bracken.

Caille scrambled over with an oath, laid hands on her.

She could not ease the seizure.

Her shine flowed into the flesh, suffused it, strengthened it. She gave the woman vitality and warmth. She fed her, from herself, from her strength, thinking that maybe the problem was malnutrition or dehydration, though she felt no lack in the flesh. Nothing helped, nothing worked. The seizure passed on its own. All she could do was hold the woman still so she didn't harm herself. She could only use her ordinary body. Her shine was no use at all.

She reeled back, sitting hard on her rear. *Anything,* she thought. *I can do anything. But I can't do this.* She tried again. She laid her hands on, and sent her shine through every particle of matter that constituted that body. It was healthy. It was perfect. There was nothing to fix. All that was left to try was unnatural things, changes that would tax her past exhaustion, taking years off her own life: repairing time's decay, making the body younger, stronger. Twisting matter in ways it did not want to go. A dark man might prefer to have fair hair, and prove his desire by bleaching it; but if she changed the pigmentation at the roots, it did her harm. The same man might build scrawniness into musculature through hard work, but if she did a working to increase the muscle, it did her harm. The flesh had intent of its own, separate from the will of mind or spirit. She didn't know why flesh accepted healing but resisted improvement; she didn't know why it seemed determined to age—determined, in the end, to fail and die. Death was the climax of aging, and she could heal neither. But this woman wasn't dying. This woman wasn't dead.

She was only seizing, again, her body trying to tear itself into pieces. It took both of them to hold her still this time. Caille cried out as she felt the woman bite through her own tongue, and healed it as Eilryn jammed a stick between her teeth.

Rage swept through Caille. Her shine had dominion over air and water, over metal and stone and wood, over flesh, over bone. It would kill her if she misused it, but the choice was hers. How could it have failed her?

"It's not your fault," Eilryn said, as the seizure passed. "I saw what you did. I know you did everything you could."

Caille realized that every thought and emotion was passing across her face. She collected herself, smoothed her features. *Not my fault.* She was being childish, taking failure as personal affront. She had healed the woman. The seizures were not a physical impairment. They must stem from something else.

The seizures only started in the night, Eilryn had said. The siege had ended in the night. "Is she a shielder?" she asked him.

"A what?"

"A shielder, a fighter. That scabbard is for a fighter's blade. Was she in none's-land?" Nothing she was saying seemed to make any sense to him. "Was she on the coast, Eilryn, at any time in the past three years?"

He hesitated, then said, "For an eyeblink."

Whatever that meant, an eyeblink wasn't long enough to attach someone so strongly to none's-land that she would convulse at its dissolution. It was a wild idea anyway. But the woman had been profoundly unconscious when the veil of delusion was lifted. Caille had sensed it in her sleep, but maybe the woman was in too deep a place to reach. Maybe delusion was still pouring inland, invisible to those newly immune to it. Maybe it could still affect her.

This woman could be dying for the simple reason that she believed she was.

If so, the only person who could help her was the one who ended the siege.

"We have to take her down to the holding," Caille said. "We have to find out what happened last night. We have to find—"

"No!" Eilryn said. "No one else." He went to his knees beside the woman, drew the cloak over her and tucked it close, weighted it with the scabbard, put her hands back on the scabbard as though that would anchor her to the world somehow. It only made her look as if she were lying in state, waiting for the bonefolk to come. He put her arms back at her sides, then replaced them where they'd been. He untucked the cloak and tucked it again tighter.

Caille knelt beside him and took his hands to stop their fitful fretting. Without even thinking, she healed a hairline fracture in one of his ribs, the holes in his back teeth, bruises and strains all over him. She only realized she was doing it when her shine came up against a colony of infection in his lungs and an infestation of worms deep in his belly. She killed them. It hurt her. They were only doing what worms and infections did. Somehow she managed not to cry out. He was staring at her, deeply flushed. "Thank you," he whispered.

She turned him to face her. He seemed calmed by the healing. This might be the only time she'd find him receptive. "Listen to me, Eilryn," she said. "If this is Liath Illuminator, then there are friends of hers in town. People who knew her a long time ago. People in authority, people with resources and power, people smarter than you or me. They might know who ended the siege, or be trying to find out right now. I think that person might be able to help her. Or mages might." He went stiff, and she clutched his hands tight. "Eilryn . . . please. It's only down the hill, it's not far. You should let her friends try to help her."

"I don't know," he said, anguished. "I don't know how to tell. If they're all right."

Caille smoothed the tousled hair off his brow. It was damp. He'd broken a sweat. "Then let me," she said softly. "Let me tell you who you can trust."

With a groan, he nodded.

Caille got up. "We can't leave her here. Are any of those blankets long enough for a sling?"

"I made a . . . a thing. To carry. I don't have a word." He said that as though he ought to. When he tugged at another pile of hazel boughs and two poles came up, connected by a rectangle of canvas sewn around the poles like a sail, Caille blinked and said, "A litter. That's a sort of litter. Traders use something like that to carry goods." She didn't want to think about how being dragged around in that had exacerbated the head and neck injuries.

They got the woman onto it, her travel pack laid in with her, her cloak and the blankets tucked around her. Eilryn had tied her in before, standing between the poles and dragging only the front. Now Caille took the rear. Eilryn wore his own pack and two others he'd dragged from the underbrush—old, threadworn packs, one holding tools, one weighted with hard, square objects.

A carter ground his team to a halt as soon as they came out onto the road. In town, she had him leave them at the Bootside. On this clear, chilly morning there were only children playing in the field. She called to one and sent her to fetch Dabrena and Adaon. Then she left Eilryn there, with an impulsive kiss that mortified her after she'd done it, and went to fetch her sisters. Elora would be in the Greenhill Cloister, and she'd know where Pelufer was.

A Heelwoman was tethering her horses to the block in front when Caille came running up to the massive, carven stone front doors. The doors were open on the skylit greenness within. Elora was just coming out, with Pelufer behind her.

Caille stared at the head and arms dangling from the off side of the Heelwoman's farther horse. Close-cropped red hair, with a tail in the back. Skin a webwork of puckered white scars.

"Where's Eilryn?" she said to the Heelwoman. "Why did you move her like that? What *happened* to her? I healed her!"

The Heelwoman raised her hands, told her to slow down. She couldn't wait through words, she couldn't wait for answers. She lunged to make sure Liath was all right. The Heelwoman caught her up in muscled arms. She struggled. She heard Elora's command to let her go, the Heelwoman's reasonable protest. She gave her body a vicious twist in the woman's grip and appealed to Pelufer.

"Let her go," Pelufer said, a hand dropping to a sheath at her belt. "She's a touch, she can't harm your friend."

The Heelwoman opened her arms and stepped back to the other side of Liath. Elora said, "Caille, wait," uncertainty spiking into fear. Caille went to Liath, ignoring the Heelwoman's suggestion that she help get her down from the horse. Elora said, "Pel, that's *her.*" As Caille raised her hands, Pelufer swore and said "Caille, *don't touch her,*" but moved too late to stop Caille from laying her hands on Liath's head.

A blinding blaze of agony seared her fingers and palms, numbed her wrists, shot up her arms, turned the world white.

She woke up in a chair in the big, enclosed front workhall of the Greenhill Cloisters. At first it seemed blessedly familiar, a balm of greenery. But something was missing.

The hall was full of white menders and one gray scholar, murmuring among themselves and consulting codices. All of Gir Doegre's seekers seemed to be here. There were some mages, and someone she thought might be a visant, sitting fascinated by a bit of angled glass. The Greenhill Cloisters were where the touches trained, but there was no shine except what she felt from her sisters, beside and behind. Their copper light was the strange absence she'd felt.

The Heelwoman was in the near corner, her back turned, with Liath wrapped and pillowed in blankets on a table in front of her. Adaon stood beside her. They were just standing there in silence, looking down at Liath.

I must be dreaming.

Elora, crouched beside her, said, "It wasn't a real burning. It only felt like it. Your hands are all right." She stroked Caille's hair off her face.

Caille gasped, her eyes going wide, her body folding with arms crossed tight at her chest to protect her hands. A touch's nightmare, to lose her hands.

"You weren't the first to find out the hard way," Pelufer said, gesturing. Two other people were wrapped and pillowed in blankets on tables in other corners of the hall. Two other women. Two other tall women. Two other women with red hair. She and Pel and Elora looked alike sometimes to people who didn't know them. Those women were different ages. One had no scars—

"Liath," she said, trying to get up.

"Yes, it's Liath Illuminator," said Pelufer, "and no, you're not going near her."

"I healed her," Caille said. "The scars are gone. That's the woman I healed. Except she looks younger. And the other . . . I was so sure . . ."

"You didn't heal any of these women," Elora said. "You couldn't have. You felt what happened when you touched one."

"They're all her," Pelufer said, with a humorless grin. "And if you can explain that, or why no touch can touch them, you'll save everyone in this holding a lot of trouble."

"Then they're not her," Caille said, sitting up. Still too stunned to reject the absurdity of what Pelufer had just said, she made a new kind of logic out of it. "I healed her. We brought her to the Bootside." She pushed out of the chair, wild to get back to Eilryn. "Dabrena—"

"I'm right here," Dabrena said, detaching herself from a clump of menders.

"I sent for you," Caille said. The child would have tried many other places in town before this one. "A woman—he said she was Liath Illuminator—she's sick, I healed her but I couldn't—"

"Slow down," said Dabrena. "Who said?"

The smooth rumble of the front doors opening turned all their heads before she could cry *Just come with me to the Bootside!*, and she saw Kazhe stop dead in the middle of a caged, catlike pacing, saw the jug she was holding slide from nerveless fingers, heard the clinking, crunching splash of its impact on the marble floor, saw her fall back as though from the sight of a ghost.

That cleared her view to see Eilryn, trailed by the flustered steward who'd opened the heavy stone doors, walking slowly into the hall. His face was set and grim under the strain of the burden he carried. On his back and dangling from his shoulders were all four travel packs. In his arms was Liath, the one Caille knew, the one Caille knew was the real one because Eilryn had told her. He let her head loll to the side so she wouldn't choke on the blood drooling from her mouth. He tried to keep hold of her arms, but one slid free, and Caille saw from its grotesque looseness that the shoulder was dislocated.

Menders rushed to take Liath from him, but he ordered them off, and whatever they saw in his eyes made them back away, looking to Dabrena.

"Let them take her, son," Dabrena said. "You're about to drop her." She took a step toward him; but Caille rushed past her, eeling away from her sisters' outflung hands, and helped him ease her to the floor.

"I couldn't wait any longer," he said. "She bit halfway through her tongue, she pulled her shoulder out when I tried to hold her, I couldn't—"

"It's all right now," Caille said, having healed the tongue with the first touch, now reseating the arm bone to make it easier to mend the tissue. "Just tell them who you are. They're the ones who can help us." She touched his chin to pull his gaze from Liath to her. "You can trust them."

His gray eyes searched hers. Whatever he sought there—honesty, certainty, assurance against risks she could not imagine, horrors that could make him so unwilling, in such extremity, to ask anyone for help—he must have found.

"This is Liath n'Geara, of the Petrel's Rest, in Clondel, in the Neck," he said, as though reciting words learned by rote. "Liath Illuminator. She's my mother. My name is Eilryn n'Torrin. I was born on the outer seas."

He looked at Caille, his only comprehensible link to this strange land he had never known, and said, "Is that enough?"

She leaned across the healed, unconscious body of his mother to lay her hands on his chest, press her face against his neck. "Yes," she breathed, drawing back, her eyes filled with only him. "Yes. That's who you are."

MINDS ALOFT ON their glow in Rekke's sky-high gleaning while their bodies sat cradled by tree roots in the Toes, they saw a twistedness around Eiden's body. A circumference of tortured sea and air, nine times as wide as none's-land on the coast. It made the sight ache, and it was filled with horrors.

The convex disk of the world curved away to all sides, a distant blur of other lands and other seas. It was land, like Eiden, and oceans, like the Nine Seas, with sky above. Whatever dwelled there, however alien, was the stuff of matter and its three constituent elements. Ioli thought all lands had human form, and was surprised at the lumpy, shapeless landmasses. There was no order to the outerlands. But they were earth and air and water. They made sense.

What was between—that made no sense. Where the sea swept around Eiden's body, it swept into a tangle. It was a distortion, a braid of impossibility, a vortex or a whirlpool with no discernible cause. It circled Eiden widdershins, and whatever went into it was no longer in either world—inside or out.

The wrongness of it, the tortured involution of it, was sickening. The twistedness occurred in the sea-space where the apparitions were. Perhaps the apparitions were things caught in that twistedness and unable to break free. Perhaps things born of that twistedness dwelled there, too.

Near the Fist was a black, burned place. A hole, straight through the twistedness. A burnhole, such as a hot brand would make if pressed against a canvas tarp. The twistedness was a barrier. It trapped, but it also shielded. It protected Eiden's shores. What went into it was swept around and never made landfall. Now there was a hole in it.

The hole was getting bigger. Tearing at its blackened edges. Widening. It might have been a pinhole when it began. Now, as they watched, an entire ship sailed through it. Straight for the coast.

Before too much longer, two ships would fit through it abreast.

Ioli came back into his flesh with the sense of sinking through fathoms of water, heights of sky become depths of glow. They were back in the spiritwood's roots, under the rope-linked treehomes of Edva-Gani-Teka, in Curl, in the Toes.

"Invasion," Rekke said. Blunt and harsh.

"Did we do that?" Ioli asked. "Did I burn that hole, by ending the siege?"

"No burnings," said Mauzl. "No time."

"He's right," Rekke said. "Whatever made that, it happened a while ago."

"The mages in the Maur Sleith shield talked about some arcing bright light on Candlenight. They said it scared them. No one listened."

Rekke grunted. "Now they know how it feels."

"Fixing?" Mauzl scrambled up from his rooty seat and rubbed his rear.

They couldn't fix this. Maybe mages could, or touches. Ioli took a deep breath. The morning air was sweet, filled with the jungle's perfume and bitterness, its loamy richness. It was so good to be home. "We have to tell someone what we've seen. Someone who can do something."

"Yes," Rekke said. Rekke who never agreed with him. Rekke who pushed him where he didn't want to go, then balked at whatever he tried to do. "But what I'd give for one of your sling beds, and a jug of palmheart wine."

"Going again," Mauzl said. Weary and forlorn.

The retorts were launching in barrages and Breida had deployed the bulk of fighters along the cove road to defend the landing and the approach when grapnels began coming over the cliff wall, flung from skiffs that had launched from the black ship. Shielders with axes hacked some loose, touches weakened others. They came too fast.

Monstrosities poured over the wall.

Human-shaped but spider-bodied and insect-limbed: four arms, two legs, heads studded with faceted eyes. Six blade-sharp claws on each bristling paw. Glinting armor plates were embedded like scales in tough flesh under wiry bristle hairs. Ranks of razor teeth, upper and lower, showed when they howled. Their mouths were in their bellies, protected by tusks that gnashed like teeth; plunge a spear or longblade down their throats and they spasmed and went still. Gaps in the plating allowed their legs to bend. The groins where legs met trunk were weak spots. They bled a clotting mucus instead of blood, and their hides resisted honed edges, but they could be cut. There was no breath in their unearthly howls, but they gagged on blades and spears.

They could be fought with shielders' weapons.

Three years of fighting phantasms had not slowed her shielders' steps. They began to beat the horrors back.

The short blast of a Khinish horn sounded once from the cove. The landing was under threat. From what? All the skiffs from the ship had come here.

Breida fought her way to the wall and looked out.

There were two ships now, black-sailed, black-hulled, painted with iridescent, alien symbols. Their retorts, aimed blind, had hit neither, though rocks still splashed into the sea around them. The decks of the second were bare of skiffs, bare of monstrosities, crewed by metallic stick figures, with dwarfen bowfolk tied or . . . impaled . . . along the prow's rails. How could the shortbows of those stunted things have the range of the arrows she'd seen? She heard the bows crank back. They were made of metal, and drawn by some sort of ratchets or winches. Stronger than any arm could draw.

The Khinish horn blew again, three short blasts.

Skiffs from the new ship had made the landing.

All right, Breida thought, turning back to the battle. *Now we're going to need a little help.*

An earsplitting crack announced the destruction of the largest retort, its throwing arm shattered by a weight of monstrosities massing on it. One of the others was burning.

The nearest monster was getting the better of the biggest shielder on the cliff. Breida came up on it from behind. It had eyes all over its head. It saw her and started to turn, still fending off the shielder with two of its arms. She swung her longblade over her head and on the forward sweep cut between the plates and straight through its neck. Its head tumbled away, taking the multitude of eyes with it. Viscous ichor bubbled up from the stump and sealed the opening, hardening to lacquer in a breath.

New eyes sprang out like instant-forming crystals all over its body.

Now we're going to need a lot *of help.*

THE GREENHILL CLOISTERS were full of growing things, a rectangle of vaulted, ribbed, pillared galleries where exotic plants and topiary trees could grow and twine. On the back of the hall was a greenhouse, newly glassed by touches who worked sand into great clear sheets. All the marble of the hall was carved in intricate, flourished relief. In Triennead times, this had been a bindinghouse, a confection of stone alive with cultured greenery in every nook and cranny. Now it served menders like Reiligh, who had repopulated it with herbs, and the few binders Gir Doegre had in residence, and young touches who came from far and wide to learn the use of their shine.

Elora drew strength from the ivied walls of this front workhall, the dark-leaved, enspiraled fig trees spaced along the sides, the golden fall of sunshine through the skylight warming the bank of herbs in the center.

She had sent all the touches away. The mages were useless, the visant had contributed all he could, the seekers had a silence on them, and the menders, having worked half the night and most of the morning, were at a loss.

We need Louarn, she thought without thinking, then chastised herself. Louarn was a charming wanderer whose heart would never come to rest. She'd outgrown her puppy love for him years ago. He was a passable big brother but a mediocre surrogate parent, and as a friend of the family he was unreliable at best, all too quick to be off roaming after whatever grabbed his interest. Caille adored him, and look what came of it: She fell in love with the first handsome, dark-haired, mysterious boy to cross her path. Eilryn was only another beautiful boy set to break their hearts. Pelufer adored Louarn, though she would never admit it, and worse came of that: She'd spent her girlhood pledged to haunts and blades, preparing to be kenai to that haunted man. Louarn didn't want a kenai. He didn't want a bladed bodyguard. He didn't want to be the Lightbreaker to Pelufer's Kazhe. He wanted to be wandering and learning. He'd be back before long, of his own. Elora had to give him that—he was as good as his word to return. But only eventually. Only when he was ready.

Or if they needed him. Elora had vowed never to need him again.

But he knew about putting broken things back together.

Liath n'Geara, the Liath Illuminator of legend, had come back to Eiden Myr in pieces. One was mortal, and could sustain damage, and carried clearly on its body every one of its four nines of years and one; it had taken a blow to the head from which it had never awakened. The other three had been conscious, with impaired memory and intermittent fits of temper and vague distraction, until they'd come within a few dozen threfts of each other; removing them to opposite ends of town had not revived them, nor had any menders' draughts or herbals. No touch could lay hands on them without intense pain. All three shared the apparent indestructibility Pelufer ascribed to hers: small cuts to the pads of their fingers healed as they were made. All three had appeared from nowhere. The seeker Nerenyi claimed that hers traveled through shadows, between realms; Pelufer said that hers had tried to flee through shadows. Each of the three was of a different apparent age: one two nineyears, one a hardened, scarred year older, one two nineyears older still, wind-scoured and sea-brined. All three were privy to information they could not possibly possess.

At least, not unless they could travel in a breath from place to place. Elora had the ways; she could pass through wood into the realm of the forest bonefolk, and from there to any other part of Eiden Myr she chose to go. The bonefolk didn't like to see the living go through the ways, and she'd stopped doing it; but that such travel was possible she couldn't deny, since she had done it herself. Haunts were capable of such travel, but haunts had no bodies at all. Pelufer said that the Liath she'd touched wasn't a haunt and wasn't dead.

The three incarnations of Liath were not haunts, not apparitions, not disembodied spirits. They were preternaturally alive—might even verge on immortal, if their abrupt convergence didn't kill them. The mortal Liath's seizures had begun the previous evening, before the siege delusion was lifted—the time when Kazhe and Dabrena were receiving visits from the incarnations. The seeker Nerenyi's incarnation had been fine until midmorning, when the pair of them rode into town, and then she'd passed out just like the others. The incarnations were parts of a whole—splinters, it seemed, of the boy's mortal mother—but coming close to each other had stunned them half to death. The mortal Liath's seizures had stopped as soon as they were all together in this workhall. It seemed less an improvement than a deeper slide into oblivion.

Seekers had pondered and debated, menders had administered poultices and medicines, mages had cast. Nothing helped. A visant held a faceted crystal in a ray of sunlight, angling it to throw different-colored rays on ceiling and walls. Elora believed he was right: The boy's mother was the crystal, and the incarnations were the rays of light. That didn't get them any closer to waking any of these women up. They had to find out what had put Liath in this state to begin with. But the boy was wary and watchful and closemouthed. He wanted them to fix this without his having to explain it.

Elora could understand some reticence. She'd spent her childhood hiding powers she was convinced would put her in jeopardy if they became known outside the circle of her sisters. She wouldn't even tell the boy she'd loved, who was her pledge now. The way Eilryn looked at Caille was the way Nolfi still looked at her sometimes. She'd hoped for such a love, for Caille, though Pelufer's first reaction had been to order Eilryn to get his bloody hands off their sister. Elora had drawn Pelufer aside. "She's in love, can't you see it? Let her be in love. We'll watch her. We'll manage somehow." Grudging, resentful, Pelufer had said, "She's too young to be in love." To them, Caille would always be too young for everything. Elora knew they had to let her go. Let her rove the wild woods. Knowing that didn't make it easier. She'd like to rove the wild woods herself; and as trader and touch and alderwoman, she felt pulled in three herself sometimes. She just wasn't prepared for her maddening baby sister to pick a secretive, potentially dangerous outerlands boy to fall in love with, complete with a magelight so bright it made their mages squint, and a battered mother out of history, broken into pieces.

Dabrena turned at last to the boy and said, "We can't help her, Eilryn. Not with the information we have. You're going to have to tell us how this came about, or there's nothing else we can do."

Eilryn raised his startling gray gaze to Dabrena, then dropped his dark head and spoke, in that alien accent that was part Norther Highlands burr, part holding smoothness, and mostly nothing Elora had ever heard before, a musical strangeness. "I never cast unless it's very urgent—to keep the ship from sinking, that sort of thing. It can set off the mines, and it wastes materials. The only things in the intorsion, besides what the mines release, are what people snared there brought in with them, and it's hard to trade with people who fear what your light will bring down on their heads. We had almost nothing. Her clothes, Caille . . . I'm sorry, there was nothing else to wear, they came from a—"

"It doesn't matter. Just tell your story. I understand."

"I'd warded us, but it must have worn off. A finger found us. He called the attack. He had one spikeclaw with him. We killed the spikeclaw, but the finger—they aren't supposed to fight, they always wait for the spikeclaws to come . . . It was my fault, I was slow, brainless, I didn't expect him to . . ."

"He attacked you," Kazhe prompted in a low, hard voice. It was the first thing she'd said to the boy—or to anyone since the boy arrived. She had been Torrin Lightbreaker's bodyguard, and from the way she'd reacted when Eilryn had walked in, Eilryn took strongly after his dead father. She'd been drinking all night and would not go sleep it off. "The fingers only point light out, but this one attacked you himself."

"He attacked me," Eilryn confirmed. "From behind. She must have felt it coming. She has eyes in the back of her head. But she couldn't see the angle of the bludgeon. She swept her blade around and shouldered me out of the way and took the blow. Her blade went halfway through the finger, and the finger went into the sea, and so did the blade. That was our only fighter's weapon. The rest was use knives and belaying pins and such. Once a finger calls the attack they swarm on you. There was only one of me and not enough weaponry. I had only enough materials for one casting. I could ward the ship again, but it would wear off. She was still bleeding. I had to stitch up the gash, and that needed time and quiet. I could outsail the spikeclaws, but the mawbellies and the steelbones have big ships, fast ships, and the fangwasps can fly. If I was sailing the ship, I couldn't be stitching the wound. There was only one thing I could see to do. A casting she had forbidden. It was all or nothing. The last leaf."

"You cast the two of you home," Dabrena said.

"Magecraft can't do that!" cried one of the mages.

Eilryn fixed her with his clear gray gaze. "Apparently it can," he said, "because I did." He turned back to Dabrena. "I cast us into light. I cast us through the inner braid of the intorsion. I aimed for the Fist, where she was always trying to go. But I . . . overshot. Next I knew we were in a field that turned out to be in the Boot. I suppose I should be grateful I didn't send us through to the intorsion on the other side and drown us. I didn't think I could bring the ship too, not alone, and I didn't want to . . . break anything or crush anyone, or bring attention on us, a whole ship appearing from nowhere in the middle of some village. I had no idea what would happen, really. Only that it would bring her home and get us out of there. Away from the spikeclaws and fangwasps. Somewhere quiet where I could stitch her up and get my bearings."

"You cast yourselves into light," Pelufer echoed in a flat voice.

Eilryn met her disbelief straight on. "Yes. Light can pass through the intorsion. It twists light, I think. It twists everything. But I made a bright, straight light, an arrow, a needle, a blade. I punched us through it."

"You couldn't have cast on yourself," the mage said. Yet he had.

"The arc of golden light we saw on Candlenight," another mage said.

"That was us, I reckon." Eilryn looked at his mother, in pieces all around him. "I did this to her. The casting . . . She didn't come back the way she was supposed to. She wouldn't wake up. Not even after Caille healed her."

She's dying. No one wanted to say it.

"Why would it splinter her into shards like this?" Dabrena said.

Nerenyi Seeker came out of her silence. "Magecraft is an actuation of creative spirit," she said. She had been a mage once. She'd traveled with Liath, when they were mages, when they were young. "Magelight touches the source of dreams, and fantasy, and memory. It works through what can be imagined and remembered to create a reality truer than itself. Liath was unconscious when Eilryn cast. Her spirit wasn't . . . anchored. It was roving through memories and dreams. Existing in several layers of self, as we all do when the cohesion of consciousness eases. The casting must have knocked her spirit loose, from her body and from itself. Different parts of her, who she was at discrete, intense times of her life—different selves flying in all directions."

"Made half of light," Adaon said. "A light that burns touches when they lay hands on the half that's flesh, because it's flesh that spirit made to clothe itself. Protect itself. Carry itself."

For once, no one accused either seeker of spewing mystic babble. Both were visants, and Adaon was Adaon, and Nerenyi had been keeper of codices on Senana, a position that commanded a deal of respect.

"Magelight did this," Dabrena said. "Magelight ought to be able to undo it." She glanced at the young mages, and they dropped their eyes and shifted their feet. *Mages,* Elora thought with contempt. *If it doesn't fit in their precious canon, they don't know what to make of it.*

Kazhe said, "This blade can inflict a wound. That doesn't mean this blade can heal it."

"Maybe it could, if you taught it how," Caille said softly.

Kazhe hocked phlegm and washed it down with whatever was in that jug, stashed or fetched from somewhere despite Elora's best attempts to have her barred from inn to alehouse.

Dabrena said to Eilryn, "Perhaps you might fix this yourself, with adequate casting materials." She avoided glancing at Liath's clothes as she asked, "What sort of leaf did you cast with?"

His chin lifted. "It wasn't flesh. It was a blank sheet of felted wood pulp, torn from the back of a drowned fisherwoman's log."

Elora understood only part of that, but Dabrena seemed satisfied. "You cast single-handed. Do you claim a triadic discipline?"

"I'm a wordsmith," he said. "Only a passable illuminator, and not much of a binder—I can scrounge and I can adapt, but I don't know how to make much."

"How did you learn wordsmithing from an illuminator?" a mage asked. *And one with a seared light to boot* hung unsaid at the end of her words.

"I . . . just did," he replied. "She taught me to scribe. I made up whatever I needed and didn't have, I suppose. I don't know how much is me and how much is . . . I don't have a word for it. The marks of the tradition, what wordsmiths learn here in their training."

"Canon?" Dabrena said.

His face lit up. "Yes! That's a good word. Canon."

He has no idea how foreign he is, Elora thought. *To him, what he does seems perfectly normal. He has no idea what ingrained traditions he just tossed over his shoulder, traditions that Pelkin n'Rolf fought for years to keep alive. He's a marvel of improvisation, and a slap in the face to every mage.*

"Will you try, Eilryn?" Dabrena said.

"Don't you think he already tried?" Caille said. "Don't you think he'd have fixed it by himself if he could?"

"I did try," he said. "I stole materials. They were excellent quality."

"Try with our mages then," Dabrena said. "Perhaps three are required."

They tried. The casting took forever, as castings did. The leaf just lay there. "It's no good," Eilryn announced, and rose with feline grace as he said to the other mages, "My thanks nonetheless. The fault is not in you, or in us, but in the light, or our understanding of the problem we address."

One moment he was a boy of nine-and-eight, struggling to understand and make himself understood in an alien world. The next he was a polished, gracious mage, so full of power that even someone with no magelight could sense it.

Don't break my baby sister's heart, Elora bade him with all her will as Caille went into his arms.

"Can't we just shake her, snap her out of it?" Pelufer said. It took a moment for Elora to realize she meant Liath. "If we wake her up, maybe they'll disappear, they'll go back into her."

"There's nothing in there to wake," Nerenyi said. "It's out on those other three tables. She'll wake only if we put them back inside her."

"We need someone who's good at puzzles," Adaon said. He looked straight at Elora. "Someone experienced in reuniting fragmented selves."

I'm not in love with him anymore. That ended a long time ago. He always comes back. I'm not jumping on an excuse to drag him here. Not just so I can see him again. Elora sighed, and told Dabrena, "I'll send for him."

She would never break her pledge's heart. Louarn saw her as a little girl, at best a half-grown sister. She'd given herself to Nolfi, mind and body and heart; she adored him, and always had, and the vestiges of her stupid senseless irrelevant girlish infatuation did not detract one whit from the love she felt for him. Nolfi was everything to her.

Everything but the minute, delicious, painful thrill she felt to know that Louarn n'Evonder would be coming home.

She could have called for Lornhollow by laying hands on any wooden object. But she went out through the garden court, through the sun-warmed glasshouse, into the crisp harvestmid air, to the deep stand of birches along the mill tributary. She laid hands on the peeling bark and drew into her the profound, earthy patience of the trees.

Only when she felt herself again, her purpose clear, did she send through her shining hands a call to the boneman Lornhollow. He had loved her mother once, so much that he passed her life force to her daughters to make them strong and make them shine. Prendra n'Anondry's love for the boneman had detracted not one whit from what she felt for Nimorin n'Belu, the love of her life.

I'm Prendra's daughter, Elora thought, and felt the deep answer in the wood.

The sun, approaching the height of its transit from Low Sea to Sea of Charms, reduced Haunch shadows to Headward-pointing stubs. As harvestmid tilted toward winter, the arc of the golden luminary became the province of Southers. Louarn, a Norther by birth and blood, lay down alone on Keiler's bed, and prepared to dream.

Dreams had used to come on him the moment he opened himself to the force of sleep that was his constant adversary. Now, rested and alert, he would have to acquire the dreaming state through an act of meditation. Traveling through dreams had never seemed a skill before, rather a wild talent kept barely under control—a rushing flood checked by the wall of his will. Now it was a flow into which he sought to release himself.

He had not slept safe since he was a boy named Mellas in the care of the stableman who'd fostered him after Flin, the small child he'd been, had woken from his safe bed to see his parents murdered by the Ennead. One day Mellas woke from his dream of safety to find that not even Bron could shield him from that Ennead—or from himself. No sleep was safe thereafter.

No beds were safe, until he came to Keiler's.

Now he would leave it.

The three visants he'd met in Sauglin were in the Toes. He'd sensed their gleaning like a beacon in the night. They had ended the siege. Louarn was not entirely surprised. When he'd met him, the visant Ioli had already triaded his two friends, already traveled through Rekke's gleaning. They had escaped the warded sleephall through their glow. Louarn had known they had the power to do in one great gleaning what Ioli had pleaded with the runners to do. But he had not known how, and they had fled before he had made time to help them, caught up in his own concerns. He had not thought to see them again. Then there they were, a beacon in the dark of night, conferring immunity on the world. A gleaning so powerful that it pulled him from the depths of his own dreams.

He knew where they were. At any moment, they might move somewhere else. They might never glean so powerfully again. They wanted to hide. If he was going to find them, it had to be now, while he had a bead on their location.

It meant risking the treacherous realms between waking and sleep. It meant leaving Keiler. Keiler had known he would go sometime. . . . *Am I only indulging in wanderlust and curiosity?* In all these years, he had still never been to the Toes. He had always wanted to go. He wanted to find these visants and learn how they had crafted their great gleaning.

He wanted to know if he could still travel through dreams.

By Keiler's side, he slept deeply, restfully, trusting. Though he had learned to be grateful for half a night's fitful slumber, he had not known true, healing sleep in half a lifetime. He had not known how it would restore him. He had not known how drained he'd been by fighting his own powers. The need for sleep was a nagging misery he'd suppressed for so long he didn't recognize its ravages. He hadn't understood that denying dreams only made them harder to control when they came. After abstinence, dreams surged in on engulfing waves, coarse and ravenous, ungovernable. Over time—just a few days, he'd found—sufficient sleep calmed that flood into natural tides, a diurnal ebb and flow, a manageable cycle. *"Dreams are offal,"* someone had told him once. *"They excrete the things our minds can't bear."* They also accreted the things that minds were meant to keep. They wove impression into memory, spun decision out of doubt, knitted raveled skeins of perception into a fabric of certain consciousness. Sleeping ill for most of his life, he had known only impaired wakefulness. He had forgotten what true waking was—the clarity, the renewal.

He had never learned to control his dreams, only to contain them. He had never learned to dream at all—not ordinary dreams, whole-cloth subjective narratives. He had never let his mind alone to do what it needed to do while he slept. He had never permitted full submergence into the muscular flow of the imagination, never surrendered to the deep currents of the subconscious mind, the storied, luminescent depths of the interior.

He had never released himself into the care of his own mind, until Keiler.

"Stay," Keiler had said, feeling the bed shift under his weight, their first night back on the farmstead. "Stay, Louarn."

"It isn't safe." He meant for Keiler. He didn't know what his dreams might do, if he let himself slip past the first light doze. Conjure horrors. Whisk him away. Melt reality and re-form it in some abhorrent configuration. He longed with all his soul to stay in that warm, drowsing bed. But it wasn't safe.

"I'll watch you," Keiler said. "I'd rather sit up all night than wake to find you gone, never knowing whether it's to huddle by the fire, or for good."

"It's you I'm—"

"I know. I'll watch, Louarn. If need be, I'll wake you." Keiler coaxed him back, covered him in blankets still warm from their bodies, caressed his weary head. "I won't let you harm the world."

He'd given in, and slept. He did not know if he half roused during the night, if Keiler's hands and voice soothed him back under, if all he'd needed was someone he trusted to reassure him that all was well, that razor shadows didn't shriek around the room, that he wasn't disappearing, wasn't falling. He did not remember what he dreamed, that first night. He only knew that he woke after dawn for the first time in three nineyears, in a golden bath of sunshine, Keiler leaning on the headboard just where he'd left him, regarding him with that crooked grin. "And not before time," Keiler said, his hand sliding from Louarn's head as he sprang up. "We Highlanders can hold our water, but much longer and you'd have woken to the tragic rupture of a noble bladder."

Keiler had stayed by him, unharmed, through all those dreaming hours.

As he did the next night, and the next. In the mornings,

Louarn would emerge from sleep as from a passage casting. "I dreamed," he'd turn to tell Keiler, awed and thrilled and humbled. "I *dreamed . . .*" His parents, his homes, all the folk he had loved without admitting it, all his crafts, all the places he'd roamed—all his selves, woven on a loom of ordinary dreaming. Keiler would chuckle and say, "You dreamed. And here we are. Whole and hale." By the fourth morning Louarn could not stop talking about his dreams, recounting every odd turn, every seamless illogic, every rediscovery, until Keiler silenced him with passion; and only in its aftermath did Louarn sit up and say, "You slept"—accusation warring with relief at the realization. "I slept," Keiler acknowledged, hands behind his head, smug and charmingly self-satisfied. "Though I roused at every hitch in your breathing, I slept unscathed beside you. You're no danger, Louarn. Not unless you choose to be."

His dreams had always taken him where he most wanted, or needed, to go. He'd never considered what they would do when he was already there.

He was happy on these acres in the Haunch, but for the first time in his life he lacked a challenge—an obstacle to surmount, a puzzle to solve, a craft to learn. With the siege ended, Herne's mages need not give their lives to recast Galandra's warding. Graefel's work on the embeddings in the wordsmiths' canon would become an academic pursuit. Both the hauntrealm and pethyar would remain accessible. Louarn had learned the binder's craft, what he set out to do a dozen years ago. Now no craft remained to him to learn but the visant's.

The bed molded to his shape. Its scents murmured of all he was leaving behind.

He relaxed his body muscle by muscle—tension, then release. He emptied his mind of guilts and cares. He remembered a shack outside Gir Mened, where he'd tried to sleep and thought he'd forgotten how, and the way sleep had taken him in an eyeblink, in midthought. He thought about what he'd heard of the Toes: dark, vine-choked jungles, fermented palm sap, bright-plumaged birds that mimicked human speech. He pictured the wild Ankleman with his lazy eye, all dark scowling threat and kind heart; the scrawny grasslands boy with the scent of ages on him; the young Toeman with his ghostly mist of hair, his dark gaze that absorbed the soul's reflections. What would he ask them? What did he want from them? They had a triad; he had none, not mage nor touch nor visant, nor did he want one. *You are one,* Jhoss said, from the head of the table, which was the Head of Eiden, a table wrought in the shape of Eiden, a bonewood table white as bleached sedgeweave, old as time, rooted deep in the earth. He touched the near foot of the table, the Toes, and Jhoss said, *Don't tickle him. Your door is there,* and pointed behind him. It was: the crystalline passageway stood open to receive him. He turned to enter it, with a troubling sense that he had bidden Jhoss inadequate farewell, failed to convey the thanks he deserved for pointing to the doorway— that there was something he ought to have said. Then Lornhollow was prodding him, pressing urgent words into the flesh of his upper arm with the handspeech of the bonefolk, and he sat bolt upright, still in Keiler's bed.

"Lornhollow," he said, gripping the covers hard. "What is it?" The bonefolk resisted being used as messengers. They resisted taking the living through the ways. The more humans learned of them, the more reclusive they became. Had something happened to one of the girls? Lornhollow would not have come on a minor errand—

"Liath Illuminator," Lornhollow said aloud, in dry, rasping tones, with the stiff precision of a foreign utterance. All their names were foreign words to him. He would not have been able to make the first word with his hands; the symbols their handspeech mimed were only consonants. "Prendra's daughters have need of you."

If I don't go now, the visants will move, and I'll never find them.

Louarn could not fathom how Caille, Pelufer, and Elora could have become involved with Liath Illuminator, but he didn't need to understand a call for aid to heed it. *"I don't know where I am,"* Liath had said, in the attic refuge of her mind. *"If I find out, I'll let you know."* Perhaps she was letting him know.

He would have to find those visants another time.

The crystalline passageway would still open to him. He had not traded his dreaming powers away for a good night's sleep. He would dream himself to Gir Doegre. He thanked Lornhollow and said he would follow. Lornhollow transited through the cottage wall. Louarn made for the door, to tell Keiler where he was bound. Pelkin had thought to return to his pledge upon his death, but his path had taken him elsewhere. Louarn would not again let any farewell fall short.

A dream had told him that, and Keiler had given him back his dreams.

Rekke moved them through the watery luminescence of their glow toward the last destination he would let the grieving monkey talk him into before he had a jug, a meal, a woman, and a good night's sleep, in tidy visant order.

Ioli had insisted on going back to the head runner and telling him what they'd seen—the twistedness, the burnhole, the invading ships, the lot. Well, now they knew that magecraft couldn't fix the bloody thing. Herne took the nine mages he'd held ready to recast Galandra's warding and set them to darning the hole, and all their vaunted light had only torn it wider open.

Then Ioli had insisted on going to the Fist—to see for himself, he said, but they could have seen for themselves from a safe distance, and Rekke knew full well that what Ioli wanted was to maneuver him into mending it. "It isn't none's-land anymore," Rekke had told him. "You won't be immune to the things that are attacking that place, and neither will I, and neither will the runt." But off they went to the cliffs of perdition, and saw the shield hanging on by a thread. Rekke *saw* the hole, in person, gleaned the scorched rift in the seascape, and he tried, then, despite himself—tried to drag those burnt, frayed edges together, tried to plug the forsaken thing, tried to close it like the lips of a wound. He saw, then, in person, the rift widen, the grasped edges peel back, the exacerbation his attempt at operant gleaning had produced.

Ioli begged him, then, to go back to Jhoss—pestilent Jhoss, who'd tried to cage them like rats the last time he'd seen them. Rekke would not go back to Jhoss. He would go to Louarn. Louarn wanted things from him, too; but Louarn was a prettyboy, a smatterer, a dabbler. Rekke could disdain that frozen glow.

So they slid into the permeation of their glow, and sought Louarn. And where they came was into a realm that did not exist, had not existed scant breaths ago and would not exist mere moments hence: A realm of prismatic brilliance, crystalline extrusions, shimmers and spangles of light that tickled like the bubbles in sparkling wine. A realm that had no dimension beyond its own hollowed length. A tube, a tunnel, a white passageway. A conduit.

Louarn was walking through that conduit, a pellucid silhouette casting shadows of ruby, sapphire, and topaz. Sensing their presence, he turned, a figure of liquid diamond, corporeal ice. He paused; Rekke waited for Ioli to glean him, to glean how Louarn saw them in this place, what he took them for, why he paused; but Ioli gleaned nothing, and it came to Rekke that he didn't, either: he had no idea where they were. No idea whatsoever. He always knew where he was. He knew without thinking, and so he hadn't thought about it, but now that he did, he realized he didn't. They had gone beyond the realms he knew, into a realm he had never even glimpsed. A nauseating vertigo swayed him, and he clutched the monkey and the runt to keep himself upright. Louarn turned and continued on, a cold translucence receding into coruscation.

Behind was nonexistent. Rekke would not look behind. He dragged Ioli and Mauzl forward in desperate, stumbling pursuit, eeling past razor-edged extrusions, ducking under plunging stalactites. He threaded a needle's eye of crystalline constriction. They did not belong here. The farther they fell behind, the more the passage tightened. It was not their passage. It remained open only so long as they kept the figure of ice and tricolor shadow in view.

Louarn slipped out of sight.

Rekke hurled the other two ahead of him, then dove through the closing iris of the passage.

He sprawled into a scrape of knees and elbows and a faceful

of tufted herbs. Ahead of him, the runt and the monkey were scrambling to their feet. Ahead of them, framed by them, Louarn was shrugging his long coat back into alignment and stamping his boots tight. He looked up and said, in a mild tone, "That is the most dangerous thing I have ever seen anyone, anywhere, do."

Rekke didn't need Ioli's gleaning to know that the iceheart had seen people do some very dangerous things. But Rekke had Ioli's gleaning. He had it all the time now, just below the threshold of awareness. His glow wasn't his own anymore. It was one-third of a greater glow. Through the mingled powers of that glow, he gleaned that Louarn was concealing relief at the sight of them, come safe through on the coattails of his transit. "Couldn't you *see* us?" Rekke bellowed, bouncing to his feet. "Couldn't you wait one *grieving* breath?"

"No," Louarn replied, and set off for the nearest building, a pillared hall of white marble veined with malachite. "It's a dream, not a realm," the iceheart called over his shoulder. "Don't ever take yourselves there again."

"Not in thrice nine nonned years," Rekke grumbled, following in a stubborn stroll as Ioli ran ahead, crying the crisis, and Mauzl trotted after, into the cloisters of the Strong Leg holding.

Liath Illuminator lay in shards around the cluttered, overgrown workhall, and in the midst of her the brightest magelight Louarn had ever seen, the sun rising to spear a deep cavern through the minute aperture of a crack in the rock—light rationed, light occluded, light choked down to its minimum diffusion, and so radiant he winced in its glare. "You only focus it by trying to cut it off that way," he said to its owner, a pale, dark-haired boy too tall for his body, too composed for his age. "I suppressed my light for nine years. It only makes the shadows darker."

"Where I come from," the boy replied, bristling invisibly behind his calm gray gaze, "a magelight condemns its possessor to death. You see to your shadows, I'll see to mine."

Louarn felt a genuine smile push at his face, and let it bloom.

There were curt, pragmatic introductions then, urgent explanations; he set the Toeman's pent desperation loose and let him expand upon the fractured account he'd called out as they walked here. Mauzl took immediately to Caille and Eilryn, who were of an age with him, and they to him; it put the most intense blue glow beside the strongest shine and brightest magelight, an arrangement that had marked implications. With his puzzler's eye, Louarn watched the pieces interlock, while he puzzled over the dual problems of broken Liath and burned intorsion.

Ioli could not glean the unconscious illuminator, or lift the siege delusion from her mind if it had hold of her. Caille could not heal the burnhole in the intorsion, and Rekke gleaned that her efforts had worsened it, as had his own and those of the mages.

While they were engaged in their efforts, four bonefolk emerged from the florid marble of the walls to stand in tattered silence by Liath and her incarnations. Louarn knew two of them, Writhenrue and Irongrim, but not well. He said their names, inclined his head. A chill settled on the hall. The bonefolk sensed imminent death. The bonefolk avoided observation. This looming death must be strange and powerful, to draw them into a crowded hall. Even comatose, even broken, Liath was a lodestone. The harbinger was clear.

At the sight of them, Kazhe slung her jug of spirits to Rekke and demanded transit to the Fist to fight the invasion. Irongrim sent her from the hall in a storm-scented pungency of phosphorescence and a clinking rain of small blades and metal bindings, then melted into the nearest marble wall. The remaining three bonefolk would not explain their presence to Louarn.

Louarn believed that there was only one way to put Liath n'Geara back together again. They must combine the powers of all three lights.

He endured a few breaths of debate. Two lights had never been effectively combined; lights tended to work against each other; when lights worked toward the same end at all, their means were too different to blend. To put an end on it, he said,

"I bind the three lights in myself. No attempts have ever included me." He looked to Dabrena, who was in charge here.

"All right," she said. "Yes. We have to try."

Elora spoke for her sisters and Ioli for the visants. They agreed. Eilryn agreed to be wordsmith; Louarn would be binder, and a young local mage named Tofro would illuminate.

Louarn drew a casting circle on the floor with a piece of charcoal. Just behind the triadic point where he would sit, he bade Dabrena's menders set Liath's mortal body, with its three incarnations beside it. While he sang, he would reach back, and he and Caille and Elora would lay hands on Liath. Pelufer would have to endure the pain of touching the incarnations, but pain held little sway over her after a dozen years of the blade. He directed the visants to form a loose circle around the lot; their power required the least physical proximity and the best vantage. "I'm not familiar with your methods," he said to them, "but your glow fills this hall down to the smallest crack. If there is a focus or a linkage you employ, please prepare it. Glean me, if that will do it." Then he gestured the mages to the other triadic points of the casting circle.

As Eilryn sat, Dabrena, who had been a wordsmith in the time of the old light, handed him a long sedgeweave leaf. "These are the passage and birth strophes," she said, "and what I know of the hein-na-fhin—the one-of-three, the casting the last Ennead did to combine their leading triad into one mage. They're the only applicable canon I can offer."

Eilryn scanned the lines. The dilation of pupils, the flesh prickling on his forearms attested to the beauty and power of what he read. "I know them now," he said to Dabrena, and handed the leaf back. "Thank you. This will help."

Rekke said, "You're going into that grieving white-quartz nightmare again, aren't you."

"Something like it, I think," Louarn said. "More mist than crystal. More waking than dream. Don't follow me there. Make a bridge, if you can. Make a way back, for me to point her to. Offer her a choice. A . . . path."

Then Louarn was handing Eilryn casting leaf and binding

board, and the rock-dove quill and lampblack ink he requested, and the casting had begun.

As Eilryn scribed and Tofro drew, as the glorious swell of their magelights joined with his, Louarn opened his shine to the shine of Prendra's daughters, felt the current of life force that connected them: through the marble they sat on, through the air they shared, through the link of Liath's flesh. Opened his glow to the aqueous glow of the visants, invited their silvered indigo and slate and sky to know his own glow—his cold glow, he gleaned from their gleaning, his glow the blue of deep ice. That was a harder opening, and a hard gleaning—to see how they saw him, the iceman, the iceheart, and not shrink from the intimate scrutiny. Elora and Pelufer and Caille were warm and known, heartwood and copper and love, as familiar to him as his own breath. Rekke and Ioli and Mauzl were a sea tide, a moon tide, slate shifting on quicksilver, a limitless blue-morning sky, and in their eyes he was a coldness, a stranger to himself. Too open, too known, too delved—he could not bear it—

Open yourself, Louarn. As he began to sing, as golden light surged into the shine and the glow filling the hall, he let go of his own shadows—released into the casting the affections and memories of Mellas, the runner boy sent to fetch the Ennead the most promising mage in generations: Liath Illuminator.

The workhall of the Greenhill Cloisters flooded with shine and glow and light until to Louarn the space seemed filled with white mist. He wondered if the spectators saw it as white, or if the mages among them saw only magelight and the visant seekers only glow and the rest of them nothing at all. He wondered what the bonefolk saw.

He could not see any of them.

He could not see the other mages, either, though he felt their light joined with his; he could not see the visants. He could not turn to look for the touches. His voice rose to the peak of its range, but he was not singing the note—his body was singing it, somewhere beyond him. The white space in which he existed was not the same as the one he and Pelkin had passed through. The hue and tint of the whiteness were different, complex, flavored by others' lights. It was intoxicating. So much power . . . so much *light* . . .

The attic refuge of Liath's mind came around him in a dizzying rush, angled wooden walls and beams coalescing as though they'd rushed inward from a great distance, swooping in to surround him.

Liath stepped up to him, young and plain-clothed, righteous and unscarred, the Liath he had fetched to the Holding.

Liath stepped up to him, a year older, scarred and Ennead-garbed and bladed, the Liath who had appeared to him and Keiler, the Liath who had fought her way free of that black mountain and gone on to save the world.

Liath stepped up to him, shorn and seaworn, vested in death, her scabbard empty: Liath as she had been when she lost consciousness, hardened into an indomitable spirit by two nineyears at sea defending herself and her son.

None of them was the Liath whose mortal body lay beyond this attic, beyond the white mist. Caille had healed that Liath. That Liath bore no scars, only years and the salt scouring of the sea. That Liath wasn't here.

That Liath was where these three had to go.

"Hello, Mellas," they said—stepping *into* each other until they occupied one oscillating form, different features gaining and losing prominence, clothes and accoutrements shifting and blending. Three into one: Eilryn had scribed enough of the hein-na-fhin to reunite them. But they could not settle on one form, because that form was a destination they had not yet reached.

"Your head is bleeding," he said.

She put up a hand. It came back smeared. "It's all right," she said, in an eerie trebled dissonance of voices. "Heads bleed a lot for nothing."

"You didn't show the wound before. You're getting closer to what you are."

"I'm lost, Mellas," she said. The wound healed, the blood vanished. She picked up the pigeon feather, in a strangely blurred, elongated motion. The feather looked remarkably like the quill Eilryn had requested. She drew a kadra in blue light against the sepia shadows, a kadra that trailed and echoed itself as three of her drew it. "I found so many people I knew, but none of them could tell me the way. I think Nerenyi got me close, but I lost her somewhere. I'm trying to go home. I'd like to stay here—I'm safe here, I love this place—but it isn't home. It's only a memory of home. That's not enough." She dropped the feather in a long, suspended blue sparkle that snapped into clarity as it settled to the floorboards and became one feather again. "I'm trying to find my son. He knows where I am. Do you know the way, Louarn?"

"That's the way," Louarn said, pointing. In the far wall of the blurring attic, a blue glow was seeping in, widening, taking on firm dimension. Not a passage, not like the crystalline tunnel he walked through; a gateway. Blue freedom. His icy heart ached to see it. "That's the way back to yourself, and your son. That's the way home, Liath."

A strange smile spread across her faces. "It's a guider. Mine were blue."

He gestured her toward it. She took three steps, then paused. "What about you?" she asked.

"I have my own way back."

"Lucky boy," she said, and stepped, all of her, into the blue.

"And three become one," Louarn murmured, letting go of the attic, letting go of the mist, rejoining the highest note of his bind-song, easing his throat off its sustained reach, easing back into his body seated cross-legged and chilled on the marble floor.

The white mist separated into copper, silver, gold.

The casting leaf had dissipated.

The visants stood blinking. Tofro sat gape-mouthed and Eilryn was surging to his feet. Louarn twisted to see Pelufer clenched and pale, Elora touching her own belly. The three incarnations were gone. Caille was lifting her hand from Liath's face.

The illuminator's eyes opened.

LIATH N'GEARA L'DANOR gazed up at a starburst glare. Bone-white ribs arched into it. The belly of a whale? Strange, to find the inside of a whale so bright. The glare resolved into a sky-light. No skylights in a whale. A marble hall. Ceilinged with carved faces peering from stone foliage. Her nostrils flared at a heart-melting redolence of herbs, humus, stone. How long since she had smelled earth so near? Half a life. Shadows hovered close. Nothing odd in that; they always had. Nothing nearer than the vaulted ceiling would focus.

The sun slid out of the frame of the skylight. One shadow lightened into a girl with a round face, fawn skin, blond-streaked brown hair, hazel eyes glazing with tears. The other resolved into a man too dark to be Evonder, too old to be Mellas. Some dreamlike melding of the two. A man of white light and black shadow. A dream. A death-dream. Death was white.

Flat stone drenched her with chill through a scratchy weave. This was no dream. This was no afterlife. She fought free of a tangle of wool. Groped for her longblade, found a dim, tangible memory of it torn from her grip. "Where's my son?" she said, low and hard. "Where's my ship?"

The white shadow said, "Your ship is lost. Your son is here."

Eilryn came into view. She drove herself to her feet. He embraced her. She did not embrace him back. She checked him, compulsively, hands firm on head and neck and arms and back, seeking breaks, wounds, blood, probing for injury. Finding him sound, she scanned the hall. Dyed clothes, awed wary faces, most human from the looks of it, most unarmed. Bonefolk—she'd always wondered if there were bonefolk in the outerlands.

The finger had captured them. Why hadn't he killed them? Why had he brought them here? Where was he?

"What land is this?" she said.

"It's home," Eilryn said. "You're home, Mother."

An alien architecture of green-veined white marble. "This is no bloody home of mine. What *is* this place?"

"One of the Triennead holdings," a petite, authoritative, familiar woman stepped from the periphery to say. The shadows were all standing now, all expecting something of her. "We found the other two while you were gone."

"You took a blow to the head," said a woman with night-black hair in piled braids as tight and intricate as a rope flourish—a woman the very image of someone she had loved. "You've just come to. Give it a moment."

"No one here will harm you," said a girl like a thin, wiry double of the round-faced, streak-haired girl, older by a few years, harder by many orders of magnitude. She was dangerous, that one, and bladed. Another, the oldest, stood fey and shining in angled sunglare. The sight of the three young women side by side, carved from the same substance and yet so different, sent a queer jolt through her.

Liath stared at her son. *"What did you do?"*

"I did that casting," he said. "The one you forbade. I made us into light, sharp and bright enough to cut through the intorsion. I brought us back to Eiden Myr. Because you were knocked out when the finger clubbed you, it split off three . . . projections of you. They all found their way here, somehow. Those visants and these touches and Louarn and Tofro and I . . . we cast them back into you. I'm still not sure how it happened. But you're home, Mother. All those years, you were trying to go home. I brought you home."

"You idiot," she breathed. She gripped his shoulders, pulled him roughly against her. "You mindless, *reckless* fool! You could have gotten yourself killed!" Shouting at him, berating him, while her callused hand cradled his daft, precious head. *I've become my mother,* she thought. "Never, *never* again." She palmed the tousled black hair from his eyes. "Never, Eilryn."

He stared back at her, unyielding; then his face broke into a rare, full smile, the smile that pierced her heart because it was his father's smile. "Never until the next time it's down to me to save your life."

She swore at him and let him go, and turned to the crowd surrounding them. People she'd been with at the same time in different places. People changed from those she'd known; in her half life she had accepted those changes the way one accepted the skewed logic of dreams, but now she fought profound estrangement, to see how the years had molded them into folk she no longer knew.

Well, I can only imagine how I must look to them. She shook it off and said, "You have to warn your shield. The intorsion is a trap that surrounds Eiden Myr. It's full of things that hate the light. Our transit made a hole in it. Those things will exploit that hole."

"The invasion began at dawn," said Mellas—no, Louarn. Louarn who was Evonder's son, as old now as Evonder had been when she had known him.

"Where's Kazhe?" she said, scanning the hall. No warriors here except the bladed girl who was Kazhe's prentice. The prentice who sparred with shadows Kazhe couldn't see. They needed someone who understood large-scale battles.

"Fighting the invasion," the girl said. "In the Fist, where the hole is."

The Fist was Breida's post. *She didn't want to know me*— She shoved the memory away hard. "I don't suppose you can mend that hole."

Louarn said, "Three lights have failed in respective attempts. Using all three in tandem is the next order of business." With a strange, cold smile, completely alien to the Mellas she had known, he said, "I don't suppose you can tell us what this intorsion *is.*"

She looked at Eilryn, blinking. Hadn't he told them?

"He only explained how he cast you free of it," said the round-faced girl, the youngest of the three sisters. "And about fingers and spikeclaws . . ." She and Eilryn shared a glance. *Oh, bollocks,* Liath thought. *The first pretty girl he sees . . .* Well, she'd worry about young love later.

"The intorsion is a buffer the outerlanders created around Eiden Myr to keep themselves safe from it," she said. "Galandra's warding folded the world around it. There were gales, earthquakes, seaquakes, floods. I don't know how far the effect extended, but it ravaged the lands nearby. They wove a fence around it, threw a blanket over it—however you want to think of it. They protected themselves. Years passed. Generations. Their civilization recovered. Then something else happened, a cataclysm, a great war—something like a magewar, I think, but that's guesswork. I couldn't piece too much together from the Outer Shores folk." She paused to master frustration—at the difficulty of expressing the complexities of intorsion culture, and at the deficits in her own understanding. She concluded, with harsh simplicity, "The details of the intorsion's making are lost. I can't tell you what it's made of."

"They were defending themselves," the oldest sister said, almost to herself. She had an ethereal beauty, like sun-dappled woods, but when she spoke, even in a murmur, there was a startling power in her voice, and others listened. "We hurt them, and they were just trying to stop us from hurting them more."

"They hurt us," said one of the folk in white. Menders, Nerenyi had called them. Liath couldn't help but see them as the warders she remembered, folk who'd in the main tried to make her do things she didn't want to do. "They drove us out. They persecuted us. Galandra's warding was our last defense, and there's nothing in any codex to imply that she knew it would do harm on that scale."

Liath said, "The people Galandra's warding hurt are long gone. What's deadly in the intorsion was planted there by those who made it. The folk trapped there were people just like us, descendants of a conflict that happened more than twice nine nonned years ago, with only memory to rely on."

Dabrena said, "We have three triads here and fighters dying in the Fist. Let's get that hole closed up."

Only one voice raised objection: that of the youngest sister, the gentle one who reeked of unseen powers, the one who'd captured Eilryn's affection. "But the sealost," she said.

"Some survive," Liath said. "They're stronger than the outerlanders were. At my best count, there are still a dozen ships of your folk out there."

"We'll send mages to cast them home," Dabrena said. "Eilryn can teach them how. The shield has only a few coasters, unreliable in high seas, but the Khinish were refitting their fleet to fight the siege. We'll message the headwoman to see if she'll mount a rescue mission instead."

"Casting them home will make more holes," the middle sister said.

"And we'll mend them. First we mend the one there is."

Kazhe cut down the last of them and wiped her blade on its bristle-brush hide. The weapon drank blood, but wouldn't absorb the stinking snot these things were filled with.

The surviving shielders and their stewards and other support had dropped exhausted to the stony ground on all sides. Only their commander remained on her feet. Kazhe had barely acknowledged her when she arrived; the shield was overwhelmed, there was work to be done, she did it. Her blade sliced through the armor plates of the enemy's hide. She just lopped off the limbs, the head if she had a spare moment, and moved on to the next. Cleaved her way down to the landing, where shrieking, skeletal reinforcements massed. Mowed that field of metallic stalks, then worked her way back to clean up the cliff. She'd thought it would be exhilarating to be in the thick of battle again. She might as well have been practicing flourishes.

"You're Kazhe n'Zhevra," the leader said. A solid, redheaded Highlander, as thick as her older sister was thin, she was torn and bloodied, her armor scored and dented. She walked with a limp. Her touches were all dead.

Kazhe nodded, pulling a glove off and wiping her face.

The Shipseer was still coming. No halt three respectful paces away, no hand extended in thanks. She bore down on Kazhe with all her height and breadth and landed an open hand square in her chest, hard enough to drive the wind out before her fingers closed on the sweat-soaked shirt. Kazhe was lifted off her feet and slammed against the rock wall. She tucked her chin, protected her head. The scabbard of her blade jammed hard against her spine. She could have struck, kicked, kneed; she didn't know what stopped her. Fatigue, she told herself. Consideration—she wouldn't take down a leader in front of her command. Curiosity, to see what had the bloody woman so riled. But it was none of those.

"You could have melted every enemy weapon," the Shipseer said, straightarming her against the stone. "How many deaths bought you that hour's entertainment, *blademaster*?"

Kazhe dragged in air. "It would have disarmed you all. I stopped your puking invasion and left you bladed. Get off your high horse, stoutslinger."

The Shipseer shoved away, eyes on the sea; Kazhe stepped up on an archer's block to look over the wall. Three black-hulled ships sailed toward them in angled formation. Larger than the two that drifted crewless, with different sigils on their sails. Their decks seethed with slithering things. Masses of them boiled over the rails, dropping into the swells. The sea churned, then combed into a spread of approaching ripples.

"Maybe better dead," Kazhe said softly.

"Those are weapons," the Shipseer said. "Metal or hide or scales, they're deployed as weapons, like any spear or arrow. Try. See what your powers can do."

"Your fighters—"

"—will rearm." She ducked, and barked warning at the ragged shield behind her moments before a flight of arrows arced over the wall. "*Now*, Kazhe."

Kazhe drew her blade in a sweep over her head. She released her shine into it as it cleared the scabbard. One arrow split like a hair on the blade. Then the blade blazed with ruby light, and there were no more arrows. A peek over the wall showed shrunken archers along the ships' bows waving irate, empty hands. Cries came from the shield behind her. She had disarmed them, too.

The sea was still streaked with oncoming worms. Her shine had no effect on them. Two more ships were tacking to follow their fellows through the hole.

The Shipseer was back with her siege engines, ordering runners inland to procure whatever tools could double as weapons—spades, mallets, anything.

Around the next headland, from the Sea of Storms, three other ships were surging into view. Good pine-sided Eiden Myr coasters, gaff-rigged fore-and-aft, crewed by figures of flesh and blood. At the same moment, Kazhe heard the horns of overland reinforcements—two full, sustained blasts, perhaps a mile away.

The worms would make landfall before any of them arrived.

At a dead run, she could make it down the cove road to head off the worms. She didn't know if they could scale the rocky cliff. She'd have to take that chance, and defend the landing. She was halfway to the break in the trees when the Shipseer's shout and a rumble of weight on wooden casters stopped her.

"Back!" the Shipseer ordered. "To me, Kazhe!"

They were aiming a siege engine at the cove. *You're going to hit your own poxy ships.* Kazhe couldn't make herself understood for the racket. With an oath, she trotted over to tell the Shipseer she'd cover the landing.

"I'm taking the landing out," the Shipseer said. "Stay put."

"Shielder ships are coming from Headward," Kazhe said. "They won't—"

"They'll head off the new ships, engage at sea. You don't melt boathooks, do you, or chains, or grapnels?"

"Only if they're wielded with intent to kill," Kazhe said. It was the same reason her shine had not turned the dormant siege engines to sawdust. This one's sling was loaded now. The Shipseer pushed her back a step as the arm released and called out a word Kazhe didn't know, some warning to her folk. A deafening coveward explosion lifted rock and sand and wood debris high into the air.

"Back to the wall," the Shipseer said to Kazhe. "That's your post. If I signal you, you release that shine again. No backtalk, no bright ideas. Understood? On my signal." Then she was gone to position her remaining fighters. Kazhe was no more than another weapon, strung and drawn against the coming attack. There was no question who was in command here.

A grin spread across Kazhe's face. She strode back to the wall. The sea rocked in swells, no more worm streaks cutting its surface. The shielder ships would meet the enemy ships in moments. One black ship had been hulled by a shielder missile. More black ships were approaching the hole. More plainwood coasters were coming round the other headland, up the arm from Maur Aulein.

Now, this is a battle, Kazhe thought.

A worm twice her length and breadth came surging over the wall. Its segmented body had moved eel-like through the water, then sprouted horny barbs for scaling the rock. She cleaved it lengthwise and came up under the head of the next, hopping back to avoid a spray of acid or poison as the writhing tentacles on the falling head thrashed wildly. There were no eyes, but translucent hairs stood up all over each chitinous segment, shedding water, tasting the air, gauging its currents.

Shielders with rocks and sledges were smashing at its fellows as they slid over the wall. Kazhe killed another two and sensed her own movements attract more. She fell back to head off the rest, her blade spinning and slashing, and heard the Shipseer calling orders to form the line into clumps. The blind worms responded to motion. Back-to-back in tight groups, the shielders drew the massing creatures to defensible points and kept them from overrunning the battleground. Now Kazhe scythed through targets grouped for her convenience. Battle lust flooded her weary limbs with hot blood. Drenched in sweat, spattered with poison, she danced through the teeming foe. She was no longer aware of the blade in her hand or the movements of her limbs. They were one and the same.

She was still hacking at the last one when all were felled.

Some writhed in half-death, heads smashed. The cliff was piled with disarticulated segments. One shielder lay crushed or trampled; two more had fallen to poisoned wounds, and menders were trying to draw the poison out with poultices. Kazhe let someone squirt cool water into her mouth from a linen bag, then went to look over the wall. The Shipseer came to her side as she stepped up on the archer's block.

"Reinforcements are here," the Shipseer said. "I stationed them back beyond the camp to keep them out of your power's reach." She looked out at the launches rowing in from the parent ships. Metal ladders were lashed along their sides, folded into themselves, ready to be unfolded and braced on the seafloor. They carried eight-foot human forms, not wearing armor but made of armor, wielding spiked maces and double-headed battle-axes whose blades fanned nearly as wide as Kazhe was tall. "I can't leave them there. Do your working."

Kazhe shook her head. "It'll take their weapons, too. I don't know how far it reaches. Farther than you've put them."

The shielder ships had engaged the parent ships. The sea rang with shrieks and cries, the clang of iron on unknown metal, the crunching splinter of stove wood as a plainwood ship rammed a black hull. Several craft were in flames. There would be no more support from seaward.

"I have to deploy those shielders," the Shipseer said.

Kazhe ground her teeth, nails scoring the rock.

"You know what you have to do, Kazhe." The Shipseer hadn't come over to seek Kazhe's advice. She was determining that an order would be carried out. Her voice remained level, her demeanor calm. She was a rock. Kazhe found herself filled with an uncharacteristic warmth. Pride, she realized. She was proud to serve under this rock of a commander. But she couldn't do what the woman wanted her to do. She didn't have that kind of control of her power.

"It's all or none," she said, watching the enemy close the distance. In her mind she heard Pelufer's cry of surprise and outrage as her new longblade slagged in her hands because Kazhe was trying to destroy Liath's. She hadn't even told this woman her sister was home.

"Firewarding one building doesn't fireward them all," the Shipseer said. "Powers can be targeted."

"Mine are. They target any weapons in my awareness." She was spouting menders' words. That was how they'd characterized what she did. She had never tried to describe it. She just did it.

"Then split your awareness. When you fight, you don't cleave your allies. You know who's with you and against you." She turned Kazhe by the shoulder. Their eyes locked. Kazhe didn't shrug out of the shielder's grip, though it dug into nerves. She wanted to take direction. She wanted to be wielded. She wanted to be *aimed*.

"Deploy your fighters," she said, and stepped back from the wall, and drew her blade in a silken sigh. Back another step, as the Shipseer ordered fresh fighters into position. Back, and back, until she stood in the center of the battleground, midway between the shield and whatever would come over that wall, whatever could claw its way up the path from the cove. If she failed, she would be the only blade left. If she failed, she would be the first to fall.

I am kenai, she thought, releasing her crimson shine like a flow of blood into the transcended metal of the blade. *I am kenai. I am the blade. I strike where my will directs me.*

Ladders clanged on stone. Armored hulks with wicked axes and spiked flails swarmed over the wall. Kazhe aimed her shine at what she could see.

The maces and chains and axeheads slagged. The flails and axe poles dusted. The armor was part of their bodies and resisted the shine, but they were disarmed. Goaded past fury, they charged.

Kazhe cleaved the ones she could reach, turned to sweep her blade through the ones that had got past her—and was deafened by the ring of iron weapons on metal skin, the roar of two nonned shielders meeting the charge.

Meeting it, and holding.
She had focused her powers. She had not unbladed the shield.

Nerenyi moved off to the side as the three lights prepared to
mend the hole in the intorsion. She'd watched Liath try and
fail to shrug back into the culture she'd come from. She was
hard, distant, driven. Not the old comrade who had returned to
pull Nerenyi from the brink; not the struggling friend Nerenyi
had traveled with. This Liath was more than the sum of her
parts.

The bonefolk remained where they had stood since the
mending of Liath had begun—by the wall farthest from the
door, blending into the shadowed foliage of ivy and trained fig
trees. She seemed to be the only one who noticed, or cared, that
they had not gone.

Louarn drew a perfect circle on the marble floor in chalk of
ochre, rose, and robin's-egg. The mages, touches, and visants
arrayed themselves along the trebled line, preparing to sit;
everyone else backed toward the walls, as much on the fringe as
the bonefolk.

Nerenyi sidled closer to the bonefolk.

Kazhe rappelled down the cliff to dispatch a boatload of metallic stalk-things packing the rocks with sacks of powder meant
to turn the cliff into a tumble of stone. She'd sent the sackers
into the sea in pieces and dumped most of the powder when another boatload of the things came toward her. Gripping the slick
rope with one hand, she groped in the rocks with the other. If
there was one more sack . . . Hah—there. She dragged it out.
Something spilled over her hand like a stream of water. A
jagged stone caught at the sack. Not too big a hole. Enough
powder should be left by the time it reached its target. She saw
a dull glimmer in the rocks and ignored it, trying to brace her
feet on barnacles when a wave swept the slippery seaweed

back. Finding purchase, she hurled her sack. It wobbled through the air, spewing powder, and caught the skiff at the midships rail. The contact explosion cut the skiff in half; an eyeblink later, the forward half exploded, too, sending the last of the crew out over the waters in a glittering black metallic burst.

Faces popped into view at the top of the wall. Kazhe couldn't hear what they were saying. She couldn't hear anything. The Shipseer mimed tying a knot and hauling. Kazhe lashed the rope around herself. Only when they were starting to lift her, in fits and jerks, did she look over and see what had glinted at the corner of her eye when she pulled the last sack free.

A pewter triskele. As her body was hauled past, she snagged the chain with the tip of her blade. It slid down to the guard. She looped it around and sheathed the blade with the pendant dangling from it.

"It's Torrin's triskele," she told the Shipseer, when she could hear again, when she was huddling herself dry by a pathetic fire. The place was crawling with shielders now; she could sleep before she was needed again.

The Shipseer touched a fingertip to dull, dented, salt-encrusted pewter. "My sister's felt alive, the time I touched it. That just feels like pewter."

Kazhe dropped pendant and chain into an inner pocket of her coat. She'd have to find someone to take the thing to the Strong Leg. It wouldn't travel through the bonefolk's ways, and they'd bloody well better return her the way they'd brought her, when this was done. If it ever was. She didn't know how many enemy ships were out in that twistedness, but the twistedness was many leagues wide and circled the entire coast of Eiden Myr. That could be a lot of ships.

I was hanging where he died, she thought. *Right where he died, crushed in the rockfall. Right where I almost fell to join him. Right under where that bloody illuminator pulled me back.*

She shook herself. Scrabbling feet had probably knocked the thing loose from somewhere else, or the sea had worked its long fingers in to pull it from a deeper place. It didn't matter.

That was all a long time ago, a lifetime ago, down a long dark swallowhole.

"It is just pewter," she said, offhand. "His light was seared like all the rest. It's as dead as he is. So is that pendant."

The Shipseer's red head turned toward the sea, a reflexive movement, abruptly checked. Kazhe said, "Your sister's come home, Shipseer. She's in the Strong Leg holding, with her son. Torrin's son. The grieving likeness of him. You have a nephew. His name is Eilryn."

The shielder stared at her for long breaths.

"Don't slam me against the wall again," Kazhe said. "How was I to tell you, in all that? Did you really want to hear it in the middle of a battle?"

"She's come home," the shielder said, without emotion, testing the sound of the words.

Abruptly Kazhe understood why this particular commander had chosen this particular post. She remembered the tales of the first mirage sightings—the young shielder who had seen one of the Eiden Myr ships trying to make landfall, just before Verlein had seen the first ship of invaders. She realized how the Shipseer had come by her shieldname. *She's waited a long time,* she thought.

And then, *At least her mage lived to come home.*

"Isn't there any bloody beer to be had on this forsaken rock?"

"I need you sober," the Shipseer replied, her mind elsewhere.

"Eiden's bloody balls—I was drunk when I got here, woman."

The Shipseer called for drink. Kazhe, expecting some none's-land dregs, was surprised to taste a fine Neck ale. "Tell me about my sister," the Shipseer said, "and then I'll let you sleep." Kazhe told all she knew, and the Shipseer said, "I saw her. The night my mages reported a streak of yellow light in the sky. I thought it was a sign of siege. But it was her. Them. Then she was here." Muscles in her neck tightened. "I denied her. I thought I was seeing things."

"It wasn't really her," Kazhe said on a yawn. She strapped her blade on over bare flesh, then pulled the blanket tight and lay down with her head on her folded arm. Just before sleep submerged her, she fumbled through her wet coat and drew out Torrin's triskele to drape around her neck for safer keeping. It was only dead, dull pewter, and she'd never shied from a little sacrilege.

Liath watched the three lights try again and again to mend the intorsion. The nine of them were linked through Louarn, who was binder of so much more than casting materials now— binder of lights. Even lightless, she could sense the tremendous powers focused through him. Again and again, their attempts failed.

"I can't *touch* it," said the youngest touch, and the youngest visant whined and pulled his hands into himself to hug his knees and sit rocking back and forth, and Eilryn said, tight-lipped, "We're making it worse"—but Dabrena said, "Try. Try again. Try a different seating."

They tried again. And again. Numerous casting leaves lay wasted. The mouselike visant fell into a swoon and the mad Ankleman leaped to his feet and roared, "We're going to rip the thing wide open! I won't be party to more of this!" The circle fractured. Menders and seekers erupted into debate. The hall resounded with angry voices. Louarn said, "We cannot mend this, Dabrena."

Dabrena was furious. Light should achieve any end it set itself. Dabrena had never sat in a casting circle in her home village with Graefel Wordsmith grinding her down under attempt after attempt to do what she was incapable of doing. Liath tasted the humiliation of that night afresh, even as she remembered Dabrena, the day she earned the ring, telling her to go to Crown, to wait for them, they would find her, they would fix her. Dabrena had forged these menders from the pure conviction that anything broken could be fixed.

The breach in the intorsion could not be mended. The touch of light only widened it. This wasn't a thing that light could fix.

Every motion has a consequence. Galandra's casting, Torrin's casting, Eilryn's casting—twice nine nonned years apart and two nineyears apart, and only now converging to cast the future.

Nerenyi ignored the uproar. Their path was not her path. She approached the bonefolk. She had watched them speak to the others with their fingers. She had seen them gesture at Liath when she was in pieces and sign, *She is like us.*

She knew the runes called Stonetree. She knew that they originated in a system of hash marks on the corners of hewn stones. She recognized the patterns of those hash marks when she saw them formed by the long-fingered hands of the bonefolk. With her illuminator's sense of path and pattern, her visant's gleaning of detail, and her knowledge as former keeper of codices, she could communicate in that handspeech, if they were patient.

They trembled at her approach. She steepled her hands in front of her and, with great care and intense concentration, signed her wish to converse. The one on the left—Writhenrue, Louarn had called him—closed his eyes, held them closed for a breath, then opened them. She took that for a nod.

You said you are like her, she signed, and pointed unobtrusively to Liath.

No longer, Writhenrue signed back.

Are you in pieces? Nerenyi signed.

We are between, Writhenrue signed back. *The others of the forgotten naming are between. To go where they are is to sleep.*

To sleep, Nerenyi thought. *To fall unconscious, the way Liath's fragments did when they came close to each other.*

"There are other bonefolk," said Adaon, coming up beside her. "These are stone bonefolk. There are also wood bonefolk. They passage bodies to different realms. For ages there was no interaction between realms. Dabrena persuaded them to make contact with each other. They thought some ill would come of it, but none did. Their reluctance boiled down to superstition, or cultural taboo, or etiquette. I read that as 'sleep,' but he might have meant 'transgress.' They frequently speak in metaphors. They still avoid each other's realms."

Nerenyi liked Adaon; he was a kindred spirit, a seeker like herself, a fellow-visant, and the man who unearthed the Triennead holdings. But there was more to the bonefolk than what the menders had learned. The folk of this holding had grown too familiar with the bonefolk—took them for granted, now, without really knowing them at all. "I don't think it's a metaphor," she said, and then signed to Writhenrue, *Where are the others of the forgotten naming?*

In their realms, Writhenrue replied.

What kind of realms? she asked. When he didn't answer, she signed, *Your realm is stone. Another is of wood. You do not sleep in the realm of wood.* Before she could ask what sort of place *would* make him sleep, he replied, *Our ways are the earth. Their ways are the air. Their ways are the water.*

The three elements, she thought. *They split into the three elements the way Liath split into three times in her life. They can travel through shared matter into realms based on different elements. But it puts them to sleep. . . .*

Does there exist a Writhenrue of air? she signed. *Does there exist a Writhenrue of water?*

After a long moment, the boneman's eyes closed and opened—no eyelids to slide down, more like lips pressing together and then parting again. He signed, *Not in your naming. I am Writhenrue, in your naming. I do not know the others. To know the others is to sleep.*

Nerenyi rounded on Adaon. "Didn't any of you ask if there were airfolk and waterfolk to go with these stonefolk and woodfolk?"

"We assume there are," Adaon said in a mild tone, "but there was never any reason to—"

"I have a reason." She scorned his facile assumptions. This was what holding life did to seekers—made them lazy, made them rest on their preconceptions. That was what island life, placid and accepting, had done to her. To Writhenrue, she signed, *Why do you tarry here?* He took a jittering step back toward the stone wall, toward the safety of his own realm. Unrelenting, Nerenyi signed, You saw the woman made whole. You want that for yourselves. You wait to see what you can offer in exchange for wholeness.

Writhenrue signed, Irongrim took the bladed one through the ways.

"That's a start," Nerenyi said out loud. "Now take me."

"What are you *doing*?" Adaon gripped her arm. "It's one thing to talk to them, Nerenyi, but—"

"I'm going to this realm of theirs," Nerenyi said. "Then I'm going to the sea bonefolk. I'm going to find my pledge's body. I'm going to the air bonefolk. I'm going to find out what the bonefolk are."

Adaon argued. He couldn't help it; he was a seeker. As a seeker, he also had to respect her personal search.

The bonefolk were signing among themselves, far too fast for Nerenyi to follow. One left, melting into the wall; the other removed himself several steps from Writhenrue and crossed his arms against his chest in stubborn silence.

I do not wish to sleep, Writhenrue signed. I wish to wake. I wish to know the others. You may know the others. You may tell me.

"We'll make seekers of them yet." Nerenyi winked at Adaon, then handed him the drawstring bag with her triad's triskeles.

Adaon didn't smile. He glanced at Dabrena, who was starting toward them. "Go if you're going. Dabrena did something just as daft, once, but . . ."

Writhenrue lifted Nerenyi in his spindly arms as though she weighed nothing. As her vision rarefied into a pinpoint clarity through a green-tinged mist, Nerenyi thought, *That's the color of my own bones dissolving.* She could no longer speak. Adaon would explain it to Dabrena.

Adaon would explain it to Liath.

I guess I'm jumping off the cliff after all.

LIATH'S BODY HAD not been outdoors since her spirit's roving. Leaving the Greenhill Cloisters, she found the marble-halled metals town bathed in the cool, edged sunshine of a late harvestmid afternoon. The air was a shock. Full of noise—hammers banging metal, vendors hawking wares down the long streets, dogs barking, *birdsong*. Full of scents—Eiden Myr food, Eiden Myr tin and copper, Eiden Myr rivers and trees and soil. It smelled of all the things the sea did not; it rang with all the sounds the sea did not. She stood alone in a sensory onslaught. She was waiting for Louarn, who'd promised to fill her in on the history of the visants and the touches while they ate; they were all to get some supper and reconvene in a structure more suited to a large assembly. Eilryn had gone to share a meal in Dabrena's rooms. *Caille,* she thought, the name still ringing in her mind after Eilryn's shy, belated introduction. *That was Galandra's mother's name. Do they even know?*

Liath Illuminator was no longer her name; she was Liath Stormwind of the Inner Shores, named for her vessel and her provenance. Eiden Myr was a blur, a twist of light, a mystery; a memory faded into legend. She felt she'd walked through a veil into one of the lands-beyond—into one of the stories she'd told her little boy at night under the stars, the world of her youth become a teller's tale, insubstantial as a dream. The projections of her spirit might have fallen into these folk's arms, but she was a far cry from such softness. She'd lived hard for too long, in a realm beyond their imagining.

She missed her ship. It was part of her, an extension of her; she was naked without it. She'd put her heart and soul into its upkeep for half a lifetime. To envision it drifting, masterless, till storm or surge took it down was a gall on her heart. She missed the continuous movement, the subliminal sense of being under way. To survive was to keep moving. Stillness was terror. She felt becalmed here, helpless, no wind to move her onward. She was in irons. Nerenyi's mad disappearance into the bone-folk's arms filled her with more envy than terror. Nerenyi was continuing her journey. Nerenyi was still moving.

Caille's middle sister emerged from the hall and stood for a moment beside her, watching the sun drop low and red to stain the clouds. Kazhe had called this one Pelufer. She was unaware of the cacophony, the multiplicity of sounds and smells. She was embedded in her world, as thoughtless of it as of her own heartbeat. In her earthiness, the girl seemed to Liath to be all Eiden Myr incarnate, right down to the otherworldly cling of haunts. Liath felt herself to be all outer seas and no Eiden Myr at all.

"You wanted to find your haunts," Pelufer said at last.

"And Kazhe forbade it," Liath replied.

"Spirits take Kazhe." The wiry girl was brimming with pent energy. "She broke her vow. I didn't promise her anything. I'll find your haunts."

"No," Liath said—too fast, too sharp, raising her hand to block the hand the girl had raised to touch her with. For a tense, frozen moment it was as though they had drawn blades. Then Liath lowered her voice and her arm and said, "No. It was my heart that asked you that. Forget anything I said to you."

The girl fixed keen hazel eyes on her. More than a girl, at two nines and five, but not yet come into full possession of adulthood. "You can talk to them," she offered. "You can make your peace with them, through me."

"That's your trade, is it? Mediating between the living and the dead?"

Pelufer regarded her with a mixture of caution and curiosity. "Most people find it helps them to say goodbye."

Liath indicated the scabbard on Pelufer's back with a jerk of her chin. "And do you say goodbye to those you kill? Or do you only duel with the dead?"

The girl went pale. "You saw them?"

"I tried to pass through them. I never felt anything so cold in twice nine winters at sea."

"They're the stain," Pelufer said. "When people kill, it leaves a mark on them, a burned place. Those shadows are what's left when time has taken everything else. I think they're what's left of the Triennead soldiers. I think that when the Triennead fell, there was battle everywhere—huge forces, a clash of arms across all the world—all of Eiden, I mean—"

Liath understood the slip. She had once believed that Eiden's body and the nine visible seas were the world's entirety. It wasn't even a slip; for this earthy girl it was the truth. This was her world. This was *the* world. Liath felt a stab of protectiveness, an urge to shield that intrinsic innocence.

Pelufer did not continue. She'd been bursting to tell someone, and now that she had she seemed to realize that the person she'd told was an outerlander, a stranger to her. "I should tell Adaon," she said. "That's his bailiwick, Triennead history."

"Yes," Liath said. "And I think it's time for you to put away your deadly playmates. If you're bound to die for something, die for something real. You've sparred enough with shadows."

She'd lost her blade and no longer wore its sheath, only her old pack and the two others she'd carried for so long; but in its way the blade was nearly as much a part of her as the triskele. Pelufer saw the blade on Liath, and she said, "I'm going to the shield. Tonight. After the meeting."

Liath nodded. "And Kazhe forbade that, too."

"Yes," Pelufer said. "But there's a man there. Videsal Bladesmith. He was Auda Bladesmith's prentice. Auda—"

"I knew Auda," Liath said. "She resurrected the craft of forging blades, back when it was all but forgotten. Her skills armed Verlein's horde."

Pelufer pulled up with slightly widened eyes, recalling that she was talking to history itself. *I'm a haunt of another age,* Liath thought. *This girl has spoken to haunts from generations past, but I'm the first living haunt she's ever seen.* "I never met

Auda," Pelufer said. "Kazhe still talks about her. She died of some ague in the dark years."

"Then I grieve her," Liath said. "She was a bawdy woman, full of life, for all she crafted tools of death. I'm sure her prentice will do well by you."

Pelufer was still staring at her—jaw slightly agape, eyes narrowed. "You hate the blade," she whispered.

Liath nodded with a twist of the chin. "I hate the blade with all my heart. But I love my son, and I value my neck, and a blade saved both of them more times than I can count. My scabbard won't be empty long." She grinned. "Neither will Kazhe's, I warrant. That big visant's a lunatic, but a finer exemplar of manhood I haven't seen in twice nine years. He'll help her work off her outrage when she comes back to find you gone."

"She misses Benkana," Pelufer said. "She's got a mouth like a midden, but it's all talk. She never bedded anyone else. I know he would have forgiven her, but she wouldn't let me touch her haunts, either. I used to try every time we grappled, and she'd cuff me and set me a dozen extra drills."

Benkana gone then, too, and through some lapse of Kazhe's, or even at Kazhe's hand. Liath didn't want to know who else had died while she was gone.

Pelufer was twitching to be away, but still she hesitated, frowned. "Your son. He's . . . Is he . . . I mean, of course you wouldn't . . . but . . ."

"He's a sound lad, Pelufer. He grew up in a brutal place with his heart intact. I envy any girl he gives that heart to."

"Let me try, Illuminator." Pelufer was urgent now. "They're on you. I felt them when I pulled you out of the shadows. Let me try, before I go."

In case I don't come back, Liath heard at the end of that. Rescuing the sealost would burn dozens of holes through the intorsion, at points that could not be predicted. Liath knew full well that this girl was going to the shield to use the blade she would forge with Auda's prentice.

I couldn't bear it, she thought. *I couldn't bear to hear him speak through this girl's lips.* She found herself stepping forward. She heard her own guarded "All right." She couldn't seem to pull back into herself, pull her limbs away from the hauntspeaker's touch. She remembered being hauled from the shadows. She remembered the sick pain. She remembered the horror and the pathos that came into the girl's eyes as they fell. Still she endured the touch.

For long moments, the noise of the world receded, and all Liath could hear was the sound of their breathing.

"I can't find them," Pelufer said. "They're haunts, all right. Unpassaged. They're on you—they're on those packs, too. It's like spidersilk, a sticky filament, but it leads . . . it leads off to . . . I don't know." She stepped back. "I'm sorry. They've gone somewhere my shine can't follow."

Liath released a shaky laugh. "Don't fret, girl. I don't think I'm ready to hear whatever they'd want to tell me, if there's even anything at all."

"There is," Pelufer said. "There always is." Then she was off, to arrange for a mount or whatever she had to do before her older sister came out and captured her, leaving Liath alone with the bloodied sky, wondering whether she would ever get over the feeling that the land was locking her in.

Pelufer stowed her pack in the public stables with the horse she'd bargained for just before the stableman had knocked off for supper; she could go through the ways, as Elora did, but her ways were metal, leading to the stonefolk's realm, and the stonefolk wouldn't like her passing through. They'd transited Kazhe and that seeker Heelwoman, but on their terms. To get to the Knee, she had to ride like anyone else.

She made the rounds of the five main holding structures. They were steeped in Triennead haunts, and the haunts of all those who'd died on top of them when they were hills that townsfolk lived on. Now they were silent, abandoned. Only the living dwelled there now, prentices and other holding folk not involved in the big doings at Greenhill and Lowhill, engaged in the ordinary activities of the end of a harvestmid day. She walked along the river, which sometimes carried the haunts of the drowned, and there was nothing but the whisper of its currents. At last she went up to Woodhill—at a run in the waning twilight—and stood for heaving breaths in the bonefolk's glade, the spirit wood.

Nothing. Nothing at all. Only a silence at the heart of the world.

She found Louarn already in the Lowhill Assembly, seated across a trestle table from Liath, sharing bread and stew and cider he'd gotten on Harvest Long.

"The haunts are gone," she said. It just came out of her, the way the names of the dead used to. "I started feeling it a few days ago—something missing that I couldn't pin down. I didn't really think about it. So much was going on that I didn't have a . . ." It didn't matter now. "The Triennead haunts are gone. The Gir Doegre haunts are gone. I'll ride to the Menalad Plain if you ask me to, but it will be the same. The haunts—they're gone, just *gone*. Not passaged. Disappeared." She sank into a chair, the strangeness of it overwhelming her. The terrible nothingness in the air, the stone, the wood.

Louarn and Liath looked at each other for a long time.

"What?" Pelufer said. "Nothing's—*happened* to them, has it? Louarn—"

"They went to the hauntrealm," Louarn said. "There was a conflict brewing there when Pelkin n'Rolf made his passage. The runners' plan had been to cast a corrected version of Galandra's warding that would cut us off from all the realms by Longdark. They were proceeding on word that Graefel has since recanted, but as far as Pelkin knows, we're planning to strand them. They must have all chosen, to the last of them, to join the battle there. Even if it meant leaving everything familiar behind forever."

What hauntrealm? Pelufer stopped before she asked. There was a place haunts went when they were done with this world. She'd thought it was something like pethyar. Or something like a passing place, what the bonefolk's realms were to the bodies they passaged—a refuge, a holding place, eternal by the standards of the living but temporary by the standards of eternity. Her father and mother had left the realm of flesh; they didn't haunt Gir Doegre anymore, or her. They had gone into a kind of stillness. Other haunts went, too, after they had made their peace. But they did it in ones or twos or threes, after she'd spoken for them, and sometimes they didn't go at all—they lingered in raindrops and mist, in floors and walls, in scents and shafts of light. Some of them loved the world too much to be parted from it. For them to just *go* . . . for *all* of them to go . . .

"It was an extraordinary act of sacrifice," Louarn said.

Pelufer got up. She couldn't help rescue the sealost. There were no dead left to speak through her. There was only one thing of any use that she could do: provide Eiden Myr another kenai. Kazhe was the last. If Kazhe got herself killed, there would be none. She had to forge her blade.

"Don't leave without telling your sisters." Liath's quiet words carried an odd weight. "Don't go without saying goodbye."

She tore her pack open, rummaged within. "They'll try to keep me here. They hate what I'm going to do. No." She fumbled out a linen bag and shoved it across the table at Liath. "These are hers. She'll want them back."

"Wait—" Louarn said, and his voice almost made her turn, even though it was only his Louarn voice, not the voice of any of the seemings he put on to get people to do what he wanted them to. She almost turned, because it was him—but if she was going to be his kenai, she had to *become* kenai, and that would never happen if she stayed here sparring with shadows.

Liath opened the linen bag to find an assortment of metal accoutrements and minor blades missing their grips, and something else—a hooked dagger. It came into her hand like ice so cold it burned. She dropped it to the tabletop.

"That's Kazhe's cheit," Louarn said. "The kenai blademaster's smallest weapon."

"Small?" Liath said. "I've seen what these things can do."

"I wonder why the bonefolk didn't transit the grip?"

"This blade was magecrafted. The grip may not be what it seems." Did Louarn even know what horn was, or ivory? Her eye was drawn by the hypnotic swirls in the metal blade, and a strange, chill wind blew through her. Without knowing why, she slipped the dagger into a sheath sewn inside her boot. It would keep there, till Kazhe returned. She put the rest in her pack.

While they waited for the assembly to convene, she requested materials and scribed a message home.

I have returned unharmed from the outer seas. Your grandson Eilryn brought us to the Strong Leg holding. Though some tasks require our attention, spirits willing we shall be in Clondel soon. You have heard by now that Pelkin passed. Know that his spirit lives on, gone to a realm of his choosing. I send congratulations to my niece Oriane for earning the triskele. She is all I could have ever hoped to be, and has my envy and my blessing. I was with you that night in spirit. I remain with you always in spirit. Your daughter, Liath.

A stilted message. Scribing was not her medium. Perhaps she should draw them a picture. . . . No. Eventually she would summon the courage to face them; to confront the transformed Petrel's Rest; to bear the unbearable joy of their arms coming round her again. Any picture she sent would reveal fear, hesitation, heartache in naked pigment. Better the shadow garb of inked glyphs, the excuse of awkwardness with words. Better, for now, the safety of distance.

To seal the leaf, she pooled candle drippings and leaned down to impress the triskele shape into the wax, from the pendant she still wore around her neck. Dabrena and her menders no longer wore their triskeles. She'd worn hers since the night she got it. Though it no longer hummed with the vibrancy of magelight, though it was no longer cool when she was hot and warm when she was cold, though it was only body-temperature pewter now, it was part of her. She'd lost the use of her light before, and worn it then. Lightless she might be, but her triskele would come off her only when the bonefolk passaged her corpse.

The Lowhill Assembly was a triangle, a single hall of uncarved marble—smooth, luminous, polished to a high gloss. The stone was webbed with delicate, smoky veins. All eight holding structures had that hairline venation, each of a different cast—moss in the Greenhill Cloisters, honey in the Highhill Comb, charcoal in the Woodhill Repository, mauve in the Pointhill Torus, teal and rust and iris in the residence halls of Heelhill, Boothill, Grazehill. In the flickering light of candle lanterns and the flames from the opposing hearths, the marbled stone of the interior seemed to writhe and twist. Lowhill, two stories high and empty of all but the temporary furniture, bounced echoes at odd angles, yet held a hush of timeless peace. An enneagram veined the floor along points cast by the sun's beam through the skylight at particular times of year. All the Triennead halls were magecrafted, but in this one Louarn felt it most.

As the assembled took their seats, Adaon approached Louarn to offer belated congratulations. "I hear you've pledged Keiler n'Graefel," he said.

"Bound in private, not pledged," Louarn said, longing stirred afresh by the sound of that name. He wouldn't subject Keiler to a pledge casting for all the world. The touch of light on lightless mages brought only pain. Adaon nodded, then winced, his pale eyes changing focus.

Louarn found Elora standing behind him. She put on a beautiful smile that he hoped she hadn't learned from him. "Congratulations, Louarn." She leaned in for a brief, light embrace. "You should have told us."

Now he had also to tell her of Pelufer's rude departure. As she left him to go sit with Caille, he swore softly under his breath. He was startled to feel Adaon's hand on his shoulder, the firm squeeze of bone into bone.

"She's happy, Louarn," Adaon said, blue glow flaring, then

went to take his own seat with some resident seekers. He meant that she was happy with Nolfiander, her pledge, and that Louarn should be happy, too.

Dabrena never stood on ceremony. "We failed to mend the intorsion," she said. "We've messaged Khine for assistance retrieving the sealost. If they can't sail back in through the hole off the Fist, they'll have to be cast home. That will burn more holes, and possibly destroy the intorsion outright."

"Good," said Corle Mender. "That will give us back our ocean."

"At what cost in shielder lives?" said Selen Mender.

"And what else might it let in?" said Ronim Mender.

To Liath, Dabrena said, "Can you tell us what's on the other side?"

"Horrors," Rekke answered. He straddled a chair with his back to them and his chin on his arms. "Fire and death. Monstrosity. War."

"There's a world recovering from disaster," Liath corrected. "Much of it is wasteland. Most of it is wild and dangerous. But some of it thrives."

"And hates us," Narilyn Mender said.

"We don't know that," Liath said. "None of us have been there."

Dontra Mender turned to Rekke. "Can't we find out?"

Clapping his hands together and beaming with flattered delight, Rekke said, "Go to that blasted netherworld and risk my neck to have a look?" His dark face went black: "We can't see that far beyond our bodies, or Eiden's, and I wouldn't realmwalk there if I could."

"Outer Shores folk came from there in our lifetime," Liath said. "Some were marauders looking for lost lands to conquer, but others were peaceful fisherfolk. They're dead now, and we'd only just started to understand their languages—they steered well clear of us as soon as they learned there was light on board our vessel."

"Because they hated it—"

"No," Liath said. "Because they feared what it attracts." She waited for complete silence, and got it. "The use of magecraft has a price, in the intorsion. We know the intorsion was made to contain what the outerlands experienced as the disastrous effects of light. Magelight, at any rate—I don't know about these other two lights. When we broke Galandra's warding, a blast of light was released. It seared us all. It also spawned armadas of those black ships. The sea took some, over the years. Some we destroyed. We didn't know what they were or where they came from, not at first. My thinking ran along the lines of yours. The ships were there when I sailed out; I thought they'd always been there, circling, waiting their chance. They hadn't. The folk of the Seas There Are—the intorsion folk—said they'd appeared in the last few turns of the moon. Since I left these shores. They thought I'd brought them. I believed the magelight was gone forever, so I thought that if the horrors were some result of our breaking Galandra's warding, that was it—there would be no more of them, and we had only to survive the ones there were. Outsail them, outsmart them, outlive them."

Years passed in the brief moment Liath paused to wet her throat with cider. Years of outsailing those ships, fighting them, perhaps even destroying them—in a one-woman vessel with a small child aboard. No way home, no way out, few opportunities to resupply or rest. Louarn had begun to see the Liath he had known, resurfacing in glimpses; he had begun to settle back into Mellas's friendship with her, Mellas's view of her. Now he saw again the salted, sea-hard stranger cast back to their shores.

"One day when he was eight," she went on, "my son mended a torn sail with a casting, and I knew there was a light in him that had escaped the searing. I let him cast. Why not? No one could see. But after every second or third casting there were more shadow ships. After every second or third casting there was a shadow ship nearby within a day, when I had them plotted in my mind and I *knew* we were nowhere near one. Every second or third casting spawned a shadow, a stain, that grew into a warship. Every use of magelight risks bringing into existence one more horror bent on its destruction. The more you cast, the more they come. The more of your people you cast home, the more enemy you're going to have to fight." Her gray eyes went as cold as a winter sea. "We made the black ships that killed the Outer Shores folk and the folk of the Seas There Are."

"You didn't know," Ronim Mender said.

"You didn't kill them," Corle Mender said, "and neither did magelight. The blind hate of the intorsion's makers killed them."

"This morning, Eilryn spoke of mines," Adaon said. "Is that how you conceive the cause and effect between magelight and horrors? As dependent on location?"

"Eilryn does," Liath said. "It might also depend on the intensity of the casting, the materials used, the time of day—anything, really. Maybe it takes two or three castings to make a black ship. It's a risk you have to weigh."

"We can't leave our folk out there, now that we've the means to bring them home."

"We could lose a ship for every ship we save."

"We could destroy the barrier between ourselves and the outerlands, and sacrifice our world to save a dozen ships."

"The Khinish were prepared to risk their lives to fight invasion. Invasion is ongoing—once they know that, they'll go out there regardless. They might as well be saving the sealost while they're about it."

"Can they escort them all safely to the Fist? Then no light would be required at all, and their fleet would be massed at a single entry point."

"Then the shield and the fleet would have a finite number of enemy to fight. One concentrated battle to end it all."

"And an intorsion that's still ripping apart. What happens when it's gone? We might refrain from casting sealost home, and lose them on their way to the Fist, only to lose the intorsion anyway. Why not save the sealost the moment they're found?"

"Because every casting makes more black ships."

"A dozen more ships, in the scheme of things—"

"—could mean a dozen more shielder deaths, or nine times that, or more. And it might take several castings to send a full ship's complement of sealost home."

"They'll have to try for the Fist and take their chances. We can't risk our mages out there. We can't add the burden of more entry points to a shield already stretched to its limit."

Louarn listened to the debate through an expansion of blue glow. The visants had been gleaning; now Rekke sat up straight from his affected slump and said, to the wall, "Cast them home. It won't make any difference to your war, but it'll bloody well make a difference to the ones you save."

"Now what's he on about?" Corle asked Louarn.

Rekke, who could speak for himself, said, "I've been looking at that burnhole. Puking pounding headache it's giving me, too, but I can tell you this: *They're coming from the edges of the hole.* I don't think it's your light that creates those things. I think it's damage to the twistedness. Maybe light damages it, so mostly it amounts to the same thing—but it's not. Scarcheek says the thing was made to contain the effects of light—quakes and storms and surges. It was meant to surround light, not have light inside it. Once light got in, it weakened it, like water freezing in the cracks in rocks. If its makers thought it might fail, what would they build into that failure? Counterattack. A last-gasp defense against whatever breached it. Maybe it made ships because there were ships inside it. Maybe it made shadows because there was light inside it. Maybe it was made to be a mirror—to reflect back whatever threatened it—and the more it cracks, the more reflections there are." He humphed, and put his head back down. "Go on and shatter it," he said, in a sullen slur with his chin against his forearm. "That tear was getting wider long before we poked our light at it. Either way we'll be overrun. You might as well fetch those sealost home for a decent meal before they die with the rest of us."

"A viable theory," Adaon said. "But it doesn't take into account the mirages or the siege. Nor does what Liath's told us."

"What *about* the siege?" Selen said. "That wasn't shadow ships. *Someone* sent that wave of delusion."

"The intorsion's makers, generations back," Elora said.

Adaon said, "Then why did the delusions begin only three years ago?"

"Maybe it took a while to grow," Elora replied. "The black ships didn't spring up on the instant. Maybe it took nine years and six for the wave of delusion to grow strong enough to affect us."

"No," said Ioli, from his seat not far from Rekke and Mauzl—on his coat, by the hearth, a swamp dweller unaccustomed to chairs, chilled and uncomfortable here. "I know what started it now."

"These visants are mad," said Corle, "I don't know why we entertain—"

"They're here because they can see things we can't." Dabrena gestured for Ioli to continue.

"It was Asrik," Ioli said. "Do you remember him, Louarn?"

Louarn nodded, and for the menders' benefit said, "A young illuminator who instigated the mages' uprising in Sauglin. He advocated using darkcraft to harrow the outerlands and end the siege."

"You wondered if he was playing for power, or if he believed in what he was doing," Ioli said. "He believed in it. He lost a brother to the siege. He lost . . ." He paused, perhaps examining his memory of the gleaning. "He lost a triad to the siege. His brother and his friend, a wordsmith and binder. They had family on one of the explorer ships. They kept seeing it try to sail home. When they felt their magecraft was strong enough, they tried to cast it home. They lived on the coast. The shield there knew them. No one questioned them when they went down to the shore. They sent a casting out into the twistedness, to make a way for that ship to come home. What they got back was—horror. Some kind of unspeakable attack. It was a blur to Asrik when I gleaned him—I'd have to see him again to get it clear—but it was awful. It was a delusion. They sent a casting out and got delusion in return. The brother drowned. The binder too. Asrik ran." Ioli looked straight at Louarn. "They were nine-and-six."

"Asrik is two nineyears old," Louarn said. "That puts their casting three years ago. And Asrik is from Maur Bolein. On the Dreaming Sea."

"The first reports of siege came from the Dreaming Sea," Dabrena said.

Corle stared at Selen. "Magecraft started the siege. The touch of magecraft on the intorsion."

"Good thing you had mad visants to end it for you," said Rekke, coiling around to bare his teeth at Corle.

Corle ignored him, and said to Liath, "You see? It was a trap, laid by vengeful folk twice nine nonned years ago. Anyone could have tripped it."

"Nonetheless," Liath said, "my son and I had a part in it. There were good and decent folk in those seas. I grieve them. I always will."

Adaon said, "That's the siege and the invasion explained. But not the mirages. Liath says that the black ships destroyed everything in the intorsion except, so far, for a few of our sealost. Yet one glance off any shore shows outerlands ships. Are they haunts? What are they?"

Dabrena allowed a silence to stretch for several long breaths. Then she said, "We've debated the mirages for a dozen years. We can't solve that mystery here. I propose that we accept Rekke's assessment of the intorsion and work under the assumption that it will fail, catastrophically. We've got to bring the sealost home and find a way to shield ourselves from its collapse."

"Can't the bonefolk bring them?" one of the seekers said.

Elora's face went flat. "Lornhollow has stopped responding to our calls. Irongrim was summoned back to his realm. There's trouble there, I think. Since that Heelwoman went on her jaunt, the others have closed off. They were lured into meddling with the living once, and it didn't turn out very well. Lornhollow . . . I think they may have washed their hands of us."

"Could a wood touch still go through the ways?" asked Dontra.

"What," Elora said, "to a ship at sea?"

"To tell them to sail for the Fist. So the Khinish wouldn't have to hunt for them." Cowed by Elora's expression, Dontra said, "All right then. Could Ioli . . . glean a message like that to them? Let them know where they should go?"

"Not into the twistedness," Ioli said, his gaze on the ceiling.

"So Rekke couldn't locate those ships for the Khinish," Dontra said, and Rekke said, "Rekke can't see into the grieving intorsion and Rekke can't realmwalk onto those ships, though Rekke would be amused by the reaction of a crew stranded two nineyears at sea to three daft mismatched walleyes appearing from nowhere on their decks to babble about burnholes—so don't bother asking."

"They'll need armed escort in any event," Adaon said. "They might do best to abandon their vessels and transfer to the Khinish warships. All assuming the Khinish even agree to this at all."

"They will," Liath said, watching Ioli. "Hanla will."

Dabrena was already scribing messages, to the holding at Sauglin and the runners' new Maur Gowra headquarters. Louarn asked what she was advising them.

"To prepare their best mages," she replied. "They'll be needed to cast the sealost home if the Khinish can't bring them round to the Fist, and then . . ."

"You can't recast Galandra's warding," Liath said. Her eyes left Ioli for only a moment. "You can't do that to the outerlands. They aren't what's trying to kill you. What's attacking you was put there twice nine nonned years ago."

"We don't know how to recast the warding," said Ronim. "That casting died with Galandra's triad."

"If we could reconstruct it, we might alter it to reduce its destructive effects," said Dontra.

"We can't reconstruct it," said Selen. "Graefel thought the information was in the canon. He was wrong. Ordinarily, I would relish that. But it was the last hope of retrieving the casting."

"Not quite the last hope," said Liath. She had been staring at Ioli since he described his gleaning of Asrik, and he had been staring anywhere but back.

"That's not a thing we've ever done," he said.

Liath tongued an incisor. "Nothing we do from here on in will be anything we've ever done," she said. "Are you game, Ioli?"

Mauzl had stirred from his curled-up nap by the hearth and was regarding Liath with what looked like fear. Rekke was grumbling into his arms. After a moment, gaze skidding past Liath's, Ioli nodded.

"What are you *talking* about?" Corle cried.

This time, Louarn answered for them. "Liath is the only

mage left alive from the triad that cast Galandra's passage.
Mages can't retain their passage visions. But the memory is in
the deeps of Liath's mind. Ioli might glean it."

It took courage for Liath to offer to relive the day her light
was seared, the day she lost her wordsmith and binder to the
cliffs and the sea. Or perhaps she thought on that day each day
of her life. Kazhe did, he knew. Kazhe saw that endless fall in
the bottom of every tankard. Somewhere inside Louarn, a small
boy was always reaching for his burning mother, an older boy
was always weeping as his broken horse was put down, a boy
older still was always dying of thirst inside a labyrinth, a young
man was always finding his kindly mentor brained on the floor
of his brick house. *Our darkest moments are never far below
the surface. What she saw during the passage, though—that
will be very deep indeed.*

"We're going to find out how Galandra cast her warding,"
Liath said. "Then someone is going to work out how to cast it
without destroying the world. And without killing the mages
who cast it, since one of them will be my son."

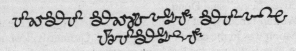

IOLI HAD BEEN in this white stone place for only half a day.
Not nearly long enough to know it. Yet he knew it with Rekke's
assurance of *where* and Mauzl's assurance of *when*. He was always looking partly through their eyes now, experiencing their
familiarities as his own. Rekke, though weary, was in his rocky
element, soothed and enlivened by marble. Mauzl was fatigued
after his fit—the overwhelming glimpse of path after path lead-

ing to annihilation, brought on by their attempt to glean the intorsion, exacerbated by the invisible but potent effects of shine and magelight—but he was keeping the past-paths open, and this place was drenched in the past. Ioli could glean here.

What mages did, when they cast passage, was as close as they ever came to gleaning another mind. It was as different from Ioli's gleaning as Eilryn's arc of golden light was from Rekke's bluesilver sphere turning inside out or a touch's copper-bathed flesh merging with the earth's flesh and squeezing through to somewhere else. Ioli could glean how it felt for a touch to go through the ways, Mauzl could glean when she'd gone, Rekke could glean where she'd gone, but none of them could know, really *know,* how she'd done it. Not to explain to someone else. Not to help someone who was looking to do it.

The young mages in Sauglin had gleaned Pelkin n'Rolf as they passaged him, and afterward all they remembered was that they had seen—not what. This outer-seas Neckwoman had gleaned the mothermage and her triad as she opened the way to pethyar for them. What she remembered of it was a misty white blur. She wanted Ioli to look into that blur and glean her gleaning. Not what had happened; Galandra's knowledge of what she had done to make it happen.

The illuminator sat cross-legged on the floor in front of him, her back to the hall. Griping and swearing, Rekke lowered himself down beside them, his heavy frame a weariness, his belly a weight of Strong Leg food, a slosh of Strong Leg wine. Mauzl was yawning, rubbing his eyes, tucking in next to Ioli in the kind of waking that was only a lighter sleep. They were tired and drowsy. That was all right. It relaxed the glow into a wider openness.

Ioli sensed Louarn glean that openness. The iceheart wanted to learn the visant's craft from them. There was no visant's craft. There were only visants. He had only to be what he already was.

Their glow made of the marblevein fireflicker hall a submarine domain of shimmer and lightdance. All glows sought to join with theirs, and learned from theirs how to join. Far off in the Belt, in the Heartlands, in Shrug, glows were melding. The seeker Adaon resisted it. He was more seeker than visant, and liked to discover his pasts and futures on his own. Though unaware of it, he was engaged in a great delving even now. Ioli wished him well. Ioli wished all visants well. What he and Rekke and Mauzl had done for them, they'd done without knowing, and they could do no more. They were only another ripple in the pool.

Ioli looked at the coarse, good-hearted publicans' daughter, the illuminator tangled in dense knotwork and saturated with the hues of history, the bristly-brined bladesharp salt-cured shipwoman, and gleaned. Her troubles, her loves, her hopes, her regrets, the elements of any human life—and then more, much more, too much—power and circumstance that had made her what she was and yet were vastly greater than her lone mortal soul—anguish and relief, victory and despair, courage, heartache, brutality, tenderness—all the triumph and tragedy of an ordinary life magnified by extraordinary confluence and condition. All the things he'd known he would see, all the reasons he'd looked away. There was a scent of destiny on her so strong it choked him. But nowhere was there more than a passing hint of what she'd seen in that passage casting.

"Well?" said the illuminator. "What do I do?"

She had just sat down. No one except Louarn and Adaon knew that the gleaning had already happened, already failed. The rest had seen three visants shudder—a wince from him, a whine from Mauzl at pain suffered and pain to come, a grunt of recognition from Rekke for a woman who'd tried to shield what she loved in the curve of her powers—and assumed it was just their daft tics.

There had to be more. There had to be a way in.

"I . . . don't know," he said. "Remember, I suppose."

The lightless illuminator closed her eyes as if expecting to see guiders form on the canvas of her mind's eye. Ioli was startled at how blue those guiders were in her memory—how like the blue of a visant's glow.

He hesitated, struck shy. Though he'd gleaned her—though

he knew that deep down she felt herself to be an artless publican, peripheral now—he wasn't any less an awkward walleye from the swamps in the presence of this commanding figure. Finally he said, "It might be better with your eyes open."

Liath looked him straight in the eye. He swayed back. What he saw, in the unguarded breath of the eyes' first opening, was more than power, more than command. He hung on, and looked back, and waited for her to summon the memory.

The sea the cliff the air the reckoners' warding the distraught bodyguard the binder the wordsmith the leaf the *light*—

Bonefolk had slid through the walls at the far corner of the hall. Louarn slid over to join them. Irongrim, he saw, and two of his fellows. No Writhenrue. No Lornhollow. Louarn stood with them and watched the gleaning from the side.

Liath's eyes glazed. Her body remained relaxed, her hands draped on her knees. Her face betrayed nothing, not even control of its expression. Mauzl watched Ioli; Rekke looked through Liath, at some far point; Ioli cried out once, very low, a sound of softest heartbreak—then broke eye contact and scooted back, giving Liath space to come out of their ineffable joined trance.

"I saw," Liath murmured, her eyes coming back into focus. Like a young mage after casting passage, she said, "I *saw* . . ."

"She knew," Ioli said. Louarn thought he meant Liath, but as he went on—in a flood of words, like a dam breaking, he spoke less than Mellas ever had but when he started the words flowed like water—it was clear that he meant Galandra. "She saw the words inside the other words, the words hidden by the ancient mages, about the giants and the whiteness and the spirits. But she had only mages. Nine mages, with herself. Six when her triad became one-of-three. They didn't know about us. They didn't know about touches. They wanted to make a safe place for lights to grow, so there could *be* other lights. She didn't know the world would wake. The world was dead, the world she brought them to. It was dead and they were going to make it live again with their seeds and their light. They didn't know how alive it would become, soaked in light for all those years. How much more alive than it had ever been." He let out that cry again. "They died but they didn't die. They were here, all those long, long years, surrounding us. The warding was them. The three of them." He pulled into himself, hugging his knees to his chest. "They sat down, all nine of them. They sat by gender. They passed a leaf from one to the next. All scribed, then all drew. Then the red one and the dark one and the fair one got up and danced a circle in the center while all the others sang. They crossed their arms and gripped each other's wrists and spun, faster and faster, until they were one and the leaf was gone. The other mages made them into the warding. They didn't know it would hurt the world. They had no idea." He clenched tighter, his white hair falling forward to obscure his face, while Rekke sprawled on his back and fell into a snore, and Mauzl crept over to Caille and Eilryn. "They were proud of what grew inside the protection of their light. They knew, a little. Not much. They knew more when they were passaged—they—it was like a gleaning. They knew from the mages who passaged them. That was a gift. To see their children." He lifted his head, shook back his hair, and glared at the menders as though they had forced him into this. "Is that enough? Is that what you wanted?"

"Alas," said Dabrena, "it is. The craft has changed profoundly from what you describe. We can't reproduce that casting. They all inscribed, they all drew, they all sang except some who danced. . . ."

"If Ioli can be believed," Selen said.

"You can trust his gleaning," Louarn said quietly.

"I saw," Liath said again. She grinned, half fierce, half mischievous, a startling sight to those who'd grieved the pain she would endure reexperiencing that day, and said with relish, "I *saw.*" She got up and went back to her chair, and straddled it with one leg jiggling, two fingers tapping the other thigh.

"Do you remember what Ioli just described?" Dabrena asked.

"No," Liath said—almost sang, in blithe cheer. "Not a bit of it, except that we passaged them. Amazing, eh, that all that was in my head?"

"If dance was ever part of magecraft, we lost it long ago," said Narilyn.

"We've overspecialized," said Corle. "Have I not warned of that for years?"

"Torrin could cast alone," Liath said. "So could Evonder. So could most of the Ennead. But Torrin said it was never as strong with one as with three."

"Or with nine," said Dontra. "But this requires nine mages each with all three triadic disciplines. That's eight more than we've got, with only Eilryn."

"And to recast it with any precision, we'd have to do it on the sowmid equinox," said Selen. "We'd have to hang on till Ve Galandra when we're more than two ninedays shy of Longdark."

"What was all that about giants and whiteness and spirits?" said Ronim.

Ioli frowned. "I don't know. They didn't know. They didn't understand what they had read. They wanted to do what the hidden words said, but they . . . didn't have what they needed. They had one light, not three. They had no giants, or spirits. I think . . . I think the spirits might be our spirits. Eiden and Sylfonwy and Morlyrien. But they weren't *their* spirits. There were other—things whose help they beseeched. There was no Eiden then. Eiden's body was a wasteland. They didn't know what those spirits were, because . . . they weren't, yet."

"They used your canon," Adaon said to Dabrena. "Whatever Graefel Scholar saw in there, they saw it too."

"I'll send to him," Dabrena said, "but it's unlikely he'll reply. He never has. We're still warders, to his reckoning."

"Send *for* him," Liath said.

"You're joking."

"Do it. Tell him I'm here, I'm back in one piece, and I did what he wanted. I looked into the passage of Galandra. Don't tell him what Ioli saw."

"Make a bargain of it," Elora said. "What he sees for what

Ioli saw. A fair trade. How can he refuse?" She looked at the bonefolk, but Lornhollow had not joined them. Louarn was signing to Irongrim, asking if he'd fetch the scholar from the Head. Irongrim folded his arms against his chest.

"It'll take him three ninedays to ride down here," Ronim said.

Dabrena said, "It'll take the Khinish two ninedays to refit their fleet, and more than that to find the sealost and get to the Fist. We can't recast Galandra's warding, but maybe we can find our own way to the casting she *meant* to do. If it's in that scholar's arrogant head, I'll wring it out."

Liath was bursting with what she had seen. Galandra's spirit and her triad's spirits gone one way; their light gone another. It was an effort to keep her peace. Ioli walked slowly across to her and said, in an outraged whisper, "Do you know what you're going to have to *do?*"

"Nothing I haven't done before," she replied. Ioli was a good lad; he reminded her of Mellas in some ways that Louarn no longer did, with his facile tongue and easy pretenses. Ioli was both much older and much younger than he was. All three of these had a soft agelessness to them that Nerenyi and Adaon lacked, having come into their glows later in life. It was beautiful—but everything was beautiful to her right now. The world was rarefied and new, surreal and luminous, all its colors more intense, all its angles sharper, its patterns more vivid. She hadn't felt this alive since she had cast passage with Nerenyi's triad for a tough old oyster diver on the Isle of Senana. She hadn't felt this alive since the night she lay with Torrin, and that was tinged with heartache; she hadn't felt this alive since Eilryn was born, and that was tinged with terror. She wanted to dance with wild abandon, drink and brawl. She could barely keep still. Ioli was backing away from her, returning appalled to his triad—he'd finally met someone madder than his Ankleman, she supposed, and that must be quite a thing to take in. She tried to stop grinning, and couldn't. She put her forehead down on her arms to hide her face. Let them think she was lost in her grieving memories. Let them think she was mourning Torrin, as though she didn't mourn him with every breath; let them think she was mourning Heff, as though that grief weren't a part of her as close and tight as her skin.

She hadn't felt this alive since the day they died.

She hadn't *been* alive since the day they died, except for the jolt of life that was bearing Eilryn, and then she was living for him, not herself.

She hadn't been alive in two nineyears.

What a time to start.

Eilryn's voice said, from very close, "I'm going to Khine. I'm going to sail with that fleet."

She looked up slowly. "No. You're not."

"You should too. They'll need us both. They'll probably split up—half round one side of Eiden Myr, half round the other. We saw some Inner Shores ships down by the lesser sink, do you remember? They might still—"

"Scribe it. Send a message to Hanla. Give her my regards."

"They need us. They don't know those seas, they don't know what—"

"Scribe it. You're good at that. Have one of these menders make you a map. Chart the perils for them."

"It's not the same as being there."

"We all find our own way through the intorsion. You know that. No two courses are the same. Every ship meets its own terrors."

Eilryn's jaw set. "But—"

"You'll be more use here training their mages. If you go back out there and get yourself drowned or shredded, they won't have your light to help cast their warding."

"This is my fault," he said. "I can help make it right."

"This is an opportunity they wouldn't have had if not for you, and that's the last I'll hear of blame. What is, is." She stood to face him eye-to-eye. "You'll stay where you're needed."

"I could fetch *Stormwind.*"

Ah. Well aimed, lad—nearly hit the heart. But no. "And what would we do with it? Putter around the coast? That's a seagoing ship. Leave it at sea, where it wants to be."

* * *

Maur Gowra and Sauglin sent three nines of their brightest mages to Gir Doegre straightaway. Eilryn trained them, then watched them ride for Khine. Their aptitude surprised him. Their appreciation for his shipgrown technique flattered him. Their destination—the seas that were his home—galled him.

The Khinish fleet launched on the full moon, three days before Longdark, bladed and maged. Touches sailed with them to improve the winds and heal their injured. Eilryn stood listening to Rekke describe the sight of the ships heading out. He heard Kara n'Dabrena—Caille's best friend, returned from her self-imposed journey year as the menders' youngest master cartographer—whisper excitedly to Caille about something of no interest to him. He watched his mother, turning and turning an ancient magecrafted blade in her hands.

Her hands were never still. On shipboard, one was always armored in a ropemaker's palm, the other armed with fid or spike or pricker to stitch canvas, wind grommets, splice line; or both were gloved as she tarred the shrouds or decking with the remains of mawbellies heated over a fire of black-ship driftwood; or both were bare as she fluffed chafing gear or leveraged seizings tight with a heaving mallet. Here there was nothing useful for those hands to do. Here they busied themselves with trifles, braiding hemp wristlets and chokers, turning and turning an old adversary's hooked blade until the light running in the metal's currents became a captured flow of braided waters.

They could be out on the real waters doing some good. Instead they were here, turning makework in their hands.

He'd never wondered before if his mother, the hardest, staunchest person he'd known in a sea filled with hard, staunch survivors, was afraid. He'd never considered that feeling the solid safety of home under her feet would careen her for good.

At midnight on Longdark, with the Khinish three days at sea under command of Hanla n'Geior on the high side and Evonder's brother Evrael on the low side, with Graefel n'Traeyen on a horse perhaps halfway to Gir Doegre, with a gibbous, waning moon bleaching the kadri in the sky, Liath Stormwind of the Inner Shores lay on the living earth and let her spirit sail the silent sea of stars.

She was waiting for Nerenyi. To do what she planned to do, she needed help. Someone who would understand her plan, and aid it. Someone who could keep the others from intervening too soon. But it didn't look as though Nerenyi would return in time. She felt an echo of old memory of that, and smiled sadly.

Kazhe might do. No doubt Kazhe would happily wield the blade herself. But it didn't look as though Kazhe would be back in time, either. It was possible that neither Kazhe nor Nerenyi would come back at all.

That left only Louarn. But he would want to tell the others first, and he wasn't strong enough to keep them from stopping her. He would try to use wiles where only muscle would serve. If it was Louarn, she'd have to do it fast, before he had the chance.

"Come back, Kazhe," she said, to the heedless stars. "Come back, Nerenyi. I can't wait much longer."

Rekke gripped the sides of the table. An eyeblink later, as Ioli gleaned what he saw, he said, "They've burned another hole."

Kara swore. They were only nine days under way. They shouldn't be that desperate yet. She was frustrated at not being able to see into the intorsion.

"Tell my mother," Kara said to an older mender nearby, as the news murmured from table to table around the long curved hall of the Pointhill Torus. The first batch of casthomes had appeared in a huddle in the middle of the Menalad Plain, several leagues from the Gir Doegre target. They might have to search for these new ones, send word through the runners to keep watch for them.

Rekke's left eye rolled wild, then froze. "They're in Maur Lengra."

They'll drown, the hallful of menders thought, *no one will notice them floundering in the middle of the maur they'll drown—*

"Bloody spirits!" Rekke said. "They cast *the whole ship* there."

At least they're safe, Ioli thought. It was the menders' thought, and Kara's, interpreted in words as his mind gleaned it from their smoothing faces and unclenching hands, but he thought he was glad too.

Ioli and Rekke stood around Kara's big map while Rekke gleaned for her, filling in details with an accuracy it would have taken her and the other menders years to match with ground-based surveys. Now her sure hand slashed another charcoal mark from intorsion to coast. The first had cut Handward from the High Sea, and widened since then. This one came in from the Dreaming Sea. At least it gave a rough indication of the fleet's position. The high ships had been halfway to the Fist three days ago. The low ships were two-thirds of the way there now—assuming any of them remained intact, beyond the one in the maur.

The map of Eiden's body and the surrounding waters, spread on the rosewood table like a human body, had already been a wonder when they started. One huge sheet custom-made for cartography by a master sedgelayer in Dru Myrle, it was a copy of the master map in the Woodhill Repository, traced by assistants onto translucent leaves, which were then chalked on the reverse and traced again, section by section with a stylus, onto the large sheet for inking.

Kara n'Dabrena l'Tolivar was supposed to be a mage. Ioli could see it, off at the edges, where Mauzl's past-paths veered into woulds and shoulds. That was a new thing, those shadow paths. Mauzl's powers were growing, or he was growing into them, or the continual blending of their glow was making all of them more than they had been. Kara was meant to be an illuminator, and triad her binder father and wordsmith mother one day as a warder. The searing of her light when she was an infant had let no other light shine forth; she was neither a touch nor a visant. She had made an illuminator of herself in spite of it, lighting the heights and depths of the physical world with her maps.

Now Rekke's bird's-eye gleaning hovered over and around her rendering, the apparent height of their view adjusted to make Eiden's body, below them, match the size and orientation of the table map. Ioli passed the blurred shadow of that gleaning to Kara. She chalked in details with uncanny realism, correcting where Rekke indicated. Rekke couldn't draw maps himself. In their time here, with the endless assortments of ink and brush and pigment, he had made pictures that made painters tight with envy. But they were all places he had seen from ground level—places as they looked to those who dwelled in them. Cartography, it seemed, was a different skill.

Rekke's admiration for Kara made Ioli admire her more.

Mauzl liked Kara, too, but Mauzl wasn't with them. At first he'd been fascinated to see the world and the inked image of it merge. But before long he'd grown bored with all the pointings of fingers and scritchings of chalk. He'd gone off with Caille and Eilryn to roam the woods and fields, more contented, with them, than he had ever been. The touch girl and the mage boy found Rekke unsettling and Ioli hard to get to know, but they'd loved Mauzl from the start, and in their company he bloomed. It was strange to think of Mauzl having friends. It was strange to think of people with no blue glow accepting his quirks and oddities, becoming fond of him for what he was, learning to see beyond his shyness. Caille and Eilryn found things in Mauzl that not even Ioli had seen there. Caille and Eilryn brought out qualities in Mauzl that Rekke and Ioli did not. *We make him powerful,* Ioli thought. *They make him human.*

Powerful or not, Mauzl still could not control the opening of the paths, and fits came upon him without warning. Caille liked to keep him close, to soothe the harm his body did itself, and under her care he was filling out, looking less the runt and more the silky, cosseted mouse. His eyes remained huge and hollow and depthless. His powers took a toll on him that Caille couldn't heal, Ioli and Rekke couldn't share. They themselves were a blind spot in the paths. Mauzl could sense which paths were mostly good or mostly bad, but he could never say why, and Ioli couldn't glean it on him. The more their glow blended, the more that blind spot included him and Rekke, as though the three of them were becoming one person, moving with one will through the world.

Ioli still felt like Ioli, from inside the confines of his solitary skull. He didn't want what they wanted. He didn't have to be where they were. They could go wherever they liked now; the glow came with them no matter how far apart they were. Mauzl wanted to be with Caille and Eilryn. Rekke was itching for the bladed Girdler to return—wary and parched, a man craving strong drink he knew was poison—and when he felt Ioli glean it on him he'd summon images to his mind's eye that made Ioli blush purple and slam his own mind shut. Ioli stayed close to him only because Rekke was helping with the maps and Ioli liked the mapmaker. Not the way Rekke liked the bladeswoman. Not the way the mage boy loved the touch girl, though he was living with her in her grotto now and their happiness, deep in the living wood, made Ioli yearn for something that sweet and uncontainable, that tender and fierce, that soft and surging. Ioli wanted to be home with Jalairi. But Kara was here.

Kara was the first person he had met who didn't mind him gleaning her at all. She'd look back at him, and smile, and never ask him what he saw—never even wonder. Kara treated happiness the way Rekke treated belief, like the most delicate crystal. She knew how suddenly baby girls could be deprived of their fathers, how suddenly children could be snatched from their homes—how one day there could be a Triennead, and the next day a slag heap and a mound of hills. She mapped the earth because it changed more slowly than anything else, because for the most part you could rely on it; but in the end even mountains changed, even the course of rivers and the shape of the world. She mapped what was against the day it became what had been.

"All right, Ioli?" Kara said, pausing with a piece of charcoal over the intorsion by the Fist, blackening and extending the ragged marks there to show how the hole had widened just in the last day. It was tearing in diagonal striations, an eye-aching, unnatural decay, and the rendering had to be done over with increasing frequency. The gum she used to lift the charcoal marks from the sedgeweave came from a spiritwood tree somewhere in the Toes.

You map what was against the day it changes to what is, he thought, staring at the gum. Lift the old day from the leaf, mark the new day on top, but the old day was still there, an impression, a shadow. "That other map," he said.

Her brows disappeared under honey-colored bangs. "I have a lot of maps."

"Your journeying. The last year."

"Ignore his nonsense," Rekke said. "This bit here's wrong. The mountains come farther down."

"I was talking to people on the coast," Kara said. "Shielders, saltmongers, kelpmongers . . . I was trying to understand the mirages. I'm a mender. I logged them. Every sighting, the position and description of every ship. We sent copies of all that to Khine for their fleet."

"It won't help them," Ioli said.

"How do you know that?"

"I don't. You do."

"Well, I know the sightings aren't recent—they're years old, some of them, but . . ." Her brown eyes went wide. She stared at the map on the table, touched a fingertip to the marks of the Fist burnhole. "A dozen years old . . ."

Rekke opened his mouth, and Ioli made a savage gesture to silence him.

Kara said, "A dozen years ago, Breida Shipseer saw Liath Illuminator's ship try to make landfall. A dozen years ago, Verlein Who Watches saw the first black ship try to attack. A dozen years ago, coastfolk everywhere started seeing the mirages. But our explorer ships went out two nineyears ago. For six years there was no sign of them. We thought they'd just sailed beyond sight. Then they were there again. Coming about, as though they'd just gone out but they'd run into trouble and were trying to get back. They never made landfall. We thought we'd gone mad, or the ships were haunts, or . . ."

For Ioli, it was like seeing a mind fight clear of the delusion of siege. He didn't need to glean her. Anyone could see it, in the flush of her cheeks, the fevered glitter of her bright brown eyes. A mind lighting with comprehension. It was beautiful. It made his heart hurt.

"Light," she said. "It's light."

"*What* is?" said Rekke. He was twitching, tapping. He liked making the map clearer. He liked being in the hall and in the sky at the same time. He came back, all of him, into the hall, and it was too much glass and not enough stone, and he didn't understand. What Kara was doing was lightless visantry.

"What we see," Kara said, with breathless awe. "What we see when we're not daydreaming or imagining or remembering. What our eyes see, our ordinary eyes—my eyes. It's light. The intorsion twists light. That's what the mirages are. Light that the intorsion twisted around and around until finally it seeped in to us. The locations I plotted—that's where everything *was*. That's why we didn't see our ships right away. That's why we didn't see the black ships right away. We didn't see any of them for six years, because that's how long the intorsion trapped that light. It took six years to reach us. When we look at the intorsion, *we're looking into the past*."

"Not for much longer," Rekke said.

He'd sent his wild eye back up to its perch in the sky. He was looking at the three burnholes. Widening. Tearing. Soon they would reach the outer side of the intorsion. Soon they would tear all the way through, and everything that had been trapped in there, twined in there, torqued in there—air and water and light and ships and all—would burst apart.

What would happen to the coast? How far in would it reach? *What was is about to become what is.*

* * *

Louarn roamed.

Within the touchcrafted glass walls of the Pointhill Torus, one long circular hall around an open-air garden, Dabrena and Karanthe pored over reports. Karanthe had come as the runners' liaison, but in truth to see Liath. Keiler had not come. Louarn's longing was painful and deep. He'd expected Keiler to join him here, if not for him then for Liath, but Keiler had his own obligations and concerns. Folk did not always choose the same paths.

Down the hall a quarter-turn, Ioli sat with Kara by the completed map. The only emendations they made now were to the burnholes, long black scars on the sedgeweave. Rekke lay supine on the next table, as though he'd gleaned Eiden's body for so long that he felt he'd become it.

At the table farther on, Eilryn and Caille sat across from each other, Mauzl at the end, eating a modest breakfast. Their three lights formed a perfect triangle. Louarn's eye sought by habit for her sisters, but Pelufer was long gone to the bladesmith in the Knee, and Elora was still home with her pledge. It was only just gone dawn, a cold small sun rising in the frozen sky. He did not know whether all these folk had sat up the night—the last night of the old moon—or found their way here at first light. He had not slept sound since he left Keiler's side, but he had roamed the longstreets during the dark hours, filled with foreboding he did not want to inflict on the holding's sleepless.

Liath sat in the center of the hall's rotunda, no coat on her in the frigid air. The garden was planted in a pattern of three arms radiating outward from a shared center—a circular stone bench in a depth of ivy. Pointhill formed the shape of a triskele. Liath still wore her triskele, and made no effort to hide it, with her penchant for billowy shirts loose-laced at the top. Liath still wore her scars. To Caille's dismay, three of them had reappeared over the days following her healing: one of the Ennead's triangular scars, on the back of her right hand; the scar over her kidney where Kazhe's blade had repaid her betrayal of Torrin; and the long scar from temple to lip, which Liath would not explain and Eilryn said she'd had as long as he could remember. Perhaps the triskele, to her, was another mark of a loss that made her who she was.

Dabrena still wears warder's white, Louarn thought, *and Karanthe still wears reckoner's black. We incorporate our wounds into our strengths as we can.*

He had come to the hall's second set of doors, opposite the first. One led outward, in the direction of the Blooded Mountains. One led inward, to the garden. He took the second, and said, "Tell me what you saw in Ioli's gleaning. Tell me why, or I won't help you. You can't do it alone."

"Do what?" Liath said, intent on something she was twisting in her hands.

Louarn waited. He had been waiting for more than three ninedays, and she had not come to him. He knew what she planned.

She made a face at the hemp in her hands. Nine strands twisted into a braid so deft and complex that his puzzler's eye could barely follow it. "I forgot," she said. "You have that bloody blue glow, don't you."

"I'm not Ioli. But I've known you a long time, Illuminator."

Liath was silent, working her braid. At last she said, casually, as though they sat by a warm fire at leisure to ask idle questions, "Did you see a light in your father, Louarn?"

"In the hauntrealm? No. Nor in Pelkin." He hesitated. "They were dead."

"And your kenai-to-be? The middle girl, the one you won't let yourself—"

"Don't," he said, quickly.

She grinned. "I've known you a long time, runner boy." The strands of twine went under, over, across, under, over, across. "Did she ever see a shine on any of her haunts? Did her Triennead haunts ever intimate they had a light?"

"Not to my knowledge." He made himself relax. The price of old friendships would always be thoughtless gestures that sliced too close to the bone.

She finished the length of braid and looped it to splice, producing a penknife with which to shave the ends increasingly fine as she tucked them in. In moments, there was an intricate circle with no visible beginning or end. "I don't remember any of what Ioli described in Galandra's passage. It wasn't for me to hold. That's as it should be. But I remembered what I saw when I was there. I always remembered it, but it was mixed up with everything else that was happening—the Ennead launching through the warding, Portriel in the middle of them, the world . . . unfolding itself. Afterward, I went over it and over it, trying to think how I could have saved them. It wasn't until Ioli opened up that memory again, let me *be* there, *in* it, that I saw. I saw the faces of Galandra's triad splitting off from hers—the hein-na-fhin undone, their joined selves parted. I saw them fade as the casting leaf dissipated. It went into the earth, and they went on, and then their light went on." She gestured him to join her on the ice-cold bench. He had to climb over the back; it was a joined circle, too. She slipped the wristlet over his hand and snugged it on his forearm. "They went on, Louarn. *Their light followed after.*"

"It only seemed that way—"

"No. There was a delay. They were passaged. We nearly went with them. I had time to look out at the Storm, time to think about all the beautiful things that would be lost if the world ended. I had time to see Portriel's will and spirit drive the Ennead from their target. I had time to know that we were being passaged too. And then we were seared. The searing was their light going out of this realm. *Separately,* Louarn. After they had gone."

"That doesn't mean . . . You don't know for certain . . ." He swore.

"I know, Louarn. I remember."

Louarn remembered the young mage girl with a blocked light—the girl he was supposed to call to the Ennead. She failed in a casting; he did not call her. She came anyway, attached herself to him and came along, and after all that befell them on that journey, injury and shadows and Southers with cruel hooked blades, she still would not turn for home. So he had taken her into that dark mountain, even though by then he'd have given anything to keep her from it.

"What about your son?"

"My son is fine. Look at him. He's happy, though at the moment more than peeved at me for keeping him here. He's the brightest bloody light who ever lived and ever will. He's found the love of his life. I fought to protect that life for twice nine years. He's safe now. He's where he belongs."

Louarn took Liath's chin in his hand, holding firm against the reflexive jerk of her head. *"You are not the second coming of Galandra."*

Her gray eyes were cold. "No. Like this, I'm *nothing*."

"All right," he said. "I'll take you to a place where you can start." *Though right now I think I'd give almost anything to keep you from it.* He looked through the glass into the hall. "We have the materials. Caille is here. I'm afraid you'll have a job talking them all into it, but I can help with that. We'll have to send for an illuminator." Something caught at the edge of his eye. He started to turn. "When do you . . ."

"Now," she said, and drew a dagger from a sheath in her boot.

Kazhe's cheit.

"No—"

Fast, faster than he would ever be, she plunged the hooked blade into her gut, and twisted, and drew it upward.

Caille's shriek came strangely muffled through the transparent wall.

Louarn's hand shot toward the dagger's hilt.

"It's hooked," she warned, teeth gritted. "Don't pull it out."

He blanched to hear her speak through that much pain. No groan, no cry. He knew what the Ennead had done to her, he'd imagined what she'd survived for all those years at sea, but he had not known till now how hard she had become.

"Eilryn!" he shouted, lifting her in his arms, planting one foot on the bench, another on the back, taking the impact of doubled weight in both knees as he landed—trying to run for the door, managing only a stagger across the composted, leaf-

mulched, winter-dry garden beds. Why call for Eilryn? Why not Caille? *Because this is what she wants. This is how it had to be. But she should have warned me, warned them, gotten their—*

Permission. Approval. They would never have given it. His most potent, manipulative persuasion could not have engineered that kind of acquiescence.

"Put coats or cloaks on that table," he ordered, *"now,"* and menders jumped to obey him with no comprehension of why he asked. Eilryn had bolted round the end of the farther table to Caille when she cried out, thinking the pain was hers, ignoring Louarn's shout, and was only just turning.

"We have no illuminator, you bloody fool," Louarn grated to Liath as he laid her on the hasty pile of cloaks, pillowed her head on someone's hat. Within the shock and the outcries, Eilryn's voice, Dabrena's, Karanthe's, the fluttering hover of distraught menders, the two of them seemed suspended in a sphere of near silence, a bubble of elongated time.

Liath grinned red, and rasped on a froth of blood, "Of course you have. You have my son. I trained him."

A blow from the side knocked Louarn staggering into the chill flow of time and panic. In the moment that Eilryn stood torn between ministering to Liath and killing him with the knife coming out of his belt, Liath said something that Louarn couldn't hear for the hubbub—telling Eilryn that Louarn hadn't done this, telling Caille to stand off, she'd done this for good reason.

"Don't heal her, Caille," Louarn said, snatching casting materials from worktables, one part of his mind calculating how long she could last with a grievous belly wound in hall air insufficiently warmed by braziers, one part of his mind listing the inks and pigments Eilryn would require, trying to work out what he could substitute from the stores that lay to hand. *My soul for a rotting binder's truss,* he thought—and then a jar marked with the warning symbol for quicksilver came into his hand. He looked up to find Karanthe sorting through cartographers' backings for something suitable to use as a binding board. She understood, then. She understood that once you reached out to see how that light felt, you never stopped reaching, no matter how far—

He tore himself from the gleaning to block Caille's hands. "She wants passage," he said, "not healing. She means to come back. Let her go."

Caille cast a wild, desperate look at Eilryn.

"Going . . . find . . ." Liath said, in a horrible breathless slur as her torn gut seized and failed to push out air for speech, then fell into a lolling swoon, hands sliding from where they'd protected the blade's grip.

"Do you understand?" Louarn said to Eilryn, laying the binding board across Liath's thighs to free him to take Eilryn by the shoulders. The boy was pale with shock and dawning horror. "It's you and me, do you understand? The passage strophes. Don't improvise. Scribe what Dabrena showed you. Your love, your fear, save all that for the illumination, and render it the way your mother taught you. Yes?" He shook the boy. "Yes?"

Eilryn nodded.

Caille said, "No," and laid a hand on the dagger's grip. In the next moment she was on the floor and clawing her way back up the table to stand.

"It won't let me," she said, staring at the blade with an unspeakable expression. Then she snarled, and laid hands on it again.

This time Louarn saw the pressured burst the blade gave out when Caille's flesh touched it. She was braced this time, but her hands were flung wide. *Lodestone on lodestone,* Louarn thought. It didn't matter what or why—only that the kenai's magecrafted dagger had protected the casting subject.

"Eilryn," Caille pleaded, but Louarn came round to her side of the table and moved her gently aside. Her shine, swelled to bursting by the fight to heal a mortal wound, flowed through him instead, a nearly debilitating sweetness. "It's all right, love," he said, but she would not withdraw until Eilryn looked across at her, his face set in stone but his eyes—large gray eyes, Liath's eyes—imploring her to understand.

"I thought she'd given up," he said. Louarn tacked the sedgeweave to the binding board with a wince as the sharp tips entered woodflesh. "I was wrong."

"But why . . . ?" Caille's face was wet with tears, her body anguished by the pain of the body just a hand's breadth away.

"Because her light is all she ever wanted besides home, and her dead restored," Eilryn said, tears spilling disregarded onto his own, indurate face.

Louarn handed the casting leaf across, then the jar of quicksilver and a dove's-wing quill. Karanthe already knew, the visants already knew, Dabrena and the menders were just seeing it now, but Caille still could not comprehend why a vibrant woman would choose this grisly, seeping, agonizing death, wrought with a tool that would thwart her tender healing.

"She's going to find her light," Louarn said, and then Eilryn laid dipped quill to leaf, and the casting began.

Eilryn was engulfed in a mist of white. No sense of space, no orientation. He was standing, as he'd been for the casting. Louarn stood at three times arm's length. He could still hear Louarn's bindsong. It was rising to a climax, then subsiding, gentle and slow as a broad leaf through thick fog—falling, lower, and lower still. He could still see Caille and Mauzl, but they were diaphanous shadows, fading, unable to hang on to him.

Between him and Louarn stood his mother. She was restored to a slender, youthful vitality he'd never seen on her or any of her incarnations—wistful, with a glint of humor, but still commanding, still his mother: his mother at her best, his mother the way she must have felt herself to be, inside.

This is where we were, she said to Louarn. Her mouth moved, and Eilryn could hear her, but her voice registered in his mind more than his ears, a thought more than a sound. *One of me, with you and Pelkin.*

Yes, Louarn replied, in that same unearthly voice. He looked at Eilryn. His dark blue eyes were filled with the scintillating mist of this place. It was unearthly. He was so much more powerful than Eilryn had been able to see, with his one light. *I'm glad you stayed*, Louarn said to him. *You can wait with me.*

I don't understand, Eilryn whispered.

We'll find our way, Louarn replied. *Where do you most want to go, Liath? That's where this passage will take you.*

Eilryn went cold. Louarn was asking if she wanted to die. He must have wondered that, too. Eilryn had. He'd wondered if in the end what his mother wanted was to join Torrin and Heff in death. She'd seen him safe home. She'd seen him grow up. Maybe she felt that her work in the world was done and it was time to move on. She'd told him once that she should have died with her triad, that she didn't understand why she hadn't. Then she'd been angry at herself for saying that to him. He opened his mouth to tell her, *No, it isn't time yet, don't leave me, don't go—*

Two figures were resolving out of the mist inside the crystalline tunnel.

One was tall, as tall as he was, as tall as his mother. He was garbed in black linen and silk, a black cloak swirling around his calves as he walked toward them, like a shadow—like one of the reckoners of old, as though in this realm where you were what you felt yourself to be, he felt himself to be a shadow, a dark revenant of a black mountain, a proxy for something larger than himself, a messenger, a rover. Black hair swept in waves to his shoulders. *Just like mine*, Eilryn thought. His lips curved up in a closemouthed smile. *Just like mine*, Eilryn thought. His eyes burned amber, the color of magelight.

With a cry that tore through Eilryn's heart, a cry that echoed down all the long ages, Liath took three steps forward and was in his arms.

They melted into each other, faces pressed into each other's hair, bodies fit tight all up and down their long, spare length until no space remained between, until it seemed they were one body that had come back the way it was meant to be, like someone cast into pieces and now made whole.

Time went still around that embrace. Nothing moved; for a moment that was a lifetime, nothing could. Then the other figure came into the mist-white space where Louarn and Eilryn stood.

A big man, bigger than any of them, with a gentle face that blurred down one side so that Eilryn couldn't make it out, though his eyes filled in a symmetry of features. Dressed in dun and beige and brown, chestnut-haired, hazel-eyed—earth incarnate. *You are their son,* he said. *We didn't know there was a child. This is a great gift.* Eilryn heard no words; the man's hands had moved rather than his mouth. Eilryn had understood them. He glanced at Louarn, whose brows lifted in a shrug: he hadn't.

This is Heff Farrier, and I understand him, just like my mother did.

Heff smiled. He'd heard Eilryn's thoughts as though he'd spoken them.

That's my father, he thought. His father, whom he'd never seen, except through his mother's eyes, brought to life in the stories she told of her youth, in the portraits she painted when they had materials enough to spare for paintings that were not castings.

Liath drew back from the embrace, and confirmed with casual formality, *Torrin, this is Eilryn. Your son.*

Torrin n'Maeryn l'Eilody looked on him for the first time, and smiled. *A handsome lad,* he said, laughter dancing in his golden eyes.

Of course, Liath said with an answering grin. *He looks just like you.* She turned to look at Eilryn, too, a look of unguarded affection such as she rarely bestowed. *I named him for your parents.*

Torrin cocked his head, then said, *He does them honor.*

Eilryn wanted to go to him, greet him, embrace him—but he was a stranger, and like a child struck abruptly shy Eilryn just stood there, unable to move, unable to do anything but stare at this haunt of the man who had sired him.

Liath was looking at Heff. Just looking at him, and he looking back at her. Then his hands came up, and moved: *I said I'd always find you.*

It was meant as apology. Heff meant that Liath had had to find him—that he had failed. But she said, *And so you have. Louarn opened a way, and there you came, out of all the realms and all the years. I wouldn't have known where to begin.* Then she embraced him, hard, not long, a crushing hug of fierce relief. She wanted to stay in those arms, safe and soothed; Eilryn could feel that longing like a poignant warmth suffusing the space they stood in. But she had come here for a reason. Not to die. Not to experience this profound reunion, and stay. Back in the world, a hooked knife pierced her flesh. She had only as long as the last note of Louarn's bindsong. There was no knowing how long that was.

I would embrace you, Eilryn, Torrin said. *But you should not be brushed that close with death. Spirits willing, we'll meet again, in another place.*

Eilryn nodded, unable to speak—unable even to think.

There's a realm, Louarn told them, stepping forward. *A ghost of the bonefolk's realm, from the time of their glory. Populated by the unpassaged dead. Do you know it?*

Torrin shook his head. *We have been caught between realms. A long time, from the looks of it—the span of this boy's life. It felt much longer.*

You have a passage out now, said Louarn. *I don't know where it will take you. That's up to you. You'll find aid in that hauntrealm, if you go there. Folk you knew in life. But tread carefully. The old Ennead haunts it, too. Your old friends are fighting it. They may ask your help, and I don't know if you'll have time to give it. We'll be waiting here. We'll wait as long as we can.*

This isn't your passage casting? Torrin asked Liath, taking a step back. *I would not have—*

Too late, Liath said—almost sang, she was so full of joy. Eilryn felt forgotten, seeing the three of them together. Rejoined, after the span of his whole life. *You've already brushed me with death. I've been brushed by death more times than I can count. I'm dying right now. That's why I'm here.*

She can return to the world, if she chooses, if you're in time, Louarn said. *You must go. I don't know how much time there is.*

You're the runner boy, Torrin said suddenly, focusing on Louarn. *Bron's fosterling. The boy Liath befriended. The boy with the powerful dreams.* He seemed to see more than that in Louarn, but couldn't place it.

Louarn gave a brief, wry smile. *You're in one of them now.*

Who are you? Torrin asked, quietly but with an intensity driven by something that looked like pain.

Louarn seemed to understand the question. Just as quietly, he replied, *I am Louarn n'Evonder. Your friend Evonder's son.*

Then part of him lives on, as well, Torrin said. *Heff spoke truly. These are great gifts.*

We're just swimming in sons today, Liath said. *But I have a light to find, and I think you might, too. We've got to go.* She looked at Heff. *You don't have to come, Heff. I think you can go anywhere you like from here.*

Heff had hated his magelight; it had eclipsed his shine. Eilryn hadn't understood that before they left the seas. He'd grown up believing that his magelight, his great danger and his great gift, was the most important thing about him, no matter what lip service his mother gave the importance of his life, his self. He'd never sympathized with what she told him about Heff and his earthcraft. How could anyone want *not* to have a magelight? How could anyone seal magelight off on *purpose*? But now there was Caille. Her shine was beautiful, and precious, and it didn't matter one whit whether he could see it or not—he would die to keep anything from harming that shine, or her. He understood why his mother would want to spare Heff this task. It wasn't his task. Heff wouldn't accept his light back if someone handed it to him on a bed of flowers.

That's why you've come? Heff asked Liath. *To find your light?*

Liath nodded.

Then let's go find it, Heff said, and started toward the crystalline passageway.

Thank you, Louarn, Liath said. And to Eilryn, she said, *I'll be back. But if you have to go, you go. Don't wait for me.*

He'd heard her say things like that before, when she was risking her life to save them both. Going on deck to battle horrors, making him stay below, hide himself. Telling him she'd be back when what she meant was that she might not, but she loved him and she'd try. He knew how to sail the ship. He could sail the ship himself from the time he was eight. He was meant to carry on, to survive, to keep sailing, even if she could not come back.

I understand, he said. *Spirits shield you—*

She was gone into prismatic iridescence, gone into pure, white light. The three of them walked abreast, with Liath in the middle.

Within the mist of passage, the last note of the bindsong lengthened, and deepened, sinking almost past the reach of hearing. One long, low wave, longer than the slow pulse of the sea, deeper than the deepest dream, slower than creeping ice; lower than the fathomless depths of time, and still descending.

Eilryn locked eyes with Louarn, and listened as the note went down, and down, and down.

Louarn did not know how long they waited in the mist of passage, a stillness in a dream. He did not know how long he and Pelkin had roamed the realms, or how long they had stood in Liath's attic refuge, or how long he had stood frozen at the edge while Pelkin made his foray into the hauntrealm. He did not know how long it would have seemed to someone awaiting them in the whiteness. Longer than the last breath of his song, but shorter than the daylong journey it seemed to the wanderers? It felt he and the boy had stood a nineday vigil. The note had long ago dropped past hearing, but he could sense it—a vibration in the whiteness, a tremor in the depths of his chest, a roundness in the back of his throat. Now it was no more than aspiration. A memory of sound.

His breath was running out.

She'll come, Eilryn said.

She had not come. Louarn did not think she would. Perhaps they had fallen, all three of them this time, together, into one of the cracks between waking and sleep, between life and death. Perhaps they had joined the battle in the hauntrealm, and given themselves in defense of the realm of the dead—finished the battle they had waged against the Ennead all those years ago. Perhaps that battle never ended, and they would remain locked in strife forever, protecting the world from hate at the cost of their eternal souls.

Or perhaps they had found pethyar, and gone on.

She's not coming, lad, Louarn said. *We can't stay.*

The passageway was closing. The boy lunged for it. Louarn tackled him, dragged him back into blank white safety. *Let her go.*

I'll find her! Eilryn cried—a pure cry of heartbreaking heroism.

Your path is not her path. Louarn gripped him in iron-banded crafter's hands. *You cannot follow where she has gone. I know. I tried. It's not for us.*

Eilryn wailed, and thrashed, but Louarn held him fast; and that wailing grief of a child for his mother became its own eternal, inexorable song, and wove back into the echoes of the bindsong, and brought their flesh around them—Louarn standing on one side of the table, his lungs spent, his belly contracted to his spine to squeeze the last air out; Eilryn's hands gripping his across the body, hard enough to break bone, his face blank and hard, fleeting wisps of iridescence clearing from his seagray eyes to reveal the harrowed vacancy of despair.

The casting leaf was gone. The passage—to where, there was no telling—was complete. The sun had not yet cleared the Highhill Comb.

Louarn did not release Eilryn's hands. "She's back with the people she loves," he said. "She went where she wanted to go. Respect her choices, Eilryn. Honor her memory by going on."

With a snarl, Eilryn wrenched free.

Dabrena shoved free of Karanthe to slap Liath's face, clear her airway, massage her chest, bring all her mender's skills to bear in bringing that life back. She'd tear the blade from her belly so Caille could touch her, heal her—

Louarn put her back into Karanthe's keeping. "She's gone, Dabrena."

"Then where are the stinking bonefolk?" Dabrena said. "Have they washed their hands of our dead and all?"

"We have to bring her to the spirit wood, so," one of the menders said.

"I promised her help," Dabrena said.

"And you gave it," said Karanthe. "Your folk healed her. This is on her. Her choice." She met Louarn's gaze. "She's Pelkin's granddaughter."

Rekke had not moved from his sprawl on the table round the curve of the long hall. He could see through the gleaning, Louarn supposed—through Ioli, standing wide-eyed well to the side, and Mauzl, creeping through the background behind Caille and Eilryn. Now Rekke's heavy, lanky frame surged upright and he said, *They're at the Fist. I can see them!*"

For the split of a breath, everyone thought he meant Liath. Then Dabrena muttered, "Grieving spirits, what a time," and asked Rekke how many.

"Half a dozen Khinish ships," he said. "No—seven now. More coming, I think. From maurward. They beat the ships that took the high route."

"There's nothing we can do for the Fist." Karanthe touched Dabrena. "Let's take her to the spirit wood. We can't just leave her on a table. Bre. Come on."

"The hole is belching black ships," Rekke said, his roving eye pointed Fistward. "It's clogged with them. The Khinish won't get through."

"Only warships, or explorer ships?" Dabrena asked.

"Tall. One square sail, banks of oars, a staysail aft," Rekke said. "Those are Khinish. But—two more—one's sailing in, straight in, the fools—" He winced, and swore, and spun around, shaking off whatever he'd seen.

Eilryn pressed Caille at Mauzl. "And the other?" he said.

Mauzl didn't know what to do with Caille, didn't know how to put his arms around her; she pulled him close instead, without a glance, hugging him to her side as though he were the one who needed comfort and protection. She wasn't looking at Eilryn. She was looking out into the garden.

Through the glass, whence a boneman emerged as though coalescing from the winter air.

"Frostworn," Louarn said, with some surprise.

The boneman didn't answer, only took one long storklike step to close the distance to Liath's body, and reached down for it.

Something like a choked sob came out of Eilryn's throat.

Frostworn reared back. In a distressed flutter, his hands said, *I cannot take this one through the ways.*

"It's that poxy blade," Caille said, and tried to reach for it, but Mauzl whined and clung to her and would not let her near. "Dabrena, pull it—"

"No!" cried Mauzl.

"Leave it," said Louarn. "Leave her. This is beyond our understanding. Leave it lie for now." He moved to slide her eyes closed, pull the trailing edges of cloak up, and said, "Frostworn, will you . . ."

But Frostworn had backed into the glass and was gone. Not here to help them, then. Nothing changed. The bonefolk didn't want to know them.

"What about the other ship?" Eilryn said to Rekke.

"It was nothing," Rekke said. "Not in play."

"What do you mean?"

Rekke made a series of mocking faces. "Not in play! Anchored. Abandoned."

Eilryn strode toward Rekke as though ready to take him by the throat.

"No," said Ioli, backing away. "I know what you're going to—"

"And you know you can't stop me." He stood toe-to-toe with Rekke, if not quite eye-to-eye. "Look at that ship," he said. "Look close."

"It's gaff-rigged. One of ours. There's no one aboard, I tell you, or if there is they're dead on deck or below—"

"Look at the figurehead. Tell me."

Rekke snarled, overwhelmed by the fighting, the ripping hole, the growing fleet of shadow ships, unwilling to turn his eye to one small motionless vessel.

Ioli answered for him. "It's Galandra's face," he said.

"That's *Stormwind*. I left it anchored off the Fist. Ioli, show me what he sees."

Rekke said, "I won't be party to some fool—"

"I cast us back here blind. I'll cast myself blind at where my ship was if I have to. I'm not one of your visants, Ankleman, but if you want to protect me, you'll show me where to aim."

"A ship's a smaller target than a field in the Boot, boy."

"That's none of your concern." Eilryn was pulling sedgeweave from the nearest side table, examining and discarding quills. "*Show me*, Ioli."

Mauzl whined, and hid his face in Caille's shoulder. She stroked his flaxen hair. She did not try to intervene in Eilryn's rebellion.

His mother had told him not to go. But she had left him. He was done answering to her.

That didn't stop Dabrena or Karanthe from trying to head off what they saw as a mad grieving flight from a loss he couldn't bear. He shook them off and arranged his materials on the table where Rekke had lain. Louarn had never seen anyone cast single-handed. In spite of everything, he found himself awed by Eilryn's choice of inks and pigments, the mesh sedgeweave he had seemed to find by feel, the competence with which he served as his own binder. *This must be what it was like to watch Torrin Wordsmith cast,* he thought.

And then, *The young fool is going to get himself killed, and all his mother's striving will have been for naught.*

"That ship is part of her," Eilryn said, trimming the point of a reed pen, dipping it, blotting it—holding it poised over the leaf. "If she lands anywhere in this world, if she haunts anything, that will be it. I'm not leaving it out there to rot, or be blown to bits when the intorsion rips apart, or be cast away forever when you ward this land again."

"You're grieving, son," Dabrena said. "You're not thinking clearly. She wanted you here, she wanted you safe. Don't flout her wishes—"

Eilryn's gaze was so cold it froze the words in Dabrena's throat. "*She's dead.* She can't stop me now, if she ever could."

Louarn stood still clutching the cloak-shroud close around Liath Illuminator's cooling flesh as her son scribed and painted and sang himself into a figure of living golden light, and lifted free of the fragile glass hall to fetch back the only thing that he had left.

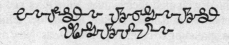

COPPER KILLED THE shadows that helmed the black ships. Kill the things at the helm and you killed the ships. Hitting them was the trick. They surrounded themselves with semblances of flesh to block the shot. Hanlariel ti Khine had never dreamed that the point of her life would come down to the tip of an arrow.

Nonetheless, she was Khinish, and Khinish made themselves useful. She was no seawoman; the ship *Pulchritude* was commanded and sailed by others. She was no mage; the ship's contingent of sealost would be cast home by others, if the commander could angle them through that rent in the air, that place where sea and sky went ragged as untrimmed selvage, and head the ship in one direction for the duration of one casting. She was still headwoman, but there were no orders left to give. Her ships had come in sight of each other and could communicate by pennant and semaphore. No complexities could be conveyed that way, but none remained to be conveyed. *Prevail, or die with honor.* She didn't need to send a bird for that, and their foredeck cages were nearly empty as it was.

The last message she'd received from the menders gave them only till the new moon before the intorsion failed completely—if they didn't burn any new holes through it in the meantime. From the looks of things, they wouldn't have till the end of the spirit days. Two days, she thought, perhaps one. They were lucky to have gotten here so fast. They were lucky to have gotten here at all.

An ordinary Khine-to-Fist passage took nine days and one in fair weather—without delays to take on passengers from unconventional craft in recalcitrant seas, without delays to fight free of black ships along the route. They owed their speed to the touches who'd wrangled their winds. Nine days ago and four they had set out from Khine, shoulder to shoulder, a line of two dozen ships spreading to comb the twisted seas. Now nine ships and five remained of hers, a dozen of Evrael's. One of his had been cast entire to Maur Lengra. All but one of the ships that carried sealost were intact.

She could see Evrael's fleet, in tattered glimpses, growing clearer as hers came up on the tornness. Between them was a teeming seaway of black ships.

Between them and the shores of home.

Well, she'd never expected to reach those shores. Three fleets the size of hers and Evrael's combined remained at home awaiting deployment. If the failure of the intorsion spawned more monstrosities, those fleets would sail to meet them. The rescue ships were no less an attack force, with no less intent to go down fighting. *Pulchritude* would stay at sea and fight until only Khinish ships were left, or only black ships, or until the fracturing intorsion took them all.

"We're going in," the commander told her now, as she tried to draw a bead on the helm of any black ship. The range was closing fast. "Shoulder to shoulder, as we set out. We'll shove ourselves right down their throats."

The black ships were oblique. They liked to come in on an angle. Head-on confrontations made them veer off. They were creatures of this twistedness; straight courses were not to their taste. It was her folk's only advantage.

We'll be surrounded, she thought. *They'll swarm us from the sides, the back. More keep coming out of the sides of our corridor in.*

So long as they held course long enough to cast their human

cargo home, she'd count it a victory. Every black ship they took with them was a garnish.

Long since seared, Evrael te Khine could not see the golden light arc from the deck of his ship to the Fist. "Raise the peak, and hard alee!" he bellowed, voice punching through the smoke and the din, and heard his orders translated into the creak of sheaves in blocks, the rhythmic chant of haulers on halyards, the groan of wood as the great sail filled and the mast and keel responded. He ordered the fore trimmed. The ship turned just in time, and just enough, to avoid collision with the black ship bent on ramming it. To allow the mages to aim their folk home, they had heaved to under luffed sail as long as they dared. If he had waited for the mages to follow, his vessel would be stove and boarded.

The ship stuttered, paused; the ramming ship, in its close passage, had snatched their wind. Spears and arrows flew; one took the touch who could have summoned wind. He ordered both jibs sheeted in. Black deformities leaped across the narrowed gap to grapple with fighters stationed along the rails. A shout and a rolling rumble of blocks announced the enemy boom released to swing into their mainmast. It crashed to at the length of its sheets—three fingers short. The heavy sheets had swept fighters to the deck, both Khinish and enemy. Other Khinish hacked at the sheets with axes. Two leaped onto the boom and crossed to the black ship, hurling spears into its archers' backs, then running up the shrouds, quick as spiders, to cut the enemy sails loose.

His vessel found the freedom of air and surged forward.

As they came out into relative clarity, away from the flaming skeleton of the Khinish vessel *Alacrity* and the smoke and the dust and the spray of missiles, Evrael looked into the scared faces of the mages huddled at the foot of the mainmast, and said, "We'll get you home."

They were the last. Within his fleet, all but one ship's complement of sealost had been cast home down the length of the existing burnhole, along with the mages who'd cast them. He'd had that last ship's complement aboard his vessel: a dozen tattered, starving High Arm folk who had survived in this twisted netherworld for twice nine years. His borrowed mages had cast them home, and the runner and the bird with them, and several injured Khinish who were no more use to Evrael. The young mages were terror-stricken, and managed their complex castings despite it. He had not seen such courage in years.

The moment those mages were gone, his ship would become an attack vessel for as long as his crew would follow him.

Three black ships had come about. Evrael cast his eye along their new heading to find out why, and saw a little battered sealost ship, one man at the tiller, limping under torn sails toward the center lane of the burned seaway. It had somehow threaded its way through the battle. He could not imagine how it had achieved its current position, but there it was.

His ship must be either anchored or on an undeviating heading for the mages to aim their castings accurately. In a melee, with the ship required to come about hard and often, chances were they'd cast themselves out to sea.

Hanla's ships were bearing into the sealane now, nine-and-five of them abreast. If not for his mages he could sail out and around to flank them and draw fire. They would not reach his location in time to save the straggling sealost vessel. To anchor safely, or to sail a straight course, Evrael would have to sail away from the closing battle. The three converging black ships would have the little sealost craft in range of arrows and missiles before that craft made landfall. No other warship of Evrael's fleet was in position to intercept. From his position, Evrael could do better than intercept.

"Don't," said Prill Wordsmith, seeing his decision in the grim set of his face. "Let us cast you to safer waters."

Brave mageling, he thought. There was no safer distance. Not for them. He didn't mind, for himself. He'd lived eight nineyears and three, a long, illustrious life. It was his crew he grieved for. But they would not forgive the dishonor if he made them flee when they could fight.

His seaman's heart, long constrained to the ribbon of safe

waters around the coast, had soared as they entered the seaways. Despite the intorsion's perversity of crosswinds, its perilous whirlpools and contrary currents, its seas that bucked without warning and its distortions of what the eye perceived, he had exulted to be truly seaborne at last. These were no seas that he had ever known, but the thought of giving them up twisted his heart the way the intorsion twisted wind and light and current. Nine days and four was not long enough.

He ordered the ship to come up into the wind.

"How many can you take?" he asked Prill.

"Only three others, if we go ourselves," she replied. It was more involved for them to cast on individuals than on the entire ship. That was no excuse for the laziness or panic that had taken one of his ships off to Maur Lengra against its commander's orders. "Oh, please, Evrael, let us cast the ship home!"

There wasn't time for his crew to draw lots. He called for volunteers and, as expected, received none. He ordered the youngest to the mainmast, and the oldest save himself, and the one who had left the most children back on Khine. He had to order them twice; to dishonor them into complying he would have declared them severed from his crew for insubordination, but it would not dissuade last-breath heroics, so there was no point.

The limping craft was making its best speed shoreward under headsails. Not fast enough. The three black ships had come abreast, bearing down on the wounded ship at a good nine knots. Evrael guided his ship in between them.

"Heave to!" he called, to halt his headway. "Drop anchor!" And then, to the mages, as his commands echoed back to him up the length of the ship: *"Now."*

The wordsmith was already scribing, the illuminator was prepared with pigments held steady in the curve of her legs. The binder grabbed at the youngest sailor when she rose to rejoin her fellows, and forced her back down into the tarred casting circle.

Evrael ordered his archers to let fly. From high in the crow's nests, sailors whirled long slings over their heads and flung stoneweight rocks in long, deadly arcs at the oncoming ships. Arrows rained on them in answer; some clinked off the mainmast-mounted tarp that protected the casting circle, warded against metal in an invention of Prill's.

Such brave, bright children. He was glad they would live.

He felt the conflicted currents of the intorsion trying to turn his ship. He ordered the drogue dropped as well. Now both bow and stern were firmly chained. His vessel blocked the seaway crosswise. The enemy would have to sail through him to catch the wounded craft, around him to reach Eiden's shores.

The black ships came off the wind and slowed in palpable hesitation. That gave the wounded craft sufficient lead. It would make it safely inshore before enemy missiles reached its decks. Evrael could still pull his ship out of here.

The mages were not finished casting. The illumination was complete, but the bindsong had just begun. If he moved his vessel now, they would have to start again. He would not have moved it anyway, except to rise to the attack.

"Stand to," he called. "Prepare for impact."

Two of the three black ships broke off to circle round. Farther warships from his fleet surged on touchcrafted winds to meet them, to clear some room for Hanla's fleet. The third black ship embraced the wind and bore down on him.

The mages and his three crew dissolved into clarity and were gone.

"Strive well, and die with honor!" Evrael te Khine called to his sailors, and heard the command echoed back to him from every throat.

The black ship rammed his with a bone-aching crash, its blade-sharp prow carving straight through his hull, his deck. The mainmast split with an earsplitting crack and toppled to port in slow, inexorable majesty, draping the sea with canvas. Under it all threaded the roar of Khinish voices as his crew poured onto the aggressors' ship and engaged the bristling monstrosities on its deck. Evrael stepped to the aft cache of javelins stored upright by the wheel housing. He hurled them into the deformities clinging to the shrouds and rigging of the enemy craft. When they were gone, he took up a fallen archer's bow.

One after another, the Khinish voices fell silent.

He could feel his ship begin to sink. A grievous angled wrongness in the deck below his feet. The vibration of water rushing into the holds.

Dead strewed the decks of both ships, clearing his line of sight to the enemy's stern. He braced his feet, drew the bow left-handed to compensate for the right elbow ruined in the last skirmish, and aimed for the black stain at the silver wheel of the black ship. His eyes could not resolve its details, but he sensed its sentience, he sensed its regard, and he could see enough of it to aim at. The head of his arrow was copper; copper, they had found early in their passage, killed the shimmering shadow stains that helmed those ships. They were the guiding intelligence and malevolent motive of each vessel; he believed they spawned their ships to suit their purposes, clothing themselves in wood and deformity to become a force of death in the realm of flesh.

He had a clear shot.

On the crooked rail of the enemy's smashed bows, one tortured, dwarven archer came out of its battered shock and cocked its ratcheted metal bow at him. Its arrow, released point-blank, drove straight through his heart, out the back of his chest, and deep into the skin of his dying ship.

I join thee in honor, Streln, his cleaved Khinish heart called out into the next life.

He let his arrow fly, and took the black ship with him.

The Fist was deeply, brutally cold, the footing icy and treacherous. Bare trees carved the indifferent sky like the claws of an invader lying dead and frozen on its back. Breida scanned the sea, her keen eyes aching with the strain of peering through the shredding veil of the intorsion. Most of the battle was clear enough—a widening lane aswarm with blackships, lone Khinish warships nipping at its edges, a rank of Khinish rescue ships bearing down in one great all-or-nothing shoreward advance. But some of the battle took place where the intorsion was tearing. That, she suspected, was where more blackships would slip through to attack her position. The raveled places themselves seemed to give birth to blackships. She'd posted two other sentries and ordered everyone else to wrap up where they could and sleep. The Khinish wouldn't keep those ships busy for long. Soon their shore's defense would be her shield's job again. It always came back to that, and always would.

Below her position on the cliffwall, high seas smashed crewless blackships against the rocks. The waters shimmered with seething stain. The blood of blackships, she thought.

The headland was a stinking slaughterground. Crew after crew, the blackships' complements had stormed her cliff. She and her shield and the kenai had held them off, wave after wave, for more than three ninedays. The gaping locals, at no urging from her, had taken up scythes and froes and pickaxes and joined her shield in a mass of unexpected reinforcements. Eiden's folk had surprised her, and they'd held their own against impossible odds.

But what was out there now . . . If even a third of those ships survived to attack the shore, her post would be overrun.

One Khinish warship, aflame, crumbled into itself in a gout of smoke and embers; another had been sliced in two by a ramming ship, and now she saw the split halves engulfed by waves. The ramming ship melted into a glittering stain and was lost to her sight, probably an oily smear on the swell. She squinted. Why weren't all the blackships maneuvering to engage the Khinish?

A handful were coming around the place where the rammed ship had been. Were they making for shore? She twitched, about to call her shield to duty. Then she saw that those blackships had seized on something, like a pack of dogs. One tiny ship with a torn, scorched main and fore, limping in under headsails. The rammed warship had taken the arrow for it, like a shielder. A lone sealost ship. Where had it come from?

She lost it for a few breaths. As the intorsion failed, it took on the consistency of fog, wisping across her field of view, dragging ragged glimpses of the past across the clear battle lanes of the present. For a few breaths, her sight of what-is was obscured by torn shreds of what-was—a section of raft-up here, a streak of patrolling blackship there. The menders had messaged her about the mirages. Explained that what she'd seen from this very vantage point a dozen years ago was Liath's first attempt to make for shore, six years after it happened. Hard to countenance—yet hard to dismiss, with two realities right in front of her, one passing like tendrils of windblown fog across the other.

She'd have to wave that sealost ship round the far headland, toward the Sea of Sorrows. There was no port for it here. She'd blown the landing up. Like as not, her next view of it would be a smoking hulk anyway. Then the misty billow of what-was blew past, and as in a dream, one of those bloody ensnaring dreams where the same thing kept happening over and over, events turning back on themselves, an intorsion of the mind, the sealost craft came clear.

A snub two-master. A woman's face for a figurehead. A tall, lean body at the tiller. It was Liath's ship.

Two blackships had come from nowhere—disgorged by the edges of the burnhole. They would converge on the little ship just before it made the cliff. If it veered off in either direction, one of the blackships would have it. Its only chance lay in a headlong run, and it was too damaged for that. Who steered it? Not Liath—body too broad-shouldered, hair too dark. No matter. That ship had to come in. It had to make landfall before the intorsion ripped apart.

She kicked her second where he lay bundled in blankets and the coats of the dead. "Wake them," she said—but she didn't wait for shielders to come out of their stupor to work the retort. There'd be no following those fast-moving ships to aim it. In moments the maurward one would pass through its bearing.

The hurling arm was winched down tight, but the sling was empty. She loaded it with what came to hand—stones, stray iron balls, a bag of powder that might be explosive or might be chalk. Last she put in an ironsmith's anvil that she could barely lift. The counterweight was four of the same.

She released the retort. Its great swinging arc was a thing of beauty; the ground-jarring impact when the arm crashed into its cradle would wake the dead.

One chance in twice nine nonned that the projectile would find its mark. She raced back to the wall, watched the weighted missiles spread in the air, watched the maurward blackship sail right under where they would fall . . . a few more threfts . . . almost there . . .

The balls and stones peppered the blackship's decks, knocked down a couple of crew. The bag of powder exploded against the mainmast in a pale smoky billow of harmless chalk. The anvil plunked into the waves two threfts short.

Neither blackship had slowed. If anything, they'd picked up speed. The sealost ship had shed speed. It made no sense. The canvas it had was well filled with wind; it had dropped its useless main and fore to reduce drag. It should have gained, not lost, while she was working the retort. Had they hulled it? A lucky shot from just inside the limit of their range?

The blackships altered course to compensate. They'd be on it in breaths now. *"Come on!"* Breida shouted.

It would not squeak past. There was no arguing with course, heading, speed. Nothing she or that brave little craft could do would change it now.

The figure at the helm resolved into a black-haired boy on the threshold of manhood. Dressed in loose clothes tight-cinched with a broad belt—outerlander garb. Lean, like Liath. Tall, like Liath. Sitting in that aft steering well just as Liath had sat on every approach, from the angle of the hand on the tiller to the cock of the opposite knee, the drape of the arm.

Grieving spirits. That's her son. Her eyes widened. *What is he* doing?

He'd thrown a leg over the tiller—steering with the hollow of his knee. He was lifting an axe. Reaching back. Cutting a line. A line to a drogue.

Released from the dragging weight, the little ship surged forward, keel carving the waves.

One blackship came in from the right, one from the left, far enough to clear each other's sides, close enough to catch the target craft at bow and stern and spin it to crunch between them.

The boy slammed the tiller over as his ship leaped shoreward; hauled in the headsail sheets; heeled his craft onto its beam ends, and eeled from between the closing jaws, into clear seas.

A deafening cheer went up from the shield, startling Breida down to her siege-hardened bones. She had not felt them come around her at the ramparts. For those last breaths, it had been just her and the doomed craft.

Fioral hefted rope and grapnel. "Give him a ride up, Shield-master?"

Breida shook her head. "He's a mage. He could have cast himself home with the rest of them. He brought that ship in to salvage it." To her stewards, she called, "We'll need a launch!" She found her stone touch in the crowd, sent him running down the coveward path to smooth a way through the rubble for one of the drydocked rowboats to be carried down and put in the water. Save beaching, which they could not do, that boy's ship would be safest anchored under bare poles in the middle of the cove. Her stewards would row out and bring him in.

Liath's son, she mused in amazement. *Who'd have ever bloody thought it.*

She turned her gaze, as ever, back to sea. The rank of Khinish warships had borne down into the seaway. Blackships were moving to surround it. Her mages cried out in wonder; a glance over her shoulder showed them gaping at the sky. She could only imagine the array of golden arcs they must see, a glowing skyful of them, as the mages on those warships cast themselves and the rescued explorers home.

The rescue ships became warships. Turned on a breath, fanned out stern-to-stern to face the surrounding foe.

Outnumbered nine to one. Twice nine to one. More.

"Take your posts," she ordered her shield. "It's coming."

The burnhole became as good as its name, filling with

smoke, missiles, flaming debris. Even from this distance, it was an ugly battle.

"Shipseer."

She turned. Fioral had the sealost boy in hand. Breida nodded acknowledgment, and Fioral went off to her own post.

"Eilryn, is it?"

A nod.

"I've a mount you can take. Or go find the mages."

"I'll stay."

"Can you fight?"

The barest hint of smile. "I can."

"Your mother will skin me if I let you come to harm."

A flicker in the eyes. A dinged nerve. She waited. He would tell her if he chose. If not, not. Shielders didn't nose into each other's carrysacks.

He chose not.

She nodded. "We'll just have to live, then, eh?"

"More than the Khinish are doing," said Godill, from the wall.

Breida sent a steward for weapons and protective gear for the boy. Her eye caught on Kazhe, stationed where she was told to be, up the rise where she could see to aim her powers. The kenai saluted the boy, though the boy didn't see it, then swigged from a cask of Neck brandy. The stuff fired her blood, made her twice the fighter she already was. Breida stiffened. Beyond the blademaster, at the far fringes of the encampment, stood rank upon rank of bonefolk.

At least a nonned of them, pale as bleached linen in the stark daylight, tatters fluttering in the sea wind. Facing the cliff. Waiting to claim the dead.

A little early, aren't you? she thought at the forsaken things. She hated the sight of them. So many just standing there in eerie silence curdled her blood. *Spirits take the lot of you. We'll die when we're bloody ready to.*

She considered putting the boy in Kazhe's care, but in the end let him stay beside her as she joined the vigil at the wall.

It was a death watch, no less than the bonefolk's.

The Khinish had stones, she'd give them that. They were fearless, cunning, inventive, skilled, and brutal. They should have been indomitable. Blackships massed on them—so many that all that could be seen of the Khinish warships was the pennants whipping on their topmasts.

"Our turn," Breida said.

LIATH PLUMMETED INTO open space. No air whistled past. Torrin's hand tore from hers, then Heff's. They were there—she could sense them, she was not alone—but she was falling, her arms flailing through void, her shout making no sound. Was this the fall, the fall from the cliff, had she stepped into the death she should have died with them all those years ago?

Something slammed into her. She thought she felt an arm or leg brush her, Torrin's or Heff's, but then she was tumbling away, swept sidewise on a gust or in a flood. Heff and Torrin were swept along with her.

She was flying, and she was home in the circle of her triad, and they were slowing, falling, easing into a realm of wonder, infinity drenched in gold. Magelight drifted in soft, shining mist, fleeted in streaks and wisps, angled in widening rays that diffused into distance. The realm of magelight was a golden vastness stitched with radiance, wormed through with undulating luminosity. They hung suspended in that light as three figures of fluid reflection—the shape of themselves without substance, their forms become animate mirrored contours. Could the light sense them, or were they apparent only to each other? In the realm of matter, light was apparent only to itself.

Here light was elemental, the quality of being, and she and Heff and Torrin were mere echoes of that quality: reified by what they displaced. They floated in glory.

I could go, Liath thought. *I could go, now that I've seen this. I could go, knowing my light lives on in this place. I could go, and be no less myself.*

She knew these lights with a sweet, heart-piercing recognition of spirit. Tolivar's light, sailing golden seas without end. Pelkin's light, burnished, abiding. Graefel's light and Hanla's and Keiler's, joined in a triadic bond no personal estrangement could weaken. Triads remained connected until magecraft dissolved their bonds. Not even the searing could burn through those bonds.

Not even the searing could burn through lights. She discerned no difference between the lights of the seared living and the lights of the unpassaged dead. These lights weren't dead. These lights weren't ghosts of light. The searing wasn't a searing. The searing was a wholesale displacement.

What she'd seen in her gleaned memory was true. Their lights *had* gone somewhere. That where was here.

She saw the light Kara would have shown if she hadn't been shorn of it in infancy. Liath was astonished, not so much that she could recognize a light she'd never seen in life but that it was as bright as any adult's. *We're born with our full lights,* she thought. *We don't grow them inside us as we grow. They're there from the beginning. It's a matter of us becoming . . . vessels worthy of them. Wise enough, experienced enough,* awake *enough for them to come forth through us.*

She saw Imma's light, and Gisela's, and if her mirrored seeming could have wept here, it would have wept for joy to see Nerenyi's with them—to see that clear, fierce light she'd never thought to look upon again. *You're with her, Nerenyi, wherever you've gone,* she thought. *Your light and hers will never be parted. That much, at least, is forever.*

The same should be true of her own and Heff's and Torrin's. Where were they? She'd given her life for this. She could move on without one last, hard-won glimpse of the blazing incandescence that had served Torrin Wordsmith. She could leave without one last, poignant taste of the sweet golden warmth Heff Binder had sealed away. But she would not leave without seeing the one thing her rash self-inflicted death had earned her, the one thing no living mage ever got to see: her own light.

She saw the lights of all the mages she'd encountered in her journey year. The lights of warders and reckoners she'd met in the Holding. All passed her without knowing her—passed Torrin, a shining scion of that Holding in his day, without knowing him. The three of them were transparent here. In an infinity of lights, it must be more than coincidence that they should see the ones they knew; but they were not seen in return.

Drawn by Heff's thoughts, or Torrin's, the magelights of the Ennead came into view. Lerissa's light chased Freyn's, or Freyn's chased Lerissa's, in an endless circle around the central, stolid light of Worilke. No telling if the two circling lights were trying to break free, trying to embrace, or trying to destroy each other. Liath pitied them. She was unmoved by the sight of the leading triad's lights, tangled into a chaotic, inextricable tumble, rolling oblivious through golden light they could have joined.

Some change in Torrin drew her attention. Though they hung motionless, he'd gone still, as when he'd come upon her in Louarn's crystalline mind. Pulled up short by emotion so old and so deep that it stunned him.

She knew before she looked. It was Evonder's light.

Drawing hue and tint from the lights around it, taking first one form, then another, that chameleon light was unmistakable. Among the brightest of any they had seen, but smoky, guarded—ever changing to protect itself, never settled, never easy. Torrin might have been the only soul in all the realms Evonder trusted. Evonder's light showed not the slightest recognition.

It was trying to find Torrin, but it couldn't see him.

Liath couldn't stand to witness either Torrin's torment or his joy. There had to be a way to move, to will herself to her light and then lead them out—

She found herself facing Torrin's light.

Heff's light was behind it. Her light was at its side.

Nothing was as bright as those three lights. Evonder's light was still shuttered by stealth, but Torrin's had cast off its baffles and shone in all its blazing spendor. Hers was almost its match. Heff had spoken truly, all those long years ago, when he'd said that there was only one light, anywhere, brighter than hers.

She had no more than that one glimpse of it, no more than one whiff of its rain-fresh scent, before that desperate, yearning light seized upon her, drove through its own reflection in the mirrored surface of her seeming, and filled her in a burning convulsion of relief.

She had no lungs, no mouth, no means of gasping or crying out. Worse than someone reaching in and ripping her innards out—someone plunging them back in.

The golden colors around her exploded. Haze and murk cleared away. Her own magelight flooded her senses, drenched her spirit, filled every crack and crevice of her soul. The other magelights became visible as they truly were.

She could not look straight at Torrin's. She had to squint as it approached. Its advance was circumspect. They regarded each other with mutual respect and mutual wariness. Assessing. Considering.

Choosing. In a fierce, dizzying rush, Torrin's magelight swept into his liquid contour, shaped itself to his shape and illuminated it from within. Made of him a figure of blinding brilliance.

Evonder's light could see them now. It brushed her; it painted across her light-acute senses a smoky distillation of aged, golden wine. Then it tried to go to Torrin.

The magelights behind it would not allow it. The lights of the remaining triad of the last Ennead. The lights of Evonder's triad—Naeve, his mother, and Vonche, his mother's pledge. They withdrew, dragging Evonder's writhing, struggling light after them in one last bid to keep it away from the light of Torrin n'Maeryn.

No one light on that Ennead had matched Torrin's. Now Torrin was made of magelight. He had substance in this realm. All the power of his light could be brought to bear.

Torrin reached out, took hold of Evonder's light, and ripped it free of its triad.

The lights of Vonche and Naeve stretched into wicked pointed spears and launched themselves at Torrin. Torrin pivoted. Their burning trajectory missed him by a hair. They streaked off into infinity on a silent shriek.

Evonder's light had been flung free. Now it twisted itself into a chain and settled around Torrin's neck, shaped like a pendant triskele cast in light. Startled, Torrin held it with something like reverence. In his hand, the pendant flared so bright that pain lanced through Liath's eyes.

She averted her gaze. It came to rest on Heff's light.

Heff's had been a sweet light, gentle and expansive. Now it was contracted into a fever-bright point, so dense and hot it burned nearly white. As Heff looked on it, it shrank back.

Heff's light knew he didn't want it. It had dragged behind its triad like a ninestone weight. Straining, in despairing futility, to avoid the moment when its bearer put it back into its prison.

Heff extended open hands. Liath didn't know what power of heart it took to will his apparition to move. His magelight crept forward, hesitant, watchful. It brushed his knuckles and drew back. A mistreated creature sniffing an offer of kindness, ready to bolt.

Heff's hands said, *I'm sorry.*

His light was a free light. No triskele had ever been cast to bind it or anchor it. A wild light, too wild now to come back into the keeping of a human will, it trembled upward and settled, quivering, onto Heff's upraised palms. Heff tried to touch it with a fingertip. Some memory, perhaps, of the flesh he once had and its ability to soothe. He could not touch the trembling light.

He let it go. It hovered for a moment, then curled around his head, his neck, twined around his legs. It circled him, flitting in and then away—testing its freedom. The intensity of its glow increased. Heff smiled.

The light swelled to twice his size. It engulfed him. He let himself be swallowed. He let himself be known.

His light blazed.

It swept upward and outward in a joyous sparkle. It fountained over them, collected into a ring, spun around them three times, then broke its circle to fly off into the gold. Relief, gratitude, and happiness shimmered in its wake. The last Liath saw of it was a faraway flare, gamboling and cavorting with lights like Kara's—the lights of seared infants, wild lights that had never known training, never known the harness of the human will, never known anything but this glorious, eternal liberty.

Liath's light-filled form shuddered at a jolt of dislocation. *That was our triad dissolving.* Grief threatened to well up. A limb cut off. Their heart cut out. She tried to say Heff's name, but he raised to the shape of his lips a finger of liquid reflection and shook his head. His hands said, This is its home. I am still part of you. I always was.

Torrin said, in strange voiceless words like the speech of fire, *Your quest is complete, Illuminator—you and your light have found each other. The fondest wishes of Heff and his light have come true. Now I have a charge to carry out.*

Liath looked at the chained triskele of living magelight around his neck. *I know the place,* she said, and held out her hands. *Help me find the way.*

Torrin's palm slid across hers on a current of lightning. Heff laid his liquid hand on hers; she could not grasp it, for her shining fingers sank through, but the weightless contact was sufficient to anchor them in each other.

With the taste of his light on her tongue, she willed herself to where Evonder was. Torrin and Heff went where she went. Draped around Torrin's neck, Evonder's light came with them. She had the powerful sense that this transit was not their doing—that it was the lights of the magelit realm, sensing their intent through the goldenness and sending them where they wanted to go.

She came into the hauntrealm as into the memory of a dream.

Dressed respectively in black linen and silk, undyed homespun, and loose, broad-sashed sea garb, they stood under a fire-opal sky on an expanse of turquoise moss shading to plum, in sight of a hill topped with frosted pavilions, in walking distance of flared, prismatic towers that grew like an impossible mushroom forest in the lee of that hill. She remembered this place as she remembered everything that had happened when she was divided: blurred, unreal, as though she'd traveled not physically but through the visions a teller's tale conjured in the mind. She was once again a manifestation of spirit, the shell of her body left behind on another shore. But the air of the place did not force her to her knees. She occupied space here as someone entitled to it. This realm did not resist her.

That meant she was dead. "Bloody bollocks," she murmured.

A black stain was seeping up into the sky. A malevolence that sensed their presence, and feared it, and hungered for it.

"Move!" Tugging at Torrin and Heff, she started for the nearest canopied white tower at a flat-out run.

The shadow was larger than the hill. Far larger than it had been, and slower than when it had attacked Pelkin. It cast no shadow in the sourceless light; it *was* shadow, animate shadow. It was almost on top of them.

Figures were emerging on either side of it. Not as a buffer, but as decoys to lure it in another direction. *They have no defenses,* she thought. *They have no weapons.* She kept running. She caught Torrin when he twisted an ankle, waved Heff on, and supported Torrin under the arm as they stumbled back into a run. She could feel the pain each time his weight slammed onto his left foot. *We can be injured here,* she thought. *We can tire. We can flag.* "Faster," she gritted to Torrin. He grunted response. They were going as fast as they could.

Darkness blotted her vision to the left. The shadow was not taking the bait. She heard calls, taunts. The shadow, undeviating, came on. *It wants our light,* she thought—but it wasn't her the shadow seized on, and it wasn't Torrin. It was Heff.

The shadow touched him. It was ponderous and he was running full out, but when it touched him he froze in midstep. It covered his left arm and shoulder, his left hip and leg. It was al-most to his head. Almost to his heart.

Torrin pulled Heff's right arm over his shoulders and braced his left leg between Heff's feet. Liath crouched down and wrapped her arms around Heff's rigid right leg. The shadow was less than a foot from her face. It was silken smooth, nonre-flective, bitter cold. It gave off an astringent odor. Her gorge rose. Her flesh prickled at the sound of it, so low it was nearly inaudible, like the hum in a ship's rigging—the sound of count-less human voices screaming.

They put all their strength into wrenching Heff free of the shadow's grip. Heff did not weigh what he had. The three of them reeled back, tripped, and landed in a tangle. Liath scrab-bled to her feet to face the rolling hill of shadow. Torrin strug-gled to stand Heff up. People were everywhere, shouting, but she couldn't make it out for the roar in her ears.

There wasn't time. The shadow was slow, but not that slow. Torrin couldn't drag Heff away faster than it could move.

"Take me," she said, and stepped toward it.

She thought it hesitated. She took another step.

It fell back.

A glance behind her found people coming to Torrin's aid, bearing Heff off in their arms. She took a third step. The shadow sank straight down. No trace of it left behind but that unnamable reek—somewhere between linseed oil and wood turpentine, she thought, but then it was gone and she couldn't remember it.

"*Now* we have a weapon," she said, to empty space.

Pounding footfalls made her turn. She was jerked half off her feet. "Come *on,* you bloody fool," Evonder said. "It could sur-face right underneath you."

"It—" She resisted him. "It doesn't like—" She broke his grip on her arm. Swearing, Evonder rounded on her. She said, *"It doesn't like light."*

His youthful face went flat under its shock of sandy hair. He said, "You have no idea what you're toying with. Follow me now, or die." He turned and made for the tower, scanning the terrain for any sign of the shadow's reemergence.

Heff, she thought, and ran after him.

Evonder walked through the wall of the nearest tower. Liath followed. It was like bursting through chill slush. The space inside was vast and dim. An undulation of curved, spectral walls filled her with nausea and sent her groping into the interior. Torrin's light was a serene yellow beacon. When she reached him, her eyes had adjusted to the eerie darklight. She could see Heff, sitting on the floor, braced on Torrin's arm.

Half of Heff's body had been scoured of flesh.

I'm all right, his hands said. Both hands—one unmarred, one a bloody mass. It doesn't hurt. This body is a seeming.

Mine's not, she thought, but didn't argue with belief that deadened pain.

"My ankle is healed," Torrin said. "These bodies are semblances. Heff's will heal as well."

"His spirit won't," Evonder said.

Torrin looked up, and for a long moment no one was there but the two of them—not the silent, growing crowd, not even Liath. Before Torrin died, they had not seen each other in at least a year. What she sensed pass between them—what passed in depths profound beyond her understanding—filled her with desire and an ache of jealousy. In another time, in another life . . .

Evonder said, "You're wearing two triskeles."

In the crystal passageway of Louarn's mind, Torrin had not worn any, and Liath had not noticed after that. Now he did. One was pewter, the image of the one he'd worn in life. The other was gold, and glowed with a sooty light.

"So I am," Torrin said, sounding as surprised as Liath felt. He stepped to within a breath of Evonder. "One of them is yours," he said. "Do you want it?"

Evonder's eyes hadn't left the golden pendant that shone from inside the lacings of Torrin's shirt. He nodded, once.

Torrin lifted it over his head and draped it on Evonder.

The triskele flared like phosphorus cast on a brazier. Chain and pendant burrowed into Evonder, burning. Evonder collapsed at the knees; Torrin caught him. Their lights bridged, melded, like one light too long divided; then Evonder's became wholly his again, a smoky wine-gold glow at the core of him. He staggered back and put his hand to his chest, speechless.

"Now we have three weapons," Liath said.

A hand fell on her head, slid down to tug on the tail of hair at the nape of her neck. She rose, and turned, and was in her grandfather's arms.

"No time for prolonged reunions, I'm afraid," Pelkin said. "Not unless we use these weapons you've brought us."

"What did you mean about Heff?" Liath said to Evonder. He only gestured to Heff, who was rising to his feet, no sign of unsteadiness, no sign of the scouring his flesh had suffered. Two hazel eyes regarded her from a symmetry of rounded features. She ran her hands down chest and arm, felt plain skin with muscle beneath. The rumpled topology of burns was smoothed away. She reached around herself to probe her back, then touched her cheek, her hand. The scars that had reappeared after Caille's healing were still there. They were part of her—marks of what her spirit had suffered, no more eradicable than the experiences themselves. Heff's scars had been a part of him he'd allowed no mage to heal. That part of him was gone.

"They consumed it," Evonder said. "They thrive on pain. Their hunger is insatiable. All souls bear old sorrows and griefs and hurts, wounds and bereavements, regrets and failures. All bodies are made of soulstuff here. The shadow hunts us to consume us. There's no return from that kind of death. It eats, and grows fat on us. It seeks to burst the boundaries of the realms that haunts are heir to and find its way into the outer realms—if not their physical plane, then the realms where their haunts dwell."

"The leading triad," Torrin said. "What they became, in the one-of-three."

"Gondril was voracious beyond any extreme of human gluttony," Pelkin said. "Seldril was trained to feel pain as pleasure. Landril was ingrained with his makers' thirst for vengeance. Now they are one being, with all three needs."

"What about your parents?" Liath asked Evonder.

"Naeve and Vonche tried to harness the power of the shadow to their own ends," Evonder said. "They were among the first it devoured. Freyn lasted longer, but it had her in the end. Worilke came later, and Lerissa."

Heff tapped Liath, and said with his hands, How many others?

The price for losing the private bitterness that made him Heff was to seem whole again. He could have spoken. She wished he would; she longed to hear the warm, beautiful voice. But he was still Heff. He would remember his losses in every gesture, in every silence.

"How many others?" Liath translated.

"Too many," Evonder said, with the curt brevity of a commander losing a war.

"No reckoning is possible," Pelkin said. "This realm is the size of Eiden's body, and populated with twice nine nonned years of unpassaged dead. We have seen nonneds fall. Many times that number have fallen unseen."

Shadowy throngs milled around the periphery. These shades had been fighting for a long time. They were weary of huddling in their strange, dark-lit shelters; weary of the constant fear, weary of the failed attempts to destroy what stalked them. In their ranks, she saw faces she knew, but they were swallowed by the crowd before she could make contact. She wanted to greet them. She grated on the obligation that kept them distant.

"They had tried every conceivable weapon before I came here," Pelkin said. "We've tried everything we could think of since. Even forgiveness. Compassion." He paused. "Everything but magelight."

"Then let's walk our magelights down its throat," Liath said. She looked at Torrin, who stood with arms folded, then at Evonder, who was pacing. "You died once to defeat that triad. Will you do it again? For real?"

"It won't be enough," Pelkin cut in. "I remember your lights. A nonned of you would not be enough to vanquish the black thing that triad has become."

"How do you know?" Liath said. "Have you tried? Have you touched it?"

I know, Heff signed. I touched it.

"Where does it go when it fades from view?" Torrin asked.

"As it leaves one part of this realm, it appears in another," Evonder said. "Part of it goes into the earth, part rises somewhere else. Unpassaged seekers have their theories. It is always somewhere in this realm. These structures are safe, but limited."

"You can go back into the realm of life," Liath said. "Graefel didn't find what he thought was in the wordsmiths' canon."

Pelkin sat up straight. "What did he find?"

"They didn't know yet, when I . . . left." No one had asked her how she'd died. Inquiry was bad form here. She was just as happy not to say. "Graefel was still on his way to the menders' holding."

"Then we must continue to assume that isolation is imminent," Evonder said. "The unpassaged dead have forgone their haunts in the world of life, to fight the shadow here."

"It seems to me they're only feeding it," Liath said. "Send them back! If they've got to be trapped in one realm, why shouldn't it be the safe one?"

Evonder's pacing paused, and he and Pelkin exchanged a glance.

"What?" Liath said. "Why not just let the cursed shadow rot here?"

"We may be what keeps it here," Pelkin said.

"There is one way to kill it," Evonder said. "It becomes ill when it overfeeds. It has no choice but to consume whatever enters it, and it can't grow fast enough to easily accommodate a surfeit. The larger it grows, the slower it moves. If every spirit in this realm converged on it at once, it would . . . choke."

"Shoving ourselves down its throat is the last expedient," Pelkin said. "But we have exhausted all other options. The spirits present here are those who volunteered for the first wave.

The rest await our word. The ghost of the makers' realm will be covered from head to foot in souls. There will be no stretch of ground where the shadow can emerge in safety. How many remain after the shadow falls . . ." He knuckled his forehead, then let the hand drop. "Some may survive. That is our hope."

"We made the thing," Evonder said. "We made it out of vengefulness and rancor. We brought it with us into exile, and we fed it, and in stripping it of light and life we transformed it into what it is now. We're responsible for it. It's our burden."

"It's our shadow," Pelkin said.

"It has to be destroyed," Liath said. "Not just banished."

"Have you casting materials?" Torrin asked.

Heff said, A casting to destroy it would require deathcraft.

"We're haunts," Evonder said. "We have only what we bring with us—our conception of ourselves. No inks, no quills, no sedgeweave; no tools to produce them if we had the raw materials, no materials with which to fashion tools. We inhabit the ghost of a realm. Nothing here is changeable. Or malleable."

Nothing to change. Nothing to make. Nothing to do.

Truly this was a realm of death.

What did that make pethyar? More changeless, more still, more static even than this? Given a choice, she'd take this hauntrealm and eternal cat-and-mouse with soul-eating shadows—

"Could we passage it?" she asked suddenly.

The four men stared at her, as silent as the thronging shades.

"Not to pethyar," she said. "I wouldn't unleash a thing like that on the only safety we have left to believe in." *Even if I don't believe in it. Even if I think it's more likely oblivion than joy. Even if it seems to me that pethyar must be an agony of stillness, an intolerable boredom of peace. Even if I wonder whether a few shadows wouldn't liven it up.*

"Where, then?" said Evonder.

Liath looked into Torrin's amber eyes. "It doesn't like light," she said. She turned to Pelkin. "You said a nonned of us wouldn't be enough. What about a nonned times nine nonned?"

Pelkin blinked. "You found the hauntrealm of magelight."

"We only theorized such a place," Evonder said.

"It's not a hauntrealm," Liath said. "Magelight can't die. If it could, the Ennead's lights would have destroyed each other years ago. The lights there are alive. They're everything the shadow isn't." She grinned. "They're its antidote."

"You cannot lure it there," Pelkin said. "It will not follow. Before I arrived, haunts escaped the shadow by moving back into the realm of life as bodiless spirits. The shadow would not chase them there. True flesh may prevent them feeding, or perhaps it was the copper light, the blue—"

"There was always magelight there," Liath said. "Even in the dark years. I've seen the lights of those who died as infants. They're as strong as any adult's."

Pelkin raised a silver brow. "That explains a great deal. And assures that the shadow will not be baited into the fire."

"We'll bring the fire here," Liath said. "Torrin brought Evonder his light. We'll go back and fetch yours, Pelkin, and as many others as we can . . ." She paused as Heff's hands moved.

They will not come with you, he signed. He pointed at Evonder, then at Torrin: That light was an exception. That light cleaved to him for love.

"All right," she said. Her words came slowly. Her eyes were fixed on Heff's hands. Her mind was fixed on the way Heff's hands moved through space to make his thoughts known. "We can't fetch light here. We can't lure shadow there." When Heff's hands shaped concepts in the air, they altered the course of her thinking, affected the way she behaved—acted on the world around him. "We'll have to *send* shadow there. We'll have to cast."

"We have no materials," Evonder repeated with forced patience.

"We do. We have the only thing we brought with us. Ourselves."

They would send one scout ahead and one observer after. Bron took the vanguard, stepping out of the ranks of the dead. "So much fuss about light for all these years," he said. "Old Bron won't miss a chance to get a look at the stuff for himself." Liath knew better; she saw the long-banked anger in his dark Khinish eyes, and knew that it was Gondril who had killed him. After a moment, he said, "I promised him I'd be there when he looked death in the face. I don't suppose this death will have a face, but if we can give it one, best it be mine." Bron didn't think he was coming back. Heff didn't think he was coming back. The stable-master had been the closest thing Heff ever had to a father. Their embrace was both reunion and farewell, as fierce as it was brief.

Evonder drew an invisible casting circle on the dark expanse of the tower's floor. Torrin tore a fingertip open and scribed in blood on the smooth alien substance of the floor. Several rendings of his flesh were required, as it healed in a matter of breaths, and the fluid Celyrian he scribed was nearly lost in the spectral darklight, but the motion of his fingers burned a trail across Liath's vision, like a glowing brand through dark air.

There was no ritual handing over of casting leaf and binding board. When Torrin finished, he nodded to her. She bit her finger—it was harder to draw blood than it had looked—and reached out to begin the illumination.

Her guiders burned a clear, heart-piercing blue. She had not seen them in half a lifetime. She had not felt magelight swell in her for twice nine years.

On the seeming of a floor in the seeming of a tower in the ghost of the makers' realm, she drew the kadra Light.

Joy flooded her. Magelight flooded her. She drew passage kadri, and strengthening kadri, and warding kadri to keep Bron safe in a strange realm. A torn fingertip was too coarse an implement with which to historiate, so she drew her patterns dense and strong, representing Bron's steadfast quality of spirit with pure shape instead of portraiture. She had only one color to work with, so she worked in contrasts: angles and corners to buttress the curling glyphs of Torrin's scribing, a straight border of equal line and space to frame the whole and secure the passage. When she had finished, she nodded to Evonder. He gestured Bron into the circle, and reached for their hands.

Magelight flowed into her and out of her, then blended into continuity. As Evonder sang, the smoky reticence drained from his light and left only the sweetness of golden wine, a heady draught of pleasure and potency. Torrin's light had the intensity of the sun, the nerve-tingling crackle of skyfire.

Evonder's voice echoed from the tower's vastness only when his bindsong trailed to an end. Bron's seeming faded to a clear shimmer, and he was gone.

"How will we know we delivered him safely?" Liath asked, as the surging magelight subsided to its resting state—dimmed and guarded in Torrin, smoky and veiled in Evonder.

"We won't," Evonder said. "There are no guarantees." He and Torrin rose with the same feline grace, and Liath with them. "Now comes the hard part."

They left the safety of the tower and awaited the shadow.

It did not come.

"It senses our lights," Evonder said. "It won't come near."

Liath said, "We'll cast from inside—I can see through those walls now—"

"No," Torrin said, and turned.

Behind him, shades were emerging from the tower in droves. Shielders and stewards, villagers and vocates, warders and reckoners—so many familiar faces, in among scores of folk who moved like fighters, some small portion of all the fighters who must have died during the magewar and the Strong Leg battle, the siege and the invasion. They filled the mossy sward of plum and azure, surrounded the tower, arrayed themselves to shield the triad with their lightlessness and draw the shadow with their numbers.

The shadow obliged. It consumed a dozen of them in its ascent. The others gave no ground. They hemmed it—sacrificing their eternal lives to keep the shadow in one place while the mages cast.

Torrin was already scribing in long, sure strokes of his fingers on the moss. His nails would not score it, but the motion of pattern had power, and he was scribing with his own spirit. Liath, stunned by the shadow's mindless consumption of souls, its engorgement, had to force her eyes to follow the paths of his glyphs. She did not see Torrin's nod when he was through, only his hand drawing back. She mastered her horror. Stroked passage kadri and binding kadri across the mossy mat. She put her pain into the casting, her rage, her grief at the loss of those souls. The shadow hungered for hurt and sorrow. She hurt. She sorrowed. It was the only means of connecting with the darkness. Her borderwork was fast and angry, a three-cord knot with the ends turning downward and inward where they met: encirclement, and passage. The shadow would go where that border forced it—into the invisible, ornamented verse that led to light.

The anguish in Evonder's bindsong shocked her. The voice of his soul sang all the years of imprisonment and misery in that Ennead's Holding, a lifetime of terror and loneliness. That voice held no insurgency, no subversion. It was the voice of a child lost in the labyrinth, impaled on the impossible choice between the horrors his dark elders demanded from him and the tortured ethics of his own heart. The shadow was helpless to resist a voice so beautifully wounded. The shadow was desperate to be away from their magelight. The shadow strained, and broke—not sinking down into the earth, but surging up into the air, a glutted, noxious, shapeless enormity that blotted out the opalescent sky, writhed in torment as it struggled against its passage, then vanished.

No cheer went up from the remaining shades. They stood silent. Waiting. Liath's eyes roved over them in a panic to find the ones she knew. Heff was there. Pelkin was there. Tolivar was there. Terrell was not—Terrell the big ox of a vocate whose gentle simplicity hid wisdom deeper than the glib wit of his peers. Benkana was not—Benkana, who'd been Kazhe's lover, the only soul who could warm that blade-cold woman into something halfway human.

Terrell's death and Benkana's, the deaths of all the others the shadow had taken—those deaths were forever. A body become worm castings was beyond any bonefolk's reclamation. A soul gone to feed the shadow was gone for good.

Liath drew her knees up and covered her face.

Evonder's voice was hoarse, his throat blown out by his bind-song and not yet healed. "They bought the lives of countless others, if this succeeds."

Liath was sick to the deeps of her heart of such accountings.

"Are you ready for me?" said a young voice.

Liath dropped her hands and looked at the youth named Solly, who'd volunteered to be sent behind Bron and the shadow to observe and report. His face, as he walked from the safety of the tower, was somber and brave. He'd had a light, before the searing. He'd been a boy then, a struggling prentice illuminator she met on her journeying, the first she'd ever shown her knotwork to. He'd died during the dark years, at the age of nine-and-eight. Her son's age. His death, however obliquely, was on her hands, and Torrin's. To defeat the Ennead, they'd broken the warding and released the power that seared the light that would have saved him. He was keen to go to the lightrealm; still she felt she was piling new harm on top of old, by sending him on such a journey.

They cast him through, and waited.

Time passed at different rates in different realms. Liath wondered if time wasn't a dimension described by the collective awareness of those who experienced it. Time for one alone in an isolated realm passed more quickly than time in a realm thick with consciousness. For Torrin and Heff, wandering lost in realms between, two nineyears had felt like many more. Would Bron's experience, and Solly's, slow to a crawl relative to the time the hauntrealm spent awaiting them? Would their sojourn there be days to the hauntrealm's breaths?

Solly came racing down the hill from the frost-sparkle pavilions.

"It's done!" she heard him call, when he was close enough for her to make out words—and to be certain that what she saw in him was in truth a gentle glow of magelight. "It's over, the thing is dead, it's done, we're safe!"

Now the cheer rose from the assembled shades. Now Solly had to fight his way through embraces, backslaps and congratulations. Torrin, Liath, and Evonder rose to greet him and were themselves pulled into the crowd, hugged and handshaken, praised and thanked. Liath felt Tolivar's arms come round her, felt the wicked sweetness of his lips on hers, and forgot, for a moment, about failure and success, time and realms. When last she'd seen this sailor from the Knee, he had been tossed dead into her cell in the Holding's bowels. She'd tried to put him back as he ought to be—make him a semblance of the free-spirited binder who craved the ecstasy of magelight. She'd tried to cast passage for him, scribing kadri on his flesh in his own blood. She'd failed. He'd become a haunt. She had grieved that, terribly—but now he was here, young and whole and beautiful again, and the triad that had killed him was destroyed.

She wanted to tell him about Dabrena, about Kara, tell him they were happy. But there was too much to tell, and not enough—she didn't know if they were safe, back in the realm of flesh. This was why haunts avoided an initial rush of reunions. This was why haunts avoided questioning each other. It took time to tell the story of a death, longer still to tell the story of a life. They should have all eternity for that unfolding.

"And I could barely see him but I know what I saw and he was gone, that's what happened, I'm certain of it," Solly was telling Pelkin and Evonder. Pelkin, though he looked shaken by whatever Solly had been saying, took him in hand, bade him calm himself and start at the beginning, for everyone to hear.

The lad licked his hands, smoothed back his hair, pulled up his sagging hose, tugged his tunic down. "I thought I was falling, when they cast me through," he said. "I thought I was done for. But the light . . . caught me. As though it found me somehow and cushioned me. An ocean and a sky of fire. It goes on forever, that realm, and you can't move, but your light finds you. My light *found* me. It was dim, I might never have seen it, but there it was, leaping on me like my dog at home, happy and sloppy and—coming back where it wants to be. I could see better after that. I could just see Bron in the distance. I saw the shadow as soon as I got there, I should have started with that—

There was me, and there was the shadow, and in between the shreds of the shadow was Bron. The shadow was in tatters. The light . . . The lights weren't doing anything to it, they didn't seem to care if it was there or not, any more than they cared if I was there or Bron, but it was like . . . I don't know what it was like. Watching a raft break up in a river, except nothing moved, really. The shadow stayed in one place. It just . . . tore apart. It took forever. I guess it must have fought. I think Bron was talking to it. I saw . . ." He went pale and said, on a swallow, "I saw their lights. The triad's. Rolled up like a ball of yarn. But that sounds silly, and they were . . . terrible. Bright. Like knives. Cruel. They wanted their triad back. The shadow twisted and ripped to get away from them. It wanted them too, it wanted their power, but they hurt it. They hurt it more than any of the other light did. I think . . . I think in the end it was their own light that killed them, really. Once their light found them the end came very fast. It unraveled and it twined through the rips and shreds, trying to match itself up to them, to go back into them. The shadow wasn't a shadow there—it was a kind of ripple, a reflection, like water. When its light touched it, it burst into bubbles. Nonneds and nonneds of little droplets spraying everywhere. Like a great sack of marbles flung loose. Everywhere the droplets went was a kind of . . . white glow. They disappeared. I felt . . . I saw . . . Oh, it doesn't matter. The shadow burst! It's destroyed! It's gone!"

He seemed ready to split his seams, drunk on his restored magelight, thrilled past coherent speech by the adventure he'd survived. Liath stared at Torrin and Evonder and Pelkin. It seemed too much to hope . . .

Let's find out, Evonder seemed to say. He clapped Solly on the shoulder, squeezed. "Good lad. Now tell us what became of Bron."

That was a longer, more halting tale, doubling back on itself after false starts, full of guesses and partial images and visions only half described. But there was no doubt. What he described was the passage of a spirit into pethyar.

"I saw," he said. "I *saw.* The white . . . The light . . . I know what I saw, and you can't tell me any different. I saw Bron go."

"They sent us here," Liath said to Torrin. "They could have sent him on. It's possible. They could have sent them all—"

"They may have simply sent him back," Evonder said. "This realm is large. He may turn up far from here."

"No," Pelkin said, dismissing a black-clad man he'd been conferring with. Still running his reckoners in the afterlife. "Every circle has reported in. Unless he's hiding, Brondarion te Khine is nowhere in this realm."

"Perhaps he went back into the world," Torrin said. "Or to some realm of his own making. Do we know what he wanted?"

"He wanted to bring down the Ennead," Liath said, "and he wanted justice for his stewards who were killed, and he wanted his fosterlings to grow up in safety."

"Then he got what he wanted, inasmuch as it is possible. Perhaps he did go on."

"I *saw* it," Solly insisted. "I saw a whiteness in the deeps, something bigger than . . . bigger than itself. I saw things . . ." He swore. "I saw!"

"All right, lad." Pelkin paused, closed his eyes, swayed. Liath had never seen her grandfather overcome by emotion before. "We believe you."

The magelights had passaged the spirit of Bron Steward into pethyar. The magelights had passed into pethyar all the spirits the leading triad's shadow had consumed. An effervescence of passage through the realm of light.

Quietly, Torrin said to Pelkin, "Will you be the first, Illuminator? The first to go fetch your light, and go on?"

Pelkin opened silver eyes full of yearning and said, "No. I've got to see the rest of them through. I'll be the last."

Torrin smiled. "I'm afraid Evonder and I demand the dubious honor of fighting for that position. You cannot cast single-handed. You must go before us."

"You're a leader, Pelkin," Evonder said. "Lead them into glory."

Liath couldn't follow their leaping logic, their unsaid words. She didn't want to follow it. She wouldn't accept it. They couldn't *go*, not now, not after she'd just found them all again. . . .

Pelkin folded her into his arms. "Your gran is waiting for me, pet," he murmured, for her ears alone. "She's waited a good while, and so have I. I never thought I'd see her, once I chose this path. Gift me with this, will you? Gift me with this final passage, to my light and to my love."

It took a long time for Liath to stop crying. Pelkin held her through the wretched sobs. Then he thumbed the tears from her face, wiped at his own, and pressed her casting hand between his hands, her tears against his tears. "A pledge of flesh and humors," he said. "That is all I can leave you in the end, child of my child: the promise that we will meet again, in a sweeter place."

They set about the task of passaging the dead.

Pelkin went bearing an expression of sublime expectation. Tolivar went with a wink and a smile. Others looked frightened; some looked relieved. Some wept and some grinned from ear to ear. All but Pelkin—who was dissuaded from it with effort—promised that if they could find it in their hearts to do so, they would come back here to aid in the castings, then permit themselves to be cast onward by Evonder's triad. With each spirit that failed to return, Torrin issued graver warning to the next: Wait and see. Wait and be sure. But most were too eager to wait. Then Tolivar returned with a young journeymage named Farris from the time of the Triennead, and one of Pelkin's folk, a man named Coldur. Not far behind them were three more of Pelkin's reckoners. Liath noted the looks shared between Tolivar and Farris, the palpable pleasure they received from the first blending of their lights. *Who'd have thought that haunts could fall in love.*

Given the option to go on, not one spirit in the hauntrealm chose to remain. Not one mage chose to remain lightless. Not one haunt, light or lightless, went back. Every one of them went on.

Soul by soul, the three triads passaged all the long procession of the dead. Days might have passed, or ninedays. Because the sun never rose or set, Liath lost track of time. There was no physical fatigue. Her light did not tire. Every casting into peth-yar opened eternity to her, opened all understanding to her, then slammed the door of her memory. She might be accumulating the wisdom of the ages in increments, or driving herself mad. It didn't bother Evonder or Torrin. *I'm different,* she thought, but did not know in what way.

I'm grieving, she thought, but did not know why.

The stream of haunts became a trickle. In all the ghostrealm of the makers' world, only her triad and two others remained—and Heff. Tolivar, Farris, and Coldur passaged the reckoner triad, and her triad passaged them.

Liath melted into Heff's arms. She drank in the soothing peace and strength of him as if storing comfort for a long haul. Time had ceased to have meaning; she might have stood a life-time in those arms. They made no move to let her go. *I could stay here forever,* she thought. *Truly, forever. But I'm keeping him.* Serle and Bron were waiting. She drew back and cupped his broad, sweet face in her hands, drew his big head down to press a tender kiss between his eyes. "Heff," she said. "Oh, Heff. I wish you peace, where you are going. I wish you love. It can't be too late for that."

He touched his brow to hers, closed his eyes; stepped back, laid his hand on his heart for a long breath, then opened it to her.

Inside the casting circle, his expression was serene. Torrin scribed in a semicircle on one side of him; Liath completed the circle by linking the last glyph to the first in a twining foliation in which kadri nestled like ripe fruit. Evonder sang, and the white realm opened, and just before Liath was subsumed in the all-knowingness that never lasted, Heff said, aloud, in a mel-lifluous voice, "Fare you well, my friend. I love you dearly."

Next she knew, her triad's hands were dropping from hers, and the clarity of passage was slipping from her memory like a leaf borne away on a brook, and Heff was gone into eternity.

Liath said, almost without breath, "Why is it so hard? Why do I grieve a passage into joy?"

Torrin rose, and drew her up. "Because you don't believe in it," he said.

Evonder threw an arm around her shoulders and said, as he and Torrin set off walking with her between them, "Because you're next. And because deep down, through all these castings, you've known you weren't going to follow them."

"I don't understand," she said.

With a wry twist, Torrin said, "You have a habit of conveniently failing to understand what you don't like." She found his eyes full of warmth. "It's part of what makes you strong, Liath. Stronger than any of us ever were."

They strolled down the gentle curves of flower-bordered paths in the endless summer of the afterlife, arms around each other. Sensing imminent endings, unwilling to face them, Liath didn't press for a better answer. She didn't ask where they were going; she reveled in the feel of their bodies against hers. The next thing she knew, they had come onto a plain of velvet turf, and mountains carved the distance with the outline of the Elfelirs.

"This is the Strong Leg," she said.

"You're not finished, Liath," said Evonder. "You're not done with your life. Truth to tell, you make a terrible haunt." A boyish smile lit his storm-green eyes. "You're going home."

"You can give them back their lights," Torrin said, as Evonder moved off a ways. "Evonder's light showed us how, when it hitched a ride on me. The way spirits haunt the realm of flesh in raindrops, shadows, the creak of a stair, magelight visits the triskeles. It is accessible through those pewter conduits."

"Torrin, I can't—"

He silenced her with his lips. The kiss was deep, plundering, a kiss of hunger and adoration, a kiss deferred for twice nine years and many times that. It was a kiss of farewell. She tore free of its implications and said, "Can't we stay here? *Be* here, be together, just for a while, or even forever? What difference would it make, what harm would it do, why shouldn't we take the pleasure of this beautiful realm we've saved, we've earned—"

"You aren't finished, Liath."

"Let them find their own bloody lights! Given time, they'll—"

"They may not have time. They need you to make certain they do. Evonder and I are bound for pethyar, and you are not. We just cast unnumbered souls into that realm—don't think I failed to apprehend your feelings about the place."

She frowned, searching through the veil of words he draped between them. Evonder hid behind his face. Torrin hid behind his tongue. "You're lying," she said. His cat's eyes flickered. "You're not going to pethyar. You're going to stay here. You're going to watch, aren't you. To make sure the shadow doesn't return, to make sure nothing like that ever grows again. To passage any unpassaged haunts who find their way here in the future. Eternal vigilance . . ."

With a sigh, Torrin nodded. "Yes. One of us will stay. It remains to be determined which. One would have to stay in any event, to cast the others on. It cannot be you. Like your grandfather, you can cast passage only with a triad."

"Then I'll stay with y—"

He laid a finger on her lips, made the gesture a caress. "Death doesn't suit you, love. You're far too alive to be here. That's the difference you felt between us. We're dead, Liath. You must let us go."

She winced her eyes shut. She'd had enough of tears. "One more day, then. One more night. We had only one night, Torrin." She looked straight into his weary, handsome face. "We have bodies here . . ."

His smile was heartbreaking. "And do you think I could let *you* go then?"

Evonder reappeared. Anger flared. Just a little longer, and she might . . .

No. She would never talk Torrin into anything, least of all embracing what he knew he would lose. And he was right: She had no use for pethyar. Not yet. To stay here, even with someone she wanted, someone she loved, with only themselves and this unchanging place for aeon upon aeon . . .

She hadn't braved death to get her light back on a whim. She could hardly remember her reasons now—death leached those reasons away—but they were there, waiting for her. Tasks waited for her to come back and complete them.

Life waited for her to come back and complete it.

"Well, you're dead," Evonder said cheerfully, strolling up to them. "I took a peek. They're in quite a taking, your friends. You're dead, but the bonefolk won't have you."

"My body . . ." Liath said, struggling to remember. "I chilled it, before I killed it. To slow it down. Buy myself more time."

"I think there's something else at work, but yes, that might have been enough. If not, we'll know soon enough, when you land back here." Evonder looked at Torrin. "Shall we cast this passage?"

They were going to send her back into her body.

I don't want to leave them, she thought. *But I want to live.*

She sat between them, and as they sent her out of the unchanging light of the ghostrealm, she looked into Torrin's eyes, and knew:

He hadn't denied her because he was afraid he wouldn't be able to let her go. He hadn't denied her because he couldn't bear to have a thing he must lose.

He had deferred her. He knew that it was Evonder who would stay, and watch, just as he'd done before. He knew that it was he who would go forth into mystery, just as he'd done before. He believed that in that mystery they would meet again, and there would be no more partings then.

Gazing through eternity in his golden eyes, Liath believed it too.

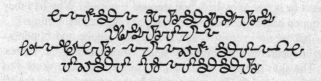

HANLA LET HER last copper-headed arrow fly as the shadow ships converged on hers and crushed it against the Khinish warships around it. Her ship was pressed back into the center of the throng. Wood groaned, yielded with a shriek, a crunch as of bone. The commander was shouting at them to move midships. The crush around her eased. She groped an iron-headed arrow from the quiver on her back and let fly through blinding smoke and screams. Sensed more than saw or heard it find a target. Knew it was futile. Reached for another arrow anyway.

The deck took a violent lurch, and she went to one knee. The ship was sinking. All the ships were sinking. The sounds of death were terrible—Khinish dying, touches dying, vessels dying. The ships to either side were in flames, fire running up tarred rigging, licking through taffrails. Invaders boarded them anyway—why bother? Because they wanted everything dead. Maybe themselves most of all. No explaining that. But they were strange, these invaders who walked through fire. They didn't seem to come from the enemy ships. Pale as the teeming, crawling slugs, but upright on two feet. Tall as the armored axemen, but half as thick. Almost delicate. They seemed to float rather than walk, but they didn't fly or hover like the huge fanged insects. Even killing them, the black ships invented a plague of new horrors.

Spirits, she didn't want to drown. She fought a panicked impulse to climb the shrouds, though they were burning now, or shimmy up the nearest mast, but it was tilting, angled horribly, unnaturally, like a limb bent backward at the joint. Better to die under a blade than drown. Better to take an arrow through gut or heart or lungs. Why had they stopped shooting? Why had they stopped hacking? Where *were* the grieving, pestilent things?

"Come and get me!" she roared into smoke and blindness and unbearable heat. Freezing water swirled around her ankles.

The ship settled with something like a thud. The water was nearly to the rails. The raked masts broke sternward, and the aft end of the ship dipped beneath the surface, making the deck an angled terror. She clawed from tackle to bitt, fought her way forward against grasping frigid swirling seawater. Anything to stave off that endless slide to icy death. *"Take me!"* she raged at the black monstrosities she knew were all around her.

Her arm banged wire mesh. The birds' cage. They were shrieking within, the three that remained. She fumbled the latch open with numb fingers and pulled them off the sides of the mesh where they clung above the water. Flung them into the air. Flung them home.

Tell them we died with honor.

The cage broke from its lashings and skidded aft. She grabbed wildly for purchase. Felt the prow come under her hand, a triangular joining like the tip of a kadri, and crawled past it onto the bowsprit. "Kill me, you perverse, *stinking* things. . . ." She drew a blade and slashed from side to side, hoping to irritate something into beheading her to have done with it.

The sea sucked the ship down in one endless, stomach-dropping rush.

Hanla smashed through the water. The surface tried to wrench her from the bowsprit and only tangled her in its netting. Silence roared around her. She thrashed free of the netting, then in a spasm locked her legs and arms around the spar, gripped with her knees. A wild thought skated through her mind of the wooden spar cracking off, floating back to the surface. But the abrupt submergence in winter waters shocked her limbs loose. She lost the bowsprit. For one heartbeat she was suspended in buoyancy and thought the surface might still be within her grasp. Then the sucking slide of the ship pulled her down after.

She realized the air had gone out of her only when she inhaled the sea.

The sea was luminous. Green as the glow of bonefolk feeding. A mesmerism of bubbles. Death was agony, and green light, and the strangest sense of arms coming round her. The embrace of the sea. It felt like the embrace of a man.

Graefel? she tried to say.

It was only the ocean's depths, squeezing her tight.

Through the open smithy door in Ulonwy, Pelufer could just barely hear the voices outside. Two shopkeepers, she thought, crossing paths on noonday errands. Their words were lost in the low thunder of the forge fire, the bubbling of flux, the hissing song of metal fired hot enough to weld, the ringing blows of Videsal's hammer. Then the high urgency in the voices cut through. Tending the fire, Videsal's young prentice girl looked over at her, eyes wide.

Pelufer stood at the tempering barrel, swirling a blade gently through a brine quench. The quench was cooler than the heated air of the smithy, but warmer than the winter air outside. Pelufer was damp with perspiration and the steam that had billowed up when she first slid the blade into the quench. She could still feel the vibration of the metal through the tongs. When that stopped, it would be safe to touch the blade with her bare hands.

Videsal Bladesmith never wore gloves. He claimed it made you complacent—that one day, unthinking, you'd pick up something hot bare-handed. Working gloveless made you remember what you could touch and what you couldn't.

He was looking at the door. He looked at her, then bent again to his work.

"I tell you, we have to get out of here," said a voice outside.

"And where would we go? Where's safer than where we are?"

A whistle that might have been some faraway townsman signaling crisis, or gas escaping a flawed piece of charcoal in the fire.

Videsal's hammer rang on the singing metal.

Pelufer's shine flowed gently through the tongs into the hardening metal, seeking warpage, cracks, blisters. She found none. Videsal had told her to draw a hard temper, promising that the nickel would bond the iron layers. She was doubtful, but did as he said. She had never worked with pure nickel before. After an acid etch, its indurate silver-whiteness would take a fine polish, a striking contrast to the iron's satin gray. Pelufer didn't care about the pattern. It was the strength and flexibility of the blade that mattered, how well it held an edge.

"And what are you going to do about it?" said a voice outside, raised in anger now. "Run into this smithy, snatch up a blade, go off to join the shield?"

"I'm going to close up shop and get my family out of here, that's what!"

Videsal cared very much about the pattern of her blade. He was a patterner, a master of the pattern-welded blade. That the layering of metals in his specialty produced weapons and tools of exceptional toughness was secondary to him. *"This blade will have a pattern of pools,"* he had said, after the first stack of twice nine layers had been welded and folded, as he chiseled holes down to one-third of the stack's depth. When he forged it flat, the holes spread into small ovals that elongated with each repetition of welding and folding and forging, pools within pools. Kazhe's blade, familiar to Videsal from long ago, had a waterfall pattern, but Pelufer had been adamant: She didn't want Kazhe's blade. She wanted her own. After repeated folding and forging, this blade had more than four nonned layers, each layer a ripple in a pool. The pools swirled around each other, sinuous, undulating. At the center of each pool was the small oval of one of the last-punched holes.

"Your blade has eyes," Videsal had said as he handed it to her for tempering, fixing her with a black-hot stare that sent a chill up her spine. Though he worked metals, though his prentice was a metals touch like Pelufer, Videsal was a visant, as complex and edged and cool as one of his blades. *"Mind where they look."*

"What makes you think this is my blade?" Pelufer had asked. She'd been here in the Knee for three ninedays. She didn't know how many blades she had forged, and watched him forge, and watched his prentice forge. When she rushed up here from Gir Doegre, she'd half thought he would take one look at her

and just hand her the perfect blade. She'd also fancied herself quite the bladesmith. Videsal put paid to both notions in short order. He made her work for what she wanted. He would not let her near the forge when she was angry or impatient. For years, she had stormed off to her forge at any provocation, putting her rage into the blades. Videsal broke that habit. He demanded a cool eye and a cooler heart. But she could not help the leap her heart took now. Invasion was coming, right to this Knee shore, half a mile away. This was her calling. This was her time. She would have to go. But this blade wasn't ready, he wouldn't let it go without grinding and polishing, and all the other blades they'd made had gone straight to the shield to replace inferior weapons.

She had to go to the shield, to become a weapon.

She had to go now.

Videsal drew the next wire-bound billet from the charcoal fire and ladled borax over its edges. The yellow billet cooled to cherry red in the five breaths it took him to flux it. He rotated it to drop the excess, gave it a tap with the ladle, and slid it back through the hole of the closed fire. It would sing and sparkle its readiness to be welded. "I don't think it's your blade," he said at last. "I think it's about to become your blade."

More voices sounded outside. Pelufer heard Tarunel's name—Tarunel Highguard, lead shielder on the coast of the Knee. Pelufer was half in love with him just from what she'd heard, and desperate to meet him, fight for him, *fight*.

She looked around the smithy. "Don't you have some weapon stashed away, something you'd be willing to let me have till this one's ready? I have to go—"

"You remember the conditions," Videsal said, immovable. He pulled out the billet, bubbling with flux, and inspected the distribution of melted powder through the layers. Satisfied, he laid the billet on his anvil and hammered, in sure, fluid, over-lapping strokes, to weld the layers tight and straight.

Pelufer ground her teeth. She remembered. If she went to the shield, he was finished with her. He crafted weapons of death, but for some unfathomable reason he held her back from using them. Poxy visants and their poxy eyes. Nothing they ever did made sense.

She gripped the tongs so hard she felt them gouge the tang of the hardening blade. Eiden's *balls,* she was sick of masters. Sick of deferring. Sick of doing what other people thought she should do. She could leave now, leave this grieving half-tempered blade in its brine bath. At a dead run, she'd be up at the beach in no time. Someone would have a weapon to lend her. No one could stop her. Not her sisters, not Kazhe, not Videsal. She could go anywhere, do anything she wanted to.

Shouts and cries came from the road outside. The tempered blade had stopped vibrating. She reached in and pulled it from the quenching barrel with her bare hand. The nervous cries outside tore into shrieks of terror.

Something hurtled through the open smithy door. Something huge, black, buzzing, fanged.

The prentice choked down a scream and shrank against the wall.

Videsal turned his black-hot gaze on Pelufer.

The fangwasp, a wicked arch of thorax and abdomen dangling bristled legs under a deafening drone of wings, circled once inside the walls like a trapped bat, then hovered, fixed on the red-hot metal billet in the bladesmith's hands, and struck.

Pelufer plunged the new-tempered blade into its body.

Dripping fangs snapped at her face. Veined, transparent wings hard as tin sheets buffeted her head. A sound like escaping steam came out of the impaled, writhing body. Pitting all her weight and muscle against inexplicable resistance, Pelufer dragged the blade free with a long teeth-grating scrape of metal on gritty innards. Through her shine, through the flesh of her hand on the unwrapped tang, she felt the blade scoured, as by caustic sand. There would be nothing left. She would look down to find a poker in her hand.

She could not tear her eyes from the fangwasp as it fell. Acid poured hissing from its riven body, smoking where it ate through the forge's stone foundation. Still its wings beat, its head thrashed from side to side. It did not want to die.

"Finish it," Videsal said, in a low voice.

She couldn't finish it. He had a hammer in his hand. Let him bludgeon the thing out of its misery. She was holding a poker, a stripped iron leaf, what was left of an unground, unsharpened—

She looked at what she held in her hand.

Three feet of gleaming, swirling metal, ripples within silver ripples standing out in stark brilliance against a blade of satin gray, edge honed to a razor sharpness.

She raised the blade, and brought it down behind the fangwasp's head, stopping just short of the floor with a control honed by years of practice. Decapitated, the creature jerked once, and was still.

"Did you foresee this?" she breathed at Videsal. He had plunged his billet back into the fire and turned to rummage through a drawer in one of the workbenches. He did not answer, except to tell her to lay the blade on the workbench. Then, almost too fast to follow, he'd slid a bar-stock guard down the tang, clapped on ash fittings for a grip, wound the whole in linen, and tapped on a plain ball pommel. It was all temporary, thrown-together; given the time and care he ordinarily put into preparing the complexity of fitted and soldered hilts, she wouldn't have believed him capable of such crude expedient if she hadn't just seen it for herself.

"If the grip jars apart, rewrap the tang as you can and do without the guard." He handed her the blade, and a shoulder belt with a ring in lieu of a scabbard. "Spirits shield you, shielder." The prentice, a pair of gloves in her mouth, was guiding her loose arm into her coat sleeve.

The fangwasps seemed attracted by the forge's combination of heat and darkness under the cold winter sun. She cleaved them fast to save the blade from further etching, flowing through guards as though she were fighting shadows in the field at home. Acid spattered her coat but did not eat through; it congealed to a stickiness in the icy coastal wind. She fought her way out into the silent street, feeling the eyes of Ulonwy townsfolk on her through the louvers of every shuttered window. After untold breaths, the black buzzing things stopped coming. The shield must have headed off the rest, or she'd killed all that there were.

It was a queer silence. Not right. As if all the breath had been sucked out of the world. At the center of it, an unearthly wail came from the direction of the sea. She covered the half mile to the beach at a dead run. Her first sight of the shield was a disarray of fighters standing stunned, their blades dragging, forgotten, in the sand. Only Tarunel Highguard turned at her dune-muffled steps, her rasping breath in the dead, keening silence. Younger than everyone said, but as rugged and handsome—long otter-brown hair, slim-hipped muscular build, brown eyes both sharp and wise.

Behind him, the sky and the sea were tearing apart.

Breida's left fist was raised to signal the retorts. The blackships had demolished the Khinish fleet and were swarming on her position. The spreading tear in the intorsion had become audible, a sustained shriek. It spewed abominations—flying things, swimming things, shapeless things that rolled across the crests of six-foot swells as though the sea were flat as glass. Then the wind died, and for a moment everything was perfectly still. Perfectly silent, except for that distant, metallic, edge-on-edge shriek. The blackships sat becalmed. The shapeless things rode the swells, undulating. The flying things hovered. The swimming things backed water.

The current *tore*. At the borders of the hole in the intorsion, the seas had never met; the discontinuity of the waters had been a constant strain on credulity and vision. Now the seas fractured, like imperfect crystal under strain. The sky crazed into a webbing of faults, and split apart to reveal the sky behind it. From every crack, from every fracture, oozed more blackness. Everything the intorsion had spawned before now deliquesced into a glittering, oily blackness, smearing the air, staining the waters.

"Eiden's teeth," Breida swore softly, her left arm falling limp.

Before their eyes, the intorsion devolved into chaos. Shreds of past and present whirled on impossible, incomprehensible winds, indistinguishable, all rushing past in a nauseating disassociation. Shielders around her bent and vomited. Kazhe was shouting from the rise behind them. Breida couldn't turn. She couldn't tear her eyes away.

"Down," the boy beside her was saying. "Down. She says get down—"

Breida felt the first breath of disaster brush her face, and bellowed to her shield, *"DOWN!"*

The wind that swept over them as they ducked below the wall might as well have been a hurtling granite block. Shielders slammed flat. Trees cold and winter-brittle cracked and toppled. Retorts crashed onto their sides. Supply-laden tents whipped skyward and were gone. Even the bonefolk, impervious, indestructible, only partially in this realm, swayed back like stalks of grain.

After the first burst had swept past them, blasting toward the Sea of Sorrows, Breida grabbed the top of the wall and hauled herself standing.

The seaward sky was black. The stain had risen in the wake of that blast of wind. It filled the air. It blotted the light.

"Eiden's *puke!*" said Fioral. "It's like the grieving siege!"

"Maybe it isn't real," said Simry.

"It's real," Breida said with quiet conviction.

"How do we *fight* something like that?" said Godill.

"We're about to find out," said Breida, and turned to form up her shield, ready archers, get the retorts hauled upright.

The curtain of shadow was coming in.

The forward ranks of the Highguard's shield were still scrambling to their feet and shaking off sand after the winds unwound in one buffeting backlash and half buried them all. The front edge of the advancing stain engulfed them.

The stain was not as easily sated as the siege had been. The stain kept coming. Pelufer drove forward to meet it.

Her blade tore with ease into the bank of glittering blackness, gouging it. A good cut—but in the blade's wake, the wound sealed itself. She hacked pieces of thick shadow substance off, carving holes in the wall, trying to separate it into sections, but there was more beyond. Pressing into the gaps she carved, she sought for the other side, but couldn't find it, and got out just before the blackness closed around her. It was like hewing wet sand. Her eye created monstrous insectile figures moving within it, but when she cut it there was nothing but stain. Nothing to engage; nothing to kill. In all directions, thick, floating stain was moving inexorably inland.

I have to stop this. That's why I'm here.

She raised her blade and willed her shine to fill it. This noxious black mist was the last offensive of the intorsion. It was a weapon. She was trained kenai. She was meant to destroy it.

Her shine did nothing. The shield kept dying.

"Tell them to fall back!" she cried to Tarunel. "It's not like the siege—they're not saving anyone!"

He ordered his shielders to form up beside him. They backed away from the creeping mass, step by step, futile blades brandished. Pelufer fell back, too. Not as far. Keeping herself between them.

Missiles and arrows had no effect. Tarunel ordered all his resources brought to bear, to no avail.

The shadow embraced the coast to the limits of vision. A noose tightening on Eiden Myr. It would take everything, destroy everything. Not just lights, not just shielders—everyone. *That's what it was meant to do if we attacked it,* she thought. *That's what it was meant to become if we broke it.*

That's what it is.

The intorsion was created of stain, fueled by it. Its makers had summoned all murderous thoughts, all destructive will, and woven them into that braid. Severing that braid, magecraft released the pitch black hatred it was made of.

Only one of her. Only one of her against a darkness that would consume the world.

She had sparred with shadow. She was filled with shadow. All the deaths folk wrought were shadows. Shadows, like the shadow rolling inexorably inland, a black death mist. Stains, like the stain spreading toward them, a black death tide. Stained shadows, like the ones she had sparred with all these years in Triennead fields. The fields of old battles. The shades of ancient battles, nothing left but the will to fight, the imperative to kill.

"I don't want Kazhe's stinking blade," she had told the bladesmith. *"I want my own."*

Pelufer raised her blade. Her shine flooded it. No ruby glitter, no crimson light the color of fresh arterial blood. Her blade went dark, dark red. The red of spent blood. The red of stained blood, pooling in the eyes.

Pelufer's blade looked into the shadows. Pelufer's shine summoned them.

They came from the Kneeside field in Gir Doegre. They came from the Bootside field. They came from the ground around every Triennead hall. They lifted free of the blood-drenched ground of the Menalad Plain. She wrested them from the spirits of stained shielders, purging the darkness that sent some into exile and the darkness that others acquired there. Stain gathered in her glowing dark red blade, and in one sweeping slash she flung it out again.

It engaged the enemy.

Stain fought stain in a roiling clash of darkness. Deep in the oily blackness flashed the semblance of blades, the semblance of brawling bodies, engaging and breaking apart, forming and re-forming, a seething mass of death's desires and death's consequences. Stain wanted nothing more than battle. Stain wanted nothing more than death. Two fronts of stain collided with thunderous reverberation, and rolled off seaward.

To either side, Armward and Bootward, the shadows of the intorsion still advanced.

Pelufer drew deep upon herself. Deeper than she'd known she could. She pushed every last ounce of her shine into that blade. The blade that was hers, not Kazhe's. The blade of a haunt touch, not a kenai. She would never be kenai. That was not her shining. Only one kenai remained in all the world, and would until the day Kazhe died. Pelufer's shining was shadows.

Pelufer's craft was metals. Pelufer's training was blades. Here, at long last, the three combined.

She drew stain from mile after mile of Eiden's shores, and flung it out, spreading back along those shores, to fight this last, dark, glorious battle. The stain seized freedom with savage rapture. The freedom to kill without restraint. The freedom to die unhindered. To die for real. To die for good. No more cold, dry, hungry half life devoid of spirit long passed on. No more bitter consignment to the wretched corners of the living soul.

From behind her, as though infinitely distant, Pelufer heard the cries of shielders as their stains tore free of them. Some staggered and fell; some dropped their weapons and stumbled up the dunes, away from the conflict of smoke and sickness and rancor. Others bore only secondhand stain, the seepage from their fellows, the seepage from the intorsion, the contagion that had spread through none's-land for three long years. They looked to sea: *That was in me. Now it's gone.* They looked to Pelufer: *You did this. You took that out of me.*

The way animals long used to aching hurts looked up at Caille after she'd eased their pain.

She drew out Risalyn's stain, and Yuralon's, where they tended shielders on the Maur Alna coast. Over all the distance and all the years, the two fighters-turned-healers sensed her touch with deep recognition. Risalyn shrugged as her stain went; Yuralon's gratitude was shining, his easement profound.

She drew out Ioli's stain, and Mauzl's, and Kara's; she drew the undeserved stain from all who'd entered none's-land with intent to help, not harm. Much of that was the intorsion's stain, which had leaked into the edges of the land over the years; there was a heady justice in flinging it back. Some of the intorsion's stain had goaded men to stain themselves, to terrorize and hurt what frightened or diminished them, and she drew that stain out like a thorn, a splinter, leaving bewilderment and humbleness in its wake.

She drew out the stain of the inlanders who had left folk on the coast to die. They could not have seen the stain if they were not stained themselves. They'd as good as killed those they'd abandoned to certain death, those they'd refused to readmit to safe inland life. They were all complicit in sending the severed to their doom. That stain was thin, dilute, but bitter and wide-spread; she took it all, for all it was worth, and flung it outward.

Mile after mile, league after league to each side, she sent her shine around the coast, and filled her blade with dripping shadow, and shook it clear. Only when her encircling powers had reached the Fist did she find the one soul that would not give up its stain.

Her master's.

Breida felt the stain tear free of her as though she'd been turned outside in and her skin ripped out through her intestines.

She had never taken a human life. After grinding years of war, that was strange realization. But she had killed, and killed, and killed, with grim and abiding satisfaction, and she did not surrender those kills easily. She had slaughtered monstrosities, abominations, things made whole-cloth of stain themselves, things bent on her destruction. But life was life, whatever form it took, and she had killed it. She would do it again. She hadn't asked for expiation. She carried her burden with austere pride. It made her who she was. She did not know who was hauling it from her, but she fought with all the rending teeth and nails of her staunch spirit to hang on—and she could not.

The battle for her own stain was the first battle she had ever lost.

Pelufer felt Kazhe raise her blade to block.

A kenai weapon was the only weapon another kenai could not destroy.

Pelufer had never understood that Kazhe's murderous rage was as much her weapon as the blade. She had never under-stood that Kazhe's tortured grief was as much her shining as Caille's love and her own hauntsense were theirs.

A world apart, they locked blades, guard to guard. Kazhe's stain reached back into the ages, carried by kenai after kenai until at last it settled into her. Kazhe's shadow was deep, cast by the blinding brightness of Torrin Wordsmith's light and all the dark deeds she had done to shield that light. Kazhe's torment was profound. She would not give it up.

Their duel was silent and invisible and ferocious—Pelufer bound and determined to cleanse the depths of Kazhe's rage and pain, Kazhe fiercely bound to keep them. There was no sparring now. There was no teaching. In the darkest depths of their souls, that night-blind fight played out at full intent. Pelufer had discovered the power of her blade. Kazhe's blade sought to annihilate that weapon to protect her own. Kazhe sought, in those endless moments, to annihilate Pelufer. If she could not destroy the blade, she would destroy the wielder.

Pelufer hung on. She held her own. She leaped and danced, instinctive and agile. She could not prevail. Kazhe was older, harder, craftier, and far more vicious. In the end it was a stand-off. That meant that Pelufer had lost. She had failed to extract the most potent stain of all—the stain that would drive the ancient shadows of the intorsion from their shores for good.

She came back into herself gasping, lowered her blade with trembling arms. Her heart pounded with the afterterror of a dance on the edge of the abyss. She had been one breath, one eyeblink, one misstep away from obliteration. In all her years of bladeplay with shadows, she had felt nothing so burning cold, so merciless, so deadly as Kazhe n'Zhevra.

"Kenai."

She startled to find Tarunel Highguard beside her. He looked out at the pall of smoky darkness hanging over the sea. No wind would sweep that darkness away. The shadows were evenly matched. They would watch this battle rage for the rest of their lives. *At least we'll have lives,* Pelufer thought.

In a young, melodious voice tempered to a hardness by the rigors of command, the Highguard said, "For three years I waited for you. For three years of siege I dreamed of you. Dreamed of the day you would be ready, and put an end on all this. Today you came, a breathless girl scrambling over the dunes waving a brand-new blade in the face of catastrophe, and my heart soared."

She tried to take that in. Ran her eyes over the curve of his jaw, the sleek fall of his hair. Blinked when he turned his wise, bright gaze on her to say, "And then you gelded me."

"What? I don't . . ."

"I was a boy of nine-and-four when they fought the battle of the Menalad Plain, but I heard the stories of what your master did. Took all their blades away, all their spears, their bows, their axes. That was the power of a kenai, I thought. The power to disarm. I never knew it could be used like this. I never knew how deep that gelding cut might go."

"I saved your stinking life."

"And took all its strength in the bargain. I might rather have died, kenai. I pledged my life to defend these shores. This land has been my charge for as long as makes any difference. The stain inside was what I fought with. There's nothing now."

"There's nothing left to fight. It's all out there, fighting itself. You're done. It's over."

He laughed beautifully, a flash of pearl teeth, a depth of dimples. "Is it, kenai? Is it really?" His laughter vanished. *"Is it ever?"*

Save them, cleanse them, and they whined that it had unmanned them. Pelufer shook him off and strode to the waterline, where the jagged pilings of the sunken wreck that had been the trading docks cast shortening shadows on the waves in the approach of noon.

There was one more set of shadows to disburse.

Her own.

She had never taken a human life, but she was filled to brimming with the marks of those who had, and the marks of those they'd killed.

She didn't have to raise the blade now. She had merely to touch it, and murmur: "Ardis, Traig, Bendik . . ." Dead of the old Ennead's Holding, so far from her experience. "Deilyn, Niseil, Astael, Sowryn . . ." Haunts whose killing was no doing of hers, but whose deaths had brushed her, shadows of shadows, and left their marks on her. "Croy," she murmured, "Elya . . ." Limb by limb, she pruned the haunt tree in her mind, until no murders were left on it, only the gentle, ordinary dead. She cast the galled limbs into driftwood upon the waters, for the tide to take out to join the other stains.

She did not feel cleansed. She felt cored.

She turned to hard, beautiful Tarunel—without apology, without conclusion. He would stay and watch the coast as he had always done, for incursions that he did not trust would ever end. "Send your people home."

He didn't tell her to keep her nose out of shielder business. He looked past her, his tanned face gone chalky as white lead, his pupils wide and dark, the pulse in his throat jumping. "Drevala," he murmured. "Asmar. Sobasil."

Pelufer's gut clenched. It was like listening to herself uncontrollably spouting the names of the dead.

"Hadesal," he said. Then, louder, "Timonis!" In the next blink he was shoving past her, striding down the sand-drifted plankway his shield had laid for firmer footing, his arms opening.

Pelufer turned. Standing dazed were all the shielders she had seen the stain take. Tarunel *was* saying the names of the dead. But they weren't dead. He was hauling a living dead man into a rough hug, pounding him on the back. From one to the next he went, shaking them, clapping their shoulders. Each one of them said the same thing: "A boneman saved me."

Pelufer was left gaping on the fringe as these folk who'd lived and died together found each other again in the realm of life.

Breida kept one eye on the offshore clash of darkness as she listened to a Khinishman recount how bonefolk had come through the smoke and the flames of the end of the blackship battle and saved him and several score of his fellows who now stood in her encampment. On the fringe of that encampment, bonefolk stood silent and motionless, responding to no human who spoke to them.

"Why change their ways now?" a mender asked. "Why transit the living when all they've done for twice nine nonned years or more is passage the dead?"

"Nerenyi," Eilryn breathed.

Perhaps only Breida heard him; the other Khinish and shielders and menders and touches and stewards were all talking over each other, at cross-purposes. She had no reason to pull them into line. As near as she could tell, their stains were doing the fighting for them now. Kazhe knew something about it, but she wasn't saying. And Eilryn wasn't saying who this Nerenyi was or why she should have anything to do with cracked, miraculous bonefolk.

She snugged her thrice-shrunk wool closer against the bitter cold, and considered when to tell her shield what they didn't seem to fathom yet:

They could go home.

Some would stay. She would stay. At any moment that ring of smoky offshore madness might contract again and try to kill them. It was creeping up into the sky now, moving up instead of in, as though the outer stain were trying to surmount the inner, and being countered. At least she would be on duty to sound the alarm. At best she would figure out how to fight it. Perhaps whoever had dragged their stain from them and cast it at the enemy had found the way. Or perhaps not. She wouldn't turn her back on what else might come, now that their last protection from the outerlands was gone. In truth she'd only come round to where she'd started, with Verlein a dozen years ago. Scanning the horizon. Keeping her lone watch. No idea what might come.

Kazhe strode through the encampment, straight to Liath's son.

"This is yours," she said, lifting the chain from around her neck. It had grown as heavy as her blade was light. "It can't go where I'm going."

The boy didn't reach for the triskele she held. Well aware of whose it was, she supposed. She didn't care. "I'm going with you," he said. "It won't travel the ways with me either."

His voice was his father's. The years turned back; she might be glaring up at the father, not the son, arguing routes and tactics, arguing safety, arguing futility. The grieving man had never made it easy to keep him alive.

She'd lunged on tiptoe to drape the chain around the boy's neck before he could react. "Then you'll find your own way back." She turned, but the boy said, "Kazhe"—the first time he had ever said her name, and so much the way his father used to say it that a blade went through her heart.

"What?" she snarled, rounding on him.

Anyone else would have stepped back. He didn't budge. But when his mouth opened, nothing came out. He glanced at his aunt the shieldmaster and tried again. Still nothing.

Didn't make wordsmiths like they used to.

"I'm done here," she said, and addressed the shieldmaster. "Live, Shipseer. Live forever. Who's to stop you?"

She startled to find her arm gripped forearm to forearm. "Live, kenai," the Shipseer said. "Live longer than that. No one can stop you."

She returned the grip, then turned on her heel and strode past celebrating shielders and resurrected Khinish, past cookfires scrabbled from windblown debris, past the shambles of a camp that bloody alemonger had kept alive and intact through years of impossibility. She strode right up to the rank of bonefolk, poked one hard in the chest, and said, "Now you'll take me back."

Without acknowledgment, the thing complied. Took her through emerald greenness into the glimpse of a coal-hilled, amethyst-vaulted infinity, then sent her on alone to walk straight out of a marble pillar into Gir Doegre's copyhall. *I could get used to this,* she thought—and came face-to-face with the prentice who'd tried to rip her guts out not an hour past.

Blades were drawn and one-slice bouts began and ended a nonned times in the space of that startled confrontation. Kazhe won most of them. In two or three she faltered, and the prentice lived, and she did not. That was interesting. That was new.

"Quick trip from the Knee," she said, in a level voice. The glass-walled copyhall wasn't, anymore. The bight end of the in-torsion had whipped through here as well. Not nearly so cold as in the Fist, even so. They'd righted and relit the braziers and were all clustered around something.

"Stone's close enough to metal," Pelufer replied, shifting with the angle of Kazhe's gaze, "and so is sand. They've plenty of that up there."

"Should have gotten a ride from a boneman. They're moving folk like stones on a board these days."

"That's why they didn't care that I went through their ways."

Kazhe's eyes narrowed. The girl was blocking her view of something. How long had she been back? Long enough to put herself between Kazhe and something she didn't think that Kazhe should see.

Pelufer said "No—" but Kazhe had already elbowed her aside.

The edges of her vision took in the menders, the visants, the other touch girls, the birdmaster, the lad-of-all-lights. The edges of her awareness took in the passage gloom, the stink of despair. The center of her gaze riveted on the yellowed grip pro-truding from the belly of that forsaken publican.

"What have you done with my grieving cheit?"

Boots crunching on broken glass, she bulled past fending arms to lay her hand on it.

Caille cried, "Don't pull it out!"

She couldn't have let go if she wanted to. This was worse than Pelufer tugging at her stain like some fool trying to jerk a cloth out from under a table setting. Her shine flared with a warmth that left her weak-kneed and humiliated. The little touch girl fell back a step and gaped.

"Don't pull it out," Louarn commanded. "We don't know what that will do."

"This is my blade," Kazhe said, "and she's dead. It won't hook anything she has a use for, where she's gone."

"She's not dead," Elora said. "The bonefolk won't take her."

"Looks puking dead to me," Kazhe growled, but she was trying now in earnest to release the blade, desperate to be free of that repulsive, debilitating warmth. The blade wouldn't let her go.

She would bloody well yank it out and make it let her go.

Adaon drew in a sharp breath. He had seen blades enter and leave flesh before. No reason for this to shock him so. Yet it did. His vision tunneled.

Tunneled, and expanded, into a gleaning, or a seeker's epiphany, or both.

If the bonefolk were refracted into three unwoundable, realmwalking, preternatural incarnations of spirit, the way Liath had been, they had refracted *from* something. Liath's mortal flesh had been the base from which her indestructible, otherworldly forms roamed—a shell her spirit vacated when it was cast in trine. The bonefolk had to have left shells somewhere.

Liath had fractured into herself at different ages. She had cracked along temporal lines. The bonefolk had cracked along material lines. Each incarnation had taken on the properties and affinities of one of the three elements of matter: Water, air, earth. Liquid, gas, solid.

Driven by ineffable imperatives, the bonefolk passaged flesh to their own realms for safekeeping. But they could not or would not take metal or stone.

Metal flowed inside the earth like deep, incalculably slow water. Metal was a form of stone. Colored quartzes flowed in veins within the white stone of this holding. Lightstone flowed in veins within the Aralinn Mountains—in the holding there, a fastness that predated the mages' exile, crafted by the indigenous inhabitants of Eiden Myr, the fallen race that many believed had crafted all Eiden Myr in its image.

Louarn's father Evonder believed that lightstone's whispers were echoes of the minds of that long-lost race. Louarn believed that the bonefolk were the remnants of that lost race. Bonefolk reacted palpably and inexplicably to lightstone. Louarn's mother Lerissa had promised them redemption through the stone—redemption for sins they could not remember—and they had believed her.

Lightstone glowed, in the presence of mages, with a moon-white light like the sum of all lights. Lightstone whispered in dry, raspy, leaf-rustle voices that in the presence of visants became loud as surf. Lightstone, in the hands of touches, became warm as flesh, malleable as wax.

Lightstone wasn't the memory of the lost race.

Lightstone *was* the lost race.

Like the shells of crustaceans collecting on the seafloor, transforming into limestone over aeons of heat and pressure, folding and refolding, the bonefolk's shells were crushed and liquefied over aeons in the earth, flowing in molten veins into the interstices between rocks, filling the cracks and crevices, suffusing Eiden's body. Becoming part of the earthen vessel they had crafted. Resting and cooling in Eiden's deeps, taking on the consistency of stone. But waxy. Alive. Whispering memories, the dry rustle of dreams.

Cool and quiescent in the depths of the earth, lightstone lived. Its consciousness and will roamed land and air and sea, incarnate as the bonefolk of the earth, the winds, the waters. It was the repository of memory and the potential of resurrection. It was the aggregate of the bonefolk's bodies, flesh waiting to be reunited with spirit. It bided underground, oblivious, unrecognized.

Deep in the bones of his mind, Adaon recognized it.

I know where their bodies are.

Adaon released his breath as Kazhe hauled up what was hooked on her blade.

The dagger weighed as much as a human soul. It took all the strength of Kazhe's muscled arm to pull it from the deeps of flesh. Honed to a fine edge, the blade sliced with ease through viscera in its ascent—but in its shining wake left them whole and healed.

The moment it came free, with the vicious wound sealed to a puckered scar behind it, the alemonger thrashed up and grabbed Kazhe by the shoulders. The icy grip chilled her to the bone. The dead gray eyes chilled her to the soul. Then the ale-monger dragged into her chest a great sobbing heave of air, and retched blood all over both of them.

With an oath, Kazhe tore away. The menders and touches were all fluttering concern and ministration. She wanted no part of that cooing and aahing.

She wanted no part of this bloody blade. No use to her, a blade that healed what it had just killed.

She dropped the thing in front of Pelufer, who caught it on open hands with a fighter's reflex and a touch's caution. "Have it," Kazhe said. "It's yours."

The blade lay flat across Pelufer's palms. She looked up without comprehension.

"It's yours," Kazhe said, with a gesture of dismissal. "Your training is over. You fought me in the dark. A darker place than I could have found in the middle of the plains on a moonless night. You've . . . passed your trial. The cheit is yours." She bared her teeth. "My first successful prentice. And my last."

Pelufer's fingers started to close over the hooked blade.

"Mind that, now," Kazhe said. "It might heal you, all right, but it will still cut you first."

Without a look to the illuminator, she strode out of the broken glass hall, snagging the Ankleman as she passed him. "Come on," she said. "If there's a tavern left standing in this stormblown town, you can trust me to find it."

In that moment of distraction—Mauzl watching the paths branch from the astonishing softsharp coldwarm blade, struggling against incipient seizure, fascinated and aroused and shamed by the savage anticipation they gleaned from Rekke—

Ioli broke through Mauzl's lockdown and got a clear, straight, stomach-dropping view of the paths that branched from him.

He looked across at Mauzl's depthless, pleading eyes, and shook his head.

Very slowly, Mauzl nodded.

Liath returned to the realm of flesh inside a shell of misery. This flesh was cold down to its bones, so cold it hurt. This flesh was sick and racked with heaves, its mouth putrid with blood. There was a choking smell of bowel on it. Though numb, groping fingers couldn't find the gaping wound she'd carved in the gut, though something had healed the damage—*Kazhe,* she thought, but that was insane, it must have been the young touch girl Eilryn loved—this flesh had its own memory of pain, and its belly was a convulsion of agony. *Sorry,* she thought. *Wrong realm. Wrong body. I'll just be going now.*

Against her breastbone, her triskele burned.

She fell into a swoon. There was some sense of hands touching her, sending waves of warmth through her, easing clenched muscles; she stayed submerged, not yet ready to try that body again. There was a distant sense of being bundled, carried; immersion in warm water, *touch-warmed, now, that is truly a strangeness;* a yielding bed and pillows of sheddown, like sinking into clouds. She dreamed of floating on healing airs in a bath of golden light. She woke into a lamplit sleeproom and the delicious idleness of Caille's fingertips combing through the tail of hair at her nape. Across from her was a window. Outside the window was an afternoon sky darkened to charcoal by something like storm clouds.

Eilryn's faraway voice grew louder with the opening of an outer door. "... to every hall in this holding, no one knew where you'd brought her ..."

She'd always thought he had his father's voice. She'd never realized how much he sounded like her, or how wholly like himself.

Caille's fingers slipped away.

"No, don't stop," Liath murmured, and turned onto her back, as her son pushed through the slightly open sleeproom door.

Her heart came up into her throat.

He was radiant. A golden splendor, dimming the lamplight to shadow, flooding the room. Making of it a realm of magelight, as wondrous and as beautiful as the realm of light itself.

Yes, she thought. *Oh, yes. This was worth dying for.*

He stopped in his tracks. "Mother . . ." he said. "Your *light* . . ."

"It's nothing," she said. The same as the haunt of light she sensed in the battered triskele around his neck. She could taste its beloved, familiar flavor from across the room. Bright, so beautifully bright, but . . . "A dappled drop of sunlight, compared with yours."

He shut it down. She saw it happen. Becoming aware of his light, he tried to hide it. She blessed the lands of home, that had made him safe enough to forget to hide himself, even for a breath.

All lives started with a breath.

"But," he said. "But . . . *Your light* . . ."

Her face cracked into a beaming smile, and she looked on the fearless, articulate boy struck stammering by what he saw, and thought that whatever he was feeling right now, it could not hold a candle to the joy of seeing her son's magelight for the first time.

Caille left the sleeproom to give Eilryn and his mother some time alone together. She walked out of the Heelhill residence hall, into the grassy triangle it formed with the Boothill and Grazehill halls. She sat on a bench, warming its chilled, sleeping wood with her shine.

The stain was creeping upward, the sun lowering to meet it. Clouds slid out of the stain on one side, delivered a shaded gray promise of snow as they crossed the sun in their transit across the heavens, then slid back into the stain. The transit was growing shorter. Come dawn, the sun would have to fight its way halfway up the sky to scale the ringwall of darkness.

This morning, when Pelufer came back, they couldn't see the

curtain of darkness from ground level. Now they could. The darkness was rising. If it didn't stop, it would cover them, and kill them.

They had reserves. The land could do without sunlight for a little while. Till Greenfire. Maybe.

Mages had immense powers. There was a time when folk believed that there was almost nothing magecraft couldn't do. She had immense powers, and there was a time when she believed that there was almost nothing she couldn't do. But she had found that there were things her shine simply could not mend or heal or change. There were things that magecraft simply couldn't ward against or smooth or fix. Hatred was one of them. Vengefulness was another. Tortured guilt. Murderous rage. The lust to kill. The wish to die.

Those were what the stain was made of. Unless the visants could glean it away, she didn't know what they would do. But so long as some little shine remained, she would hold out against the darkness.

3

Aiden's Light

❧

At what seemed to be dawn, Pelufer found Kazhe standing on their practice ground in the Kneeside field, staring up at the constricting circle of cloud.

"Walleye's asleep." Kazhe twitched the jug in her hand. "Needed more of this. Needed to hear silence instead of those wretched snores."

"You can stop this." Pelufer's hand dropped to her longblade.

"*Look* at it." Kazhe gestured skyward with her chin. "How could one stain more or less make any difference?"

The menders and seekers hoped it would consume itself. Pelufer knew it wouldn't. "It's not one stain, the stain you bear. It's the stain of all the kenaila who came before you. All the darkness cast by all those bright lights through all the aeons."

"Not all. My father's. His mother's. Her father's."

"One lineage," Pelufer acknowledged. "A dark lineage. A powerful one." She paused. "A brave one."

Kazhe snorted and said, "You won't bait me with your exquisitely subtle hints of cowardice," with the clear articulation she produced when she had been drinking hard for a prolonged period.

Pelufer touched the dagger that Kazhe had given her. The cheit, the tooth, smallest of the kenai's three blades. It could heal flesh, perhaps bring souls back from the dead. Kazhe's longblade could melt weapons. "Your tain," she said. "It might have powers, too. It's on the Menalad Plain somewhere. I can find it."

"It's not mine," said Kazhe. "It was Benkana's. Leave it where he fell." Quietly, she added, "Maybe he seeded a child somewhere I didn't know about. If you can find such a child, send her for the blade, or him. No one else."

With full intent, Pelufer said, "Benkana's death wasn't your fault."

One moment there was no use knife at her throat, the next there was, and Kazhe had her in a grip there would be no striking free of.

"Of course it was," Kazhe said. Her tone was mild. "So was Torrin's. If I didn't think they were, there'd be no kick to my stain, now, would there. You wouldn't be looking to pour it down the dark's throat." She pushed off, leaving Pelufer standing, balanced, as though nothing had happened. "It's my stain," she said. "It's going to stay that way."

Looping up the jug Pelufer hadn't seen her drop, Kazhe strode across the graying, shadowed, sunless field toward the taverns and alehouses that lined Bronze Long, and whatever floor or table she'd left the snoring Ankleman on.

Pelufer wiped the first spit of icy rain from her face, and started back for the holding.

Karanthe had not worn her triskele in two nineyears. She had not sat in a casting circle, as mage or subject, in two nineyears. When she was small, being cast upon had made her wail for the light she could not yet touch. Once she was seared, she could not bear the touch of light. She could not bear it now; it filled her with unanswerable longing. She held herself still inside the circle in the Lowhill Assembly, held her heart tight against the parched misery, the isolation in the center of power she could no longer sense.

The triskele was lifeless on her breastbone. Two nineyears ago she took the thing off and wrapped it in cloth inside a bag so she would never again have to feel the deadness there. But as Eilryn Wordsmith handed the inscribed casting leaf to Louarn Binder, who then handed it to Liath Illuminator in an extra step performed only for the major castings, Karanthe felt something stir within the chill pewter. Something dim, something vague. Something turning over in its sleep. Something in the depths of that pewter . . . reaching out to her.

Her imagination. *I'd rather be outside watching visants and touches fail to bring light back to the sky than be in here watching mages fail to bring light back to me.*

Karanthe was knifed with jealousy at the expression on the illuminator's drawn face when she cast with her son for the first time. Karanthe's hand cramped with desire to be the hand ornamenting those wordsmith's glyphs. To shape the leaf, bestow dimension, open a window on possibility and mold it into change. She drew a deep breath of relief when the leaf passed to Louarn.

He set it in front of her. The triad clasped hands. Karanthe smelled smoke and catsclaw resin on the binder, sweat and pigments on the illuminator, forest and earth on the wordsmith. Not the slightest whiff of magelight.

She'd heard Louarn's singing voice only once before. Hearing it again recalled for her a stavewood holding, a stale room, an interminable vigil. That had been a different song—a canonical melody, the passage melody, adapted to celebrate Pelkin's life, speed his spirit on its way, keen his departure. This melody was new. An original creation, for a first-time casting. A song that painted colors with sound, wove a tonal canvas of dark and light. It was a joyous song, a paean to art, a paean to creativity itself—a paean to light.

A song to summon light.

Her triskele went so cold it burned. She gasped. Laid her hand on it. Felt it open, like a cage—like a door. She swayed, dizzy with the intimation of vastness. Any hint of what lay beyond was swept away in a rush of great soft wings. Unfolding within her. Filling her.

Like candles lighting of themselves at dusk, Liath's light and Loaurn's and Eilryn's swelled into goldenness. She scrambled to her knees, looked around the hall, saw an array of young lights that were three times brighter than the ordinary lights of old. She said, "Dabrena—" But when her eye found Dabrena, she saw no light in her old friend, and it was as though the searing had just happened—the shock of it, the bereavement.

"Good, is it?" Dabrena said, with warm amusement. "It's all right. Karanthe, don't look so stricken. I'm right behind you." Her hand fell to her little son's pale head, and Karanthe saw the light in him.

Former warders were touching drawbags and lockets and trinket boxes stashed about their persons. "Good thing I hung on to this." "I thought I was only being sentimental." "Who'd have thought I was carrying my own light around all this time?" The young mages demanded instruction from the casting mages. Watching the new casting enter the living archive of the craft, Karanthe was struck with a memory of Pelkin, in the early days of the archives, painting his powerful illuminations onto permanent sheets for binding in codices—

The taste, the scent, the texture of his light suffused her senses with an intensity no casting could have provided. His powerful, precious, intoxicating light, as golden as afternoon sunset on a wheat field, as smooth and redolent and burning as the finest brandy. She had known it, before the searing, but not like this. She had joined with it, in the reckoners' casting in the magewar—but not like this. She groped her way to a table and sat down heavily, overwhelmed. No memory was ever this strong. She had sensed the sublime intensity of mages' lights blending when she cast them triad, and that was not this strong.

Her heart's desire granted—to touch that light. To be filled with that light, to know it as she knew her own. His light had not returned in her; she knew her light as she knew her skin, and only her light was in her now. But the moment she thought of him, there it was—the flood of sensation that brought him alive for her as though he were standing beside her chair.

She became aware of Louarn's eyes on her. His frown, as he crouched beside her. "I wanted so much from him," she said. "I thought I wanted so many things. But in the end it was only this.

To know his light. To know how that light felt." She raised her gaze to Louarn's. "I missed him so. Now I feel as though I just spent eternity with him."

Louarn's frown lifted. Her happiness must be infectious indeed, to drag a genuine smile from Louarn n'Evonder.

She looked across at Liath, sitting now with her back to the wall, a picture of profound fatigue, and within it that unflagging, burning light. "Does she feel this?" she asked, thinking that Louarn the visant might glean it. "He was her grandfather. Her light was with his in the realm of magelight, too."

Louarn shook his head. "I think this was a gift intended only for you."

She swiped at her eyes, embarrassed. "His family . . . they're the ones . . ."

"No." He patted her knee and stood up, and she stood beside him, becoming aware again of the day that was darkening to night. "No, Reckoner. Believe me on this. It was meant to be you."

She looked at him sidelong, seeking a sign of double meaning, but his face was so open, so sincere and warm and pleased, that she could only smile in appreciation of his friendship— grateful for the presence of another soul who had known the man she'd known and could remember him with her.

At midday, the stain closed overhead like a drawbag strung tight. One point of daylight remained, the size of a star, the shape of an eye.

The eye winked out.

"It's gone bloody dark." Kazhe, bruised and aching and soaked, dragged herself to the window and craned her neck to see up and down the longstreet. She had no idea which inn this was. They'd unrolled a carpet of worn-out welcomes all down the row of public houses. Three stories below, the street was slushy, lamplit, thronged, silent. Through the sleeting twilight, Gir Doegre was barely visible, a maze of shops and homes; the pale marble of the holding structures stood out in the gloom, an array of odd shapes rendered glaucous, alien. Above and beyond it all was nothing but the dirty gray of heinous acts and soiled thoughts. The rising curtain of dark conflict had smoothed into standoff.

"Go," Rekke said from close behind her. His voice was hoarse, graveled. "Don't leave them wallowing in their own midden."

With a snarl, she turned and bore his big frame back to the bigger frame of the bed, collapsed onto its own slats, mattress bursting sodden featherdown at the corners. He met her fierce goading madness with muscle and madness of his own, smothering and rending, insatiable. Nails gouging, mouth plundering, she drowned herself in him until the drowning world was banished.

In late afternoon, Elora left the menders to their magecastings in Lowhill, the alderfolk to their meeting in the Muted Swan, the touches to their futile efforts to clear the skies. The bonefolk had saved the Khinish and then gone; no one could reach them. They couldn't sign to bonefolk they couldn't see.

She went home through lamplit streets, past battened stalls. Hail pummeled her; she clutched her weatherwarded cloak at the neck and kept her head down.

The house was a reproach. She groped through clutter on the side table to get a lamp lit, then looked at the sitting room as if she'd never seen it. Drapes and upholstery wanted washing. Nolfi had cleared the plates she'd left out when she staggered off to sleep, but neither of them had done anything about the ashes overflowing the grate, the dust on moldings and furniture. The mess made it looked lived-in; the cobwebs by the ceiling made it look long abandoned.

She swept out the hearth, ran a duster into the corners and a cloth over the surfaces, picked up stray silks and socks and bagged them with the bedding in what had been Caille's room, set the half-filled kettle on to boil. She remembered the years she'd lived in a worm-eaten shed with her little sisters, and thought, *I can't raise my child in the bonefolk's realm.*

A flurry of fluttery movements in her belly surprised her. Ordinarily he was lulled to sleep by her activity during the day, and woke only when she lay down to rest. "It's all right," she told him, smoothing a hand over where he lay, high in her long-waisted body, still growing more up than out. Caille said he'd be able to hear her in another nineday, but she'd been talking to him since Moonfire, the night he was conceived. "It's all right"—but it wasn't all right, and all she wanted was to lie pillowed before the hearth and feel the body growing inside hers—this miniature, precious life that needed her more than all the other lives in all the world did. Right now, she was his world.

Pelufer had once complained that if they could make their own passing place, they wouldn't have to trouble the bonefolk by passing through theirs. They could move at will, as often as they liked. If they'd pursued the idea, they might have somewhere to flee. But making a place like that would be abandonment of the trees, the mountains, the plains, the rivers, the animals, the spirits, no less than an exodus to any bonefolk's realm.

We can't leave them to the darkness. We can't.

She laid her hands on the stonewood table and called for Lornhollow one last time. Only silence answered. The loneliest silence she had ever heard.

Nolfi's hands slid over her shoulders. Deep in the wood, she hadn't heard him come in. She turned, arms tangling in his until she got them around his waist, and pressed her face into the solid warmth of him, inhaled.

"He's not coming," Nolfi said, stroking the long fall of her hair.

"No," she said, muffled against him.

She didn't want to let him go, but he pulled gently free and drew a chair close to sit by her. The kettle was coming to a boil, filling the space with a hint of steam that sang of home and comfort. Nolfi took her hands in his and leaned in close, elbows on his knees. His sandy hair fell into his brown eyes.

"You have to go there, Elora," he said. "You've known that for a long time. I can't see it harming the baby. How could it? The wood is part of you, the child is part of you, you're part of them. Go tell Lornhollow you love him. Don't let the bone-folk's rules stand in the way. Don't make excuses about the baby. Don't bring a bargaining board. Just find Lornhollow and tell him. It will make all the difference." He raised her hands to his lips. "Tell Louarn, too, if it will help you—but whatever you do, do it because it's what you want, what you love, not what the rules say is right or wrong. You've tried so long to be every-thing to everyone except yourself. I can't watch that anymore."

A dozen responses formed and died on her lips—defenses, denials, declarations of fidelity. Nolfi went to the fire, loosed teacups from their hooks above the working-strewn mantel, poured water over cinnamon and cloves and citrus molasses. Elora watched the quiet way he handled breakables and scald-ing things, then said the only words that mattered: "I love you, Nolfi."

"I know," he said, stirring the sweet spiced tea. Then he turned, with a quiet smile. "And that makes all the difference."

She drank the hot drink he handed her, and warmed herself in his arms; then she pulled her boots back on, and donned her cloak, and walked again into the dark and hail and freezing rain, leaving Nolfi to tend their hearth.

She went out the back this time, and only as far as the garden wall. Where its stone corners joined was an ancient oak, wide and densely burled. She touched her belly, murmured assur-ance, and melted into the tree. Became the ancient patience of its roots, its woodflesh; felt it become in turn the soft young blaze of life that was herself. Then she was stepping into the woodfolk's realm, standing knee-deep in scarlet grass strewn with white petals, among trees of silver striation thick with cop-per leaves and heavy with impossible fruit.

"Lornhollow," she said, into the shy hush, and there he was, wading toward her through the feathery grass on his stork's legs, luminous in his own realm.

"You seek our help," he said, with his mouth instead of his hands, denying her with the small refusal to sign in his own way.

No, she answered, in the hand shapes that the menders knew as Stonetree. I've come to say that whatever we've done to anger you, I love you, and I always will. Not because my mother did. Because I do. That's all.

When she turned to go back, he bade her wait.

They strolled the groves for a long time. Other woodfolk came and went, tall and silent. They passed countless preserved bodies glowing with perfection. The bonefolk didn't know why they held the dead safe in their infinite realms.

Lornhollow told her why they'd begun to save the living.

It was Nerenyi. The seeker, Lornhollow called her, as though he did not have knowledge of her intimate enough to permit the use of her name. Elora had raged at Nerenyi for two turns of the moon, believing it was her willful incursion on the bonefolk's sanctuaries that had estranged them from the living.

The bonefolk were shy folk, reclusive, protective of their privacy—deeply shamed by an ancient act they could not recall. They feared that the illuminator's redemption would bring their transgression to glaring light. They longed with all their old, dry spirits to know what they had been, but feared to remember what they had done. Their ranks divided. They withdrew.

Only Writhenrue was more curious than afraid. Only Writhenrue had the temerity to defy restriction and respond to the seeker. Lornhollow had had that kind of courage once. Lornhollow had defied convention when he befriended the woman Prendra in the realm of flesh, when he passed her ways on to her daughters. That was all the courage Lornhollow had. Writhenrue went farther. The curiosity in Writhenrue responded to the curiosity of the seeker, and he opened his realm to her, then gave her into the keeping of his counterparts in the airfolk's realms, the waterfolk's realms. Writhenrue came to love the seeker as Lornhollow had loved Prendra. The folk had considered Lornhollow an aberration, even an abomination. As all the Writhenrues in all the realms became known to the seeker and knew her in turn, the folk relented.

"Each Writhenrue loved her," Lornhollow said aloud, "and so all Writhenrues were one. All the living are one. We could not love one of the living and let the others die. You are all the seeker. You are all Prendra now."

"Why didn't you come to me and tell me this?" Elora cried. "Why did you stay away when I called for you? Why hide a thing as wonderful as this?"

It was a gift, Lornhollow signed.

"But we can help you. We put the illuminator back together. We can do it for you. Adaon found your bodies, Lornhollow, they're the lightstone in the mountains, the bones of the earth. I don't know how we'll keep the ground from quaking or caving in, we'll have to put every touch in Eiden Myr to work, I think, to heal the land as the lightstone leaves it—or maybe you'll go into the earth, maybe that's where you dwelled long ago? We can work it out now. We can save you. Reunite you with yourselves and . . . your memory . . ."

Bindlegore and Thorngrief, Lornhollow's old comrades, came up beside him in the grove where they had paused, a stillness of golden-leaved, ebon-trunked trees. Sourceless light lit the bonefolk's tatter-clothed bodies in pearl.

"It can't have been that bad, what you did," she said softly. "Wouldn't you rather know?"

They stood without expression. Others gathered, forming a circle within the trees. Just standing, regarding her with their brimming dark eyes, arms folded loosely before them as though cradling a body, or a baby, or a secret held so close they no longer knew it anymore.

Louarn would know how to persuade them, she thought.

Nolfi's sweet face rose in her mind, fawn-skinned and warm, eclipsing the distant, pale face of Louarn. *"Don't bring a bargaining board. . . ."*

It was a gift, Lornhollow had said. A gift, not a trade. If they had come back to the living after saving the dying fighters, it would have implied that they deserved something in return.

No trades. No persuasion. Only gifts, freely given.

"I love you, Lornhollow," she said. "Caille loves you all.

Pelufer loves you. My mother loved you, and through us she loves you still. Loving one of you, we love you all. Whatever you did. Whatever you choose. Will you tell the others?"

What one knows, all know, Lornhollow signed. What one tells, all hear.

Elora left the gilded grove for the living flesh of Nolfi's oak tree in its winter sleep. She didn't know what they would choose. She didn't know what had happened to the seeker. She didn't know what to do about the dark if the bonefolk didn't come to help. But she knew that she'd done the right thing, and returned to the right place. She raised her hood against the icy downpour and started for the warmth and light of the house.

Only then did she feel the new shine swell in her belly.

She hurried inside, to tell her pledge.

Ioli sat in the center of the enneagram wrought in living stone on the floor of the silent, vacated Lowhill Assembly. Alone, and never less alone.

It was early evening. The menders and the mages had departed, their castings complete. Ioli had gleaned their awe through the iceheart's glow. Seen their lights return to them, through his eyes. Felt his yearning to fly through dreams back to his pledge and restore his light. Ioli didn't think that Highlander would accept his seared light back, but there were no visants near him where he dwelled, so Ioli couldn't be sure.

The world was full of visants. No place, however new, would ever again be too alien for Ioli to negotiate. He had only to let the visants' world seep into the edges of his eyes. Knowing wasn't pushing your mind against. Knowing was reception. Letting the knowing of others in. Most visants were still gathered in enclaves, and like as not they always would be. But there would always be wanderers and some who preferred to live out in the world. Their diverse knowing formed a cool, clear pool from which any of them could drink.

Ioli didn't have to see the sun to gauge the time. Countless visants knew the time without thinking. Ioli didn't have to squint through the ice storm to see the ashen shroud of stain. Visants stared at it from places where the weather was clear and winter-crisp. Through him, through others who'd served on the shield, they had intimate knowledge of that stain. They knew the fists, the boots, the stones, the blades. From Rekke, from Mauzl, from him. From their memories of Yorlmen and Fyldur, from their memories of gleaning shielders, from the intensity of Rekke's coupling with the last living flesh to bear the stain. Rekke sought to drown in that savage union the ever-present company of gleaning. Without knowing it, he sought to take that stain into himself, dissolve it so the torment could pass to him and spare the bladeswoman.

His heart was far too soft for such a burden.

The hall would fill again, and soon. Mauzl was already rising from his spot in the touch girl's grotto, starting out into the hail-battered woods. Ioli did not call Rekke. Ioli was in no hurry for what was to come.

He slid again into Mauzl's gleaning of the paths Jalairi trod. Thus far all led to happiness. Only Mauzl could glean as far as Mauzl could, though others were gaining ground. What Ioli gleaned of Mauzl only confirmed Jalairi's futures. The discoveries she would make as seeker. The young man who would come into her life, and always be there to catch her when she fell. The depth of knowledge she would acquire about the jungle, the secrets in its plants and soil, the wonders of its creatures. Even now she was watching a flying lizard swoop from tree to tree, marveling at the skin stretched between back legs and front, struggling to divine the principles of flight—how the glide of a flying lizard or rodent differed from the feathered lift of birds, the membranous flight of bats. She was wondering about Ioli, too. She was about to ask the village visant if there was news of him. "Do you know how he's faring under this canopy of stain?" she said to the visant a moment later.

Of course he did.

Tell her I love her, Ioli thought, more in feeling than in words. *Tell her I know she knows. Tell her I said to tell her anyway.*

He felt the message pass, and let the gleaning go.

* * *

The streets of Gir Doegre, long and short, filled with bonefolk.

They came from the trees, from the walls, from the earth. They formed from the sleet, rose from the slush, flowed out of the flowing river. They slid down the winds, coalesced from the exhalations of chimneys, took shape in the still air under the awnings in the lee of inns.

The folk of the earth, the folk of the water, the folk of the air, they stood unaffected by the hail and icy rain, oblivious of the deepening cold. They made no move to walk, or speak, or gather. They came, and they waited.

The streets were empty. Families were home at their supper, loners tucked into the camaraderie of public houses. Blue evening was black as a moonless midnight. Hail had iced the roads and was yielding to a windswept snow. The keepers reduced their rounds to once an hour, but inclement weather stretched those hours out of shape. The creak of iron-hung signs, the moan of loose tin on a stall were the only sounds. The bonefolk stood alone in the swirling darkness.

Dogs lay down inside their doors with curled-under tails and did not bark. Cats crept to deeper shelter. Children peered through shutter slats to see bonefolk standing still and silent and could not find the breath to call their parents. A little girl padded into the cookroom to tug on the hem of her father's tunic and say, "Padda? Did somebody die?" A lone runner afoot, caught out when the snow began, veered off the Boot Road to the lights of the Highhill Comb, where menders pored over codices in lamplight, forgoing supper in hope of finding some marginal mention of anything like a pall of stain. "Your high street's full of bonefolk," he announced to the mender who answered his knock.

In the mounting snow, the bonefolk waited, still as death.

Dabrena struggled through snowdrifts in a swinging sphere of lanternlight to collect Adaon and Louarn and Liath and run the macabre gauntlet of bonefolk. They found Lowhill bright and warm. Ioli had laid a fire in one hearth, and Rekke—clean, tidy, his wet hair streaked with ice—was busy at the other. Kazhe was nowhere to be seen. Caille, Eilryn, and Mauzl sat close in the center of the enneagram on the floor. The walls were lined with stonefolk, Writhenrue among them. "Where's Nerenyi?" Dabrena asked him. Bending her neck back to look him in the face was like looking up at the shrouded sky.

Where she wishes to be, the boneman answered, with his long, bleached, facile hands, in the language of stone and trees.

Liath shrugged. Dabrena did not pursue it. Elora arrived, beating snow from her clothes. Louarn fetched binding materials from the cupboard at the back of the hall. This was Louarn's casting, Elora's working. Dabrena didn't know which visant would lead the gleaning. She wished that Jhoss had taken her advice and turned back for the Heel instead of forging on to the Head. She'd have liked easier access to him right now.

"He's coming with Graefel," Ioli said. He made a small bow in apology for gleaning her thoughts—the way you'd offer back a ball you'd caught after someone accidentally hit it at your head. "They're still two days away. The wind delayed them, then the dark. They've rallied visants and mages to fight it. They'll resume their journey once they learn what's happening here."

A chill crawled up Dabrena's backbone. *Visants,* she thought. *Like nails on slate. But it's bloody brilliant information.*

Ioli smiled, and the chill begat a shiver.

Caille had scrambled to her feet and rushed to lay hands on Elora's belly. Elora was laughing. "Yes, he has a shine. Isn't it beautiful? He got it in Lornhollow's realm."

"He's perfect," Caille breathed. "He's bright."

"I know." Elora permitted herself one moment of beaming, then said, "And he'll sleep if we leave him be." To Louarn, who was crossing the enneagram with an armful of sedgeweave topped with a box, she said, "Touches should be in place within an hour of the visants' . . . gleaning . . ."

Her voice trailed off. A hushed pause descended upon the

hall. Understanding hovered just beyond mind's reach. Offering itself. Unformed, but there for the taking.

Dabrena seized on it with her mender's mind. What they were going to try to do for the bonefolk. The effect it might have on lightstone deposits throughout the land. Where those deposits were, who might be affected by the potential upheaval, what local touches and mages could do to minimize it. The strangest certainty that it would all come right, as though there were any way of knowing what the future held, past all the gaping pitfalls. . . .

This is how it felt when the siege lifted, Dabrena thought. She looked at Ioli. Everyone looked at Ioli. This was his doing. He dangled comprehension before them in a package as concise as thought. No words, no lengthy scribings or spoken explanations, no runners pounding overland on horses or birds winging wearily through storm, not even a cadre of touches sent through the ways. Reach for the knowledge, and it was yours. Turn away, and it would fade, a half-formed notion discarded. Everyone in Eiden Myr must be feeling this. No demand, no control, no forcing—only invitation. The teasing sense that something important shimmered at the edge of awareness, something to do with the earth and the bonefolk, and it would come to you if you let it.

Elora blinked. "Well. That saves some time and trouble."

The chill in Dabrena's spine spread to her gut. She had not yet articulated, even to herself, the ramifications of such power when Ioli looked at her and said, "Yes. I could. But I won't."

With the intuition acquired over years of training prentices, Dabrena assessed him for signs of deceit or smug superiority. She did not find any, but neither did she find solace—except in that she had not thought, for certain, *No, he won't.* He could have put that thought in her. He was letting her decide.

That in itself could be manipulation. The truth, she realized, was that if he meant to manipulate her she would never be aware of it. Left uncontrolled, his opening of himself should have leaked his own personal concerns, but he remained stubbornly opaque. Left uncontrolled, his opening should have opened the deepest motives of his triad, but she was treated to no insight into Mauzl and subjected to no visions of whatever went on in the Ankleman's mad head. He showed them only what he meant to show.

Perhaps, she thought on a swell of pity, that meant he need not see what he did not wish to see.

Pelufer came in, frowned at Kazhe's absence, then brightened at the new shine inside Elora. Kara and Reiligh brought the twins; Adaon got them seated by the fire. A couple of seekers poked their heads in, hoping for permission to observe, and Dabrena granted it, but posted the next arrival, a warmly dressed mender, outside the doors to turn any additional comers away. She wanted a clear path of egress in case anything went wrong. She wanted elbow room in case lightstone bonefolk started rising out of the floor.

That's it, she thought. *That's all I can do.* As head of this holding, she was in charge here, but must now accept with grace the role of host. Louarn was seating the three triads on the points of the enneagram—one mage, one touch, one visant, then the same twice more around the circle. At Elora's direction, touches throughout Gir Doegre and its environs stood ready to ease the earth during the lightstone's waking, and Ioli reported that mages and touches were prepared in kind from Toes to Crown. Dabrena bit down on an urge to bid them wait. *Slow down, let's think this through, you have no idea what you're doing, this is madness, it's the middle of the night, this is a critical casting of vast scope, we must take more care with it*— There would be no morning unless the bonefolk were restored to power that could dispel the stain, and the human lights had always worked better by feel than by rote.

The visants had pulled their powers up by the bootstraps. The training of touches had more to do with teaching them to trust their instincts than with drilling them in technique. Mages trained for years in their craft, learning to scribe and sing and paint, memorizing verse and melody and pattern, but canon, in the end, was only a starting point; each casting was a fresh discovery. At their best, the lights worked just as they would work now—flexing and adapting to meet the requirements of unexpected circumstance.

This is what they do, she thought. *This is what they are.*

She could only let them do it, and watch, and hope.

Rekke delved the lightstone in Eiden's body. It was everywhere—in veins, in deposits, in fragments. Some of it lay in chunks on mantels, in stonemongers' sheds; one rounded piece, set in a ring of strange metal that resisted his gleaning, gathered dust under the stone platform of a bed in a bluestone house on Khine, and another piece, rough and irregular as though hacked out of the ground by an incompetent miner, sat on the floor in front of Louarn, who'd had it in his pocket. How it would all come back together he didn't know, or what form it would take when it did.

He felt hacked from the ground himself. His back and flanks were scratched, neck and chest and shoulders teeth-scored, muscles gouged with bruises; the tenderness he felt for the blademaster was a deeper bruise. He enjoyed a handful now and then, but ordinarily preferred his women pliable, responsive, forgettable. This one was ruthless, ravening, not forgettable at all—and only the glow could have torn him from her. A plunge into the icy river and a roll in fresh snow had cooled the fire in his blood only enough for him to dress and depart instead of plunging back into that bed. Sore and spent and aching, he still hungered. Sorest of all was his puking, cretinous heart.

He didn't know what he would do, after this. He wouldn't go back to the mines. He had become everything Jhoss had dreamed of and more; he had helped the monkey fulfill his grieving mission; all his walleye charges had come into their own, and there was no longer any none's-land to keep them out of. Only the stain, still, to protect them from, and if the blademaster wouldn't save them from it then the bonefolk would. Only this last bit of purpose left to him, to lend his glow to the greater glow in aid of the iceheart's white-light redemption. To pull the lightstone from the earth and return its spirits that it might live again. After that, his future was the blank face of an impenetrable rockwall. Not even the runtling's paths gave him any help in delving that wall.

"Let's not be all night about it," he grumbled at the binder's preparations. The marble tried to welcome him and his gleaning, and he could only wriggle to ease his sore tailbone, cross and uncross his legs, lean back on his hands then hunch forward over his lap. He wondered if he had ever been comfortable in his own skin, then glared around the hall, his wild eye seeking the source of the thought that the monkey had gleaned.

Grieving visants, he thought. *Can't leave a man a moment's peace to settle down inside his own head.*

The iceheart sat to his right, his back to the doors, facing the shadowed angle at the back of the triangular hall. Except for the circle that connected the points of the enneagram they sat on, the hall was all angled opposition. The iceheart sat at the apex of a triangle on the floor, but along a base of the triangle that was the hall. To the iceheart's right was his bodyguard-in-training, the conduit of stain who was never stained herself. Past her was the monkey, then the illuminator who had passed through realms of death and light he would never have dared enter; then the touch who was with child, the runtling, the outer-seas boy; the circle came round to the little touch girl, on his left, and then himself. The mage triad sat at the points of one triangle of the enneagram, the touch triad at the points of the next, his own triad at the points of the last. A pretty scheme. An arrangement typical of the iceheart, connecting them to their triads while interspersing their lights around the circle. The iceheart believed it would make for a powerful casting; so did the stump of a seeker warming his turquoise glow by the hearth, the one who'd delved the nature of lightstone as not even Rekke could. The little one, beside him, she had a powerful glow, just starting to reach out to her father's. Rekke wished her a safe, sunlit world to grow up in, then smacked his own face, hard, to drive the soppy sentiment away. No one in the circle flinched. He leered at them and rolled his eye. They were too used to his mad antics. When this was done, he would strike off into the world, see what new mischief he could concoct, find fresh blunts to unsettle and appall.

Strike off into the wide world—quick, the moment this was finished, before that blademaster sliced straight through his bloody tender heart and left the pieces rotting on the ground behind her.

Louarn handed sedgeweave and binding board to his left, then brush and pigment pots. The casting materials had to pass through Rekke's hands and Caille's to reach Eilryn. Mauzl and Elora would pass them on to Liath, and Ioli and Pelufer would return them to him. He passed deasil, for an entry to the world, as in a birthing. The touch of each light's hands on the materials would bind the casting; when he clasped hands with Rekke and Pelufer, the contact of flesh would travel around the circle and allow the touches to bind them into the working. In the circle, the visants could keep all participants in view. Casting and working and gleaning would weave together, spirit and flesh and mind. Through stone and air they were connected to the bonefolk—the ones in this hall and the ones beyond. Through marble and earth they were connected to the lightstone sleeping deep in Eiden's body.

Eilryn laid quill to sedgeweave, and the casting began. Eilryn's magelight reached out to Louarn's and Liath's. Ioli's gleaning passed the mages' experience of that reaching to Louarn even as his own magelight reached back. Shine flowed through the marble Louarn sat on, linking him to the touches' bodies. Ioli's gleaning of the touches linked him to their minds.

Eilryn passed leaf and board to Mauzl, who handed them with reverence to Elora, whose shine flared briefly in the wood as she passed them to Liath. In response to Liath's requests, Louarn mixed pigments and again passed deasil. The materials passed from hand to hand, giving the casting a prolonged solemnity.

As Liath's powerful, gleaned kadri radiated through the circle, Louarn surveyed the surrounding bonefolk. Writhenrue, Irongrim, Frostworn, Hoarspike . . . He had known some of these folk, when he had fled to the stonefolk's realm to escape the labyrinth and the searing. He had learned the bonefolk's hand-speech from them as if as a first language. He had felt he should be one of them, had passed back into the world with no compre-hension of his stunted, hairy, cartilaginous form. Bonefolk had fostered him as his harrowed mind and injured body regained their strength. It seemed as in a dream that he had bided in their realm. It also seemed another home, another loved place lost.

The leaf passed to him. He laid the piece of lightstone in the middle of the leaf and laid the board inside the enneagram. He had to go forward onto his knees to slide it centered. When he settled back cross-legged, he opened his hands to either side and received the rough miner's grip of Rekke's hand, the blade-callused grip of Pelufer's. Flesh linked to flesh around the cir-cle, shine flowing into shine, magelight flowing into magelight, all knowing and known within the gleaning—

The enneagram began to glow. It glowed white, moon-white, like lightstone, though any lightstone was far below; white as death's antechamber, silver-white as the nimbus of clouds around a full moon. The angled lines connecting the triads flared up in white flame. The flame spread to the circle, cool as mist.

"Don't let go," Louarn said. He looked at each one of the eight faces. He drew breath, opened his throat, and sang the gleaning: the love of the three touch girls for the boneman Lornhollow, their mother's love living on through her heirloom shine; his fostering in the stonefolk's realm, the heartbreak when the time came to pass through; what it was like for Liath to be severed from her body, split in three, reunited. His voice was made of breath but flowed like water. His voice was firm and malleable as the richest soil. He wove in melodic lines from the birth and passage songs. He fulfilled the highest demands of his craft. And then, through the song, through the gleaning, he opened himself. A full nakedness of the soul. To redeem the bonefolk, who so feared the exposure of their great transgres-sion, he must reveal it all. To buy their trust and pay their way forward to the spirits, he must give himself, with no reserve.

There was much that Prendra's daughters didn't know about

him, even Pelufer, who had touched his haunts. There was much that Liath hadn't guessed, for all she'd known him of old. Even the visants had not gleaned everything. Manipulation. Inappropriate desires. Complicity with the last Ennead. How close he had come to seducing control of the reborn light from his own mother in order to use it for his own ends. The three lights combined begat such shadows as would make a boneman quail. Whatever the forgotten crime of the bonefolk, it could be no worse than any crime that he had considered, or abetted.

In a rush of purest vision, he felt the bonefolk open in return, and he brought his song to an end.

The hall had gone glaring white over an expanse of shadow in which the enneagram still burned. He was awake; he was in Lowhill, not the dimensionless misty place where he had brought Pelkin and Eilryn and Liath, or the crystalline corridor the visants had followed him through. He could feel the bluesilver glow, the ruddy copper shine, the golden magelight, but he could no longer see them as discrete lights. All was white, subsumed in the white casting.

The bonefolk were gone. Not passaged through the stone, not fled back to their realms. Taken by the glare.

"Don't let go," he said again. It seemed a breath and a lifetime since he had said those words the first time.

Another breath, another lifetime passed. Silence hung suspended in the hall. The silence of stars burning white and chill on the ocean of night. The glare in the hall faded. The enneagram subsided to a flat smoke gray.

A figure shimmered into view in the shadows at the back of the hall. Another appeared off to the side, another in the center. Made of air, made of water, made of flesh, made of light—they were bonefolk, but not bonefolk at all. They were figures of living lightstone. They burned as white as the symbol on the floor had, luminous and silvery and cool. Tall as trees, older than mountains, sinuous as rivers. No more the long-limbed stalk, the brimming eyes. Their motions were fluid, almost floating. Their dark ancient eyes were filled with wisdom and an alien power.

Across from Louarn, bathed in that moonsilver glow, Elora

seemed to melt. She looked up at the creature of light in the center and breathed, *"Lornhollow?"*

The creature made a beautiful sound, musical as the flow of brookwater, hushed as a fall of snow. A weave of tones and shapes that no human lips or tongue or throat could produce. "That is our name," it said. Its voice and aspect were masculine and feminine, and both, and neither. "There is no equivalent in your naming. We were the rivenfolk. We are the folk of the ways. The folk of the dream. To you, we are . . . whatever you would call us." It leaned down and brushed her hair with silver. Not a human gesture, yet charged with tender affection. "I am still your Lornhollow," it said. "Lornhollow of the Wood. I would not lose that naming."

The folk of the dream, Louarn thought.

Caille laid her hands flat on the marble floor. "It's quiet," she said. "The ground. There's . . . no harm."

"Your dreamers and weavers were not needed," said Lornhollow of the Dream. "We soothed the earth as we rose from it. No . . . harm." A drift of murmurs surrounded each utterance— soft voices speaking in different tongues, a whispery emanation of flesh or light.

The doors, behind Louarn, blew open on a snowy gust. No one moved to close them. Caille's shine drew on Elora's and Pelufer's and his and warmed the air before it chilled them. Liath rose and walked to the first creature, standing in the far shadowed corner of the hall. She reached out to touch it, and her hand disappeared into light, yellow-gold into silver-white. *So like what happened to me,* Louarn gleaned from her, through Ioli. *So like. But not like me at all.*

"Are you the makers?" Adaon asked.

The second creature, closest to him, turned, bathing Adaon's dusky face in silver and awe. "I too would not lose your naming. I have been Writhenrue in all my forms, and Writhenrue I would remain, for that is who the seeker loved." Asked about themselves, they answered for all of them; asked about all of them, they answered first for themselves. Writhenrue's hand lifted in a supple shimmer to brush Adaon's eyes. "The place we made is gone on without us. We did not make this earth. We could not make this earth. We wove its shape. We could not carry it. We erred. We reached too far alone."

"I don't understand," said Adaon, his pale eyes dazzled with silver.

"I know," said Writhenrue, in a rustle of whispers.

The makers, Louarn thought. *The folk of the dream.* So much to ask, so much to learn—but no assurance that these ascended folk would linger. Urgency pressed in on midnight's shifting, the whirl of the world toward dawn unseen beyond the skin of stain. "Can you dispel the darkness?" he asked.

The first creature, refulgent in shadow it did not illuminate, said, "We drove the darkness from the place we made. It does not live."

They aren't human, Louarn thought. *They are the folk of the dream.* How to make oneself understood to an incarnate dream?

"The stain," Dabrena said. "The darkness above the darkness and below the light. Can you lift it from us?"

The three silvery forms scintillated, a suggestion of the insectile jitters of agitated bonefolk. The whispery murmurs grew louder, like a wind rising, then subsided. "That was done," Lornhollow said.

"It's still there," said Pelufer.

Lornhollow brushed her head. "You lifted it."

"Not far enough," she replied, head bowed.

The visants could not glean these folk. Rekke's wild eye saw infinite realms, a cascade of silver shadows; Mauzl's eyes saw a blur of aeons. Ioli's eyes could make nothing of them; his gleaning drew on Prendra's daughters, who had known the bonefolk best, and on Louarn's gleaning and Adaon's.

The folk of the dream.

At last it was Eilryn who said, "Can you banish the stain that has engulfed our land and blocked it from the sky?"

The dreamfolk quivered, and Lornhollow said in its many-voiced voice, "It is your darkness. We can do nothing."

Through the gleaning, Louarn felt the swell of hopelessness. They could not tear their eyes from the marvel of these shining, risen folk. They could not take in that there was anything these folk of incandescent power could not do. Louarn felt the pleas rise, the raft of questions: Were the passing places still accessible, could they go there to save their lives? In their fear of refusal, Louarn felt the dismal alternative loom: that they sail into the outer seas, return to the outerlands, return the way they came twice nine nonned years ago, count their sojourn in the realm of light a happy dream gone dark and make their way in the world they had fled.

It was a dream, he thought. *A beautiful dream. And now it's ending.*

The anguished bellow that came from his left seemed no more than the despair of his heart given voice.

His visant's eyes, his puzzler's eyes, could not take in what he saw as he wrenched his gaze from the luminosity of makers and tried to focus on the stain-drenched ugliness that had swept in on the last freezing gust of snow.

Caille was clutching at her chest. Eilryn had hauled her from the circle with such violence that they were still skidding backward on the marble. She scrabbled to get free. His grip was iron, his gray eyes hard as steel.

Motion drew Louarn's gaze closer.

Rekke, who had been sitting on his heels with his knees on the floor and his hands on his thighs, was a paralysis of agony. Shoulders back, chest thrust forward, head thrown back, spine arched. His head rolled toward Louarn. His wild eye fixed on Lornhollow. His ordinary eye fixed on Louarn. Agate. Glittering. Through the gleaning came its command: *Protect.*

A blade wrenched out from just inside his left shoulder blade.

Louarn flung his arms wide to shield Pelufer from the shadow and bladegleam that leaped across the circle.

Ioli made no move to defend himself. As though he'd known this moment would come. The shadow's arm cocked back at the elbow. Louarn fought to propel himself forward and tackle the shadow. Pelufer was gone from behind him, and he was falling. The shadow's blade thrust through Ioli's heart. Wrenched out.

Turned for him.

He looked up into black eyes, swart skin, oiled hair. A blue-silver glow constricted by bitter hatred. A stain as fresh as a fresh spill of blood.

It wore off, he heard Ioli think, in words as clear as if he'd spoken aloud. He understood, through the gleaning, with the speed of thought, who this man was and what Ioli had done to him in the jungle. He could not understand why the voice of Ioli's mind, Ioli's heart, spoke relief. Spoke joy.

The blade arced overhand, down to his ice-blue heart.

The blade vanished, melted, leaving a fist clutching a wooden grip.

The fist flew open, the stabbing arm flew wide as Pelufer's eye-swirled longblade cleaved the man from crown to sternum. Her boot caught the body at the hip and sent it spinning so that no part, not even a spatter of blood, would touch Louarn. The body flopped to the floor with a sickening crunch of skull. The gush of blood was quickly spent. Pelufer had sliced the heart in half.

Liath's running dive from the back of the hall pulled up short inside the circle. A spray of blood dotted her shirt. She dropped the handle of a melted knife. The linen-wrapped wood made a dull sound on the marble in the silence.

Rekke was slumped, still balanced over his legs. Just starting to fall. Caille tore free of Eilryn—or Eilryn, seeing Fyldur die, let her go—and eased Rekke to the floor. Blood pooled beneath him. His eyes were milky, sheened with death. They'd fixed on the same point. The wild look was gone from him.

"No," Caille said when her shine had no effect. *"No!"* She made for Ioli, but the cleaved body lay across her path. Liath caught her up and lifted her over it.

Ioli lay supine. His visant's inkdrop eyes were sightless. His lips bore the suggestion of a smile.

Pelufer fell to her knees, staring at her blooded blade.

Mauzl. With Lornhollow blocking his view, Louarn thought

of him only now. He got to his knees and looked across the circle to where Mauzl and Elora sat. Mauzl's head was bent between his knees, his arms over his head. Elora had covered his body with hers in reflex as instinctive as Louarn's had been to shield Pelufer. Now she drew back, staring at the head and torso Pelufer had cut in half. Her hand kept contact with Mauzl, smoothing down his flaxen hair, but slid off as he uncurled, and straightened.

As though releasing a cry he had held pent for ninedays, Mauzl threw back his head, and howled.

"They're dead," Caille said. "They're dead. There's no healing this. They're dead."

To Lornhollow, Elora cried, *"Can't you do anything?"*

"It is your darkness," the creature said. It had not moved from inside the circle. It had stood still and luminous as violence erupted and subsided around it. Now it bent over the grisly mess that had been Fyldur, brushed its flesh with silver, and passaged it, blood and all, in a sparkle of green, on a scent of storm.

Still bonefolk, then, Louarn thought. As though it mattered. But it did.

Because the gleaning carried shock and horror no different from his own, he hadn't realized it was still open. The same aqueous bluesilver luminosity, slate and indigo and morning sky in equal parts. Still filling the hall.

"We've got to passage them." He staggered to his feet. The materials cupboard seemed a mile away. "I can still feel their glow. It's not too late."

"No."

Louarn couldn't tell who had spoken. Two folk of the dream moved with weightless grace, one to Rekke's body, one to Ioli's. Reiligh and Kara had fled with Dabrena's children. Adaon had gone after them, found the mender clubbed unconscious outside the door, and hauled her inside. Caille was healing her. Pelufer was watching the door. Kazhe stood there, bareheaded, crusted with snow, her longblade a ruby blaze. She had felt the stain of Fyldur come skulking into Gir Doegre. She had sought it, found it—disarmed it. But not in time. The blade dangled from her hand, shine fading.

Louarn's gleaning shattered against what it found in her as she stared at the fallen body of the Ankleman.

"No," came the voice again, strong and clear. Too strong, too clear to be Mauzl's, but in Mauzl's voice it said, "No passaging. You'll break me. You'll tear the glow in three."

Pelufer walked to Mauzl as if in a trance. As the combined glow condensed around Mauzl, Louarn lost the clear gleaning of her, but he could imagine. She had the hauntsense. She had taken a human life for the first time. She had protected him— become his kenai in fact as she had always been in spirit. The stain on her was the color of torment. Her longblade was still in her right hand. She reached out her left, touched Mauzl's cheek. "They're on him now."

With a swipe at the blood leaking from her nose, she came back to Louarn. "It's too late to passage them to pethyar," she said. "They're haunts. They went where they had to. Leave them be." She looked down at her blade as if seeing it for the first time. Louarn would have pulled her close, offered the only human comfort left when words could not reach, but she stepped back. "Maybe it will be enough," she murmured to the blade, and sheathed it.

She strode to the door. Kazhe barred the way. They faced each other for what seemed an age but was an eyeblink, grief and guilt and stain and failure between them like a clash of blades. Then Kazhe stepped aside, and Pelufer was gone into the blindness of snow. A breath later, with one last look at the dead, Kazhe was gone as well, faded into the white.

"It's all right," Mauzl was saying, as the dreamfolk passed Rekke's body and Ioli's through phosphorescence into wholeness. "It was the only path."

Mauzl's triad was preserved in the unity of its glow. But Louarn did not have Mauzl's gleaning. Mauzl's paths did not propagate through the collective visant glow in any comprehensible way. The shining wonder of the dreamfolk, the marvel of redemption that his white-light ennead had effected, was stark, almost intolerable against the vicious, ugly acts committed on its heels.

Pelufer bore her stain until she reached the sandy coast of the Knee.

She held it cupped in her hands like a bit of black ash sheltered from the blizzard. Whiteness swirled around her, blinded her so that only the tip of her longblade could tell whether there was road before her or snowdrift or ditch or wall. When she took off her gloves to blow hot breath on her hands, white spots on the flesh would not rub off. Her frosted eyelashes clicked with every blink; frost cracked off her eyebrows when she squinted, and ran down her cheeks, below her scarf, like half-melted tears. She forged on, refusing to take her stain through the ways, uncertain if the stonefolk's realm even existed anymore. Step after frozen, footsore step, refusing to bring a mount out into this darkness and white storm. She didn't know if she had missed the upland town she had aimed to reach before she froze. She didn't know how many times she fell as the snow got deeper. She didn't know when she fell and did not get up, when she fell down and fell asleep. She didn't see the face of the luminous silver-white creature that reached through the snow to send her on. *Not yet,* she thought. *I can't die with this stain on me. Please, not yet.*

"Then you shouldn't have bulled off on a three-day journey in the middle of the worst snowstorm we've seen here in my lifetime," a voice said to her, and she was in Tarunel Highguard's tent, a fourbody whose canvas sides sagged under the weight of snow. She tried to say *How . . . ?* and produced only a rasp.

He smiled his perfect, dimpled smile under brown eyes hard as kiln-fired brick. "The dreamfolk brought you, so. They'll take anyone anywhere. Some are saying they'll take us out from inside this stain, but then we'd have to leave our homes behind." He regarded her with curiosity and no pity. "I think you've come to drive that stain away."

"Not enough," she managed to say. He reached across to

squeeze warm water into her mouth from a linen bladder. "A lot . . . of stain for me. Not much, in all of that. But . . . I'm . . ."

"But you're going to try. Good on you. Just wait for the storm to pass."

"How long?" she managed, before comfort smothered her.

"Last my visants told me, it was a day since the dreamfolk came. The storm will last as long as you can sleep. I'll warm some soup when you wake up."

He did, but she didn't eat it. She dragged herself, stiff and clumsy, from the tent in fumbled-on boots and stared in awe at a hushed realm of wonder. Snow blanketed the shore down to the tide line, an eerie glitter in the twilight that passed for day under the shroud of stain. The sea was flat and silver-gray as hammered tin. The tide was ebbing, the water little more than a lacquer coating on the sand, bordered by a thin frill of breakers. A handful of shielders were rolling tarps from the tops of beached rowboats and hauling them down to the water. The shieldpost was reduced to a scattering of tents, three sailless craft, a cadre of fighters she could count on her fingers, but still they readied themselves to row out and meet invasion if it came.

Someone healed me, she thought, looking at those fingers, which should have gone black with frostbite after she fell in the snow. Then she remembered that one of the lightstone beings had transited her. The dreamfolk, Tarunel called them. She had no memory of passing through the bonefolk's realms. Maybe the transit itself had healed her. Maybe the cheit at her belt had done it.

Her stain rose up and doubled her over. She groped for her longblade. It was still on her back. She heard Tarunel come out of the tent. She straightened herself and struggled down past the edge of snow. The wet sand was like mud. Her boots were water-warded. She let the sea swirl around them, and drew her blade.

It was the same motion she had used to kill Fyldur n'Drav. A blade in a back-mounted scabbard drew forth into the strike of wrath. Kazhe had taught her long ago never to draw a lazy blade, never to draw a leisurely blade. The drawing of a blade was a cut to be made in earnest, and if all it cut was air then it must cut each particle of air right down the center. Her arms remembered the cut, remembered the blade's passage through skull and brains and cartilage and bone, through the muscle of the heart, through the yielding viscera. Her arms remembered the scrape of edge on pelvic bone as she drew the blade free, back into guard, her boot already lifting to spin the body away from Louarn.

I protected him as I was supposed to. But Kazhe had already saved him.

Pelufer had not killed the Greasehair to save Louarn. Kazhe had melted his blade. Louarn had no longer needed saving. She had killed the Greasehair because he killed Ioli. She had killed him because he killed Rekke. She had killed him because he *would* have killed Louarn, to destroy his ice-bright glow. She had killed him because she was supposed to become kenai.

She had trained in the blade for nine years and three. She could pull her stroke at any point. She could drive an axe to the precise layer of grain in a piece of wood, stop a club swung at full intent when it touched the hairs on a man's nose. She could have pulled her stroke. She had followed through.

He was inside her now, this Fyldur. She knew him better than she knew her sisters. The demanding childhood pocked with failure. The moons with Jhoss, learning to hate Rekke's name, learning to hate Rekke, learning to hate anyone with a brighter glow than his. The spines that Ioli had picked from his mind, the blessed relief from hatred. The past that had crept back up on him as the moon turned and turned again. The spines that had grown back. The stain that had bloomed again where she had torn the stain from him with everyone else's. His old stain was in that shroud. His new stain was in her. It was the same stain. Seeded by inadequacy, fed by memory, watered by guilt, it had grown back.

He would have gone on killing visants as long as he lived. But that was not why she had killed him. She had not known that about him until she killed him. She had killed him because she could.

She had killed him because she had trained for nine years and three to be a killer.

She wanted to hurl her blade at the shroud instead of her stain. She did not want to let go of the black bitter taste of that stain. She did not want to forget what she had done and why. She did not want to be shrived. Fyldur's haunt would find its way to Evonder n'Daivor and he would passage it. The scorched mark of his death should stay on her forever.

One stain more or less would not tip the balance. But she could not be sure of that. She had to try.

Not so easy, is it, she imagined Tarunel saying. *Now you know what you robbed us of.* But he had left her to stand alone at the water's edge.

Invasion might come at any moment. Rain and snow fell through the shroud. Seabirds flew into and out of it. It would not stop ships brave or cruel or angry enough to venture in. All it stopped was sunlight. If attackers swarmed their shores, they would need killers. They would need every killer she had purged of stain, and every death they dealt would start it all again.

That's why we have to go, she thought, and then had no idea what she meant. They couldn't abandon their world to the darkness.

Perhaps they would need killers again. Perhaps she would even be called upon to train them. But she would never again draw a longblade in this life.

In the eerie half-light, the nickel-silver eyes of her blade were a baleful glare against the matte iron finish. The nickel never lost its polish. The blade was feather-light. The blade drank blood. But it was not a kenai blade, and never would be.

She swung it back and down with a step into left tail guard, and released her shine into it. Her stain followed, ripped from her innards like a scab. She grunted, swayed, but maintained her stance. She looked down at the blade, saw the swirled eyes stand out in lurid silver against the black of stain. "Fyldur," she whispered. Then: "Pelufer."

She looked out at the shroud. She swung the blade up, a clean true-edge cut. The blade's edge whistled through the air, sliced each particle straight down the middle. The cut's force flung the stain out over the sea and into the shroud. The cavern in her mind emptied with a thud that left her ears ringing. Earth and sea appeared to tilt at different angles. She maintained her stance. She followed through and brought the blade into inside right guard.

She opened her fingers, spread her palms, and let it drop.

A hand snatched it up a bladelength from the sand. Kazhe sprinted past her, boots pounding a froth of surf. She circled round to one of the rowboats and tossed the blade in. Then she got behind the transom and with a roar of effort pushed the craft out of the sucking sand and into the sucking tide.

Pelufer could not understand what Kazhe was doing. She looked up the beach at Tarunel. He stood before his tent, legs spread, arms crossed. No move to intervene. She looked across the hammered-tin sea at the blank gray shroud. A swirling ripple like one of the eyes in her blade was the only sign of the stain she had cast into it, and it was whirlpooling down to nothing.

Kazhe wouldn't let go of her stain. She was taking her stain to the shroud.

"No!" Pelufer shouted, and burst into a run to catch the rowboat.

She was too slow and far too late. Kazhe had pushed it out till the water was up to her thighs, then straightarmed up and over the transom. She had oars in now and was stroking deep. Moving fast, with the tide, as she found a rhythm. Her body was all muscle, driving the wooden shell in great thrusts across the water. No swells to slow her. Nothing but gulls between her and the shroud.

"Come back!" Pelufer shouted across the water. "Kazhe! *Come back!*"

How many taverns had she fetched Kazhe out of, how many alleys, how many ditches, dragging her off to a bath and a bed and a meal? How many menders' draughts had she poured down her throat, how many healings had she begged from

Caille, from other touches, to reverse the ravages of Kazhe's headlong dive toward death? How many times had she dangled herself as bait? *You can kill youself after I'm trained,* she'd say. *You can kill yourself when there's a kenai to take your place. You can kill yourself when I'm grown. But not before.*

Kazhe had trained her. Kazhe had bestowed her cheit. Kazhe had seen her safe into adulthood. There was nothing to hold her now.

She drew breath to call again, then let it out a ragged groan. It was no use. For as long as she had known her, Kazhe n'Zhevra l'Keit had been trying to drown herself—in drink, in storm, in blood. But never in the sea.

Never in the stain itself.

"It won't do any good," she moaned. Her stain, with Fyldur's on its back, had been a droplet in the ocean. Not even Kazhe carried enough stain to counteract this. It was vast. It covered the world. Kazhe would die for nothing.

"Maybe she won't die," Tarunel said, walking up to stand beside her with one hand on his cocked hip, the other resting on his blade. "She could just row into the thing, dispel it or not, and come back."

The boat was small in their sight when the prow entered the shroud. Kazhe backed water, then shipped her oars. The clunk of ash on thwarts carried clearly across the winter stillness.

She's not even wearing a coat. Pelufer had spent her adolescence warming the chill from that drunken body, pulling it in out of the cold. *I kept you alive, you puking sot. Don't do this. Don't do it this way.*

Kazhe stood up. Stepped onto the seat. The boat rocked. She rode it like a grasslands horse. She brandished Pelufer's blade.

The despairing cry ripped out of Pelufer's throat the way the stain had ripped out of her heart: "Kazhe! *NO!*"

With a fierce whoop that cracked the stillness like the launch of a siege retort, Kazhe dove into the shroud.

There was no splash. The shroud swallowed it—or swallowed Kazhe. A ripple went through it, only just large enough to see, only a little larger than the ripple Pelufer's stain had made. *No use,* she thought, *no use, it was all for nothing*—but the ripple was spreading. Widening, and swirling, becoming a hungry whirlpool, inhaling stain. At its heart was a black pinpoint, swelling—enlarging to become a throat, a deepening vortex like a whirlwind laid on its side, undulating within its own rotation.

"Stand away," Tarunel warned, but Pelufer resisted the arm he threw across to shield her and bear her back, resisted the command in his voice—rolled away from the arm so that it pressed empty air. With an oath, Tarunel ordered his shielders to fall back beyond the dune. He did not leave her side.

The shroud writhed. It resisted the sucking vortex. The whirlpool spanned a third of the visible horizon now and was still growing. Its throat was a blackness deeper than dark, deeper than the absence of light. A density of striving stain spun tight. The mass of a black linen shroud spun down to the diameter of a single flaxen thread. Somewhere at the other side of the world, the tortured fabric tore. There was no sound—no thunderclap, no tearing shriek and rush of wind as there had been with the intorsion. Just the silent, spinning whirlpool, and the shroud of stain sucked down its throat.

Sunlight blinded them, sunrise come in an eyeblink in the middle of the morning. Pelufer could almost hear the cry go up from the world. Shock, fear, dawning delight. The sky was a depth of clear blue ice. They shielded their eyes from the sun. The shroud whirled over the sea like a strange gray hole in the daylit sky, a tunnel into the black of night beyond. It flattened and diminished as they watched, the black eye at its center drawn to a point. Spinning now too fast to see, it whirled down into a tight gray knot, a burl on the sky, a canker. Then it sucked itself through its own black center, and was gone.

Pelufer stood blinking beside Tarunel. The shoreline was a powdered confection of sunlit snow, trampled in long swaths by shielders stumbling down the dunes to join their leader at the waterline and gape at the horizon they had watched for three years or

a dozen years or two nineyears but hadn't seen, straight and clear,
unwarded and untwisted and unshrouded, ever in their lives.

The sea, a pure blue dancing with sungleam, was almost, but
not quite, empty and still. Directly underneath where the stain
had vanished, a lone rowboat drifted out with the tide.

MAUZL WAS STILL howling. Mauzl had not stopped howling. It
was partly Rekke's howl, but mostly his. The lankbones loved
his big loose strong body. Losing it enraged him. Fyldur enraged him. He almost went tearing off after Fyldur's haunt. He
knew that haunt would go to the realm of white towers, he knew
from the scarcheek that a mage there would passage him, so he
almost followed, to wrench the Greasehair back from pethyar.
Ioli kept him here. In the end, Rekke always did what Ioli
wanted. But Rekke howled.

Mauzl howled too. No one to hide behind now. No one to
speak for him when his small Mauzl-mind and dumb Mauzl-
mouth could not express the vision of the paths. It should have
been Rekke who lived, the realmwalker, the strong loose body
big enough for three, the wild mind full of layers where another layer or two wouldn't make any difference. It should
have been Ioli who lived, the sane one, the one who brought
them together, the mind stable enough to bear two other minds.
But paths could not be twisted. Paths could only be chosen.
The iceheart seated Mauzl farthest from the door. The Greasehair hated the monkey and the lankbones more than he hated
Mauzl.

Mauzl howled, and the glow did not comfort him. The glow
was not compassion or friendship. The glow reached every blue-

silver mind, but the glow was a cold unity. The glow could not smooth the pain away. Mauzl did not understand the pain he felt. It was not a pain of the mind. It was a pain of the heart, and he had never understood his heart, and the glow did not reach there.

The scarcheek recognized the seatings of the lights, with her lightless gleaning, and went to walk the realms of death. *The shine goes with a touch's body into the bonefolk's keeping. The glow stays with a visant's haunt, a quality of consciousness. Unpassaged mages lose their light when they become haunts. That light goes somewhere. I'm going to find it.* She took the hardest path of all, and became the vessel for her light again. Mauzl took the hardest path of all, and became the vessel for his triad's glow.

It was so much more than his small Mauzl-self could bear.

They were in him now. Thinking their thoughts, mulling their notions. Trading thoughts and notions, in and out, back and forth. Like shiny balls. That was a good game. Mauzl could watch that game if he liked. Lose himself in it. That was soothing. That almost made them all forget the howling. They could burrow in, if they liked, and just watch the shiny thoughts flit to and fro. They could burrow to the deepest shiniest in, where the howling wasn't.

But the threelight had to raise the world. He had to do his part. He couldn't be weak Mauzl now. He couldn't go back to being the hideabout boy. He couldn't lose himself inside, where it was pretty. He had to stay outside.

Outside, where the howling was.

"It's hard out here."

The mage boy folded onto the snowy riverbank, longbody and coalhair and catgrace. No shine to warm the ground for them. No gentle touch to ease the howling. No stroking from the sea-eyed boy. Only thereness. Thereness was better. Stroking hurt. Soothing made you think about the terrible pain. Thereness was just there.

"It's hard on deck when all you want is to go below, and you can't, because there's no one else to sail the ship. It's cold. You're drenched in spray and storm. Your joints and muscles start to feel like crumpled foil. You don't remember what warmth was, except to want it. Sailing the ship, you have to watch, all the time. Feel, all the time. No slacking. No looking away. Always on watch, always thinking, never resting." He tossed a rock down into the flow of river, into the middle where the ice hadn't reached. He couldn't see the minute change in the flow. Then he could. Ioli gave him that, from Rekke.

Mauzl sat with the mage boy for a long time, looking at the river.

The mage boy understood how it was to be Mauzl. The touch girl understood too. Not even the iceheart or the scarcheek could understand. Not even the monkey or the lankbones. In the mage boy's thereness was knowing that it didn't take a glow to see. Alone with his light on the nine seas the way Mauzl was alone with the paths on the ocean of grass, the way the touch girl was alone with her terrible shine inside her sister-circle. Love was not enough to cross those gulfs. Light was not enough to plumb those deeps. Only thereness. Only knowing. Only knowing there was someone else. A thereness there. Like you.

"I could watch for you, sometimes," Mauzl told the mage boy.

The mage boy smiled a widewhite trueheart smile. "And I'll watch for you, and Caille for us. We'll watch for each other." He got up, chilled and stiff, and dusted snow off his seat. "Come on now. You've been out here since dawn."

You can't freeze the pain away. I know. I tried. The mage boy didn't mind being gleaned when it was Mauzl doing it, even though it was Ioli. He knew that nothing he could say and nothing he could think would make the howling stop. He wasn't trying to make the howling stop. He was only being a thereness.

All Mauzl could say was *I hurt,* and all Eilryn could say was *I know.*

The head scholar's red hair and beard stood stark against pale skin, the crystalline blue of his eyes softened little by his gray garb. He tugged dove-colored gloves off, finger by finger, and tucked them in his belt to warm his hands before the fire. *He doesn't look like so much,* Eilryn thought, comparing this aging man with the hard master who loomed so large in his mother's stories. She was sitting back, hands dropping into her lap, head cocked—the reaction of most in the Grazehill dining hall to the entrance of Graefel n'Traeyen and Jhoss n'Kall. A clink of utensils on stoneware, a swish of napkins, and then silence.

"The message embedded in the wordsmiths' canon was not a set of instructions for a mage ennead to recast Galandra's warding," Graefel said, as Jhoss—slight, skeletal, pink-eyed— drifted off to stand in what shadow he could find between the hearth and the weak sunshine of a winter's morning. "It was not a set of instructions for a mage ennead at all."

No demand to know who's restoring magelights, though that tight high collar can't disguise the triskele underneath, Eilryn thought. *No demand to hear what we know before he'll tell what he knows.*

Graefel flung his cloak over a chair and carried the chair up to the far end of the dining table, where Dabrena sat across from Herne—the first runner to be transited by the dreamfolk. The etiquette in this hall was to leave the ends of the tables empty. Eilryn himself had broached it—humbly, and with permission, so that he and Caille and Mauzl could sit together in full view of each other. He regretted that now. The subtle politics of holdings was alien to his experience, but the inadvertent opposition spoke clear enough.

The scholar placed a quire of sedgeweave on the table. The top leaf bore an arrangement of verses in lines so flawless they might have been scribed along a straightedge. Eilryn couldn't make the words out, but the flowing Celyrian was a seduction, inviting him to read it, copy it—carry out its directives. He'd never sensed such resonance in a permanent scribing. Caille lifted her hands off the table as though it had gone hot—as though, impossibly, she'd felt some transfer of that power through the medium of flamewood. Mauzl abruptly left off sneering over his shoulder at Jhoss on Rekke's behalf and pinned his gaze on the scholar. Dabrena and Herne, and Adaon and Karanthe beside them, had to visibly restrain themselves from leaning over to get a closer look. Louarn, on the other side of Mauzl, stared across at Liath as they both stiffened.

"Extraordinary," the scholar said, and glanced at Jhoss, who nodded. "I can't feel it, myself, but then I have no magelight."

"All three lights respond to it," Louarn said.

Cutting Louarn dead, Graefel said to Dabrena, "Are your folk versed in the historical codices?"

"As well as they need to be," Dabrena said.

Caille had no use for codices, historical or otherwise, and Mauzl couldn't read. "I'm not," Eilryn said.

"Nor am I," Louarn said, his quiet delivery a challenge.

Graefel said, "The senders of this message—the embedders, if you will—were the first mages. The founders of a craft that evolved into the magecraft practiced by Galandra. At the time when they were beginning to codify the verses that became the core of our wordsmiths' canon, they had just emerged from an age of ignorance and illiteracy following the fall of an age of giants."

"Giants," Adaon echoed.

Graefel nodded, assessing Adaon. "Sometimes called weavers, sometimes called hearkeners, most often referred to as the ancients—powerful beings of indeterminate provenance and foggier demise, and apparently quite real, though their history had passed into legend by the time scribed records were made."

"So old. So pretty," Mauzl murmured. Eilryn said, "The dreamfolk."

"Perhaps," Graefel said, and went on. "Those first mages lived at the dawn of an age of light—the ancient past, as reckoned by the oldest of the Head codices, which are very old indeed; but the urgent present for the canonical embedders. They knew the potential in their fledgling light—and its dangers. They believed it could make the world bloom; they knew it could inspire such persecution as would extinguish it forever. They accepted the risks and did their best by a hard world—a world vastly larger, by the way, than our grandest estimates of the extent of the outerlands. They also created a plan of escape should they one day be forced to flee for their lives."

"Galandra's exile," one of the menders said.

"No," Graefel replied, tapping the edges of the quire into alignment. "The exodus Galandra led was of her own design. The question is whether she and her folk conceived it—or modeled it on the canon's message as best they could."

"She saw the words inside the other words, about the giants and the whiteness and the spirits," Mauzl said in a soft voice— very nearly Ioli's voice, and almost exactly the words Ioli had said after he gleaned Liath's memory of Galandra's passage. "But she had only mages. They didn't understand what they had read. They wanted to do what the hidden words said, but they had one light, not three. They had no giants, or spirits."

A hollowness shivered through Eilryn's limbs. Only in the four ninedays since he came to this holding had he learned their canon. They called him a prodigy for getting nine nonned verses by heart so fast. They didn't understand how hungry he was. His spirit was parched, his mind ravenous for verses of time-tried artistry. Now it came home to him that he had learned the same lines Galandra had learned. He had all the core materials Galandra had had. *I could do almost anything with that. She did. She saved her people.* And whatever he couldn't do, Caille could, and whatever she couldn't do, Mauzl could, and . . .

Graefel's crystalline eyes had speared Mauzl squirming. "You gleaned that on my pledge's prentice?"

A bit of Rekke surged up in Mauzl then, but before he could spit any seething blasphemies Liath said, "He did. What happened to those first mages?"

Graefel bestowed a cold smile upon the sedgeweave before him and said, "For untold generations, the world thrived in their light. Then it fell, as they knew it would, into darkness and corruption. That was the world Galandra fled, leading our ancestors to safe haven here. All they had left of the hopes, the dreams, the knowledge of their forebears was what survived within the canon after years of fear and ignorance had destroyed most of the texts they had made. In the end, the only safe place was inside their heads."

Mauzl's body clenched as the paths opened all around him. Sometimes the only safe place was inside your head, but sometimes there was no escaping the inside of your head, or the inside of your self when the abyss yawned open on all sides. Now Rekke was here. Now Ioli was here. Ioli would not let him fall. Rekke delved the abyss and neutralized its terrors. Mauzl only swayed a little, and not even the touch girl noticed, not even the mage boy. Their minds were full to bursting of other things.

Pelufer said we should make our own passing place, the touch girl was thinking. Not in so many words, she hadn't made it into words yet, but it was a shape in her mind, a texture, a thing she could touch, and once she touched it she would understand. They were all so close to understanding. *Pel always said the first way to counter an attack was to void it by stepping aside.*

We could do Galandra one better, Eilryn was thinking, though he did not yet know how. *We could make a safer place. A place we're wholly responsible for, good and bad.* Then he grew distracted, thinking: *When did it become "we"?*

Eilryn and Liath and Louarn are powerful and inventive enough to recast Galandra's warding, Dabrena was thinking. *If we ask them, they'll find a way. They could be the second coming of Galandra. But it would harm the world, and start it all again.*

Would we destroy the world, or risk the world destroying us? Adaon was thinking, aware of his pledge's thoughts with the kind of gleaning that didn't require a glow, only years of close association.

The only child who ever defeated a game of would-you, Liath was thinking, *is the child willing to say, "I would do neither."*

The paths bent toward the iceheart. Mauzl had never seen the paths do anything like that. He gleaned Jhoss's gleaning, paths drawn on a fabric, the fabric weighted by people of destiny. Ioli had been one, the Illuminator had been one, the Lightbreaker had been one. Now it was the iceheart. His glow was deep as an ocean abyss, wide and cold and clear as the winter sky.

"Stop," the iceheart said, as the scholar drew breath.

He had it. Jhoss saw that he had it, Ioli then Mauzl saw that he had it. Not even Graefel had it, and Graefel hadn't finished saying all his words.

The endless ebb and flow of stain. The endless cycle of the realms, peace and prosperity falling into decay and darkness, rising again into light and life—only to fall, again, and rise, again, and again, and again, and again. In each rising were new wonders to replace and supplant what was lost in each fall, but suppose, just suppose, just imagine there could be only rising. . . .

Graefel's silence was frost. It spread to fill the hall. Into it, Louarn said, "I know what they meant us to do."

"Do you?" Graefel said, with one brow raised.

Louarn produced his most disarming smile. "Not how, scholar. Not even what, precisely. I would not presume to achieve in a day the vision you earned through four nineyears of dedication. But unlike you, perhaps—unlike you, and Dabrena, and Herne, for all the respect I bear them; unlike anyone who has ever held authority in this land or assumed it in order to save us from imminent threat—I will not see it imposed on Eiden Myr. I want the word of each of you that what comes next will be the choice of every soul who lives in this land."

"How would you ask them?" said Herne. "Can you wait the year it would take my runners to canvass them? How loud can you shout? Would you assemble them all on some mountainside, every last person, and take a show of hands?"

"I have any number of visants who could count them at a glance," Jhoss said from his shadow, with a cadaverous smile. "But that will not be necessary."

"I have Ioli's gleaning," Mauzl said. He had to tear the words out of small, scared Mauzl. Ioli's power was the one that frightened everyone. When people were afraid they sometimes hurt. "I can show them. The way Ioli showed the siege." He fought to keep his head up. He looked at Caille and Eilryn. They were excited and afraid, but they made themselves calm, to help him.

"This is a new world now," Herne Runner said, confronted with a power that could make his runners obsolete—perhaps already had, in conjunction with dreamfolk who'd willingly transit any who asked. He turned his scowl on Louarn. "I haven't known you long or well, Louarn, but Pelkin trusted you as he trusted few folk in this life. I'll take your blind vow."

Dabrena was remembering the old headman of Khine and the fiasco on the Menalad Plain. "Our folk have always done best when left to sort themselves out," she said softly. "Or make their own decisions." She looked up. "All right, Louarn. I promise."

"I vow as well, for what it's worth." Graefel looked directly at Louarn for the first time. "I suppose my son may have seen something in you after all."

Everyone in the dining hall took the vow, though most held no claim to authority over any group or holding. Caille and Eilryn took it, too, though Caille felt that if the touches had a head it was Elora, who wasn't here, and Eilryn feared that as the brightest of a generation of bright lights he would be called upon to lead the mages in some way. Jhoss took the vow, though he made no claim to be the visants' head, for they had none. Mauzl himself took the vow, though he felt like a fool. And so did Liath Illuminator, though she was looking at her son when she spoke, and thinking along other lines.

"Now," said Graefel. "The embedders knew the limitations of magecraft, though they did not foresee this realm of Galandra's making, where magelight could bloom unencumbered, and I do not know how bright our reborn light is by comparison with the original. The embedders knew that the most powerful things come in threes; they knew that where there was a yellow light, there must also be a red and a blue. But the white light of those three human lights combined is only one element of the grand triad they foresaw. One of the others, confirmed by your young visant's gleaning, is the ancients—and the ancients, it appears, are what has so whimsically been dubbed the dreamfolk. Our island must have been the haven they withdrew to when they passed out of history's eye, just as it later became a haven for Galandra's people."

"The other is Eiden," Caille said. She'd been speaking to herself, but when she felt the attention of the hall come on her she cleared her throat and said, "It's Eiden. Eiden and Sylfonwy and Morlyrien. Those are the spirits Ioli was talking about."

"Ioli said they didn't exist, either in the embedders' time or in Galandra's," Liath said.

"They do now," said Adaon.

"The earth woke," said Elora. She came in with Pelufer, with a grizzled one-armed shielder, and with one of the dreamfolk, too tall and wide for the entry, passing through doorposts and lintel. "Steeped in light for nine nonned years, the earth and the winds and the waters woke. This is Lornhollow, scholar. One of your ancients. Lornhollow is asleep. The folk of the dream are their own dream of themselves. That's why they glow silver-white. Like your dreams, Louarn."

"My white dreams have been known to cast black shadows," Louarn said, reevaluating Lornhollow.

"You're a mage," Elora said. "And a visant, and a touch. Those black shadows are yours, not the dream's."

Mauzl asked permission, from the hall and from the new arrivals, and Ioli gleaned to them what had passed here—to all but the dream creature, whom no visant could glean or glean to.

Herne gestured to Lornhollow. "And when he wakes? Will that be his death?"

"He's a she, and she's a he," Pelufer said with a grin, pulling a chair up behind Caille and Liath and straddling it backward. "Maybe one of you wordsmiths can think of a word that's both, and neither. If not, he doesn't care what you call her."

"Finish, Graefel," said Louarn.

The scholar inclined his head and said, "In these leaves is a set of directions for the . . . conception, the creation of a new realm. A realm of matter, just like ours; a mortal realm, just like ours; but in all other ways a realm of infinite possibility. Only the grandest triad could create such a thing, the embedders believed: a triad of triads, a transcendent ennead. Three spirits, three ancients, and three human lights. The three lights have blossomed. You folk in this holding have resurrected the ancients. The spirits are awake and alive. Three forms of life; three immeasurable powers. It is within our grasp. To leave this world, and start a new one. To leave behind whatever ancient enmities we fear. To ward ourselves without harming the outerlands. To leave not a scar or trace behind, and ascend . . ." He gave a wry shrug, and half a smile. "Into glory," he said, and laid his hands on the pile of sedgeweave before him.

Everyone spoke at once. At last Dabrena pounded her mug on the table for silence, and pointed to Louarn, who said, "When would this event take place, should all agree to it?"

"I would suggest Ve Galandra," Graefel said. "In extremity, it could be done in a day, and that day could be today. But the embedders suggest careful preparation, and the equinox as the time of actuation. The sowmid equinox being nearest, that would be noon on the balance day of Ve Galandra."

"How long will it take?" Eilryn asked. "Is it like a casting, or a gleaning, or a working?"

"All three of those, and more, though you will forgive me if in my old mage habits I tend to refer to it as a casting. The preparations could take a nineday. The casting itself would take as long as any magecasting, no more; all the powers of the ennead are expected to work in tandem. The results, the first mages believed, would be more gradual than instantaneous—incremental through afternoon, faster through evening, culminating in full transcendence by midnight. Of course, they never attempted it in practice."

Caille asked, "Would we still have bodies, still eat and drink and sleep, bear children—die? Would we be like haunts in the realm Louarn described? Or creatures of light, like the dreamfolk? Or something else?"

"We would be everything we are now, and more. We might conquer death, if we wish it—or discover death, learn it, integrate it into something new and unimaginable to us as we are now. I can only guess. But we need not lose anything we cherish, including the joy of bearing new life and perhaps the joy of leaving it. The constraints are few, and the possibilities are limitless."

Herne said, "We'd be staking everything on the beliefs of primitive mages untold generations ago. And on your translation of those beliefs."

Graefel slid the sedgeweave quire toward the table's center. "I fully expect—in fact, I demand—that my work be questioned and tested by as many folk as possible. Not only my decoding, but its content and the embedders' intent. Judge for yourselves whether they were primitive. They may only have dreamed of the existence of the elements required to achieve their goals, but they lived in a time of powers we can barely imagine."

Elora said, "It sounds as though we'll have to leave this world behind. Many of us grieved that prospect when we thought we might have to flee the shroud into the bonefolk's realms."

"Eiden Myr would ascend entire. All of it, just as we know it now. But . . . healed. Like the bodies of the dead when the bonefolk passage them."

"You imply that this will be a realm of matter—a physical place," Adaon said. "You say we might conquer death. Pelufer has long hoped for some way we might reunite haunts with the bodies preserved in the bonefolk's realms. This transcendence holds promise toward that end. Liath said our haunts are passaged to pethyar now, but if there's still a chance, if the dead might *want* to return, if they still exist in any form that would have any use for the bodies they had . . . well, how would there be room for us all?"

"The bonefolk's realms are limitless. They will be accessible. Our own realm could be expanded, replicated, or new lands established around it—our own outerlands. The canonical embedding implies infinity and eternity. Whatever we need, we would make, including space, even time. We would colonize our dreams."

"Speaking of the bonefolk's realms," Herne said, "you told Pelkin that we would be cut off from the realms of our dead."

"I was wrong," Graefel replied. *Words I never thought would pass those lips,* Mauzl gleaned from several minds. "We would be cut off from the realm we inhabit now. That was the great caveat in the canon, which I initially misread. We, not our dead, would be cut off from the world that gave us birth. That is the protection this ascension offers. It is also its greatest price."

Karanthe said, "You say we'd bring Eiden Myr with us. But

you can't just pull a great chunk of land and air and sea out of the world without catastrophic consequences to that world."

Adaon said, "Bodies are flesh our spirits make to garb themselves. If the spirits are fully a part of this transcendence, they would make the land and air and sea anew."

Liath said, "We don't know how much hatred is left in the world, now that what the intorsion trapped is gone. There may be only sad, backward folk who could use our help."

Mauzl said, "Rekke gleans horrors out there."

Liath said, "Perhaps they deserve our pity, and our aid."

"That, I think, is a judgment best left to the greater debate," Dabrena said, and pointed to the shielder, who had raised the arm he had. Purlor One-Arm, after a gruff introduction, said, "There's no sign of aggression as yet, and all lead shielders are in place and on watch—the dreamfolk have taken each on the rounds of the other posts, so we can see for ourselves, meet the folk we've fought beside all these years and never met. That's quite a thing, you ask me. It means I can tell you what I saw with my own eyes: What's left of the shield can't fend off much. We need fresh, trained fighters. We need new siege retorts, new armor, new tents, new everything. We need a decent meal and more than one good night's sleep, too, but that's our problem. What's your problem is the resources required to mount an effective, flexible defense after nearly four years of siege. I don't know if you want to be sending your children and your lights one after another to that coast, none's-land or no. I don't know if you want to stain this land again. I don't know if you menders can't think up some way of keeping shielders ready inland and reclaiming the coast in times of peace. But whatever you do, don't ever say again that maybe nothing will come. Maybe it won't, this year, or next. But it did this time. It will again." He gave a sharp dip of the head, the shielder equivalent of a holding bow, and said, "I've left my post long enough." Lornhollow transited him on the spot—a thing most folk were still getting used to seeing—but the long silence in the wake of his words had nothing to do with amazement.

Like a frond rising through water, Lornhollow's arm went up. Blinking, Dabrena pointed.

"It was our great crime, dreaming so far," said the creature of silver-white light in its rustling echo of many voices. "We dreamed beyond ourselves alone, and lifted only a shadow into the new place. The golden light was a spark in mortals then. We had seen other sparks, flaring and dying in the lifetime of mountains. We had seen much, in the world that birthed us, and molded much in our weavers' hands. We had hearkened to land and sea and sky and heard a silence. We were old, and weary, and full of hubris. We wove this land from dust and embers and mud and sand. We molded it in our likeness. We painted it with mountains, chalk and jet and gold and copper. We shaped its surface in beauty, and then we sent it through the ways. But only the dream of it went. We were torn asunder. Without our dreamers, our weavers, our hearkeners, the land lay inert. It was not silent. It was our hearkening that failed. The land lay where it wished to be, and would not go on. We had transgressed. We thought we owned the land we molded, the air we wove, the waters we spun. But lands and airs and waters belong only to themselves. They will as they wish."

Herne said, "Is that warning us to disregard what Graefel's found?"

"They couldn't do it alone," Elora said. "What they were trying to do is what those ancient mages wanted to do. It means that that's a thing that life aspires to, whatever form it takes. To make a place of its own. To go beyond itself, to reach its branches up into the canopy. To become greater than it is, or realize the greatness it's capable of. The beauty, the creation. Like making a child. The dreamfolk failed, because they tried alone. In the realm of realms, it takes three."

Karanthe said, "Why couldn't they see that, and wait until the conditions were right?"

Pelufer said, "Their hearkeners are like our visants. Their dreamers are like mages, and their weavers . . . are like us. They thought they had the three they needed."

"How do you know all this?" asked Herne.

Elora smiled. "Lornhollow came to us, and told us. Last night, while Pel and I were sitting up, after Caille left. I think . . ." She made a gesture dismissive of her own sentiment, then went ahead and voiced it: "I think the dreamfolk hoped that by confessing to Pelufer their transgression, they could ease the . . . what she was feeling about what happened to . . . about the stain. But I'm embarrassing her, so I'll shut up now."

"They'd have told anyway," Pelufer said. "When they heard about this, they'd have told. But not to warn us not to do it. Only to warn us not to try to do it alone."

Herne said, "Suppose the human folk of Eiden Myr agree to attempt this thing, and the dreamfolk agree to try again. How can we know what the spirits will, or don't?"

Louarn said, "Mauzl will glean them."

This was too much for new strong Mauzl, with Ioli quailing within him and Rekke bellowing. He scrunched down in his chair and put his arms over his head. His whine was stifled but audible.

Sharply, Eilryn said "What makes you think he can do a thing like that?" at the same moment that Caille cried "Why do you keep putting every visant thing in the world on him?"

Louarn met Caille's gaze, then Eilryn's, and said, "Because I am beginning to be able to glean the dreamfolk. Because that leads me to believe such gleanings can be learned. And because, of all the lights, the mages' light of spirit was ever closest to the spirits, and the touches' shine of life was ever closest to the elements. Mauzl's dearest friends are the most powerful mage and most powerful touch in the world we know. You are a triad, the first true triad of the three lights, and you will represent the human lights if we undertake this task. Gleaning the will of the spirits can serve as your trial."

"Gleaning the will of the world is Mauzl's first task," Eilryn said, not backing down a hair. "The one he volunteered for."

"Don't try to make him do more than he can do, Louarn," Caille warned. She realized that she sounded just like her sisters when they tried to shield her powers from a greedy world. Pelufer and Elora realized it, too. The looks on their faces were strange—looks she'd never seen there before. They looked the way parents looked when their children left on their journey year. Sad and happy and lost and free, all at the same time.

"I'll do it," Mauzl said, coming out from under his arms, brushing his hair off his face. "I'll try." He looked at Eilryn, then Caille. "We'll try. But the other first. If this isn't what the world wants, it won't matter, will it?"

Don't you know?

The question came so clear and loud that Mauzl startled. It was Jhoss. Genuine curiosity. Mauzl thought, very slowly so that it wouldn't be lost in the gleaning, *All futures are always possible. The world wants everything, and nothing, until we take the first step down the path of finding out.*

Dabrena looked at Graefel and Herne, who nodded, then around the table, around the hall. "Any more questions? Basic questions that will inform the debate?" No hands rose. "All right, then," she said. "No time like the present. Will it take long, Mauzl?"

To offer the knowledge would be a matter of heartbeats. For them to choose to look, or not—that would be longer. For them to think about it, talk about it, decide and change their minds and decide again until they were certain . . . "I don't know," he said. "Days. Ninedays. Tonight's the new moon. The next new moon is Greenfire, yes? By then, maybe."

"Good enough," Dabrena said. Then, feeling that something official was required of her, she waved a hand and added, "Have at it."

What will the world decide? The collective question bubbled up from the stew of thoughts in the dining hall. Mauzl shut his mind against it, shut his eyes to keep it out, clamped down tight against the opening of the paths. He did not want to know. He did not want to pass his knowing, however unknowing, on to them. He did not want to bring it into being with his knowing.

If he looked, he would glean the paths. He would see, with the all-seeing that was not focus and was not sight but was pure unarticulated knowing, which paths were almost mostly good. He would try to take those paths. He always had. Walking blind, tapping his way, feeling his way along the not-bad paths. He could do nothing else; he had to walk in what he believed was the right direction. But right, and good, and mostly good, and not-bad—all those were Mauzl-choices, Mauzl-judgments.

He wanted, with all his will and all his heart, for the world to choose its own path. The paths could not be twisted. The paths could not be hammered like metal or braided like twine. All paths existed, always; for every infinity of paths that the next step, the next breath, the next eyeblink collapsed into one path, an infinity of new paths came into being. He had changed the paths already, merely by looking away. Denying the vision of the paths was in itself a path. Anything he did changed the paths. Everything he did, even nothing, was a choice. Clamping down tight on his own vision was a choice. A choice he'd never had before—something new that came with Ioli and Rekke but was equally new to them. The first choice he'd ever made without using his path-vision itself.

He rested his mind in the soothing pathblind dark, and let Ioli open the gleaning to make their offering to the world.

In the menders' holding in the Strong Leg, debate went on, day after day, in every workshop and room and corridor of every hall. In the town that hosted that holding, debate went on in every public house, every shop, every field; it surrounded every trader's stall, ran up and down the longstreets and the short, seeped into every home, simmered in every sleeping mind.

In the scholars' holding in the Head, debate echoed down the passageways in moving conversation, hushed into whispers muffled by the hangings on sleephall walls, rang in scriptoria and pillared galleries, drifted from cliff-face balconies to merge with the crash and ebb of surf. The scholars pored over codices they'd read a dozen times, seeking enlightenment, paradigms. They sought the chambers that visants occupied, though of those who had come nearly all had left again, and sought to plumb their gleanings; most ended up in meditation, calmed by the visants' whirling, sparkling, spinning things, the complex simplicity of objects arranged by size or shape on tabletops and floors, and found in that meditation a lightless gleaning of all they had read and all they had learned, and went out again to renew discussion with their colleagues.

In the runners' holding by Maur Gowra, reports came in from every region describing village meetings, town halls whose rafters trembled with raised voices, a festival air on village greens as crowds fell to trading and feasting while they argued. For every runner who went out again, two or three returned, and stayed. As they debated among themselves, they began to think of going home, folding their black garb into the backs of drawers or wardrobes, putting their footsore horses out to pasture.

Debate ran around the coast and back like a polishing cloth on a shield's iron rim. Some said, We could be safe; we could put up our blades for good and live with our families and tend our farms and workshops. Others said, We only want an excuse to abandon our posts; weariness and terror is a craven reason to favor ascension. Still others said, We're running away; to leave this world and its dangers would be cowardice. Still others said, Favoring ascension is an insult to us, as good as saying that we can't be trusted to hold this coast; and some among those added, We fought too hard to hold this ground, sacrificed too much to retreat in disgrace now. Still the words "home" and "peace" and "safety" flowed up, and back, and around. Don't look to fight for the sake of it, some began to say. It will take time, but we'll remember how to be inlanders again. We've done our duty for twice nine years. We've earned our rest. Let's be the last of us. The last to ever raise a blade on these shores.

In a visant enclave on an ice-girt island in Lough Grendig, a seeker moved a stone in an arrangement and asked a visant a question. The visant moved a different stone in answer. The seeker moved another stone, and asked another question. The visant shrugged. They played the game to its conclusion, which resulted in no win for either side, and the seeker said, "Then it really is up to us. How many lands are gifted with the freedom to choose their own fate? Given that choice, how can there be any choice at all but to go on?"

"Imagine the journey it will be," said an aging woman named Ailanna to her pledge as they sat rocking by the fire. Their grown children looked after them now, easing their dotage, but Ailanna's mind was sharp and craved the new experiences her body could no longer carry her to find. She missed her journey-mage days—had missed them since she settled down and tri-aded, no less since her light had gone and she'd turned her hand to herbcraft. Bordill had always been content with hearth and home, and she expected him to contradict her, in his quiet way. Tell her that nothing would change, they'd be the same old fools they were now, rocking by the fire in their slope-roofed longhouse. But he grunted, and said, "I'd like to find out," and as she described all that she imagined might come to pass, he smiled, and imagined with her.

Among cottages and tiny crofts in the forested crook of that same arm, a logger named Jiel said to himself, "The pinecones open to reseed the ground only if we let the forest burn. In that blaze of heat the trees are created anew, and the forest stays healthy and strong."

"We don't know enough about our world to make it over again somewhere else," said a woman in the town dancehall of Umbril. "Why does the sun shine? Why does the moon wax and wane? What makes the seasons change? For all our scholars and our seekers and our menders, we don't know *anything*." A man named Elfinnin, sitting with his grandchildren, said, "But the world does. The world knows. It has only to want to make itself again—and I think it will." He looked at his daughter, bouncing her youngest on her knee, and then at his pledge. "There's a lot to be said for third chances."

The Golden Swan, in Ardra, in the Haunch, was packed from wall to wall, with the local teller and her piercing voice on hand to restore order when the debate got out of hand. As the publi-can was doing a brisk trade in his mint-flavored house ale, the arguments became spirited. But in a low voice a local wright complained, "It's like one of your tales, Eldrinda, one of your tall tales about some land-beyond"—and in a somber voice she replied, "That's exactly what it is, Lonn Saddler. It's the tallest tale of all. The grandest tale. A tale we can make come true. How many of my tales can you say *that* about? How often do you get a chance to live in the land beyond imagining?"

In the Lark and Sparrow, nearby in Gulbrid, Beilor the taverner said, "If we can make our own way, I say we should do it." Daglor, playing standstones with his pledge, Leskana, said, "But suppose we're the only place left in the world with things like scribes and menders and scholars. Forget magecraft and touchcraft and visantry; suppose we're the only ones who could bring knowledge back to a dark world?" Beilor said, "Mages gave it knowledge before, and it went dark all by itself. Let it pick itself up this time." Daglor said, "I wouldn't leave my neighbor to freeze in the winter or go thirsty in the summer." Leskana said, "You're a fine man, Daglor, and you never shirked a duty. But they've done without us for a long time, out there."

Between Lough Cara and Lough Harin, in the Belt, Gintha n'Dorn and Pierren n'Larr had a similar conversation, as the townsfolk of Haringar helped the folk of Caragar to raise a new grainhouse on the site of one the great wind had knocked down a nineday ago. "Suppose they need us to help raise them up again?" said Gintha. "How can we turn our backs?" Salda Baker—whose winceberry cobblers turned tongues inside out—said, "Perhaps *they've* gone on without *us*. All we can do is leave a legacy that others can follow."

"So long as the world has someone to save it, it will never grow up," said a woman named Shalana, in the meeting tent of the Jhardal band in the Girdle a few days later, rocking her crying toddler on her lap. She had pulled his hands back from the brazier three times with a firm admonition about getting burned, and then had let him touch it. They had just come back in with a bowl of snow to soak his sore fingers in. "We've looked after ourselves for more than twice nine nonned years. We've fallen into darkness and pulled ourselves out. The outerlands can do the same. Any favors we could do them would do them no favor."

"They tried to kill us," said a man through a mouthful of boiled barnacles in the Oriels, and a woman in the Heartlands said, between breaths to cool her soup, "We have to protect our lights, and protect our children, and protect ourselves from stain, and so long as we stay in this unpredictable world, we can't possibly do all three." A man tending a furnace on a river delta between two Toes told his fellows, "If we don't go, we'll never know what we might have become. If I thought we'd get the chance again, I'd say we should stay awhile, get the lay of the outerlands. But it's the outerlands that will deny us that chance. They'll never let us rest. They'll never let us rise. They'll drag us down, and we'll never get free. And if I'm misjudging them, then there's no reason for us not to go, because they're doing fine just as they are."

"What would we do, to redeem a corrupt and violent world?" said a sheepherd in Salmer Leng, warming himself with a cup of mulled wine while his dog lolled by the fire. "Take it over? Bend it to our will? We aren't suited to be conquerors. Cast on it, twist its mind? Who are we to say our way is right and theirs is wrong? We would have to force our will and our ways on it, and that would corrupt us past any right to tell anyone what to do."

In homes all over Khine, landholders met with tenants and stewards and itinerants with no regard for station and no intention of distilling consensus for presentation in hall. No halls would convene; that in itself was determined by consensus, but consensus of whoever Hanla Headwoman happened to meet on the road, and it was enforced passively, through her failure to call a mountaintop gathering. "We tried being conquerors again," she heard during day after day of travel around the island by foot. "We tried to conquer the mainland, and repented of it. We did a fine thing, rescuing the sealost—and I'm glad to see you back safe, Headwoman, if I may be so bold as to say—but if it's down to me, I'd rather tend my groves than take up a blade again, and three will get you nine that's what I'll have to do, and my children, and theirs, if we stay in an ailing world." Day after day, Khinishman after Khinishwoman told her, "If they need us, they're better off without us. If they hate us, we're better off without them. If they're thriving out there, let's wish them fair weather and be on our way." Hanla wanted nothing more than to keep from Eiden's shores the stain she nearly drowned in. She owed the bonefolk—the dreamfolk, now—a profound debt for saving her life, and the best way to repay it was to help them achieve their ascension. And she'd like to see her pledge's life-work come to fruition. She had always been the one to mend the rifts between them, until he rejected her attempts to mend the last and worst, so she would make no offer of reconciliation. She was happy here on Khine as she had never been on the mainland. But it was his arms she'd felt come round her in death.

In Sauglin, on their journeys, in their local triads, mages and prentice mages agreed that a realm where all lights could shine would be a glorious creation—and, they hoped, just the beginning of higher achievements. In fields and groves and workshops, touches agreed that a realm where all life could thrive was the most wonderful thing they could imagine. In their enclaves and deep in their solitary thoughts, visants suffused the glow with hopes for a place of safety and clear vision.

In Caille's grotto, deep on the eve of Greenfire, with Pelufer sprawled asleep in a pile of dogs by the hearth and Caille and Eilryn dozing in each other's arms, Mauzl murmured, "They've decided. They've decided we should go."

He did not wake them. In the end-of-winter stillness, he opened his glow and let it spread to bathe their drowsing minds. Pelufer's hauntsense steeped like spiritwood leaves, Caille's gentle fearsomeness like elderbark and cinnamon, Eilryn's vigor and boyish eagerness like dandelions and saxifrage.

The spirits were there, in them. The spirits were in the wood of the bedframe against his back, the planks of the floor, the flames of the fire. The spirits were in the cooling water in the teakettle, the vapor in the air, the air itself. The world was a medium of spirit. It was both one spirit and three; Eiden was also Sylfonwy and Morlyrien and Eiden. It was the essence of living matter, and its distillation. It was deep in the earth and stone beneath him, where the dreamfolk had lain awake and helpless. It was high in the night sky, in the moondark, in the starlight.

This was the last of the spirit days. Not an absence of light. A *clarity*.

A clear light, as vivid as the whitesilver light of dreamfolk.

Already he felt excitement stir in the greater gleaning, as visant seekers turned in their beds or woke with a sense of just having had the most terribly significant dream. Already, dimly, from beyond the glow, he felt recognition—awe, pride, vindication—stir in the lightless. The stewards they had relied upon for all these many years, to support the light, to husband the land, to shepherd its creatures, to collect the harvest of its seas . . . the farmers, the wrights, the herders, the crafters, all the lightless they had loved and pitied and overlooked as the ordinary, common folk . . . They weren't lightless. They had the spirits' light—pristine, unpigmented, uncolored. They were the spirits' familiars. They were the spirits' purest incarnation in human form. Dusted with no gold or copper or silver, saturated with no yellow or red or blue. Just the clear and potent light of being. The clear and perfect light of awareness.

That potency was strong in shielders and farmers. That clarity was strong in seekers and tellers. Vocations that no mender or runner or scholar included when they defined the three human disciplines to complement the three human lights. He remembered the iceheart's pledge, whose clear light was powerful and tender enough to bring tears to the eyes. No wonder Ioli suspected he wouldn't accept his magelight back. For twice nine nonned years, the magelight had outshone the shine of touches and the glow of visants. For twice nine years, the light and shine and glow had continued to eclipse the clarity. Perhaps it was seeing the dreamfolk drenched in their milky silver luminance that prepared the eye to see that clarity. Or perhaps it was simply a gift.

Thank you, Mauzl said to the spirits, for himself and Ioli and Rekke. *Thank you for this vision.*

It was in you all along, they seemed to say, through the wood, the vapor, the soil and roots that embraced this dwelling, through space itself. *Or maybe we're just a clutch of cracked walleyes hearing voices,* he thought—and smiled, because he knew whose thought it was, and he wasn't howling anymore.

They wanted to go. He knew it with a certainty more direct

than gleaning, because it came from the particles of his own body, the particles of the mind and eyes that did the gleaning.

A soft sparkle grew in the air before him. A delight to his visant's eye. Cats stirred on the bed; one leaped softly onto the floor to sit staring up at empty space and batting gently at the nearest sparkles. They danced, for all the world like laughter.

"Those are wraiths," Eilryn whispered, just as Mauzl felt him rouse from his doze. "My mother saw those in the Aralinns."

"They're the spirits," Mauzl said, as Caille sat up rubbing her eyes. "I think they're saying hello."

A dog opened one eye, took a dim interest, then snapped lazily at the scintillation that drifted to greet it. The sparkles danced, and it humphed back into its dog dreams.

"That's the wood of the floorboards," Caille said in awe, reaching slowly to touch a sparkle with her fingertip. It hovered, submitting to her touch with what must be vast patience for such a quick bright thing, then shimmered back to its fellows. "And that's the iron of the kettle, and that's the clay of the mugs, and there and there are bits of the bedding, the smoke from the fire . . ." She pointed, and pointed, and it was like watching someone touch the stars in the sky, one by one, and name them, and make them dance. "Oh, Mauzl . . ."

"They're light," Eilryn said. "The essence of light. There's no color, only . . . brightness."

Pelufer sat up with care so as not to startle the wraiths, and said, "You did it. You gleaned the spirits."

"They showed because they wanted you to see them," Mauzl said.

Pelufer grinned, cupping her hands, watching sparkles pool there. "Did they tell you what else they want?"

Mauzl nodded. "They want to go. Everyone wants to go. They want to make a place where the lights can shine bright. The spirits are strong here now, but they need room to grow. They want to . . . *be*, more, in the world. It's hard for them in this realm. The kind of . . . substance that's possible here. It could be more. They could be more. They're . . . bigger than where we are now?" He had more words than before, he had Ioli's words and Rekke's, but they weren't enough. He appealed to Eilryn, but Eilryn only nodded encouragement. "Everything is alive," Mauzl said. "Stone as much as trees, still air as much as winds, a bucket of water as much as the sea. But we made them . . . aware."

"I'll go tell Elora," Pelufer said, and Caille said, "Take a lantern, Pel"—but Pelufer was already slipping out the door, her grin hanging in her wake as a curve of sparkles. Mauzl lay down where Pelufer had been, safe on the warm stones of the hearth, surrounded by dogs who didn't mind his glow at all, and the soft dance of wraiths lifted the three of them gently into dreams.

GIR DOEGRE RECKONED sowmid as beginning on Ve Galandra. But Gir Doegrans were Southers, and in the southmost regions sowmid had begun on Greenfire and was moving toward its Ve Galandra climax. The river had thawed. Fields were plowed and sown. The land was ankle-deep in aconite and crocuses, white with the blossoms of dogwood and damson. The winds had softened as the moon waxed, and carried the scent of greenness. The arc of the sun's path through the sky moved Headward as the world tilted toward equinox.

Dreamfolk were everywhere. They roved the forests of night in silvery shining companies, stalked down roads in long single files, haunted the smoky corners of taverns, sat on village greens amid scores of tumbling children. They answered seekers' endless questions with patience and what some took to be humor. They were fascinated with the work of wrights and crafters, and would stand for half a day watching wheels take shape, or barrels, or shoes. They were in every field at lambing time, and never missed a birth, whether they stood by a sheepdog's ample whelping box or crammed their great frames down for a view of the most awkward corner a queening cat could crawl into. The animals didn't mind them; after a while, neither did the people. It was considered good luck for a child to enter the world under the dreamfolk's benevolent gaze.

Wraiths were everywhere. They sparkled in the rain, shimmered in the furrows of tilled earth, ran deep and shining in the flow of rivers, clustered like tiny stars around the roots and budding branches of trees. Trail your hand through still water in bucket or trough, and wraiths would sparkle in its wake. Lay a friendly hand on the shoulder of a neighbor, the weary flank of a mule, the back of a dog, and like as not you'd lift it to find an iridescent handprint there. Wraiths sparkled in middens, in smoke, in lovers' smiles, in the steam off oxen's sweaty backs in morning chill. Children played hideabout with them in yards and alleys, stuck out their tongues to collect them like tickly snowflakes. Just when a task seemed its most dull and pedestrian, a flock of wraiths would rise from some ordinary object to delight the spirit.

We are already more than we were, Louarn thought, roaming the illuminated world. *We needed no austere enneadic casting to raise us to this. Only an unveiling of what already was.* The bloom of sowmid was fresh reminder of the vibrancy that had bided dormant through winter. The vibrancy was there all along, resting, awaiting the right conditions for resurgence. Shrubs that had grown larger last summer now bloomed more profusely than they had a year before. Life waited to burst forth from every surface, every crack.

Transcendence had begun with the redemption of the dreamfolk. Transcendence had been well under way on Greenfire, when the wraiths came out and the stewards learned to see their own clear light. But transcendence had been in progress since the first mage set foot on Eiden Myr. Transcendence was emergence; transcendence was waking; transcendence was reaching. They had outgrown their island body, the dreamfolk and the spirits and the creatures of mortal flesh. Transcendence was repotting, replanting; it was the hermit crab creating a larger shell for itself to live in.

For four ninedays after Greenfire, Louarn had roved the land to watch it thaw and watch it shine. Sometimes he accepted the dreamfolk's freely offered transits; sometimes he dreamed himself from place to place. Upon arrival he walked, and bedded down wrapped in his old travel cloak in fields and under hedges as he had used to do. He went to the Toes, swung through the canopy, sipped fermented palm sap, warmed his winter-sore bones in the humid jungle, sniffed the stink and perfume of flowers as big as his head. He went to the Fist, to look across at the scorched and abandoned shores of Ollorawn, and look out at the clear empty seas where the last battle of the coast had been fought. He went to the Head, to walk the nightstone corridors of the holding where he had grown up, to roam the deep labyrinths that had been his father's sanctuary, to find the chambers that his family had occupied when he was a boy and make his peace with all that had happened there. He paid a visit to the Petrel's Rest, where Liath n'Geara, home at last in the bosom of her family, glowed with a golden happiness both coarser and gentler than the magelight she had given her life to reclaim. He arrived in daylight, to watch the pledging of Eilryn and Caille cast by Eilryn's cousin Oriane's triad, with Mauzl and Caille's sisters at their sides and a retinue from Gir Doegre in attendance; he waited until after dark to enter the public house for the celebration, so that he could look at the golden light of safety spilling through the open door, and walk inside. He found Mauzl sitting shyly in a corner, as the boy Mellas had done all those years ago. They toasted the couple's future with fine Neck ale. To Louarn it felt that a circle had been completed, and he himself could now move on—could now transcend his dark beginnings and see his dreams come true.

Keiler had gone to meet his brother and Graefel on Khine and find out what reconciliation might be possible for their family. Louarn had seen him for only an afternoon before he left, and when he was gone Louarn had lingered on the farmstead, rummaging and poking until he found the triskele wrapped in soft flannel at the bottom of a storage crate in the bindinghouse. He had held that triskele for a long time, tasting the faint remembrance of sweet light. Then he had wrapped it again, and put it away, and returned to his roving. Keiler had refused the retrieval of his magelight, preferring to think of it flying free in its own realm. Louarn tried not to grieve that; Keiler's pure, clear, potent light complemented his tricolor light in ways he would be a lifetime discovering. But he grieved Keiler's absence, and he roamed alone, and as the moon waxed to its last fullness before Ve Galandra, he turned for Gir Doegre, and the company of his family.

He and Eilryn labored to produce the materials the embedders' casting required. They sang as they worked, composing and discarding melodies; in the event, Louarn said, the moment itself would inspire Eilryn, and he would sing a bindsong of his own making, fresh from his own heart. Louarn enjoyed their nineday working side by side, speaking through movements rather than words, and through song when they used their voices. In life, their fathers had been closer than brothers. They themselves were sometimes taken for cousins. That pleased him, and eased the work, and gave added power to the quills and reeds they gathered and cut, the powders they ground, the leaves they laid and pressed.

Now the first dawn of the three-day celebration of Ve Galandra streaked the wisped clouds with gold and rose, limned the horizon in silver against the bluing sky. All was in readiness for the casting on the morrow. The dreamfolk had chosen Lornhollow for their weaver, Spinegale for their hearkener, Mistmourn for their dreamer. Those three would transit them to the Fist, where the casting would take place. The materials were packed in Eilryn's bindsack, the glyphs and melodies in his mind and heart. Caille was plump and happy, having eaten her way up one end of Harvest Long and down the other. In the last three ninedays she had spent more time with her sisters than they'd spent together in the last three years. She and Eilryn, together or apart, glowed as only the newly pledged could. After the celebration in the Neck,

Mauzl had realmwalked to the Girdle to embrace his own family, assure them of his safety, recount his adventures—and then he had gone journeying. In the company of dreamfolk he had roved Eiden's body, learning its trunk and limbs and head, learning its people, watching its wraiths dance in mountains and valleys, lakes and grasslands, forests and rivers; in the company of his haunts he had realmwalked through the old bonefolk's places, and returned with marvelous tales of realms of wind, realms of depthless seas, realms where the hills and trees were made of flesh and bone. Now Louarn watched the three of them set off into the morning light, with arms linked and strides matched, to wander the hills and forests and vales around Gir Doegre as they had used to do when they first met. The tall, spare, coal-haired boy on one end, the slim, ethereal, tawny-haired boy on the other, and between them the plump, shining, streak-haired girl; the golden yellow, copper red, and silver blue of their powerful lights merged almost into white as distance took them from Louarn's view. The easy conversation of close companionship murmured in their wake, then wafted off on the cool, scented breeze.

Nothing will be lost, Louarn thought. *Nothing that is beautiful will pass from the world. Eiden Myr will come into the summer of its days, and there it will thrive. And what a wonder that I have lived to see it.*

"It's a great honor to be one of the ennead's three dreamfolk," Elora said to Lornhollow. "I envy you. They didn't need all three of us, only Caille. It's right that it should be her, but it's going to be hard to just watch, I think."

"I'd rather watch," said Pelufer. "I'd rather be on guard in case something goes wrong, than all tangled up with the thing itself, and the one needing help instead of doing the helping."

Elora smiled. "You're still a shielder at heart."

Straightfaced, Pelufer said, "I am not."

"You are."

"I'm not."

"You are!"

Pelufer couldn't hold back the laughter. "All right I am. I was a shielder all our lives. At least, I did my best to be one."

They sat with Lornhollow on the greensward inside the corner of Bronze and Copper Longs, where they'd pitched their scrounged wares when they were children. Wraiths danced around them and hovered like midges around Lornhollow.

Pelufer turned to him and asked a question long held in. "Why do you send the bodies of the dead through the ways?" He let her run her dwarfed, fawn-dark hand over and between and around his glowing spindly-strong fingers. Beneath the aura of silver-white he was the consistency of warm wax. His flesh was translucent; the glow emanated from within, as though he were as hollow as his own name and liquid light had been poured in to fill him. She would touch him, and in breaths forget how he had felt, and touch him again, to remember.

"For the same reason you do that," he said. Elora heard his whispering voices as a disturbance of dry leaves. Pelufer heard them as a hush of silver echoes. "To know, and to remember."

"But you remember everything now, and you still do it," Elora said.

"Each knowing is different. Each knowing is new."

"It's how they learn us," Pelufer said. She drew her hand back and was immediately possessed of the desire to reach out again. "By making us anew. Will you learn the world that way tomorrow?"

"It is our greatest hope."

"Did you always learn the world that way?" Elora asked. "Did you passage the dead in ancient times?"

Lornhollow closed his great dark eyes slowly, opened them again; his fingers fanned up and back. "We did not know the world. We did not know the dead. We wove the earth, the mist, the mountains. We did not know. It was our crime, our error. To use and not to know. In all the lives of mountains, we never learned the ways. We made. We molded. We wove. We sent. We did not know."

"That's why the earth didn't go, when they tried this before,"

Elora said, sitting up, excited by this new understanding. "They were trying to . . . use it, like a tool. Carve it, like someone hacking wood into a shape it doesn't want to take, instead of working it with their shine. It was an object to them."

"What changed?" Pelufer asked. "What . . . showed you the ways?"

"The gold lights came. They sent their spirits to another place at the parting. They knew them, in that sending. We saw. We learned to know the flesh. There is knowing in the flesh even when the spirit is gone. It was our joy, to learn that knowing. It was our sorrow, to know our loss."

"They copied the exiled mages casting passage," Elora breathed.

"We preserved the flesh as a gift," Lornhollow went on. "A thing we could do when nothing else remained to us in our brokenness. We found the ways, and knew the bodies through them."

"You preserved them," Pelufer said. "You could have just learned them and let them go. You kept them safe in your safe places. Why, Lornhollow? Because somewhere deep inside you knew that there would be a use for them someday? That they could still be vessels for the spirits that parted from them?"

"We preserved them because we could," Lornhollow said, in a rustle of many voices. "What you do with them is for you to choose."

"Your dream could come true, Pel," Elora said. "In the new place. I know you've been afraid to think it, but it could."

"I was thinking of haunts, before," Pelufer said. She shifted. The ground had become uncomfortable. "I can't think why any passaged spirits would want their bodies back. Caille says bodies die no matter what you do. Eilryn says we weren't meant to know what pethyar is. And anyway . . . Mamma's body went to feed our shine. We can't ever have her back, even if all the rest come back, even if there's a reason to come back, even if there's room for all the new and all the old. That was her sacrifice. There's no undoing it."

"There is," Elora said. "I know there is. It was a brave and shining sacrifice because she didn't know there might be a second chance. The Khinish gave their lives to bring our sealost home. That heroism remains even though the bonefolk saved them. Acts like that *matter*. But it doesn't mean we have to leave them as they are. They don't have to stay a tragedy to count."

"Adaon keeps saying that flesh is a vessel the spirit makes to carry it through the world. Do you think . . . if she wanted it enough . . . if Padda came back, and we were all there, and . . ."

"Yes," Elora said. "That's exactly what I think. And I think we could help her, too. Lornhollow of the Wood gave us her shine. I think Lornhollow of the Dream could help us give some back to her."

"That's a beautiful thought," Pelufer said, but her own thought was *Let's get there first and have a look round before we start to hope.*

"You have the ways," Lornhollow said. He collected his long limbs and rose to tower over them. Looking up, Pelufer saw from the sun's position that it was just gone noon. Her shadow and Elora's were very slight, and very slightly canted Head-ward. Tomorrow was the day of balance. The day when the shadows at noon would be almost no shadows at all. This time tomorrow, they would be in the Fist, and the ennead's work would begin. Her pulse raced.

Lornhollow cast no shadow no matter the angle of sun. He inclined his head deeply. The others must be calling him. "Pass through," he said, in silver echoes, and dissolved from under the sunshine and the wraiths.

" 'You have the ways,' he said. That means it can be done, Pel. You and Caille can do it. You can help her come back, if she wants to come."

Pelufer shrugged, stroking the grass, her fingers still seeking the vanished memory of lightstone. "Maybe. But why Caille and me? Why not you?"

Elora gave a sad smile. "You're the ones who do things, Pel. You're the ones with destinies and grand adventures and powers that change the world. You made an impossible blade and mus-tered an army of shadows to battle the stain. Caille saved the world when she was five years old; tomorrow she'll help do something even bigger. I just sat here through it all, just sat at home worrying about Lornhollow, pining over Louarn, showing young touches what they don't realize they already know in their bones, trying to keep my food down, trying to keep the alderfolk and traders and menders and touches from falling out."

You risked yourself and your child to approach Lornhollow and make peace, Pelufer thought. *The dreamfolk would never have got their bodies back if not for that. You've made a child, a new life that will be born in the new realm. How can any dark deed of mine compare to that?* She didn't say those words. They didn't answer what Elora really meant. Instead, with quiet intensity, she said, "You did the most important thing of all. You minded your home and your work and your family. You rose above your private troubles and you kept order—in your own house and your own heart. That's what living is, in a world that's right. Whatever else we discover and whatever else we might become, that's the reason we're making this new realm. So we can see to our trades, our crafts, our farms, our lives. So we can raise our children and explore our past and find out how our world works, so we can love each other and make discoveries and explore new places and make beautiful things. No war, no invaders, no ancient vengeance coming back to corrupt us. No rulers, no cataclysms. Just people living their lives, for good and for bad. That's the place we're going to make. Kazhe took away my blade because blades have no business in a place like that. She gave her life as the bodyguard for all of Eiden Myr. All I did was wrangle some shadows. Now that I'm done with that, I have to figure out how to be what *you've* been all along. I have to find out what I would have been . . . if I could have been you."

Pelufer was more than a little appalled at herself for saying so much. Then Elora's face opened into a smile she had almost forgotten, a smile like the one that came over her when she was shining in the deepest greenwood. "I'm proud that you're my sister," she said at last, "but I'm glad that you're my friend."

Pelufer made a face and applied herself to smoothing down the grass. Then she looked up from under her bangs, and grinned.

"Mother was a coppersmith," Elora said.

Pelufer slapped her knees. "Then that's what I'll be. Or a nickelsmith. Nickel is a wonderful metal. Pure and silver and shining. I'd like to see what I could do with a metal like that, instead of making it into blades."

"And that has nothing to do with the fact that Tarunel n'Selinir comes from a family of nickel miners," Elora said.

"He does?" Pelufer said. Then she laughed, because of course she knew.

Suddenly, Elora said, "You're her daughter, Pel. You're the one she haunted. You have her grin, her laugh. You have her way with metals. *You're* her heir. Don't ever forget that."

"You're the one who looks like her."

"You don't know that. You don't remember her face."

"I do." "You don't." "I do!" "You don't," said the children in their memories. Pelufer smiled, letting them argue themselves out, and then she said, "I don't have to." She picked a strand of wind-brushed hair off Elora's cheek and smoothed it back in its place. "I can look at yours."

The domed skylight in the Lowhill Assembly had been unboarded and reglassed. At noon, Dabrena and Adaon stood with their children observing the focused rays of sun crawl a fingersbreadth from the enneagram's point of equinox. The four of them came here on all the major holidays to watch the rays hit their marks, but tomorrow they would be in the Fist; this was the closest they could get this year. They stood for a long time, watching the shaft of light cross the floor and begin to climb the wall, feeling the turning of the world's disk, the great slow dance of the luminaries.

Dobran clutched a slate with a hole in one corner and a piece of chalk tied to it on a string. He would not be parted from the thing, and Dabrena had taken to dressing him in white not to make a miniature warder or mender of him but because it kept the incessant erasures from showing on his sleeves. Blowing his nose was the most use he could remember to make of his pocket cloth.

"These are the glyphs for 'sun,'" he said, scribing them in Ghardic on his slate. "And this is 'moon,' and this is 'star.'" Then his little hand executed an astonishing flourish, and his name appeared in curled Celyrian script beneath the blocky glyphs. "And that's me. I'm a luminary too."

Dabrena stared agape at Adaon, then said, as casually as she could manage, "That's quite lovely. Where did you learn it?"

He pressed his lips together, appealing wide-eyed to Andri, who shrugged and said, "She'll figure it out."

"Kara taught him," Adaon said—with some surprise, as though the knowledge had come from nowhere. Then he looked down at Andri.

"Look, Padda," Andri said. "Look at that. That's both our lights together. Look how it makes a new color of the glow!"

She said it to distract him. He didn't need to be a visant to know that, only a father. But he saw the change in the hue of her glow. It was tinged with his own. He was seeing what his glow looked like through his daughter's eyes. Their glows were blending. Her glow was blending with the greater gleaning.

"He's going to be mad and scared now," Andri told Dobran. "He's going to wonder what all the grownup visants might glean to me."

Dobran was more interested in whether Dabrena would be angry at him or at Kara for jumping ahead in her strict order of lessons. Dabrena just blinked. Trust Kara to know that a child could handle more than she'd ever expect.

"You're going to have to work harder now, you know," Adaon said with a chuckle, and for a moment Dabrena thought he was talking to her. But he was looking fondly on Dobran, whose eyes had gone wide again as he understood what he'd let himself in for. "She'll be setting you Celyrian every day now, instead of that simple Ghardic you've been riding on."

Dabrena, in turn, was looking at Andri. She had never been frightened of her younger daughter. She wasn't now—but she had to admit to some discomfort at how exposed she would be before the eyes of this extraordinary child. How could they possibly raise a child with that kind of vision? A child who could see through all their ploys, a child who sensed their every change of mood?

And how is that different from any other child? she asked herself. *It's like the shine that all young children have but lose as they get older. All young children have that clarity of sight. The difference in the blue ones is that they hold on to it.*

"Give Andri your slate," she said to Dobran. "Clear it first."

She expected an outraged, pouting refusal, but he just said "Why?" as he rubbed his marks off and handed it over.

"Because from now on, what one learns, both learn," she said. "You'll teach each other anyway, and I expect that to continue. Scribe 'sun' and 'moon' and 'star,' please, Andri—and if you can sign your name, you do that too." As Andri worked her impromptu assignment, Dabrena knelt on the marble floor, said, "And because I want to do this," and pulled Dobran into a squirming hug.

Let me never damp the light in this child, she thought, her face buried in his silken moonlight hair, her spirit drinking in the sweet goldenness of his magelight. *Let both of them shine in all their ways for all their lives.*

Adaon cocked his head at her, and smiled, then bent to check Andri's work; and from the slate and the chalk and the stone around them burst a sparkling shower of Eiden's light.

Late afternoon bathed the veined marble halls in shades of burnt orange and dark gold. "You should learn to cast single-handed," Eilryn said, finding his mother on the stone bench in the center of the triskele formed by the Pointhill Torus. She'd been back from Clondel for a sixday, rested and healthy. The top of the glass wall behind them blazed in reflection like a second sun.

Liath laughed. "Me, sing a binding?"

"We sang all the time on *Stormwind*. Take this. It's a start."

Liath accepted the wood-bound sheaf of sedgeweave he handed her. It felt weatherwarded, permanent, heavy. She opened it onto leaf after leaf of verses scribed in his vigorous hand. Setting these down must have been a meditation for him.

And proof of the craft he had mastered in his time here. Her son had grown up a journeymage; she'd never expected him to undergo, and pass, his trial at home, but she was glad for it. And painfully proud.

"This is the canon, isn't it. The wordsmith's canon."

He nodded. "All of it, core and extended. I had to scribe a bit small to keep the codex manageable. I wouldn't read it in bad light if I were you." His grin gave way to a distant look. "It was an odd experience, making this for you. Not just the wraiths that clung to the quill and sparkled in the ink, or that the dreamfolk kept coming round while I worked. With each strophe it felt that the leaves were trying to become a casting. As though . . . as though they were soaking up my light. I was half surprised they didn't dissipate. I'd rather not think what would have happened. Every casting there is, done all at once."

"I can feel your light in this." Liath stifled an impulse to press the codex to her breast. It would only embarrass him. "I will treasure it."

He smiled again, shyly now—still her adolescent son, changeable as the sky. "Don't treasure it too much. Use it. Learn it. That's what it's for."

Abruptly she was swept by memory. His father, the day they met, teaching her to scribe her name. Herself, teaching Eilryn to sail the ship, responding to every cry of *I can't reach!* and *I can't do this!* with "You must. It's as important as breathing." The two of them toe-to-toe after her journey through death, berating each other for the risks they had taken, when she found out that he'd run the gauntlet of every black ship in the intorsion to salvage *Stormwind.* Herself, crushing his father's haunt against her with all her strength and crying out, *I want you back!*

His father, the night she lay with him, the night he filled her with the seed that bided within her until the warding was broken and the light seared and the first freedom lifted, bided those hours inside her body and then made a child of the new light, a child she would not know she carried until she was at sea with no way home, not knowing that the way home was that very child—his father, murmuring against her ear, *Perhaps there is still something of me left. If there is, my love, I give it into your keeping.*

"Spirits, Mother, don't *cry*. It's not *that* great a gift."

She ran her fingers through his tousled black hair, cupped his strong, wise, shining face in her rough hands, and said, the codex forgotten on her lap, "It is, Eilryn. Oh, it is. It is the greatest, sweetest gift in all the world."

"Blue evening," Jhoss said, his albino face lurid in the twilight seeping through the nonagonal windows of the Highhill Comb. He had lit no lamps in this section. Mauzl had found him by his glow. "Our time of day. Blue morning even more so."

"The passing times." Mauzl hadn't wanted to come to Jhoss. He wanted to be at supper with Caille and Eilryn. But the two of them needed to be alone, and he had felt Jhoss's call through the gleaning. "When anything might happen. But anything might always happen. There's no certainty in light. No safety in dark."

"There's no safety anywhere but what we make, and even then we still have ourselves to reckon with." He gestured around the hive-shaped hall, the nonagonal cubbies filled with the honey of maps and codices. "I was a beekeeper, before I heard Torrin Wordsmith speak on my village commons, and left my home to follow him. Beekeeper, not hivemaster. I believed I was the tender of the bees; I believed I knew full well that no one could master them. But still I established their hives where I reasoned they should be. Still I learned their ways that I might bend them to my will." He produced a parchment smile, surveying the combed space. "I never saw till now that I was only one of them." He looked at Mauzl. "We are swarming. Establishing a new hive."

"It's a good path," Mauzl said. "I know that's what you want to know. But you already know." He grimaced. "I don't like these conversations."

"If Rekke could know," Jhoss said. "If he could understand."

"He knows. You know he does."

"That is not my gleaning. Neither are haunts."

"It's there in the greater gleaning," Mauzl said, for Ioli. And then: "Haunts are the grabblers' bailiwick. Naught to do with us." He shook his head, hard, to shake Rekke into silence, but Rekke was going mad, and the movement only puffed his hair out wild and made him less himself and more the lankbones.

"You must let them go," Jhoss said. "In the new place."

"I know," Mauzl said softly. He didn't know whose tears sprang to his eyes. *And I will. But what will I be then? The runt. The damaged walleye, lost in my spinners and sparklers. Would that be so bad? Staring mesmerized at wraiths for the rest of my days?*

"You will never again be what you were, Mauzl n'Shefen," Jhoss said. "My blue mind cannot contain what you might become."

Mauzl rounded on him. "You made Fyldur. *You* created him. You and your impossible demands and your rejections. You killed us! It was your stinking enclave in the Heel behind that blade!"

"As I made you, by that reasoning," Jhoss said. "Yet you know very well that I did not. You made yourself. All of you. No precedent to follow. No model. No one to guide you. A staggering achievement. I am in awe. Does that flatter your Ankleman, Mauzl? To know that he has awed me? To know that with you and your Toeman he achieved what I could not? Ordinarily such realizations come when the prentice no longer cares what the master thinks. But I have told you I was no master. *You* seeded the greater glow, you three. You wakened the visant light to its potential. You made a passive power operant. You yourselves became the precedent, the model, the guide. Through courage and intuition you effected in a season what I could not through years of study and rigorous thought. The glow is intuition. It cannot be logicked. It cannot be reasoned. You are proof of the error of my methods and fulfillment of my highest aspirations. And you are not finished. Tomorrow only clears the way for continuing expansion."

Deep inside, Rekke was sobbing. That was crampgut throat-close. That was worse than howling. A boy, a brokenhearted boy, that's who was in there.

"I was never meant to sire a child," Jhoss said, in his soft, rasping voice. "A son like Rekke would have appalled me. The more because he so badly needed a father. But sometimes things come upon us of their own." He rose and laid his hand on Mauzl's head. Visants didn't like to be touched. But Jhoss knew that Rekke was an exception who craved touch. His hand was cool, and dry as old bleached vellum, bones light as a bird's. "I am proud," he said. "I have no right to pride, for I had no part in this, but I am proud. Yet perhaps, here at the end of the world, not too proud to tell you. You did well, my boy. Know that, if nothing else. You are everything I dreamed you would be, and more."

"He knows," Mauzl said, as the hand slid away and the sobs ceased.

"I know," Jhoss said from the darkness. He was only glow now, viscous and sweet, like spiritfruit preserves. "I know. And now I know that sometimes it needs also to be said."

Liath walked through gathering darkness down the candle-girt path to the Greenhill Cloisters. They'd told her Graefel Scholar had taken to working here. He planned to go back to the Head when this was done, she knew, to resume his scholar's life; Hanla had made a brief appearance at Eilryn's pledging celebration in Clondel, and told her that. She found him by his hard, bright light, reading beside the fire in an upstairs workroom. He looked comfortable alone, as though he'd always been that way and always would. It was hard to remember him as a village wordsmith with a family. Hanla had her light back; she said she might as well be able to use the kadri that constantly formed in her mind's eye. Liath was glad to see Graefel's as well. He would never be entirely alone, or entirely ascetic, in the company of that living light.

At the sight of her, he closed the codex he was reading and set it aside. "Illuminator," he said, inclining his head.

She sat herself down cross-legged by the hearth and pulled a travel-worn pack into her lap. "This should go back to the Head," she said, drawing out a codex wrapped in waxed canvas. "The dreamfolk will transit it with you."

He unfolded the cracked canvas with great care to reveal a stained and dented binding, velvet over boards. He opened the codex with greater care, and his russet brows rose in his vulpine face, carved by the firelight into planes of restrained astonishment. "This is Luriel's codex. We have been searching for this for more than two nineyears."

"It was with Torrin's things." To Graefel Wordsmith, Torrin Wordsmith would always be the great betrayer of his craft.

"The hopes and dreams of Galandra's daughter have journeyed far," he said to the tearstained leaves. "Now they will journey into a realm beyond her dreams." He looked up. "Did you ever learn the significance of the shadow glyphs in your name?"

"Yes," she said, with mild surprise. "And found the names they led to, and lost them, and found them again. But you had already told me what they meant."

"An extra portion of pain in your life—and luck, and joy," he said. "And you met it head-on. In that much, at least, I told you true."

Liath looked down at the battered pack, hesitated, then handed it up to him. "Bring this back to the Head as well. That's where it came from, codices and all."

"I'm better at sending than at bringing," Graefel said. "But I will bring this, and store it safely there." He opened the pack to slide Luriel's codex back inside, and said, "I hope I meet its bearer someday."

I hope so too, Liath thought. Then she left him alone with the codices, the warmth and brilliance of the fire, the suggestion of pattern in the embers' molten depths.

Night deepened into folds of silken darkness, into river murmur and nightbird trill, the winged whisper of drowsing minds. The waning gibbous moon was an insinuation of silver on the unseen horizon of the Dreaming Sea. The patient stars in their slow spangled passage blued the dreaming town.

Anifa n'Bendri dreamed she grew an eye in the back of her head, which she thought would be terrifically useful. Mireille n'-Jenaille dreamed of ousting Elora n'Prendra from her place among the alderfolk. Beronwy n'Fiorin dreamed of her buried longblade melting and flowing deep beneath the earth, feeding the roots of majestic trees whose silver leaves she mashed into a poultice that cured grief. Pelufer n'Prendra dreamed of her father, young and strong and tending his stall, trading hopes instead of copper. Toudin n'Melfo dreamed that one of his stews rose out of its pot and spoke wise words to him, and knew that when he woke he would not remember what it had said. Caille n'Prendra dreamed that she slept in soft drifts of wraiths. Denuorin n'Amtreor dreamed of a whining and a scratching at the door, and knew that it was the little buff dog he'd lost when he was a boy, and rushed joyfully to let it in. Elora n'Prendra dreamed that she was at work in Greenhill, and went to fetch something, and found that there were many more rooms than she had realized.

Eilryn n'Torrin dreamed that his ship was sailing seas of molten light. He woke to the feel of a hand squeezing his shoulder. "It's only me, Eilryn," his mother said, and he was at a table in the Woodhill Repository. "I fell asleep," he said.

"I can see that." His mother closed the codex he'd been slumped over. "Let's get you home and warm."

He groped at the cloak she snugged on him. "It's too far," he said. "The ship's in the Fist." Then he remembered that dreamfolk could transit them there.

"Home is with your pledge," his mother said, tying the cloak at his neck. He was already wearing his coat. He'd put it on when the heatstones cooled. He remembered. It was too much trouble to warm another batch in the firehouse. No flames were allowed inside here. Wraiths lit the chamber but did not warm it. An enchantment of them, so many that there was light enough to see, to read.

"Come, love," his mother said. "It's just around the hill."

Bleary and confused, he let himself be led. The soft

starlight cast a glamour, made the path and the trees into another kind of dream. Soft, dim nightwraiths rose from the woods around them. As they approached the grotto, he asked why his mother had a pack on, and she said, "I'm going to see your aunt."

Breida hadn't been at his pledging. She wouldn't leave her post. Mother hadn't seen her at all since their return. They'd all be there tomorrow anyway. It made sense for Mother to go up first for a private reunion. "I couldn't tell her you were dead." His mother gave a soft knock on the door. "I tried, and no words came out. It was the strangest thing. But I'm glad for it now."

Caille opened the door, all warmth and sleep and relief. He wanted nothing more than to surrender to the dreaming tides. "Thank you, Mother," he managed. "I'll see you tomorrow."

"See you," she said, and kissed his brow.

As Caille ushered him inside, Liath whispered, "Sweet dreams, my love," and gently shut the door.

When she turned, the wood was filled with dreamfolk. They stood silent, otherworldly, as the bonefolk used to do, but she had the strangest sense of . . . homage. She bowed to them, and said in a low voice, "I'm bound for the Fist. Are there any who can speed my way?"

Every head inclined toward her. The nearest stepped forward, and brushed a moon-bright palm across her brow. The world dissolved into a pinpoint clarity so beautiful it made her heart hurt, and made her wonder whether perhaps they hadn't transited her at all, but re-formed the world around her so that the ground she stood on was the Fist.

The Fist, where Galandra's ennead had cast their warding; the Fist, where Torrin and Heff had died. The ground she had tried for twice nine years to reach from sea. She had dreamed of this moment. The soil and stone beneath her boots. The scent of land. But it was the scent of the sea that struck her. She had been away from it for five turns of the moon.

A broad silhouette blotted out the starry heavens by the cliff-wall. Liath took a step out from the scorched and hacked trees. The sentry had already sensed a presence, was already turning.

For a moment it froze. Then it called a low order to the sentry at the other end, and strode toward her.

"Breida," Liath said, as she and her sister came into each other's arms.

The embrace was crushing. Her plump, comely sister was harder than the rock she guarded now, all muscle and height and weight, but she felt like Breida, smelled like Breida, laughed like Breida as she took Liath by the shoulders and lifted her half off her feet. "It took you long enough, you grieving wretch," she said. "I've been waiting up for you."

"I don't think you ever sleep," Liath said. They went to the wall and stood the rest of Breida's watch, leaning close, speaking in low voices. When Breida's relief came out, in the slender hours between midnight and dawn, Liath said, "Sleep now, Brei. Sleep a little. You don't have to watch for me anymore."

"Don't I?" Breida said, with a hard, sad cant to head and voice.

Liath smoothed her hair and said, "Sleep, and dream of paradise, and tomorrow it will come true."

Breida Shipseer surrendered at last to exhaustion so profound her sleep was pure and dreamless, the deepest sleep she'd had in years, while Mauzl n'Shefen could find no sleep at all. He roamed the empty, battened streets and alleys of Gir Doegre, listening to the murmurs of his haunts, wondering why he felt so lonely when two people lived inside him. At dawn he found himself on the roof of a residence hall, watching the deep blue of sky lighten in advance of the rising sun. Kara n'Dabrena came up beside him, and they stood in what he thought must be companionable silence until the molten disk of the golden luminary rose out of the Lowlands.

"We'll never know what's out there," she said.

"We know what was. Some of it."

"We'll never know what becomes of it."

"Do you want to?"

"Not enough to go there." She smiled. "Not enough to miss finding out what happens here. Or seeing Andri and Dobran grow up. Or meeting my father." Her smile widened. "Someone's going to have to map the new realm."

Of all the minds his joined glow had gleaned, hers was the most open to expansion. Hers was the most open to everything. Fierce and hungry, gleeful and unguarded. To him she seemed the clearest of clear lights. A pure incarnation of spirit, of awareness. A child of Eiden and Sylfonwy and Morlyrien. A steward of existence. A cartographer of transcendence.

"I don't know what I'll be, in the new place," he said. He wanted to offer her himself, but what he was today would be something different tomorrow. Ioli and Rekke were the ones she had befriended. Without them, he might become a creature of surpassing strangeness, his glow expanding down the paths until he was not even human anymore. Or he might lapse back into hiding, barely able to speak, his humanity profoundly damaged by powers too great for it to contain.

She looped her arm through his. He startled, because he hadn't seen it coming, and because he didn't mind it. "No one ever knows what they're going to be," she said, and drew him to look down at the grassy triangle where dreamfolk had begun assembling to transit them. "Shall we go?"

So many paths lay open. So many shining paths, serene and possible, rising into all the bright, clear futures. "Yes," Mauzl said. "Let's go."

The luminaries aligned.

Eilryn, Caille, and Mauzl sat cross-legged on Galandra's ground—close enough for knees to touch, close enough for Eilryn's elbow to nudge Mauzl as he worked. They were encircled by dreamfolk as by a stand of argent trees. Mistmourn, their dreamer, wove Stonetree symbols in the air with graceful fingers as Eilryn scribed, a casting outside a casting; as Eilryn illuminated, Mistmourn's fingers made moonsilver patterns in the sunlit air, arcane yet archetypal, alien yet intuited by all who watched; when Eilryn began to sing, Mistmourn sang with him in an ethereal echo of many voices, dissonance within harmony, counterpoint within unity. Eilryn handed the leaf to Mauzl as he sang; Mauzl's haunts read the first mages' verses, and gleaned them to the world, and Louarn gleaned them to the dreamfolk, and gleaned in turn the dreamfolk's deeper gloss. Mauzl's glow surged to rival the intensity of Eilryn's magelight as the world began to understand the change being worked upon it—and asked of it. The dreamfolk's hearkener, Spinegale, widened that knowing, dispersed it among the dreamfolk on every mountain, in every vale, in every lake and river and field and arbor, in the breakers crashing on every shore. Through the conduit of Spinegale, the dreamfolk added the wisdom and sadness and wonder of the ages, and Mauzl's joined gleaning enlarged it still more, parting the veils of time and realms and mind for everyone to see. With Eilryn and Mistmourn still singing, Mauzl handed the leaf to Caille, and at her touch it fountained with wraiths. Lornhollow, the dreamfolk's weaver, bent to lay hands of moonsilver light upon her shining shoulders as she held the leaf. Their power flowed through them, through the ground, the air, through Caille's body to Eilryn and Mauzl, and outward to every limb of Eiden's body, suffusing its waters, filling its winds, surging through rock and soil and up again into what grew on them, meeting itself in every meeting of elements.

Caille laid the glittering leaf on the rocky turf. Eilryn sang the last note of his bindsong. Mistmourn's echoing harmonies gave way to the harmony of wind and surf and leaves. The dreamfolk backed slowly outward to join their fellows as Caille and Eilryn and Mauzl rose to join their friends and families; the circle within circle opened to include the world. The casting leaf dissipated into wraithsparkle that spread through the grass and up and out to the limits of sight in all directions. Every particle of matter shimmered. Winds and currents became visible, stillness became motion, motion became clarity.

Sight became limitless. All realms were visible, layered one inside another, one beyond the next—the realms of the waterfolk and earthfolk and airfolk, the realm of haunts where only Evonder dwelled, the realms of light and darkness in between.

All realms became one, an infinity of realms, an infinity of paths, there for the choosing, there for the joining.

The world was alight, agleam, its spirits a joyous scintillation. The light of the casting mage, the shine of the working touch, the glow of the gleaning visant did not subside when their tasks were completed, but surged the brighter as all the human lights joined with them. The dreamfolk were so luminous they blurred, and their moon-bright radiance made the blaze of day both stronger and rounder—softening it, deepening it, intensifying it.

Across Eiden Myr, there were troughs to fill, sheep to herd, bowls to turn, seeds to sow. Though the world might be alive with light, though dreamfolk might stand in silent, ecstatic worship at every milepost and headland, there was still work to do. The world was transforming before their eyes, but folk would not waste a perfectly good sowmid afternoon. They were the stewards of the world. In the midst of transcendence, they went on with their lives.

That's their shine, Mauzl thought, through the gleaning. *That clear light actuates this casting as much as any saturated light.*

At the moment of equinox, when all shadows were most diminished, the lights of Eiden Myr were their brightest. A tremor went through existence.

"It's begun," Graefel said, in a low voice.

"How long?" said Breida Shipseer, from her post by the cliffwall, where Pelufer and Tarunel also stood.

"By moonrise it should be done."

"How will we know?" said Karanthe, from a cluster of runners.

Graefel opened his hands, shook his head, looked to Louarn; Louarn gave a slight shrug and said, "I suppose we'll know when we get there."

The runners and the scholars and the menders sat where they had been standing and pulled provisions from packs and scrips and wallets; after a few breaths, a runner with extra cheese offered to trade some for a scholar's extra bread, a scholar traded oatcakes for a mender's marmalade, and the boundaries began to blur, white and black and gray congregating to share the food they had brought. Seekers and shielders did the same; at one end of the headland, someone pulled out a drum and sketched an idle rhythm, and at the other end someone pulled out a flute and improvised a melody. Other instruments joined in, and other voices. As the sun angled downward, a teller launched into a tale of the lands-beyond, and a tale of the world's beginnings followed from a different teller, and tales flowed of olden times in Eiden Myr, recapitulating their past with the music and birdsong and wind and surf a gentle background.

Louarn stood alone, off to the side. In a mesmerism of tellers' tales, he barely registered the sound of footfalls behind him, and startled when arms slid round his waist; then he flushed hot, and smiled hugely, and laid his hands on Keiler's arms, leaned his head into the hollow of his neck.

"You didn't think I'd let you bask in the center of all this without me, did you?" said the Norther burr.

"The center is probably somewhere in the Heartlands or the Belt," he replied, basking in Keiler's clear, pure light.

A warm chuckle resonated through his back and into his chest like a binder's song. "Where you are is the center of everything," Keiler said.

Eilryn walked to his aunt at the cliffwall, to ask her where his mother was. Seeing him approach, she only pointed.

His stomach lurched three ways at once.

I never thought to look, when we got here. I never checked. How could he have forgotten his own ship, the ship he'd risked everything to salvage, the ship he'd been born on, grown up on?

Because this is home now. Because this is the home she wanted for me, and this land, not the sea, is where my eyes first turn.

"The craft is sound," the Shipseer said. "We spent the last nonned days refitting it. It's wooded, watered, and provisioned, not to mention armed. And weatherwarded, and stocked with casting materials. A better start than she had before, and she made a miracle of that."

The ship looked so small, sailing back around the far point. She would not have sat at anchor. She must have sailed back and forth out there all morning while he prepared and while he cast, then all afternoon while the land and air and sea became suffused with light. Coming about, again and again, there at the border of the sparkle in the seas. Waiting for the sight of him. *This isn't right*, he thought, his heart breaking. *Mothers watch sons go off into the world, not the other way round.*

"She was saying goodbye." The words tore out of him as he remembered their parting. It felt as though he'd dreamed it. She'd left him in a dream, she'd said she would see him tomorrow but it was tomorrow now and *this* was the seeing she'd meant, this distant farewell across the sunset waters—

Breida laid a firm hand on his shoulder, and with the other disengaged his fingers from their death grip on the wall. "As best she could," the Shipseer said. "She doesn't like goodbyes. They hurt too much." She turned him toward her; her hands were iron, her eyes were kind. "She always comes home, son."

"But this last time . . . it was I who brought her . . ."

"She made you," Breida said. "You were her way home. She'll make a way again, you mark me. She'll find us, when it's time."

Eilryn turned to the sea, and waved—hesitant at first, disoriented to be here on shore with his hull and his sails and his masts out there on the water, and then with vigor as the flame-haired figure at the tiller waved to him.

Fare you safe and well, he bade her, deep in his cracked heart, perversely joyous at the eager fierceness with which *Stormwind* came about and seized the wind. *Spirits speed your journey, and bring you back to me someday.*

He stared after the dwindling ship until the sun sank into the Highlands and twilight claimed the Forgotten Sea. If he cast his eye just to the side, he could still make out the pale blur of bleached sails. He would have watched until that too was gone, but Caille touched his arm, and said, "Look, Eilryn. Look."

He turned from the sea, and found Caille and Mauzl to either side of him, and Louarn and Keiler with Graefel behind Breida, where all of them had stood to watch his mother sail away; and they were made of light, and the rocky plateau was made of light, and the battered trees along the cove road and up the rise, and the bogs off toward the Elbow; and off in the Head, across the Sea of Sorrows, the Aralinn Mountains rose into peaks of light, and the chalk Oriels, and the pink-and-gray Gerlocs in the High Arm, and the Blooded Mountains and the Elfelirs and the Cor Range far to Bootward, and all the hills and vales and downs below them, and the nine colored lakes of the Belt, and the silken grass-lands of the Girdle, and the lowland marshes and the deep jungles of the Weak Leg; and he understood how it was that he could be seeing all this, and at the same time seeing just the shining headland, just the shining slope, just the edge of the shining sea, because he could sense it in every bone and muscle of his body, he could see it with the vision shared by every soul in Eiden Myr.

He drew Caille and Mauzl tight against him. He listened to the stillness of the birds, the change in the sea's breathing, the shift in the wind's song. He smelled the freshness of sowmid rain in the air, the strange warm scent of the dreamfolk's bodies, the earthy fragrance of Caille, the grassy scent of Mauzl. He felt alive, savagely, jubilantly, ravenously alive; he was infused with aching love for this precious land and its spirits and its creatures.

"Do you see?" Pelufer whispered into the stillness, on a breath of light. "Do you *see*?" And Mauzl came out of all the long paths of the past and all the long shining ways of the future to say, in his own soft Mauzl-voice, "What we are and what we'll be. That's what's coming."

We can no longer turn back, Louarn thought. The casting bore them upward like a tide that had no ebb, just flow. A tide rising into wonder, into infinity. He gripped Keiler's shoulder hard, bone on bone, flesh on flesh.

They rose, and rose, into the ages.

THE NINE SEAS

Liath heaved *Stormwind* to under luffed sails on the dark waters and watched the landmass of Eiden Myr subsumed in light.

She was already farther than she had ever sailed from those shores, in seas too deep to anchor in. She could no longer see the cliffwall that topped that headland on the Fist, or the figures that had been arrayed along it, but they had turned away before she lost them to angles and distance—the broad red head of her sister, the coal-dark head of her son, the familiar shapes of Louarn and Graefel and Keiler. They were watching their own transcendence. Facing into the future. Not following the diminishing speck of the past that she had become.

To avoid the harrowed shores of Ollorawn, she had sailed Headward into the Sea of Sorrows, well out past the shimmering wraithtide that would only carry her back inshore. She had not yet chosen her ultimate course; first she would see this through to the end. Soon she would no longer be able to reckon direction in terms of Headward and Bootward, Fistward and Fingerward. Even trapped in the intorsion, she had been able to navigate by sight of Eiden's body. Now she would have to fall back on the ancient directions of east and west, north and south. She would always have the kadri in the sky.

I was never meant for paradise, she thought. Or perhaps she wasn't ready for it yet; or perhaps, and most likely, she had lost the capacity to accept it. She had grown up in paradise—in a peaceful realm where milk always flowed, calves and kids were born sound, crops grew tall, blight vanished, where there were no floods or drought or accidental fires, where no illness persisted or spread, where old age was comfortable, wine never turned to vinegar in the cask, water was always pure and fresh; a realm that had no memory of longblades or of war, a realm that had forgotten the words "murder" and "army." She had believed in that realm down to her bones, and the shattering of that belief had changed her forever. Paradise had become a legend, a myth, a tellers' tale—a land-beyond. Now Eiden Myr was transforming into that land-beyond in fact. Burning with pure, bright light, forging in the fires of its power and its love a new realm, a better realm, a realm made on the beliefs of those who dwelled there.

She would have been a heretic in such a realm.

From out here, on the dark seas, she could believe the transcendence she beheld. An island realm, alive upon the waters, lifting itself into light. A realm in which the elements and the ancients and the folk of light had joined into the truest, highest triad, and gained the power to make themselves anew. From out here, once home was gone, she could believe in home again.

They'll be safe there, she thought, of her family and her friends and her dead. *All the old darkness has been vanquished.* Any trouble, any strife would be their own, in their own place, to conquer in their own way. Fyldur's spines grew back. There would always be darknesses in folk's hearts; there would always be new stains. But the stains would be theirs, and new, not the old stains of a world locked forever in a circle, an intorsion, of risings and fallings. The great hope was that they would find, or make, a better way to be the flawed, brave, tragic creatures that they were. Perhaps even to rise above those flaws. If all they ever achieved was a realm where folk could live and die in peace, then it was more than the rest of the world had ever managed, and she would laud it. It would be the world of her childhood come true.

Out here, in the dark, she might see her way clear to return one day. She might learn to believe in paradise again. One day, out here in the dark, she might come at last to understand that it was time for her to go home. If that day came, no severing of realms would stop her. If that day came, she would seek to find her way home, or make her way home, or learn her way home. That day, if it came, if she lived that long, would be the greatest challenge of her life, and she would meet it as she'd met the others, head-on. In her heart she did not believe that she would fail, if that day came.

That day was not today.

The mountainous Head, the crags of the Low Shoulder, the bogs and downs and seaside cliffs of the Low Arm had grown so bright, in their bright shimmering pool of water, that land and ocean blurred. Was the new realm already forming? Birthing itself and its luminaries, laying down its seas, positioning itself at the nexus of infinities? Did her son exist in two realms now, was he both partly here and partly there? It was hard, to watch him go. Hard, to watch home go. Much harder than she had expected, and far more lonely.

I will be the only remaining mage of Eiden Myr in all the world. The last flesh of Eiden Myr, the last living memory of those fine, strong folk.

She cut the thought off. It would make her too precious to herself. She could not survive if she had to guard herself that close. *You are going into hard places,* Heff had said to her once. He hadn't known the third of it.

Or perhaps he had.

Her eyes were so filled with Eiden's dazzling light that for long breaths she ignored the mote of color that danced at the edge of vision. Then it irritated her enough to look, and it was not a trick of the eye, not some odd reflection—there was something there. Something that winked out, then reappeared. Something floating on the gentle swells off toward the Sea of Storms. Something made of colored light.

She grudged out of her trance and moved the tiller, sheeted in. Found a breath of air in the still, spangled night, enough to nudge her craft toward the ruby glow. Toward where it had been, when it dimmed and vanished—then where it was, for she had come alongside it.

Barely able to believe her eyes, she tossed a boathook down, and hauled Kazhe n'Zhevra's crimson longblade over the rails and aboard her craft—with Kazhe herself attached, soaked and sputtering and swearing.

"Stain spit you out?" Liath said, when the woman had coughed the nine seas all over her clean-swabbed deck.

Kazhe got to her knees, dragged an arm across her mouth, tried to speak, endured another spasm of great racking coughs, and stayed on all fours, panting. Her answer was a curt nod that flung water from her draggled white-blond head.

"Well, you're going to have to row back, and I won't thank you for costing me my lifeboat," Liath said. "But you might have time yet. Their casting has taken all day to get this far. The end will probably keep till moonrise."

Kazhe shook her whole body, like a dog, spraying seawater. "No," she rasped. "I don't bloody know what's going on there, but I'm not rowing anywhere near it." She sat heavily on the deck. "I never felt so naked in my life. Isn't there anything to kill on this forsaken sea? Something dark and deadly?"

"You can't stay here." Liath offered the blademaster fresh water to clear her throat and explained what had happened after she dove into the shroud.

"I'm not going into any realm of grieving light. I just spent nine lifetimes in a realm of shadow. Took it long enough to consume itself, and you'd think it would take me down with it when it went, wouldn't you? But this forsaken blade dumped me back in the waters here. I've been trying to drown myself since, but the bloody thing won't let me. Cast it away and there it is, smack on my chest like a clinging babe. Too smart to go into its sheath on my back and leave me facedown in peace. It *floats*. The puking piece of offal *floats*." The dimming and vanishing of the blade under the swells had been Kazhe rolling on top of it, trying to weight it into the depths. She doubled over coughing, then lifted her arm and hurled the blade spinning over the side. Liath's eyes followed the ruby arc, then lost it; she heard the splash, but when she looked at Kazhe, the grip of the blade peeped over her shoulder.

"Huh," Liath said. "You can't just run yourself through?"

Kazhe huddled shaking on the deck. "I tried to kill myself with this blade once, but I had to be blind drunk to do it, and even then the wretched thing only cut a hole in my belly to drain the drink out. You'd need a hold full of pure spirits to get me anywhere near that state."

"I could do it for you."

Kazhe's red-rimmed eyes focused on her, burning. "The blade would kill you first. And it would be my hand wielding it."

Liath grinned. Not so determined to die, then. "I thought you vowed never to take another human life with that blade."

Kazhe grabbed a belaying pin, hauled herself up, spat over the side, then sat hard on the cabin housing. "Grieving blade took a vow, not me," she said. "But this one didn't." She pulled a dagger from her boot. "This one didn't." A use knife from a side sheath. "This one—"

"All right," Liath said. "So long as I don't have to protect you, you can stay aboard." She ignored the perfunctory snarl. "But you'll pull your weight."

"Not sure I want to stay on this floating tallystick," Kazhe said, but the look she cast the molten glowing mass that had been their home was plain. "If I do, I'll pull my weight as what I am. You're a mage. You'll be wanting a kenai."

Liath laughed outright. "You taught me to use a longblade."

"Not the way I can." Kazhe pointed to one of the weapons mounted along the bulwark below the rails and over the scuppers. "And you've plenty of those didn't take any stinking vows."

"I still won't have you aboard if you can't work lines." She had launched into her speech about every able body knowing how to sail the ship when some difference in the substance of the foredeck drew her attention. It resolved into a tall, dark form, emerging from the foremast like the shadow of a boneman.

"I'll crew for you," said a familiar voice, and Nerenyi extracted the last of herself and a bulging pack from the mast and padded down the decking on bare feet. "I helped build this boat, as I recall. I should remember how to sail it."

Liath left the tiller for the briefest, fiercest embrace, cursing Nerenyi up and down. "Call the dreamfolk and tell them to send you where you belong!"

"Too late," Nerenyi said with blithe nonchalance, although there was a hint of sadness in her velvet eyes. "It was only at the last moment that Writhenrue granted me transit here. She loved me enough to let me go. I'll never forget her for that, never mind everything else. There's no going back. They've gone too far. The winds and the waters no longer connect."

"Bloody seekers," Kazhe grumbled.

"Hello, Kazhe," Nerenyi replied.

"But why, Nerenyi?" said Liath. "There's a whole new realm being born over there . . . somewhere. Don't you want to see it? Aren't you curious?"

"Why why why," Nerenyi chided—then relented, and said, "I spent a dozen ninedays in realms of infinite wonder. I still don't know why *this* sun rises and sets, why *this* day sky is blue, why *this* moon waxes and wanes. There's a lifetime's worth of questions for me right here."

"But Gisela . . ." Liath said, and couldn't finish.

"But Torrin," Nerenyi said gently. "But Heff." She turned to Kazhe. "But Benkana."

"Leave him out of this," Kazhe growled.

"They're gone to pethyar," Liath said, and the dark head and the fair head lifted sharply. "I've been to the realm of the dead. The antechamber, anyway. All our haunts are safely passaged." She looked at the vast shimmering blur of light, which no longer resembled land or sea. "And all our living, near enough."

"One of each light left," Nerenyi said.

Kazhe replied, "And not a soul left who can see a blessed one of us."

"Which will very likely save our lives," Liath said. "Kazhe, there are blankets in the cabin. Lay a fire in the stove, strip down, and wrap up warm before the chill kills you." To her surprise, Kazhe moved to do just that.

"You're sorry you left your son," Nerenyi said, "now that your solitary martyrdom's been invaded by noisy irritants."

"You fell in love with one of the dreamfolk and couldn't bear it and ran away," Liath countered.

Nerenyi grinned. "Not quite. But their realms . . . It's like intoxication, being there. Far too delicious to be good for me." She gestured at the shining marvel their home had become. "I'll tell you all about it, if you'll tell me how on earth *that* came about." Her smile turned wicked. "And I want to hear, syllable for syllable, exactly how Graefel Scholar admitted he was wrong."

"Plenty of time for all that," Liath said, moving the tiller to compensate for drift and maintain a position where she didn't have to twist around to see.

"If we live," Kazhe called up from below. Liath could smell the fire going in the stove. Wood from a tree that grew on Eiden's body. It would burn for a while to warm them, blazing bright behind the iron grate, and then be gone to ashes. *Well, the whole ship's made of Eiden,* she told herself. *And so are we, come to that. We'll be living in Eiden's shine for some while still.*

They drifted on swells smooth and long enough to reflect the stars. Kazhe came up wrapped in blankets and curled herself beside the tin stovepipe. Nerenyi sat cross-legged on a deckbox, long night-dark hair flowing down her long, straight back. The light of transcendence grew so bright they had to squint, but it did not shine on their faces, or illuminate sky or sea. It was a light seen by the spirit. There seemed to be no solid matter left within it; it was all light and no substance, a portrait painted upon the sea, a luminous vision of what had been, a shining dream. When they could see it even through tight-shut lids and fending hands, it began to fade—a watertight lantern dropped into a clear, dark, depthless sea, falling and falling through the fathoms, still burning, still bright, but sinking into silence, sinking past sight, sinking steadily until it was only a memory of light, until only the mind's eye could conjure a vision of it, still and silent and shining in the deeps.

Only dust and sand and ashes remained, subsiding into the sea, where Eiden's body had lain sprawled across the waters. Three long, slow swells rocked the ship, three quiet slaps against the hull; a breeze sprang up, a slight displacement of air, then died. The nine seas were become one sea again, smoothing seamless, barely a ripple to mark the passage of a world. The nine winds were one wind again, or nine times nine winds, or none.

I never learned their names, Liath thought.

They sat becalmed for some time in the great stillness. The moon rose huge and pale out of the sea off their starboard quarter, paving the ocean in liquid silver. The faraway shores of scorched, dead Ollorawn became dimly visible, no longer blocked by Eiden's Fist. Then a wind came out of the moon and over the sea. A southeasterly wind, Liath judged, trying the new reckoning on for size.

"Which way?" she said, as Nerenyi went to raise the headsails and Kazhe moved onto a bitt well below the swinging boom.

Kazhe and Nerenyi flung arms out at random, in opposite directions.

Liath split the difference. She brought them up into the wind and sailed straight down the road of liquid silver light.

acknowledgments

Special thanks to: Russell Galen, Teresa Nielsen Hayden, Patrick Nielsen Hayden, Eric Raab, Liz Gorinsky, Kenneth J. Silver, Milenda Lee, Jim Kapp, Nathan Weaver, Rob Stauffer, Becky Maines, Gary Ruddell, Carol Russo, Ellen Cipriano, and Ellisa Mitchell. John Clements, Rich Estok, Gary Gryzbek, Louis Leibowits, Todd Sullivan, and the rest of ARMA (www.thearma.org) and ARMA-NYC. Michael Blitz and everyone who trains at Krav Maga Long Island (www.kmli.com). Angi-Kate, Carlee, Carmel, Juan, Julianna, Kalnaur, Karin, Missy, Nick, Robert, Shirleen, Whyette, and the other loyal denizens of the Proxy Circle message board, for their thoughtful posts and for hanging in there through the long wait; Randy Reed and John Flint, for support from the earliest days. Adam Throne, Bob Stacy, Dan Persons, and Michael Yolen, for reading and commenting on all or part. Kevin Broderick, for love and support through some particularly interesting times. My mom, for whom no dedication could ever be enough appreciation.

And, always, Jenna Felice.